Kingdoms in Peril

Volume 2

Kingdoms in Peril

Volume 2

The Exile Returns

Feng Menglong

Translated by Olivia Milburn

UNIVERSITY OF CALIFORNIA PRESS

University of California Press
Oakland, California

Cataloging-in-Publication Data is on file at the Library of Congress.

ISBN 978-0-520-38102-5 (cloth : alk. paper)
ISBN 978-0-520-38103-2 (pbk. : alk. paper)
ISBN 978-0-520-38104-9 (ebook)

Manufactured in the United States of America

32 31 30 29 28 27 26 25 24 23
10 9 8 7 6 5 4 3 2 1

Contents

The Zhou Confederacy circa 500 B.C.E. Adapted from *Map of the Five Hegemons* by SY, CC-BY-SA 4.0

List of Main Characters

Volume Two

The persons included in this list are characters who appear in multiple chapters of *Kingdoms in Peril*, and whose deeds would continue to be referenced long after they themselves were dead. Some of these historical individuals appear under various different names during the course of the book, as they inherited titles or achieved honors. In each section, rulers are listed first, followed by other important personages.

CAO (Ji clan; marquis)

The ruling house of Cao was descended from Prince Zhenduo, a younger brother of King Wu of Zhou (r. 1049/45–1043 B.C.E.). This tiny state was rarely of great political importance, and was ultimately destroyed by the armies of Song in 487 B.C.E.

Lord Gong (r. 652–618 B.C.E.), personal name Xiang: his disrespect to Lord Wen of Jin during his time in exile resulted in much subsequent violence.

Xi Fuji: a senior advisor to Lord Gong of Cao who attempted to mitigate the effects of his lord's quarrel with Jin.

CHU (Xiong clan; king)

The kingdom of Chu, based along the middle reaches of the Yangtze River, became an increasingly powerful state during the early Eastern Zhou dynasty, and its monarchs declared themselves kings. Although frequently in conflict with the Central States, the Chu kings were nevertheless part of the Zhou world, and the power they possessed reached its apogee under King Zhuang, the third hegemon.

King Cheng (r. 671–626 B.C.E.), personal name Yun: a clever, competent ruler who was to prove Lord Xiang of Song's nemesis and played an important (if ambiguous) role in Lord Wen of Jin's rise to power as the second hegemon; murdered by his son, Crown Prince Shangchen.

King Mu (r. 625–614 B.C.E.), personal name Shangchen: a violent and bellicose man who seized the throne by assassination.

King Zhuang (r. 613–591 B.C.E.), personal name Lü: in the early part of his reign an idle monarch, who then reformed and established himself as the third hegemon, under whose enlightened rule Chu reached a peak of power and prestige.

King Gong (r. 590–560 B.C.E.), personal name Shen: spent his reign locked in conflict with the resurgent power of Jin, culminating in the Battle of Yanling in 575 B.C.E., in which King Gong lost an eye.

Cheng Dechen (d. 632 B.C.E.): one of King Cheng of Chu's senior generals, in command of many major campaigns during his reign, committed suicide following his defeat at the Battle of Chengpu.

Dou Ban: son of Dou Ziwen, a senior minister in the Chu government personally beaten to death by King Mu.

Dou Bo: one of King Cheng of Chu's most important generals, forced to commit suicide after being slandered by Crown Prince Shangchen.

Dou Yuejiao (d. 605 B.C.E.): cousin of Dou Ziwen and a senior military figure under both Kings Cheng and Mu of Chu; eventually executed by King Zhuang for treason.

Dou Ziwen, personal name Guwutu: served as a senior minister under King Cheng of Chu.

Sunshu Ao (d. c. 593 B.C.E.): the sagacious and wise minister who served King Zhuang of Chu.

JIN (Ji clan; marquis)

The ruling house of Jin was descended from a younger brother of King Cheng of Zhou (r. 1042/35–1006 B.C.E.). After a long and messy period of political instability, Jin became enormously powerful in the reign of Lord Wen, the second hegemon. The uneasy alliance between Jin and the neighboring state of Qin established by Lord Wen did not survive him, and the two states were quickly locked in conflict.

Lord Hui (r. 650–637 B.C.E.), personal name Yiwu: was held as prisoner-of-war in Qin, his life spared only by the intercession of his half-sister, Lady Mu Ji.

Lord Huai (r. 637 B.C.E.), personal name Yu: son of Lord Hui; held hostage in Qin for some years, eventually murdered by his uncle, the Honorable Chonger, in a coup to put himself in power as Lord Wen.

Lord Wen (r. 638–626 B.C.E.), personal name Chonger: second hegemon following on Lord Huan of Qi; succeeded to the title after many decades in exile and went on to become the most powerful aristocrat of the age.

Lord Xiang (r. 627–621 B.C.E.), personal name Huan: succeeded his father, Lord Wen, as Master of Covenants and as such continued to dominate diplomatic relations between the Central States, but was soon locked in conflict with Lord Mu of Qin.

Lord Ling (r. 620–607 B.C.E.), personal name Yigao: installed in power by Zhao Dun on the death of Lord Xiang, he turned out to be a sadistic lunatic and was murdered at the Peach Garden by Zhao Chuan.

Lord Cheng (r. 606–600 B.C.E.), personal name Heitun: installed in power by the Zhao family after the murder of Lord Ling.

Lord Jing (r. 599–581 B.C.E.), personal name Ju: attempted to restore the hegemony to Jin, and was persuaded by Tu'an Gu to massacre the powerful Zhao clan in revenge for the death of Lord Ling.

Lord Li (r. 580–573 B.C.E.), personal name Zhoupu: an idle, dissolute, and incompetent ruler who brought the state of Jin to the brink of a civil war before being poisoned by rebel ministers.

Lord Dao (r. 573–558 B.C.E.), personal name Zhou: a member of a junior branch of the ruling house in exile for generations, attempted to bring overly powerful ministerial families under control and restored the Zhao clan to its former honors.

Bo Di: a eunuch assassin employed by a series of Jin rulers, including Lords Xian, Hui, Huai, and Wen to remove inconvenient persons.

Jie Zitui: one of Lord Wen of Jin's companions in exile, who was killed by his ungrateful lord after he came to power; these events are commemorated in the annual Cold Food Festival.

Han Jue (d. 566 B.C.E.): played a key role in saving the life of the sole survivor of the Zhao clan, and was the founding ancestor of the Han clan, which would eventually partition Jin at the beginning of the Warring States era in 475 B.C.E.

Hu Tu (d. 637 B.C.E.): Lord Wen of Jin's maternal grandfather and a senior government minister, for many years his eyes and ears in the Jin capital city.

Hu Yan (d. 622 B.C.E.): son of Hu Tu and thus Lord Wen of Jin's uncle; a loyal supporter during his exile.

Lady Mu Ji (d. c. 637 B.C.E.): half-sister of Lords Hui and Wen of Jin, and wife of Lord Mu of Qin, played an important role in trying to stabilize a series of civil wars in Jin.

Tu'an Gu: a loyal supporter of Lord Ling of Jin, subsequently presided over the near annihilation of the Zhao clan under Lord Jing of Jin.

Zhao Cui (d. 622 B.C.E.): one of Lord Wen of Jin's senior companions in exile, related to him through marriage first as brother-in-law and then as son-in-law, and founder of the Zhao clan, who would eventually partition Jin in 475 B.C.E.

Zhao Dun (d. 601 B.C.E.): Zhao Cui's son and a dominant figure in the government of Jin for many decades.

Zhao Wu (598–541 B.C.E.): a descendant of Zhao Dun, who would be the sole survivor of the massacre of the entire clan in the reign of Lord Jing of Jin.

LU (Ji clan; marquis)

Lu was founded by a son of the first Duke of Zhou, a younger brother of King Wu of Zhou (r. 1049/45–1043 B.C.E.), who held enormous power at the beginning of the dynasty as regent to the infant King Cheng. With the state of Qi, Lu dominated the political scene on the Shandong peninsula, and the two ruling houses frequently intermarried, with disastrous results. However, the demand that peace be preserved in the region outweighed all other considerations.

Lord Xi (r. 659–627 B.C.E.), personal name Shen: brought order to the extremely chaotic situation in Lu following the murders of Lord Min and other claimants to the dukedom.

Lord Wen (r. 626–609 B.C.E.), personal name Xing: his court was dominated by collateral lineages of the Lu ruling house, leaving him with little authority.

Lord Xuan (r. 608–591 B.C.E.), personal name Jie: installed in power following the murder of his half-brothers by his mother and Dongmen Sui after the death of Lord Wen.

Dongmen Sui (d. 601 B.C.E.): a son of Lord Zhuang of Lu by a concubine, dominated the government of the state through the rule of several lords of Lu, and was a key coconspirator of Lady Jing Ying (d. 601 B.C.E.), the mother of the future Lord Xuan of Lu, in the murder of other claimants to the title.

QI (Jiang clan; marquis)

The Jiang ruling family of Qi were descended from Jiang Ziya (dates unknown), a key advisor to King Wu of Zhou during his conquest of the Shang dynasty. His descendant Lord Huan of Qi dominated not just the Shandong peninsula, but the whole of the Central States, a position that was ultimately recognized by the Zhou king with his appointment as the first hegemon. The fighting among his sons as to which one would inherit his honors caused prolonged and damaging political instability to the state.

Lord Huan (r. 685–643 B.C.E.), personal name Xiaobai: first hegemon of the Eastern Zhou dynasty. Coming to the title following the assassination of Lord Xiang and attempts to seize power by his cousin the Honorable Wuzhi and his older brother the Honorable Jiu (d. 685 B.C.E.), Lord Huan went on to dominate the political scene for decades.

Lord Xiao (r. 642–633 B.C.E.), personal name Zhao: installed in power by the forces of Lord Xiang of Song following a brief interregnum by one of his half-brothers, the Honorable Wukui, in the chaos following the death of Lord Huan.

Lord Zhao (r. 632–613 B.C.E.), personal name Pan: came to power following the death of his bellicose and abrasive half-brother, Lord Xiao.

Lord Yi (r. 612–609 B.C.E.), personal name Shangren: usurped the title in a coup following the death of his half-brother Lord Zhao. His debauched lifestyle and brutality resulted in his murder by two relatives of his victims.

Lord Hui (r. 608–599 B.C.E.), personal name Yuan: came to the title after the murder of his half-brother, Lord Yi.

Lord Qing (r. 598–582 B.C.E.), personal name Wuye: fought against the state of Jin and was badly defeated by them at the Battle of An in 589 B.C.E.

Bao Shuya (d. 644 B.C.E.): a friend and contemporary of Guan Zhong, and a long-serving minister in Lord Huan of Qi's administration.

Guan Zhong (d. 645 B.C.E.), personal name Yiwu: the mainstay of Lord Huan of Qi's government, and important early Chinese political thinker.

Shu Diao: a eunuch in the service of Lord Huan of Qi, and with Yi Ya, an ally of the Honorable Wukui.

Yi Ya: Lord Huan of Qi's cook and a key player in the conflict at the end of his reign.

QIN (Ying clan; earl)

The origins of the Ying ruling family of Qin remain highly obscure and very controversial. However, during the reign of Lord Mu, Qin was drawn into preserving peace in Jin following a succession of coups and civil wars. After the death of Lord Mu, a highly intelligent and competent ruler, Qin resumed its isolationist stance, and its rulers had very limited contact with the Central States.

Lord Mu (r. 659–621 B.C.E.), personal name Renhao: presided over a major expansion in the power and prestige of Qin. Through his wife, Lady Mu Ji, he played a significant role in the establishment of a succession of Jin rulers, and was closely allied with Lord Wen of Jin.

Lord Huan (r. 603–577 B.C.E.), personal name Rong: in conflict with Jin, and defeated by them in the Battle of Masui of 578 B.C.E.

Baili Xi: a senior minister under Lord Mu of Qin, was claimed by Qin as a slave in the dowry of Lady Mu Ji of Jin.

Lady Huai Ying (d. 620 B.C.E.): the daughter of Lord Mu of Qin, married first to Lord Huai of Jin, and then to his uncle, Lord Wen of Jin. Her family connections and personal army were instrumental in protecting her second husband following his return from exile.

SONG (Zi clan; duke)

The dukes of Song were descended from the Shang dynasty royal family, and they received lands and honors in order to allow them to continue to perform ancestral sacrifices for the Shang kings. Lord Xiang of Song would attempt to become hegemon and repeatedly tried to assert dominance over the political life of the Central States, only to be outwitted at every turn by the clever, ruthless, and charismatic King Cheng of Chu.

Lord Xiang (r. 650–637 B.C.E.), personal name Zifu: a very silly and stubborn man, whose determination to become hegemon brought disaster on his state and resulted in his own untimely demise.

Lord Cheng (r. 636–620 B.C.E.), personal name Wangchen: inherited a devastated state following his father's death from a wound received at the Battle of Hong in 638 B.C.E.

Lord Zhao (r. 619–611 B.C.E.), personal name Chujiu: a neglectful ruler only interested in hunting with his boon companions.

Lord Wen (r. 611–589 B.C.E.), personal name Bao: usurped the title following the murder of Lord Zhao, thanks to the machinations of his paramour, Lady Wang Ji, the widow of Lord Xiang of Song.

Honorable Muyi: Lord Xiang of Song's older half-brother and regent during his time in captivity, kept fully occupied by trying to prevent the worst from happening during Lord Xiang's rule.

WEY (Ji clan; marquis)

The Wey ruling family were descended from a younger brother of King Wu of Zhou. Although very important in the founding of the Eastern Zhou dynasty, a succession of decadent and incompetent rulers reduced Wey to a condition of near terminal collapse, and it struggled to survive as an independent state within the Zhou confederacy.

Lord Cheng (r. 634–632, 632–600 B.C.E.), personal name Zheng: suffered considerable political problems and experienced his country being invaded thanks to his disagreements with Lord Wen of Jin.

Honorable Shuwu (d. 632 B.C.E.), Lord Cheng's brother, governed the state as regent during Lord Cheng's captivity, only to fall victim to his political rivals.

Ning Yu: a key supporter of Lord Cheng and instrumental in the machinations to extract him from captivity and restore him to power.

ZHENG (Ji clan; earl)

The state of Zheng was founded when King Xuan of Zhou (r. 827/25–782 B.C.E.) granted these lands to his younger brother, Prince You. During the course of the Eastern Zhou dynasty, Zheng would find themselves perilously placed between the rival states of Chu and Jin; however, at the same time, Zheng repeatedly intervened successfully in the affairs of the Zhou kings, always in support of the regnant monarch.

Lord Wen (r. 673–628 B.C.E.), personal name Jie: a strong ally of King Cheng of Chu, married to his sister, Lady Wen Mi, and thus increasingly alienated from the rest of the Central States.

Lord Mu (r. 627–606 B.C.E.), personal name Lan: a strong ally of Lord Wen of Jin, after serving many years in his government while in exile from Zheng.

Lord Ling (r. 605 B.C.E.), personal name Yi: murdered in the first year of his reign in a stupid argument over food.

Lord Xiang (r. 604–587 B.C.E.), personal name Jian: came to the title unexpectedly following the murder of his half-brother.

Lady Xia Ji: the daughter of Lord Mu of Zheng, was widely regarded as the most beautiful woman of her time, as a result of which she was treated by a succession of powerful men as a prize to be captured.

ZHOU (Ji clan; king)

The Zhou dynasty was founded in 1046 B.C.E., when the future King Wu of Zhou and his ally Jiang Ziya (founder of the state of Qi) defeated the last monarch of the Shang dynasty at the Battle of Muye. The Zhou kings went on to create the Central States by rewarding family members and key supporters with significant grants of land, which they ruled with considerable day-to-day independence. During the course of the Eastern Zhou dynasty, the kings were increasingly sidelined and politically irrelevant; however, they retained an important religious and ceremonial role, which was not yet challenged by rival kings.

King Xiang (r. 652–619 B.C.E.), personal name Zheng: his reign was overshadowed by constant conflict with Prince Dai, which resulted in long alternating periods of exile for both of them.

King Qing (r. 618–613 B.C.E.), personal name Renchen: a monarch with an uneventful reign, of little authority following the upheavals caused by his father and uncle.

King Kuang (r. 612–607 B.C.E.), personal name Ban: succeeded his father but produced no heirs.

King Ding (r. 606–586 B.C.E.), personal name Yu: succeeded his older brother, and attempted to play a more active role in the affairs of the Central States.

Prince Dai (d. 635 B.C.E.): younger brother of King Xiang of Zhou, and a highly charismatic figure, whose attempts to seize power were forgiven by his long-suffering relatives until he was finally executed by Lord Wen of Jin.

Prince Hu: a major figure in diplomacy in the reign of King Xiang.

Chapter Thirty-one

Lord Hui of Jin is angered and kills Qing Zheng.

Jie Zitui cuts flesh from his thigh to feed to his lord.

Lord Hui of Jin was imprisoned at Mount Lingtai, a situation that he blamed entirely on Lady Mu Ji, for he did not know anything about the servants in mourning clothes or her defiant determination to force her husband to free him. He complained to Han Jian: "When His Late Lordship was discussing the prospect of a marriage alliance with the state of Qin, a divination was performed by the Grand Astrologer Su, which said: 'The neighbor to the west reproaches us for not keeping our word and there can be no amends.' If my father had followed this advice, I wouldn't be in this situation now!"

"His Late Lordship made many mistakes, but the marriage alliance with Qin was not one of them!" Han Jian retorted. "If Qin didn't care about the alliance, would you ever have been installed in power? You repaid them by attacking them, thereby turning an ally into an enemy. There is no reason to blame Qin for what they have done. You ought to look to your own behavior for the source of the problem!" Lord Hui fell silent.

A short time later, Lord Mu of Qin sent Noble Grandson Qi to Mount Lingtai to ensure the Marquis of Jin had made himself comfortable and announce that he would soon be going home.

"We are none of us particularly pleased with you," Noble Grandson Qi told him. "However, His Lordship has decided to support the alliance created by his marriage and thus did not allow his wife to carry out her threat of committing suicide. When you have handed over the five cities west of the Yellow River and sent Scion Yu here as a hostage, you can go home!"

Lord Hui now realized what he owed to Lady Mu Ji and felt deeply ashamed of himself. He instructed Grandee Xi Qi to return to Jin and ordered Lü Yisheng to arrange for the transfer of the land and hostage.

Lü Yisheng made a special journey to Wangcheng, where he had an audience with Lord Mu of Qin. He presented maps of the five cities and an account of their taxes, grain levies, and population. He also expressed his willingness to give hostages to ensure the return for the Marquis of Jin.

"Why has the scion not arrived yet?" Lord Mu asked.

"There have been civil disturbances in our state, so the scion at the moment cannot leave the capital," Lü Yisheng explained. "On the day that His Lordship returns, the scion will leave!"

"Why have there been such problems in Jin?" Lord Mu inquired.

"Our more educated subjects are well aware of how badly His Lordship has behaved towards you and now thinks only of how to requite the kindness shown to us by the state of Qin," Lü Yisheng replied. "However, ordinary people do not understand this, so they want to take revenge against you. That is why there have been problems."

"So your people are still looking forward to the return of the marquis?" asked Lord Mu.

"Gentlemen understand that His Lordship will certainly be coming back, and so we will have to send the scion to Qin to secure our alliance with you," Lü Yisheng answered. "However, ignorant people think that he will not be coming back, so they are demanding that the scion should be established as our new ruler to prevent any further invasions by Qin. In my humble opinion, establishing His Lordship in the first place demonstrates your might, while setting him free will demonstrate your magnanimity. Both might and magnanimity are necessary if you wish to become hegemon over the lords of the Central States. What is the advantage for Qin in offending both the elite and the common people in Jin? I do not imagine that Your Lordship would be prepared to lose all the gains that you have made so far and give up any chance of ever becoming hegemon!"

Lord Mu laughed and said, "You and I are in absolute agreement."

He ordered that Mengming should go and settle the new borders of the five cities and arrange for officials to take charge. He also arranged that the Marquis of Jin should be moved to a guesthouse in the suburbs of the capital, where he was treated with all the rituals due to a distinguished visitor, including being honored with the sacrifice of seven animals. He ordered Noble Grandson Qi to command the military escort that would protect the Marquis of Jin and Lü Yisheng when they returned home.

At a basic sacrifice, a cow, a sheep, and a pig were slaughtered. The sacrifice offered to the Marquis of Jin was the most lavish kind, at which seven animals of each species were killed. This shows that Lord Mu wanted to reaffirm the alliance between their two countries.

Lord Hui was defeated in battle in the ninth month. Then he was imprisoned in Qin and was released in the eleventh month. Of the ministers captured with him, all followed him home to Jin with the exception of Guo She, who had died of illness in Qin and was buried there. When Yi Xi heard that Lord Hui was coming home, he said to Qing Zheng: "You prevented Han Jian from capturing the Earl of Qin because you were so desperate to save His Lordship, and as a result the marquis has spent months in captivity. Now His Lordship is coming home, and you will not be able to escape the effects of his wrath. Why do you not go into exile abroad to avoid it?"

"According to military law, a defeated soldier and a captured general both deserve to die," Qing Zheng said. "It is my fault that His Lordship has endured imprisonment and humiliation—what crime could be greater than this? If His Lordship had not returned, I would have taken my family and servants to seek punishment at his hands in Qin. Now that His Lordship is returning home, he can execute me here. I have stayed with the intention of allowing the letter of the law to be applied: that will please His Lordship and will show his subjects that there is nowhere for a guilty man to hide. Why would I run away?" Yi Xi sighed and left.

When Lord Hui arrived at Jiang, Scion Yu met him beyond the suburbs in the company of Hu Tu, Xi Rui, Qing Zheng, Yi Xi, Sima Shuo, and the eunuch Bo Di. Lord Hui spotted Qing Zheng from his chariot and his anger began to rise. He ordered Jiapu Tu to summon him into his presence and asked him, "How dare you come to see me?"

"If Your Lordship had followed my original recommendation to requite the kindnesses that you had received from Qin, you would never have been attacked," Qing Zheng pointed out. "If you had taken my advice later on and made peace with Qin, you would not have had to do battle. If you had ever listened to a word that I say, you would not have hitched Petite to your chariot, in which case you would not have been defeated. I have been completely loyal to you, my lord. Why should I not come to see you?"

"What do you have to say to me today?" Lord Hui demanded.

"I have committed three crimes that merit the death penalty," Qing Zheng replied. "The first is that I gave loyal advice but could not find the means to make Your Lordship listen to me. The second is that when the divination showed that I should serve as your bodyguard, I could not make you agree. The third is that when I went to summon your generals to come to your assistance, I could not prevent Your Lordship from being taken prisoner. I ask that you punish me, so that everyone should know the crimes that I have committed."

Lord Hui could find nothing to say in return, so he ordered Liang Yaomi to recite the list of his crimes.

"None of the 'crimes' that you have mentioned deserve the death penalty," Liang Yaomi said. "On the other hand, you have indeed committed three crimes that do deserve death, did you know that? The first is that when His Lordship became stuck in the bog and called out to you for help, you paid no attention. The second is that when I was about to take Lord Mu of Qin prisoner, you called me off to rescue His Lordship. The third is that when we were all taken prisoner and placed in chains, you did not fight or face any danger, but ran off home."

"The officers from the three armies are all here, and so I ask you a question," Qing Zheng said. "Is a man who sits here calmly awaiting the death penalty the kind of person who would refuse to fight or face any kind of danger?"

Yi Xi remonstrated: "Qing Zheng has done nothing to avoid punishment. He is clearly an extremely brave man. If you would pardon him, my lord, I am sure that he will expunge the humiliation that you suffered at Hanyuan."

"He has already been comprehensively defeated in battle," Liang Yaomi sneered. "If we send him out to avenge our defeat, will not everyone laugh at us and think that Jin has no competent generals?"

Jiapu Tu also offered remonstrance: "Qing Zheng offered loyal advice three times: this ought to outweigh any other consideration. It would be better to pardon him, thereby demonstrating His Lordship's benevolence, rather than to execute him to show how strict the laws of Jin are."

"The reason why our state is so strong is because our laws are properly applied," Liang Yaomi proclaimed. "If people go unpunished, who will ever respect our laws again? If you do not execute Qing Zheng, you will never be able to discipline your army again!"

Lord Hui turned his head to look at Sima Shuo, ordering him to begin the execution. Qing Zheng stretched out his neck for the knife.

An old man wrote a poem bemoaning Lord Hui's shortsightedness, which made him unable to forgive Qing Zheng's errors. This poem runs:

On whose instructions were the granaries closed and treaty obligations ignored?
Who listened to flattery and executed those who offered loyal advice?
Lord Hui was a narrow-minded and vindictive man,
Who should have been imprisoned forever at Mount Lingtai!

When Liang Yaomi had Lord Mu of Qin encircled, he thought that he could not possibly escape from his clutches. Just at that moment, Qing Zheng shouted, "Save His Lordship!"—so he had to let him go. He loathed Qing Zheng because of this and was determined to see him executed. When Qing Zheng was beheaded, the sky grew dark and the sun ceased to shine. Many of the grandees present had tears running down their cheeks. Yi Xi asked permission to collect his body for burial, saying, "I do so to repay all the kindness I have received from him."

When Lord Hui returned to his state, he immediately handed over Scion Yu to Noble Grandson Qi, to go to Qin as a hostage. At the same time, he requested the return of Tu'an Yi's body, which he buried with all the ceremony due to a senior grandee. His son inherited his office as a middle-ranking grandee.

One day, Lord Hui said to Xi Rui: "During the three months that I was in Qin, the one thing that I was worried about was Chonger, because I was afraid that he would take advantage of the situation to launch a coup. Now I can relax on that front."

"As long as Chonger survives in exile," Xi Rui said, "he poses a terrible threat to you. You will have to get rid of him before he really causes trouble."

"Who can kill Chonger for me?" Lord Hui asked. "I will reward him most generously."

"Many years ago, the eunuch Bo Di attacked Pu and got close enough to Chonger to cut off his sleeve," Xi Rui said. "He has always been terrified that one of these days Chonger will come back, at which point he will be severely punished. If you want Chonger dead, he is the man to do it."

Lord Hui summoned Bo Di and gave him secret instructions to murder the Honorable Chonger.

"Chonger has been living with the Di people for twelve years," Bo Di said. "When the Di attacked Jiuru, they took his two daughters prisoner: Lady Shu Wei and Lady Ji Wei. Both of them are supposed to be very beautiful. Lady Ji Wei is now Chonger's wife, and Lady Shu Wei is married to Zhao Cui. Each of them has given birth to children. Since Chonger and his principal advisor are happily married to their wives, they have stopped thinking about us. If I go and attack them, the Di will certainly help Chonger by mobilizing their armies and going to war, in which case we may not be victorious. I would prefer to take a couple of knights and travel secretly into Di territory, to wait until Chonger goes out on a journey, and then kill him."

"That sounds like an excellent plan to me," Lord Hui said happily. He gave Bo Di one hundred ingots of gold, with which he could hire the knights to accompany him. Afterwards, he told him to set off: "I am expecting you to leave within three days. You will receive the rest of your money once you have returned."

As the old proverb has it: "If you don't want other people to know about it, don't do it; if you don't want other people to hear about it, don't say it." Even though Bo Di was the only person who was present when Lord Hui issued his instructions, there were still plenty of palace servants who were well aware of his plans. When Hu Tu heard that Bo Di was spending money like water, trying to recruit knights into his service, he became suspicious and made secret inquiries. Hu Tu had long held the highest rank in the government, so were there any palace eunuchs whom he did not know personally? It was impossible to keep this conspiracy from reaching Hu Tu's ears. He was deeply alarmed and immediately wrote a letter, which a servant took out to the Di under cover of darkness, to tell the Honorable Chonger what was afoot.

That day it so happened that Chonger was out hunting along the banks of the Wei River with the Di chief. Suddenly someone broke through the circle of guards and begged for permission to see the two Hu brothers, saying, "I have a letter from Old Minister Hu."

"Father never sends letters abroad," Hu Mao and Hu Yan said. "If he has written to us, there must be a crisis in Jin."

They immediately summoned the messenger into their presence. He presented the letter to them, kowtowed once, turned around, and left. The two brothers wondered what on earth could be going on! They opened the letter and read it:

> His Lordship is planning to assassinate the Honorable Chonger. He has already given the eunuch Bo Di his orders, and he will set off within the next three days. You must inform Chonger of this and go into exile somewhere else as soon as you can. If you delay, it will be disastrous.

The two Hu brothers were deeply alarmed and immediately reported the contents of this letter to Chonger.

"My wife and children are here," the Honorable Chonger said. "This is my home. If I leave, where could I go?"

"When we came here originally," Hu Yan reminded him, "it was not to set up home, but to make plans for getting back to our country. At that time we did not have the resources to go much further, so we settled down here temporarily. Now we have been here for ages, and it is high time that we moved on to a bigger country. Bo Di's arrival shows that Heaven is speeding you on your way!"

"Since it seems that we have to go, where should we be heading for?" Chonger asked.

"Even though the Marquis of Qi is old," Hu Yan said, "he is still the hegemon. He is well-known for his sympathy and support for other lords and his employment of intelligent and brave knights. Since Guan Zhong and Xi Peng are dead, he has been left without any wise advisors. If you were to go to Qi, His Lordship would certainly treat you with great generosity. If there is any change in Jin, we can make use of Qi's authority to put you in power."

Chonger thought that this was good advice, so he called off the hunt and went home. He informed his wife, Lady Ji Wei: "The Marquis of Jin is going to send someone to assassinate me, and I am afraid that I am in serious danger here. It is my plan to make a tour of the major states such as Qin and Chu, to see if any of them will help return me to my own country. I hope that you will make every effort to raise our sons well. If you do not hear from me for the next twenty-five years, you should marry someone else."

Lady Ji Wei burst into tears. "I understand that you are an ambitious man, and I am not expecting you to stay here with me. I am twenty-five years old now, so if I wait for you for another twenty-five years, I am going to be pricing my coffin rather than thinking about getting married again! I will wait for you however long it takes. Do not worry about me!"

Zhao Cui had his own instructions for his wife, Lady Shu Ji, which do not need to be given here.

. . .

Early in the morning the following day, Chonger ordered Hoo Shu to arrange for transportation, and told his treasurer, Tou Xu, to collect all the gold and silk that he owned. Just as he was giving these instructions, he caught sight of Hu Mao and Hu Yan running towards him. They said: "We have just received another message from our father, saying that Bo Di set out the day after receiving his instructions. He was afraid that you would not have left yet, and would be caught off guard. Father did not even have time to write a letter for you; he just instructed the fastest messenger that he could to come here, traveling day and night, to tell you to leave at once! You must not lose a single moment!"

When Chonger heard this news, he was profoundly shocked. "Bo Di has come quicker than I would have believed possible!" he exclaimed.

He did not bother with packing, but ran out of the city on foot with the two Hu brothers. When Hoo Shu saw that the Honorable Chonger had gone, he prepared a single oxcart, chasing after him to make him get inside. Zhao Cui, Qiu Ji, and the others caught up with them one by one. There was no room for them to sit in the oxcart, so they all had to walk.

"Why hasn't Tou Xu come?" Chonger asked.

"All of Tou Xu's baggage has disappeared, and I don't know where he has gone," someone replied.

Chonger had already lost his home, and now he discovered that his money was all gone too, but in the circumstances he did not seem particularly upset or depressed. Such was the situation, and he had no choice but to carry on. He was as much at a loss as a dog at a funeral, moving as quickly as a fish escaping from the net. It was fully half a day after the Honorable Chonger had left the city that the Di chief discovered that he was gone. He wanted to send some money and gifts to him, but it was already too late.

There is a poem that testifies to this:

After twelve years spent among the barbarians,
This caged dragon had still not found an opportunity to soar.
Why should one brother turn against another?
Why force him to hurry from pillar to post?

Lord Hui had originally given the eunuch Bo Di a deadline of three days to set off for the lands of the Di, but on the second day he had already arrived. Now, this Bo Di was a eunuch who had always been much favored for the efforts he made to carry out his lord's wishes. In the past, Lord Xian of Jin had sent him to attack Pu, but he had missed Chonger and only been able to cut off his sleeve. He could well imagine how much the Honorable Chonger hated him for this. Now he had been ordered by Lord Hui to do exactly the same thing. He was very keen to kill Chonger, not only because this would establish his credit with Lord Hui but also to eliminate a potential source of future problems. He therefore collected together a small band of knights and set off at the earliest possible opportunity so that his intended victim would have no warning and it would be easier to kill him. He did not know that Hu Tu had already sent not one but two messages and that all was revealed. Thus, when Bo Di arrived among the Di and asked after the Honorable Chonger, he was long gone. The Di chief had always been very fond of Chonger, and so he ordered that all border crossings should be closed. Anyone who wanted to come into the country was subject to a very harsh interrogation. In Jin, Bo Di was a highly valued palace eunuch; now he had come here to murder the Honorable Chonger at the head of a band of assassins. If he were questioned, how should he answer? Under the circumstances, it was impossible for him to cross into Di territory, so he had to go home and report this to Lord Hui. Lord Hui could not think of anything to do about it, so he had to give up his plans for the moment.

. . .

It was Chonger's intention to go to the state of Qi, but in order to get there he had to travel through Wey. As the proverb has it: "If you want to climb socially, you have to be ready to humble yourself, and if you want to travel far from home, you have to be prepared to suffer." It goes without saying that after leaving Di territory, Chonger was reduced to terrible poverty. A couple of days later, when they arrived at the border with Wey, the official there questioned them as to where they had come from.

"My master is the Honorable Chonger of Jin," Zhao Cui announced, "who has been forced into exile. We want to go to Qi, so all we require is permission to pass through your territory."

The border official opened the gates to let them through, and he also sent a hasty message to this effect to the Marquis of Wey. The senior minister, Ning Su, asked permission to welcome the party into the capital.

"When I established my state at Chuqiu," Lord Wen of Wey said, "Jin did nothing to help me. Although the ruling houses of Wey and Jin are members of the same clan, we have never sworn a covenant together. Besides which, these people are exiles—why should we greet them with lavish ritual? If you go out to welcome them, I will have to offer them a banquet and give them appropriate presents, which would be a waste of time and money. It would be better to throw them out of the country." He gave orders that the gatekeepers not allow the Honorable Chonger of Jin into the city, so he had to make a detour to skirt it.

Wei Chou and Dian Jie came forward and said, "This man, Hui of Wey, has been really rude to us. While you are here, you ought to make a formal complaint."

"A powerless dragon is no more than a snake or slow-worm," Zhao Cui told them. "Our master will have to put up with this, for we cannot expect other people to treat him with ceremony."

Wei Chou and Dian Jie complained: "If they fail to fulfill the duties of a host, why don't we rob a few villages to pay for our expenses? They can hardly blame us for that!"

"Such a robbery would make us criminals," said Chonger. "I would rather starve than lower myself to that level."

That day, the Honorable Chonger and his followers ate no breakfast: they simply continued their journey, enduring their hunger. Early that afternoon, they arrived at a place named Wulu, where they caught sight of a number of peasants sitting on the side of a hill, eating their meal. Chonger ordered Hu Yan to beg them for some food.

"Where do you come from?" the peasants asked.

"We come from Jin," Hu Yan explained. "The man on the cart is our leader. We have been on a long journey and run out of food, so please, could you give us something to eat?"

The peasants laughed and said, "What kind of man comes to us and begs for food rather than working for it? We are farmers: we have to eat our fill or we will not have the strength we need for our work. Why should we give any extra food to you?"

"Well, if you cannot give us any food, then please give us something to eat out of," Hu Yan said.

For fun, one of the peasants picked up a lump of earth and handed it to him, saying, "You can make a food bowl out of this."

Wei Chou was furious: "How dare you humiliate us in this way!"

He picked up the peasant's bowl and smashed it on the ground. Chonger was also very angry and was going to give the man a good whipping. Hu Yan rushed in to stop him, saying, "It is easy to find food, but it is difficult to get land. Land is the fundamental basis of the state, and Heaven has borrowed the hands of these peasants to give you your land. This is an omen that you will be returning in glory to Jin, so why are you so angry? You should get down from your chariot, bow, and accept this gift!"

Chonger did indeed do as he said, getting down from his chariot to make his bow. The farmers did not understand what he meant and they laughed heartily about it: "These people are all mad!"

Later on someone wrote a poem, which reads:

Land is the basis of the state;
August Heaven borrowed these hands to console them in adversity.
The intelligent man realizes at once that this is an omen,
The stupid peasant still thinks that this is a joke.

They moved on for another ten *li*, by which time they were all too hungry to proceed any further, and lay down to rest under a tree. Chonger was so exhausted by lack of food that he lay down with his head pillowed on Hu Mao's legs.

"Zhao Cui is carrying our food stores, but he is right at the back," Hu Mao said. "We will just have to wait for him."

"Even though he is carrying our grain, there is not even enough for one person to eat his fill," Wei Chou complained. "I reckon there won't be anything left."

They picked some wild herbs and cooked them up, but Chonger could not swallow them. Suddenly he saw Jie Zitui bringing him a bowl of meat stew. Chonger ate it and thought that it was absolutely delicious. When he had finished, he asked, "Where did you get meat from out here?"

"This is flesh from my thigh," Jie Zitui told him. "I have heard it said that a filial son will kill himself to serve his parents, and a loyal subject will kill himself to benefit his lord. You have not had anything to eat, so I cut flesh from my thigh in order to fill your stomach."

Chonger burst into tears and said, "I have caused you unimaginable pain! How can I ever repay you?"

"I hope that one day soon you will be able to return to the state of Jin," Jie Zitui told him. "That is all I want. What more recompense could I possibly wish for?"

An old man wrote a poem in praise of his actions:

A filial son should keep his body intact;
Any damage to him brings shame upon his family.
Ah! Jie Zitui
Cut his thigh in order to fill his lord's stomach.
Loyal servants are sometimes called "his arms and legs,"
His trusted confidents may be called "his heart."
Even though he remembered his duty to his parents,
The conflicting duties of filial piety and loyalty can be impossible to
reconcile!

If you only care about your own family,
How can you expect ever to enjoy emoluments from your ruler?

After a long, long time, Zhao Cui finally turned up. Everyone asked him what had delayed him, and he explained: "I picked up a couple of thorns in my foot, so I couldn't walk very fast." He took out their remaining rice, packed into a bamboo tube, and presented it to Chonger.

"You must be suffering terribly from hunger," Chonger said. "Why didn't you eat it yourself?"

"Even if I were starving," Zhao Cui replied, "I would not dare to steal food from my lord."

Hu Mao then joked to Wei Chou: "If that rice had fallen to your lot to carry, it would be in your stomach by now." Wei Chou felt so embarrassed that he moved away from the rest. Chonger handed the cooking pot to Zhao Cui, who washed it in the river and cooked their food. Everyone then had something to eat, and Chonger was deeply impressed by how equitably they shared it. For the rest of the journey to Qi, Chonger and his companions had to search for food along the road. Sometimes they got something to eat, other times they found nothing.

Lord Huan of Qi was well aware of the Honorable Chonger's reputation as a clever man, and the moment that he was informed that he had entered his borders, he sent an envoy to meet him at the suburbs, to welcome him to a guesthouse suitable for the reception of members of the aristocracy. He also held a banquet in his honor. On this occasion, he asked, "Have you brought your family with you?"

"I have barely been able to look after myself," Chonger answered, "let alone bring my family with me!"

"For me, an evening alone feels like a year," Lord Huan said. "You, sir, are on your travels and have no one to keep you company. I am most concerned about this."

Accordingly, he selected a beautiful girl from his extended family and presented her to Chonger, together with twenty chariots and teams of horses. That meant that in future all his companions would be able to ride. Lord Huan also ordered his majordomo to ensure that a set allowance of grain and meat be delivered to them every day. Chonger was delighted with this, and he said with a sigh: "I have often heard that the Marquis of Qi enjoys treating people generously—now I believe it! It is only too appropriate that he should have become hegemon!"

This all happened in the eighth year of the reign of King Xiang of Zhou, which was also Lord Huan of Qi's forty-second year in power.

• • •

Lord Huan of Qi, from the time that he entrusted the business of government to Bao Shuya, followed Guan Zhong's dying words to the letter and sent away Shu Diao, Yi Ya, and the Honorable Kaifang of Wey. However, now his food was no longer tasty, he did not sleep well at night, he had nobody to talk to, and he looked very unhappy.

"Since Your Lordship sent Shu Diao and the others away," the senior Lady Ji of Wey said, "the state has not become noticeably better governed, but you have become more depressed by the day. Since your current staff obviously does not suit you, why don't you summon them back again?"

"I miss them terribly," Lord Huan said, "but having dismissed them once, if I were to summon them back to my service, would this not annoy Bao Shuya?"

"And does not Bao Shuya have a staff of his own?" the senior Lady Ji of Wey retorted. "You are an elderly man, my lord, so why should you suffer this distress and inconvenience? Since you have been so badly affected by the change in your diet, why do you not summon Yi Ya back first? The Honorable Kaifang and Shu Diao will then return of their own accord."

Lord Huan followed her advice and summoned Yi Ya back to cook his food, only to meet with remonstrance from Bao Shuya: "Have you forgotten the advice that Guan Zhong gave you on his deathbed, my lord? Why have you brought him back?"

"These three men make my life more comfortable," Lord Huan said, "and they present no danger to the state. Do you not think that Elder Zhong was perhaps being overcautious?" He paid no attention to anything that Bao Shuya had to say, and insisted on summoning the Honorable Kaifang and Shu Diao. The three men returned to work at the same time, in close attendance upon their lord. Bao Shuya was so worried by the whole situation that he fell sick and died. This precipitated a great crisis in the affairs of Qi.

Do you want to know what happened in the end? READ ON.

Chapter Thirty-two

Having climbed over a wall, Yan Er commits suicide.

A host of heirs cause trouble at court.

As has already been explained, Lord Huan of Qi ignored the advice that he had received from Guan Zhong on his deathbed and recalled Shu Diao, Yi Ya, and the Honorable Kaifang of Wey to his service. Bao Shuya remonstrated, but His Lordship paid no attention, after which Bao Shuya became sick and died. These three men were utterly out of control; taking advantage of the fact that Lord Huan was now extremely aged and in poor health, they were able to monopolize power in Qi. Those who went along with them were honored with noble titles and wealth; those who disagreed were either killed or forced into exile. However, for the moment we will have to leave this part of the story here.

. . .

In those days there was a famous doctor from the state of Zheng whose name was Qin Yuan, styled Yueren, who happened to be living in Lu Village in Qi. As a result, he became known as Doctor Lu. As a young man he had owned a little hostel, and at one point Changsang Jun came to stay there. Qin Yuan realized that he was no ordinary man and treated him very generously, refusing to allow him to pay for his board and lodgings. Changsang Jun appreciated this and gave him a miraculous medicinal herb. If you took this herb with dew, your eyes became like mirrors. You could see all sorts of strange things in the darkness, and even look through walls. If the person you were looking at had some kind of illness, even if it was hidden deep in the body, you could see it clearly. It also gave you a supernatural ability to understand the changes in a person's pulse. In ancient times there was a physician named Bian Que, who lived in the time of the Yellow Emperor and knew all about medicinal herbs. When people saw that Doctor Lu was so brilliant, they thought that he could easily rival the abilities of that earlier physician, so he became known by the epithet Bian Que.

Some years earlier, this modern Bian Que had been traveling through the state of Guo when he heard that the scion of that state had suddenly collapsed and died. This Bian Que then went to the palace and announced that he could cure him.

"The scion is dead," the palace eunuch told him. "Can you bring him back to life?"

"I can try," Bian Que said.

The eunuch reported this to the Duke of Guo. His grace had cried until his tears soaked the front of his gown, but now he summoned Bian Que into his presence. Bian Que instructed his disciple Yang Li to use acupuncture on the scion, and a short time later he revived. Afterwards he gave him a medicinal soup, and within two weeks the scion was back to his normal health. After that, everyone said that Bian Que could raise the dead.

Bian Que traveled all over the place, saving the lives of countless people. One day, his travels took him to the city of Linzi, where he had an audience with Lord Huan of Qi. He presented his opinion: "Your Lordship has a disease of the epidermis. If you do not treat it now, it will get much worse."

"I am not sick," Lord Huan told him, and Bian Que left.

Five days later he had a second audience with Lord Huan and presented his opinion: "Your Lordship's illness has now reached your bloodstream. It has to be treated." Lord Huan refused.

Five days later he had a third audience with Lord Huan and presented his opinion: "Your Lordship's illness has now reached your intestines. You must have it treated immediately." Lord Huan still refused.

When Bian Que left, Lord Huan sighed and said, "Really, doctors do like to see disease everywhere! I am not sick, but he insists on saying that I am."

Five days later, Bian Que again demanded an audience. When he caught sight of Lord Huan in the distance, he withdrew. Lord Huan sent someone after him to ask the reason.

"His Lordship's illness is now affecting his bone marrow," Bian Que explained. "When it was his epidermis that was affected, it could have been treated with moxabustion. When it reached his bloodstream, I could have used acupuncture. When it reached his intestines, it could have been cured with herbal cordials. Now that it has reached his bone marrow, there is nothing that even the God of Longevity could do. That is why I left without saying a word."

Five days after that, Lord Huan did indeed fall ill. He sent someone to summon Bian Que, but the people at the guesthouse said, "Master Qin packed up and left a couple of days ago." Lord Huan was extremely upset by this.

. . .

During the course of his long life, Lord Huan of Qi was married to three wives: a princess of the Zhou ruling house, Lady Ji of Xu, and Lady Ji of Cai, none of whom gave birth to a son. The Zhou princess and Lady Ji of Xu both died young, while Lady Ji of Cai was divorced and sent home. He had six junior consorts whom he favored, and who were treated with the same ceremony as if they had indeed been his principal wives. They were spoken of as if they had been marchionesses. Each of these six women had a son: the senior Lady Ji of Wey was the mother of the Honorable Wukui; the junior Lady Ji of Wey was the mother of the Honorable Yuan; Lady Ji of Zheng was the mother of the Honorable Zhao; Lady Ying of Ge was the mother of the Honorable Pan; Lady Ji of Mi was the mother of the Honorable Shangren; and Lady Zi Hua of Song was the mother of the Honorable Yong. Lord Huan of Qi also had numerous sons by concubines or maidservants, but they are not counted here.

Of these six women, the senior Lady Ji of Wey had been married to him the longest. Of his six sons, the Honorable Wukui was the oldest. Lord Huan of Qi's favorite servants, Yi Ya and Shu Diao, were both on excellent terms with the senior Lady Ji of Wey, and they repeatedly suggested to the marquis that he should appoint Wukui as his heir. Later on, Lord Huan came to appreciate how clever the Honorable Zhao was, so after discussion with Guan Zhong, at the meeting at Kuiqiu he instructed Lord Xiang of Song to support Zhao's accession. The Honorable Kaifang of Wey was a close friend of the Honorable Pan and was a mainstay of every plot to make him the heir. The Honorable Shangren was a friendly and generous man, much loved by the people of Qi. Given that his mother, Lady Ji of Mi, was greatly in His Lordship's favor, he naturally came to have his own plans concerning the succession. The Honorable Yong was aware of the fact that he held the lowest status of any of the six, so he was the only person in the palace who was happy with his present lot. His five brothers were all busy building up their own factions and suspecting each other, just like tigers that hide their teeth and claws until some prey comes into view.

Lord Huan had once been a good ruler, but even the finest sword becomes blunt with age. He had now been hegemon for many decades and had satisfied every ambition. Even at the height of his powers he had always had strong appetites for women and wine. Since as a young man he had been incapable of caution and restraint, it was hardly to be expected that in his old age he should suddenly be able to keep a clear head. Besides which, he now had a host of flatterers and toadies working for him, who made sure that he was kept in the dark about what was going on. They ensured that he was kept amused and entertained, and that he was told only what they wanted him to hear. His five oldest sons each sent their mothers to beg that they should be appointed as the scion, and Lord Huan promised all of them that this would be done, but no public announcement was ever made. As the proverb goes: "If you don't plan for the future, you can guarantee that there will be problems in the short term."

Suddenly, Lord Huan of Qi became seriously ill, to the point where he was bedridden. Yi Ya had observed Bian Que's abrupt departure, so he was sure that this illness would be impossible to cure. He then came up with a plan in concert with Shu Diao, in which they hung a message—framed as if it were from Lord Huan—from the gates of the palace. It read:

> I have been struck down by heart disease, and in my current condition I need peace and quiet to recuperate. I do not want any of my family or government officials to come into the palace. The eunuch Shu Diao will now be responsible for guarding the palace gates. Yi Ya can take charge of security within the palace complex. Any matters of state will have to wait until I have recovered.

After Shu Diao and Yi Ya had forged this missive and hung it from the gates of the palace, they allowed the Honorable Wukui to stay, sending him to live in the senior Lady Ji of Wey's palace. When Lord Huan's other sons came to the palace to ask after his health, they were not allowed to see him. Three days later Lord Huan was still alive, so Shu Diao and Yi Ya expelled all of his servants and bodyguards—male and female—from the palace. The gates were then sealed. They ordered that a wall, thirty feet high, should be constructed around Lord Huan's residence, to cut him off completely from the outside world. There was a small hole left in this wall, about the size of a dog flap, and every morning and evening a little eunuch squeezed through to see if Lord Huan had died yet. Meanwhile, they drilled the palace guards to prevent any of his other sons from attempting a coup. This does not need to be described in any detail.

• • •

Lord Huan was lying in bed, unable to raise himself up. He shouted for his servants, but no one responded. He looked around, but there was nothing to see. Then he heard a faint thud, as if someone had fallen down from quite a height. A short time later, whoever it was pushed open a window and came in. Lord Huan opened his eyes wide—it was one of his concubines: Yan Er.

"I am hungry and would like a bowl of porridge," Lord Huan said. "Could you go and get some for me?"

"There is no way that I can get you some porridge," Yan Er told him.

"Well, at least you can bring me some water to quench my thirst," Lord Huan said.

"I am afraid not," she replied.

"Why, what is going on?" His Lordship asked.

"Shu Diao and Yi Ya have taken power," Yan Er explained, "and they have closed the gates of the palace, building a wall thirty feet high around your apartments to prevent you from communicating with anyone outside. How am I supposed to get you any food or drink?"

"How did you get in here then?" Lord Huan asked.

"You favored me once," Yan Er said, "and I am mindful of that grace, so I risked my life to climb over the wall. Having seen Your Lordship, I can rest in peace."

"Where is the Honorable Zhao?" Lord Huan asked.

"He is being kept out of the palace by that horrible pair," Yan Er told him, "and they have stopped him from getting in."

Lord Huan sighed and said, "Elder Zhong was indeed a sage! He could see much further than any ordinary man. My own muddle-headedness has brought me to this pass." He shouted out angrily: "Heaven! Heaven! Is this how I am going to die?" Having repeated this several times, he spat a mouthful of blood. Then he said to Yan Er, "I have six favorite wives and more than a dozen children, but where are they now? You are the only one who has come to see me off. I feel deeply ashamed for not having appreciated you more before this."

"I hope that you will look after yourself, my lord," Yan Er replied. "If you die, then I will die with you."

Lord Huan sighed and said, "If the dead have no awareness, then this is the end. If they do, how will I face Elder Zhong in the Underworld?" He covered his face with his sleeve, breathed deeply a few times, and died. Lord Huan succeeded to the title in the fifth month of the twelfth year of the reign of King Zhuang of Zhou and expired in the tenth month of the ninth year of the reign of King Xiang. He was in power for forty-three years and died at the age of seventy-three.

Master Qian Yuan wrote a poem praising Lord Huan of Qi's good qualities:

After the Zhou capital moved to the east, rules and regulations slackened.
He directed the lords to show their respect to the king.
He campaigned to the south so that arrogant Chu presented tribute of sweet herbs;
He fought against the vicious Rong on the edge of the Gobi Desert.
He preserved the states of Wey and Xing with benevolence and magnanimity;
He laid down clear prohibitions, and his reputation for justice was known to all.
To his uprightness the *Spring and Autumn Annals* can attest,
He was the best of the Five Hegemons.

An old man wrote a poem bewailing the fact that Lord Huan of Qi's glorious rule ended in such a debacle. This poem reads:

For more than forty years he was a hegemon,
Without equal anywhere in the world.
But bedridden, he allowed Shu Diao and Yi Ya to take control,
And there was nothing that the Elder Zhong could have done about it.

When Yan Er saw that Lord Huan had passed away, she wept bitterly for a time. Then she thought that she would like to call to the people outside, but she could not make herself heard beyond the high wall. She tried to climb over it, but there was nowhere to get a foothold. She considered the matter for a while, then sighed and said, "I have already stated that I would die for my lord. After all, women are often killed as sacrificial victims at funerals." She took off her gown and laid it on top of Lord Huan's body before manhandling two of the shutters off the window frames, because she wanted to cover his corpse completely. She then kowtowed at the foot of the bed: "Your soul cannot have gone far, my lord. Please wait for mine to catch up with you!" She dashed her head against a pillar, killing herself by cracking her skull.

What a virtuous woman!

Later on, someone wrote a poem about Yan Er's virtues, which runs:

Favored concubines usually act out of selfish motives;
The only one who accompanied her lord in death was Yan Er.
When planting flowers, a moment's incaution will ensure no blooms;
When picking willows, inattention means you miss the willow-floss.

That night, the little eunuch entered through the hole in the wall, only to find a body covered in blood at the foot of one of the pillars in Lord Huan's bedroom. He ran out in a panic and reported to Yi Ya and Shu Diao: "His Lordship has committed suicide by dashing his brains out on a pillar!"

Yi Ya and Shu Diao did not quite believe this, so they ordered some of the palace servants to break through the wall. The pair then entered to see for themselves, only to discover that the body was that of a woman, which surprised them greatly. One of the eunuchs recognized her and said, "This is Yan Er." Looking around, they noticed that a pair of shutters that had previously been covering the windows was now on top of the bed, and beneath the shutters was the inanimate body of Lord Huan of Qi. Alas! No one knew exactly when he had died.

Shu Diao wanted to discuss how they would conduct the funeral. "Slow down! Slow down!" Yi Ya told him. "We must first see that the Honorable Wukui succeeds to his father's title, and then hold the funeral. That way we can avoid any dissension."

Shu Diao thought that this was a very good idea. The two of them went together to the palace occupied by the senior Lady Ji of Wey, where they made a secret report: "His Lordship has already passed away. The succession should now proceed to his oldest child: that is your son. However, during His Late Lordship's own lifetime, he instructed the Duke of Song to install the Honorable Zhao as the next ruler and formally appointed him as scion. All the ministers know this. When Lord Huan of Qi's death is formally announced, they will certainly support the scion's accession. In our opinion, your best option is to take advantage of this one night's grace to send your guards to murder the Honorable Zhao, followed by a quick ceremony installing your son in power. In that way you can present everyone with a fait accompli."

"I am just a weak woman!" the senior Lady Ji of Wey told them. "I will have to leave everything to you!"

Shu Diao and Yi Ya then spearheaded the attack on the East Palace, each in command of several hundred guards, with the intention of taking the scion prisoner.

Scion Zhao was extremely upset that he was excluded from the palace and had no news about the state of his father's illness. That night he was sitting alone next to a lamp, caught up in a reverie. He did not think that he was dreaming, but he must have been, because a woman appeared to him and said, "If you do not leave now, they will kill you. My name is Yan Er. His Late Lordship ordered me to come and warn you." Scion Zhao wanted to kowtow to her, but she pushed him away. He felt as though he was falling into a vast gulf, and this woke him up with a start. The woman had disappeared.

Such a strange omen could not be ignored. He immediately ordered his servants to bring lanterns to light the way. Opening a side door, he went on foot to the nearby home of the senior minister, Gao Hu, and knocked urgently on the door. Gao Hu opened it and asked why he had come. Scion Zhao told him what had happened.

"His Lordship has been sick for two weeks," Gao Hu said, "during which time those wicked men have cut off all communication with the outside. Your dream is extremely inauspicious. Your father was referred to as 'His Late Lordship,' which suggests that he must already have died. In the circumstances it would be best to treat your dream seriously, as it would be very dangerous to ignore it. You will have to go into exile abroad before they kill you."

"Where should I go?" Scion Zhao asked.

"His Lordship entrusted you to the care of the Duke of Song," Gao Hu replied, "so now you had better go there, for his grace is sure to help you. I have always served in domestic posts, so I cannot go with you. However, I have a client named Cui Yao who is responsible for keeping the keys of the East Gate to the capital. I will send someone to tell him to open the gates so that you can leave the city tonight."

Before he had finished speaking, his porter came in to report: "Guards have surrounded the East Palace." At this news the blood drained from the scion's face, leaving it a sickly grey. Gao Hu instructed Scion Zhao to change his clothes, so that he would look like an ordinary member of his household. He instructed his most trusted servants to escort the scion to the East Gate, with a message for Cui Yao to unlock it and allow him to leave.

"His Lordship's death has not yet been formally announced," Cui Yao said. "In opening the gates for the scion, I am committing a crime for which I will be severely punished. You have no servants with you, sir, so if you have no objection, I will accompany you to Song."

"I would love to have you come with me," the scion said happily.

He opened up the gate and they walked out of the city walls. Cui Yao saw that he had brought a chariot with him, which he now assisted the scion to climb into, while he himself took the reins. They traveled as quickly as they could in the direction of Song.

. . .

Now to go back to a different part of the story. Yi Ya and Shu Diao led the guards to surround the East Palace and search every nook and cranny, but they could discover no trace of Scion Zhao. When the drums sounded the fourth watch, Yi Ya said: "In surrounding the East Palace, we were trying to catch him off guard. If we are still hanging around here when it gets light, Lord Huan of Qi's other sons will find out what is going on. Should one of them be the first to get to court, we will really have messed things up. We had better go back to the palace now and prepare for the ceremony installing the Honorable Wukui. When we have seen how people react to this, we can decide what to do next."

"You have taken the words right out of my mouth," Shu Diao said.

The two men then gathered their troops. However, before they reached the palace, they saw that the doors to the main hall of audience were open wide and a mass of officials had gathered there—a host of hereditary ministers from the Gao, Guo, Guan, Bao, Chen, Xi, Nanguo, Beiguo, and Lüqiu families—more than I can possibly name. When these officials heard that Yi Ya and Shu Diao had taken a large number of guards out of the palace, they realized that something important must have happened, and so they had rushed around to the court to find out what was going on. News had already leaked out from the palace that Lord Huan of Qi was dead. Then they heard that the East Palace had been surrounded and they instantly proclaimed that wicked men were taking advantage of this opportunity to launch a coup.

"The scion was chosen by His Late Lordship. If anything were to happen to him, how could we call ourselves subjects of the Marquis of Qi?" The one theme running through this hubbub was asking what could be done to save the scion. It was just at that moment that Yi Ya and Shu Diao came back with their troops, and the officials advanced en masse, shouting and screaming: "Where is the scion?"

Yi Ya raised his hands and said, "Scion Wukui is safe and sound in the palace."

"Wukui was never formally invested as scion," the ministers shouted, "so he cannot become our ruler. We want Scion Zhao!"

Shu Diao drew his sword and screamed: "Zhao has already fled! According to His Late Lordship's deathbed instructions, we will install the Honorable Wukui as the next ruler of Qi. Anyone who does not agree to this will die by my sword!"

The anger of these officials could not be contained, and they yelled and cursed: "It is all your fault that His Lordship is dead—you murdered him! Now you are trying to monopolize power here and dispossess the rightful heir. If you establish the Honorable Wukui, we swear that we will never condone it!"

Grandee Guan Ping stepped out from the crowd and said, "Let us begin by beating that pair of murderous swine to death, for that way we will get at the root of this disaster. Then we can discuss what we are going to do next."

He began hitting Shu Diao about the head with his ivory staff of office, and Shu Diao raised his sword to ward off the blows. Other officials began to crowd around him, wanting to join in.

"Guards, kill them!" Yi Ya screamed. "Why do you think I have been paying your wages all these years?"

There were several hundred armed guards present, and they now attacked the officials at will with their weapons, hacking them to pieces. The officials were not armed, nor were there enough of them to withstand this onslaught. How could they defend themselves? As the proverb says: "When fighting breaks out on the white marble steps of the palace, it is Yama, King of Hell, who presides over the court." About one third of the ministers present died at the hands of these murderous soldiers, and most of the remainder were injured. They fled the palace any way that they could.

By the time that Yi Ya and Shu Diao had killed or put to flight the assembled ministers, the sun was already high in the sky. They then brought the Honorable Wukui out of the palace and held a ceremony of accession in the main hall of audience. Eunuchs sounded the bells and beat the drums, while armed soldiers stood on guard in two long lines. However, instead of an enthusiastic crowd acclaiming his accession, only Yi Ya and Shu Diao stood below the palace steps. The Honorable Wukui felt angry and humiliated.

Yi Ya respectfully informed him: "No formal announcement has yet been made of His Late Lordship's death. Since his ministers did not even know that they should have come to court to offer condolences, how can you expect them to know that they should be acclaiming your accession? You must summon the heads of the Guo and Gao families to court, for then you can use their name when assembling all your more junior officials. Their reputation can be used to put pressure on the others."

Wukui agreed to this and ordered his servants to go and collect Guo Yizhong and Gao Hu. These two men held hereditary senior ministerial appointments conferred by the Zhou Son of Heaven, and they were much respected by all the other officials. That is the reason why they were selected for this summons. When Guo Yizhong and Gao Hu heard the command brought to them by the palace eunuchs, they knew that the Marquis of Qi had passed away, and so they dressed themselves in hemp mourning robes rather than wearing court dress. They went to palace to take charge of the funeral.

Yi Ya and Shu Diao met them at the gates to the palace. "The new marquis has already been installed," they said. "You should go and congratulate him."

Guo Yizhong and Gao Hu were both appalled. "To proclaim the new ruler before the old ruler has even been buried is not ritually correct. We have no right to appoint anyone who was not approved by His Late Lordship. There is only one person who has the right to preside over the funeral, and we support him." There was nothing that Yi Ya and Shu Diao could say to this.

Guo Yizhong and Gao Hu took their places outside the gate, looking out into the distance. They bowed twice, in tears, before walking away.

"We can't hold a funeral," Wukui complained, "and none of the ministers are prepared to obey me. What do we do now?"

"This is just like fighting a tiger," Shu Diao told him, "the strongest will win. You must occupy the main chamber in the palace while we patrol the perimeter. We will wait and see if any of your brothers come to court and if they do, we will arrest them."

Wukui followed their advice. The senior Lady Ji of Wey sent all her own guards to join them and made all her eunuchs put on armor, as well as all the more powerfully built palace maids, to swell the number of soldiers. Yi Ya and Shu Diao took command. Each patrolled one half of the outer palace complex. There is no need to say more about this.

. . .

When the Honorable Kaifang of Wey heard that Yi Ya and Shu Diao had installed Wukui, he discussed the situation with Lady Ying of Ge's son, the Honorable Pan. "No one knows where Scion Zhao has gone. If Wukui can launch a coup, then so can we!"

He gathered together all his servants and his own private army, making camp in the Right Hall. The Honorable Shangren, the son of Lady Ji of Mi, also discussed what had happened with the Honorable Yuan, son of the junior Lady Ji of Wey. "We are both His Late Lordship's sons, and we have an equal right to succeed to his title. The Honorable Pan has already occupied the Right Hall at the palace, so we should occupy the Left Hall. If Scion Zhao comes back, then we can yield our claims in his favor. If he does not come back, then the state of Qi should be divided into four."

The Honorable Yuan thought that this was a very good idea. They all had not only their own guards, but also their own private armies, who now assembled. The Honorable Yuan camped in the Left Hall, while the Honorable Shangren made camp for his followers at the main gate to the palace, having agreed that they would help each other out if there was any trouble. Yi Ya and Shu Diao were afraid of the forces at these men's control, so they occupied the main hall but did not dare to come out and fight. The others were equally frightened of the forces under the control of Yi Ya and Shu Diao, so they made sure that their men stayed inside the camps, to prevent conflict. Indeed, the court became enemy territory and there were no passersby on the streets.

There is a poem that testifies to this:

Tigers and leopards fight in the phoenix belvedere and the dragon hall,
Arms and armor are everywhere to be seen on the palace marble steps.
Here four wild beasts fight to the death over a scrap of meat;
Which will make the decision to surrender and survive?

At this time, only the Honorable Yong was afraid of becoming involved in a civil war, so he fled into exile in the state of Qin. Lord Mu of Qin appointed him to the office of a grandee. Now let us to return to the main story.

When the officials discovered that the scion had gone into exile, they refused to go to court and simply stayed at home. The loyal old ministers, Guo Yizhong and Gao Hu, felt as if they were pegged out on a bed of nails. They racked their brains for a solution but could not come up with a viable plan. This impasse endured for more than two months.

"These young men are only thinking about fighting over the marquisate," Gao Hu complained. "No one seems to have considered the fact that His Late Lordship is still unburied. Today I will reason with them, even if it kills me."

"If you talk to them first, I will second you," Guo Yizhong said. "Even if they murder both of us, at least we will have done something to justify our hereditary titles and emoluments."

"If it is only the two of us who speak out," Gao Hu reminded him, "no one will pay any attention to us. Anyone who took a salary from the government should count as an official in His Late Lordship's regime. If we were to collect as many of these people as we can and go to court together, perhaps we can persuade the Honorable Wukui that he ought to bury his father?"

"By law the title should go to the eldest son," Guo Yizhong remarked, "so there is a precedent for accepting the Honorable Wukui as our new ruler."

Thus they made the rounds throughout every corner of the capital, gathering up officials from the old regime, with the express intention of demanding Lord Huan of Qi's burial. When the officials saw that these two old gentlemen were prepared to take charge, they pulled themselves together. They went to court in a huge delegation, all dressed in mourning clothes. The eunuch Shu Diao tried to prevent this, questioning them as to their purpose: "Why have you come here?"

"The situation seems to have reached a stalemate with no end in sight," Gao Hu answered. "We have come here specially to request that the Honorable Wukui presides over his father's funeral and for no other reason." Shu Diao then allowed Gao Hu into the palace.

Gao Hu waved his hand and Guo Yizhong and the other officials all filed in after him, walking towards the main hall. They told Wukui: "We have heard it said that the generosity shown to you by your parents is as great as Heaven and Earth. As a child, you should show respect to your parents when they are alive, and bury them properly when they are dead. It is completely unacceptable that you should be fighting for wealth and power while your deceased father lies unburied. A ruler should be a model for his people; if you are not filial, how can you expect us to be loyal? His Late Lordship died sixty-seven days ago and his body has still not been put in its coffin. How can you rest easy on your throne?"

When they had finished speaking, the officials all prostrated themselves on the ground and wept bitterly. Wukui also shed tears: "I have been unfilial. This is a terrible crime. I would be perfectly happy to hold a funeral for my father, but I do not want to appear to have been forced into it by my brothers."

"The scion has gone into exile abroad," Guo Yizhong reminded him. "You are the oldest son. If you can preside over the funeral and see that

His Late Lordship is respectably interred, you will indubitably become the next Marquis of Qi. Even though the Honorable Yuan and his cohort have occupied the side wings of the palace and the main gate, we can deal with them. Who would dare to quarrel with you?"

Wukui wiped his tears and got down to bow to them. "That is what I would like to do."

Gao Hu ordered Yi Ya to take control over all parts of the palace. If any of Lord Huan's sons arrived to take part in the funeral wearing appropriate hemp garments, they would be allowed into the palace. If they turned up with armed men, they should be arrested and punished. Shu Diao was sent to Lord Huan's private apartments to prepare the body for burial.

Lord Huan's corpse was lying on the bed all this time, with no one to take care of it. Even though it was the depths of winter, the body started to decay and a whole host of maggots came out of it, crawling out past the walls. To begin with no one knew where these creatures came from, but when they entered the bedchamber and opened the shutters covering the windows, they discovered that the body had pretty much been reduced to a skeleton—a deeply shocking sight! Wukui started screaming, and the ministers present broke down in tears. They immediately brought the coffin in and tried to put the body into it. However, the corpse was so badly decayed that it could only be bundled up in a robe and belt in a very perfunctory manner. Yan Er, on the other hand, looked just as she had when she was alive, and her body appeared totally incorrupt. Gao Hu and the other men present knew that she had martyred herself out of loyalty, and they all sighed with admiration. Orders were given that she too should be encoffined. The ministers then assisted Wukui with performing the necessary rituals as he presided over the funeral, and all the mourners wept and wailed in turn. That night they stayed beside the coffin of Lord Huan.

At this time the Honorable Yuan, Pan, and Shangren were all holed up in their own encampments. They saw the senior ministers Guo Yizhong and Gao Hu lead the other officials into the palace, dressed in mourning, but they had no idea what was going on. Later on they heard that Lord Huan had been buried and that the officials had allowed Wukui to take charge of the funeral, thus accepting him as their new ruler. They then sent messages to each other, as follows: "Guo Yizhong and Gao Hu have taken charge. We cannot carry on fighting."

They dismissed their forces, put on mourning clothes, and hurried to the palace to take part in the funeral. When the brothers caught sight of each other, they burst into tears. If it had not been for Guo Yizhong and Gao Hu persuading Wukui to do the right thing, who knows what would have happened!

Master Hu Zeng wrote a poem bewailing these events:

Having ignored your loyal advisors and favored flatterers,
Who can be surprised that your sons fought over the succession?
If it had not been for Guo Yizhong and Gao Hu's sensible agreement,
Your bones would have stayed on the bed and never been buried!

Scion Zhao of Qi fled to the state of Song, where he had an audience with Lord Xiang of Song. He bowed down to the ground and wept as he described the chaos unleashed by Yi Ya and Shu Diao. Lord Xiang of Song then summoned his ministers to discuss the situation: "Ten years ago, Lord Huan of Qi entrusted the Honorable Zhao to my care at the same time as he appointed him as scion. I have kept this matter secret, but I have never forgotten it. Today, Yi Ya and Shu Diao have launched a coup in Qi and the scion has been forced into exile. I wish to bring the feudal lords together for an interstate meeting that will punish the criminals now in power in Qi and install the rightful ruler, Zhao. All I want to do is to see him settled in his proper place. If I succeed in this, I will become famous among the lords, and in the future it will be much easier for me to convene meetings and covenants. It is my intention to take over as hegemon now that Lord Huan is gone. What do you think?"

Suddenly, a man stepped forward and presented his opinion: "There are three ways in which we do not match up to Qi, so how can you become the new hegemon?"

Lord Xiang looked at him; the speaker was the Honorable Muyi, styled Ziyu, his oldest half-brother born to a concubine mother. The Honorable Muyi had refused to take the title of Duke of Song when their father died, and Lord Xiang had rewarded him for standing aside by appointing him as a senior minister.

"When you say that there are three ways in which we do not match up to Qi, my brother, what do you mean?" Lord Xiang inquired.

"Qi is guarded by Mount Tai and the Bohai Sea, and it has extensive areas of good farmland at Langya and Jimo," the Honorable Muyi explained. "We have only a small area of territory, a tiny army, and few natural resources. That is the first way in which we do not match up to Qi. They have the great hereditary ministerial houses of Gao and Guo, which form the backbone of the administration, in addition to which they have people of the caliber of Guan Zhong, Ning Qi, Xi Peng, Bao

Shuya, and so on. We have no civil or military figures that come even close to rivaling their abilities. That is the second way in which we are inferior to Qi. When Lord Huan went north to campaign against the Mountain Rong he was directed by the Yuer, while when he went hunting outside the suburbs the Weituo appeared to him. In our case, in the first month this year five stars fell to earth and were transformed into stones, while in the second month there was an unusual wind and six crows flew backwards. These are omens of surrender and regression. That is the third way in which we cannot equal Qi. Given these facts, it is as much as we can do to look after ourselves. How can we possibly be expected to look after someone else?"

"I have always tried to live my life according to the principles of justice and benevolence," Lord Xiang proclaimed. "If I do not save this wretched man, I will not be benevolent. If I abandon someone who has been given into my care, I will not be just." He then circulated a message about installing Scion Zhao in power among the other aristocrats, and they agreed that they would meet at the suburbs of the Qi capital in the first month of the following year.

When this message reached the state of Wey, Grandee Ning Su of Wey came forward and said: "If you have a son by your principal wife, then he should be appointed your heir. If you do not, then you should pick your oldest son. That is perfectly normal. The Honorable Wukui is the oldest son, and he has treated us with great generosity in arranging for us to have a garrison here. I hope that you will pay no attention to this."

"Everyone in the world knows that the Honorable Zhao was appointed as the scion," Lord Wen of Wey told him. "Giving us the garrison was a private benefit; installing the scion is a public duty. I cannot ignore the cause of public good for purely selfish reasons."

When the message arrived in the state of Lu, Lord Xi said, "The Marquis of Qi entrusted the Honorable Zhao to Song and not to me. Personally, I go by the principle that the oldest son should succeed to his father's honors. If Song attacks Wukui, they will do so over my dead body."

. . .

In the third month of the tenth year of the reign of King Xiang of Zhou, which was also the first year in power of the Honorable Wukui of Qi, Lord Xiang of Song took personal control over an allied force consisting of the armies of the states of Wey, Cao, and Zhu, and attacked Qi in support of the claims of Scion Zhao. The soldiers made camp in the suburbs of the capital. Yi Ya had by this time been promoted to a mid-level grandee and had also become the marshal in command of the Qi army. Wukui sent his forces out of the city to meet the enemy, while the eunuch Shu Diao coordinated information at headquarters. The two ministers, Guo Yizhong and Gao Hu, took responsibility for defending the city walls.

"We installed Wukui in power purely because His Late Lordship was lying unburied," Gao Hu said to Guo Yizong, "not because we supported his candidature. Now the scion has arrived with support from Song. His legal position is unassailable; his strength is more than we can possibly match. Yi Ya and Shu Diao have murdered many officials and illegally seized power: this is certain to bring disaster down upon Qi. We should take this opportunity to get rid of this precious pair, welcome the scion back, and support his claim to become the new ruler, for that will prevent any of his brothers from plotting further coups and ensure that the state of Qi is as secure at Mount Tai."

"Yi Ya has already taken the army out to station them in the suburbs," Guo Yizhong said. "I will summon Shu Diao under the pretext of discussing the situation with him, then I will kill him. Once we have led the officials out to welcome the scion and he has taken the Honorable Wukui's place, there will be nothing that Yi Ya can do about it."

"That is a wonderful plan!" Gao Hu exclaimed.

He arranged for a number of knights to set an ambush at one of the towers on the walls. Having announced that he had something of great importance and secrecy to discuss, he sent someone to summon Shu Diao for a meeting. As the saying goes: "Having set a good trap, you can capture a tiger; having arranged delicious bait, you can hook a leviathan."

If you don't know whether Shu Diao fell for this or not, READ ON.

Chapter Thirty-three

The Duke of Song attacks Qi and installs the Honorable Zhao.

The people of Chu set an ambush in which the Master of Covenants is captured.

As mentioned above, Gao Hu took advantage of the fact that Yi Ya had taken the army out of the city to set a number of knights in ambush at one of the towers on the city wall. Then he sent someone to summon Shu Diao to discuss the situation. Shu Diao arrived at once, completely unsuspicious. Gao Hu had arranged that wine should be served in the tower. After they had drunk three cups, he opened the discussion: "The Duke of Song has united the feudal lords to raise a large army to install the scion by force. How are we going to defend the capital?"

"Yi Ya has already taken the army out of the city to intercept the enemy," Shu Diao told him.

"A tiny force cannot withstand the onslaught of a massive army!" Gao Hu said. "We need you to save Qi from disaster."

"What can I do?" Shu Diao asked. "If you have any ideas, I would be happy to listen to them."

"I need your head," Gao Hu exclaimed, "for then we can make our apologies to Song!"

Shu Diao got up in alarm. Gao Hu glanced back at his entourage and shouted: "What are you waiting for? Get him!"

The knights came bursting out from their places of concealment and seized Shu Diao to behead him. Gao Hu then ordered that the gates should be flung open and sent people to circulate around the city, calling out: "The scion is outside the walls. Anyone who wants to go and welcome him, come with me!" The residents of the capital loathed Yi

Ya and Shu Diao, which is why they had never given their allegiance to Wukui. When they heard that Gao Hu was heading out to welcome the scion, they all waved their hands and shouted for joy. Nearly one thousand people followed him out of the city.

Meanwhile, Guo Yizhong went to court and knocked on the palace gates. When he had an audience with the Honorable Wukui, he presented his opinion: "The people support the scion and have gone to welcome him; there is nothing I could do to prevent it. You had better prepare your plans for going into exile at the earliest possible moment."

"Where are Yi Ya and Shu Diao?" Wukui asked.

"I do not know what has happened to Yi Ya," Guo Yizhong told him. "However, Shu Diao has been killed by the people of the capital."

Wukui was very angry and said, "If the people of the capital have murdered Shu Diao, how could you not know all about it?" He gestured to his entourage to arrest Guo Yizhong, but he managed to slip out of the palace.

Wukui got into a small chariot and drove out to do battle with a drawn sword in his hand, accompanied by a couple of dozen servants. He gave orders that young men should be encouraged to enlist in the army, to defend the city against the enemy. Although the palace eunuchs shrieked this message from one end of the city to the other, no one was prepared to sign up. In fact, it simply attracted the malevolent attention of his enemies.

You could say:

Virtue and benevolence are always requited in the end,
Vengeance and enmity create an endless cycle of violence.
Having once acted in concert,
You will rise and fall together.

These enemies were the ministerial families of Gao, Guo, Guan, Bao, Ning, Chen, Yan, Dongguo, Nanguo, Beiguo, Gongsun and Lüqiu. Since it was members of these families who had refused to submit to the Honorable Wukui's authority, they had been massacred by Yi Ya and Shu Diao; the survivors hated them more than they could say. Now they heard that the ruler of Song had escorted the scion back to his country and that Yi Ya had gone out to do battle. On the one hand, for their own private reasons, they wished to see Yi Ya's army defeated; on the other hand, they had no wish to see the capital put to the sword when the Song army arrived. No one was sure what to do. When they heard that the venerable Gao Hu had killed Shu Diao and set out to welcome the scion back to the city, they were all delighted and cried, "Today Heaven has finally opened its eyes!" Having taken the precaution of arming themselves, they rushed to the East Gate to discover if there was any news of the scion's arrival, only to bump straight into the Honorable Wukui's chariot. When they spotted him, their eyes became fixed upon him; one man having drawn his sword, the rest followed suit. They surrounded Wukui, their weapons in their hands.

"This is your lord!" his servants shouted. "How can you behave like this?"

"He is nothing of the kind!" they screamed.

They began to attack the servants, and the Honorable Wukui found that he could not withstand the assault. He abandoned his chariot and tried to escape on foot, only to be cut to pieces by the mob. The area around the East Gate was in tumult, but fortunately Guo Yizhong came and calmed the situation. The crowds then dispersed. Guo Yizhong arranged for the collection of Wukui's body and had it buried at an official guesthouse. At the same time, he sent a messenger to report this news to Gao Hu as soon as possible.

Yi Ya camped his army at the East Pass, where he was holding the Song army in a stalemate. Suddenly, in the middle of the night, the army mutinied. They proclaimed: "Wukui and Shu Diao are both dead. The venerable Gao Hu has led the people of the capital to greet Scion Zhao and install him as the new ruler. We are not prepared to help you anymore in your treasonous activities."

Yi Ya realized that the army no longer supported him, which felt like a knife through the heart. He immediately sent several trusted servants to travel under cover of darkness to the state of Lu, to ask for help. By dawn, Gao Hu had arrived to pacify the rebellious soldiers under Yi Ya's command. Then he went directly to the suburbs of the capital to meet Scion Zhao and conclude a peace treaty with the states of Song, Cao, Wey, and Zhu. These four armies then turned back home. Gao Hu escorted Scion Zhao to a guesthouse outside the city walls of Linzi and arranged for someone to take a message to Guo Yizhong that he should prepare a state coach and join them at the head of a delegation of officials.

When the Honorables Yuan and Pan heard what had happened, they met with the Honorable Shangren to discuss their next move, suggesting that they should all go out of the city walls to greet their new ruler. The Honorable Shangren looked mulish and said, "We were there when our father was being buried, but Zhao was nowhere to be seen! Now he is threatening us with Song's army, which is basically stealing the state of Qi by forcing all his older brothers to give up their rightful claims to the title. This is completely illegal. Furthermore, according to my information, the armies of the feudal lords have already left. We ought to take our own soldiers out and kill Scion Zhao in the name of taking revenge for Wukui. We can then ask the ministers to pick one of us to become the next marquis, thereby avoiding a situation where Song has us in shackles and we lose everything that our father gained when he was hegemon."

"If we were to do that," the Honorable Yuan replied, "we would require an official order from the palace, to ensure the legality of our actions."

He went into the palace to inform the senior Lady Ji of Wey of their plan. The senior Lady Ji of Wey wept and said, "I would sacrifice my own life to avenge the death of Wukui."

She immediately summoned all of Wukui's servants and old cronies to join forces with her three stepsons, so as to prevent the accession of the scion. Shu Diao had many clients who wanted revenge for the death of their master, and they too came to help. They were divided into groups and sent to guard the gates of the city of Linzi. Guo Yizhong was frightened of the forces under these men's command, so he sealed the gates to his official residence and did not dare to show his face abroad.

Gao Hu said to Scion Zhao: "Although Wukui and Shu Diao are dead, their supporters are still alive and well. Your half-brothers are in control of the city, and they have closed the gates so that we cannot get in. If we were to try and force them to open the gates, this would spark a civil war. If you were to fight and lose, you would also lose everything that you have gained up to this point. You had better go back to the state of Song and ask them for help."

"Whatever you say," Scion Zhao agreed.

Gao Hu then assisted Scion Zhao to go into exile in Song for the second time.

. . .

Lord Xiang of Song had only just arrived at the border himself when Scion Zhao caught up with him. He was most surprised at this development and asked him what he was doing. Gao Hu explained exactly what had happened.

"This has come about because I stood down my army too soon," Lord Xiang said. "There is nothing to worry about. As long as I am here, I will get you into Linzi by hook or by crook!"

He immediately ordered General Gongsun Gu to hold another muster of chariots.

In the first campaign he had been assisted by the three states of Wey, Cao, and Zhu, so he had only contributed two hundred chariots to the allied army. This time, however, he would be alone, so he wanted to muster a further four hundred chariots.

The Honorable Dang took command of the vanguard, while Hua Yushi took control of the rearguard. The Duke of Song himself commanded the central army. He escorted the scion back out of the borders of Song into the outskirts of Qi. Gao Hu had traveled on ahead to use his prestige as a former senior minister to make the border officials open the passes. Thus, one gate after another opened until they were making camp at the foot of the city walls of Linzi.

When Lord Xiang of Song saw that the gates to the capital were sealed, he ordered his three armies to prepare for a full-scale assault on the city. The Honorable Shangren then said to his half-brothers Yuan and Pan: "If Song actually attacks the city, that will leave us vulnerable to uprisings by our own people. We should make a concerted attack on the Song army before they have had time to get settled into a siege. If we are victorious, then everything will be fine; if we are so unlucky as to be defeated, then we can each head off into exile to make our own plans for the future. That would be better than insisting upon trying to hold the city, for what would we do if another coalition force were to arrive here?"

The Honorable Yuan and Pan thought that he was absolutely correct. That very night, they ordered that the gates should be opened, and they led their forces out to attack the Song encampment. Since they did not know what they were doing, they only succeeded in plundering the camp made by the Honorable Dang, who was in command of the vanguard. Since the Honorable Dang was taken by surprise, he had to abandon his encampment and flee. When General Gongsun Gu of the Central Army heard that the advance camp was under attack, he immediately sent his forces out to rescue it. Hua Yushi from the rearguard, together with the Grandee of Qi, Gao Hu, also led their forces in to assist, and the two sides fought a series of skirmishing battles right up until morning. Yet throughout, they had no idea whether they were winning or losing. As the poem says:

Marching through the forest with swords and lances—here come great warriors,
Moving through thickets with sabers and spears—a parade of heroes.
No battle can ever end in a draw,
The outcome will soon determine victory and defeat.

Although there were a great many more soldiers on the Qi side, they were all answerable to their own leaders and had no understanding of how to cooperate with each other, as a result of which it was impossible for them to withstand the onslaughts of the Song army. Having fought throughout the night, the Qi forces had been cut to pieces by the Song troops. The Honorable Yuan was afraid that Scion Zhao would be able to get into the city, in which case his situation would indeed be parlous. He took advantage of the chaotic situation to run away into exile in the state of Wey, accompanied by a couple of his most trusted servants. The Honorable Pan and Shangren gathered together the tattered remnants of their army and made their way back to the city, with the Song soldiers in hot pursuit. There was no time for them to shut the gates, so Cui Yao drove Scion Zhao straight into the city. When the senior minister Guo Yizhong heard that the armies of the Honorable Yuan, Pan, and Shangren had been defeated and that the scion was actually already inside the capital, he gathered together all the officials and they installed scion Zhao in power. He declared this to be the first year of his rule and took the name Lord Xiao. Once Lord Xiao had formally assumed the marquisate, he rewarded his supporters, promoting Cui Yao to the position of grandee. He also gave vast quantities of silk and gold to reward the Song army. Lord Xiang stayed for five days in Qi, then went home to Song. Lord Xi of Lu had raised a huge army to rescue Wukui, but when he heard that Lord Xiao had already succeeded to the title, he simply turned them around and went home. These events created a serious rift between the states of Qi and Lu.

The Honorables Pan and Shangren discussed the situation and decided to put all the blame for sending out the army to intercept the enemy on the Honorable Yuan. The venerable old ministers Guo Yizhong and Gao Hu knew that four of the scion's half-brothers had been involved in conspiring against him, but they wanted Lord Xiao to prevent the situation from becoming any worse. Therefore, they placed the blame entirely on Yi Ya and Shu Diao and executed every member of their faction. Everyone else involved was pardoned, with no questions asked about exactly what they had done. In the eighth month, a great triple-mound tomb was built for Lord Huan at Mount Niu. Yan Er was buried beside him, so a further small mound was erected above her grave. In order to warn off the Honorable Wukui and Yuan's mothers, all of the senior and junior Lady Ji of Wey's eunuchs and maidservants were killed and buried with Lord Huan, a total of several hundred people.

At the end of the Yongjia reign era of the Jin dynasty, the empire collapsed into civil war and local people broke open the tomb of Lord Huan of Qi. There was a lake of mercury inside the tomb, which gave off cold vapors that assaulted the nose, so no one dared to go in. A few days later the vapor had dispersed, so they went into the tomb with their dogs. They discovered several dozen bushels of gold cicadas, a pearl-encrusted shroud and a jade suit, as well as more weapons than could possibly be counted. The tomb was also stuffed with skeletons, the bodies of the sacrificial victims. You can imagine from that how lavish the funeral that Lord Xiao arranged for his father was! But what was the good of it all?

A bearded old man wrote a poem:

Above the tomb are three mounds as large as mountains;
Gold cicadas and a jade suit are there hidden away.
Lavish funerals have always attracted the attention of grave-robbers;
There is nothing wrong with being buried modestly.

• • •

Let us now turn to another part of the story. After Lord Xiang of Song had defeated the Qi army and installed Scion Zhao as the new ruler, he believed that he was the most important man in the world and started to think that he should call all the other feudal lords together so that he could take over Lord Huan of Qi's role as the Master of Covenants. However, he was afraid that the rulers of the greatest states of the Zhou confederacy would not come, so he only invited such small states as Teng, Cao, Zhu, and Zeng, and a covenant was sworn south of the capital city of Cao. It was only after the rulers of Cao and Zhu had arrived that Yingqi, Viscount of Teng, finally appeared. Lord Xiang of Song did not allow him to attend the blood covenant and went so far as to imprison him. The ruler of Zeng was afraid of Song's military might and hurried to this meeting, but even so he arrived two days late. Lord Xiang of Song summoned his ministers and asked them about this situation: "I have just recently summoned my allies. Zeng is a tiny state, but they have still felt free to humiliate me by arriving two days late. If I do not punish them severely, how can I demonstrate my authority?"

Grandee the Honorable Dang came forward and said, "In the past, Lord Huan of Qi campaigned to the north and the south, but the only people he was never able to make submit to his authority were the Eastern Yi. If you wish to be obeyed by the Central States, you will have to bring those people under your control. If you want to do that, you will have to employ the Viscount of Zeng."

"How do I employ him?" Lord Xiang asked.

"The floods and droughts of the Sui River are under the control of a god that sends down rain and wind," the Honorable Dang explained. "The Eastern Yi have set up altars to worship this deity, at which sacrifices are performed in all four seasons. You should use the Viscount of Zeng as a sacrificial victim to the god of the Sui River, not only so that this god may favor you, but also because the Eastern Yi will hear about it. Who can fail to tremble before someone who has the power to execute one of the feudal lords? In the future, with military support from the Eastern Yi, you can campaign against other feudal lords and make yourself hegemon."

The senior minister, the Honorable Muyi, remonstrated: "No! You cannot do this! Since antiquity the rule has been established that you cannot sacrifice large animals over a minor matter. Each animal represents a life, not to mention a human being! Sacrifices are performed in order to allow people to pray for blessings. If you kill someone in order to pray for a blessing for yourself, the gods will turn against you. All the standard sacrifices for the good of the country are performed by the minister of rites. The god of the Sui River is nothing but a demon! It is the custom of the Eastern Yi to perform these dreadful sacrifices, but if you, my lord, were also to carry them out, not only will it appear as if the Eastern Yi has won you over, but nobody else will ever be willing to submit to your authority. Lord Huan of Qi was the Master of Covenants for forty years, he rescued ruined states and saved the lives of many people in danger—his magnanimity brought peace to the world for decades! You have merely presided over a single covenant, and now you are threatening to torture a feudal lord to death in order to garner blessings from a demon. I can well imagine that the other aristocrats will turn away from us in disgust and alarm; I have the greatest difficulty in picturing them respecting our authority!"

"The Honorable Muyi is talking rubbish!" the Honorable Dang proclaimed. "His Lordship's plan for attaining hegemony is completely different from that undertaken by Qi. Lord Huan had been in power for more than twenty years when he became the Master of Covenants—can His Lordship wait that long? If you are prepared to go slowly, then you make a show of virtue; if you want it quickly, then you use force. You have to think about the different methods to obtain results in these circumstances! If we do not follow Eastern Yi customs, then they will suspect us of duplicity; if we do not strike fear into the hearts of the other lords, they will ignore us. If we are suspected and ignored, how can His Lordship ever become hegemon? King Wu of Zhou executed the last king of the Shang dynasty and hung his head from his battle standard—that was how he established his new dynasty. That was how he treated the man who was his king! Why should we hesitate to execute another feudal lord? Just go ahead!"

Lord Xiang was in a fever of impatience to establish his authority among the other aristocrats, so he paid no attention to what the Honorable Muyi said. He sent Lord Wen of Zhu to arrest the Viscount of Zeng, kill, and cook him. His meat was then offered in sacrifice to the god of the Sui River. He also sent envoys to invite the Eastern Yi chiefs to join him in the ceremony at the Sui River. The Eastern Yi were not used to the idea of obeying the Duke of Song's orders, so none of them actually turned up. Yingqi, Viscount of Teng, was terrified by this development and sent someone to arrange for lavish bribes to be offered, after which he was released from imprisonment.

Grandee Xi Fuji of Cao warned his ruler, Lord Gong: "The Duke of Song is a vicious and cruel man, who will never accomplish his overweening ambitions. You had better go home."

Lord Gong of Cao then made his farewells and left, but he did not carry out the full ceremonies due to the host of an interstate covenant. Lord Xiang was annoyed by this and sent someone to upbraid him for this omission: "In the past when aristocrats met, the guest would offer the host a gift of dried meat, grain, live animals, and sacrificial meats as a token of his esteem. I have now spent many days within the borders of your state, and yet you have failed to make it clear that at this covenant I was the host and you the guest. What do you plan to do to rectify this situation?"

"A gift of dried meat, grain, live animals, and sacrificial meats is offered as standard when an aristocrat sends a formal embassy to another court," Xi Fuji responded. "You, my lord, have set up camp in the south of our country on official business, and His Lordship obeyed all your orders as quickly as he could—this is quite sufficient to demonstrate his allegiance. Now you are blaming us for not having performed all the ceremonies due to a host, which has upset His Lordship deeply. However, what you are asking for is totally inappropriate, and we are not prepared to offer it!" Lord Gong of Cao then returned home.

Lord Xiang was furious at this and gave orders for his army to move to attack Cao. The Honorable Muyi was forced to remonstrate for a second time: "Lord Huan of Qi's covenants and meetings bound the Central States together. He was generous to everyone else and yet did not expect a lavish recompense, he did not blame other people for problems, he did not execute people for not turning up, and that is how he got the best out of others and gained their affections. You have not lost anything by the fact that Cao refuses to provide these ritual gifts, so why do you insist upon attacking them?"

Lord Xiang did not listen. He sent the Honorable Dang in command of a force of three hundred chariots to besiege the capital city of Cao. Xi Fuji was well-prepared, so although the siege lasted for three months, the Honorable Dang was not able to defeat them. At the same time, Lord Wen of Zheng went to pay court to Chu for the first time, after which he arranged with the rulers of Lu, Qi, Chen, and Cai that they should swear a blood covenant with King Cheng of Chu within the borders of Qi. When Lord Xiang of Song heard this, he was deeply alarmed. In the first place, he was worried because if either of the rulers of Qi or Lu became hegemon, Song could not possibly dispute this; secondly, he was worried that the Honorable Dang had lost the initiative in the attack on Cao, damaging morale and making him a laughingstock among the other feudal lords. He summoned the Honorable Dang back home, whereupon Lord Gong of Cao sent an ambassador to present formal apologies, for he was afraid that the Song army would simply come back again later. From this point on, Song and Cao resumed their original good relations.

Lord Xiang of Song was desperate to become hegemon. When he realized that the lords of the little states did not submit to his authority and the lords of the big states had all gone off to attend this blood covenant with Chu, he went into an absolute panic and summoned the Honorable Dang to discuss the situation.

The Honorable Dang came forward and said: "Today, Qi and Chu are the most important states. Even though the Marquis of Qi used to be the hegemon, the state still has not recovered from the damage inflicted by Lord Huan's sons fighting over the inheritance. Chu has usurped the title of king and is now jockeying for a new position in the Central States. The other aristocrats are all terrified of them. If you were prepared to humble yourself and offer lavish gifts, my lord, you could ask that all the lords that have covenanted with the king of Chu should also swear a blood covenant with you. The king of Chu would most likely be happy to agree to this. Having used Chu's might to make the feudal lords agree to this, you can then use their combined might to put pressure on Chu. That will place you in a very powerful position."

The Honorable Muyi remonstrated yet again: "Chu has an unassailable position; why would they be prepared to do anything to help us? If we have to ask Chu to use their might to force the other feudal lords to swear a blood covenant with us, is it likely that they will subsequently be willing to subordinate themselves to us? You are just going to end up dragging us into pointless warfare."

Lord Xiang did not agree with him, so he ordered the Honorable Dang to take lavish bribes to Chu and ask for an audience with King Cheng. After asking why he had come, King Cheng agreed to meet the Duke of Song at Lushang in the spring of the following year. The Honorable Dang returned home to report this to Lord Xiang.

"Lushang is in Qi," Lord Xiang said, "so this must all be known to the Marquis of Qi."

He sent the Honorable Dang out again on a formal embassy to Qi, to explain that he would be going in person to meet the king of Chu. Lord Xiao of Qi agreed to this. This happened in the eleventh year of Lord Xiang of Song's rule, which was the twelfth year of the reign of King Xiang of Zhou.

The following year in the first month, Lord Xiang of Song was the first to arrive at Lushang, where he constructed a sacrificial altar and then settled down to wait for the rulers of Qi and Chu. Lord Xiao of Qi arrived in the first week of the second month. Lord Xiang was proud of his success in installing Lord Xiao of Qi in power, so when the two of them met, he felt very pleased with himself. Lord Xiao deeply appreciated the assistance that he had received from Song, so he did everything that a host could to make Lord Xiang feel welcome. Another twenty days later, King Cheng of Chu arrived. When the two rulers of Song and Qi went to meet him, they decided to conduct the ceremonies by order of precedence. Now, although the ruler of Chu had usurped the title of king, officially he was just a viscount. That made the Duke of Song the most senior person present, followed by the Marquis of Qi, with the Viscount of Chu bringing up the rear. The decision to go by order of precedence was Lord Xiang of Song's idea. When the time came, they ascended the altar. Lord Xiang proudly took the place of the Master of Covenants, grabbing hold of the sacrificial oxen's ear, and obviously had not the slightest intention of politely offering to yield his place to anyone else. King Cheng of Chu was not pleased, but he forced himself to smear his mouth with blood with an appearance of complaisance.

Lord Xiang made a respectful gesture with his hands, and said: "The dynasty in which my ancestors ruled as kings has collapsed, forcing me to become a subject of the Zhou. In spite of my humble abilities and meager strength, I am hoping to host an interstate meeting, but I am afraid that other people will not take it very seriously. That is why I am hoping that you two lords will permit the use of your names and reputations to encourage the feudal lords to meet at Yudi, within my humble state, in the eighth month. If you are prepared to assist me in bringing the aristocracy of the Zhou confederacy together and reaffirming our alliances through a blood covenant, a fraternal friendship can be maintained between our states for many generations to come. Although the dukes of Song are direct descendants of the kings of the Shang dynasty, I can assure you that I and my descendants will be fully aware of all that we owe you!"

Lord Xiao of Qi waved his hand to indicate that he wanted King Cheng of Chu to go first; King Cheng waved his hand to suggest that Lord Xiao go first. The two of them insisted on yielding precedence to the other to the point where the whole ceremony ground to a halt.

"If you do not mind my suggestion," Lord Xiang said, "why don't we both sign it at the same time?" He then took out the text of the agreement and handed it over to King Cheng of Chu to affix his signature, completely bypassing the Marquis of Qi. Lord Xiao was offended by this. King Cheng of Chu raised his eyes and their glances crossed. The text proclaimed that the signatories wished to convene a meeting that would reaffirm existing good relationships among the feudal lords by a further blood covenant, which would follow the model of Lord Huan of Qi's "plain-clothes" meeting, which took place without any military escort. The Duke of Song had already signed his name at the bottom of the document.

King Cheng of Chu laughed inwardly, though he spoke mildly to Lord Xiang: "The lords of the Zhou confederacy will come to this meeting if you call them, so why do you need me?"

"Zheng and Xu have been your allies for many years now, while Chen and Cai have made several blood covenants with Qi," Lord Xiang said. "Without your assistance, I am afraid that these rulers would not attend the proposed meeting. I hope that you will help us out here."

"If that is the case," King Cheng of Chu remarked, "then the Marquis of Qi ought to sign first, followed by me."

"I obey the Duke of Song's orders," Lord Xiao said. "Any lords that refuse to attend will have to be brought around by Chu's fearsome reputation."

The king of Chu smiled and signed his name. He then handed the brush to Lord Xiao, who said, "If you have Chu on your side, you don't need Qi. I am very lucky to have survived my recent troubles and been able to return to my state safe and sound. In the circumstances, I would be grateful to be allowed to occupy even the last place at a blood covenant; why should I care about my placement? What has signing this bamboo document to do with me?" He resolutely refused to put his name to this letter.

In fact, Lord Xiao of Qi was angry because the Duke of Song had asked the king of Chu to sign first, making it quite clear that he despised Qi and gave much more priority to buttering up the Chu monarch. That is the reason why he refused to sign.

Lord Xiang of Song was preening himself about the fact that the Marquis of Qi owed everything to his kindness, and he thought that everything that Lord Xiao said was the result of his sincere gratitude. Therefore, he packed up the letter that he had written and put it away. The three lords spent a further couple of days at Lushang, before leaving in a flurry of expressions of mutual appreciation.

An old man wrote a poem that bewails these events:

The feudal lords were originally all members of the Chinese race;
Why should they humble themselves before the king of Chu?
It is a mistake to imagine that all branches from one root are the same tree,
But who would have guessed that each was working to his own advantage?

When King Cheng of Chu got home, he told Grand Vizier Ziwen about what had happened.

"The ruler of Song is a nasty piece of work," Ziwen declared. "Why on earth did you agree to help them convene this meeting, Your Majesty?"

The king of Chu laughed and said, "I have been planning for a long time to put myself in control of the central states. My slow progress has been irritating me, but fortunately, now the Duke of Song wants to hold a 'plain-clothes' meeting. I am going to make use of this to unite the feudal lords under my leadership. What is wrong with that?"

Grandee Cheng Dechen came forward and said, "The Duke of Song is trying to establish a reputation that his abilities and resources cannot support; he is stupid enough to believe that he can trick people into accepting his authority. If we were to set an ambush for him, we can take him prisoner."

"That is exactly what I had in mind to do," the king of Chu said cheerfully.

"If you agree to meet him and then take him prisoner, people will say that Chu is untrustworthy," the Grand Vizier remarked. "How can we expect the feudal lords to submit to our authority?"

"Song wants to be the Master of Covenants," Cheng Dechen said. "That means that the duke always treats his peers with the greatest arrogance and condescension. They are not used to being bossed around by Song, and none of the aristocrats are prepared to take this kind of behavior from him. If we take him prisoner, we can demonstrate our military might. Having captured him, we will then release him, for that will demonstrate our generosity. When the feudal lords are feeling covered in shame because of the Duke of Song's uselessness, to whom will they give their allegiance if not to Chu? It would be stupid to refuse to carry out the whole scheme simply because you believe you should keep faith in such a minor matter."

Ziwen then presented his opinion: "Cheng Dechen's plan is much better than anything I have come up with."

The king of Chu appointed Cheng Dechen and Dou Bo as generals, and each selected five hundred chariots to be under his command. They then ran a series of exercises and settled upon the best plan of campaign for how to capture the Duke of Song. This will not be described in detail now, for you can read all about it below.

. . .

When Lord Xiang of Song returned home from Lushang, he was delighted with the way that things had gone, so he told the Honorable Muyi: "Chu has agreed to my hegemony over the feudal lords."

The Honorable Muyi remonstrated with him: "Chu is a barbarian country; you have no idea what they are really up to. They may tell you what you want to hear, but that does not mean that they have any intention of actually carrying it out. I am afraid that they are lying to you."

"You are too suspicious," Lord Xiang said. "I have treated them with sincerity and loyalty. Why should they lie to me?"

He did not listen to a word that the Honorable Muyi said, giving orders that the invitations to the proposed interstate meeting should be circulated. First he sent someone to Yudi to build the sacrificial altar, together with the necessary official guesthouses, which were exceptionally well-appointed. He stockpiled grain and food in his storehouses, so that there would be enough for the soldiers and their horses to eat. He would also be offering a series of banquets, each one more lavish than the last, which had to be prepared long in advance.

In the seventh month, Lord Xiang of Song ordered his chariot to drive him to this meeting. The Honorable Muyi remonstrated yet again: "Chu is a very powerful country that treats its enemies without mercy; please take the army with you!"

"I have agreed with the other aristocrats that this should be a 'plain-clothes' meeting," Lord Xiang said crossly. "If I go with my army, then I will be responsible for violating the terms of the invitation. In the future the feudal lords will have no reason to trust me again!"

"You can go in an unarmed chariot, my lord, thereby keeping your word," the Honorable Muyi suggested. "However, I will arrange for a hundred chariots to be waiting in hiding three *li* away from the site of your meeting with a view to helping you out in an emergency. How does that strike you?"

"What is the difference between me arranging for the troops to be waiting in hiding and you doing so?" Lord Xiang retorted. "Neither option is acceptable."

When he was about to set off, Lord Xiang became afraid that the Honorable Muyi would ignore his prohibitions and secretly mobilize the army, thereby ruining his reputation for trustworthiness, so he insisted that the two of them should travel together to Yudi.

"I am really worried about your safety," the Honorable Muyi said. "I am happy to go with you." The pair of them then went to the meeting place together.

The rulers of six states—Chu, Chen, Cai, Xu, Cao, and Zheng—all arrived at the appointed time. Neither Lord Xiao of Qi nor Lord Xi of Lu was present, the former because he was unhappy about the snub administered by the Duke of Song, the latter because he had never had anything to do with the king of Chu and was not about to start now. Lord Xiang arranged for senior officials to greet the rulers from the six states and see them safely ensconced in their respective guesthouses. The report came back: "All participants have arrived in civilian chariots. The king of Chu has by far the largest retinue, but none of them came in military vehicles."

"I knew that Chu would not lie to me," Lord Xiang said.

The Grand Astrologer made a divination to determine an auspicious day for the blood covenant, and the result was circulated to the representatives of each state present. A couple of days in advance, servants were sent to prepare the altar. Before dawn on the appointed day, torches were lit on the altar and the steps leading up to it, making everything as bright as day. There was an area set aside for resting to one side of the altar, where Lord Xiang took up position before the proceedings began. Five lords arrived one after the other: Gu, Lord Mu of Chen; Jiawu, Lord Zhuang of Cai; Jie, Lord Wen of Zheng; Ye, Lord Xi of Xu and Xiang, Lord Gong of Cao. They had to wait for a long time after daybreak before Xiongyun, King Cheng of Chu, deigned to arrive. Lord Xiang greeted him with the formal rituals due to a guest by his host, offering to allow him to ascend first to the altar. The pair of them went up the left- and right-hand sets of steps at the same time. The guests were supposed to go up the right-hand set of steps, and given that none of the lords would dare to offend King Cheng of Chu, they let him go first. The two generals, Cheng Dechen and Dou Bo, ascended in his wake, and indeed every single aristocrat was attended by a couple of followers, who do not need to be listed in any detail. The left-hand set of steps was reserved for the use of the host of this meeting, so only Lord Xiang of Song and the Honorable Muyi were allowed to use them. The rituals for the ascent of the steps was determined according to host and guests, but once they had ascended to the altar platform where the blood covenant would be sworn, it was time to select the Master of Covenants. He would preside over the sacrifice of the animals, the smearing of mouths with blood, and the swearing of the oath and would head the list of the participants.

Lord Xiang of Song was hoping that the king of Chu would open his mouth, so he stared at him. The king of Chu hung his head in silence. The rulers of Chen and Cai stared at each other. No one dared to be the first to speak. Lord Xiang could not stand it one moment longer, so he declared: "We are gathered here today because I want to carry on the good works undertaken by the first hegemon, the late Lord Huan of Qi. I want us to respect the king and bring stability to our people, preventing conflict and putting away our weapons, so that everyone can enjoy the blessings of peace. What do you think of my plan, my lords?"

Before any of the other lords had had an opportunity to answer, the king of Chu got up and came forward. "You are absolutely right, your grace. But who should be the Master of Covenants today?"

"I have done the most to bring this meeting about," Lord Xiang said, "and I also have the most senior title of anyone present, would you not agree?"

"My family have now assumed the title of king for a couple of generations," the king of Chu reminded him. "Although you are the most senior duke in the Zhou confederacy, you do not outrank a king. I am afraid that I take precedence over you." With these words he took the seat of honor.

The Honorable Muyi tugged at Lord Xiang's sleeve, hoping that he would put up with this insult in the first instance and wait until later before giving vent to his rage. Lord Xiang felt the position of Master of Covenants, which had almost been in his grasp, slip from between his fingers. How could he be anything other than furious? He tried to force himself to quell his rage, but he could not prevent himself from looking cross and speaking hastily: "Thanks to the beneficent influence of my ancestors, I hold the appointment as the most senior duke in the realm. Even the Son of Heaven has to treat me with respect! You speak of your ancestors having 'assumed the title of king,' which means they have usurped the prerogatives of the Zhou monarch. How can a false king be put ahead of a real duke?"

"If I am a false king, why did you invite me to come here?"

"You are here because you took part in the meeting at Lushang," Lord Xiang retorted, "and not because I invited you to attend."

Cheng Dechen, who was standing to one side, shouted, "Let us ask the lords present: are you here because of Chu? Or because of Song?"

The rulers of Chen and Cai, both of whom paid their allegiance to the king of Chu, immediately spoke out: "We are here because Chu ordered us to come. We would not dare refuse."

The king of Chu laughed heartily and said, "What do you have to say to that, Your Grace?"

Lord Xiang realized that he had been caught at a disadvantage and did not want to carry on the discussion. This was no time to be debating who was right and who was wrong—he needed a plan to get away. Unfortunately, he did not have any guards with him. Just as he was hesitating, Cheng Dechen and Dou Bo took off their ceremonial robes to reveal that they were wearing armor underneath, and each had a small red flag hanging from his belt. They waved these from the edge of the platform, at which point the king of Chu's entourage, more than a thousand men in all, also took off their clothes to reveal their hidden armor and reached for the weapons that they had concealed about their persons. They stormed up to the altar like a swarm of wasps. The feudal lords were all scared witless. Cheng Dechen held Lord Xiang of Song so tightly by the arms that he could not move, while Dou Bo directed the soldiers under his command to steal all the silk, jade, and bronze objects laid out at the altar. The Duke of Song's servants ran away in confusion, desperate to find somewhere to hide.

Lord Xiang caught sight of the Honorable Muyi, keeping close beside him, and whispered: "I really regret not listening to your advice. Given the current circumstances, you must get back to the capital as soon as you can. Do not worry about me."

The Honorable Muyi thought that there was nothing he could do to improve the situation if he stayed, so he took advantage of the chaos to steal away home.

Was Lord Xiang of Song able to get away? READ ON.

Chapter Thirty-four

Lord Xiang of Song's mistaken benevolence loses him popular support.

Lady Jiang of Qi sends her husband on his way while he is drunk.

Although King Cheng of Chu had pretended to arrive unarmed at the meeting at Yudi, in fact all of his entourage were knights with armor hidden under their clothes and weapons concealed about their persons. They had all received strict training under the auspices of Cheng Dechen and Dou Bo, and they were both brave and ferocious! The main army, under the command of the two generals Wei Lüchen and Dou Ban, had followed on behind and were spoiling for a fight. Lord Xiang of Song, completely unaware of this, had fallen into their trap. As the saying goes: "When a naive man meets an able plotter, by the time he realizes what is going on it is far too late." Once the king of Chu had Lord Xiang under control, his soldiers stole all the fixtures and fittings from the guesthouses and all the grain and food from the storehouses. Even the duke's entourage and his chariots and horses were now taken over by the Chu army. The five lords from Chen, Cai, Zheng, Xu, and Cao were so terrified that none of them dared to protest.

King Cheng of Chu invited the aristocrats back to his guesthouse, where he enumerated the six crimes Lord Xiang of Song had committed to his face: "You attacked the state of Qi in a time of national mourning to remove the newly established ruler in favor of your own candidate; that is your first crime. The Viscount of Zeng went to attend an inter-state meeting that you had convened but arrived late, whereupon you treated him in an exceptionally humiliating and brutal manner; that is your second crime. You used a human being to replace an animal in performing a heterodox sacrifice to a demon; that is your third crime. Cao failed to treat you with the ceremony that you felt to be your due and did not apologize, for which you laid siege to their capital for months; that is your fourth crime. As a direct descendant of the kings of Shang, you have failed to comprehend that you lack both virtue and military might and that no auspicious omens have been vouchsafed to you, yet this has not prevented you from longing to become the next hegemon; this is your fifth crime. You have made use of my position to bully the other feudal lords into accepting your leadership and behaved with the utmost arrogance to both of them, while showing no understanding of the fact that you ought to yield the place of honor to me; this is your sixth crime. You must be very stupid to have come to this meeting without your guards. I have a thousand chariots under my command, and each of them is ridden by a battle-hardened warrior; they will crush your capital city of Suiyang under their boots and take revenge for what you have done to the states of Qi and Zeng. Please get onto your chariots, my lords, that you may watch me take the Song capital. When I have done so, I will hold ten days of feasting for you."

The feudal lords all agreed to this. Lord Xiang opened his mouth, but no words came out; he looked just like a statue carved from wood except for the two lines of tears rolling down his cheeks. A short time later, the entire Chu army had assembled. Although King Cheng had claimed that he had one thousand chariots, in fact there were only five hundred. King Cheng of Chu rewarded the army officers who had shown particular valor, then they struck camp and moved towards Suiyang, killing anyone in their way and dragging Lord Xiang of Song with them. The feudal lords all remained in the encampment at Yudi, just as the king of Chu had instructed them to, for they were far too frightened to go home.

A historian wrote a poem criticizing Lord Xiang of Song's mistakes, which runs:

> Your immoderate flattery of the king of Chu brought disaster down upon you;
> The city of Suiyang became a battlefield.
> In the past Lord Huan of Qi brought the feudal lords together nine times,
> But he did not allow Chu to set foot beyond their borders.

The Honorable Muyi escaped from the covenant platform at Yudi and made his way back to the capital city. He explained to Marshal

Gongsun Gu that the Duke of Song had been taken prisoner: "The Chu army will be here any minute now. You must muster the army at all possible speed and set them to defending the battlements."

"The state cannot be even a single day without a ruler," Gongsun Gu said. "You must temporarily assume the mantle of the duke, for that will allow you to give orders to the army and issue rewards and punishments. That way people will take you seriously."

The Honorable Muyi whispered in Gongsun Gu's ear: "Chu will be bringing His Grace along with them when they attack us, in the hope of putting us under more pressure. You must do the following and then they will release him."

"You are absolutely right!" Gongsun Gu said. He instructed the ministers: "His Grace may never come home. Let us appoint the Honorable Muyi to take charge of the government."

The ministers were all aware of what a clever man the Honorable Muyi was, so they were happy to agree to this. The Honorable Muyi made a report to this effect to the ancestral temples, then he took his place at court facing south as befitted the acting ruler of a state. He gave his orders to the three armies and enforced a strict curfew. The walls and streets of Suiyang were all guarded by men armed to the teeth.

Just as they made the final touches to their preparations, the main army under the command of the king of Chu arrived and immediately set up camp. His Majesty sent General Dou Bo forward to parlay: "His Grace is now in our hands, and we will decide if he lives or dies. If you surrender now, you can preserve his life."

Gongsun Gu responded from the battlements: "In the interests of our state altars we have already appointed a new ruler. You can kill our old lord if you want, but we will never surrender."

"Your ruler is in our hands," Dou Bo demanded. "What do you mean you have a new one?"

"Lords are appointed in order to preside over the altars of soil and grain," Gongsun Gu proclaimed. "They need constant supervision, so how could we not appoint a new duke?"

"If we let His Grace go home, how will you repay us?" Dou Bo asked.

"His Grace has humiliated the state altars by being taken prisoner," Gongsun Gu replied. "Even if you send him home, he can never be our ruler again. It is entirely up to Chu whether you allow him to come home or not. If you want to do battle, our whole army is waiting here inside the city walls, and we do not think that we will lose."

Dou Bo was impressed by the firmness of Gongsun Gu's replies, and he reported this back to the king of Chu. The king of Chu was furious and gave orders for an attack on Suiyang. Arrows and rocks fell from the city walls like rain, and many Chu soldiers were injured. After attacking the city for three days in succession, there were still no obvious signs of progress.

"Since they don't want the Duke of Song anymore, how about we kill him?" the king of Chu asked.

"Your Majesty has already blamed Song for murdering the Viscount of Zeng," Cheng Dechen replied. "If you now kill the Duke of Song, it will clearly be six of one and half a dozen of the other. To make matters worse, Lord Xiang has now been reduced to the status of an ordinary resident of Suiyang, so killing him will not only be useless for your efforts to attack the city but will also arouse the enmity of its residents. You had better release him."

"How do we put a good face on the fact that we have failed in our attack on Song and released their former ruler?" the king of Chu asked.

"I have a plan," Cheng Dechen told him. "The rulers of Qi and Lu are the only lords who did not attend this meeting at Yudi. Qi is a long-term ally of ours and can be forgiven; Lu is a country in which ritual and justice are paramount, and they consistently supported the hegemony of Lord Huan of Qi. They have never had any time for us. If we present the prisoners whom we have captured in Song to Lu and request the presence of the marquis at a meeting at Bodu, Lu will be frightened into attending by the sight of the Song captives. Lu and Song have been close allies since they swore a blood covenant together at Kuiqiu, in addition to which the Marquis of Lu is a most benevolent ruler. He is sure to ask us to be merciful to the Duke of Song, and we can then release Lord Xiang into the Marquis of Lu's custody as a gesture of goodwill. Thus, at one stroke we can gain the support of both Lu and Song."

The king of Chu clapped his hands and laughed heartily: "You really are a clever man."

He withdrew his troops with a view to setting up camp at Bodu. He sent Yi Shen to lead an embassy to the Marquis of Lu and present a number of Song captives and their chariots to him.

When Yi Shen arrived at Qufu, he presented these spoils of war and his letter of credentials, which read:

> The Duke of Song has behaved with exceptional rudeness and arrogance to me. I am presently encamped at Bodu. I have no intention of dealing with my prisoners without consultation, so I respectfully present some of our booty

> to you, my lord, and request that you will join me in the deliberations over what to do with the remaining captives.

When he read this, Lord Xi of Lu was very alarmed. As the saying goes: "When the rabbit dies, the fox is sad; even animals can understand the death of a member of a different species." He understood perfectly well that Chu was trying to frighten him into submission, in spite of the respectful wording and their presentation of the spoils of war. However, Lu was weak and Chu was strong; if he did not go to attend this meeting, he had every reason to be concerned that they would turn their army against him and there would be nothing that he could do about it. He therefore treated Yi Shen with the utmost generosity and immediately wrote a reply, which he had conveyed to the king of Chu posthaste. This letter said:

> I have received your message and will join you immediately.

Lord Xi of Lu set out on the heels of the messenger, attended by Grandee Zhong Sui, and soon arrived at Bodu. According to the instructions that he had received from Yi Shen, Grandee Zhong Sui had a private audience first with Cheng Dechen, at which lavish gifts changed hands. The wheels having been thoroughly greased, Cheng Dechen then arranged for the meeting of the Marquis of Lu with the king of Chu, at which both parties said only the most flattering things about each other. The five lords of Chen, Cai, Zheng, Xu, and Cao had all come to this meeting from Yudi, and they took the opportunity to discuss the situation with Lord Xi of Lu. Lord Wen of Zheng opened the discussion with the suggestion that the king of Chu should be appointed as the Master of Covenants. The other aristocrats hemmed and hawed about that.

"A Master of Covenants ought to have a reputation for being benevolent and just, so that other people are happy to submit to his authority," Lord Xi of Lu said crossly. "The king of Chu is backed up by his enormous army, which has allowed him to take the most senior duke in the Zhou confederacy prisoner. He can clearly command great military might, but he has acted in a completely unprincipled manner and everyone is terrified of him. We have all sworn blood covenants with the Duke of Song; if we do not save him but just suck up to Chu instead, will we not be scorned by every right-thinking person? If Chu is prepared to release the duke from captivity, not only can we swear a blood covenant here, there is also no reason that we should not obey their commands in the future."

The other lords said, "The Marquis of Lu is absolutely correct in what he says."

Grandee Zhong Sui had this message conveyed privately to Cheng Dechen, and he reported on it to the king of Chu.

"The feudal lords complain that I have not behaved with the justice that they expect from a Master of Covenants," the king of Chu said. "Why should I disappoint them?"

He had another sacrificial altar constructed in the suburbs of Bodu and set a date on Kuichou day in the twelfth month for those present to smear their mouths with blood. At the same time, he would pardon the Duke of Song.

The day before the covenant was due to be held, the Duke of Song was released from captivity and he had an audience with the other feudal lords. Lord Xiang of Song was humiliated and angry, with a thousand complaints to make about the way in which he had been treated, but instead he had to thank each of his peers personally for their help. When the day of the meeting dawned, Lord Wen of Zheng deputized for all the other aristocrats present when he respectfully requested that King Cheng of Chu ascend the platform to take the position of Master of Covenants. King Cheng held the ear of the sacrificial ox, then the rulers of Song and Lu smeared their mouths with blood one after the other. Lord Xiang was furious, but did not dare to say anything. When the ceremony was over, the feudal lords went their separate ways.

• • •

Lord Xiang of Song had heard gossip that the Honorable Muyi had usurped his title, so he intended to flee to the state of Wey to avoid him. However, a messenger from the Honorable Muyi now arrived and stated, "The reason why a regency was instituted in Song was to ensure that Your Grace's position was secure. The state is yours; why do you not come home?"

A short time later, a fully appointed official carriage pulled up to carry Lord Xiang back to his state. The Honorable Muyi went back to his old position.

When Master Hu Zeng spoke of the release of Lord Xiang from captivity, he was full of praise for the Honorable Muyi's plan and the way in which he kept his nerve when claiming to have replaced his former ruler. If he had made even the slightest mistake when arranging for the return of Lord Xiang, Chu would certainly have become suspicious of what he was up to and refused to release him.

His poem of praise reads:

If you have to gamble, it is better to use tile tokens rather than golden ones.
The new ruler was able to extract the old ruler from danger.
That he first took the title and then abdicated it for the sake of his lord
Is the reason that a thousand generations have extolled the Honorable Muyi.

There is also a poem that discusses how the lords of six states gave up their hereditary powers and privileges in order to curry favor with Chu. How could they expect that Chu would give any consideration to the Central States under these conditions? This poem reads:

The fox is always sad once the rabbit is dead.
Who was the prisoner here and who the guard?
They were completely unashamed of their actions in flattering this barbarian,
Thinking that they had done well in gaining the release of the Duke of Song.

Lord Xiang's ambition of becoming hegemon resulted in his being held prisoner by Chu for a while, which he found profoundly humiliating. His hatred of them entered the very marrow of his bones. However, he was certainly not powerful enough to be able to avenge this insult. He was also furious with the Earl of Zheng for suggesting that the king of Chu should become the Master of Covenants. This was more than he could swallow, so he determined to attack the state of Zheng. In the third month of the fourteenth year of the reign of King Xiang of Zhou, Lord Wen of Zheng went to Chu to pay court to their monarch. When Lord Xiang of Song heard this, he was absolutely furious and raised an enormous army to punish Zheng, which he commanded personally. He ordered his senior minister, the Honorable Muyi, to help Scion Wangchen run the country in his absence.

Muyi remonstrated with him: "Chu and Zheng have been allies for many years. If Song attacks Zheng, Chu will go to their rescue. In those circumstances you cannot possibly win. It would be much more sensible for you to devote your time to improving the running of the country and waiting for a better opportunity."

Marshal Gongsun Gu also remonstrated, but Lord Xiang responded angrily: "If you don't want to go, I will go on my own." Gongsun Gu did not dare to say another word.

The army advanced in the direction of Zheng. Lord Xiang was in control of the central army with Gongsun Gu as his deputy. He was assisted by Grandees Yue Puyi, Hua Xiulao, Xiang Zishou, and the Honorable Dang. Spies informed Lord Wen of Zheng what had happened, and he was very alarmed. He quickly sent someone to report this emergency to Chu.

"Zheng has always served me with loyalty!" King Cheng of Chu proclaimed. "I must rescue them!"

Cheng Dechen stepped forward and said, "If you want to rescue Zheng, you had better attack Song."

"Why?" King Cheng asked.

"The residents of Suiyang's nerves cracked when the Duke of Song was captured," Cheng Dechen replied. "Now yet again he has bitten off more than he can possibly chew by attacking Zheng with an enormous army—his capital must be empty. If we take advantage of that to go and attack them, they will be terrified. We do not have to wait until we do battle to know that our victory is assured. If the Song army turns back to save Suiyang, they will be exhausted by the effort and we can take advantage of that too. Is it possible that we can fail?"

The king of Chu was much impressed by this advice. He immediately appointed Cheng Dechen as commander-in-chief with Dou Bo as his deputy, and they then mobilized the army and attacked the state of Song.

• • •

Lord Xiang of Song was locked in a stalemate with Zheng when he received news of the mobilization of the Chu army. He turned around and went home. He made camp south of the Hong River, with a view to intercepting the attack of the Chu forces. Cheng Dechen sent a messenger with a letter provoking battle.

Gongsun Gu told Lord Xiang, "The Chu army has come to rescue Zheng. If we apologize to Chu, pointing out that we have withdrawn our troops from Zheng, they might be amenable to just going home. We are in no fit state to do battle."

"In the past, Lord Huan of Qi raised an army and attacked Chu," Lord Xiang responded. "Now Chu has invaded us, and we are not going to fight them. What kind of a way is this to continue Lord Huan's hegemony?"

Gongsun Gu tried again: "I have heard it said that the same clan does not rule two dynasties. Heaven abandoned the Shang dynasty a long time ago. You may want a revival, but is it going to happen? Our armor is not as hard as that of Chu; our weapons are not as sharp as those of Chu; our people are not as strong as those of Chu; indeed, the inhabitants of Song view Chu as being as frightening as a nest of cobras. How on earth are you going to defeat them?"

"Chu has many soldiers, but lacks justice and benevolence," Lord Xiang retorted. "I may not have many soldiers, but I have virtues to spare. In the past King Wu of Zhou had merely three thousand Agile Tiger guards at his disposal, and yet he defeated the Shang dynasty with their tens of thousands of soldiers; that is the effect of benevolence and justice. As a good ruler, I would rather die than run away from a bastard like the Chu king."

He made a note at the bottom of the letter provoking battle, stating that he was prepared to fight on the north bank of the Hong River on the first day of the eleventh month. He ordered that a great flag should be hoisted above his battle chariot, with two words on it: "Benevolence" and "Justice."

Gongsun Gu was deeply pained by these developments. He spoke in secret to Yue Puyi: "Victory in battle is determined by killing the enemy, and yet His Grace is yapping about benevolence and justice. Sometimes I think that he has gone completely mad! We are all in terrible danger! We must be very careful to try and minimize the damage to our country."

On the appointed day, Gongsun Gu got up before cockcrow and begged permission from Lord Xiang to put his troops into strict battle formation.

. . .

Meanwhile, the Chu general, Cheng Dechen, had camped north of the Hong River.

"Let us assemble the army at the fifth watch to prevent the Song troops from stealing a march on us," Dou Bo requested.

Cheng Dechen laughed and said, "The Duke of Song's only talent is believing his own fantasies. He knows nothing at all about military matters. If we assemble the army early, then we can do battle first thing; if we assemble the army in the evening, we can do battle overnight. What is there to be afraid of?"

As it got light, the Chu army began to ford the river.

"The Chu army has waited until now to cross," Gongsun Gu told Lord Xiang. "That means that they do not think of us as posing any threat to them. Let me take advantage of this situation and make a sudden attack while they are still wading across. That way we can deploy the whole of our army against the part that is in the river. If we wait until they have all assembled on this side, there will be too many of them for our small army to stand a chance. What will we do then?"

Lord Xiang pointed to his great battle standard and said, "Have you noticed those two words: 'Benevolence' and 'Justice'? I am going to live up to them! How could I possibly attack an army before it is ready?" Yet again Gongsun Gu was left speechless.

A short time later, the entire Chu army had made its way across the ford. Cheng Dechen was wearing an official hat hung with jade beads and an embroidered silk gown with armor on top; he had a bow and quiver hanging from his waist and a whip in his hand. When he had given his orders to his officers, they began to move into battle formation. He seemed totally confident and behaved as if the enemy did not exist.

"Chu is going into battle formation, but they have not yet lined up properly," Gongsun Gu said to Lord Xiang. "If you sound the drums for an immediate attack, we can put them to flight."

Lord Xiang spat in his face and said: "Bah! You only seem to care about winning this one battle, rather than ensuring that my reputation as a benevolent and just ruler lasts for a thousand years. Since when has it been acceptable to drum your army on against an enemy that has not yet gone into battle formation?" Gongsun Gu had to bear his humiliation and worry in silence.

When the Chu army was drawn up in full battle array, their fearsome warriors and well-prepared horses filled the mountains and spread out over the plains. Every single Song soldier looked terrified. Lord Xiang sounded his drums, and then a similar reverberation could be heard from the Chu army. Lord Xiang of Song held a long spear in his hands. He headed the first attack aimed directly at the Chu formations, followed by the Honorable Dang and Xiang Zishou and their officers. When Cheng Dechen noticed the speed and ferocity of their advance, he discreetly gave orders to allow his battle formations to open a route for the attackers. Lord Xiang and his accompanying chariots advanced well past the Chu front line, and by the time that Gongsun Gu brought up reinforcements from the rear, the Duke of Song was already entirely surrounded.

He saw a single general standing beyond this melee, who shouted: "Come and fight if you have the guts!" This was Dou Bo. Furious, Gongsun Gu wielded his halberd to stab Dou Bo, who parried with his sword. Before the pair of them had fought more than a few rounds, the Song general Yue Puyi arrived with his troops. Dou Bo was now clearly under considerable pressure, but fortunately Wei Lüchen broke free just at that moment and came to fight Yue Puyi. Gongsun Gu took advantage of this momentary panic to plunge into the midst of the Chu army, slashing from side to side. Dou Bo held tight to his sword and went after him, but then the Song general Hua Xiulao arrived, and the two of them started fighting just in front of the main body of the Chu army.

Gongsun Gu found himself trapped in the middle of the Chu battle lines. He made a feint to the left; then he attacked to the right, and as this went on, he noticed that he was surrounded by more and more soldiers pouring in from the northeast, pressing ever closer. He made haste to leave. Just then he bumped into the Song general Xiang Zishou, his face covered in blood, who shouted: "Go at once to rescue His Grace!"

Gongsun Gu followed Xiang Zishou as the pair cut their way out of the encirclement. He caught sight of a group of officers, all of whom had sustained serious injuries, fighting to the death with the Chu soldiers in a battle in which they had not retreated a single inch.

Lord Xiang had always treated his subordinates extremely well, and so they were prepared to die for him.

The Chu soldiers knew of Gongsun Gu's bravery, so they gradually retreated. Looking straight ahead, Gongsun Gu spotted the Honorable Dang lying slumped in his chariot, severely injured. The great battle standard reading "Benevolence" and "Justice" had been stolen by the Chu army. Lord Xiang had sustained a number of wounds, of which the most serious was the arrow stuck in his right thigh, piercing the tendons in such a way that he was unable to stand.

When the Honorable Dang caught sight of Gongsun Gu, he opened his eyes wide and said, "You must help His Lordship. I am going to die here." Having said this, he passed away—a devastating loss for Gongsun Gu. He lifted Lord Xiang into his own chariot and bravely cut his way out of the encircling forces, shielding the Duke of Song with his own body. Xiang Zishou brought up the rear as the officers guarded Lord Xiang's retreat, fighting every step of the way. By the time they had finally gotten clear of the Chu army, every single officer who had followed the Duke of Song into battle was dead. Eighty or ninety percent of the Song army had been killed. When Yue Puyi and Hua Xiulao realized that the Duke of Song had left the tiger's den, they too made their escape.

Cheng Dechen followed up his victory by pursuing the defeated army, which abandoned chariots and equipment the whole way along the road. Gongsun Gu helped Lord Xiang to escape back to his capital under cover of darkness. An enormous number of Song soldiers had been killed, and now their parents, wives, and children were rioting outside the palace gates, furious that by ignoring Gongsun Gu's advice

Lord Xiang had brought about this dreadful defeat. When Lord Xiang heard this, he sighed and said, "A gentleman should not compound the troubles of others. I will always behave according to the principles of benevolence and justice. I have no intention of taking advantage of my people!" Everyone laughed sarcastically at this.

All the stories told later on about how Lord Xiang of Song lost the support of his people and was defeated in battle, simply because he was trying to be benevolent and virtuous, refer to the events of the Battle of the Hong River.

A bearded old man wrote a poem bewailing these events:

Oblivious to the pain suffered by Teng and Zeng, you chose to worry about Chu,
Happy to endure a wounded leg for the sake of an empty reputation.
If Lord Xiang of Song can be described as benevolent and just,
There is no difference between Robber Zhi and good King Wen of Zhou!

The Chu army won a great victory, crossed back over the Hong River, and returned home singing songs of triumph. As they left Song territory, a mounted scout reported: "The king of Chu has come in person to meet you at the head of his army; he is camped at the Ke Marshes."

Cheng Dechen immediately traveled to the Ke Marshes, where he had an audience with the king of Chu and presented his booty.

"The Earl of Zheng and his wife will arrive here tomorrow to congratulate us on this victory," King Cheng told him. "I want them to see a grand display of our captives and the ears you have taken from the dead."

Lady Wen Mi, Lord Wen of Zheng's principal wife, was the younger sister of King Cheng of Chu. Since she had decided that she would like to see her older brother, she traveled in Lord Wen of Zheng's train to the Ke Marshes, riding in a closed carriage. After having an audience with the king of Chu, he treated them to a magnificent parade of his captives. Lord Wen of Zheng and his wife both offered their congratulations and gave lavish gifts of gold and silk, which were distributed among the soldiers as rewards. Lord Wen of Zheng respectfully requested permission to offer a banquet in the king of Chu's honor the following day.

Early the next morning, Lord Wen of Zheng came out of the city to escort the king of Chu into his capital, whereupon they attended a ceremony at the main ancestral temple in which a full nine sets of formal gifts were presented, just as if the Zhou Son of Heaven were present. At the extravagant banquet that followed, several hundred different dishes were served on bronze platters and tureens. Such an extravagant meal had never been seen before among the states of the Zhou confederacy. Lady Wen Mi had given birth to two daughters named Bo Mi and Shu Mi, respectively. Neither of them was married yet, so both were present on this occasion. Lady Wen Mi introduced her two daughters formally to their uncle, and the king of Chu was very pleased. Lord Wen of Zheng and his wife and daughters took turns in offering toasts, to the point where the banquet lasted late into the night and the king of Chu became extremely drunk.

"The generosity with which you have treated me is already far more than I deserve," King Cheng told Lady Wen Mi. "However, I would really enjoy to be escorted on the journey home by you and your daughters."

"As you wish," she replied.

Lord Wen of Zheng accompanied the king of Chu out of the city walls and said goodbye. Lady Wen Mi and her two daughters then rode to the army camp on the same chariot as King Cheng. The king of Chu was much taken with his nieces' beauty, so he dragged them into his tent to enjoy the pleasures of the bedchamber. Lady Wen Mi paced up and down outside, unable to sleep a wink but also too frightened of her brother to kick up a fuss.

For an uncle to abuse his nieces in this way shows that the king of Chu was no better than an animal!

The following day, King Cheng bestowed half the booty captured by his army upon his younger sister, Lady Wen Mi, and then turned his chariot homeward, taking his two nieces with him. He installed them in his harem.

Grandee Shu Zhan of Zheng sighed and said, "How can the king of Chu end well? Up until now he has behaved very properly, but this time he has shown an utter disregard for all rules. It is such a shame!"

. . .

Let us now consider something other than the conflict between the states of Song and Chu. The Honorable Chonger of Jin had gone to live in Qi in the seventh year of the reign of King Xiang of Zhou. It was now the fourteenth year of King Xiang's reign, and the Honorable Chonger was still there. After the death of Lord Huan, his sons fought among themselves over the succession, embroiling the state in a civil war. After Lord Xiao had inherited his father's title, he pursued a very different line of policy from that of his predecessor, since he truckled to Chu at the expense of the alliance with Song. As time went on, more and more feudal lords found themselves opposed to the new Marquis of Qi.

Zhao Cui and the others discussed the situation in secret: "We came to Qi in the hope of being able to use Lord Huan's status as hegemon to restore the Honorable Chonger to his state. The new lord has lost the hegemony, and the feudal lords are in open revolt against him; it is clear that he can do nothing to help our master. We had better go somewhere else and find someone who can put him in power."

They went to see the Honorable Chonger, to tell him the fruits of their discussion. However, he was completely besotted with his wife, Lady Jiang of Qi, and spent his whole time in parties and drinking, paying no attention to what was going on around him. His loyal followers waited for more than a week without being able to have an audience with him.

Wei Chou was furious and said, "We all believed in him: that is why we have suffered in his service, following him into exile. Now he has spent the last seven years in Qi with each day slipping past as he enjoys himself in comfort, while we have to wait ten days without being able to clap eyes on him. How will he ever achieve anything if he carries on like this?"

"This is not a place where we can speak openly," Hu Yan said. "Please come with me."

They went some way out of the East Gate of the city, to a place named Sangyin, where there were lush old mulberry trees as far as the eye could see, so overgrown that the sun could not penetrate. Zhao Cui and his nine companions sat down in a circle in a grove.

"What plan do you have to offer?" Zhao Cui asked.

"It is up to us to get the Honorable Chonger on the move again," Hu Yan replied. "We can arrange everything in advance, pack up our luggage and so on, then we invite the Honorable Chonger to go hunting outside the suburbs. Once he is out of the city, we can force him to leave with us. The only problem is to decide which state we should head for."

"The Duke of Song wants to become hegemon, and he has a good reputation," Zhao Cui remarked. "We should go to him first, and if that does not work, we can move on to either Qin or Chu. Sooner or later we will be successful!"

"I am an old friend of Gongsun Gu," Hu Yan said. "He might be willing to help."

Having discussed various different aspects of the problem in some detail, the men dispersed. This being such a dark and isolated place, they were not aware of anyone else around them. They did not think of the old saying: "If you don't want anyone to hear, then don't say it; if you don't want anyone to know, then don't do it." Lady Jiang had more than a dozen maidservants working in the mulberry trees, picking leaves to feed to the silkworms. When they saw these men sitting down to discuss matters, they stopped picking to listen. When it was all over, they went back to the palace and reported every word that they had said to Lady Jiang.

"Impossible!" Lady Jiang exclaimed. "You should not repeat such gossip." She ordered that her silkworm maids should all be arrested and imprisoned in a single room. In the middle of the night they were murdered, so that this would be kept secret. She then kicked the Honorable Chonger awake and said, "Your followers want you to move on to another state. My silkworm maids overhead their plot, and I was afraid that they would reveal all. This might have placed an obstacle in your way, so I have killed them. You had better finalize your plans to move on as soon as possible."

"I am happy here, and that is all that I care about," Chonger said. "I am planning to spend the rest of my life in Qi. I swear that I will never go anywhere else."

"Jin has not known a moment's peace since you went into exile," Lady Jiang reminded him. "Your brother Yiwu is a nasty piece of work and his people hate him, he has led his army into defeat, and he has no allies among his neighbors. Everyone is waiting for you. This time you must put yourself in power in Jin; you cannot drag this out any longer!" However, the Honorable Chonger was so deeply in love with Lady Jiang that he refused to leave her.

The following morning Zhao Cui, Hu Yan, Jiu Ji, and Wei Chou presented themselves at the gate to the palace and sent in the message: "We would like to invite the Honorable Chonger to go hunting in the suburbs."

Chonger was still lying in bed, so he sent one of the palace servants to take back the message: "I am not feeling very well, so I have not yet gotten dressed. I cannot possibly go with you."

When Lady Jiang heard this, she quickly sent someone to summon Hu Yan into the palace for a private meeting. Lady Jiang dismissed her entourage to the far side of the screen; then she asked him why he had come.

"When the Honorable Chonger was staying with the Di, he harnessed his horses to his chariot every day and went off hunting foxes and rabbits," Hu Yan explained. "Now that he is living in Qi, it is ages since he last went out hunting. I am afraid that he is getting lazy, so I came to invite him out. There is nothing else going on."

Lady Jiang laughed quietly to herself and said: "I gather that this hunting will take place in either Song, Qin, or Chu . . ."

Hu Yan was deeply alarmed. "Why would we go so far on a hunt?"

"I know all about your plans to make my husband leave here," Lady Jiang told him. "There is no need for pretense. I have spent half the night arguing with him, but he simply will not agree. This evening I will throw a banquet in his honor and get him drunk. You can then carry him out of the city under cover of darkness. That way nothing can go wrong."

Hu Yan kowtowed and said, "For you to be prepared to break up a happy marriage to see your husband make his reputation is something that very few women have ever been capable of, no matter how supportive and virtuous they might be." He then said goodbye.

Afterwards Hu Yan informed Zhao Cui and the others of what had happened, and they packed up their luggage, prepared provisions, and assembled their chariots and men. Zhao Cui and Hu Mao left the city in advance of the rest of the party, with a view to waiting for them outside the suburbs. Hu Yan, Wei Chou, and Dian Jie stayed behind, hidden in a pair of small chariots parked on either side of the palace gates. They were waiting for a message from Lady Jiang to go into action. As the saying goes: "If you want to make a name for yourself, you will have to go much further than other people."

That evening, Lady Jiang held a banquet in the palace and invited her husband to drink a cup.

"Why are you holding this banquet?" the Honorable Chonger asked.

"I know that you are a very ambitious man, so I offer you this toast to send you on your way," Lady Jiang said.

"Human life is short and hard. Having found a comfortable billet, what more can I ask?"

"A man should want more than just a comfortable billet," Lady Jiang told him. "Your followers are advising this for your own good; you ought to do as they say."

Chonger looked unhappy and cradled his cup in his hands without drinking from it.

"Do you really not want to go? Or are you simply lying to me?" Lady Jiang demanded.

"I am not going anywhere," Chonger said. "Why should I lie to you?"

Lady Jiang laughed. "Your ambition prompts you to go; your love for me prompts you to stay. I arranged for this party to be a farewell banquet, but now I realize that it has served to persuade you not to go anywhere. So let us enjoy ourselves!"

The Honorable Chonger was delighted. The pair of them drank toast after toast to one another, as the palace servants sang and danced and served more wine. Chonger was already drunk, but they insisted over and over that he have some more, until in the end he collapsed on his seating mat. Lady Jiang covered him with a blanket and ordered someone to go and fetch Hu Yan. He realized that the Honorable Chonger was dead drunk, so he quickly summoned Wei Chou and Dian Jie into the palace. They carried him out, sandwiched between his mat and the blanket. Then, as Hu Yan said goodbye to Lady Jiang, they rolled him up in a carpet like a baby in swaddling bands and bundled him into a waiting chariot. His wife wept silent tears.

There is a poem that testifies to this:

The Honorable Chonger just wanted a happy life,
It was his wife who sent him on his way.
To see him achieve his ambitions,
She was prepared to break up a loving marriage.

Hu Yan set a cracking pace as the two chariots sped away. They made their way out of the city walls as dusk was falling, then rendezvoused with Zhao Cui and the others. Under cover of darkness, they traveled fifty or sixty *li*. When they heard a cock crow and the dawn started to show in the east, the Honorable Chonger started to shift around at the bottom of the chariot, calling for a servant to give him a drink of water to slake his thirst.

Hu Yan reined in his chariot and said, "If you want water, you will have to wait until it gets properly light."

Chonger felt that he was lying on a jolting surface and said, "Help me to get out of bed."

"This isn't a bed," Hu Yan told him. "You are on a chariot."

The Honorable Chonger opened his bleary eyes and asked, "Who are you?"

"It's me, Hu Yan."

Chonger was startled and realized that he had fallen into some kind of trap that Hu Yan had laid for him, so he threw aside his blankets and sat up, cursing: "Why didn't you tell me what was going on? What do you mean by dragging me out of the city?"

"We are going to help you take power in Jin."

"I don't want to go!" Chonger said. "There is no guarantee that I will achieve anything in Jin, and I don't want to jeopardize my position in Qi."

Hu Yan told him a lie: "We are already more than one hundred *li* from the Qi capital. When the Marquis of Qi discovers that you have run away, he will send the army in pursuit. There is no way that you can go back."

Chonger was extremely angry. Having noticed the spear that Wei Chou was carrying, he grabbed it out of his hands and tried to stab Hu Yan.

Did he survive? READ ON.

Chapter Thirty-five

The Honorable Chonger of Jin travels around the Zhou confederacy.

Lady Huai Ying of Qin marries two husbands.

The Honorable Chonger was so furious at Hu Yan's plan to get him out of Qi that he grabbed the spear that Wei Chou was holding and stabbed at him. Hu Yan got out of the chariot as quickly as he could, but Chonger leapt down and chased him with the spear. Zhao Cui, Jiu Ji, Hu Mao, and Jie Zitui all got out of their chariot to help try to calm him down. Chonger threw the spear onto the ground in a fury. Hu Yan kowtowed and apologized: "If killing me would help you to feel better—go ahead!"

"If this journey ends with me becoming the Marquis of Jin, then we will draw a line under these events," Chonger told him. "If, on the other hand, I have to spend the rest of my life in exile, I swear that I will eat your flesh!"

Hu Yan answered with a laugh: "If we do not succeed, I will be leaving my corpse exposed in the wilderness somewhere, in which case you are hardly likely to want to eat it! If we are victorious, you are going to be eating the finest of delicacies served in beautiful bronze dishes. In that case, what would you want my rank old meat for?"

Zhao Cui and the others came forward and said, "We have abandoned our families and left our homes to travel far away, simply because we believe that you, sir, have a great future ahead of you. We have given up everything to follow you because we are hoping that our biographies will one day be recorded in books of bamboo and silk. The present Marquis of Jin is a wicked man; every single one of his subjects would be happy to see you become their next ruler. If you do not show that you are willing to take the title, why should anyone come to the state of Qi to escort you back to Jin? We were all involved in plotting to get you away; this was not just Hu Yan's idea. You should not make him take full responsibility for this."

Wei Chou also said in a loud voice: "A man ought to work hard to establish a good reputation and to become famous. What is to be done about the kind of person who only cares about enjoying family life rather than considering his duties to his people?"

Chonger's expression changed as he said, "Under the circumstances, I have to go along with what you have arranged."

Hu Mao then presented him with some coarse rice, while Jie Zitui gave him a cup of water to drink. Chonger and his followers ate and drank their fill. Hoo Shu and the others cut some grass to feed the horses, before harnessing them up again. The chariots were then put back on the road and they continued along in the same direction.

There is a poem that testifies to this:

When the phoenix leaves the flock of chickens, it soars high into the air;
When the tiger departs from the wildcats' lair, it roams deep in the mountains.
If you wanted to know if Chonger could become hegemon,
You need only to observe his journey through the Central States.

Within one day's journey, they arrived in the state of Cao. The only thing in this world that Lord Gong of Cao cared about was having fun. He paid no attention whatsoever to any matter of government, and he surrounded himself with small-minded flatterers and oily courtiers, at the expense of real gentlemen. He treated the hereditary aristocracy of Cao like dirt. He had more than three hundred cronies at court, to whom he had given the right to wear the official robes of grandees and to ride in fancy carriages. These men were all scum drawn from the marketplace and bars of the capital, but they knew how to amuse and please His Lordship. When they saw the Honorable Chonger of Jin arrive with an entourage of exceptionally brilliant knights, this really was an instance of how oil and water can never mix. They were terrified that these people might stay in Cao, so they were determined to prevent Lord Gong from having anything to do with them.

Grandee Xi Fuji remonstrated: "The ruling houses of Jin and Cao belong to the same clan. The Honorable Chonger is a poor man and he is passing through our territory, so we should treat him generously."

"Cao is a little country and we are sandwiched between great states," Lord Gong of Cao said. "There are a great many men in Chonger's position coming and going through our lands. If I have to treat all of them with full ritual, it is going to be really expensive. How am I supposed to cope?"

"The Honorable Chonger is famous around the world as a wise and good man, in addition to which he has double pupils and fused ribs: these are the signs of greatness," Xi Fuji said. "You cannot treat him as an ordinary junior member of an aristocratic house."

Lord Gong of Cao was very childish; on being told of the Honorable Chonger's wisdom and goodness, he could not have cared less. On the other hand, once his double pupils and fused ribs were mentioned, he said, "I have heard of double pupils before. But what are fused ribs?"

"Fused ribs mean that these bones have grown together," Xi Fuji told him. "This is a most remarkable thing."

"I don't believe it!" Lord Gong of Cao said. "Let him stay at the guesthouse, so that I can watch him in his bath."

He ordered his people to take the Honorable Chonger to the guesthouse, where he was served with water and ordinary food. No stipend was offered and no banquet was served, nor were the normal ceremonies between a host and a guest performed. Chonger was angry and refused to eat. The servants at the guesthouse prepared a bath and invited him to wash. The Honorable Chonger was filthy from his journey and was delighted with the idea of bathing, so he took off his clothes and got into the bath. Lord Gong of Cao and a couple of his cronies went to the guesthouse in plain clothes. They burst into the room where the Honorable Chonger was having his bath and insisted on scrutinizing him closely. They got a good look at his fused ribs and discussed the matter thoroughly. Having reduced the guesthouse to chaos, they left. Hu Yan and the others heard that some strangers had come and rushed to see who it was. Then they heard the sound of laughter and joking, so they asked the servants at the guesthouse what was going on. This was when they discovered that it was the ruler of Cao. Both Chonger and his companions were furious.

Xi Fuji had remonstrated with the Earl of Cao, who paid no attention. He then went home, and his wife met him at the door. Observing his depressed expression, she asked, "Did something happen at court?" Xi Fuji explained that the Honorable Chonger of Jin had arrived in Cao and that Lord Gong had been rude to him.

"Today I was picking mulberries out beyond the suburbs," his wife said thoughtfully, "when I saw the chariots of those people from Jin passing by. I did not get to see the Honorable Chonger properly, but his companions are all exceptional men. I have heard it said that you can tell a man by the company he keeps. Judging by his followers, the Honorable Chonger will have no problems in returning to the state of Jin in glory. When that happens, he will raise an army and attack Cao. The good here will then be destroyed along with the bad, but by that time it will be far too late for regrets. Since the Lord of Cao does not listen to loyal advice, you will have to make your own private approach to the Honorable Chonger. I have already prepared several dishes of food. If you were to conceal a white jade disc among them as a first meeting present, you can establish good relations before you have even met. You had better do this as soon as possible."

Xi Fuji followed her advice and visited the guesthouse that very night. Chonger was both furious and hungry, so when he heard that Grandee Xi Fuji of Cao was wanting to see him and had brought food, he summoned him in. Xi Fuji bowed twice and apologized for His Lordship's rudeness, while also making it clear that the food was intended to show his own great respect for the Honorable Chonger.

Chonger was very pleased, then he sighed and said: "I did not know that Cao had ministers like you. If I am so lucky as to gain power in Jin, one day I will find a way to pay you back for all your kindness." While he was eating, Chonger discovered the white jade disc, and he told Xi Fuji: "You have been very kind to me and prevented me from starving to death here. That is enough; you do not need to give me such a lavish gift."

"That is just a little token of my esteem," Xi Fuji said. "I hope that you will not refuse to accept it." However, Chonger absolutely insisted that he could not take it.

When Xi Fuji finally left, he sighed and said, "The Honorable Chonger is a very poor man in an extremely difficult situation, and yet he is not greedy for my jade disc. Such a man will achieve anything he sets his mind to!"

The following day, the Honorable Chonger set off on the next stage of his journey. Xi Fuji escorted him some ten *li* out of the city, though this was done in a private capacity.

A historian wrote a poem about this:

He made the mistake of thinking that this tiger was nothing but a moggy;
The ignorant Lord Gong of Cao had no idea what he was dealing with.
How sad that in his entourage of three hundred men,
There was not one to match Xi Fuji's wife.

On leaving Cao, the Honorable Chonger arrived in Song. Hu Yan rode on ahead in his chariot to meet Marshal Gongsun Gu.

"His grace completely overestimated his capabilities and ended up trying to do battle with Chu," Gongsun Gu explained. "Our army was defeated and his grace injured in the leg; in fact, right up to the present day he still has not recovered from this injury and cannot get out of bed. However, he has long been aware of the Honorable Chonger's brilliant reputation and a guesthouse has been specially prepared for your reception, with room for your chariots and horses."

Gongsun Gu then went into the palace to report this to Lord Xiang of Song. He was eaten up by his hatred for the kingdom of Chu, and day and night he prayed for someone to come and help him plan his revenge. Now he heard that the Honorable Chonger of Jin had arrived on his travels. Jin was a great state and the Honorable Chonger had an excellent reputation, so he could not have been more pleased. However, there was nothing that could be done about the fact that the wound in his knee had still not healed, so it was impossible for him to go and meet his visitor. Instead he ordered Gongsun Gu to go to the suburbs to meet him there and escort him to the guesthouse, performing all the rituals of a host on the Duke of Song's behalf. He even ordered that seven sets of animals should be sacrificed in Chonger's honor.

The following day the Honorable Chonger wanted to continue on his journey, but Gongsun Gu begged him to stay over and over again, just as he had been instructed by Lord Xiang. He also inquired privately of Hu Yan: "When you first arrived in Qi, what did Lord Huan offer him?" Hu Yan told him that the Honorable Chonger had been given a wife and a gift of horses. Gongsun Gu reported this to the Duke of Song.

"There is already a marriage alliance between Jin and ourselves, so I cannot possibly give him one of my daughters," Lord Xiang of Song said. "On the other hand, a gift of horses would be perfectly acceptable."

He then presented him with twenty teams, and the Honorable Chonger was more pleased than he could say. He stayed in Song for a couple of days, during which an endless succession of banquets and feasts was held. Hu Yan realized that no one held out any hope of the Duke of Song recovering from his injury, so he discussed with Gongsun Gu which state they should go to next.

"If the Honorable Chonger was looking for a respite from his troubles, even though Song is only a small state, it would offer him a comfortable asylum," Gongsun Gu said. "If, on the other hand, he is ambitious, we have just suffered a terrible defeat in battle and cannot possibly help him, so you had better go to one of the other great states that is in a position to assist you."

"I appreciate your honesty," Hu Yan told him.

He immediately reported this to the Honorable Chonger, and they began their packing. When Lord Xiang of Song heard that the Honorable Chonger was leaving, he gave further gifts of food and clothing, which really pleased his companions.

After the Honorable Chonger left, Lord Xiang's arrow wound festered more badly with each passing day, and not long afterwards he died. On his deathbed, he told Scion Wangchen: "I got into this position because I did not listen to Gongsun Gu's advice. When you become the Duke of Song, you should entrust him with the business of government. Chu is our enemy; you must never ever make an alliance with them. If the Honorable Chonger returns to Jin, he will become the marquis. If he becomes the marquis, he will unite all the other feudal lords under his authority. As long as you remain on the same side as Jin, Song will be at peace."

Scion Wangchen bowed twice and accepted his father's commands. Lord Xiang died after fourteen years in power. Scion Wangchen presided over the funeral and then succeeded to the title as Lord Cheng of Song.

An old man wrote a poem explaining that Lord Xiang of Song was neither a virtuous nor a powerful ruler and so he should not be ranked among the Five Hegemons. This poem reads:

He got himself severely injured before ever achieving anything,
Yet he was proud of his idiotic attitudes and poses.
This weakling paid no attention to inconvenient facts,
Yet still people rank Lord Xiang of Song among the Five Hegemons!

When the Honorable Chonger left Song, he went to the state of Zheng, and his arrival was immediately reported to Lord Wen of Zheng. He discussed this situation with his ministers: "The Honorable Chonger rebelled against his father and fled into exile, circumstances that make it impossible for any of the other states to install him in power now. He has been reduced to near-starvation on many occasions. This is not a good person, and there is no need for us to treat him with full ritual propriety."

The senior minister Shu Zhan remonstrated with him: "The Honorable Chonger of Jin is assisted by three things that demonstrate that Heaven is protecting him. You must not treat him rudely."

"What are these three things?" the Earl of Zheng demanded.

"As we all know, if two members of the same clan marry, their offspring will not prosper," Shu Zhan replied. "But Chonger is the son of a woman from the Hu family, and they are members of the Ji clan. In spite of this handicap, he has an excellent reputation as a most worthy man and has traveled all over the place without coming to any lasting harm. That is the first sign. Since the Honorable Chonger went into exile, the state of Jin has not known a moment's peace, which surely means that Heaven intends to see a capable man installed in power there! That is the second sign. Zhao Cui and Hu Yan are both remarkable men, and yet they have been prepared to subordinate themselves and serve the Honorable Chonger. That is the third sign. Just based on that, Your Lordship ought to treat him with full ritual propriety. It is well to behave properly to a member of your own clan, to show sympathy for someone in trouble, to show respect for a brilliant man, and to accord with the wishes of Heaven."

"The Honorable Chonger is an old man," the Earl of Zheng said. "What can he do?"

"If you are not going to treat him properly, then you had better kill him," Shu Zhan replied. "You do not want to leave such an enemy alive to cause trouble for you in the future."

The Earl of Zheng laughed and said, "That is going a bit far! First you want me to treat him with full ritual propriety, then you want me to kill him! Why should I be nice to him? Why should I be so cruel?" He ordered the gatekeepers in the capital to close the gates and not allow the Honorable Chonger into the city.

When Chonger realized that Zheng was not going to let him in, he spurred on his chariot and traveled to the kingdom of Chu, where he sought an audience with King Cheng. King Cheng treated him just as if he were indeed the Marquis of Jin, offering him a banquet and holding a sacrifice in his honor in which nine sets of animals were killed. Chonger did not want to participate in this on the grounds that his position did not warrant it.

Zhao Cui was standing by his side and said, "You have been in exile for decades and now even small states think that they can bully you, not to mention the large ones. This is Heaven's will. You cannot refuse." The Honorable Chonger then agreed to attend the banquet. The whole way through, the king of Chu treated him with the utmost respect, while the Honorable Chonger showed himself to be suitably modest. The two men got along very well together, and Chonger decided to stay in Chu.

One day the king of Chu was out hunting with the Honorable Chonger in the Yunmeng Marshes. The king of Chu was showing off his martial prowess and shot at first a deer and then a hare, killing both of them. The generals present prostrated themselves on the ground and congratulated him. Subsequently they happened across a bear, which charged the chariot.

"Why do you not shoot it?" the king of Chu asked.

The Honorable Chonger held firm to his bow and nocked his arrow, praying silently: "If I am going to return to my country and become the new lord, may this arrow lodge in the beast's right paw." He then let fly a single arrow, which did indeed strike the animal in its right paw. The officers captured the bear and presented it to His Majesty. The king of Chu was amazed and impressed: "You, sir, are truly a wonderful shot!"

A short time later, some of the beaters started shouting. The king of Chu sent his servants to investigate. They came back shortly and reported: "Out in the mountains, the beaters put up an animal that is somewhat like a bear. It has a trunk like an elephant, it has a head like a lion, it has paws like a tiger, it has fur like a leopard, it has bristles like a wild boar, it has a tail like an ox, and it is about the same size as a horse. Its fur is patterned in black and white spots, and neither swords nor spears nor arrows have been able to wound it. Its jaws can cut through iron as if it were butter, and it has crunched its way through the metal fittings on our chariots. It is much more powerful than we can deal with. We have lost control of the situation, and that is why we started shouting."

"You have lived for a long time in the Central Plains, sir, and know many things," the king of Chu said to Chonger. "You must know what this animal is."

The Honorable Chonger turned his head to look at Zhao Cui, who stepped forward and said, "I know. This animal is called a 'Mo.' It is born from the collected essence of Metal. It has a small head and tiny feet, and it loves to eat bronze and iron. Wherever its urine or excrement lands, there you will find the five metals, but they will instantly melt away into water. Its bones do not have any marrow, which means they can be used to make pestles; if you make its skin into a cloak, it will ward off damp and disease."

"How does one capture this amazing animal?" the king of Chu asked.

"The skin and flesh of this creature are made of iron, so the only point of attack is by stabbing it with a pure steel weapon through the nose," Zhao Cui said. "Alternatively, you can kill it by burning it—as this creature is Metal, the only thing it really fears is Fire."

When he had finished speaking, Wei Chou shouted: "I will capture this beast alive without using any weapons. Let me present it to Your Majesty!" He jumped down from the chariot and ran off.

The king of Chu said to Chonger, "Let us go and see what he does." He ordered that his chariot should be driven after him.

Wei Chou had run to the northwestern corner of the encirclement, and the moment that he caught sight of the animal, he rushed in and punched it a couple of times. The beast was not at all frightened but made a cry somewhat like the lowing of a cow. It got up and licked the golden belt buckle at Wei Chou's waist. Wei Chou was furious and shouted: "Pestiferous animal! How dare you be so rude?" He leapt back about five feet, while the animal rolled into a ball and came to a halt some way away, squatting down. Wei Chou became even angrier and launched himself towards it. With all his might, he leapt up on top of the beast and put his two hands around its throat. The Mo did its best to throw him off, but Wei Chou hung on, never losing his grip. After struggling for some time, the animal became exhausted. Wei Chou was more than strong enough to keep hold of it and exerted more and more pressure on the animal's neck, so that it could not breathe or move. Wei Chou jumped off and rubbed his well-muscled arms a bit. Then with one hand on the Mo's elephant-like nose, he brought it in front of the king of Chu's chariot, leading it just as if it were a lamb or a dog. What an amazing man! Zhao Cui ordered the officers present to light fires and sedate the beast with smoke; the Mo then collapsed in a heap. Wei Chou let go of it completely, and, taking the precious sword from his belt, he tried to behead it. The sword flashed but the animal was unhurt.

"If you want to kill this animal and take the skin," Zhao Cui said, "you will have to light fires all around it and roast it to death." The king of Chu followed his advice. The Mo had flesh like iron, but as the fires built up around it raged ever hotter, it gradually softened to the point where you could cut it.

"Your followers really are remarkable!" the king of Chu exclaimed. "They are skilled in every art. I am sure that they are a match for ten thousand of my men!"

The Chu general, Cheng Dechen, was standing next to King Cheng when he said this, and he did not look at all pleased. He immediately said to the king of Chu, "You have praised this man's martial abilities; let me fight a bout with him!"

The king of Chu refused, saying, "He is just as much a guest of mine as the Honorable Chonger, so please show him some respect."

After the hunt was concluded, a great banquet was held. The king of Chu asked Chonger: "If you come to power in the state of Jin, how will you repay me?"

"You already have more than enough maids and servants, jade and silk, Your Majesty," Chonger replied. "Likewise, the kingdom of Chu produces vast quantities of fur and feather goods, ivory and leather. What can I do to pay you back?"

The king of Chu laughed and said, "Nevertheless, you must do something to repay me, and I want to hear what it will be."

"If thanks to Your Majesty's beneficent influences I am fortunate enough to be able to return to the state of Jin, I hope that our two countries will be able to coexist in harmony, allowing our people to enjoy a lasting peace," Chonger said. "If that proves impossible and you invade the central plains, I will withdraw three days' travel."

On an average day, an army would advance thirty li *before camping for the night, so three days' travel represents ninety* li. *What the Honorable Chonger meant by this was that should Chu and Jin go to war, he would retreat ninety* li *before he would turn around and do battle. This was his way of requiting the kindness that he had received in the kingdom of Chu.*

When the banquet that evening was over, the Chu general, Cheng Dechen, spoke crossly to King Cheng: "You have treated the Honorable Chonger of Jin with great generosity, but look what he said to you today! If in the future he goes home, he will certainly betray all the kindness that you have shown him. I ask your permission to kill him."

"The Honorable Chonger is a good man, his followers are all exceptionally brilliant, and Heaven seems to be on his side," the king of Chu said. "Do you think that I am stupid enough to go against the will of Heaven?"

"If you will not have Chonger murdered, Your Majesty, then you should keep back Hu Yan and Zhao Cui, to prevent trouble in the future," Cheng Dechen told him.

"If I make them stay here, they won't work for me, so I would just be storing up resentment," the king of Chu said. "I have been doing my best to get on good terms with the Honorable Chonger. I am not going to wreck that now!"

From this point onwards he treated Chonger with even greater liberality.

• • •

To turn to another part of the story: It was now the fifteenth year of the reign of King Xiang of Zhou, which was also the fourteenth year that Lord Hui of Jin had been in power. That year Lord Hui became seriously ill, to the point where he was no longer able to attend court, but Scion Yu was still being held hostage by the state of Qin. Scion Yu's mother came from the ruling house of the state of Liang, but her father was an unprincipled man who paid no attention to the sufferings of his people and ordered them to work on grandiose building projects for him. His people hated him, and many fled as refugees to the state of Qin so that they would not have to work as forced labor on these schemes. Lord Mu of Qin took advantage of this alienation from his populace to order Baili Xi to raise an army and make a surprise attack on Liang, which resulted in the destruction of this state. The ruler of Liang was murdered by his rioting subjects.

When Scion Yu heard that Liang had been destroyed, he sighed and said, "Qin has ruined my maternal family; that means they don't care what happens to me!" He developed a profound loathing for the Qin regime. On hearing that Lord Hui of Jin was sick, he thought to himself: "I am a hostage here, without any support from Qin, and I have lost contact with people at home. If something happens to my father, the ministers and grandees will establish one of my brothers as the next lord, in which case I will have to spend the rest of my life here. Am I really doomed to be just a pawn in other people's machinations? I had better run away and go home, where I can look after my sick father and ensure my position among the people."

That night he explained his ideas to his wife, Lady Huai Ying, while they were in bed together: "If I don't go home immediately, someone else will inherit the marquisate of Jin. But if I do go home, it will break up our marriage. How about you go with me to the state of Jin, for that would be the best of all possible worlds?"

Lady Huai Ying began to cry, and replied: "As the scion of an important state, you have been consistently humiliated during your time here as a hostage, so it is entirely natural that you would want to go home. His Lordship married me to you so that I could help you settle down. If I were to follow you home, then I would be betraying His Lordship's trust in me. I cannot do that. You will have to make your own decision. Don't discuss it with me! Although I do not dare to go with you, I will not reveal your secrets to anyone else." Scion Yu then escaped and went home to Jin.

When Lord Mu of Qin heard that Scion Yu had left without saying goodbye, he cursed him roundly: "You traitorous bastard! May Heaven strike you dead!" He then told his ministers, "Yiwu and his son have both betrayed me. I must have my revenge!"

He really regretted that he had not installed the Honorable Chonger in power years ago, and he now sent someone to find out what had become of him. Thus he discovered that the last few months he had been living in Chu. Lord Mu of Qin then sent Noble Grandson Qi on an embassy to the king of Chu, with a view to bringing Chonger back to Qin to put him in power.

Chonger was deliberately mendacious in his discussions with the king of Chu: "I owe my life to Your Majesty. I do not want to go to Qin."

"The kingdom of Chu is a long way away from Jin," King Cheng reminded him. "If you want to succeed to the marquisate, you are going to have to go somewhere else. Qin and Jin are neighboring states, and it takes less than a day to get from one to the other. The Earl of Qin is a very sensible man, who loathes the present Marquis of Jin. This is your great opportunity and you have to go!"

Chonger bowed and bade him farewell. The king of Chu gave him generous presents of gold and silk, horses and chariots, to ensure that he would travel in style. It took several months for the Honorable Chonger to make his way to Qin. Even though he had to pass through the territory of many different states on the way, all were subordinate either to Chu or to Qin; moreover, he was traveling in the company of Noble Grandson Qi. This easy voyage does not need to be described in any detail.

When Lord Mu of Qin heard the news that the Honorable Chonger had arrived, he was absolutely delighted. He went out to the suburbs to meet him in person and escorted him to an official guesthouse, where he was treated with the utmost ceremony. Lord Mu of Qin's principal wife, Lady Mu Ji, had always been fond of Chonger, and she loathed Scion Yu, so she encouraged her husband to bestow Lady Huai Ying on him as his wife, uniting the two countries by a marriage alliance.

Lord Mu sent his wife to suggest this to Lady Huai Ying, who said, "I have already lost my virginity to Scion Yu, so how can I marry again?"

"Scion Yu is not coming back," Lady Mu Ji told her. "The Honorable Chonger is a wise man who has many supporters, so he will become the Marquis of Jin one of these days. When he comes to power in Jin, you must be his principal wife to affirm the alliance between Qin and Jin from one generation to the next."

Lady Huai Ying was silent for a long time, then said, "If what you say is true, how can I begrudge myself when I could be affirming this alliance?"

Lord Mu sent Noble Grandson Qi to speak to Chonger. Scion Yu was the Honorable Chonger's nephew, which made Lady Huai Ying his niece by marriage, so Chonger refused the marriage alliance on the grounds that it represented generational incest.

Zhao Cui came forward and said: "I have heard that Lady Huai Ying is a beautiful and intelligent woman who is much loved by both the Earl of Qin and his wife. If you do not marry this woman, you cannot cement your alliance with Qin. I have heard it said: if you want other people to love you, you must first love them; if you want other people to obey you, you must first obey them. You cannot refuse a marriage alliance with Qin and still expect them to support you. Do not say no!"

"It is forbidden to marry someone of the same clan, and generational incest is even more taboo!" the Honorable Chonger said.

Jiu Ji came forward and said: "When people in the past forbade intermarriage among members of the same clan, they were referring to people with the same spiritual qualities and not to being part of the same bloodline. The Yellow Emperor and the Red Emperor were both sons of the ruler of the state of Youxiong, a man named Shaodian. The Yellow Emperor was born at the Ji River and the Red Emperor at the Jiang River. However, since these two men had different spiritual qualities, the Yellow Emperor took the clan name Ji and the Red Emperor took the clan name Jiang. The Ji and Jiang families have intermarried for many generations. Of the twenty-five sons of the Yellow Emperor, fourteen established their own clan names, but of them only Ji and Qi count as having the same moral values and principles. If your spiritual values and your clan name are the same, no matter how distantly you may be related, you cannot get married. If your spiritual values and your surnames are different, no matter how closely you are related, you can still get married. The sage-king Yao was the son of Diku and hence a grandson in the fifth generation of the Yellow Emperor. The sage-king Shun was a grandson in the eighth generation of the Yellow Emperor, which made Yao's daughters Shun's great-aunts. Nevertheless, Yao proposed that his daughters should marry Shun, and Shun did not refuse. These are the principles by which people in antiquity regulated their marriages. Are you telling me that you have the same spiritual values as Scion Yu? Are you telling me that marrying Lady Huai Ying is worse than marrying a great-aunt? You are marrying your nephew's abandoned ex-wife; you are not stealing her from him. Who is getting hurt?"

Chonger discussed this further with Hu Yan. "Do you think I should do this, Uncle?"

"When you go back to Jin, are you planning to work for the marquis?" Hu Yan asked. "Or do you want to replace him?" Chonger did not reply, and Hu Yan continued. "Scion Yu is just about to become the next marquis. If you are planning to work for him, then Lady Huai Ying should be treated as the future Mother of the Country. If, on the other hand, you are thinking of replacing him, then she is the wife of your enemy. Any more questions?"

Chonger still looked worried. "Since you are planning to wrest the state of Jin from his grasp," Zhao Cui said, "why do you balk at taking his wife away from him? What is the point of fussing about a minor matter when you are determined to accomplish great things?"

The Honorable Chonger then made his decision. Noble Grandson Qi reported back to Lord Mu of Qin. Chonger selected an auspicious day for the wedding, which was held in the official guesthouse. Lady Huai Ying turned out to be much more beautiful than his previous wife, Lady Jiang of Qi. She had also carefully selected four women from her clan who would serve as junior wives, all of whom were very lovely. Chonger was so pleased that he completely forgot the travails he had suffered.

A historian wrote a poem discussing Lady Huai Ying's marriages:

Can a woman have two husbands?
Can she marry both an uncle and a nephew?
Provided that this wedding cemented the alliance with Qin,
They did not care that people criticized this violation of ritual propriety.

Lord Mu of Qin had always admired the personality of the Honorable Chonger of Jin, added to which they were now doubly related by marriage. The friendship between these two men flourished as they attended banquets together every three days and met for dinner every five days. Scion Ying of Qin also had a great deal of respect for Chonger and went to see him regularly. Zhao Cui, Hu Yan, and the others became very closely associated with the Qin senior ministers like Jian Shu, Baili Xi, and Noble Grandson Qi, as they planned how Chonger should return to his state. They did not want to be premature in their attack, partly because the Honorable Chonger was newly married and partly because there had not yet been any overt signs of trouble in the state of Jin. However, as the ancient saying goes: "When the time is right, even an iron tree will put out flowers." Since Heaven had created Chonger and destined him to become the Marquis of Jin and a famous hegemon, naturally it would give him an opportunity to show what he could do.

. . .

When Scion Yu came home from Qin, he had an audience with his father, Lord Hui of Jin. His Lordship was delighted and said, "I have been sick for a long time, and it has worried me greatly that I had no one who could be trusted to carry out my duties. Now that you have been able to escape from captivity, you can take over and I can relax."

In the ninth month, he became critically ill. Therefore, he ordered Lü Yisheng and Xi Rui to support Scion Yu: "You do not need to worry about the other members of the ruling house; you just need to deal with Chonger." Lü Yisheng and Xi Rui kowtowed and declared that they would carry out his orders.

That night, Lord Hui died. Scion Yu presided over his funeral before taking power under the title of Lord Huai. The new Marquis of Jin was afraid that Chonger would launch a coup, so he issued orders: "All those subjects of Jin who followed the Honorable Chonger into exile have three months to return. If they come back within this time limit, they will have their old jobs back and there will be no reprisals. If, on the other hand, they do not come back within this time, their names will be struck off from their clan registers and they will be condemned to death in absentia. Any family members who refuse to call them back to Jin will be executed with no possibility of pardon."

The old minister, Hu Tu, had two sons who had followed the Honorable Chonger the whole way to Qin: Hu Yan and Hu Mao. Xi Rui privately urged Hu Tu to write a letter to his sons, summoning them back to the state of Jin. Hu Tu refused again and again.

Xi Rui then spoke to Lord Huai. "Hu Yan and Hu Mao are men of truly remarkable talents, and they have played a key role in supporting the Honorable Chonger. I am not sure what is going on, but their father refuses to call them back. You had better speak to him yourself, my lord."

Lord Huai sent someone to call Hu Tu into his presence. Hu Tu said his final farewells to his family and staff before he left. When he had an audience with Lord Huai, he presented his opinion: "Due to ill health, I was resting at home. I do not know what you wish to discuss with me, my lord."

"Your sons are in exile abroad," Lord Huai said. "Have you written to them telling them to come back?"

"No," Hu Tu replied.

"I have issued commands that if an individual does not come back within the appointed time, his family and friends will be punished in his stead," said Lord Huai. "Did you not know that?"

"My sons have worked for the Honorable Chonger for a long time," Hu Tu replied. "When a loyal subject serves his lord, he is loyal until death. My sons are loyal to Chonger just the same way that ministers at court are loyal to their ruler, and that is why they followed him into exile. If they were to betray him by coming home, I would kill them at our family temple. How could I possibly summon them back?"

Lord Huai was furious. He shouted to two guards to put the keen edge of their swords against his neck. "If your sons come back, I will pardon you." He had bamboo strips placed in front of Hu Tu, while Xi Rui guided his hand writing the letter.

"Let go of me!" Hu Tu shouted. "I will write it myself."

He then wrote in large letters: "A son cannot have two fathers; a subject cannot serve two rulers."

Lord Huai was very angry and said, "Aren't you afraid of the consequences?"

"I am more worried that a son might prove unfilial or that a subject might be disloyal," Hu Tu replied. "Everyone has to die sooner or later, so what is there to be afraid of?" He stretched out his neck for the sword. Lord Huai ordered that he be beheaded in the marketplace.

The Grand Astrologer Guo Yan went to see his exposed corpse and said with a sigh, "His Lordship has only just succeeded to the marquisate and his position is still highly unstable, yet he has already started torturing and executing old ministers. Can disaster be far away?" He immediately proclaimed that he had been struck down by a severe illness that prevented him from setting foot outside his house. The surviving members of the Hu family and their servants made haste to flee into exile in Qin, where they reported what had happened to Hu Yan and Hu Mao.

Do you know what they did next? READ ON.

Chapter Thirty-six

The Lü and Xi families of Jin conspire to set fire to the palace.

Lord Mu of Qin pacifies a second civil war in Jin.

The two brothers Hu Yan and Hu Mao had followed the Honorable Chonger as far as Qin. Now they heard that their father, Hu Tu, had been murdered by order of Lord Huai of Jin, and they beat their breasts and wept loudly. Zhao Cui, Jiu Ji, and the others all tried to console them.

"The dead can never come back to life, so what does it avail you to mourn so excessively?" Zhao Cui said. "Let us go and see Chonger, for we have important matters to discuss."

Hu Mao and Hu Yan then dried their tears and went to have an audience with the Honorable Chonger. Hu Mao and Hu Yan said, "Lord Hui is now dead and Scion Yu has succeeded to the title of Marquis of Jin. He has given everyone who followed you into exile a deadline to come back. If we do not go back, then our family and friends will be punished in our stead. Since our father refused to summon us, he has been killed." When they finished speaking, they burst into tears again, their hearts pierced by pain.

"Uncles, do not be so sad!" Chonger said. "The day that I take power in Jin, I will avenge the death of my grandfather."

He immediately went to have an audience with Lord Mu, to report what had happened in the state of Jin.

"Heaven wants you to take charge in Jin," Lord Mu told him. "This opportunity cannot be lost! I know what to do."

"If you want to protect Chonger's chances, you will have to move quickly, my lord," Zhao Cui replied in his stead. "Once Scion Yu's accession has been formally reported at the ancestral temple, the respective positions of ruler and subject will be fixed and it will be very difficult to overturn." Lord Mu agreed with every word that he said.

Chonger said goodbye and went home to his official residence. Just as he had sat down, the gatekeeper reported: "A man has arrived from the state of Jin and says that he has some top-secret information. He is demanding to see you."

The Honorable Chonger summoned the man in and asked him his name. He bowed and said: "My name is Luan Dun, and I am the son of Grandee Luan Zhi of Jin. This new marquis is completely paranoid and has instituted a reign of terror. The people loathe him, and none of his ministers will accept his authority. My father has sent me here secretly to throw in our lot with yours. Scion Yu only trusts two men: Lü Yisheng and Xi Rui. Old ministers like Xi Buyang and Han Jian have lost power completely. My father has contacted people like Xi Cou and Zhou Zhi Qiao; they are raising a private army together. They are waiting for you to go back to Jin to help you take power there."

Chonger was very pleased and agreed that on New Year's Day the following year he would meet him at the Yellow River. Luan Zhi then said goodbye and left. Chonger prayed to Heaven and then performed a divination using the *Book of Changes*, from which he obtained the six lines of the hexagram "Great." He was not at all sure how to interpret this, so he summoned Hu Yan to tell him if it was auspicious or not.

Hu Yan bowed and congratulated him: "This hexagram combines the trigrams that signify Heaven and Earth. It means that you will get great returns for only a small outlay. It is the most auspicious of omens. This time you will not only become Marquis of Jin, you will also become the new Master of Covenants." Chonger then told Hu Yan what Luan Dun had said.

"Tomorrow, you must ask the Earl of Qin for an army," Hu Yan told him. "You cannot delay a moment longer!"

The following day, Chonger went to court to make his request to Lord Mu of Qin. His Lordship did not wait for him to open his mouth: "I know that you are anxious to return to Jin, but I am afraid that my ministers will not stand for the army being turned over to your command. I will have to go with you at least as far as the Yellow River."

Chonger bowed, thanked him, and withdrew. When Pi Bao heard that Lord Mu was about to install the Honorable Chonger in power, he wanted to lead the vanguard of the army. Lord Mu agreed to this. The

Grand Astrologer selected the most auspicious day for them to set off, which turned out to be in the twelfth month.

Three days before this date, Lord Mu held a banquet at Mount Jiulong to see off the Honorable Chonger of Jin, at which he presented him with ten pairs of white jade discs, four hundred horses, the complete furnishings for his residence, and all sorts of other gifts too numerous to be recorded here. Zhao Cui and the Honorable Chonger's nine other followers each received a pair of white jade discs and a team of four horses. Chonger and his supporters bowed twice and thanked him.

On the day of departure, Lord Mu of Qin led out an army of four hundred chariots, in the company of Baili Xi, Yao Yu, his senior generals the Honorable Zhi, Noble Grandson Qi, the commander of the vanguard Pi Bao, and so on. Having left the protection of the city walls of Yongzhou, they turned east. Scion Ying of Qin had become a close friend of the Honorable Chonger and was very upset to see him go. He escorted them as far as the north side of the Wei River before saying goodbye with tears in his eyes.

A poem on this subject reads:

Brave generals and battle-hardened troops, like tigers and wolves,
Escorted the Honorable Chonger to the border.
Lord Huai's execution of Hu Tu was all in vain,
Just like trying to blot out the sunshine with your hands.

In the first month of the first year of Lord Huai of Jin, which was the sixteenth year of the reign of King Xiang of Zhou, Lord Mu of Qin and the Honorable Chonger of Jin arrived on the banks of the Yellow River. The boats were ready and waiting to take him across. Lord Mu had arranged a further banquet there to send him on his way, and he said solemnly to Chonger, "When you get home, do not forget my wife and me." He ordered that one half of his army should follow the Honorable Chonger over onto the other side of the river, under the command of the Honorable Zhi and Pi Bao, while he himself would remain camped with the remainder west of the Yellow River. As the saying goes: "All you could see were triumphal banners; all you could hear were shouts of joy."

The man named Hoo Shu had been responsible for the Honorable Chonger's luggage ever since he first went into exile. When they traveled through Cao and Wey, there had been many times when they had gone hungry. As a result, he took a lot of trouble to keep the very last scraps of food and the last rags of clothing in case they should ever come in handy. Now, when it came to crossing the Yellow River, Hoo Shu was packing up the luggage until every little bit of food, worn-out mat, and tattered tent was carefully stowed on board the boat. Even things like the snacks that had been served with wine at this last banquet were as treasured as if they were jade and taken to the boats.

Chonger noticed this and burst out laughing: "Today I go back to Jin as their new marquis, and in future I will be eating only the finest of foods. What on earth do I need things like that for?" He gave orders that all these items should be left on the riverbank.

Hu Yan sighed to himself and said: "Before Chonger has even become rich and noble, he has already acquired the habits of extravagance and wastefulness. In the future he will only be interested in novel sensations, treating those of us who suffered in exile with him just like those worn-out mats and tattered tent curtains. What was the point of working so hard for him for nearly two decades? I will say goodbye now before we have even crossed the Yellow River, and then perhaps in the future he will still think of me kindly."

He then knelt down and presented the pair of white jade discs that the Earl of Qin had given him to the Honorable Chonger, saying: "Once you have crossed the Yellow River, you will be in Jin territory. With the support of the ministers inside Jin and the help of the generals from Qin, your victory is assured. There is no point in my following you anymore, so it is my intention to stay here in Qin serving you at a distance. Please accept these two white jade discs as a token of my esteem."

Chonger was shocked. "I always intended that you should share my wealth and honors, Uncle," he said. "Why are you talking about leaving me?"

"I am well aware that I have committed three crimes against you," Hu Yan said. "That is why I do not dare to follow you anymore."

"What three crimes?" Chonger asked.

"I have heard it said that a sagacious servant can bring his master respect; a good servant can bring his master peace," Hu Yan replied. "Thanks to my poor abilities, you suffered great hardship in Wulu. That is my first crime. You were treated with disrespect by the rulers of Cao and Wey. That is my second crime. I took advantage of the fact that you were drunk to get you away from the Qi capital, making you very angry with me. That is my third crime. Since you were still on your travels at that time, I did not dare to abandon you. Now you have arrived back at the borders of Jin, and those of us who have followed you in exile for so many years are completely worn out. Just like those leftover bits of food, we are no longer wanted; just like those worn-out mats and tattered tents, we have no further role to play. There is no point in my staying any longer. This is the reason why I am asking your permission to leave."

Chonger cried bitter tears and said, "You are absolutely right to complain of my behavior, Uncle; this was my mistake." He ordered Hoo Shu to put back all of the things that he had just been commanded to abandon. He also swore an oath at the riverbank: "If once I get back to Jin, I ever forget what my uncle has done for me and disagree with him on a matter of government policy, may my sons and grandsons fail to flourish."

Afterwards he threw the white jade discs into the river and said, "The God of the Yellow River will act as witness to my oath."

At this time Jie Zitui was on one of the other boats. When he heard that Chonger and Hu Yan had sworn an oath, he laughed and said, "It is by Heaven's will that the Honorable Chonger returns to Jin. How can Hu Yan take all the credit to himself? I am ashamed to be associated with such a greedy man."

From this point on, he resolved upon a life of reclusion.

. . .

After Chonger had crossed the Yellow River, he advanced eastward until he arrived at Linggu. Deng Hun, the chancellor of Linggu, ordered his men to climb up onto the walls and defend the city. The Qin army besieged the city and Pi Bao led a daring attack on the walls, breaching them. He captured Deng Hun and beheaded him. The two cities of Sangquan and Jiushuai heard what had happened and surrendered without a fight. When this news was reported to Lord Huai by his spies, he was deeply shocked and immediately mobilized all the soldiers and chariots that he could lay his hands on inside the state. He appointed Lü Yisheng as the commander-in-chief and Xi Rui as his deputy; the army was camped at Luliu to block the advance of the Qin forces. However, his men were afraid of the might of the Qin army and did not dare to do battle with them. The Honorable Zhi, representing Lord Mu of Qin, wrote a letter, which one of his servants carried to Lü Yisheng and Xi Rui. This ran:

> By any standards I have behaved extremely well in my dealings with the state of Jin, but Lord Hui and his son betrayed me and looked upon Qin as their enemy. I was prepared to put up with this treatment from the father, but I am not prepared to take it from the son. The Honorable Chonger is known to

> one and all as a clever and noble-minded man; he has the support of many knights, Heaven is on his side, and everyone inside and outside the country trusts to his honesty. I have brought my army to camp on the western side of the Yellow River and have ordered Zhi to escort the Honorable Chonger into Jin, so that he may preside over the state altars. If you two gentlemen retain a sense of right and wrong, then put down your arms and surrender to us. This is your last chance to avoid disaster!

After Lü Yisheng and Xi Rui read this letter, they were silent for a long time. They wanted to fight, but they were worried that they would not be able to resist the onslaught of the Qin army, in which case they were in for a repeat of what had happened at Mount Longmen. They wanted to surrender, but they were afraid that Chonger would prove a vengeful enemy, in which case they would suffer the same fate as that of Li Ke and Pi Zhengfu. Having hesitated for ages, they finally fixed upon a plan. They wrote a letter back to the Honorable Zhi as follows:

> We know that we have deeply offended the Honorable Chonger, and that is why we do not dare to relax our guard. In fact, we would be happy to support the Honorable Chonger, provided that he agrees to treat us just the same as the men who followed him into exile all those years ago. In that case, we will all be on the same side and there will be no reason to punish us for what we have done. Then we will obey any orders that you care to give us.

When the Honorable Zhi read their reply, he realized immediately that they were feeling isolated and frightened, so he went to Luliu on his own to see Lü Yisheng and Xi Rui.

Lü Yisheng and Xi Rui were delighted to come out of the city to welcome him and explain the nature of the problem: "We would be happy to surrender, but we are afraid that the Honorable Chonger will punish us. If you would swear a blood covenant with us, we will trust you."

"If you will withdraw your army toward the northeast," the Honorable Zhi suggested, "I can report your change of heart to the Honorable Chonger and the deal can be done."

Lü Yisheng and Xi Rui agreed, and once the Honorable Zhi had departed, they gave orders to withdraw and set up a new camp at the city of Xun. Chonger sent Hu Yan and the Honorable Zhi to Xun to meet with Lü Yisheng and Xi Rui. That very day they sacrificed an animal and swore an oath with its blood to be loyal to Chonger and support his succession to the marquisate. Once the covenant had been sworn, they sent an envoy to follow Hu Yan back to Jiushuai, where they picked up the Honorable Chonger and escorted him to the walled city of Xun to join the main force of the Jin army. From that time onwards, the army was under his command.

Since Lord Huai had received no news from Lü Yisheng and Xi Rui, he ordered the eunuch Bo Di to go to the Jin army to urge them to fight. En route he discovered that Lü Yisheng and Xi Rui had withdrawn their forces to the city of Xun and that they had made a peace treaty with Hu Yan and the Honorable Zhi, thereby betraying Lord Huai and putting Chonger in his place. He rushed back to report this development. Lord Huai was very alarmed and quickly summoned his ministers Xi Buyang, Han Jian, Luan Zhi, and Shi Hui to court to discuss this matter. These old ministers were all very fond of the Honorable Chonger, and they had been deeply angered by Lord Huai's reliance on Lü Yisheng and Xi Rui. "Now that that precious pair have betrayed His Lordship, things here are almost at the end of the road. What is the point in summoning us now?"

One after the other they refused to go; this one was feeling ill, that one had urgent business to attend to—less than half actually showed up at court. Lord Huai sighed deeply and said, "I should not have come back secretly. It is because I broke the alliance with Qin that things have reached this pass!"

Bo Di presented his opinion: "Your officials have all sworn allegiance to the Honorable Chonger in secret; you cannot stay here a moment longer! Let me drive you to Gaoliang, where you can hide out until you have made plans for how to deal with this crisis."

Now, the story is concerned not with Lord Huai of Jin going into exile in Gaoliang, but with what the Honorable Chonger did when Lü Yisheng and Xi Rui sent their envoys to greet him and bring him to the Jin army. The two men kowtowed and apologized, while Chonger spoke kindly to cheer them up. Zhao Cui, Jiu Ji, and the other men who had followed Chonger into exile met with them, and they all spoke freely together. Lü Yisheng and Xi Rui were very pleased with this, so they escorted Chonger into the city of Quwo, where he held court in the temple of his grandfather, Lord Wu. A number of ministers from the Jin capital city at Jiang, with Luan Zhi and Xi Cou at their head, arrived at Quwo, with a train of more than thirty men, including Shi Hui, Zhou Zhi Qiao, Yangshe Zhi, Xun Linfu, Xian Mie, and Qi Zheng. A further group of ministers, including Xi Buyang, Liang Yaomi, Han Jian, and Jia Putu, were waiting to welcome him on his arrival in the suburbs of the capital city of Jiang. The Honorable Chonger formally succeeded to the title on his arrival in the city, taking the title of Lord Wen. Chonger was forty-three years of age when he fled to the Di, fifty-five when he arrived in the state of Qi, and sixty-one when he arrived in Qin; by the time he finally made his way home to become the Marquis of Jin, he was already sixty-two years of age.

When Lord Wen had been established, he sent someone to Gaoliang to assassinate Lord Huai. Scion Yu had succeeded to the title in the ninth month of the previous year, and now he was murdered in the second month, meaning that from start to finish he was Marquis of Jin for less than six months. How sad! The eunuch Bo Di collected his body and buried it before fleeing into exile. No more of this.

. . .

Lord Wen held a series of banquets in honor of the Honorable Zhi and issued lavish rewards to the Qin army. Pi Bao wept and prostrated himself upon the ground, begging to be allowed to rebury his father, Pi Zhengfu, in a proper grave. Lord Wen agreed to this. Lord Wen also wanted Pi Bao to stay and take office in his government, but Pi Bao refused: "I have already accepted office at the Qin court. I would not dare serve a second lord." He then traveled back to the far side of the Yellow River with the Honorable Zhi to rejoin Lord Mu of Qin. His Lordship then stood down his army.

A historian wrote a poem praising Lord Mu of Qin:

As this magnificent army swept across the plains east of the Yellow River,
They were as fine as soaring dragons or rearing tigers.
If Lord Mu of Qin had not been motivated by a sense of justice,
Could he have scored such a signal victory?

Lü Yisheng and Xi Rui had been terrorized into surrender by the might of Qin. However, they remained suspicious and on edge; likewise, when they had any dealings with people like Zhao Cui or Jiu Ji, they could not avoid feeling ashamed of themselves. To make matters worse, although Lord Wen had now been in power for many days, he had neither rewarded his supporters nor punished his enemies, so they felt sure that he was up to something. This merely increased their nervousness, so they hatched a plan together whereby they would use their own private armies to foment a rebellion in which the palace would be burned and Chonger murdered. Afterwards they would establish some other member of the ruling house as the new marquis. They thought to themselves: "It would not be safe to reveal our plan to anyone at court with the exception of the eunuch Bo Di. He hates Chonger, and now that he has succeeded to the title of Marquis of Jin, Bo Di must be very frightened that he will be executed. He is an unusually brave and daring man who would be happy to take part in our plot."

They sent one of their servants to summon him, and Bo Di came in answer to this call. Lü Yisheng and Xi Rui told him of their plot to burn the palace, and Bo Di was very pleased to join in. The three men swore a blood covenant together and decided that they would strike on the last day of the second month. Lü Yisheng and Xi Rui both went to their estates and began the work of secretly assembling their forces. This is not part of our story.

Even though Bo Di had agreed to take part in this conspiracy, he was not happy about it. He thought to himself: "First Lord Xian ordered me to go to and attack the city of Pu; then I was instructed by Lord Hui to go and assassinate Chonger. This is like Jie's dog barking at Yao—the animal was defending his master. Lord Huai is dead now, and Chonger has succeeded to the title of the Marquis of Jin. It would be a terrible thing to kill him, given that he has at long last brought peace to the state of Jin. Besides which, people say that Chonger has the support of Heaven, in which case, even if I try to kill him, I will not succeed. Supposing that I do kill him, the people who followed him into exile will not let me get away with it. I had better go and hand myself in to the new marquis and then try and talk them out of punishing me. That would be the very best plan under the circumstances."

Then he reconsidered this idea: "Given the crimes that I have committed against him, I can't possibly go straight to the palace." Instead he went in the middle of the night to talk to Hu Yan.

Hu Yan was very surprised to see him and said, "You have committed terrible crimes against His Lordship! You should be planning to get away from here as far and as fast as you can, rather than coming to bother me at this time of night!"

"I am here because I need to see His Lordship, and I am hoping that you will act as an intermediary," Bo Di said.

"If His Lordship sees you, he will kill you!" Hu Yan told him.

"I have top-secret information that I want to give to His Lordship that will save many lives," Bo Di announced. "I must see Lord Wen to tell him what is going on!"

Hu Yan took him to the palace and knocked on the door. He went in ahead of Bo Di and had an audience with Lord Wen, at which he explained that the eunuch was demanding to see him.

"What can Bo Di be up to that he is going to save many lives?" Lord Wen inquired. "This must be some excuse that he has made up to come and see me. He is no doubt hoping that you will plead with me to spare his life."

"As the saying has it: a sage can get information even from the mumblings of woodcutters," Hu Yan said. "You, my lord, have only recently succeeded to the title, and so you will have to put aside your natural inclination to be angry with this man, just in case he does indeed come to you with important and loyal advice. You must not refuse to see him!"

Lord Wen was not convinced, and he sent one of his servants to take a message out, complaining about Bo Di's past actions: "In trying to murder me, you cut off my sleeve—I still have that robe and go cold every time I look at it. There was also the time when I was living among the Di that you came to try and assassinate me. Lord Hui ordered you to leave within three days, and yet you set off on the second day. Fortunately I was protected by Heaven, otherwise your unseemly haste would have seen me fall into your hands. Now that I have come to power, how dare you come and see me! You had better run away as fast as you can, before I have you arrested and executed!"

Bo Di roared with laughter: "His Lordship has been in exile for nearly two decades but he still does not understand the way that the world works. Lord Xian was His Lordship's father; Lord Hui was his younger brother. If a father and son fell out, if a younger brother ended up being enemies with his older brother, what has this to do with me? I was just a palace eunuch, and it was my duty to serve Lord Xian and Lord Hui; how was I supposed to know that one day the Honorable Chonger would become Marquis of Jin? As His Lordship knows perfectly well, Guan Zhong shot at Lord Huan of Qi and hit him on the belt buckle under orders from the Honorable Jiu. In spite of this, Lord Huan employed him in a senior ministerial position and he became hegemon over the world. If he had borne a grudge over being shot at, he could never have become the Master of Covenants. It is His Lordship's prerogative to refuse to see me, but I am afraid that if I leave, disaster will soon overtake him!"

Hu Yan presented his opinion: "Bo Di must know something. You have to see him, my lord!" Lord Wen then summoned Bo Di into the palace.

The eunuch did not make any attempt to apologize for his crimes. He simply bowed twice and said: "Congratulations!"

"I have now been in power for a while," Lord Wen said. "Is it not a bit late for you to be congratulating me?"

"Even though you have succeeded to the marquisate," Bo Di replied crisply, "that is not yet a matter for congratulations. With my help your position is secure. That is why I am congratulating you!"

Lord Wen thought this a most peculiar thing to say and ordered his entourage to leave him so that he could hear what he had to say in private. Afterwards, Bo Di explained every detail of Lü Yisheng and Xi Rui's conspiracy: "Their people are to be found throughout the city and they have raised a private army from their own estates. You must leave the city in plain clothes along with your uncles, and then go to Qin and get them to raise an army for you. That is the only way that you can get through this trouble. I will stay behind to track down and kill the traitors inside the capital."

"In this emergency, I will have to leave with you," Hu Yan told him. "I am sure that Zhao Cui can be trusted with the day-to-day running of the country."

Lord Wen told Bo Di, "If you stay behind, I will reward you generously." Bo Di kowtowed, said goodbye, and left.

Lord Wen and Hu Yan discussed their plans for a long time, after which Hu Yan arranged that a closed carriage should be waiting at the back gate of the palace, with only a couple of people in attendance. Lord Wen summoned his most trusted servants and instructed them in what they had to do. Under no circumstances whatsoever was this information to be divulged to anyone else. That evening, he went to bed as normal. At the fifth watch, he announced that he was feeling unwell due to having caught a cold and ordered eunuchs to light torches to suggest that he had locked himself in the lavatory. In fact, he went to the back gate where Hu Yan was waiting with the carriage to convey him out of the city. The following morning news spread throughout the palace that His Lordship was ill, so a succession of visitors came to his bedroom to ask after his health only to be turned away on the grounds that he was too sick to see them. There was no one in the palace who knew that he was gone.

When it got light, Jin officials gathered at the court. On realizing that Lord Wen would not be appearing, they went to the palace gates to find out what was happening. They found the pair of vermillion doors bolted fast, with a placard hanging above them announcing that His Lordship was too ill to go to court. The gatekeeper proclaimed: "Last night His Lordship took a chill, and today he is too sick to get out of bed. He has postponed all court audiences until the first day of the third month."

"His Lordship has only just succeeded to the marquisate, and there are dozens of decisions that he has to make," Zhao Cui said. "Now all of a sudden he has become sick, really: wind and clouds come when you least expect them; good luck and bad can strike you at any moment."

Everyone believed that the excuse offered was true, so they sighed and went home. Lü Yisheng and Xi Rui also heard that Lord Wen had become too sick to leave the palace and that he would not be holding court until the first day of the third month. They were secretly delighted and said, "Heaven wants us to kill Chonger!"

Lord Wen of Jin and Hu Yan managed to make their way out of Jin territory undetected and entered the state of Qin. They sent a secret missive to Lord Mu of Qin, arranging to meet him at Wangcheng. When Lord Mu heard that the Marquis of Jin was back, he realized that a coup must have taken place. Announcing that he was going hunting, he immediately called for his chariot, driving straight to Wangcheng to meet the Marquis of Jin. Lord Wen then explained what had happened.

Lord Mu laughed and said, "You have already received the Mandate of Heaven; what can Lü Yisheng and Xi Rui do about that? I am sure that Zhao Cui and the others can deal with these bastards. Do not worry about it!" He ordered Noble Grandson Qi, the commander-in-chief of the Qin army, to go and camp at Hekou, with a brief to gather information about what was going on in Jiang and then act as he saw fit. The Marquis of Jin would be staying safe in Wangcheng.

Meanwhile, Bo Di was afraid that he might be suspected of duplicity by Lü Yisheng and Xi Rui, so some days earlier he had moved into Xi Rui's house on the pretext that they had things that needed to be discussed. On the last day of the second month, he told Xi Rui: "His Lordship has announced that he is going to hold an audience first thing tomorrow, which means that he must be feeling a bit better. If the palace were to catch fire, he would try to leave. If Grandee Lü Yisheng were to guard the front gate and you take charge of the back gate, while I lead my servants to patrol the gate that goes through to the court—all in the name of firefighting—even if Chonger sprouted wings, he would find it difficult to get away."

Xi Rui thought that this was a wonderful idea and mentioned it to Lü Yisheng. That evening, the servants brought weapons and flammable material into the palace before dispersing to take up their positions for the ambush. At around midnight fires were lit by the main gate, and in an instant the place was a sheet of flames. The inhabitants of the palace were woken from their dreams into a complete inferno, and their one thought was to escape. The place was reduced to chaos. By the light of the fire they could see soldiers rushing hither and yon, shouting: "Do not let Chonger escape!" Some of the residents of the palace had suffered terrible burns; others who ran into the soldiers were severely injured. The sound of screaming and sobbing was unbearable. Lü Yisheng searched Lord Wen's bedchamber with a drawn sword in his hand but found no trace of him; he bumped into Xi Rui, who had fought his way in from the back gate, who asked, "Have you done it?" Lü Yisheng said nothing, he just shook his head. The two men then braved the fires to search the whole place over again.

Suddenly they heard a great shout go up outside, and Bo Di rushed in to report: "The Hu, Zhao, Luan, and Wei families have sent all their servants and guards to help fight the fires. When it gets light, we are going to have every single inhabitant of the capital here, and it will be impossible for us to get away. We had better leave the city now while things are in confusion and wait until dawn has broken. When we know for sure whether the Marquis of Jin is alive or dead, we can plan our next step."

Lü Yisheng and Xi Rui had failed in their plot to kill Lord Wen and had already begun to panic about the consequences. They had no idea what to do next, so they summoned their supporters and fought their way out of the palace gates and got away.

A historian wrote a poem about this:

These flickering flames were a wicked plot to kill the rightful lord.
Who would have imagined that he had already escaped to Wangcheng?
If the Marquis of Jin had punished the attempted assassination at Pu,
Would he have been able to get away and meet his family in Qin?

When the grandees of the Hu, Zhao, Luan, and Wei families realized that the palace was on fire, they immediately summoned all their guards and ordered them to form a bucket chain. They were ready to act as firefighters, having no idea that they were caught up in a massacre. When it got light and the fires died down, questioning of the survivors elicited the information that Lü Yisheng and Xi Rui had launched a coup and that the Marquis of Jin had disappeared. Everyone was deeply alarmed.

The eunuch whom he had entrusted with his final instructions now leapt out of the flames and informed them: "His Lordship left the palace in plain clothes in the early hours of the morning a couple of days ago; I have no idea where he has gone."

"When we ask Hu Yan," Zhao Cui said, "we will know the truth."

"My younger brother went into the palace a couple of days ago, and since that time he has not been home," Hu Mao mused. "I imagine that the two of them have gone off together—they must have known in advance of the conspiracy between Lü Yisheng and Xi Rui. We had better impose martial law on the capital, repair the palace, and wait for His Lordship to come home."

"Those two bastards have launched a treasonous conspiracy against the government," Wei Chou said. "They have set fire to the palace and attempted to murder His Lordship. They cannot have gotten far! Give me an army division and I will hunt them down and behead them."

"Control over the army is the most important branch of executive power in the state," Zhao Cui reminded him. "His Lordship is not present, so who would dare to call out the army on their own authority? Even though they have run away, they will soon be forced to give themselves up."

Lü Yisheng and Xi Rui were in fact camped outside the suburbs of the capital. They now discovered that the Marquis of Jin was still alive and that martial law had been imposed by the grandees. Being afraid that they would be punished, they wanted to flee to another country, but could not make a decision about where to go.

Bo Di tricked them into making a terrible mistake: "In recent years, every single Marquis of Jin has owed his position to Qin. You two must both be old acquaintances of the Earl of Qin, so if you go and tell him that the palace has burned down by accident and Chonger is dead, you can throw yourselves on his mercy and get his support for making the Honorable Yong the next marquis. Even though Chonger is not dead, he will find it difficult to reverse this decision."

"Having made a covenant with the Earl of Qin at Wangcheng, we can throw ourselves on his mercy," Lü Yisheng said. "The only problem is whether or not we will be able to talk Qin around."

"How about I go on ahead to talk to the Earl of Qin?" Bo Di suggested. "If he is agreeable, then the two of you can join me. If he refuses, we can make other plans."

Bo Di then went to Hekou, and on discovering that Noble Grandson Qi was camped west of the Yellow River, he crossed it and sought an audience with him. He explained exactly what had happened.

"Those traitorous dogs want our assistance," Noble Grandson Qi said. "Let us trick them into joining us here and execute them for their crimes. Let the laws of our country be made clear to one and all! I am sure that they will come, particularly if they think they are getting something for nothing."

He wrote a letter that he asked Bo Di to take to Lü Yisheng and Xi Rui, which read:

> Before Lord Wen went back to Jin, he agreed with me that he would honor the original agreement to give land to Qin. Accordingly, I sent Noble Grandson Qi to camp his army west of the Yellow River, with a view to clarifying exactly where the borders between our two countries run. I have always been afraid that Lord Wen would simply repeat Lord Hui's weasel words. Now I discover that Lord Wen has been burned to death and that you intend to establish the Honorable Yong as the new marquis. I am very happy to hear this, and I hope that you will come and discuss the matter at the earliest possible moment.

When Lü Yisheng and Xi Rui received this letter, they set off perfectly happily. On their arrival at the camp west of the Yellow River, Noble Grandson Qi came out to meet them, and after a polite exchange of greetings he hosted a banquet in their honor. Lü Yisheng and Xi Rui were completely unsuspicious. They had no idea that Noble Grandson Qi had already sent someone to report this exchange to Lord Mu of Qin, who was now waiting for them at Wangcheng. Lü Yisheng and Xi Rui stayed at the army camp for three days, after which they were told that they would be having an audience with the Earl of Qin.

"His Lordship is currently visiting Wangcheng," Noble Grandson Qi explained, "so why don't you join him there? Leave your troops camped here, where you can pick them up when you come back, and then we will all cross the river together. Wouldn't that be a good idea?"

Lü Yisheng and Xi Rui followed his advice. When they arrived at Wangcheng, Bo Di and Noble Grandson Qi entered the city ahead of the main party and had an audience with Lord Mu of Qin. Lord Mu sent Pi Bao to meet Lü Yisheng and Xi Rui. He also ordered Lord Wen of Jin to conceal himself behind the tapestry hangings of the room. Lü Yisheng and Xi Rui entered one after the other, and when the formal greetings were complete, they mentioned arranging the accession of the Honorable Yong.

"The Honorable Yong is here," Lord Mu told them.

"Please let us see him!" they said.

"Let the new Marquis of Jin come out!" Lord Mu shouted. A man emerged from behind the tapestry hangings, moving with firm and unhurried steps. Lü Yisheng and Xi Rui stared at him: it was Chonger, Lord Wen of Jin. This gave Lü Yisheng and Xi Rui such a shock that they could barely stand, and they shouted out: "Spare us!" They kowtowed over and over again. Lord Mu invited the Marquis of Jin to take a seat.

"You traitorous dogs!" Lord Wen cursed. "What have I done to you that you should conspire against me? If Bo Di had not gone to the authorities, I would never have been able to escape your ambush at the palace. In that case I would have been burned to a cinder!"

Lü Yisheng and Xi Rui now realized that they had been betrayed by Bo Di. "Bo Di swore a blood covenant with us, and that makes him part of the conspiracy," they said. "He must die with us!"

Lord Wen laughed: "If Bo Di had not sworn the blood covenant with you, how would he know all the details of your plot?" He shouted to his guards to arrest the pair and commanded that Bo Di should oversee their execution. A short time later, their heads were presented below the palace steps. Poor Lü Yisheng and Xi Rui! They had served Lord Hui and Lord Huai with the utmost loyalty, and if they had fought the Honorable Chonger to the end at Luliu, they would have left a glorious reputation. However, having first surrendered and then rebelled again, they found themselves at the mercy of Noble Grandson Qi. Thus they ended up being beheaded at Wangcheng. Is that not sad to have died in such miserable circumstances?

Qian Yuan wrote a poem about this:

A man can never alter what he is like;
So few reform, so few change their minds.
Today at Wangcheng they lost their heads,
Regretting their surrender at Luliu!

Lord Wen ordered Bo Di to take Lü Yisheng and Xi Rui's heads and show them to their followers camped west of the Yellow River; at the same time, news of his victory was sent to the capital. The grandees all said happily: "Hu Mao was right!"

Zhao Cui and the others made haste to prepare an official carriage and went to the Yellow River to meet the Marquis of Jin.

If you want to know what happened after that, READ ON.

Chapter Thirty-seven

The determined hermit, Jie Zitui, burns to death at Mount Mianshang.

The spoiled favorite, Prince Dai, occupies the palace.

After Lord Wen of Jin had executed Lü Yisheng and Xi Rui at Wangcheng, he bowed twice and thanked Lord Mu of Qin for all his help. He then announced that he wished to escort his wife, Lady Huai Ying, home to Jin.

"The poor woman was married to Scion Yu before you, so I am afraid that she feels that an official appointment as your principal wife would bring shame upon your ancestors," Lord Mu said. "You had better make her one of your junior wives!"

"The ruling houses of Qin and Jin have been allies for many generations, and that fact alone makes it perfectly acceptable for her to become my principal wife," Lord Wen replied. "Please do not refuse this! Besides which, no one knows the reasons why I have left the country, and now I can tell them that it was to perform the proper ceremonies for establishing a marchioness. Is that not better than the truth?"

Lord Mu was very pleased. He escorted Lord Wen back to Yongzhou and then sent Lady Huai Ying and five other women to Jin, riding in a magnificent procession of covered carriages. Lord Mu escorted Lady Huai Ying as far as the Yellow River and gave her three hundred elite warriors as her guard. He called these men "warp and weft servants."

Right up to the present day, people call estate managers "warp and weft servants"; this expression is derived from these events.

Lord Wen and Lady Huai Ying sailed across the Yellow River to where Zhao Cui and the other ministers were waiting with carriages and horses at Hekou. They assisted the Marquis and Marchioness of Jin to get into their carriage. A vast train of officials followed them, the sky was filled with banners, the sound of drums reverberated through the skies—it was a wonderful scene. When he had left his palace, escaping under cover of darkness, Lord Wen was like a tortoise hiding his head and tail; now he returned in glory like a phoenix with the wind beneath its wings. That was then and this is now! When Lord Wen arrived in Jiang, the inhabitants of his capital all clapped their hands and acclaimed him. It does not need to be said that the officials congratulated him when he held court. Lady Huai Ying was then formally established as the marchioness of Jin.

. . .

When Lord Xian was considering marrying off his daughter, Lady Bo Ji, he ordered Guo Yan to perform a milfoil divination, and the following reading was obtained: "They are close relatives. Three times they will settle our lord." Lady Bo Ji became the principal wife of Lord Mu of Qin, and her stepdaughter—Lady Huai Ying—became the principal wife of Lord Wen of Jin; does this not refer to the family relationship between them? Lord Mu installed the Honorable Yiwu in power in Jin; later on, he also installed the Honorable Chonger in Jin. Lord Wen was forced to flee into exile and, thanks to Lord Mu's assistance in the execution of Lü Yisheng and Xi Rui, he got back his mountains and rivers. Surely this is what the divination meant when it said: "Three times they will settle our lord." In addition to that, Lord Mu had a dream in which Lady Treasure took him to the Heavenly Palace, where he had an audience with God on High. He heard God on High call his name and say, "Renhao! I command you to pacify the civil war in Jin!" He said this twice. First of all, Lord Mu pacified Li Ke's uprising; later on, he also put an end to Lü Yisheng and Xi Rui's coup. Everything in the dream and the divination corresponds to what actually happened.

There is a poem that says:

Every success and every failure is predetermined,
Our lives passed in pointless struggle as we float in the void.
Laugh at those fools who cannot peacefully accept their fate,
Forcing themselves to hunt for winter thunderbolts and summer snows.

Lord Wen of Jin loathed Lü Yisheng and Xi Rui, so he wanted to hunt down and kill every last one of their supporters. Zhao Cui remonstrated: "Lord Hui and Lord Huai lost popular support because they were so tyrannical. You will do much better by being lenient." Lord

Wen followed his advice and announced a general amnesty. Lü Yisheng and Xi Rui had many supporters, and in spite of the fact that they had been officially amnestied, they found it impossible to relax. Every day new rumors swept the city, and this caused great concern to Lord Wen.

Suddenly one day, first thing in the morning, a junior official named Tou Xu came to the palace gates and asked for an audience with the marquis. Lord Wen was washing his hair, and when he heard this request, he said angrily: "This man stole my baggage and money, which caused me enormous troubles on my journey and reduced me to begging for food in Cao and Wey. Why on earth does he want to have an audience with me?"

The gatekeeper started to send Tou Xu away, just as he had been ordered to do.

"Was His Lordship washing by any chance?" Tou Xu asked.

The gatekeeper was amazed: "How did you know that?"

"Someone who is washing his hair will be bent over, a posture that confuses the mind," Tou Xu explained. "If the mind is confused, you say things that you don't mean. No wonder that he refused to give me an audience. His Lordship escaped the consequences of the coup organized by Lü Yisheng and Xi Rui purely because he was prepared to forgive Bo Di, so why can't he forgive me? The reason I came is because I have a plan for how to bring peace to the state of Jin. If His Lordship refuses to see me, I will leave!"

The gatekeeper reported what he had said to Lord Wen.

"I have made a bad mistake," His Lordship said. He immediately put on an official hat and robe, and summoned Tou Xu into the palace for an audience. Tou Xu kowtowed and apologized for the crime that he had committed. Afterwards he said, "Do you know, my lord, how many supporters Lü Yisheng and Xi Rui had?"

Lord Wen frowned and said, "A great many."

"These people know full well that they have committed a terrible crime, and that is why they are still worried in spite of the amnesty that has been offered. You must think of some way to calm them down, my lord."

"What plan do you have for doing so?" Lord Wen asked.

Tou Xu presented his opinion: "As everyone in the state of Jin is aware, I stole your money and left you to starve. If you were to go out for a tour of the capital with me as your charioteer, everyone would hear all about it. That way they would know that you do not bear grudges and their fears will be allayed."

"That is a good idea," Lord Wen agreed. He announced that he would be going on a tour of the city and that Tou Xu would drive him.

When Lü Yisheng and Xi Rui's old supporters heard about this, they said to themselves, "Tou Xu stole all His Lordship's savings and he has been reemployed in his old job. What do we have to worry about?" The worrying rumors gradually died down. Lord Wen did indeed give Tou Xu charge over his storehouses and treasury again. It was entirely because he was so magnanimous that he was able to bring peace to the state of Jin.

• • •

Before Lord Wen succeeded to the marquisate, he was married twice. His first wife, Lady Ying of Xu, died very young. His second wife, Lady Jee of Fuyang, gave birth to a son and a daughter. The son's name was Quan; the daughter was Lady Bo Ji. Lady Jee of Fuyang died while they were living at the city of Pu. When Lord Wen went into exile, his son and daughter were very young, so he left them behind in Pu. Arrangements for their care were made by Tou Xu, who entrusted them to the care of the Sui family. Without fail, an annual income was paid to them in grain and silk. One day Tou Xu found an opportunity to mention this to Lord Wen.

He was amazed and said, "I thought they were killed long ago when the army attacked Pu. Now you tell me they are still alive! Why did you not mention it before?"

"I have heard it said: a mother is honored because she has given birth to a son; a son is ennobled because he is the child of a favorite wife," Tou Xu replied. "You have traveled all over the Zhou confederacy, my lord, and wherever you went you acquired new wives and had more children. Even though the Honorable Quan is still alive, I did not know what your attitude to him would be, so I did not want to tell you earlier."

"You should have told me!" Lord Wen complained. "I have come within a whisker of being condemned as an unnatural and neglectful father."

He immediately ordered Tou Xu to go to Pu and give lavish rewards to the Sui family, and bring his children home. He gave instructions to Lady Huai Ying to look after them. Lord Wen then appointed the Honorable Quan as his scion, and Lady Bo Ji was married off to Zhao Cui. From this time on she was known as Lady Zhao Ji.

• • •

When the chief of the Di people heard that the Honorable Chonger had succeeded to the marquisate of Jin, he sent an ambassador to offer his congratulations. He also sent Lady Ji Wei home to Jin. Lord Wen asked her how old she was now, and she replied, "We have been separated for eight years, so I am now thirty-two."

"Well, we are lucky that it wasn't twenty-five years!" Lord Wen joked.

Lord Xiao of Qi also sent an ambassador to escort Lady Jiang to Jin. The Marquis of Jin thanked her for all that she had done for him.

"It is not that I wanted to break up our happy marriage," Lady Jiang said. "However, I encouraged you to go so that you would achieve what you have today."

Lord Wen told Lady Huai Ying about the good sense and generosity that both his Di wife and his Qi wife had shown to him in the past. Lady Huai Ying admired these two women very much and declared it was not suitable that she had precedence over much more senior wives. A complete reorganization of the harem hierarchy was indicated. Lady Jiang of Qi was appointed as marchioness, with Lady Ji Wei of the Di as the secondary wife and Lady Huai Ying as the tertiary wife.

When Lady Zhao Ji heard that Lady Ji Wei had come home, she encouraged her husband, Zhao Cui, to bring back his first wife, Lady Shu Wei, and her son from the Di. Zhao Cui refused: "His Lordship gave me your hand in marriage. I would not dare think of the Di woman again."

"That is a very vulgar and unpleasant thing to say, and I really thought better of you," Lady Zhao Ji replied. "Even though I come from a noble family, Lady Shu Wei is your first wife, in addition to which she gave birth to your son. What do you think you are doing, abandoning her because you have acquired a new wife?"

Although Zhao Cui made agreeable noises, he could not come to any decision about what to do. Lady Zhao Ji then went to the palace, where she had an audience with her father, Lord Wen, and said, "My husband is not willing to bring Lady Shu Wei home, and I am going to get the blame for this. Please, can you resolve this impasse!"

Lord Wen sent an envoy to the Di to bring Lady Shu Ji and her son home. Lady Zhao Ji wanted to give up her position as the principal wife, but Zhao Cui simply would not allow this.

"She is older than I am and she married you first," Lady Zhao Ji told him. "There are rules about these things that cannot be broken. Besides which, I have heard that her son, Dun, is already grown up and has shown himself to be a most brilliant young man. He should become your heir. My place is as your secondary wife. If you do not agree, I will simply have to move back to the palace."

There was nothing that Zhao Cui could do to persuade her, so he reported what she had said to Lord Wen.

"My daughter is a very good girl to feel that she can give up her position," Lord Wen said. "I am not sure that even the mother of the founder of the Zhou dynasty could match her."

He summoned Lady Shu Wei and her son to court, whereupon she was established as Zhao Cui's principal wife and her son, Dun, became his heir. Lady Shu Ji refused resolutely, but Lord Wen explained that this was his daughter's own idea. She then bowed her thanks and left. That year Zhao Dun was seventeen years of age, an exceptionally able young man with excellent principles, as well as being both learned and good at martial skills like shooting and driving a chariot. Zhao Cui loved him very much. Later on, Lady Zhao Ji gave birth to three sons whose names were Tong, Kuo, and Ying, but none of these men were a patch on Zhao Dun. This belongs to a later part of the story.

A historian wrote a poem praising Lady Zhao Ji's wisdom and good sense:

Most women love gossip;
If they are not malicious, they are jealous.
Some are rendered arrogant by their husband's love,
Some take out their resentments upon the legitimate wife.
Causing trouble wherever they go,
They are lazy and sluttish,
They make a show to fool others,
But all they are doing is deluding themselves.
A woman of noble family prepared to accept demotion,
A woman of high status prepared to take the back seat.
A woman who promoted her stepson at the expense of her own children,
A woman who let Lady Shu Wei take precedence over herself.
Such a virtuous lady!
Such an example to us all!
The daughter of Lord Wen of Jin,
The wife of Zhao Cui.

Lord Wen of Jin wanted to issue rewards to celebrate his return, so he convened a great meeting of his officials and divided them into three groups. Those who followed him into exile were placed in the first group; those who had expressed their support were placed in the second group; while those who had surrendered to him were placed in the third group. Within each group, the contribution that an individual had made was calculated and determined the precise grade of reward that he received. Thus in the first group of those who had followed Lord Wen into exile, Zhao Cui and Hu Yan received the very greatest rewards, while other individuals such as Hu Mao, Xu Chen, Wei Chou, Hu Shegu, Xian Zhen, and Dian Jie received lesser rewards. In the second group of those who had expressed their support for the Honorable Chonger before he succeeded to the marquisate, the most important were Luan Zhi and Xi Cou, while Shi Hui, Zhou Zhi Qiao, Sun Bojiu, and Xi Man received lesser rewards. In the third group of those who had surrendered to him, Xi Buyang and Han Jian were rewarded with the greatest generosity while Liang Yaomi, Jia Butu, Xi Qi, Xian Mie, Tu Ji, and so on all received lesser rewards. Those who did not have any land were given estates; those who had estates were given titles. In addition to all this Lord Wen presented Hu Yan with five pairs of white jade discs, saying: "You threw yours into the Yellow River. Let these replace them." He also remembered how the innocent Hu Tu had been killed and established a shrine in his memory at Mount Ma'an near Jinyang.

Later on people came to call this mountain Mount Hu Tu.

His Lordship ordered that the following message should be displayed on the gates to the capital: "If there is anyone who has not yet received rewards for their hard work on my behalf, let them present themselves."

Hoo Shu came forward and said: "I followed you into exile from the city of Pu and traveled everywhere with you, my feet split and bleeding. Now you have rewarded those who followed you into exile, but I have not been included. What have I done to offend you?"

"Since you are here, let me explain," Lord Wen said. "I have given the highest rewards to those who encouraged me to behave with justice and benevolence, for they were those with whom I could discuss my innermost thoughts. I gave second-best rewards to those who came up with clever plans for how I should deal with the feudal lords whom I met, thereby avoiding humiliation. The third grade of rewards went to those who protected me, braving swords and arrows. Thus the most generous rewards went to the virtuous, followed by the clever, followed by the brave. If all that you have done for me is to follow me into exile, that is something that anyone could have done and cannot be rewarded as highly as people in the first three groups. When I have finished rewarding them, I will get around to you." Hoo Shu withdrew, deeply embarrassed.

Lord Wen ordered that large quantities of gold and silk should be given to his supporters at a more humble social level, and to his servants. Everyone who received such rewards was very pleased. Wei Chou and Dian Jie were the only ones to be unhappy because they were very proud of their martial abilities and yet they had seen civil officials like Zhao Cui and Hu Yan receive much greater rewards just for talking. They complained about this, but Lord Wen did not reprimand them because, after all, they had done great things in his service.

. . .

Of all the people who followed Lord Wen into exile, Jie Zitui was the one who had suffered the most. When they crossed the Yellow River, he realized that Hu Yan was planning to take advantage of his position, for which Jie Zitui despised him. After the first time that Lord Wen held court when Jie Zitui had to offer his congratulations, he claimed to be ill and stayed at home. He was determined to remain poor and untainted by any stain of corruption, so he took to weaving to support himself and his elderly mother. When the Marquis of Jin held the great meeting of all his officials to determine who would receive what grade of reward, he did not see Jie Zitui and thus he forgot about him, and did not even ask what had happened to him. One of Jie Zitui's neighbors, a man named Xie Zhang, realized that he had been overlooked and was very unhappy about it. When he saw the message hanging off the gates to the city, "If there is anyone who has not yet received rewards for their hard work on my behalf, let them come forward," he went to knock on Jie Zitui's door and tell him about this news. Jie Zitui simply laughed and said nothing.

His elderly mother, who was out in the kitchen, heard him and said, "You served His Lordship with dedication for nearly twenty years, in addition to which you cut your own thigh to feed him when he was starving. You have suffered so much . . . why don't you remind him of how much he owes you? At the very least, we might get a grant of food that guarantees us something to eat every morning and evening. That would be better than what you make by weaving!"

"Lord Xian had nine sons, of whom His Lordship was by far the best," Jie Zitui replied. "Lord Hui and Lord Huai were both nasty pieces of work. Heaven abandoned them, and thus the state has now come into the possession of His Lordship. The other officials fight to establish their own claims to have assisted him, without any understanding of the workings of Heaven; I am ashamed to be associated with them. I would rather spend my life in weaving than claim that something that was the will of Heaven came about as a result of my own efforts."

"Even if you do not want to be given an official post," his mother said, "you should nevertheless attend one audience at court, so they don't forget how much you suffered in cutting your own thigh."

"There is nothing that His Lordship has that I want, so why should I have an audience with him?" Jie Zitui retorted.

"Since you are an honest and uncorrupt man, I will have to be a worthy mother to you," she said. "Let us go into reclusion deep in the mountains, that we may not be spattered by the mire generated in the marketplace!"

"I have always been particularly fond of Mount Mianshang," Jie Zitui said happily. "That mountain is high and its valleys are correspondingly deep—we can go and live there."

He then fled to Mount Mianshang, carrying his mother on his back. He built a little hut in one of the valleys and they prepared to spend the rest of their lives there, living off the land. None of his neighbors knew where he had gone, with the sole exception of Xie Zhang, who wrote a letter and hung it from one of the gates to the capital one night. The official who found it presented it to Lord Wen the next time that he held court. Lord Wen read the following words:

There was a fine dragon who tragically lost its home.
A number of snakes followed it, roaming around the world.
The dragon was starving and ate the meat of one of the snakes;
The dragon returned to its pool and sank happily into its native mud.
The snakes followed it and each found its own lair;
Only one snake was left to call out in the wilderness.

Lord Wen finished reading the letter and said in surprise: "This must be a complaint from Jie Zitui. When I was traveling through Wey, we ran out of food and Jie Zitui cut a lump of meat from his own thigh for me to eat. Now I have rewarded all those who served me in exile, but I have forgotten about him. How can such a mistake be excused?"

He sent someone to summon Jie Zitui to the palace, but he was no longer living where he had been. Lord Wen had all his neighbors arrested and questioned about where Jie Zitui had gone. "Anyone who can tell me will be given an official post."

Xie Zhang came forward and said: "That letter was not written by Jie Zitui, but by me. Jie Zitui was ashamed to have to ask for a reward, so he took his mother and went to live in reclusion in one of the valleys of Mount Mianshang. I was afraid that his good deeds and suffering would go unrecognized, so I wrote a letter and hung it on the gate, so that everyone would know."

"If you had not done so, I would have completely forgotten what I owe him," Lord Wen said. He accordingly appointed Xie Zhang as a low-ranking grandee. Immediately afterwards, he called for his chariot and set off in the direction of Mount Mianshang in search of Jie Zitui with Xie Zhang as his guide. He found one peak soaring high above the next, he found lush grass and overgrown trees, he found bubbling streams, he found little wisps of floating cloud, he found birds that filled the forest with song and mountains and valleys that reechoed with their calls, but he found no trace of Jie Zitui at all. Although he must be somewhere on this mountain, he could be anywhere.

His entourage grabbed hold of a couple of passing peasants, and Lord Wen questioned them. "A few days ago we saw a man carrying an old woman on his back resting at the foot of this mountain," they said. "He had a quick drink and then picked her up again and continued up the mountainside. We do not know where he has gone."

Lord Wen ordered that his chariot halt at the foot of Mount Mianshang and sent his people to search it, but in spite of spending many days at this task, they discovered nothing. His Lordship was angry and asked Xie Zhang, "Why does Jie Zitui hate me so much? I have heard that he is a very filial son, so if I set fire to the mountains he will have to rescue his mother. That will force him out of hiding."

Wei Chou came forward and said, "We all suffered much in your service during your time in exile, not just Jie Zitui. Now he has gone and hidden himself to put pressure on you, my lord, forcing you to waste your time here with your guards. When he has been forced out by the flames, I am really going to tell him off!"

He ordered his officers to kindle fires the whole way around the mountain. The flames leapt into the air, burning everything in their path. These fires burned for three days before they finally died down. Jie Zitui was not willing to come out; he and his mother were burned to death in each other's arms at the foot of an old willow tree. When the soldiers found their bodies, Lord Wen came to see them. He wept and ordered that they be buried at the foot of Mount Mianshang, where a temple would also be established in their memory. All the fields around the mountain were given to this temple and the local peasants made responsible for maintaining the sacrifices there. "Let Mount Mianshang be known as Mount Jie to commemorate my terrible mistake."

Later on Mount Mianshang was given county status and renamed Jiexiu, a name that records the fact that Jie Zitui is supposed to have stayed on this mountain. The fires were lit on the fifth day of the third month, just after the Qingming Festival. Local people remembered that poor Jie Zitui had died in a fire, and so they could not bear to use their stoves—thus they ended up eating cold food for a month in his memory. Later on this was reduced to three days. Right up to the present day in Taiyuan, Shangdang, Xihe, and Yanmen, every year one hundred and five days after the winter solstice they prepare cold food and eat it just with water; this is called "Forbidden Fire" or "Forbidden Smoke." They celebrate the day before Qingming as the day of the Cold Food Festival, and on this day they place a willow branch on their gates to summon the soul of Jie Zitui. Some people hold sacrifices out in the wilds, or burn spirit money; all of this is done for Jie Zitui.

Master Hu Zeng wrote the following poem:

Traveling with his lord for nineteen years,
He suffered the torments of exile at the ends of the earth.
Such pain he experienced when cutting his thigh to feed his lord,
His principles so strong that he refused all emoluments and burned to death.
The fires on Mount Mianshang mark the start of a festival;
The shrine at Mount Jie commemorates his loyalty and honesty.
To the present day no fires are lit on the Cold Food Festival,
Surely that counts for more than an annual salary?

Lord Wen of Jin rewarded his supporters, instituted important reforms in the government, promoted good and able men in his service, reduced punishments and cut taxes, maintained good relations with his people, helped widows and other needy people, and governed the country well. King Xiang of Zhou sent Kong, Duke of Zhou, and the Court Scribe Shu Xing to invest Lord Wen of Jin formally as the new marquis. Lord Wen treated these men with the utmost ceremony. When Shu Xing returned to the royal capital, he had an audience with King Xiang and said, "The Marquis of Jin will become the next hegemon. You must be sure to treat him well." After this King Xiang paid less attention to Qi and became more closely involved in Jin, which does not need to be described in any detail.

• • •

At this time Lord Wen of Zheng, a man with an unpleasant bullying nature, was a sycophantic client of the kingdom of Chu who no longer maintained diplomatic relations with the other states of the Zhou confederacy. He was angry because the Earl of Hua served Wey rather than Zheng, so he raised an army and went to attack Hua. The Earl of Hua was terrified and asked for a peace treaty, and the Zheng army then withdrew. The Earl of Hua immediately restored his old alliance with the state of Wey and did not pay the slightest attention to Zheng. Lord Wen of Zheng was furious and appointed the Honorable Shixie as commander-in-chief with Du Yumi as his deputy. After raising yet another army, they attacked Hua again. Lord Wen of Wey was on excellent terms with the Zhou king, and he complained about Zheng's behavior to him. King Xiang of Zhou then sent Grandee You Sunbo to Zheng to request that they leave Hua alone. Lord Wen heard that they were coming long before they actually arrived, and he said angrily: "What is the difference between Zheng and Wey, that they are treated so generously and we get the sharp end of the stick?"

He ordered the arrest of You Sunbo the moment he crossed the border; he was planning to release him when his army had returned in triumph after crushing Hua. When You Sunbo was placed under arrest, his entourage managed to escape and make their way home. They reported what had happened to King Xiang of Zhou. King Xiang cursed and said, "Zheng thinks that they can kick me around, but I will have my revenge!" He asked his ministers, "Which of you can punish Zheng for me?"

Grandee Tui Shu and the Viscount of Tao came forward and said: "Ever since Zheng defeated the armies of our former king, they have behaved with unbelievable arrogance. Now that they have allied themselves with the barbarians in Chu, they think that they can bully us and imprison our people. However, if you were to raise an army and attack them, it is not certain that you would win. In our humble opinion, you should borrow troops from the Di. That would really frighten them."

"No! No!" Grandee Fu Chen screamed. "As the ancient saying goes: 'Do not let strangers interfere with your family.' Even though Zheng has behaved badly, their ruling house is descended from Prince You, which makes them Your Majesty's cousins. You should not forget that Lord Wu of Zheng played a major part in the move of the Zhou capital to the east or that Lord Li of Zheng put an end to Prince Tui's rebellion. The Di are barbarians . . . they are wolves . . . they are not like us. I can see only disadvantages in using barbarians to destroy a member of your own family; avenging a minor insult at the expense of what ought to be a good relationship."

Tui Shu and the Viscount of Tao said: "When King Wu attacked the Shang dynasty, nine Yi barbarian tribes fought on his side—why should His Majesty have to rely only upon his family? The campaign in the eastern mountains was launched against the states of Guan and Cai: their lords were King Wu's brothers! Zheng has now behaved just as badly as Guan and Cai did. What is more, the Di barbarians have been consistently loyal to us. Why should we not seek their assistance in punishing a rebel?"

"You are absolutely right," King Xiang said. He sent Tui Shu and the Viscount of Tao to the Di, to discuss the possibility of a joint attack on Zheng.

The chief of the Di was happy to take part, and so he pretended that he was going out hunting and suddenly launched a major incursion into Zheng territory. He attacked and captured the city of Yue, which he then garrisoned with his own troops; afterwards he sent an ambassador to report this to the Zhou king, accompanied by the two grandees.

"The Di people have done very well by me," King Xiang of Zhou proclaimed. "Given that the queen has just died, would it not be a good idea to establish a marriage alliance between us?"

Tui Shu and the Viscount of Tao said: "The Di people sing a song that goes as follows: 'The first Lady Shu Wei, the second Lady Shu Wei—both are as lovely as pearls and jade.' The Di ruling house has two women who have the title of Lady Shu Wei, and both are exceptionally lovely. The first Lady Shu Wei is the daughter of a man named Jiuruguo, and she is married to the Marquis of Jin. The second Lady Shu Wei is the daughter of the Di chief himself, and she is still unwed. Your Majesty ought to ask for her hand."

King Xiang was delighted with this news and ordered Tui Shu and the Viscount of Tao to go back to the Di to propose this marriage alliance. The Di escorted Lady Shu Wei to Zhou, and King Xiang wanted to appoint her to be his new queen.

Again, Grandee Fu Chen remonstrated: "It is one thing for Your Majesty to reward the Di people for working hard in your service. However, as the Son of Heaven you now want to marry a barbarian woman. The Di will take advantage of the fact that their success and this marriage alliance have placed you off guard."

King Xiang did not pay any attention to him. Lady Shu Wei became queen and was placed in charge of the palaces.

This Lady Shu Wei was pretty, but she was not at all modest and retiring. She came from a people who prided themselves on their horse-riding and archery. Every time that the Di chief went out hunting, she would invite herself along. She was used to behaving without any restraint when she went galloping across the plains, accompanied by her father's soldiers. Now she found herself married to the Zhou king, forced to live hidden away in the palace harem just like a bird in a cage, and she could not endure it.

One day she said to King Xiang, "From a very young age I have been used to going out hunting, and my father never forbade it. I find living in the palace so oppressive that it makes me feel physically sick. Why do you not hold a great hunt, Your Majesty, and let me attend?"

King Xiang was besotted with his new wife and did exactly what she said. He ordered the Grand Astrologer to select an auspicious day and mustered a large number of chariots and men to go hunting at Mount Beimang. A tented enclosure was erected about halfway up the mountain where King Xiang and Queen Wei could sit and enjoy the spectacle.

King Xiang wanted to make her happy, so he gave the following order: "The deadline is noon. Anyone who captures thirty beasts will be rewarded with three military chariots; anyone who captures twenty beasts will be rewarded with two light battle chariots; anyone who captures ten beasts will be rewarded with a camouflage chariot. Anyone who captures fewer than ten animals will receive no reward."

In an instant the princes and the royal grandsons, the generals and the army officers all set off shooting at foxes and rabbits, each determined to show off their abilities and gain the highest reward. After they had been hunting for a good long while, the Grand Astrologer announced: "It is now noon." King Xiang issued orders for everyone to come back, and they presented the animals that they had captured. Some had ten and some had twenty, but there was only one person who presented more than thirty beasts. This young nobleman was exceptionally handsome and strong. He was King Xiang's younger half-brother: Prince Dai. The people in the Zhou capital called him Taishu, though he officially held the title of Duke of Gan. Some years earlier he had attempted to usurp the position of his older brother and conspired with the Rong army to attack the Zhou capital. When his coup failed, he had fled into exile in the state of Qi. Later on Dowager Queen Hui had begged King Xiang over and over again to forgive him, and Grandee Fu Chen had also advised him that he should restore his younger brother's position, so in the end he had no choice but to summon him back home and restore his honors. He had done very well at this hunt; King Xiang was extremely pleased to see his younger brother take first place, and so he gave him the three military chariots. Everyone else also received rewards according to how many animals they had killed.

Queen Wei, who was sitting beside the king, noticed that Prince Dai was an unusually good-looking man and an excellent shot. Much impressed, she asked King Xiang who he was, and when she discovered that he was a royal prince, she was even more amazed. She said to King Xiang: "It is still early, and I would like to give myself a good workout by going hunting. Please give the order, Your Majesty!"

The whole point of this occasion was to please Queen Wei, so how could the king refuse her request? He immediately ordered the troops to start another drive. Queen Wei removed her embroidered silk robe. This revealed that underneath she had on a short jacket with narrow sleeves over which there was an unusual thin coat of golden mail. Her waist was clasped by a multicolored embroidered belt, and six feet of dark grey silk was wound around her head in a turban and held in place with phoenix-headed pins to keep the dust out of her hair. A quiver was hanging from her belt, and in one hand she was gripping a vermilion lacquer bow. Her get-up was complete.

There is a poem that testifies to this:

A lovely young woman with delicate fair skin
Appears as a strange vision in barbarian garb.
This amazon is proud of her martial prowess,
The most beautiful warrior in the whole of the army.

Queen Wei looked exceptionally attractive in this costume, and King Xiang smiled happily at her. His entourage brought up a battle chariot for her to ride in.

"It is quicker to ride on horseback than it is to take a chariot," Queen Wei remarked. "My servants who came with me from Di territory are all used to riding on horses; let me show you what we can do!"

King Xiang ordered that the correct number of blood-horses should be brought before him, saddled and bridled, for her servants to ride. Queen Wei was about to get astride her horse, when King Xiang called out: "Stop!" He asked his ministers and fellow clan members, "Are any of you good at riding? Can you guard Her Majesty against accidents?"

"Let me go!" Prince Dai said.

That was exactly what Queen Wei wanted. The Di servants formed a guard that set off ahead of Her Majesty. Prince Dai, riding a magnificent stallion, followed close behind them. Queen Wei wanted Prince Dai to admire her; Prince Dai wanted to show off in front of Queen Wei. Before they tried shooting any quarry, they decided to race their horses. Queen Wei whipped up her horse, which set off like a streak of lightning. Prince Dai chased her down on his own horse. As they raced around the mountain, it was hard to say who was winning.

Queen Wei reined in her horse and praised Prince Dai: "I have heard so much about you. I am happy to say that it has not been exaggerated."

Prince Dai bowed in the saddle. "I am not nearly so good a rider as Your Majesty," he replied modestly.

"Come to the dowager queen's palace tomorrow morning," Queen Wei said. "I want to talk to you."

Before she could say another word, her servants rode up behind her. Queen Wei glanced provocatively at Prince Dai, and he quickly nodded his head. Then they both rode back.

As they made their way along the mountainside, they happened across a little flock of deer. Prince Dai shot first to the left and then to the right; with just two arrows he killed two deer. Queen Wei also shot and killed her beast, and her entourage praised her immoderately. Queen Wei raced her horse back to the royal enclosure. King Xiang came out to meet her and said, "You have done well, my darling." Queen Wei presented the deer that she had shot to His Majesty; Prince Dai also presented his two deer. King Xiang was most pleased. The soldiers shot one more drive and then went home. The cooks had been hard at work preparing a banquet of venison and other game, which was now enjoyed by the court. Having feasted to their hearts' content, they went home.

The following day Prince Dai went to court to thank His Majesty for his generous gift, and then he went to Dowager Queen Hui's palace to ask after her health. Queen Wei was already present when he arrived. She had prepared bribes that would be offered to their servants, and as her eyes met those of Prince Dai, the two of them made their decision. Making some excuse for their departure, they left, to meet again in private in one of the side rooms of the palace—thus they began their affair. When a greedy man and a lovesick woman come together like that, they find it difficult to let each other go.

"Come to the palace whenever you can," Queen Wei instructed him.

"I am afraid that His Majesty will become suspicious," Prince Dai said.

"I can deal with that," the queen said. "Do not worry."

Dowager Queen Hui's servants had a pretty good idea of what was going on, but they knew that she adored Prince Dai, and the whole thing had such serious implications that they did not dare to open their mouths. Dowager Queen Hui eventually realized something of what was going on, but she simply ordered her servants not to gossip. Queen Wei's servants were heavily bribed and did everything that they could to smooth the path of the affair. Prince Dai was sometimes hidden in the palace all night, and the only person who did not know about it was King Xiang.

A historian wrote a poem that bewails this:

Prince Dai should have remembered that this woman was his sister-in-law;
King Xiang reckoned without his wife in his dealings with his brother.
This hunt became a lover's assignation,
And for the first time he regretted marrying a barbarian.

There is also a poem that says that King Xiang should never have summoned Prince Dai home and thus he brought this disaster upon himself. This poem reads:

He ought to have known that a rebellious temperament is impossible to change;
If he could not bear to execute his brother, he should have disowned him.
If you invite a tiger into your home, you must expect it to bite you.
King Xiang really was totally unrealistic.

If you have started doing something wrong, the will to put yourself right grows less, and your daring increases day by day. As the affair between Prince Dai and Queen Wei progressed, they became more and more comfortable with one another, and their relationship became so well-established that they ceased trying to conceal it from other people, in fact did not see at all why they should. Under the circumstances, it is natural that everyone came to know about it. Queen Wei was a young and luscious woman, while King Xiang was well into his fifties—even though he was deeply in love with her, they usually slept in separate bedrooms. Prince Dai was rich and powerful, so the gatekeepers and the other palace servants all said to themselves, "The prince is the beloved son of the dowager queen, and if His Majesty were to die, he would become the next king. Is there any reason why we should not take his bribes now?" Thus he was able to come and go in the palace at all hours of the day.

One of the palace maids, named Xiaodong, was extremely pretty and very good at music. One evening at a banquet, Prince Dai summoned her and ordered her to play a jade flute to accompany him as he sang. He had been drinking for a long time and was too drunk to realize how badly he was behaving. His Highness grabbed hold of Xiaodong and wanted to enjoy her. Xiaodong was terrified of Queen Wei, and tore herself from his grasp. Prince Dai was furious and drew his sword to chase after her, determined to kill Xiaodong. The maid ran to King Xiang's bedroom, banging on the door and begged in tears to be let in. She explained that the prince was rampaging around the palace harem. King Xiang was very angry and picked up the sword beneath his pillow before rushing into the harem, where he was going to kill Prince Dai.

If you do not know whether Prince Dai survived, READ ON.

Chapter Thirty-eight

To avoid a civil war, King Xiang of Zhou takes up residence in Zheng.

By keeping faith, Lord Wen of Jin arranges the surrender of Yuan.

When King Xiang of Zhou heard what Xiaodong had to say, he was overcome with anger and rushed over to his bed, where he picked up his sword, before hurrying out in the direction of the harem. He intended to kill Prince Dai. After going a couple of steps, he suddenly changed his mind completely: "The prince is the dowager queen's favorite child. If I were to kill him, given that no one outside the palace knows what is going on, people are sure to accuse me of being unfilial. Besides which, Prince Dai is very well-trained in martial arts—he might not run away. If he were to stand his ground, I would be in a very nasty position. I had better just ignore the situation for the moment, and when I have some evidence I can divorce my wife. When faced with proof of his adultery with my wife, Prince Dai cannot possibly stay here. He will have to go into exile abroad. That would be by far the best solution." He sighed deeply and threw his sword to the ground, then went back to bed. However, first he ordered some eunuchs to find out what the prince was up to. They reported back: "When the prince realized that Xiaodong had complained to Your Majesty, he left the palace immediately."

"If someone is coming in and out of the palace, why has that not been reported to me?" King Xiang demanded. "Do you want me to be murdered in my bed?"

The following morning King Xiang ordered the arrest of all the servants working in the harem; to begin with they denied all knowledge, but when he summoned Xiaodong and confronted them with her, they could no longer keep it a secret and told His Majesty everything. King Xiang confined the divorced Queen Wei in the Cold Palace, locking and bolting the doors. A small hole in the wall allowed food and drink to be passed to her. Prince Dai was well aware of his guilt in this matter, and fled into exile with the Di people. Dowager Queen Hui was devastated by this news and became seriously sick. From this time onward, she was bedridden.

When Grandee Tui Shu and the Viscount of Tao heard that Queen Wei had been deposed, they were very alarmed: "It was the two of us who asked permission to raise an army and attack Zheng in the first instance; it was also our idea to request a match with Queen Wei. Now she has been divorced all of a sudden. The chief of the Di is sure to be extremely angry about the treatment meted out to his daughter. Prince Dai has already gone into exile with the Di, and he is sure to try and mislead their ruler with all sorts of lies. Supposing that the Di army comes to try and punish us, how are we going to get ourselves out of trouble?"

They immediately called for a light chariot and set off in hot pursuit of Prince Dai. On the way, they discussed what they should do: "If we have an audience with the Di chief, we should say such and such." Within a day they had arrived in Di territory.

Prince Dai had halted his chariot outside the suburbs, thus Tui Shu and the Viscount of Tao were able to enter the city ahead of him and have an audience with the Di chief: "Originally, when we were sent here to request a marriage alliance between you and the Zhou ruling house, the prospective bridegroom was Prince Dai. However, when the Zhou king heard how lovely your daughter is, he married her himself and appointed her as queen. It so happened that she met Prince Dai while visiting her mother-in-law, the dowager queen, and they fell into conversation. The palace servants started gossiping about this, and the Zhou king believed every malicious lie they spoke. He paid no heed to the support you gave him in the attack on Zheng, but immediately ordered Her Majesty to be demoted and sent to the Cold Palace, while the prince was forced into exile. The king has betrayed his family, besmirched the reputation of the royal house, ignored all the demands of justice, and let down everyone who has helped him. Please raise an army and attack the capital! You can put Prince Dai on the throne, rescue the queen—the Mother of the Country—and thus complete the good work that you have begun."

The Di chief believed what they said and asked, "Where is Prince Dai now?"

"He awaits your orders outside the suburbs."

The Di chief then welcomed His Highness into the city. Prince Dai asked permission to perform the rituals due to a senior family member, which deeply pleased the chief. He raised an army of five thousand men and commanded the senior general Chiding to attack Zhou and put Prince Dai on the throne, in concert with Tui Shu and the Viscount of Tao.

. . .

When King Xiang of Zhou heard that the Di army had arrived at his borders, he appointed Grandee the Earl of Tan as his ambassador. He went to meet the Di army and explained to them exactly what Prince Dai had done. Chiding killed him and hastened his army on until they reached the foot of the walls to the royal capital. King Xiang was furious and appointed the minister, Yuanbo Guan, as the commander-in-chief of the army with Mao Wei as his deputy. He left the city with an army of three hundred chariots to meet the enemy. Yuanbo Guan was well aware of the fearsome reputation of the Di cavalry, so he insisted that the army should be encamped in a series of interconnecting stockades, which stood as hard as a rock. Chiding assaulted these encampments many times, but he was not able to break through. Day after day he attempted to provoke battle, but the Zhou army did not respond. Chiding was enraged, so he came up with a plan whereby he ordered his men to construct a tower on Mount Cuiyun. The banners and flags of the Zhou Son of Heaven fluttered from the top of this tower, and he ordered one of his officers to dress up as Prince Dai and hold banquets there, with singing and dancing. He instructed Tui Shu and the Viscount of Tao to take one thousand cavalry each and wait in ambush on either side of the mountain. They were ordered to hold off until such time as the Zhou army arrived. When the signal was given from the top of the tower, they were to launch their attack. He instructed his son, Chifengzi, to take five hundred horsemen to the Zhou camp, where they were to shout insults at the men inside, in the hope of annoying them. If they came out of the encampment to do battle, his son was to pretend to be defeated and lead them in the direction of Mount Cuiyun. Chiding and Prince Dai withdrew the main army with a view to using them later on, and everything was ready.

Chifengzi led his five hundred cavalry off with a view to provoking battle. Yuanbo Guan inspected his force from the top of the stockade, and, realizing that they were few in number, he wanted to go out and fight them. Mao Wei remonstrated: "The Di people are very tricky. Since we are in a position of strength, all we have to do is to wait for them to get bored, then we can attack them."

By noon, the Di cavalry had all gotten off their horses and were sitting on the ground, shouting out curses: "The Zhou king is a right bastard and he clearly has completely useless generals. You won't surrender and you won't fight, what is the point of that?"

There were even some people who were lying around yelling insults. Yuanbo Guan could not stand it anymore and gave the orders to open the gates of the camp. When they were thrown wide, some one hundred chariots poured out. A senior general was riding in the very first one, wearing a golden helmet and an embroidered silk robe, and grasping a huge sword; that was Yuanbo Guan himself.

"Get back on your horses, lads!" Chifengzi yelled. He picked up his iron spear and went to do battle, but before they had even crossed swords ten times, he turned his horse's head to the west and fled. There were many of his men who had not been able to get onto their horses in time, and the Zhou army was busy rounding up all the loose animals. Chifengzi rode back and fought again, gradually leading the Zhou army in the direction of Mount Cuiyun. He abandoned his horse's heavy armor as he and a couple of other Di horsemen headed around the back of Mount Cuiyun. Yuanbo Guan raised his head and saw a red banner with a design of soaring dragons fluttering from the top of the mountain. The man beneath the embroidered baldachin would have to be Prince Dai, who was drinking great gulps of wine from the cup in his hand.

"I am going to kill that bastard!" Yuanbo Guan declared. He collected a few chariots on a bit of flat land at the foot of the mountain and was just about to start his assault, when siege engines started to hurl great lumps of wood and rocks at them. Yuanbo Guan had no idea how to deal with this, and all of a sudden the slopes of the mountain were boiling with soldiers. On the left there was Tui Shu, on the right there was the Viscount of Tao, and the ironclad cavalry that they commanded now started to encircle them, moving like the wind. Yuanbo Guan realized that he had fallen into a trap and hurriedly ordered his army to retreat, but the road along which they had traveled had already been blocked by logs pulled across by the Di soldiers, making it impassable for chariots. Yuanbo Guan shouted orders for his infantry to clear the way, but their morale was shattered and they fled without offering any fight. Yuanbo Guan had no clue what to do. He took off his embroidered robe and attempted to mingle with the fleeing troops.

"Come this way, General!" one young soldier called out.

Tui Shu heard this shout and suspected that the general referred to would be Yuanbo Guan, so he ordered the Di cavalry under his command to pursue them and they captured about twenty men alive. One of them was indeed Yuanbo Guan. By the time Chiding arrived with the main army, they had already won a great victory, capturing chariots and horses, together with much of their equipment. Those officers and men who managed to get away went back to the camp and reported to Mao Wei. Mao Wei gave instructions to hold the defenses of the stockade while he sent someone to inform the Zhou king at the earliest possible opportunity of this crisis, together with a request for more soldiers and another general. No more of this now.

Tui Shu tied up Yuanbo Guan and presented him as part of the spoils of war to Prince Dai. The prince ordered that he be kept prisoner in their camp.

"Mao Wei is sure to be deeply upset by the fact that we have taken Yuanbo Guan prisoner," Tui Shu said. "If we attack his encampment in the middle of the night and set fire to it, we can also take him prisoner."

Prince Dai was impressed and suggested it to Chiding. He too thought this a good stratagem and secretly gave the necessary orders. Therefore, just after the drums had been beaten for the third watch, Chiding personally led one thousand foot soldiers forward, armed with sharp axes, and they cut their way through the stockades. Having infiltrated the main encampment, they heaped brushwood onto the chariots and set light to them. In an instant the flames leapt up, racing through the encampment, and the soldiers panicked. Tui Shu and the Viscount of Tao led their forces of crack cavalry on the attack—the Zhou army could not withstand this onslaught. Mao Wei got into a little chariot and escaped through the back gate of the encampment. However, almost immediately he ran into a division of infantry, under the command of Prince Dai.

"Where do you think that you are going?" he shouted.

Mao Wei tried to make a break for it, but he was brought down by Prince Dai's spear. The Di army had won yet another great victory, and now they laid siege to the royal capital.

When King Xiang of Zhou heard that both of his generals had been captured, he said to Grandee Fu Chen, "If I had listened to you, none of this would have happened."

"The Di are now in a very strong position," Fu Chen said. "Your Majesty had better leave the city temporarily. I am sure that you can find one of the feudal lords who will be happy to put you back on your throne."

"Even though His Majesty's army has been defeated," Kong, Duke of Zhou, said, "we could mobilize our private forces to defend the city. Surely we cannot just abandon the state altars and seek protection from one of the feudal lords?"

Guo, Duke of Shao, presented his opinion: "Fighting is a very risky strategy. In my humble opinion, this disaster is the fault of Lady Shu Wei. If you start by ordering her execution and then defend the city until such time as the armies of the lords arrive to lift the siege—that would be the best possible plan."

"This crisis was brought about by my own stupidity," King Xiang said with a sigh. "Dowager Queen Hui is now seriously ill. If I were to remove myself temporarily, that would please her very much. If my people want me back, then one of the lords will be able to reinstall me on my throne." He told the dukes of Zhou and Shao: "Prince Dai has come back for Queen Wei. If he marries her, he will be worried by the gossip that this will occasion, so he will not dare to remain here in the capital. I want the two of you to hold the city for me and await my return."

The dukes of Zhou and Shao kowtowed and accepted the mission entrusted to them. King Xiang then asked Grandee Fu Chen: "My lands are bordered by the states of Zheng, Wey, and Chen. Which should I head for?"

"I would encourage you to go to Zheng," Fu Chen said. "The ancestors of the present lord demonstrated exemplary loyalty to the Zhou royal house, which the earl has certainly not forgotten. Zheng was also very unhappy when you used the Di army to attack them, and they have been waiting for the Di to betray you to prove their point. If you go to Zheng, they will be so happy to welcome you that they are unlikely to bear any grudges." King Xiang then made his decision.

Grandee Fu Chen had a further request to make: "Your Majesty will have to break through the Di front line in order to escape. I am concerned that the Di will meet you head-on with their whole army. What will you do then? Let me take my own forces out of the city to do battle with the Di, and you can escape while they are occupied elsewhere."

He assembled his whole clan and all his staff—several hundred men in total—and gave a rousing speech about loyalty and justice. After that, the gates of the city were opened and they marched straight out against the enemy encampment, forcing the Di to fight. King Xiang then slipped out of the city and headed for the state of Zheng, accompanied by Jian Shifu, Zuo Yanfu, and a dozen other men. Grandee Fu Chen fought a terrible battle with Chiding, in which many Di soldiers were killed or injured. Fu Chen sustained dreadful injuries himself.

When he bumped into Tui Shu and the Viscount of Tao Zi, they felt sorry for him: "Everyone knows about the loyal remonstrance that you have offered the king. We will spare your life."

"I repeatedly warned His Majesty of the consequences of his actions, but he did not listen to me," Fu Chen replied. "That is why things have reached this crisis. If I do not die in this battle, he will think I am angry with him." He fought on and was killed. More than three hundred members of his clan and staff died with him.

A historian wrote a poem in praise of these men:

> It is never a good idea to use barbarians to control your own people.
> If you allow your wife to have affairs, you are bringing disaster upon yourself.
> Ignoring good advice ended in a terrible battle,
> But Fu Chen's loyalty was recorded in the *Spring and Autumn Annals*.

After Fu Chen died, the Di discovered that King Xiang had left the city, but by that time the gates had closed again. Prince Dai ordered that Yuanbo Guan should be released and sent to stand outside the city walls and call out to those within. The dukes of Zhou and Shao were standing on one of the gate towers and told Prince Dai, "We would be happy to open the gates to you, but we are worried that the Di soldiers will rape and plunder the city if we do."

Prince Dai begged Chiding to set up camp away from the city, promising that the contents of the treasuries and storehouses would be given to the Di. Chiding agreed to this. Prince Dai then entered the capital and went straight to the Cold Palace, where he released Queen Wei. After that he went to visit Dowager Queen Hui. When the poor woman saw him, she was absolutely delighted; she died with a smile on her face. The prince had no time to mourn—he hurried to his meeting with Queen Wei in the inner palace. He wanted to kill Xiaodong, but she had already committed suicide by throwing herself into a well before he could punish her. How sad!

The following day, Prince Dai presented a forged will from his mother, Dowager Queen Hui, which installed him as the new king and Lady Shu Wei as queen. He went to court to receive the congratulations of his ministers. He gave an enormous bounty from the state storehouses and treasuries to the Di army. It was only once this had been done that he started mourning his mother. The people of the capital composed a song about this:

Who has time to mourn their mother when they have a wife to marry?
A sister-in-law becomes a wife, a subject marries the queen!
He is not ashamed of what he has done, but he is bothered by the gossip;
Who is going to get rid of him? Why, you and I!

When Prince Dai heard this song, he realized that he did not have the support of the populace. He was afraid that there would be some kind of open rebellion against his authority, so he decided that it would be best if he and Queen Wei moved to Wen. They built a massive palace there and enjoyed themselves day and night. The capital and the running of the Zhou Royal Domain were entrusted entirely to the dukes of Zhou and Shao. Prince Dai was a king in name only, because he actually had nothing to do with his officials or the people. Yuanbo Guan was eventually able to escape and make his way home, but this belongs to a later part of the story.

. . .

When King Xiang of Zhou left the capital, he headed in the direction of the state of Zheng, but he had no idea of what his reception would be like. When he arrived at Fan, he found a place with no official guest-houses but plenty of bamboo, hence its alternative name of Zhuchuan. King Xiang questioned the locals and discovered that he had already crossed the border into Zheng. He gave orders to halt the chariots and stayed overnight in a thatched cottage belonging to a man named Feng.

"What is your job, sir?" this man asked.

"I am the Zhou Son of Heaven," King Xiang replied. "There has been trouble in the capital, and so I am running away."

Mr. Feng, very shocked, kowtowed and apologized: "Last night my younger brother dreamed that a red sun illuminated our thatched cottage, and now Your Majesty graces us with your presence." He immediately ordered his younger brother to kill a chicken for dinner.

"Tell me about your younger brother," King Xiang said.

"My younger brother is the son of my stepmother," Mr. Feng told him. "We both live here, farming the land and looking after her."

King Xiang sighed and said, "What a delightful family! I may be the Son of Heaven, but that has not saved me from disaster at the hands of my stepmother and half-brother. My position is a great deal worse than that of these peasants." He was so upset that he burst into tears.

Grandee Zuo Yanfu stepped forward and said, "The first Duke of Zhou was a great sage, and even he got into trouble with members of his own family. Do not be sad, Your Majesty. You need to get in touch with the feudal lords as soon as possible to inform them of what has happened. They will not just sit there and let this continue."

King Xiang then drafted a letter personally, which would be sent to the states of Qi, Song, Chen, Zheng, and Wey. It read:

> Thanks to my lack of virtue, I have suffered at the hands of Prince Dai, the favorite son of my stepmother. I have now been forced into exile and am living at Fan in the state of Zheng. Please help.

Jian Shifu presented his opinion: "The only feudal lords with aspirations towards hegemony are Qin and Jin. Qin has such wise men as Jian Shu, Baili Xi, and Noble Grandson Qi in the government, while Jin is administered by Zhao Cui, Hu Yan, and Xu Chen. They will encourage their lords to restore you to your throne. There is no point in expecting help from anyone else."

King Xiang ordered Jian Shifu to report his situation to Jin, while Zuo Yanfu performed a similar office in Qin. When Lord Wen of Zheng heard that King Xiang was resident in Fan, he laughed and said, "His Majesty has found out that Zheng is a much more reliable ally than the Di." He immediately sent artisans to build houses in Fan for the court in exile, under his own personal supervision. He also provided the necessary furniture and equipment, all of which was the very finest quality. King Xiang had an audience with Lord Wen of Zheng, at which he looked very ill-at-ease. The states of Lu and Song sent ambassadors to make polite inquiries and offer gifts. The only person who made no response was Lord Wen of Wey. When Grandee Zang Sunchen of Lu heard about this, he sighed and said, "The Marquis of Wey is dying. The relationship between the feudal lords and His Majesty is like that of a tree and its roots, or a river and its source. A tree without roots will wither; a river without its source will run dry. He must be dying!"

This happened in the tenth month of the eighteenth year of the reign of King Xiang. The following year in the spring, Lord Wen of Wey did indeed pass away, to be succeeded by Scion Zheng, who became Lord Cheng. It was just as Zang Sunchen had prophesied. Of this, no more.

• • •

Jian Shifu went to Jin to report the emergency just as he had been instructed by the king, and Lord Wen of Jin mentioned the problem to Hu Yan.

"The crucial factor that meant Lord Huan of Qi could unite the feudal lords was his respect for royal authority," Hu Yan said. "Even more importantly, in recent years Jin has changed rulers so many times that people have become used to it and no longer understand that they should respect their lords. If you put His Majesty back on the throne and punish Prince Dai for his crimes, everyone will know that you are not someone to betray. This is a wonderful opportunity for you to imitate and glorify the example of your ancestors who supported the Zhou royal house and unified the state of Jin. If you do not do this, then Qin will take the initiative and they will become hegemon in your stead."

Lord Wen ordered Grand Astrologer Guo Yan to perform a divination about this, and he reported: "This is extremely auspicious. This is exactly the same omen that the Yellow Emperor received just before the battle of Banquan."

"How can I possibly be worthy of that?" Lord Wen asked.

"Although the Zhou dynasty is in decline, the Mandate of Heaven has not yet changed," Hu Yan told him. "Kings today are equivalent to the emperors of high antiquity. His Majesty's victory over Prince Dai is assured."

"Please perform a divination with milfoil," Lord Wen requested.

He obtained the trigram "Sky" with the trigram "Lake" above it, which together form the hexagram "Large." When he cast the second divination, he obtained the trigram "Lake" with the trigram "Fire" above it, which together form the hexagram "Espy."

Guo Yan gave the following reading: "The third line of the analysis of the hexagram 'Large' says: 'The lord will be offered a banquet by the Son of Heaven.' This means that you will be victorious in battle and His Majesty will reward you. No omen could be more auspicious! The trigram 'Sky' represents Heaven; the trigram 'Fire' represents the sun. To see these two trigrams together is an omen of enlightenment. The position of 'Sky' in the first hexagram is succeeded by 'Lake' in the second one; 'Lake' is associated with water. When water is found in the lower part of a hexagram, it reflects the light coming from the sun in the 'Fire' trigram. This means that the Son of Heaven's beneficent light will shine upon the state of Jin. What is there to be concerned about here?"

Lord Wen was very pleased and then held a great muster of men and chariots, which were then divided into a Left and Right army. He appointed Zhao Cui to command the Army of the Left with Wei Chou to assist him; he appointed Xi Cou to command the Army of the Right with Dian Jie to assist him. Lord Wen himself would remain at headquarters with Hu Yan and Luan Zhi, coordinating information for the two armies. As they were about to depart, one of the border officials stationed east of the Yellow River reported: "The Earl of Qin has set off in command of an enormous army to restore His Majesty to the throne. He has already arrived at the Yellow River and will cross it shortly."

Hu Yan came forward and said: "The Earl of Qin is determined to see the restoration of the Zhou king. The reason why he has been forced to make camp at the Yellow River rather than proceeding on his way is that as he travels east, he will have to go through the territory of the Caozhong Rong and the Litu Di. Normally Qin has nothing to do with these people, so Lord Mu must be concerned that they will not allow him to pass through their lands unmolested. That is the reason why he is not advancing. You will have to give bribes to these two barbarian peoples and explain that armies are on the move in order to restore the king to his throne; they will listen to you. You should also send someone to apologize to the Earl of Qin and explain that the Jin army has already set out on this mission, for then he will go home."

Lord Wen was pleased with this advice and sent Hu Yan's son, Hu Shegu, to bribe the Rong and Di peoples with gold and silk. He also sent Xu Chen to the Yellow River to apologize to Qin. Xu Chen requested an audience with Lord Mu of Qin and, as he had been instructed by the Marquis of Jin, informed him: "Your Lordship has been deeply concerned by the news that the Zhou Son of Heaven has been deposed—my lord has also been worried. He has now mobilized a huge army and plans to deal with this problem on your behalf—his victory is guaranteed. There is no point in your going any further."

"I have come this far because I was concerned that the Marquis of Jin, as a newly established lord, would be having problems putting together an army," Lord Mu said. "It is wonderful news that Lord Wen plans to put His Majesty back on the throne. I will await news of his success."

Jian Shu and Baili Xi both made representations: "The Marquis of Jin wants to use this occasion to make the feudal lords submit to his authority. He is worried that you might steal some of his thunder, and that is why he has sent someone to halt your advance. You had better carry on going and join in the efforts to restore His Majesty. Would that not be best?"

"It would indeed be wonderful if I could participate in the restoration of His Majesty, but I am afraid that the road to the east will prove impassable for us if the Rong and the Di cause trouble," Lord Mu reminded them. "Lord Wen has only just taken over the running of his state and has not yet achieved any signal success to help him in calming the volatile political situation in Jin. I am perfectly happy to give him this opportunity."

He ordered the Honorable Zhi to go to Fan, together with Grandee Zuo Yanfu, to make polite inquiries concerning King Xiang's situation, while Lord Mu stood down the army and went home.

When Xu Chen reported that the Lord of Qin had begun his withdrawal, the Jin army advanced and made camp at Yangfan. The administrator, a man named Cang Ge, came out to the suburbs to welcome the army. Lord Wen ordered the General of the Right, Xi Cou, to lay siege to Wen while the General of the Left, Zhao Cui, went to meet King Xiang in Fan. On Dingsi day in the fourth month, King Xiang returned to the royal capital, whereupon the dukes of Zhou and Shao welcomed him at court. This does not need to be described in any detail.

. . .

When the people of Wen heard that the Zhou king had been restored to the throne, riots broke out in which Tui Shu and the Viscount of Tao were killed. They threw open the gates of the city and allowed the Jin army to enter. Prince Dai and Queen Wei climbed into a chariot and tried to escape the city, fleeing to the Di. The officers guarding the gate shut it and would not allow them to leave. Prince Dai drew his sword and hacked several people to death. Just then Wei Chou came in pursuit, shouting: "Where do you think you are going, bastard?"

"If you let me leave the city, I will reward you generously," Prince Dai said.

"If His Majesty is prepared to let you go, I will think about it," Wei Chou told him.

Prince Dai was furious enough to attack him with his sword, but Wei Chou forced him down from his chariot and beheaded him with a single stroke. The officers who had taken Queen Wei prisoner now brought her forward.

"What is the point of keeping this whore alive?" Wei Chou asked. He ordered the soldiers to shoot her. How dreadful that this beautiful barbarian woman should die in a hail of arrows, less than six months after she eloped with Prince Dai!

Master Hu Zeng wrote a historical poem about her:

Having exiled his brother and stolen his wife, he took possession
of Wen;
After half a year's pleasure, all that remained was suffering and pain.
If debauchery and betrayal are not quickly punished,
By what principles can we govern the world?

Wei Chou brought the two bodies back and reported to Xi Cou, who asked, "Why didn't you drag them in front of the Son of Heaven in chains and let them be punished after a proper trial?"

"His Majesty involved us because he wants to avoid the reputation of a fratricide," Wei Chou said. "It is better to kill them here and now!"

Xi Cou sighed sadly and gave orders that the pair of them should be buried beside the Shennong River. He also made arrangements to settle the people of Wen and sent someone to Yangfan to report a successful resolution of the problem.

When Lord Wen heard that both Prince Dai and Queen Wei had been killed, he decided to go in person to the royal capital and report this to King Xiang. King Xiang held a lavish banquet in his honor and bestowed enormous quantities of gold and silk upon him. Lord Wen bowed twice and refused this gift: "I do not want any presents. But if when I die, I can be buried in a kingly tomb, I would thank Your Majesty for your benevolence for the rest of eternity!"

"When the first kings of Zhou established the ceremonial regulations that govern our lives," King Xiang remarked, "they laid down strict sumptuary legislation that distinguishes different levels of society and applies to both the living and the dead. I would not dare to interfere with these regulations simply because I owe you an enormous debt of gratitude. I will never forget, Uncle, what you have done for me!"

He then increased the Marquis of Jin's fief by four towns from the Royal Domain: Wen, Yuan, Yangfan, and Zanmao. Lord Wen thanked His Majesty for this munificent gift and withdrew. The residents of the capital, young and old, were lining the street, jostling one another for a glimpse of the Marquis of Jin. They shouted their acclamation: "Lord Huan of Qi has come back to us again!"

Lord Wen of Jin gave orders that the two armies of the Left and Right should stand down, while the main army made camp south of Mount Taihang. He sent Wei Chou to take possession of Yangfan, while Dian Jie took charge of Zanmao and Luan Zhi went to Wen. The Marquis of Jin went with Zhao Cui to take possession of Yuan.

Why did Lord Wen have to go in person to take charge of Yuan? This place had previously been the fief of the Zhou minister Yuanbo Guan; after he was defeated in battle, King Xiang took his fief away from him and gave it to Jin. Yuanbo Guan was still living there, and they were afraid that he would not accept this situation, so the Marquis of Jin had to go in person.

When Dian Jie arrived in Zanmao, he was greeted by local officials who arranged a banquet for him. The same thing happened to Luan Zhi in Wen. However, when Wei Chou arrived in Yangfan, the local official Cang Ge said to his subordinates: "Zhou has already abandoned its old capitals; not much is left now! Why should the Marquis of Jin be given these four towns? The marquis is a subject of the Zhou king just like us, so why should we obey him?"

He led the people of Yangfan to climb onto the city walls to defend them. Wei Chou was furious and advanced his troops to besiege the city, shouting: "If you surrender immediately, I will forgive you. If you force me to attack the city, you will all be butchered!"

Cang Ge shouted down from the top of the wall: "I have heard it said that virtue should be shown to the Central States, military might should be used to overawe the barbarians. These lands are part of the Royal Domain and the people who live here are the king's relatives by marriage, if they are not actually part of the royal clan. You are also a subject of His Majesty; how dare you use your army to threaten us!"

Wei Chou realized the truth of what he was saying and sent someone to report this to Lord Wen as quickly as possible. Lord Wen wrote a letter to Cang Ge as follows:

> These four cities were given to me by the Zhou king, and it would have been an act of lèse-majesté for me to have refused to accept it. If you are concerned about His Majesty's relatives living in the city, should you wish, you can all have a safe-conduct to leave and go back to Zhou.

He instructed Wei Chou to cease the attack on Yangfan and allow the people who wished to leave to do so. When Cang Ge received the letter, he told the residents of the city: "Those of you who want to move to the Royal Domain can leave; anyone who is happy to live under Jin control can stay."

More than half of the inhabitants wanted to leave. Cang Ge led them all out of the city and they moved to Zhicun. Wei Chou agreed to the border between Jin territory and the Zhou Royal Domain and returned.

• • •

When Lord Wen of Jin arrived in Yuan with Zhao Cui, he found that Yuanbo Guan had been busy spreading lies to his subordinates: "The Jin army has laid siege to Yangfan and butchered all the inhabitants." The people of Yuan were terrified and swore to defend the city to the last man when the Jin army laid siege to them.

"The reason these people will not obey you is because they do not trust you," Zhao Cui said. "If you could find some way to gain their trust, they would surrender without a fight."

"How do I get them to trust me?" Lord Wen asked.

"You must give orders that each soldier is to take provisions for three days," Zhao Cui replied. "If the city of Yuan does not fall in that time, then you must lift the siege and leave."

Lord Wen did exactly as he had said, and on the third day, the officers reported: "The soldiers only have food for today." Lord Wen did not say anything. In the middle of the night, one of the inhabitants of Yuan threw a rope over the top of the city walls and rappelled down it. "The people inside already know that the residents of Yangfan weren't butchered," he said. "They are planning to surrender the city to you tomorrow evening."

"I originally decided that the attack on the city should last three days," Lord Wen said. "If within that time you had not surrendered, then I would leave. The three days are now up and I am going to withdraw the army first thing in the morning. You have successfully defended your city, and you have nothing to worry about from me."

The army officers present pointed out, "The people of Yuan are going to surrender the city to us tomorrow evening. Why don't you stay one more day, my lord? That way you can capture the city before you go home. As for the fact that we have run out of food, we are not far from Yangfan and they can reprovision us soon enough."

"Trust is the greatest treasure that a state can have," Lord Wen told them. "People rely upon it. Everyone knows that I set a time limit of three days. If I stay for one more day, then I am breaking my word. If I lay my hands on Yuan but lose the trust of my people, how can they rely on me in the future?"

The following morning, he lifted the siege of Yuan. The people there looked at one another and said, "The Marquis of Jin would rather lose control of this city than break his word. He really is a wonderful ruler." They quickly raised the flag of surrender above the city walls, and many people climbed down to run after Lord Wen's troops. Yuanbo Guan had lost all control of the situation and ended up having to open the city gates.

An old man wrote a poem about this:

They were prepared to fight to the last man;
Who would have expected that a few words could bring peace to the country?
Having left Yuan, Yuan chased after them to surrender,
Honesty and justice proving more useful than trickery.

The Jin army had advanced three *li* before the people from Yuan caught up with them to hand over the document of surrender from Yuanbo Guan. Lord Wen ordered that the chariots stay where they were while he went back to the city of Yuan alone. The people danced and sang as they congratulated him. Yuanbo Guan came to have an audience with him, and Lord Wen treated him with all the ceremony due to a minister at the royal court and made arrangements for his family to move to Hebei. Lord Wen appointed new officials to administer the four towns that he had been given, and he instructed them: "There was a time when we were traveling through Wey, and Zhao Cui, who was in charge of my remaining food, got left behind. Being a loyal and trustworthy knight, he did not eat it. I got Yuan by keeping faith with its people, and you will administer it in the same way."

He appointed Zhao Cui Grandee of Yuan, which he would govern together with Yangfan.

Lord Wen said to Xi Cou, "In spite of the close relationship between Xi Rui and the previous Lord of Jin, you and the Luan family were the first to give your allegiance to me. I will never forget this." He appointed Xi Chou Grandee of Wen, which he would be administering together with Zanmao. A garrison of two thousand soldiers remained in each place.

Later on people said that the first step in Lord Wen's campaign to become hegemon was accomplished when he demonstrated his sense of justice in putting King Xiang back on the throne and demonstrated his trustworthiness by calling off the attack on Yuan.

If you want to know when Lord Wen finally became hegemon, READ ON.

Chapter Thirty-nine

Zhan Huo of Liuxia advises on how to get rid of the enemy.

Lord Wen of Jin attacks Wey and ruins Cao.

Lord Wen of Jin, having pacified the four cities of Wen, Yuan, Yangfan, and Zanmao, placed himself in complete control over the area south of Mount Taihang, and he renamed this place Nanyang. This happened in the winter of the seventeenth year of the reign of King Xiang of Zhou.

At this moment in time, Lord Xiao of Qi was still determined that he should succeed to his father's title of hegemon. However, his involvement in the death of the Honorable Wukui had disgusted Lord Xi of Lu; his arrogance at Lushang had alienated him from Lord Xiang of Song; and his refusal to come to the interstate meeting at Yudi had angered King Cheng of Chu. Since the lords felt alienated from him, they did not bother to send embassies to Qi. Lord Xiao was enraged by this and decided to raise an army to campaign against the Central States, to recapture the position that he had lost. He summoned his ministers and put it to them: "In the past, when our former ruler, Lord Huan, was alive, he went out on campaign every year and fought every day. Now I am sitting here at peace in my court, just like a snail in its shell. I know nothing about what is going on beyond my borders, and I am ashamed of this. A few years ago the Marquis of Lu plotted to bring the Honorable Wukui to power and caused me great trouble. I have not yet avenged this. Today Lu has concluded an alliance with the state of Wey to the north and the kingdom of Chu to the south. If they join together to attack Qi, how can we withstand them? I have heard that Lu has suffered famine this year, and it is my intention to take advantage of the situation to attack them, in order to put an end to their conspiracy against me. What do you think of this, my ministers?"

The senior minister, Gao Hu, presented his opinion: "Lu has many allies. If we attack them, we are not sure to be victorious."

"Even if we are not victorious, it is worth trying," Lord Xiao proclaimed, "for then we can see whether the feudal lords are united against us or not."

He personally led an army of two hundred chariots to invade the northern border of Lu. The people there heard this news and reported the emergency at the earliest possible opportunity. Lu was in the grip of a terrible famine, and the populace could not possibly withstand a trained army. Grandee Zangsun Chen said to Lord Xi, "Once Qi has penetrated deeply into our territory, even if we do battle, we will not necessarily be able to defeat them. I ask your permission to send an ambassador to apologize to them."

"Who would be the best person to send?" Lord Xi asked.

"I can recommend someone," Zangsun Chen said. "The man I have in mind is the son of the late minister of works, Zhan Wuhai. His name is Zhan Huo, his style-name is Ziqin, he currently occupies the post of chief judge, and he holds a fief in Liuxia. In addition to being an upright man, he is also widely learned and extremely pleasant; however, because he was so strict in his interpretation of the law when in office, he did not meet with the approval that he should have. Therefore he resigned and now lives in retirement. If you send this man as your ambassador, not only will he uphold your orders to the letter, he will also be much admired by Qi."

"I know this man," Lord Xi said. "Where is he now?"

"He is living in Liuxia," Zangsun Chen replied.

The Marquis of Lu sent someone to summon him, but Zhan Huo claimed that he was too ill to go.

"Zhan Huo has a cousin named Xi, who is a persuasive speaker, though he only holds junior office," Zangsun Chen mentioned. "If you send him to talk to Huo and ask for advice about how to conduct the mission, he will listen to his cousin." Lord Xi followed his advice.

When Zhan Xi arrived in Liuxia, he met Huo and explained His Lordship's orders.

"Qi has attacked us because they are hoping to continue Lord Huan's hegemony," Zhan Huo said. "If you want to become hegemon, the only way is by showing your respect to the king. If we upbraid them for not following the commands of the Zhou kings, we will escape disaster."

Zhan Xi went back to see Lord Xi of Lu and said, "I know how to get rid of Qi." Lord Xi had already prepared some gifts for the army, animals, grain, and clothing, which he loaded onto a couple of carts. These he entrusted to Zhan Xi.

When Zhan Xi arrived at the northern border, the Qi army had still not yet crossed it, so he advanced as far as Wennan, where he met with the advance guard of the Qi forces. Cui Yao was in command of the vanguard and Zhan Xi handed over his gifts to him. They then rode back together to join the main army. Zhan Xi asked for an audience with the Marquis of Qi, at which he handed over the gifts to the army and said, "When His Lordship heard that you had come in person to our humble country, he sent me to present these items to your soldiers."

"It would be more accurate to say that when the people of Lu heard that I had raised an army, you were all scared witless!" Lord Xiao declared.

"It is possible that some mean and humble individuals were scared," Zhan Xi replied, "but I would not know anything about that. What I know is that no gentleman was frightened."

"At present you have no ministers of the caliber of Shi Bo and no generals of the quality of Cao Gui," Lord Xiao sneered, "besides which you are suffering from a severe famine and every edible plant in the wilds has been grubbed up and eaten. How could you not be terrified?"

"If nothing else, at least in our humble country we uphold the commands of the Zhou kings," Zhan Xi replied. "In the past, His Majesty enfeoffed your ancestor in Qi and enfeoffed my lord's ancestor, Boqin, in Lu. He ordered the Duke of Zhou and the founder of the ruling house of Qi to kill an animal and swear a blood covenant. The words of that oath ran: 'May our sons and grandsons from one generation to the next support the royal house and never bring harm to one another.' This text was recorded in the archives kept by the Grand Historian. When Lord Huan of Qi brought the feudal lords together nine times, he first made a blood covenant with Lord Zhuang of Lu at Ke, because he was upholding the mandate that he had received from the Zhou king. It is now nine years since you first came to power, and everyone in my country has been expecting Qi to say, 'I am hoping to restore the hegemony of my father, Lord Huan, in order to bring peace to the feudal lords.' It struck us as most unlikely that you would be prepared to disobey the mandate given to your house by King Cheng of Zhou, to break the oath sworn by your ancestor, the first marquis, to abandon the hegemony achieved by Lord Huan, and to turn your friends into your enemies. That is why we were not frightened."

"Go back and tell the Marquis of Lu that I am willing to restore the alliance between our two states," Lord Xiao said. "I will not use troops against him again." He immediately gave orders to stand down his army.

Qian Yuan wrote a poem criticizing Zangsun Chen for knowing full well how wise Zhan Huo was and yet failing to recommend him for office at court. This poem runs:

The beacon fires far to the north proclaim the danger of Lu's situation;
To make the enemy withdraw by just a few words smacks of a remarkable talent.
Zangsun Chen was not willing to see this brilliant man succeed,
And Chief Judge Zhan Huo was left to rot in Liuxia.

When Zhan Xi returned to Lu, he reported back on his mission to Lord Xi. "Even though the Qi army has withdrawn, they still despise us," Zangsun Chen declared. "I ask permission to go to Chu with the Honorable Sui and beg them for an army to attack Qi. That way, the Marquis of Qi will never again dare to look us straight in the face. Afterwards we will be able to enjoy the blessings of peace for many years."

Lord Xi thought that this was a good idea and appointed the Honorable Sui as his principal ambassador, with Zangsun Chen to assist him, and they went on a formal embassy to Chu.

Zangsun Chen had long been friendly with the Chu general, Cheng Dechen, so he asked him to discover how the king of Chu felt about the whole situation and tell him, "Qi has betrayed the treaty signed at Lushang, while Song fought Your Majesty at the Hong River: both of these states are now the enemies of Chu. If Your Majesty wishes to punish them, His Lordship is willing to devote the whole of his meager revenues to this task."

King Cheng of Chu was very pleased by this and immediately appointed Cheng Dechen as the commander-in-chief with Shuhou, Lord of Shen, as his deputy. They led their army to attack Qi, occupying the lands of Yanggu, with a view to installing Lord Huan of Qi's son, the Honorable Yong, as the new marquis with Yi Ya as his prime minister. A garrison of one thousand soldiers was established, under the command of Shuhou, Lord of Shen. They believed that this move would have support from the state of Lu. Cheng Dechen then returned to the court in triumph. Grand Vizier Ziwen was already an old man by this time. He requested permission to retire and let Cheng Dechen take over his position.

"I hate Song much more than I hate Qi," the king of Chu proclaimed. "Cheng Dechen has now taken my revenge upon Qi, so I would like you to attack Song, to avenge what they did to Zheng. You can retire once you have returned to Chu in triumph. How would that be?"

"I cannot match up to Cheng Dechen's achievements," Ziwen said. "Let him replace me, lest I ruin Your Majesty's plans."

"Song's security is guaranteed by the state of Jin," the king of Chu said. "If I attack Song, Jin is sure to come to their aid. You are the only person who can deal with both of them, so please undertake this campaign for me."

He then ordered that Ziwen should conduct military exercises at Kui after mustering the army, in order to make sure that everyone understood their instructions. Ziwen was determined to use this occasion to demonstrate how much better Cheng Dechen was at these things than himself, so he hurried through the maneuvers and finished them before midday, without punishing even a single individual.

"How can you demonstrate your authority if you do not punish anyone during these exercises?" the king of Chu demanded.

Ziwen presented his opinion: "My talents in this direction can be compared to just the smallest feathers on an arrow. If you really wish to stamp the authority of the general on the army, you need to employ Cheng Dechen."

The king of Chu then ordered Cheng Dechen to carry out further exercises at Wei. Cheng Dechen put his troops through a fine-tooth comb. He applied military law to the letter, and anyone who made a mistake was punished. The exercises that he conducted lasted all day. In total he ordered seven people to be whipped and three people had an arrow punched through their ear, so that everyone followed implicitly the commands issued to them by bells, drums, and signal flags.

"Cheng Dechen is indeed a talented general," the king of Chu said happily.

Ziwen again asked permission to retire, and this time the king of Chu agreed. From this time on Cheng Dechen was both Grand Vizier and commander-in-chief of the Central Army.

The ministers all assembled at Ziwen's house to congratulate him on recommending such a brilliant man for office, and they held a party for him there. All the civil and military officials in Chu had assembled with the sole exception of Grandee Wei Lüchen, who was mildly indisposed. About halfway through the party, the gatekeeper announced: "There is a child at the gates who is asking for admittance." Ziwen gave orders to summon him in. The child clasped his hands together and bowed, before sitting down in the very furthest seat and starting to eat and drink, carrying on as if there were no one else present in the room. Some of the guests recognized this child: he was Wei Jia, the son of Wei Lüchen, who was then about thirteen years of age.

Ziwen was most surprised by his behavior and asked him, "I have found a great general for our kingdom. All the most senior ministers have offered congratulations with the exception of yourself. What is the reason for this?"

"The other officials may believe this a matter for congratulations, but I think that it is a disaster," Wei Jia told him.

Ziwen was furious and said, "When you say that it is a disaster, what do you mean?"

"In my humble opinion, Cheng Dechen is indeed a very brave man, but he is bad at making strategic decisions," Wei Jia commented. "He can advance, but he does not know when to withdraw. He would make a good junior general, but he cannot assume ultimate authority. If he is in charge of the government and the army, he is sure to bring about disaster. There is a popular saying that anything too stiff is easily broken; it refers to people like Cheng Dechen! How can it be a matter of congratulation that you have recommended a man who is going to bring ruin to the country? If that does not happen, then I will congratulate you!"

"The child has no idea what he is talking about," his entourage said. "Do not pay any attention to him." Wei Jia laughed and left, shortly after which the party broke up.

. . .

The following day, the king of Chu appointed Cheng Dechen as the senior general, and he took personal command over the army. He was joined by the lords of Chen, Cai, Zheng, and Xu in an attack on the state of Song, which saw them lay siege to the city of Min. Lord Cheng of Song sent his Marshal, Gongsun Gu, to Jin to report this emergency. Lord Wen of Jin then summoned his ministers to request that they come up with a plan to rescue Song.

Xian Zhen came forward and said, "Chu is the most powerful country in the world right now, and they have behaved with the greatest generosity towards Your Lordship. Today Chu has garrisoned its troops in Yanggu and attacked the state of Song, suggesting that they are determined to cause trouble in the Central States. This is a heaven-sent opportunity to win a reputation for saving other people from disaster and succoring innocent victims of trouble. This is where we start our campaign to become hegemon!"

"I want to save Qi and Song," Lord Wen declared. "How should I go about it?"

Hu Yan advanced and said, "Chu is supported by Cao and has recently concluded a marriage alliance with the state of Wey. These two states are Your Lordship's enemies. If you raise an army and attack Cao and Wey, Chu is sure to move its forces to rescue them. In that way Qi and Song will be left in peace."

"Good!" Lord Wen said. He explained his plan to Gongsun Gu and sent him to report back to the Duke of Song, telling him to hold firm. Gongsun Gu accepted this command and left.

Lord Wen was worried because he did not have many soldiers, but Zhao Cui moved forward and said, "Since antiquity, great states have had three armies, medium-sized states have had two armies, and small states have had one. Your grandfather, Lord Wu of Quwo, had one army under his command. Your father, Lord Xian, was the first to expand to two armies, and he used them to destroy the states of Huo, Wei, Yu, and Guo and open up one thousand *li* of territory. Jin today should no longer count as a medium-sized state, and so it is appropriate for us to have three armies."

"We can have three armies," Lord Wen said, "but the question is: can we use them?"

"Not yet," Zhao Cui told him. "Your people can be mustered into the army, but they are currently too easy to put to flight. Your Lordship needs to hold a great spring hunt in order to train them in the rules of ritual propriety, so that they can understand the difference between noble and commoner, senior and junior, and so that they can come to feel close to Your Lordship. It is only afterwards that you can use them in battle."

"If I create three armies, I need a commander-in-chief," Lord Wen pointed out. "Whom should I appoint to this position?"

"A brave general is not as good as a clever one, and a clever one is not as good as a learned one," Zhao Cui declared. "If Your Lordship wants to appoint a brave or a clever general, you have a great deal of choice. If you want a learned general, then as far as I can see, you will have to appoint Xi Hu. He is now past fifty years of age, and he has always been exceptionally interested in study, delighting in the *Book of Rites* and the *Book of Music* and learning from the *Book of Songs* and the *Book of Documents*. The *Book of Rites*, the *Book of Music*, the

Book of Songs and the *Book of Documents* record the laws laid down by our former kings and are a repository of information about virtue and justice. Virtue and justice are fundamental to the people's livelihoods; people are fundamental to success in battle. Only someone who has an understanding of virtue and justice can sympathize with the people; only someone who sympathizes with the people can employ troops."

"Good!" Lord Wen said. He summoned Xi Hu with the intention of appointing him as the commander-in-chief, but he simply refused.

"I know what you can do," Lord Wen told him, "so I will not allow you to refuse." Xi Hu still attempted to insist, but in the end he gave in and accepted the position.

On the appointed day, they held a great spring hunt at Beilu, at which the Central, Upper, and Lower Armies were mustered. Xi Hu was in command of the Central Army with Xi Cou as his deputy. Qi Man was in charge of the commander-in-chief's battle standards and his drums. Lord Wen wanted to appoint Hu Yan to take command of the Upper Army, but he refused: "My older brother is present. A younger brother cannot take precedence over his older sibling." Therefore, Lord Wen appointed Hu Mao as general in command of the Upper Army with Hu Yan to assist him.

Lord Wen wanted to appoint Zhao Cui to command the Lower Army, but he refused, saying: "In caution I cannot match Luan Zhi; in strategy I cannot match Xian Zhen; and in intelligence-gathering I cannot match Xu Chen." His Lordship ordered Luan Zhi to take command of the Lower Army with Xian Zhen as his deputy. Xun Linfu drove Lord Wen of Jin's battle chariot, Wei Chou acted as his bodyguard, and Zhao Cui was appointed minister of war. Xi Hu climbed up onto the platform and gave his orders. After the drums had been sounded three times, he put his troops through their paces, assuming a series of battle formations. Raw recruits were placed at the front with experienced soldiers behind them, and they had to advance and withdraw, keeping good order. Anyone who could not do this received a warning, and after three warnings they were punished. The exercises lasted for three days in total, and during this time there was a great change in the troops, who came to obey every order automatically. Everyone saw that Xi Hu knew exactly what he was doing, and they were happy to obey his commands. Just as he gave orders for the bells to be sounded to recall the army, suddenly a wind rose up from below the general's platform and ripped the commander-in-chief's flag in two. All those present were deeply shocked.

"If the commander-in-chief's flag has been ripped to pieces, that is an omen about me," Xi Hu said. "I will not be with you for much longer. However, in the future His Lordship will achieve great things."

Everyone asked the reason for his words, but Xi Hu just laughed and said nothing. This all happened in the twelfth month of winter in the nineteenth year of the reign of King Xiang of Zhou.

. . .

In the spring of the following year, Lord Wen discussed his plan to divide his forces and attack both Cao and Wey with Xi Hu.

"I have already discussed this point with Xian Zhen," Xi Hu said. "Attacking Cao and Wey should pose no problems. However, if we divide our army, we can deal with Cao and Wey, but not with Chu. In the name of making an attack on Cao, my lord, you should ask for passage through Wey territory for your army. Wey and Cao are long-standing allies, and they will certainly refuse. I will have the army stationed at Nanhe, and when they are least expecting it, I will move into Wey territory, striking like thunder. We are eighty to ninety percent assured of victory. Having defeated Wey, we can take advantage of that to put pressure on Cao. The Earl of Cao is already in difficulties with a restive population, in addition to which he will be frightened by the defeat of Wey, in which case we are guaranteed to be able to destroy him."

"You really are a most learned general!" Lord Wen said happily.

He immediately sent an ambassador to Wey to ask to borrow a road for an attack on Cao. Grandee Yuan Xuan instructed Lord Cheng of Wey: "Some years ago, the Marquis of Jin passed through our territory when he was in exile, and our former ruler treated him very badly. Now he has come to ask for his army to pass through Wey. You must agree to this, my lord. Otherwise, he will destroy us and then move on to Cao."

"Cao and I are now both allies of Chu," Lord Cheng said. "Supposing that I agree to let him borrow this road, I am afraid that I will have angered Chu before I have succeeded in cementing a new alliance with Jin. If I annoy Jin, I can rely on Chu for support; but if I annoy Chu, who will help me?" He therefore refused to lend the road, and the Jin ambassador returned home to report this to Lord Wen.

"This is just what the commander-in-chief said would happen!" Lord Wen declared. He ordered the army to head southwards. When they crossed the Yellow River, they arrived in the wilds of Wulu.

"Ah!" Lord Wen wailed. "This is the place where Jie Zitui cut his thigh!" He began to cry bitterly, and all his generals sighed sadly with him.

"Let us capture this city and raze its walls to the ground, to assuage His Lordship's feelings," Wei Chou suggested. "What is the point of just standing around and sighing?"

"You are absolutely right," Xia Zhen agreed. "Let me take my troops and capture Wulu." Lord Wen was struck by his words and agreed.

"I would like to go along and help," Wei Chou said. The two generals got into their chariots and set off.

Xian Zhen ordered his officers to bring their battle standards, and when they passed through the forested mountains, he ordered them to select promontories where they could unfurl their flags and hang them high, to show that they had made their way through.

"I have heard people say that when advancing your forces you want surprise on your side," Wei Chou mused, "but now you are using these flags to mark your position, which will allow the enemy ample time to make preparations. What is the meaning of this?"

"Wey used to be a staunch ally of Qi, but now they serve the barbarian kingdom of Chu," Xian Zhen replied. "There are many people in the state who are unhappy about this, and they have been expecting the Central States to come and punish them. If His Lordship wishes to continue the hegemony begun by the Marquis of Qi, he cannot show weakness. He has to succeed with the first strike."

The people of Wulu were not expecting an attack by the Jin army, and when they climbed the city walls and looked out into the distance, all they could see were battle standards floating high over the forested hills—they had no idea how many troops had actually arrived. The inhabitants of the city and the people living in the suburbs all panicked and ran: there was nothing that the local officials could do to stop them. When Xian Zhen's troops approached, there was no one defending the city walls. Drumming his troops on, they captured the walls. He sent someone to report this good news to Lord Wen.

Lord Wen was very pleased and said to Hu Yan, "When you said that I would get this territory, Uncle, today's events have proved you correct." He left the senior general Xi Buyang in charge of the garrison at Wulu as the main army advanced to make camp at Lianyu. Xi Hu suddenly became seriously ill, and Lord Wen of Jin went in person to see him.

"When I was lucky enough to meet with you, my lord," Xi Hu said, "I felt that even if I ended up having my brains dashed open or my guts spilled on the ground, it would be worth it to requite someone who understood me so well. However, my life is now coming to an end, and the ripped flag was a sign that my death is imminent. There is one thing that I would still like to say to you . . ."

"I am happy to listen to whatever it is that you want to say," Lord Wen told him.

"The original reason for attacking Cao and Wey was to prevent Chu from causing trouble," Xi Hu continued. "If you want to stop them from causing trouble, you must have a good plan of campaign. Before you can develop your plan of campaign, you need to create an alliance with Qi and Qin. Qin is a long way away, but Qi is close by. You should send an ambassador to make an alliance with the Marquis of Qi, my lord, stating that you want to swear a blood covenant with him. Qi hates Chu, and so they will be happy to join in an alliance with Jin. If you can obtain the assistance of the Marquis of Qi, Wey and Cao are sure to be scared into requesting a peace treaty with you. Once Qin is brought into the alliance, you have every means at your disposal to control the kingdom of Chu."

"Good idea!" Lord Wen remarked. He sent an ambassador to communicate his good wishes to Qi and to state that he wished to swear a blood covenant with them to reaffirm the alliance that had begun during the rule of Lord Huan of Qi, that together they might pacify the Chu barbarians.

. . .

Lord Xiao of Qi was already dead by this time, and the people of the capital had placed his younger brother, the Honorable Pan, in power. He took the title of Lord Zhao. The Honorable Pan was the son of Lady Ying of Ge, and being newly appointed to the marquisate of Qi, he was deeply perturbed by the presence of Chu troops at Yanggu. He was perfectly happy to join with Jin in an alliance to resist Chu, and when he heard that the Marquis of Jin was camped with his army at Lianyu, he immediately gave orders that he would go in person to meet him. When Lord Cheng of Wey heard that he had lost the city of Wulu, he hastened to send Ning Yu, the son of Ning Su, to apologize and request a peace treaty.

"You refused me permission to take my army through Wey," Lord Wen said crossly. "Now you have been scared into asking for a peace treaty, but you are not seriously intending to keep it. I am going to stamp your capital at Chuqiu flat at the earliest possible opportunity!"

Ning Yu went back and reported this to the Marquis of Wey. Rumors flew around the capital at Chuqiu that the Jin army had arrived; in the space of a single night there were five false alarms. Ning Yu said to Lord Cheng of Wey, "Jin is known to be absolutely furious with you, and the people of the capital have panicked. You had better leave the city temporarily, my lord. Once Jin knows that you have fled, they will not bother to attack Chuqiu. Later on you can beg for a peace treaty with Jin, thereby preserving the state altars."

Lord Cheng sighed and said: "It is most unfortunate that our former ruler was rude to the Marquis of Jin when he was in exile; thanks to my own stupidity in refusing to allow Jin to move their army through my country, I have brought about this present crisis and dragged my people into danger. I really do not have the face to stay here a moment longer!"

He appointed Grandee Yuan Xuan and his younger brother, the Honorable Shuwu, as regents, while he himself fled into exile in Xiangniu. He also sent Grandee Sun Yan to beg for assistance from Chu. This happened in the second month.

A bearded old man wrote a poem, which reads:

When you are in trouble, you do not expect your host to use full ceremonials;
A wife or a gift of horses would have spared much later trouble.
Who would have imagined that the victor of Wulu
Was the beggar of yesteryear?

It was in this month that Xi Hu died. Lord Wen of Jin was deeply upset and ordered that his coffin should be sent home for burial. Given Xian Zhen's success in the attack on Wulu, Lord Wen promoted him to the position of commander-in-chief. He appointed Xu Chen to take command of the Lower Army, to occupy the position left vacant by Xian Zhen. Zhao Cui had earlier recommended Xu Chen for being exceptionally good at intelligence-gathering, and that is why he was given this job.

Lord Wen wanted to destroy the state of Wey, but Xian Zhen remonstrated: "The reason that we went on campaign in the first place is because Qi and Song were under pressure from the kingdom of Chu. If we now set about overthrowing someone else's country without doing anything to help Qi and Song in their hour of need—this really is not the kind of succor for those in danger or sympathy for the weak that a hegemon should show. Even though Wey has behaved badly, their ruler has already been forced into exile by us. We should now move our troops east to attack Cao. That way, should the Chu army come to rescue Wey, we will be long gone!"

Lord Wen thought that this was good advice.

. . .

In the third month, the Jin army laid siege to Cao. Lord Gong of Cao assembled his ministers to ask them to come up with some kind of plan.

Xi Fuji stepped forward and said, "The Marquis of Jin is here to take revenge for the fact that you spied on him naked. No matter how angry he is personally about this, he is unlikely to want to go to war over it. I am happy to go and apologize to His Lordship and ask for a peace treaty, that the people of Cao may be saved from disaster."

"Jin has not taken over Wey," Lord Gong of Cao said, "so why should they do so to us?"

Grandee Yu Lang advanced and said, "I have heard that when the Marquis of Jin was in exile in Cao, Xi Fuji privately gave him a gift of food. Now he has recommended himself for office as an ambassador, which means that he is planning to betray us. Do not listen to him! Your Lordship should execute Xi Fuji! I have my own plan for how to make Jin withdraw."

"Xi Fuji may be disloyal, but his ancestors have served in the government for many generations," Lord Gong said. "I will dismiss him from office, but spare him the executioner's axe."

Xi Fuji thanked His Lordship for his magnanimity and left the court. Just as the saying has it, this was an example of shutting the door and ignoring the bright moon outside; or instructing the plum trees to flower if they felt like it.

Lord Gong asked Grandee Yu Lang, "What is your plan?"

"The Marquis of Jin has recently been victorious in his campaign against Wey," Yu Lang replied, "so he will be feeling very pleased with himself. I ask your permission to write a secret communication to him in which I agree to open the city gates at dusk. I will also arrange that some crack troops armed with crossbows will be lying in ambush on the walls and ramparts. My missive will trick the Marquis of Jin into entering the city. We will then close the gates and shoot him dead. This plan will surely mean we can make away with him!"

Lord Gong of Cao agreed to this stratagem. When the Marquis of Jin obtained Yu Lang's letter of surrender, he wanted to enter the city.

"Cao is far from being at the end of their tether," Xian Zhen said. "Do you think this could be a trap? Let me go and see."

He chose an army officer of imposing appearance and with a long beard to dress up in the hat and official robes of the Marquis of Jin and go in his place. The eunuch Bo Di requested permission to act as the driver. Just as the sun was setting, the flag of surrender was raised above the city walls and the gates were thrown wide open. The pretend

Marquis of Jin then rode into the city at the head of five hundred men, but after about half of them had passed through the gate they suddenly heard a twanging sound reverberating through the city as arrows spun through the air like hornets. Turning their chariots around as quickly as they could, they discovered that the gates had already been closed behind them. Poor Bo Di and his three hundred or so companions were butchered there. Fortunately, the Marquis of Jin was not present, otherwise it really would have been a disaster! As the saying has it: "When the Kunlun Mountains burn, jade and stone are both destroyed."

. . .

Some years earlier, Lord Wen of Jin had visited Cao, so there were many people in Cao who knew him by sight. However, in the darkness the soldiers had no way of telling that the man they had killed was not really Lord Wen. Yu Lang believed that the Marquis of Jin was dead, so he saw no reason to keep his mouth shut in front of Lord Gong of Cao, and he praised himself immoderately. When it got light and they inspected the body properly, they realized that it was not the marquis, and Yu Lang was most crestfallen. Those who had been lucky enough not to get caught inside the city walls escaped with their lives and ran back to the Marquis of Jin. He was even more furious than he had been before and attacked the city with redoubled ferocity.

Yu Lang presented a new plan to Lord Gong: "Let us display the bodies of the Jin soldiers that we shot dead along the tops of the city walls. When their army sees this, they will be very upset, and their ardor will be blunted. Providing that we can hold out for a few more days, relief troops are sure to come from Chu. My plan is to disrupt the morale of the enemy until that happens." Lord Gong of Cao followed his advice.

When the Jin soldiers spotted the bodies hung up above the walls on bamboo poles, they gathered to look more closely. They muttered and groaned in horror.

Lord Wen said to Xian Zhen, "I am afraid that this will cause a catastrophic drop in morale. What should I do?"

"The cemetery serving the capital city of Cao is located outside their West Gate," he replied. "Let me take one half of the army and go and camp among the graves. If we start digging them up, the people inside the city are sure to become distressed. Once they are sufficiently upset, there will be riots and we can take advantage of that fact."

"Good," Lord Wen said. He ordered his army to spread the word: "We are going to desecrate the Cao cemetery." He had Hu Mao and Hu

Yan lead the troops under their command and go and camp in the graveyard. Every man was armed with a spade, and they were instructed that they each had to produce a skeleton extracted from one of these tombs by midday. When the people inside the city heard this news, they were heartbroken.

Lord Gong sent someone up to the top of the city walls to shout: "Stop digging up the graves! We surrender!"

Xian Zhen had someone reply: "You tricked our army into a position where you could kill them, then you exposed their bodies on top of your walls. Our men were so horrified by your actions that we decided to dig up your cemetery to avenge this insult. If you collect the bodies of the dead respectfully and put them in coffins to be handed back to us, we will withdraw."

The people of Cao responded, "If that is what you want, you are going to have to give us three days."

"If you do not hand over the coffins within three days, you cannot blame us when we desecrate the tombs of your ancestors!" Xian Zhen replied.

Lord Gong of Cao did indeed have the bodies on top of the walls collected and counted, so that sufficient coffins could be made to contain them. Three days later, when all the bodies had been properly laid to rest, they were transported out of the city on carts. Xian Zhen came up with a plan whereby Hu Mao, Hu Yan, Luan Zhi, and Xu Chen prepared chariots and men and lay in ambush on all four sides of the city. They were waiting for the people of Cao to open the gates to send out the coffins, then an attack would be launched in which they would strike on all sides simultaneously.

On the fourth day, Xian Zhen sent someone to shout at the foot of the city walls: "Are you handing back the bodies today or not?"

The people of Cao replied from the top of the walls: "You are going to have to lift the siege and withdraw your army five *li*, then we will send out the coffins."

Xian Zhen reported this to Lord Wen, and he gave the order to move the army back. They halted five *li* away. The gates were opened and a stream of coffins proceeded out in all four directions. Before even one third had left the city, suddenly the sound of siege engines could be heard, and the soldiers placed in ambush around each of the barbicans rose up. Given that the gates were clogged with carts bearing the coffins of the dead, it was impossible to close them immediately, and the Jin army took advantage of the chaos to cut their way into the city. Lord

Gong of Cao was inspecting the situation from the top of the city walls; Wei Chou caught sight of him from the foot and leapt out of his chariot and up the walls. He stabbed Lord Gong in the chest and then took him prisoner, tying him up with cords. Yu Lang attempted to escape, but he was captured and beheaded by Dian Jie. Lord Wen of Jin ascended one of the watchtowers, accompanied by his generals, and there he received the spoils of war; Wei Chou presented the Earl of Cao and Dian Jie presented the head of Yu Lang. Each of the generals had taken many prisoners. Lord Wen of Jin gave orders that he wanted to see the list of all serving officials in the state of Cao. There were three hundred names on this list, and every single one of these men was arrested by the Jin army—no one escaped.

Xi Fuji's name was not included in the list, and someone explained: "Xi Fuji was trying to encourage His Lordship to make a peace treaty with you, so he was dismissed from office and reduced to the status of a commoner."

Lord Wen of Jin enumerated the crimes committed by the Earl of Cao to his face: "You had one truly loyal minister, but you did not make use of him. Instead you employed a bunch of fawning lackeys, who pulled all sorts of nasty little tricks. What were you expecting other than disaster?" He gave instructions: "You will be imprisoned in the main camp until such time as I have defeated Chu, at which point I will decide what is to be done with you."

The three hundred officials were all executed and their property seized, to be handed out as rewards for the army officers. Since Xi Fuji had once given him a plate of food, Lord Wen had the area around the North Gate where his house was located cordoned off, and gave orders: "No one is to touch this place. Anyone who destroys so much as a blade of grass belonging to the Xi family will be beheaded!" The Marquis of Jin instructed one half of his generals to remain behind to guard the city and the other half to follow him back to the main army camp.

Master Hu Zeng wrote a historical poem, which runs as follows:

> The Earl of Cao ignored good advice and ended up a prisoner;
> Xi Fuji's generous act resulted in his being spared execution.
> If you act according to your own principles in any given situation,
> It is only later that you discover whether you were right or wrong.

Wei Chou and Dian Jie were made arrogant by their success. Now they heard the Marquis of Jin give orders to protect the Xi family. "We captured the Lord of Cao and beheaded his commander-in-chief today,"

Wei Chou said angrily, "and yet His Lordship has not said a single word of praise. What is a plateful of food worth that he behaves so generously to Xi Fuji? Really, His Lordship does not understand how to measure the importance of things!"

"If he enters the service of Jin, he is sure to receive an important appointment," Dian Jie said, "in which case he will be in a position to order us around. We had better set fire to his house and burn him to death, to prevent him from causing trouble to us in the future. Even if His Lordship finds out, is he really going to cut our heads off?"

"You have a point," Wei Chou said.

The two men went drinking together and that night, when everything was quiet, they secretly led the troops under their command to surround Xi Fuji's house. Fires were laid at both the front and the back gates, and the flames leapt up into the sky. Wei Chou, emboldened by the wine that he had drunk, climbed up over the gate. Braving the roaring fire, he clambered as quickly as he could over the roof searching for Xi Fuji so that he could kill him. No one could have imagined that the beams and pillars would have burned so quickly that they now collapsed with a sound like thunder! Wei Chou lost his balance and fell, landing face up. Then with a crack like the sounding of doomsday, one of the beams came crashing down, falling across Wei Chou's chest. Although terribly badly injured, Wei Chou did not make a sound; he just coughed up a mouthful of blood. On every side an inferno was raging. Scrabbling out from underneath the fallen beam, Wei Chou shinned up one of the pillars and made his way back to the roof, from which he could make his escape. Since every garment on his body was in flames, he stripped himself naked and thus avoided serious burns. Even though Wei Chou was an immensely brave man, this was too much for him and he fainted. When Dian Jie found him, he took him somewhere secluded, gave him some of his own clothes to wear, and put him in a chariot. Wei Chou was then taken home to rest.

At this time both Hu Yan and Xu Chen were still inside the city. When they saw the flames burning by the North Gate, they were worried that the army was under attack, so they rushed over there with their troops, only to discover that Xi Fuji's house was on fire. They quickly ordered their officers to set about extinguishing the flames, which had begun to spread through the entire area. When the fire first started, Xi Fuji had led his servants in an attempt to put out the flames, only to be overcome by the smoke. By the time that he was rescued, he was so badly injured as to be beyond human aid. His wife said, "The Xi family cannot all die here!" She carried her five-year-old son, Xi Lu, into the garden, where they escaped the flames by wading out into the pond. The fires were finally extinguished in the early hours of the morning. Many of the Xi family's servants had been killed and several dozen neighboring houses had also been burned to the ground. When they made their inquiries, Hu Yan and Xu Chen discovered that the arsonists were none other than Wei Chou and Dian Jie. They were deeply shocked and did not dare to try and conceal it; this information was conveyed to the main camp of the Jin army as soon as possible.

The main camp was located five *li* away from the city, so even though they had noticed the fires burning in the city that night, they did not know what had happened. The following day when Lord Wen received this urgent dispatch, he realized exactly what was going on. He immediately drove his chariot into the city. First he went to the North Gate to see Xi Fuji, who glanced at him and then closed his eyes in death. Lord Wen was terribly upset. Xi Fuji's wife bowed down in tears, holding her five-year-old son, Xi Lu, in her arms.

Lord Wen was also crying. "Do not worry, my good woman," he said, "I will ensure that your son is brought up properly."

He appointed the child to be a grandee and gave him a generous grant of silk and gold. Having arranged that Xi Fuji should be buried with all due honors, he ordered that his wife and son should henceforward make their home in Jin. Once the Earl of Cao had been released from imprisonment, if Xi Fuji's wife wanted to return home to look after her husband's tomb, he would send someone to escort her back. When Xi Lu grew up, he became an important grandee of the state of Cao, but this happened much later on.

That very day Lord Wen ordered the minister of war, Zhao Cui, to execute Wei Chou and Dian Jie on the grounds that they had disobeyed his orders and set fire to Xi Fuji's house.

Zhao Cui presented his opinion: "These two men followed Your Lordship in exile for nineteen years; what is more, just recently they have achieved great things in your service. You should forgive them!"

"The reason why people trust me is that my orders are obeyed," Lord Wen shouted angrily. "If my subjects do not obey my commands, what kind of vassals are they? If I cannot make my orders felt, then what kind of ruler am I? If neither subjects nor ruler fit their proper places, how can the country be governed? There are many of my grandees who have served me loyally, but if they all start to disobey my orders and act on their own authority, I will never be able to issue another command again!"

Zhao Cui made representations for a second time: "You are absolutely right, my lord. However, Wei Chou is a most talented and brave man; he is by far the best of your generals. It would be a shame to kill him. Besides which, there were other people involved in this crime. I think that you should punish Dian Jie in order to proclaim your authority, but surely there is no need to execute both of them?"

"According to my information, Wei Chou has suffered a very severe chest injury which means that he cannot even get out of bed," Lord Wen said. "Why should he be saved from the application of the law when he is going to die anyway?"

"I request your permission to go and visit him," Zhao Cui said. "If he is indeed dying, then we will execute him. If, on the other hand, he is going to live, then I think that you should keep this brilliant general to guard against future emergencies."

Lord Wen nodded his head and said, "You are right." He ordered Xun Linfu to go and summon Dian Jie, while Zhao Cui went to see how Wei Chou was.

Do you know whether Wei Chou survived or not? READ ON.

Chapter Forty

Xian Zhen comes up with a plan for attacking Cheng Dechen.

Jin and Chu fight a great battle at Chengpu.

Having received a secret order from the Marquis of Jin, Zhao Cui got into his chariot and went to see Wei Chou. At that time Wei Chou was laid low by a serious injury to his chest, so he was lying down in bed.

"How many people have come to see me?" he asked.

"The minister of war, Zhao Cui, has come in a single chariot," his servants replied.

"He is here to find out if I am dying or not," Wei Chou said. "If I am, he is going to punish me according to the letter of the law!"

He ordered his servants to bring him a length of cloth: "Bind up my chest for me that I may go and see His Lordship's messenger."

"You are in great pain, general, and should not move," his servants said.

"It is not going to kill me, so stop yapping!" Wei Chou shouted. He emerged dressed just as normal.

"I have heard that you are not at all well; ought you to be up?" Zhao Cui asked. "His Lordship sent me to ask after your health."

"Since you are here on His Lordship's orders, I would not dare to behave with less than the utmost ceremony," Wei Chou said. "That is why I have bandaged my chest and come out to see you. I know that I have committed a crime deserving of the death penalty; should I be lucky enough to survive, I will repay His Lordship's magnanimity until my dying breath. How could I dare to try to escape?" He then jumped up and down three times, after which he performed three star-jumps.

"Please consider your health, General," Zhao Cui said. "I will go and report back to His Lordship."

He went back to see Lord Wen and said, "Even though Wei Chou has been injured, he is still well enough to be jumping about. He is determined to continue as your vassal and will never forget all that he owes you. If Your Lordship were to pardon him, I am sure that in the future he will work his hardest to requite your kindness."

"Providing that what I do makes it clear that the law must be obeyed and my people respect me," Lord Wen proclaimed. "I am not the kind of sadist who wants to kill as many people as possible."

Shortly afterwards, Xu Linfu brought Dian Jie in. Lord Wen cursed him and said, "What do you mean by setting fire to Xi Fuji's home?"

"Jie Zitui once cut meat from his own thigh for Your Lordship to eat and yet he ended up being burned to death," Dian Jie shouted. "What is so special about giving you a plate of food? How about you set up a subsidiary cult to Xi Fuji at the temple at Mount Jie?"

Lord Wen was absolutely furious: "Jie Zitui did not want to serve in the government; that has nothing to do with me!" He then asked Zhao Cui, "Dian Jie was the principal conspirator in this arson attack. He has disobeyed my orders, killing people on his own authority. What is the punishment for this crime?"

"Beheading!" Zhao Cui replied.

Lord Wen shouted out the orders for this punishment to be carried out immediately, and then the headsman dragged Dian Jie out of the main gate of the camp and cut his head off. He gave orders that the head should be formally presented as a sacrificial offering to Xi Fuji in the ashes of his home, after which it was hung up above the North Gate with the message: "Those who plan to disobey my orders in the future, look at this!"

"What punishment should be meted out to Wei Chou and Dian Jie's colleagues who did nothing to prevent this?" Lord Wen asked.

"Let them be demoted," Zhao Cui suggested, "though in future they can redeem themselves by successful service."

Lord Wen demoted Wei Chou from his position as bodyguard in His Lordship's battle chariot; Zhou Zhi Qiao replaced him. The army officers looked at each other and said: "Wei Chou and Dian Jie both served His Lordship loyally through nineteen years in exile. For disobeying one of His Lordship's orders, one was executed and the other demoted. If that happens to people like them, how will he treat the rest of us? Clearly His Lordship is completely impartial in the application of the laws of the land, and we will have to be very careful in future!"

From this time onwards, the three armies were greatly in awe of Lord Wen.

A historian wrote a poem about this:

To put an end to chaos the laws must be strictly applied,
But it is hard to balance friendship and justice.
Loyal service in the past can hardly atone for insubordination;
These men were surely not punished simply for killing Xi Fuji!

. . .

Let us now turn to another part of the story. When King Cheng of Chu attacked Song, he conquered the city of Min and advanced as far as the north bank of the Sui River, where he built a huge network of fortifications and waited for them to be forced into surrender. Suddenly a messenger arrived: "The state of Wey has sent its ambassador Sun Yan here to report an emergency." The king of Chu summoned him in to ask him what had happened.

Sun Yan then explained in detail how the Marquis of Jin had captured Wulu and forced the Wey ruler into exile in Xiangniu. "If you do not send reinforcements immediately, Chuqiu will fall!"

"How can I refuse to help my son-in-law?" the king of Chu said. He ordered the troops mustered in Shen and Xi to stay put, to continue the siege of Song under the leadership of the commander-in-chief, Cheng Dechen, and his assistant generals Dou Yuejiao, Dou Bo, and Wan Chun. His allies among the lords would also stay in Song. Meanwhile, he would personally take command of the two wings of the Central Army, assisted by Wei Lüchen, Dou Yishen, and others, and go and rescue Wey. The lords in the allied armies were all worried about what was going on at home, so they said goodbye one after the other, leaving generals in command of their troops. General Yuan Xuan of Chun, General the Honorable Yin of Cai, General Shi Gui of Zheng, and General Bai Chou of Xu were all under the command of Cheng Dechen.

While the king of Chu was still on route, he heard that the Jin army had already moved to the state of Cao. Just as he was debating how to rescue Cao, without reaching any firm conclusion, a spy reported: "The Jin forces have already defeated Cao and taken their lord prisoner." The king of Chu was deeply shocked and said, "How amazingly quick the Jin army is!" He had his army make camp at Shencheng, ordering a messenger to go to Yanggu and collect the Honorable Yong, Yi Ya, and their companions. These lands would then be returned to Qi. He also sent Shuhou, Lord of Shen, to Qi to discuss the possibility of making a peace treaty, after which he was to strike camp and head homewards. The king of Chu sent a second messenger to Song to collect Cheng Dechen's army and warn him: "The Marquis of Jin was in exile for nineteen years and he is already past the age of sixty. Nevertheless, he has been able to return to the state of Jin in triumph. Having surmounted situations of terrible danger, he seems to have gained the knack of winning his people's trust. The remaining years that Heaven has bestowed upon him will be spent on the task of bringing glory to the state of Jin. We do not want him as an enemy, so we had better give way."

When his messenger arrived at Yanggu with these orders, Shuhou, Lord of Shen, immediately came to terms with Qi and took his army home. However, Cheng Dechen was very proud of his own abilities, and he did not accept His Majesty's decision. He said to his generals, "The Song capital will surrender any day now. Why should we leave?"

Dou Yuejiao agreed with him, and so Cheng Dechen sent him back to see the king of Chu and say: "Just a short delay will see the conquest of Song, and we can then go home in triumph. If the Jin army arrives, we will fight them to the bitter end. If we are not ultimately victorious, you can punish me according to the letter of the law."

The king of Chu summoned Ziwen and asked him, "I want Cheng Dechen to come home, but he wants to fight. What should I do?"

"If Jin rescues Song," Ziwen said, "it is because they are planning to become the next hegemon. It would not be advantageous to Chu to see Jin achieve hegemony. At present the only person who can put a stop to their ambitions is Your Majesty, so they are certain to send ambassadors to us. If you show any sign of fear, their hegemony is assured. Besides which, Cao and Wey are our allies; if they see you trying to placate Jin, they will be terrified into transferring their allegiance to them. As long as your generals stand firm, Cao and Wey will be reassured. What is wrong with that? Your Majesty had better warn Cheng Dechen not to engage with the Jin army lightly, for obviously it would be best for everyone if you can withdraw peacefully."

The king of Chu followed his advice and instructed Dou Yuejiao that he should warn Cheng Dechen not to do battle if he could avoid it and to try and negotiate a peaceful settlement. When Cheng Dechen heard Dou Yuejiao's report, he was delighted that he did not have to stand down his troops immediately, so he attacked Song with redoubled vigor, keeping up the assault day and night.

• • •

Lord Cheng of Song had already received the message from Gongsun Gu that the Marquis of Jin had attacked Cao and Wey in an effort to force Chu to lift its siege of Song, so he was determined to hold firm. Now, however, King Cheng of Chu had taken half the army to rescue Wey and yet Cheng Dechen was still assaulting his capital brutally. Lord Cheng of Song was very frightened.

Grandee Men Yinban stepped forward and said, "Jin is aware of the fact that an army has already set off to rescue Wey, but they do not know that the army besieging us has not yet withdrawn. I will risk trying to leave the city to have an audience with the Marquis of Jin and beg him to help us."

"Since we have to ask them for assistance, you had better not go empty-handed," Lord Cheng of Song said. He made a list of the precious jades and rich bronzes stored in his treasury that would be presented to the Marquis of Jin while begging him to send troops to their relief. Once the Chu army had withdrawn, every item on the list would be his to take. Men Yinban wanted a companion to go with him, and the Duke of Song appointed Hua Xiulao. The two men bade farewell to the Duke of Song and then waited for an opportunity to slip out of the fortifications, passing undiscovered through the enemy stockades. As they traveled, they inquired after the whereabouts of the Jin army, that they might report this emergency. When they finally located the Marquis of Jin, they said with tears running down their cheeks, "Our capital will fall any day now! His Lordship will begrudge you none of the treasures he has inherited from his ancestors, if only you will take pity on us!"

"Clearly things in Song are in a critical state," Lord Wen said to Xian Zhen. "If we do not go to help them, Song will be destroyed. However, if we do go and assist, we will have to fight Chu. Xi Hu instructed me that I could not win unless I was allied to Qi and Qin. However, Chu has now given the territory of Yanggu back to Qi to guarantee the peace treaty between their two countries. Qin also has a strong alliance with Chu and will not help us. What should I do?"

"I have a plan to make Qi and Qin join in the attack on Chu of their own accord!" Xian Zhen replied.

Lord Wen was pleased by this idea and asked, "What is your plan to make them do battle with Chu?"

"Song has offered us most generous bribes," Xian Zhen said. "What is so virtuous about saving them when you have been paid to do so? You had better refuse to accept these gifts and ask Song to divide the objects that they have offered us between Qi and Qin. You can then request that these two states make representations to Chu, asking that they lift the siege. They will promise to say the necessary things to Chu and send ambassadors to the king. If Chu ignores them, it will create a fault line in their alliance that we can take advantage of!"

"But if Chu agrees to their request," Lord Wen said, "then Qi and Qin will have their alliance strengthened and Song will be the loser. Where is the advantage to me in that?"

"I also have a plan that will guarantee that Chu will not agree to Qi and Qin's request!" Xian Zhen assured him.

"What plan is that?" Lord Wen asked. "How can you guarantee Chu will refuse?"

"Cao and Wey are long-standing close allies of the kingdom of Chu," Xian Zhen replied. "On the other hand, Chu really hates Song. We have already forced the Marquis of Wey into exile and imprisoned the Earl of Cao. These two states are now completely under our control, and they border upon Song. Let us partition off some of the lands of Wey and Cao and give them to Song, for then Chu's hatred will be much augmented. Whatever Qi and Qin say in their representations, is it likely that Chu will listen? Qi and Qin will seriously alienate Chu by their sympathy for Song, in which case even if they do not want to ally with us, they will have no choice!"

Lord Wen clapped his hands and made appreciative comments. He then ordered Men Yiban to make two new lists in which the treasures of Song were divided equally to be presented to the states of Qi and Qin. Once they had agreed what they were going to say, Men Yiban went to Qin and Hua Xiulao went to Qi. When they had audience with the two lords, they were to stress the tragic note.

• • •

When Hua Xiulao arrived in Qi, he had an audience with Lord Zhao, at which he said: "Yours is the only state that can resolve the conflict between Jin and Chu. If you can guarantee the survival of the state altars, we do not begrudge you any of the treasures left by our ancestors and we will pay court to you every year, from one generation to the next!"

"Where is the king of Chu now?" Lord Zhao of Qi inquired.

"The king of Chu has shown himself willing to lift the siege and has already withdrawn his army to Shen," Hua Xiulao explained. "However, Grand Vizier Cheng Dechen has only recently taken control of the government, and he is determined not to withdraw until he has achieved a victory over us. He believes that any minute now we will be forced into surrender. That is why we are begging for your help."

"Just recently the king of Chu conquered Yanggu in Qi, but they have now restored these lands to us," Lord Zhao said. "They withdrew their army after we made a peace treaty. I do not think that the king of Chu is an unreasonable man, so it must be Grand Vizier Cheng Dechen who is determined to keep up the campaign. I am happy to make representations to him on your behalf."

He appointed Cui Yao as an ambassador and sent him to the state of Song to have an audience with Cheng Dechen and beg that he lift the siege. Meanwhile Men Yinban had arrived in Qin, where he said exactly the same thing as Hua Xiulao. Lord Mu of Qin also appointed the Honorable Zhi as an ambassador and sent him to the Chu army to ask Cheng Dechen to withdraw. Qi and Qin had no communication with each other about this: they sent their ambassadors off separately. Men Yinban and Hua Xiulao both rejoined the Jin army to make their report.

"I have already conquered Cao and Wey," Lord Wen said, "so now is the time to give their lands to Song. This is not the moment to be selfish!" He gave orders that Hu Yan should accompany Men Yiban to survey the lands of Wey, while Xu Chen accompanied Hua Xiulao on an assessment of the lands of Cao, with instructions that they should get rid of all the original local officials.

• • •

Cui Yao and the Honorable Zhi were in Cheng Dechen's tent discussing the possibility of a peace treaty with Song, when the officials who had been forced out of Wey and Cao arrived to complain: "Jin has made a deal with Grandees Men Yinban and Hua Xiulao of Song to let them have all our territory!"

Cheng Dechen was absolutely furious and shouted at the ambassadors from Qi and Qin: "Look at the way that Song is bullying Wey and Cao! Does it look like they want to make peace? I cannot accept your representations, and this is not my fault! You cannot blame me!"

Cui Yao and the Honorable Zhi realized that their mission was hopeless, so they immediately said farewell. When the Marquis of Jin heard that Cheng Dechen had refused the request made by Qi and Qin, he sent someone to intercept them en route and invite them to his camp, where he held a lavish banquet in their honor.

"The commander-in-chief of the Chu army is arrogant and rude," Lord Wen said. "Should he start fighting with Jin, I hope that your two states will send troops to assist me."

Cui Yao and the Honorable Zhi promised to pass his message on and left.

. . .

Meanwhile, Cheng Dechen swore an oath with his army: "Until we have restored Cao and Wey, we will not go home!"

The Chu general, Wan Chun, said, "I have a plan that will see Wey and Cao recover without having to fight!"

"What is your plan?" Cheng Dechen asked.

"Jin forced the Marquis of Wey into exile and imprisoned the Earl of Cao simply in order to save Song," Wan Chun said. "You should send an envoy to the Jin army, saying that you are willing to lift the siege providing that Jin restores the rulers of Wey and Cao to power and returns their territory. We will then cease besieging Song. That way no one has to fight anyone else. Surely that is the very best option?"

"What do we do if Jin refuses to listen to us?" Cheng Dechen asked.

"You must tell the people of Song exactly what it is that you intend to do and why," Wan Chun explained. "That way, the people of Song will be expecting the siege to be lifted and us to be heading home. If the Marquis of Jin refuses, it is not just Cao and Wey that will hate him, Song will be furious too. If we can take Jin on under those circumstances, our chances of victory are greatly improved."

"Who will go as an envoy to the Jin army?" Cheng Dechen asked.

"If you want me to do it," Wan Chun told him, "I would not dare to refuse."

Cheng Dechen then halted the attack on Song and appointed Wan Chun to be his envoy. He got into a single chariot and headed off in the direction of the Jin army. When he had an audience with Lord Wen, he said, "On behalf of General Cheng Dechen, I salute Your Lordship. Let me explain that Chu's position with respect to Wey and Cao is just the same as yours in respect to Song. If you will agree to restore the states of Wey and Cao, we are willing to lift the siege of Song. From then on we can be in peace, and no one will have to get hurt."

Before he had finished speaking, Hu Yan gritted his teeth and glared angrily from his place next to the Marquis of Jin. "Cheng Dechen is a complete bastard!" he shouted. "You have not yet been victorious over

Song, and yet you want us to restore two states that we have conquered. You are trying to take advantage of us!"

Xian Zhen quickly stamped on Hu Yan's foot, while replying to Wan Chun: "Cao and Wey have not committed any crime that means they deserve destruction; our lord is happy to restore them. However, I hope you will agree to stay in our rear camp temporarily, while we take time to discuss the matter properly." Luan Zhi then took Wan Chun away.

"Are you really going to agree to his request?" Hu Yan demanded.

"Wan Chun's request is one whereby we are damned if we do and we are damned if we don't," Xian Zhen said.

"What do you mean?" Hu Yan asked.

"Wan Chun's arrival is part of a clever plan on the part of the Grand Vizier," Xian Zhen explained, "where they will come out of it looking very good and we will take all the blame. If we refuse, then all three countries concerned are going to be furious with us; if we agree and restore the three of them, then Chu is going to take all the credit. In the current circumstances, we had better privately agree to restore the states of Cao and Wey, thereby breaking up their alliance. We should also arrest Wan Chun in order to irritate Chu. Cheng Dechen is a violent and short-tempered man; he will move his troops to attack us. That way the siege of Song will be lifted of its own accord. We will only lose Song if Cheng Dechen has the sense to make a peace treaty with them before he leaves."

"This is an excellent plan," Lord Wen said. "However, the king of Chu treated me with great generosity in the past, and I am afraid that arresting his ambassador would not be a proper thing to do."

"Chu has conquered many small states and harassed many great ones," Luan Zhi reminded him, "and this is a humiliation for all of us. If you were not hoping to become hegemon, that is one thing, but given that you do, this shame affects you directly. How can you insist on repaying this miniscule private benefit at such terrible cost?"

"Your words make me understand how wrong I have been!" Lord Wen declared. He then ordered Luan Zhi to arrest Wan Chun and take him under armed guard to Wulu, where he would be handed over to General Xi Buyang to be kept under lock and key. His charioteer and bodyguard were sent back to transmit the following message to the Grand Vizier of Chu: "Wan Chun has behaved improperly and so we have arrested him. Once we have taken you prisoner too, we will execute both of you together." These two servants scuttled off, hanging their heads.

Once Lord Wen had dealt with Wan Chun, he sent a messenger to inform Lord Gong of Cao: "You must not imagine that I want to punish you for any mistakes you made when I was in exile. The reason why I have still not released you is because you are an ally of Chu. If you would send someone to Chu to break off your alliance and make clear that in the future you will be pursuing a treaty relationship with Jin, I will immediately send you back to Cao."

Lord Gong of Cao was desperate to be released and he believed every word that the Marquis of Jin said, so he wrote a letter to Cheng Dechen as follows:

> I have been deeply concerned by the damage suffered by the state, so to avoid further destruction, I have been forced to make peace with Jin. In future, I will not be able to serve the kingdom of Chu. If you were able to force Jin to leave me in peace, would I dare to be so disloyal?

Lord Wen also sent an envoy to Xiangniu to have an audience with Lord Cheng of Wey, at which he agreed to restore his state.

Lord Cheng was thrilled, but Ning Yu remonstrated: "This is part of a plot by the state of Jin. Do not trust them!" However, Lord Cheng paid no attention to him and wrote a letter to Cheng Dechen in similar terms to that of the Earl of Cao.

Cheng Dechen had just heard the news of Wan Chun's arrest, which upset him deeply. "Chonger, you villainous old wretch!" he shouted. "Why don't you just die in a ditch somewhere? When you were visiting Chu, you were entirely at our mercy; now that you have been restored to power, you are only interested in kicking other people around! Ever since antiquity, there has been a rule: when two countries are at war, their ambassadors still have diplomatic immunity. How dare you arrest my envoy! You will account to me for what you have done!"

His anger was still at its height when a soldier reported outside his tent: "The two states of Wey and Cao have both sent letters to you, sir."

Cheng Dechen thought to himself, "The Marquis of Wey and the Earl of Cao are both in exile, so if they have gone to the trouble of communicating with me, it must be that they have discovered some trouble brewing within the Jin army that they wish to secretly inform me about. Heaven is helping me towards victory!"

When he opened the letters and read them, he realized the truth of the matter, which was that Jin had stolen a march here on Chu. Overcome with fury, beyond anything that he had experienced so far, he shouted: "That wicked old pest forced them to write these two letters!

Wretch! Bastard! One or the other of us has to go!" He instructed his three armies to lift the siege of Song and head off in search of the Marquis of Jin: "Song can wait until I have defeated the Jin army. After all, they are not going anywhere!"

"His Majesty instructed us that we should not lightly get involved in armed conflict," Dou Yuejiao reminded him, "so if you want to do battle, you really should report to the king first. In addition to that, the two states of Qi and Qin have just made representations to you about Song, and they are angry with you for not acceding to their wishes. They are sure to send troops to support Jin in any coming conflict. Even with the assistance of our allies in Chen, Cai, Zheng, and Xu, I am not sure that we can defeat Qi and Qin. You must send someone to court to request auxiliary troops and additional commanders so as to defeat the enemy."

"I am afraid that I will have to put you to the trouble of going," Cheng Dechen said. "Please be as quick as you can!"

Having received this order from the commander-in-chief, Dou Yuejiao set off for the city of Shen, where he had an audience with the Chu king and reported Cheng Dechen's intention to engage with the enemy. The Chu king was irritated by this and said, "I told him not to do battle, but the commander-in-chief is clearly determined to fight. Is he so sure that he can win?"

"Cheng Dechen has already announced that he will accept any penalties attendant on failure," Dou Yuejiao said.

The king of Chu was still not happy about the whole situation, but he ordered Dou Yishen to set out with the Western Army.

In Chu military terminology, the Eastern Army was equivalent to the Army of the Left in the Central States. The Western Army was equivalent to the Army of the Right. All the very best troops were in the Eastern Army, so when he only sent the Western Army out, comprising fewer than one thousand men and not the best troops available at that, the king of Chu seems already to have decided that his army would lose the coming battle, so he was not willing to commit any unnecessary men.

Cheng Dechen's son, Cheng Daxin, gathered together the family's own personal troops: in all about six hundred men. He asked permission to participate in the battle, and the king of Chu agreed. Dou Yishen led his troops in the direction of Song, accompanied by Dou Yuejiao. When Cheng Dechen saw how few soldiers he had been sent, he was even more enraged and shouted, "He's not sending me auxiliaries! Does this mean he thinks I cannot defeat Jin?"

That day he ordered the armies of Chu's four allies to strike their camps and join the main force. That order meant that he fell into Xian Zhen's trap.

A bearded old man wrote a poem that says:

After laying siege to Suiyang for so long, nothing was yet achieved,
When a moment's anger sent him into battle against the feudal lords.
Cheng Dechen was determined to achieve a signal victory,
But how could he escape the coils of Xian Zhen's plot?

Cheng Dechen amalgamated the troops of the Western Army with the private soldiers of the Cheng family under his own command, to form the main body of the army. He ordered Dou Yishen to form the left wing, with the troops from Shen together with the allied forces from Zheng and Xu under his command. He ordered Dou Bo to form the right wing, with troops from Xi, together with the allied armies of Chen and Cai under his command. The whole army advanced at full speed towards the Marquis of Jin's encampment, where they built three stockades facing his troops.

• • •

Lord Wen of Jin summoned his generals for a consultation. Xian Zhen spoke as follows: "Right from the beginning our plan was to neutralize Chu. They attacked Qi and then laid siege to Song, so their army is exhausted. We must do battle with Chu, for this opportunity cannot be lost."

"In the past Your Lordship promised the king of Chu that should his armies ever campaign in the Central States, you would retreat three stages," Hu Yan reminded him. "If you now do battle with Chu, you will be breaking your word. You have gone to great trouble to demonstrate your trustworthiness to the people of the Central States; you must not undo this good work by breaking faith with Chu! You will have to withdraw."

The other generals said crossly: "It would be most humiliating for a ruler to have to withdraw to avoid a subject. You must not do this! You cannot do this!"

"Cheng Dechen is a very violent and unpleasant man," Hu Yan said, "but you must not forget how good the king of Chu was to you. When you withdraw, you are showing your respect to Chu, not to Cheng Dechen!"

"And what do we do when the Chu army chases us down?" the other generals demanded.

"If we withdraw and Chu withdraws, at least they will not resume the siege of Song," Hu Yan said. "If we withdraw and Chu still attacks us, then they will be seen to be bullying us, putting themselves in the wrong. If we try to avoid them and they insist upon causing trouble, all our people will be furious with them. If they are arrogant and we are angry, can victory be far behind?"

"You are right!" Lord Wen declared. He then gave his orders: "Our three armies will all withdraw!"

The Jin forces then retreated thirty *li*, and the army officers came to report: "We have now withdrawn by one stage."

"That is not enough," Lord Wen told them.

They then retreated another thirty *li*. Lord Wen did not allow the army to make camp until they had moved ninety *li*. A city named Chengpu happened to be located exactly three stages from their original location, and here they made camp and rested their horses. Meanwhile, Lord Xiao of Qi appointed Guo Guifu, the son of his senior minister Guo Yizhong, to be the commander-in-chief with Cui Yao as his deputy. Lord Mu of Qin appointed his second son, the Honorable Yin, as the senior general with Bai Yibing to assist him. Each set off in command of a great host to assist the Jin army in the coming battle against the kingdom of Chu. They also made camp at Chengpu. Since the siege of Song had been lifted, Lord Cheng of Song sent Marshal Gongsun Gu to thank the Jin army, and he stayed with them to help.

. . .

When the Chu army realized that the Jin forces had moved their camp and were on the retreat, they were all delighted.

"For the Marquis of Jin to withdraw is a great honor for us," Dou Bo said. "You had better make this an excuse for taking your army home. Even though you have not achieved anything, at least you will avoid punishment."

Cheng Dechen said angrily, "I have already requested auxiliary troops. If I don't even fight once with them, how can I go back? The Jin army is on the retreat, which means that they are scared of us. We should pursue them!" He gave his orders: "Advance as quickly as you can."

The Chu army advanced ninety *li*, whereupon they encountered the Jin troops yet again. Cheng Dechen surveyed the terrain and selected an advantageous place to make camp, on top of a hill commanding a good view of the nearby marshes.

The Jin generals discussed his move with Xian Zhen: "If the Chu army occupy the heights, they are going to be very difficult to attack. We ought to send out troops to prevent them from building their stockade there."

"Generals pick advantageous sites like that to make camp because they are easy to defend," Xian Zhen said. "However, Cheng Dechen has come a long way and he intends to fight. Even if his camp is sited in an easily defended position, what use is that to him?"

Lord Wen of Jin was also worried about the coming battle with Chu. Hu Yan presented his opinion: "Our camp now faces that of the enemy, and we are going to have to fight them. If we win, then you will become hegemon over the feudal lords. If we lose, then our state can still rely on the natural protection of the Yellow River and the mountains that encircle it. What can Chu do to us?"

Lord Wen could still not make up his mind. That night when he slept, he had a strange dream, in which he found himself back in Chu at the time of his exile there. He was wrestling with the king of Chu, who threw him so that he lay on his back looking up at the sky. King Cheng lay on top of him, punching his head until it broke open, then he chewed on his brains. When he woke up he was in a state of great alarm. Hu Yan was sleeping in the same tent, and Lord Wen called out to him. He told him of what had happened in his dream: "I dreamed that I was defeated in a fight with Chu and they sucked my brains. Surely this is a most inauspicious omen!"

Hu Yan congratulated him and said, "On the contrary, this is a most auspicious omen! Your Lordship is sure to be victorious."

"What makes it auspicious?" Lord Wen asked.

"You lay down on the ground, looking at the sky," Hu Yan replied, "which means that you are the recipient of the light of Heaven. The king of Chu lay on top of you, which means that he will have to prostrate himself before you and apologize for his crimes. Brains are soft, and so for yours to have been consumed by Chu means that you will make them submit to your authority only by gentleness. Your victory is assured!"

Lord Wen was persuaded by this explanation.

Before it got light, an officer reported: "An envoy from the kingdom of Chu has arrived with a letter challenging you to a battle."

Lord Wen opened and read it. This letter said:

> I would like to play with your soldiers. If you lean against the railings of your battle chariot, you will be able to watch. Let us see what happens!

"Warfare is a terrible thing," Hu Yan said, "but he refers to it as 'playing,' which is most disrespectful. How can such a man not be defeated?"

Lord Wen sent Luan Zhi back with the following reply:

> I remember the kindness that the king of Chu showed to me, so I respectfully withdrew three stages. I did not confront you directly. If you are determined to fight, how can I refuse? I will see you at first light tomorrow.

After the Chu envoy had left, Lord Wen sent Xian Zhen to muster his army again. In all there were seven hundred chariots and more than fifty thousand crack troops present.

This did not include the troops sent by Qi and Qin.

Lord Wen ascended the wastes of Shen to inspect his army. He saw that perfect order was observed among the ranks, and they advanced and retreated in unison. He sighed and said, "It is all thanks to the instructions I received from Xi Hu that I can engage with the enemy today!"

He ordered his men to cut down the trees at the wastes of Shen, in order to augment their weapons. Xian Zhen then set the order of battle. Hu Mao and Hu Yan were to command the Upper Army and they were to attack Chu's Army of the Left in concert with Bai Yibing, the deputy general from Qin. This meant that they would be doing battle with Dou Yishen. He ordered Luan Zhi and Xu Chen to take command of the Lower Army; they were to attack Chu's Army of the Right in concert with Cui Yao, the deputy general from Qi. This meant that they would be doing battle with Dou Bo. Each of these men received his orders and carried them out exactly. Xian Zhen would set the Jin Central Army into battle formation, assisted by Xi Cou and Qi Man. They would be fighting against Cheng Dechen himself. He instructed Xun Linfu and Shi Hui to take five thousand men each to function as the left and right wings, with responsibility for engaging the enemy wherever possible. Guo Guifu and the Honorable Yin of Qin were told to take the soldiers provided by their own countries and flank the Chu forces, waiting in ambush behind them. When the Chu army had been defeated, their mission was to attack and take the main camp.

By this time Wei Chou had completely recovered from the injury to his chest, so he asked permission to lead the vanguard.

"It is just as well that we kept you, general," Xian Zhen declared. "If you proceed south from the wastes of Shen, there is a place called Kongsang, which borders on Liangu in Chu. If you would lead a detachment of soldiers and place them in ambush there, when the Chu army has been defeated and they are on their way home, you may well be able to bag a general." Wei Chou set off happily.

Zhao Cui, Sun Bojiu, Yangshe Tu, Mao Fa, and a whole host of other civil and military officials accompanied Lord Wen of Jin to the wastes of Shen to watch the battle. He instructed Zhou Zhi Qiao to head south of the river with a small flotilla of boats, where they were to wait for the arrival of the heavy baggage of the Chu army, which was expected to arrive any day now. The following day at dawn the Jin army moved into battle formation on the north side, the Chu army on the south side, each with three armies facing the enemy.

Cheng Dechen gave his orders: "The armies of the Left and Right are to attack first, followed by the Central Army."

Grandee Luan Zhi of Jin, who was commanding the Lower Army, discovered that the Chu Army of the Right was using troops from Chen and Cai as their advance guard. He said happily, "The commander-in-chief gave me secret instructions: 'Chen and Cai do not want to fight, so it will be easy to put them to flight.' If I deal with them first, the rest of the Army of the Right will crumble without a fight."

He ordered Bai Yibing to advance and do battle. Yuan Xuan of Chen and the Honorable Yin of Cai both wanted to establish themselves in Dou Bo's eyes, so they competed to be the first to send their troops out. Before the two armies had engaged, the Jin forces suddenly started to withdraw. The two generals wanted to set off in pursuit, but then they saw the battle lines of the enemy part. With a thunderous sound, Xu Chen came rushing towards them at the head of a line of enormous chariots. The horses hitched to these chariots were all covered in tiger fur. When the Chu horses saw this, they thought they were real tigers and bucked in terror. The drivers could do nothing to control them, so they had to turn around and retreat at all possible speed to Dou Bo's lines. Xu Chen and Bai Yibing took advantage of the chaos to launch their attack; Xu Chen cut the Honorable Yin to pieces with an axe below his chariot while Bai Yibing shot an arrow through Dou Bo's cheek. He ran away with the arrow still embedded in his face. Thus the Chu Army of the Right was utterly defeated: countless dead lay piled up in mounds.

Luan Zhi and his troops dressed up as soldiers from Chen and Cai. Keeping tight hold of their flags, they went to report to the Chu commander-in-chief: "The Chu Army of the Right has already been victorious. Please advance your troops as quickly as you can, that we may win a great victory together!"

Cheng Dechen leaned out on the railings around his chariot and looked into the distance. He could see the Jin army running off to the north in an enormous cloud of dust. He said happily: "The Jin Lower Army has indeed been defeated!" He quickly advanced the Army of the Left.

Dou Yishen caught sight of a battle standard hanging high in the sky over the enemy troops, which he guessed would represent the location of their general. He summoned all his reserves of energy and started to cut his way across. In this instance Hu Yan came out to meet him, and after they had crossed swords a couple of times, he noticed that confusion seemed to reign behind the enemy front lines. Hu Yan turned his chariot around, and the great battle standard was also moved back. Dou Yishen reckoned that this must mean that the Jin army had already begun to crumble, so he ordered the two generals from Zheng and Xu to set off in hot pursuit. Suddenly the sound of drumming shook the ground as Xian Zhen and Xi Cou led out a division of crack troops to launch a surprise attack that cut the Chu army into two. Hu Mao and Hu Yan then turned around again and advanced in pincer formation. The troops from Zheng and Xu were the first to be terrified into trying to cut and run; there was nothing that Dou Yishen could do to prevent this. He tried manfully to fight his way out, only to run into Cui Yao of Qi, who forced him to fight a second battle. In the end, he abandoned his chariot and horses and shed his weapons; mingling among the ordinary soldiers, he was able to climb a hill and escape.

The Jin army had only been pretending to run away to the north; the massive cloud of dust was generated by the trees that Luan Zhi had cut down at the wastes of Shen, which he had hitched behind his chariots and dragged off at full speed. This naturally generated an eye-catching cloud, persuading the Chu Army of the Left to do battle in the hope of an easy victory. Hu Mao had also ordered his battle standard to be advanced and then hurriedly withdrawn, trailing in the dust, in order to suggest that he was running away. Hu Yan pretended to be defeated, tricking them into setting off in pursuit. Xian Zhen had planned this from the beginning, so he had instructed Xi Man to hoist the senior general's flag and then hold the Central Army in a defensive position. Xi Man had orders to withstand whatever the enemy threw at him, but under no circumstances was he allowed to respond. Meanwhile, Xian Zhen himself led the main body of the army out through the back of the defensive lines and then circled around, catching the Chu troops in a combined pincer movement with Hu Mao and Hu Yan. That was how they would win a total victory. This was all part of Xian Zhen's plan.

There is a poem that testifies to this:

In a crisis, what did it avail to have your troops lined up in battle formation?
How could they withstand Xian Zhen's amazing plan?
By covering their horses with tiger's skins,
They put the whole Chu army to flight!

Even though the Chu commander-in-chief, Cheng Dechen, had bravely rushed into this battle, when thinking that the king of Chu had twice warned him not to fight, he was none too confident. When he heard that both the Army of the Left and the Right had been successful in battle and were in hot pursuit of the Jin forces, he ordered the drums of the Central Army to be sounded and sent his teenaged son, the junior general Cheng Daxin, out from the ranks. Qi Man followed the orders that he had been given by Xian Zhen and kept his troops closely packed together in defense, making no response. The Chu Central Army then sounded their drums for a second time; Cheng Daxin grabbed a painted spear and started giving a display of his martial prowess in front of the enemy lines.

Qi Man could not stand it any longer, so he sent someone to see what was going on, who reported: "There is a teenaged kid out there."

"What does that brat think he is doing?" Qi Man asked. "If we capture him, we will at least have done something." He gave his orders: "Sound the drums!"

As the drums boomed out, the serried ranks of the troops parted to allow Qi Man out, waving a saber. He then fought the little general, and they crossed swords more than twenty times without a clear victor. Dou Yuejiao, who was standing at the head of his line of troops, realized that the little general was not likely to win this bout, so he quickly drove his chariot out, and, nocking an arrow to his bowstring, sighting as he approached, he let fly a single arrow, which cut through the chin strap on Qi Man's helmet. Qi Man realized just what a close shave this was and wanted to withdraw, but he was afraid that to do so directly would alarm the Central Army too much. Instead, he circled around to the back of his lines.

"There is no point in chasing a defeated general!" Dou Yuejiao shouted. "Attack the Central Army and take Xian Zhen prisoner!"

Do you know what happened next? READ ON.

Chapter Forty-one

Cheng Dechen commits suicide below the city walls of Liangu.

The Marquis of Jin becomes Master of Covenants on a platform at Jiantu.

The Chu general, Dou Yuejiao, and the little general, Cheng Daxin, gave up their pursuit of Qi Man and attacked the main body of the Jin army. Dou Yuejiao caught sight of the great battle standard floating high above them and brought it down with a single arrow. When the Jin army could no longer see their commander-in-chief's standard, they were immediately thrown into complete confusion. Xun Linfu and Xian Mie arrived from opposite directions and engaged with the enemy; Xun Linfu was killed by Dou Yuejiao, and Xian Mie was killed by Cheng Daxin.

Meanwhile, Cheng Dechen ordered his army forward. Waving his arms about, he shouted: "Don't come back until not a single member of the Jin army is left alive!"

Just as they went into formation, Xian Zhen and Xi Cou brought up their troops, and both armies were involved in a confused melee. Then Luan Zhi, Xu Chen, Hu Mao, and Hu Yan also arrived, and their soldiers advanced like an iron wall encircling the Chu forces. Cheng Dechen realized that both his Left and Right armies must have collapsed. He had no wish to fight any further, so he quickly gave orders that the bells should be struck to signal a retreat. However, so many Jin soldiers were present on the field of battle that the Chu army had been broken up into a dozen groups and each was completely surrounded.

The little general, Cheng Daxin, grabbed his painted spear and moved unimpeded across the battlefield to protect his father, at the head of a force of six hundred soldiers drawn from Cheng Dechen's own family.

Each one of these men was a match for a hundred. As they fought their way out of the encirclement, the little general suddenly realized that he had lost Dou Yuejiao and plunged back to find him. Dou Yuejiao was a cousin of the former Grand Vizier of Chu, Ziwen. This man was as strong as a bear and had a voice like the roar of a tiger. He was brave enough to be a match for ten thousand men, but his greatest skill was as an archer, for he never missed a shot. Now surrounded by the Jin army, he attacked first to the left and then to the right, searching everywhere for signs of Cheng Dechen and his son. Fortunately, Cheng Daxin met up with him and said, "The commander-in-chief is over here. We must leave at once!"

Now that the two of them were together in one place, they encouraged each other to new feats of daring, in which they saved the lives of many Chu soldiers before breaking their way out of the encirclement.

Lord Wen of Jin was standing on top of Mount Shen and when he saw that his troops were winning, he immediately ordered someone to take a message to Xian Zhen: "It is enough to see the Chu army expelled beyond the borders of Song and Wey. Do not kill or capture any more people than absolutely necessary, for I do not want to damage the relationship between our two countries or let down the king of Chu who has been so good to me."

Xian Zhen passed on this instruction to the three armies and prevented anyone from setting off in pursuit. Qi Man disobeyed this order and carried on fighting, for which he was imprisoned in the rearguard to await punishment.

Master Hu Zeng wrote a poem about this:

> Having withdrawn his army three stages to requite the kindness of Chu,
> Now he prevented them from pursuing their defeated soldiers.
> If these two enemies behaved like this when they met on the battlefield,
> How could they treat each other unjustly under ordinary circumstances?

The soldiers from the four states of Chen, Cai, Zheng, and Xu, having seen their comrades killed and their generals slain, all fled for their lives back to their home countries. After Cheng Dechen, Cheng Daxin, and Dou Yuejiao broke out of the encirclement, they headed straight for the main camp. However, one of the sentries advised them: "The flags of Qi and Qin have already been hoisted there!"

• • •

The two generals Guo Guifu of Qi and the Honorable Yin of Qin had already either killed or put to flight the Chu soldiers and were now in possession of the main camp: all the food stores and baggage had fallen into their hands. Cheng Dechen did not dare to proceed any further in that direction, so he skirted behind Mount Shen and advanced along the banks of the Sui River. There he met with Dou Yishen and Dou Bo, who had collected the scattered remnants of their armies. When they arrived at Kongsang, suddenly they heard the sound of siege engines and discovered that an army was blocking their path. On the flags they held were the words "General Wei."

When some years earlier Wei Chou had visited the kingdom of Chu, his independence and martial prowess had deeply impressed all who saw him. Now they found him blocking their route in this narrow defile. On encountering such a powerful enemy, the survivors of the Chu army, who had just suffered such a terrible defeat, were all horrified and frightened. Their morale collapsed and they began to run. Dou Yuejiao was absolutely furious, and, ordering the little general to protect the commander-in-chief, he summoned up all his courage and went out to fight alone. Dou Yishen and Dou Bo eventually summoned up enough gumption to go to his aid. Wei Chou was able to fight these three generals at the same time without showing any sign of strain. Just as they crossed swords, they suddenly caught sight of a man coming from the north on a galloping horse, shouting: "Stop your fight! The commander-in-chief has received orders from His Lordship that the survivors of the Chu army should be allowed to go home unmolested, to requite the kindness that he received while in exile!"

Wei Chou stayed his hand and, ordering his troops to stand back on either side of the road, called out, "You may leave!"

Cheng Dechen and his companions made their escape. When they arrived at Liangu, the survivors were counted. Although the Central Army had suffered some losses, perhaps six or seven out of every ten had survived. However, the armies from Shen and Xi, who had been seconded to the Left and Right armies, had only one or two survivors out of every ten. How sad!

In antiquity, someone wrote a poem bewailing the prevalence of warfare:

No military strategist can ever be sure of success;
How many heroes have returned alive from the field of battle?
Herded like animals to the slaughter,
Their flesh and blood stain the razor-sharp sword blades.
Ghostly lights flicker among the tombs,
Icy winds howl over unburied bones.

When persuading a ruler, nothing is as efficacious as talking of opening new land,
Yet each general's victory costs tens of thousands of lives.

"My original plan was to make the martial might of the kingdom of Chu respected for ten thousand *li*," Chen Dechen said miserably, "so I fell into the trap laid for me by the people of Jin. In my greed for glory I have been defeated over and over again. What can I do to atone for this crime?" He then put himself, Dou Yishen, and Dou Bo in chains at Liangu, while his son, Cheng Daxin, took command of the remnants of the army.

At the audience with the Chu king, he proclaimed himself willing to accept capital punishment. The king of Chu was then still resident in Shen. When Cheng Daxin arrived, he said angrily, "Before all of this happened, your father said, 'If we are not ultimately victorious, then you can punish me according to the letter of the law.' What does he say now?"

Cheng Daxin kowtowed and said, "My father is aware of how badly he has betrayed Your Majesty's confidence, and he has expressed himself willing to commit suicide, but so far I have prevented him. Please let him be punished according to the laws of the land."

"The laws of the kingdom of Chu state that a defeated general should die," the king of Chu declared. "Cheng Dechen and his cohort should commit suicide now, to prevent me from having to sully my executioner's axe."

Cheng Daxin realized that the king had no intention of pardoning his father and left the court in tears. He went back to report this. Cheng Dechen sighed and said, "Even if the king of Chu had pardoned me, how could I ever bear to face the people of Shen or Xi again?" He bowed twice to the north, took out his sword, and cut his own throat.

. . .

At this time Wei Jia was at home and asked his father, Wei Lüchen, "Everyone is saying that the Grand Vizier has been defeated in battle. Do you believe it?"

"I do," Wei Lüchen said.

"How will His Majesty punish him?"

"Cheng Dechen and the other defeated generals will ask permission to commit suicide and His Majesty will agree to that."

"Cheng Dechen is an inflexible and arrogant man," Wei Jia said, "who should not hold supreme office. However, given how brave he is, with clever officers to support him, he could have achieved great things.

Even though he has been defeated, he remains the only person who could possibly avenge this humiliation we have just suffered at the hands of Jin. Why do you not remonstrate and save his life?"

"His Majesty is absolutely furious, and I am afraid that nothing I could say would do any good," Wei Lüchen said.

"Do you not remember, Father, what Yusi, the shaman from Fan, said?"

"Remind me," Wei Lüchen said.

"Yusi was good at foretelling people's fate by reading their faces," Wei Jia said. "When His Majesty was still just a prince, the shaman once said, 'You will not survive without Cheng Dechen and Dou Yishen.' His Majesty was most impressed by these words, and that very day he gave Cheng Dechen and Dou Yishen a tablet that would exempt them from the death penalty, so that Yusi's words should never be put to the test. His Majesty is now so angry that he has forgotten this. If you remind him, he will be sure to spare their lives."

Wei Lüchen went immediately to have an audience with the king of Chu and presented his opinion: "Even though Cheng Dechen has committed a crime deserving of the death penalty, Your Majesty has already bestowed an exemption tablet upon him, so you can pardon him."

The king of Chu was struck by this and said, "You are talking about Yusi, the shaman from Fan, aren't you? If you had not mentioned it, I would have completely forgotten about that!" He ordered Grandee Pan Wang to accompany Cheng Daxin on a fast chariot to communicate the royal command: "You have been spared the death penalty!" However, by the time they arrived at Liangu, Cheng Dechen had already been dead for hours.

The general in command of the Army of the Left, Dou Yishen, had tried to hang himself, but because he was so heavy the rope snapped—a coincidence that saved his life. It was originally Dou Bo's intention to wait until Cheng Dechen and Dou Yishen were both dead, at which point he would place their bodies in suitable coffins and then commit suicide himself. It was for this reason that he was still alive when the message arrived from the king of Chu. Cheng Dechen was the only man who died. This was his fate.

The Recluse of Qianyuan wrote a poem bewailing these events:

> This arrogant and proud general from the kingdom of Chu
> Believed that the whole state of Jin lay within his grasp.
> A single failure brought disaster upon him;
> Anyone who believes that strength is all it takes is similarly doomed.

Cheng Daxin arranged for the encoffining of his father's body. Dou Yishen, Dou Bo, Dou Yuejiao, and the others followed Grandee Pan Wang to Shen, where they had an audience with the king of Chu. They prostrated themselves upon the ground and thanked His Majesty for his kindness in sparing their lives. When the king of Chu discovered that Cheng Dechen was dead, he regretted this extremely. Once he had traveled back to the capital city of Ying, he appointed Wei Lüchen to be his new Grand Vizier. Dou Yishen became governor of Shang with the title of duke. Dou Bo, meanwhile, was sent to guard the city of Xiangcheng. The king of Chu remained deeply upset about the circumstances of Cheng Dechen's death, so he appointed both his two sons, Cheng Daxin and Cheng Jiaju, to the office of grandees.

When the former Grand Vizier Ziwen, then living in retirement, heard that Cheng Dechen had been defeated in battle, he sighed and said, "This is just what Wei Jia said would happen. My understanding cannot even reach the level of that of a small child. Really it is too humiliating!" He spat several mouthfuls of blood and took to his bed. He summoned his son, Dou Ban, and instructed him: "I am going to die soon, but I still have something that I must tell you. Ever since your uncle, Dou Yuejiao, was born, he looked like a bear and had a voice like the roar of a tiger. This presages that he will bring ruin upon our family. At the time I begged your grandfather not to raise him, but he would not listen to me. In my opinion, Wei Lüchen does not look healthy enough to last long, and neither Dou Bo nor Dou Yishen strikes me as the kind of man who is going to come to a good end. Sooner or later, the government of the kingdom of Chu is going to fall into your hands, or those of Dou Yuejiao. He is an arrogant and violent man who seems to enjoy killing people. If he comes to power, he will cause terrible trouble and may well bring disaster down upon the whole Dou family! After I am dead, if Dou Yuejiao does indeed take power, you must go into exile and have nothing to do with him!"

Dou Ban bowed twice and accepted these commands; Ziwen then died. A short time later, Wei Lüchen also passed away. King Cheng of Chu remained deeply grateful for Ziwen's achievements, so he appointed Dou Ban as the new Grand Vizier, Dou Yuejiao became the minister of war, and Wei Jia became minister of works. No more of this now.

• • •

Once Lord Wen of Jin had defeated the Chu army, he moved to live in the Chu main encampment. There were enormous supplies of food kept within the stockade, which was divided up among the various armies. They said happily, "The people of Chu are keeping us well-fed." The representatives of the states of Qin and Qi, together with the various generals, all faced north and congratulated His Lordship on his victory. Lord Wen thanked them, but appeared depressed and unwilling to accept their praise. The generals asked, "You have defeated the enemy, so why are you unhappy?"

"Cheng Dechen is not the kind of man to give in easily," Lord Wen said. "This victory is merely a temporary gain for us. How can I not be concerned?"

Guo Guifu and the Honorable Yin then said goodbye and set off homewards. Lord Wen gave them half the booty that had been seized, and the two armies departed singing songs of triumph. Gongsun Gu of Song also went home. Afterwards, the Duke of Song sent him on an embassy to thank the states of Qi and Qin for their assistance, which will not be described in any detail.

. . .

Xian Zhen dragged Qi Man in front of Lord Wen in chains. He announced that he was guilty of the crime of disobeying an order from his commander-in-chief and bringing humiliation upon the army.

"If Chu's two armies of the Right and Left had not already been defeated, would you have been able to get away so lightly?" Lord Wen asked. He ordered the minister of war, Zhao Cui, to decide upon a suitable punishment, and Qi Man was beheaded as a warning to other officers.

"Anyone in the future who is contemplating contravening the orders given by the commander-in-chief can look at this!" Zhao Cui announced. The army subsequently behaved with even greater circumspection.

The Jin troops stayed in Shen for three days, then the marquis gave the order to stand down the army. When they arrived at the southern bank of the Yellow River, one of the mounted patrolmen reported: "The boats required to transport us across the river aren't ready yet."

Lord Wen summoned Zhou Zhi Qiao, but he was nowhere to be found. He was one of the generals of the state of Guo who had surrendered to Jin, which he had now served for a long time, but he was still looking for an opportunity to establish his merit by achieving some really difficult task. When he was sent to assemble boats at the Yellow River, he felt disrespected. Just at that moment he received a letter from a family member, announcing that his wife was seriously ill. Zhou Zhi Qiao calculated that the standoff between the armies of Jin and Chu would continue for many days yet, making it unlikely that the army would be departing soon, so he decided to go home to see his wife. He was not expecting that the moment the army arrived at Chengpu in the fourth month, battle would be joined and the Chu army would be defeated. Likewise, he could not have imagined that after resting the army for three days, the Marquis of Jin would set off home. Nor could he have guessed that some six days later the Marquis of Jin would arrive on the banks of the Yellow River and his absence would severely disrupt the crossing.

Lord Wen was furious and wanted to send officers off in all directions to seize any boats they could find.

"The people living around here have all heard about the defeat suffered by the Chu army," Xian Zhen said, "and they are in a state of terror. If you send your officers out to confiscate their boats, they will just run away and hide. Why not give orders to rent the boats for proper payment?"

"Good idea!" Lord Wen declared.

The offer of payment was posted on the gates to the army camp, and huge numbers of locals fought to be selected. Vast numbers of boats were assembled in the blink of an eye, and the whole army was then ferried across the Yellow River.

"I have now expunged the humiliations inflicted upon me by Cao and Wey," Lord Wen mused to Zhao Cui. "However, I still want to take my revenge upon Zheng. How should I go about it?"

"We can route our army home through Zheng, which will force them to deal with us," Zhao Cui suggested.

Lord Wen followed his recommendation.

They advanced for another couple of days. Then, far in the distance, they glimpsed a long train of carts with a nobleman at their head, coming from the east.

Luan Zhi, the commander of the advance guard, rode out to meet this man and asked, "Who are you?"

"I am Prince Hu," he replied, "a minister serving the Zhou Son of Heaven. Having heard that the Marquis of Jin was victorious in battle against the Chu army, bringing peace to the Central States, His Majesty is coming in person to reward you. He ordered me to come in advance to give you the good news." Luan Zhi arranged for Prince Hu to have an audience with Lord Wen.

His Lordship asked his advisors, "The Son of Heaven is going to reward me for my victory. Where on our route home is there a suitable place to hold this ceremony?"

"We are not far from Hengyong," Zhao Cui said, "and there is a place there called Jiantu, which sits on a nice level plain. By working day and night, it should be possible to build a suitable palace for the reception of His Majesty there. If Your Lordship were to lead all the other lords to pay court to the Zhou king, you would establish great merit."

Lord Wen chose an auspicious date in the fifth month with Prince Hu when he would receive the Zhou king at Jiantu. Prince Hu said farewell and left. The main Jin army headed to Hengyong, only to encounter yet another train of chariots with yet another aristocrat coming to meet them. This time it was Grandee Ziren Jiu of Zheng. The Earl of Zheng had entrusted this embassy to him, because he was afraid that the Marquis of Jin was on his way to punish him. Grandee Ziren Jiu had come specially to request a peace treaty.

"Zheng has heard of the defeat of the Chu army in battle, and they are scared," Lord Wen of Jin said angrily. "They do not really want to make peace with us. Once I have met His Majesty, I will advance my army until it comes to a halt at the foot of the walls of the capital city of Zheng."

Zhao Cui came forward and said, "Since we first set out on campaign, you have forced the Marquis of Wey into exile, arrested the Earl of Cao, and defeated the Chu army. This is quite enough to establish a fearsome reputation. What are you expecting to gain from Zheng that you exhaust the army in this way? You should accept this peace treaty. If Zheng upholds it, you can forgive them. If they betray it, you can launch a campaign against them, but only once you have rested your troops for a couple of months." Lord Wen agreed to make peace with Zheng.

• • •

The main body of the Jin army made camp at Hengyong. Hu Mao and Hu Yan took the troops under their command to build a suitable palace for the Zhou king at Jiantu. Meanwhile, Luan Zhi went to the capital city of Zheng and swore a blood covenant with the Earl of Zheng. The Earl of Zheng then went in person to Hengyong with a view to apologizing for having offended the Marquis of Jin. Lord Wen smeared his mouth with blood in a second covenant, which sealed the treaty. During their discussion, the Marquis of Jin happened to praise the bravery shown by Cheng Dechen. The Earl of Zheng said, "He committed suicide at Liangu." Lord Wen sighed a long time over this.

Once the Earl of Zheng had withdrawn, Lord Wen spoke privately with his ministers: "Today I am happy, not because I have obtained the support of Zheng but because Chu has lost Cheng Dechen. With Cheng Dechen dead, we have nothing to worry about and we can all sleep easy at nights."

A bearded old man wrote a poem that says:

Although Cheng Dechen was a brutal man,
In the future he might well have done great things.
You could say that Chu suffered a double defeat
When his body was found at Liangu.

When Hu Mao and Hu Yan built the royal palace at Jiantu, it was constructed to mirror the appearance of the Hall of Light. How do we know that? There is a poem, the "Rhapsody of the Hall of Light," that testifies to this:

The magnificent Hall of Light is built north of the capital.
Rising majestically in this privileged location, it stands beyond the suburbs;
It makes manifest the power of one man, it is where aristocrats pay court.
In each direction there are three rooms, making nine in total.
Such a building is the most important at the great ancestral shrine,
It takes the central position from the founding ancestor of the clan.
In this Hall of Light there are thirty-six doors and seventy-two windows.
To left and right, older sons and younger siblings take their appointed places;
The domed roof and the square floor represent the power of Heaven and Earth.
Places have been set for officials too, the Three Dukes being the most respected,
They take their places near the center; no other ministers are granted this honor.
The marquises enter to the east, their faces turned towards the west;
Earls file through on the west, their faces turned towards their peers.
Viscounts line up east of the main gate, barons stand opposite them to the west.
Rong and Yi barbarians stand guard outside; the Man and Di peoples also attend.
The lords of border states form serried ranks on one side; the chiefs of subordinate kingdoms match them on the other.
Jade axes with vermilion handles stand proud above the throng, dragon standards and leopard banners flutter on every side.
A cacophony of noise assaults the mountains and fills the valleys.
As the morning mist burns off, the ministers and knights line up; as the sun rises, a magnificent spectacle is revealed.
As the Son of Heaven ascends the hall in his jade-bead fringed crown,

He observes the kowtows of his lords come from every corner of the country,
Then he sits facing south, behind him a screen patterned with axes.
Sure the loyalty of a myriad subjects.

To the left and right of the royal palace, further official residences were constructed, and the work proceeded night and day. It was thus completed in little over a month. Then messages were sent to all the lords: "You must all assemble at Jiantu on the first day of the fifth month." Wangchen, Lord Cheng of Song, and Pan, Lord Zhao of Qi, both represented long-standing allies. Jie, Lord Wen of Zheng, was newly subordinate to the state of Jin and was therefore the first to arrive. Apart from them, Shen, Lord Xi of Lu, was a long-standing ally of the kingdom of Chu, while Kuan, Lord Mu of Chen, and Jiawu, Lord Zhuang of Cai, had both provided Chu with troops for the recent debacle.

Since these rulers had been terrified by the recent turn of events, they hurried to attend this interstate meeting.

Zhu and Ju were both tiny states, so their attendance could be taken for granted. Ye, Lord Xi of Xu, was not willing to obey Jin because he had served the king of Chu for ages. Renhao, Lord Mu of Qin, delayed his arrival because even though an ally of Jin, he never participated in any of the covenants or interstate meetings among the Central States. Zheng, Lord Cheng of Wey, was in exile in Xiangniu. Xiang, Lord Gong of Cao, was imprisoned in Wulu. Although the Marquis of Jin had promised both men that he would restore them to power, he had still not made any move to do so, so they were not able to attend.

• • •

When Lord Cheng of Wey heard that the Marquis of Jin was going to meet with the feudal lords, he discussed this situation with Ning Yu: "Since I am not going to be able to attend this meeting, it must mean that Jin's anger has still not abated. I cannot stay here a moment longer."

"If you leave now," Ning Yu replied, "you will never be restored to power. You had better abdicate in favor of the Honorable Shuwu, ordering Yuan Xuan to help him. They can beg to be allowed to swear the blood covenant at Jiantu. Even if you do have to go into exile, if Heaven helps Shuwu, he will be allowed to take part in the covenant. If Shuwu is in power in Wey, that is no different from Your Lordship being in command. Besides which, the Honorable Shuwu is a very kind and benevolent man; he would never conspire to depose you! He will think of some way to get you back."

Even though the Marquis of Wey was very unhappy about this idea, with things having reached this point there was nothing that he could do about it. Just as Ning Yu had suggested, he sent Sun Yan with a message offering to abdicate the title in favor of the Honorable Shuwu. Sun Yan agreed to take the message and set off in the direction of Chuqiu.

The Marquis of Wey then asked Ning Yu another question: "If I am going to go into exile, which country should I head for?"

Ning Yu hesitated, unable to make up his mind. The Marquis of Wey suggested: "How about I go to Chu?"

"Although your sister is married to the king of Chu," Ning Yu answered, "they are now locked in enmity with Jin. Besides which, you already sent them a letter decisively breaking off your alliance. It would be better if you went to Chen, for they have just become allies of Jin and in the future you will be able to communicate with Jin from there."

"No!" the Marquis of Wey declared. "Breaking off the alliance with Chu was not my idea, and under the circumstances, they will forgive me. I am not sure how the situation between Jin and Chu will develop in the future. However, if the Honorable Shuwu becomes an ally of Jin and I throw in my lot with Chu, whatever happens, Wey will be secure!"

The Marquis of Wey set off in the direction of Chu. At the border, he was upbraided for his behavior by the officials, so he changed his mind and went to Chen instead, just as Ning Yu had originally proposed.

Sun Yan had an audience with the Honorable Shuwu, at which the Marquis of Wey's command was conveyed to him.

"I am prepared to look after the country as a regent," the Honorable Shuwu said, "but how could I dare to accept that my older brother abdicate in my favor?"

He set off to attend the meeting at Jiantu with Yuan Xuan, while Sun Yan returned to report what he had said to the Marquis of Wey: "When I have an audience with the Marquis of Jin, I will beg that you be restored to power."

"His Lordship is a powerfully suspicious man," Yuan Xuan said. "If I do not send one of my own close relatives back, he will never believe this!" Therefore he ordered his son, Yuan Jiao, to accompany Sun Yan. In name this was simply to make polite inquiries as to the marquis' state of health, but in fact he was to be kept hostage.

The Honorable Chuanquan spoke privately to Yuan Xuan: "We all know that His Lordship will not be coming back. Why don't you tell the people of the capital that the marquis has offered to abdicate? They will support the accession of the Honorable Shuwu, and you can become prime minister. Jin would be happy about this development and you could use their military might to quell any opposition to your plans in Wey. You and the Honorable Shuwu could then rule Wey together."

"The Honorable Shuwu finds it impossible to neglect the rights of his older brother," Yuan Xuan said. "That being the case, how could I betray my lord? Our embassy is intended to see His Lordship restored to office."

The Honorable Chuanquan's words stuck in his throat and he left immediately. He was afraid that should the Marquis of Wey be restored to power, Yuan Xuan would tell him what he had said, in which case he would certainly be severely punished. He therefore made a private journey to the state of Chen, where he secretly reported a pack of lies to the Marquis of Wey: "Yuan Xuan has already installed the Honorable Shuwu as the new marquis, and they plan to meet with Jin to confirm this appointment."

Lord Cheng of Wey believed him, and asked Sun Yan about it. "I don't know about that," Sun Yan replied. "However, Yuan Jiao is here with you. If his father has such a plan, Yuan Jiao is sure to know about it. Why don't you ask him?"

The Marquis of Wey summoned Yuan Jiao, who informed him that there was no truth in this.

"If Yuan Xuan was disloyal to Your Lordship," Ning Yu pointed out, "would he be willing to send his son to you? There is no reason for you to suspect him."

The Honorable Chuanquan had a private audience with the Marquis of Wey and said: "Yuan Xuan has been conspiring to get rid of you for a long time now, my lord. He sent his son to you, not because he is loyal, but in order to keep an eye on what you are up to so he may have fair warning. If he intends to beg for mercy from Jin and install you in power again, he will not dare to attend the coming meeting in person. If he does go openly, you should believe every word that I have said. Please investigate the truth of this matter." The Marquis of Wey secretly sent someone to Jiantu to watch for the Honorable Shuwu and Yuan Xuan.

Master Hu Zeng wrote a poem that reads:

There should have been no question of his brother's love or Yuan
  Xuan's loyalty.
How could the Honorable Chuanquan slander them so?
The rich and powerful have always been suspicious,
Good and loyal men have often ended up their victims.

. . .

On the last day of the fifth month, King Xiang of Zhou arrived in person at Jiantu. The Marquis of Jin led the other lords out thirty *li* to meet him and escorted him back to the royal palace. When King Xiang took his position in the main hall, the aristocrats bowed and kowtowed. Once these ceremonies had been completed and everyone had taken their proper place, Lord Wen of Jin presented his Chu booty to the king, including one hundred teams of armored horses, one thousand foot soldiers, and a dozen carts of armor, uniforms, and weaponry.

King Xiang was very pleased and offered his personal congratulations, saying: "Ever since the death of the first hegemon, the Marquis of Qi, the barbarian state of Chu has become much stronger and they have repeatedly invaded the Central States. Now you, Uncle, have dispensed righteous punishment as they deserve, thus showing your respect for the Zhou royal house. There are many descendants of the great kings Wen and Wu who are relying on you, not just me!"

The Marquis of Jin bowed twice, kowtowed, and said, "That I was able to defeat the Chu invaders is entirely thanks to Your Majesty's beneficent influences. I certainly take no credit for it!"

The following day, King Xiang hosted a banquet in honor of the Marquis of Jin, at which he commanded the senior minister, Yin Wengong, and the Court Historian, Shu Xing, to invest the Marquis of Jin as hegemon. He bestowed upon him a royal chariot with all the appropriate trappings, a military chariot again with its trappings, one vermilion lacquer bow with one hundred matching arrows, ten black lacquer bows with one thousand arrows, a bronze vessel containing sacrificial wine, and an honor guard of three hundred "Agile Tiger" warriors. The command given to him read: "May the Marquis of Jin be placed in sole charge of undertaking military campaigns to root out evil that threatens the king."

The Marquis of Jin respectfully declined this appointment three times, after which he finally dared to accept it. He then had this royal mandate announced to the other lords. In addition to that, King Xiang ordered Prince Hu to invest the Marquis of Jin as the Master of Covenants, with the right to assemble the aristocrats to swear such oaths. The Marquis of Jin had a sacrificial platform constructed to one side of the royal palace at Jiantu. The lords went first to the royal palace to pay their respects, then they assembled at this platform. With Prince Hu in attendance to oversee the proceedings, the Marquis of Jin was the first to ascend, holding the ear of the sacrificial ox and followed by all the other lords in order of precedence. Yuan Xuan had already assisted the Honorable Shuwu to make his apologies to the Marquis of Jin, so on this day, Shuwu was occupying the position reserved for the Marquis of Wey and he was the last to sign the covenant.

Prince Hu read out the text: "All those who swear this blood covenant agree to uphold the honor of the Zhou royal house and to cease harming one another. Anyone who betrays this covenant will be punished by the Bright Spirits unto the third generation; he will die and his ancestral sacrifices will be terminated!"

The lords said in unison: "His Majesty commands us to make peace, who would dare to disobey?" They all then smeared their mouths with blood to seal the oath.

There is a historical poem by Qian Yuan that reads:

> Both ruler and ministers of the state of Jin were part of a great plan,
> With sufficient authority to be respected by the other feudal lords as a hegemon.
> Flags fluttered over the Chengpu battlefield as they counted their prisoners;
> Let us now praise this day's covenant at Jiantu,
> Rather than heaping unmerited esteem upon the meeting at Kuiqiu.
> Lord Huan left many unresolved problems when he died,
> Or Lord Wen would have found it impossible to achieve such remarkable things.

Once the covenant was over, the Marquis of Jin wanted to take the Honorable Shuwu to have an audience with King Xiang of Zhou, which would see him succeed to the marquisate of Wey in place of Lord Cheng.

The Honorable Shuwu broke down in tears and refused this honor: "In the past, at the interstate meeting of Ningmu, the Honorable Hua of Zheng attempted to usurp the succession, but Lord Huan of Qi prevented this. Today you have taken over the glorious work of continuing Lord Huan's legacy, so how can you expect me to succeed to my older brother's title? If you really care about me, then please forgive my older brother and restore him to his original title. He will then serve you to the best of his abilities."

Yuan Xuan also kowtowed and begged for mercy, and the Marquis of Jin agreed.

If you want to know if the Marquis of Wey was able to return home, READ ON.

Chapter Forty-two

King Xiang of Zhou holds court at Heyang.

Yuan Xuan of Wey conducts a court case at the official guesthouse.

In the twentieth year of the reign of King Xiang of Zhou, he traveled to Jiantu in order to honor the achievements of Lord Wen of Jin. After the ceremonies were over, he returned home to Zhou. The feudal lords all said goodbye and went back to their own countries. The Marquis of Wey had been misled by the Honorable Chuanquan's lies, so he had sent someone to investigate in secret. When he discovered that both Yuan Xuan and the Honorable Shuwu were attending the blood covenant and their names appeared on the oath, he thought he had real evidence of a conspiracy and immediately reported this to the Marquis of Wey.

The latter was absolutely furious and shouted, "Shuwu is indeed planning to establish himself as the new ruler." He cursed: "Yuan Xuan is a traitor! He plans to bring a new lord to power that he may enjoy great honors and wealth himself, so he even sent his son here to spy on me. How can I put up with this horrible pair one moment longer?" Yuan Jiao wanted to answer his charges, but the Marquis of Wey beheaded him with a single stroke of his sword. What a tragic death for an innocent young man! Yuan Jiao's servants fled in terror and reported what had happened to Yuan Xuan.

"My son's death was his fate!" Yuan Xuan declared. "Even though His Lordship has betrayed me, I will not let him down!"

"His Lordship must suspect you of treason," Sima Man pointed out, "so you should go into exile. Why do you not resign your post and leave, to make it clear that you have no intention of taking inappropriate advantage of the situation?"

Yuan Xuan said with a sigh: "If I resign, who will look after the state on His Lordship's behalf? I am angry with him for killing my son, but that is a private matter. Defending the state is much more important. If I were to ignore a matter of paramount importance in order to avenge my son, I would indeed be betraying my country."

He talked to the Honorable Shuwu and they sent a messenger with a letter to the Marquis of Jin, begging his assistance in restoring Lord Cheng of Wey to power. However, the story of Yuan Xuan's courageous behavior will have to be put to one side for the moment.

. . .

When Lord Wen of Jin returned home after receiving the royal mandate, the "Agile Tiger" guards and the bows and arrows that he had been given figured prominently in the procession, giving a most magnificent air to the whole thing. On the day that he entered the capital, the common people—young and old—came out to welcome his army, each struggling to find a place where they could see, their hands clutching baskets of food and bottles of water. There was an amazing hubbub as they acclaimed their heroic lord. Everyone was delighted to see Jin covered in glory. As it says:

> His courage under fire proved him a worthy successor of the first Lord Wen;
> Having defeated Chu, he continues the successful hegemony of Lord Huan.
> After nineteen years of exile as an impoverished wanderer,
> Today his reputation is lauded to the skies.

Lord Wen of Jin then held court and accepted the congratulations of his ministers, after which merit was apportioned and rewards issued. Hu Yan was declared to have achieved the greatest success, and Xian Zhen was placed second.

The generals present commented on this: "Xian Zhen was solely responsible for the disposition of the army at Chengpu and the strategy that brought about the crushing of the Chu army. Why have you declared Hu Yan to have achieved the greatest success, my lord?"

"Before the battle of Chengpu," Lord Wen explained, "Xian Zhen said, 'We must do battle with Chu, for this opportunity cannot be lost.' Hu Yan said, 'We must withdraw, for otherwise we will be breaking our word.' A victory over the enemy is a temporary success; gaining people's trust ensures ten thousand generations of glory. Which is more important, a temporary success or glory for ten thousand generations to come? That is why I put him in first place." The generals happily agreed to his assessment.

Hu Yan then presented his opinion: "The late minister Xun Xi, who died in the trouble over the Honorable Xiqi and Zhuozi, showed exemplary loyalty. You should give some kind of stipend to his descendants to encourage such behavior." Lord Wen agreed to this and then appointed Xun Xi's son, Xun Linfu, as a grandee.

At this time, Zhou Zhi Qiao was looking after his wife at home. When he heard that the Marquis of Jin had arrived, he rushed to meet him. Lord Wen ordered that he be imprisoned at the back of his train, and once rewards had been issued he discussed with the minister of war, Zhao Cui, what punishment should be meted out to him. They settled upon execution.

Zhou Zhi Qiao asked for clemency on the grounds of his wife's illness, but Lord Wen said, "When serving your ruler you should not even consider yourself, let alone a wife!"

He ordered that he be beheaded as a warning to the populace. In the course of this campaign, Lord Wen had ordered the execution first of Dian Jie, then of Qi Man, and now of Zhou Zhi Qiao. All these three men were famous generals, but because they were executed for dereliction of duty, there was no possibility of clemency. The three armies were thus shocked into obedience, and all of the generals obeyed orders to the letter. Just as the saying goes: "When rewards and punishments are issued arbitrarily, nothing works; when rewards and punishments go to the right people, there is nothing that you cannot achieve." This is the real reason that Lord Wen was able to become hegemon over the feudal lords.

Lord Wen then discussed an expansion of the army with Xian Zhen with a view to strengthening the state, but they did not dare to establish six armies that would have encroached upon the prerogative of the Zhou Son of Heaven. Instead, they called their new armies the "three infantry units." Xun Linfu was the grandee in command of the Central Infantry Unit, while Xian Mie and Tu Ji commanded the Left and Right units. Given that they had three armies and three "infantry units," they actually had six armies in total, but they were avoiding saying so openly. With this increase in their military capacity, Jin became the strongest state in the world.

• • •

One day when Lord Wen was holding court and discussing the problems posed by Cao and Wey with Hu Yan and his other advisors, a servant reported: "A letter has just arrived from the state of Wey."

"This is going to be the Honorable Shuwu asking for clemency for his older brother," Lord Wen predicted. When he opened the letter and read it, it said:

> You, my lord, have failed to destroy the state altars of Wey, and you have agreed to restore our former ruler to power, making the people of every country raise their heads to admire your great sense of justice. I hope that you will soon bring your plans for the restoration to fruition.

It so happened that Lord Mu of Chen had also sent a message to Jin, expressing the repentance of the rulers of Wey and Zheng and their intention of reforming their behavior. Lord Wen sent a letter back to each of them, agreeing to allow the two rulers to return to power. At the same time, he instructed Xi Buyang to lift his blockade. When the Honorable Shuwu received this letter, he immediately sent a chariot and honor guard to Chen to collect the Marquis of Wey. At the same time, Lord Mu of Chen sent the marquis on his way with a suitable escort.

The Honorable Chuanquan said to Lord Cheng of Wey, "Shuwu has now been ruling your country for a long time, so the people of the capital are used to obeying him, and he has even covenanted with your neighbors. You must not trust these people who have come to collect you."

"I know that!" the Marquis of Wey snapped. Accordingly, he instructed Ning Yu to travel on to Chuqiu ahead of him and find out what was actually going on. Ning Yu accepted these commands and set off.

• • •

When he arrived in Wey, the Honorable Shuwu was at court discussing matters of state. When Ning Yu joined them, he noticed that the Honorable Shuwu was sitting in a seat on the east side of the grand hall, facing west. The moment he spotted Ning Yu, he got down from his seat and greeted him with the utmost politeness.

"What are you trying to show by acting as regent and yet not sitting on the throne?" Ning Yu asked curiously.

"The rightful occupant of the throne is my older brother, and my place is by his side," the Honorable Shuwu explained. "I feel uncomfortable occupying even such a position, so how would I dare encroach upon his throne?"

"I have come here today to sound out your intentions," Ning Yu said. "All my thoughts are with my older brother, and I have been longing for his return day and night," Shuwu replied. "Please encourage my brother to come home as soon as possible to take up the reins of government, for that is my dearest wish!"

He agreed with Ning Yu that Lord Cheng of Wey would make his formal entry into the capital on Xinwei day in the sixth month. Ning Yu left the court with a view to hearing what people had to say about this development. He overheard some officials discussing the situation, and they turned to him and asked: "If our former lord is able to return, he is sure to discriminate between those who stayed behind and those who went into exile with him. Those who went with him will be rewarded, while those who stayed behind will be punished. What should we do?"

"I have come here with a message for you from your former ruler—everyone has done well, regardless of whether they stayed behind or went with him," Ning Yu said. "If you do not believe me, let us smear our mouths with blood in a solemn oath."

"If you are prepared to make a blood covenant with us, clearly we have nothing to worry about!" they agreed.

Ning Yu then swore an oath to Heaven: "Those who left supported the Marquis of Wey, those who stayed behind protected the country's security; whether at home or abroad, everyone did their best. Let ruler and subjects join together to preserve the state altars. If anyone betrays this covenant, may the Bright Spirits punish him!"

Everyone went home happily, saying, "Ning Yu would not lie to us."

The Honorable Shuwu ordered Grandee Chang Zang to take charge of the city gates and instructed him: "If someone arrives from the south, no matter how early or late it is, you must immediately let him in."

Ning Yu went back to report to the Marquis of Wey and said, "The Honorable Shuwu is entirely sincere in wanting you to go home. He has no intention of trying to usurp your position."

The Marquis of Wey believed him, but the Honorable Chuanquan had already put a great deal of effort into his slanders and he was afraid that, should he be caught out, he would be punished for deliberately misleading his ruler. Therefore, he again lied to the Marquis of Wey: "The Honorable Shuwu set a date with Grandee Ning for your ceremonial entry; who knows what preparations he is going to make to bring disaster down upon you, my lord! You had better go before the appointed date, when he is not expecting you, for that way you are sure to be able to take back your country."

The Marquis of Wey followed this advice and set off immediately. The Honorable Chuanquan asked permission to go ahead of him, expelling everyone from the palace lest they cause trouble, and the Marquis of Wey agreed to this.

Ning Yu presented his opinion: "I have already set a date for your entry. If you arrive ahead of time, they are sure to be suspicious of your intentions."

The Honorable Chuanquan shouted at him: "What do you mean by trying to prevent His Lordship from going home?"

Ning Yu did not dare to remonstrate any further, but he did say, "If you insist on leaving immediately, my lord, you should let me go on ahead, to inform your people and calm their concerns."

"You can tell them that I want to get back to Wey as soon as possible," the marquis said. "There is no other reason for my early arrival."

After Ning Yu had gone, the Honorable Chuanquan said, "Once Ning Yu arrives, that really will put the cat among the pigeons. Your Lordship must not delay your departure a moment longer." The Marquis of Wey set out in full haste.

. . .

When Ning Yu arrived at the gates of the capital, Chang Zang discovered by inquiry that he was a messenger from the Marquis of Wey and immediately let him in.

"His Lordship will arrive any moment now!" Ning Yu declared.

"I thought it was agreed that he would come back in the sixth month!" Chang Zang exclaimed. "What is he doing here now? You had better go on in to report this development, while I receive His Lordship."

Just as Ning Yu turned around, the Honorable Chuanquan came galloping up and said, "The Marquis of Wey is just behind me." Chang Zang assembled a chariot escort as quickly as he possibly could and went out to welcome his former lord, while the Honorable Chuanquan entered the city. The Honorable Shuwu had just completed a personal inspection of the palace staff to check on the cleaning and maintenance of the buildings. At that time he was off duty, so he was washing his hair in his own quarters when he heard Ning Yu report: "His Lordship has arrived." He was both delighted and startled. Coming out all flustered, he wanted to ask why he had arrived so early. Suddenly he heard the rumbling sound of chariots and horses arriving at full speed, whereupon he realized that the arrival of the Marquis of Wey was indeed imminent. He was so delighted that even though his hair was still wet, he rushed out all disheveled, holding his hair out of the way with one hand. Unfortunately, he ran slap bang into the Honorable Chuanquan. He was afraid that if Shuwu survived and the two brothers met, they would discover what he had been up to. Therefore, he was lying in wait for the Honorable Shuwu's arrival, with an arrow nocked to his bow. He let fly and the arrow flew straight into Shuwu's heart. As he crumpled to the ground, he turned his head to look back. Ning Yu rushed forward to help him up, but it was already too late. How tragic!

When Yuan Xuan heard that the Honorable Shuwu had been murdered, he was appalled and cursed: "What a wicked man the Marquis of Wey is! How dare he kill an innocent man! Will Heaven let him get away with this? If I tell the Marquis of Jin what has happened, let's see how long you stay in power!" Having wept bitterly for a short space of time, he fled into exile in Jin as quickly as he could.

A bearded old man wrote a poem, which reads:

Having decided to look after the state for the sake of his older brother,
A merciless arrow put an end to the life of this good man.
If the Marquis of Wey had not been so jealous and suspicious,
Would Chuanquan have dared to have gone on ahead to attack Shuwu?

Lord Cheng of Wey was waiting below the city walls when Chang Zang came out to meet him. The Marquis of Wey asked him what he was doing, and Chang Zang explained the instructions that he had received from the Honorable Shuwu: regardless of the time of His Lordship's arrival, he should be able to enter the city immediately.

"My younger brother really has been completely loyal to me," the Marquis of Wey said with a sigh.

When he entered the city, he met Ning Yu coming the other way. With tears in his eyes, he said: "The Honorable Shuwu was so delighted to hear of Your Lordship's arrival that he did not wait to finish bathing; he just roughly bound up his hair and came out to meet you. Who could have imagined that he would be murdered by your advance guard! I have now betrayed my word to your people. My crime merits the death penalty!"

The Marquis of Wey looked ashamed of himself and said, "I am well aware of the fact that Shuwu was innocent of all charges. Do not mention this again!"

He drove his chariot to the palace, where some of his officials were waiting to meet him. Many were not present, for they were still unaware of what had happened. Ning Yu took the Marquis of Wey to see the Honorable Shuwu's body. His eyes were both open, so he looked as if he were still alive. The Marquis of Wey pillowed his head upon his knees and burst into floods of tears, stroking his younger brother's face with his hands: "Shuwu! Shuwu! It is thanks to you that I have been able to get home, but it is my fault that you have been murdered! How sad! How terrible!"

The eyes of the dead man glittered momentarily before slowly closing.

"If you do not punish his murderer," Ning Yu said, "how can you expect the Honorable Shuwu to rest in peace?"

The Marquis of Wey straightaway gave orders for the Honorable Chuanquan's arrest. He tried to make his escape, but was captured by Ning Yu's men.

"I killed the Honorable Shuwu, but I did it for you, my lord!" Chuanquan excused himself.

"You slandered my brother and then you murdered him," the Marquis of Wey said furiously, "and now you want me to take the blame for this!"

He ordered his servants to behead the Honorable Chuanquan; he also instructed them to bury Shuwu with all the honors due to a feudal lord. The people of the capital were very upset when they first heard about the murder of Shuwu, but on discovering that Chuanquan had been executed and his victim buried with exceptional honors, they calmed down somewhat.

. . .

Let us now turn to another part of the story. Grandee Yuan Xuan of Wey fled to the state of Jin, where he had an audience with Lord Wen. He threw himself down upon the ground and wept as he explained how the Marquis of Wey had become suspicious and jealous of the Honorable Shuwu and how, on his arrival back in his state, he had sent someone on ahead to murder him. As he spoke, he broke down in tears all over again; once he had calmed down somewhat, he carried on speaking. The more he said, the more upset Lord Wen of Jin became, so he said a few kind words to try and cheer Yuan Xuan up, and then arranged for him to stay in an official guesthouse.

Lord Wen summoned his ministers to discuss this situation and asked them: "It is thanks to your efforts that I was able to defeat the kingdom of Chu in battle. At the interstate meeting at Jiantu, His Majesty rewarded me for my success and the feudal lords obeyed my commands. However, my hegemony can hardly be mentioned in the same breath as that of Lord Huan of Qi. Qin did not even bother to attend the meeting; Xu does not engage in diplomatic relations with us; although Zheng did attend the blood covenant, they are hardly to be trusted; and even though the Lord of Wey has now been restored to power, he started off by murdering his younger brother. If we do not make it clear that covenants are binding, if we do not punish the guilty, the feudal lords will all simply go their own ways. What plan do you have to offer?"

Xian Zhen came forward and said, "It is indeed the responsibility of the hegemon to hold meetings and punish those who repudiate their treaty obligations. Please appoint me to command an army that will make them feel the force of your ire."

"You cannot do that," Hu Yan said. "The way in which a hegemon makes himself most respected by the feudal lords is by supporting the Son of Heaven's authority. Now His Majesty has already come in person to see His Lordship, but we have done nothing about paying court to the Zhou Son of Heaven. Since we are obviously lacking in the most basic ritual propriety, how can we expect anyone to obey us? From the point of view of the Marquis of Jin, the very best plan would be to summon the feudal lords in the name of leading a delegation to pay court to His Majesty. We can then see who does not come and put pressure on them in His Majesty's name. Paying court to the king is the most important ceremony that we can perform. Punishing those who do not respect the king will garner us an excellent reputation. If we can both perform this important ceremony and gain a sterling reputation in the process, we will indeed have killed two birds with one stone. Your Lordship ought to consider this."

"Hu Yan is right," Zhao Cui put in. "However, in my humble opinion, I am afraid that going to court will not necessarily achieve the desired result."

"Why not?" Lord Wen asked.

"It has been a long time since the last major delegation of feudal lords paid court to the Zhou king," Zhao Cui explained. "Jin is currently a very powerful state, and if we bring together all our allies and head off in the direction of the capital, we are sure to terrify all those whose territory we pass through. I am concerned that His Majesty may become suspicious of your motives and refuse to see you. If he refuses you permission to pay court to him, you will find your authority much reduced. It would be a better plan to invite His Majesty to visit Wen and then lead the feudal lords to have an audience with him there. That way there is no reason for His Majesty to become nervous. That is the first benefit. The second benefit is that it will not put any of the feudal lords to much trouble. The third benefit is that the new palace Prince Shudai built is still standing in Wen, so there is no need to build His Majesty a suitable temporary residence."

"But will His Majesty come?" Lord Wen asked.

"His Majesty seems to be happy to maintain friendly relations with Jin, and he will be delighted that you want to pay court to him," Zhao Cui replied. "Why should he not come? I request permission, my lord, to lead an embassy to Zhou on your behalf to discuss the matter of paying court, and I will try to gauge His Majesty's intentions. I am sure that he will agree once he understands our plan."

Lord Wen was very pleased and commanded Zhao Cui to go to Zhou to beg for an audience with King Xiang of Zhou. At this meeting he kowtowed and bowed twice, then presented his opinion: "His Lordship, Chonger of Jin, was deeply moved by the Son of Heaven's great magnanimity in coming in person to bestow a royal mandate upon him. It is now his intention to lead the feudal lords in a delegation to visit the capital, where he intends to revive the old ceremony of paying court to Your Majesty. He humbly begs Your Majesty's sagacious approval!"

King Xiang was silent, and Zhao Cui was ordered to return to the official guesthouse to rest. His Majesty summoned Prince Hu to discuss the matter: "I am not sure what the Marquis of Jin is planning when he says he wants to bring a whole bunch of people to court. Can I refuse?"

"Let me go and talk to the ambassador from Jin and see if I can find out what they are up to," Prince Hu replied. "If it is at all possible to refuse, rest assured that I will do so."

Prince Hu bade farewell to King Xiang. Afterwards he went to the official guesthouse to see Zhao Cui, and raised the issue of the Marquis of Jin wanting to pay court. "The entire Zhou royal house is glorified by the Marquis of Jin's wish to lead a delegation of the feudal lords to pay respectful court to the Son of Heaven, thereby restoring an ancient ceremony that has fallen into abeyance in recent years," Prince Hu proclaimed. "However, for so many states to come together at the same time means that their luggage will form mountains and they are sure to be attended by a mass of guards. Before anyone has even seen the procession, rumors and gossip will arise and perhaps both sides will end up misunderstanding and slandering each other. This would be a terribly betrayal of the Marquis of Jin's original intention. It would be better to call the whole thing off."

"The Marquis of Jin is entirely sincere in his wish to pay court to the Son of Heaven," Zhao Cui said firmly. "On the day that I set out, His

Lordship had already begun circulating invitations to the other states, announcing that they should meet at the city of Wen. If this does not come off, then it will appear that we do not take serving His Majesty seriously. I cannot accept your suggestion."

"Then what is to be done?" Prince Hu asked.

"I have an idea, but I do not dare to mention it . . ."

"You have an idea?" Prince Hu asked. "How dare you refuse to explain it?"

"In the past there was a tradition whereby the Son of Heaven would from time to time go on a royal progress to observe the people in his realm," Zhao Cui said. "The city of Wen lies within the Zhou Royal Domain. If the Son of Heaven announced that he was going on a progress and traveled to Wen, His Lordship could lead the feudal lords to pay court to him there. Thus, on the one hand the respect due to His Majesty would be in no way compromised, and on the other His Lordship would be able to carry out the ceremony that it is his loyal and respectful wish to perform. How would that be?"

"Your plan is brilliant in every respect," Prince Hu declared. "I will go right back and report to the Son of Heaven."

Prince Hu entered the court and reported Zhao Cui's plan to King Xiang. King Xiang was extremely pleased and agreed to visit Wen on an auspicious day in the tenth month. Zhao Cui went back to report this to the Marquis of Jin. Lord Wen of Jin ordered all the feudal lords to meet at the city of Wen on the first day of the tenth month, with a view to paying court to the king.

. . .

On the appointed day, Pan, Lord Zhao of Qi; Wangchen, Lord Cheng of Song; Shen, Lord Xi of Lu; Jiawu, Lord Zhuang of Cai; Renhao, Lord Mu of Qin; and Jielu, Lord Wen of Zheng, all arrived one after the other.

"I did not attend the last meeting at Jiantu," Lord Mu of Qin explained, "because I was afraid that I would arrive late, it being so far away. This time, I am perfectly willing to take last place among the feudal lords." Lord Wen of Jin thanked him for this.

At this time Kuan, Lord Mu of Chen, had only recently died and his son, Shuo, was newly appointed as Lord Gong, but he was so much in awe of Jin's military might that he came dressed in full mourning garb. All the little states like Zhu and Ju came too. The Marquis of Wey knew that he was at fault and did not want to attend, but Ning Yu remonstrated with him: "If you do not go, then you will have added one more crime to the list and it is even more certain Jin will punish you."

Lord Cheng of Wey then set out, accompanied by Ning Yu, Qian Zhuangzi, and Shi Rong. When they arrived at Wen, the Marquis of Jin refused to see them and they were closely guarded by his troops. This time only the state of Xu refused to listen to Jin's commands. Thus the ten states of Jin, Qi, Song, Lu, Cai, Qin, Zheng, Chen, Zhu, and Ju all assembled at Wen, and the following day King Xiang of Zhou arrived. Lord Wen of Jin led the other lords to welcome him and escort him to his temporary palace, as each came up in turn and took their place with a bow and a kowtow.

The following day at the fifth watch, the lords from every corner of the country assembled, dressed in their formal robes and crowns, with jade ornaments hanging from their waists. They made a most magnificent spectacle as they advanced together, each bearing tribute to the Son of Heaven as a present from their own domains. Each behaved with the utmost respect as they took their seats, as they competed to please the Son of Heaven. This meeting was conducted on even stricter ceremonial lines than that of Jiantu.

There is a poem that testifies to this:

Dressed in formal robes and crowns they gathered at Wen,
Vying with a host of other lords to be the first to advance.
Generals look up at the sky, announcing their successful commands,
Ministers fall to the ground, overcome by the honors they have received.
The palace of Feng has been abandoned since a previous generation;
The empty reputation of Jiaru has now been humbled to the dust.
Even though it is not proper to summon the Zhou king,
What was wrong with covering it up as a "royal progress"?

Once the court ceremonies were over, Lord Wen of Jin reported the death of the innocent Honorable Shuwu of Wey to King Xiang of Zhou and requested permission that Prince Hu would join him in judging the guilty parties. His Majesty agreed to this. Lord Wen then escorted Prince Hu to the official guesthouse, where they took their seats as guest and host, before summoning the Marquis of Wey in the king's name. The Marquis of Wey entered dressed in prison uniform. Grandee Yuan Xuan of Wey was also present.

"It is not appropriate for a ruler to be interrogated by a subject," Prince Hu proclaimed. "His Lordship will have to be represented by someone else."

The Marquis of Wey was then taken to a side room, where Ning Yu kept him company, not leaving his side for even a moment. Qian

Zhuangzi went to represent the Marquis of Wey at these proceedings, where he would be confronted by Yuan Xuan. Shi Rong decided to undertake the defense himself, clarifying His Lordship's position. However, Yuan Xuan's words poured out like a waterfall, and, starting with his account of how the Marquis of Wey had gone into exile at Xiangniu, he explained in detail how His Lordship had instructed the Honorable Shuwu to assume regency over the state, and how he had murdered first Yuan Jiao and then Shuwu himself.

"This all came about from the Honorable Chuanquan's slanderous accusations," Qian Zhuangzi explained. "His Lordship should not have listened to him, but these events cannot be considered entirely his fault."

"The Honorable Chuanquan spoke to me about putting the Honorable Shuwu in power long before any of this happened," Yuan Xuan retorted. "If I had agreed to that, would His Lordship ever have been able to return to his country? It was only because I so much admired Shuwu's affection for his older brother that I refused his offer, thereby offending him and bringing about this disaster. If His Lordship had not been suspicious and jealous of the Honorable Shuwu, would Chuanquan's slanders have had any effect? I sent my son, Jiao, to follow my lord into exile so as to make my position crystal-clear. I had the most honorable motives in doing so, but my innocent son was still murdered. His motives in killing my son, Jiao, were exactly the same as when he came to murder the Honorable Shuwu."

Here Shi Rong broke in and said, "You are doing all this to avenge your son's murder; this is not about the Honorable Shuwu at all."

"I have always said that the death of my son is a private matter, and protecting the country is the most important thing," Yuan Xuan returned. "I am not a particularly clever man, but I would not dare to jeopardize national security for the sake of my own private enmities. Besides which, when the Honorable Shuwu wrote to the Marquis of Jin requesting the restoration of his older brother, I actually drafted the letter. If I had just been doing this to avenge the murder of my son, would I have been willing to let it go at that? I am aware that His Lordship was laboring under a misapprehension, and I hope he now regrets what he has done. But it is dreadful that the Honorable Shuwu had to die in such terrible circumstances to bring this about!"

"His Lordship is now aware that Shuwu had no intention of trying to usurp the marquisate," Shi Rong added. "This is all Chuanquan's fault and not His Lordship's."

"His Lordship knows perfectly well that the Honorable Shuwu never had any intention of usurping the marquisate and what Chuanquan said was just baseless slander," Yuan Xuan returned. "He should have punished him for that. What was he doing letting him enter the city first? When he allowed him to come back to Wey, when he sent him into the city ahead of the main party, he was clearly encouraging Chuanquan to commit murder. How can he possibly say that he did not know?"

Qian Zhuangzi hung his head in silence, but Shi Rong broke in again. "Everyone agrees that the Honorable Shuwu was innocent, but he was a subject and the Marquis of Wey a ruler. Ever since antiquity, countless innocent subjects have been put to death by their rulers. Since the Marquis of Wey had already ordered the execution of Chuanquan and buried Shuwu with full honors, punishments and rewards have been clearly apportioned. What crime is left for which we can punish the Lord of Wey?"

"In the past, wicked King Jie of the Xia dynasty killed Guan Longfeng, and Tang, the founder of the Shang dynasty, deposed him," Yuan Xuan declared. "Wicked King Zhou of the Shang dynasty murdered the innocent Prince Bigan, and the future King Wu attacked him. At the time, Tang and King Wu were both subjects of Jie and Zhou, but when they were shocked into action by the sight of innocent men being murdered, they raised a righteous army and punished their rulers, bringing relief to the people. Now, the Honorable Shuwu was not only a close blood relative of his killer, but also someone who had achieved great things in protecting the state at a particularly difficult moment; how could Guan Longfeng and Prince Bigan compare? Wey is just a marquisate under the control of both His Majesty, the Zhou Son of Heaven, and the hegemon; how can he be compared to King Jie or King Zhou, whose realms stretched from sea to shining sea? How can you absolve him from guilt?"

That put a stop to Shi Rong's arguments on one front, but he changed tack and said, "Although the Lord of Wey is clearly in the wrong here, since you are his subject, you should be loyal to him. When His Lordship returned to his state, you immediately left without paying court or congratulating him. How can you justify that?"

"It was by His Lordship's order that I assisted the Honorable Shuwu to run the country in his absence," Yuan Xuan said. "If he had decided that there was no place for Shuwu any more, is it likely that I would have been spared? The reason I fled into exile was not because I was trying to escape just punishment, but because I wanted to proclaim the Honorable Shuwu's innocence!"

Lord Wen of Jin leaned over from his chair and said to Prince Hu, "Every point in this debate between Shi Rong and Yuan Xuan has been won by Yuan Xuan. Given that the rulers of both Wey and Zheng count as His Majesty's subjects, I would not dare to make a decision on my own authority. However, we can punish the Marquis of Wey's supporters right now." Therefore he instructed his entourage: "Execute all the Marquis of Wey's attendants and expose their bodies in the marketplace."

"I am told that Ning Yu has been an excellent grandee of the state of Wey, and he has done his very best in extremely difficult circumstances to mediate between the marquis and his brothers as well as between him and his subjects," Prince Hu said thoughtfully. "It is not his fault that the Marquis of Wey would not listen to good advice! This court case has nothing to do with him, and he should not be dragged into it. Shi Rong is the chief judge in Wey, and I have not been at all impressed by his muddled arguments in this case, so he deserves to be punished. Qian Zhuangzi has not said a word throughout the proceedings, so obviously he knows there is no point in twisting logic like this—he does not have to be so severely punished. However, it is entirely up to you, my lord, to decide."

Lord Wen followed his advice and ordered that Shi Rong should be beheaded and Qian Zhuangzi should have his feet cut off, while Ning Yu was pardoned. The Marquis of Wey was put in a prison cart and taken to have an audience with King Xiang alongside Lord Wen and Prince Hu. This pair had prepared a report on the court case concerning the ruler of Wey and his subjects, the conclusion of which stated: "Under the circumstances, if you do not execute the Lord of Wey, it goes against every moral principle and it will make the people of the realm extremely unhappy. We request your permission to have the minister of justice punish him, to make clear the penalties of disobeying the law."

"Your account of the evidence in this case is extremely clear," King Xiang stated. "However, it cannot proceed any further. I have heard it said: 'The Zhou officials established the position of plaintiff and defendant in order to allow ordinary people to have a mechanism for addressing their grievances, but two groups of people are exempted: rulers cannot be brought to book by their subjects, nor can fathers be called into court by their sons.' If a subject can bring a court case against his lord, this means that no distinctions are being observed between the ruler and the ruled. If the subject wins the court case, that puts me in a position where I have to execute a lord for the sake of a vassal, which is totally unacceptable. I am afraid that this case will not make the penalties for disobeying the law any clearer, but it will cause enormous trouble in the future. Otherwise I would see no reason to extend clemency to Wey!"

Lord Wen was terrified and apologized, saying: "I had no idea of the complex ramifications of this case. Since Your Majesty does not want to see him punished, let the Lord of Wey go back to the capital in his prison cart and you can make a decision about what to do with him later." He then took the Marquis of Wey back to the official guesthouse, where he was placed under armed guard as before. At the same time, he sent Yuan Xuan back to Wey, to put another ruler in power there instead of Lord Cheng.

When Yuan Xuan arrived back in Wey, he discussed the situation with the other ministers. He lied to them and said: "The Marquis of Wey has already been condemned to death. According to the mandate that I have received from the Zhou king, we need to select a new lord."

The ministers proposed one candidate, the Honorable Shuwu's younger brother Shi, whose style-name was Zixia, a most generous and benevolent man.

"If we establish him," Yuan Xuan said, "it will accord with the principle of fraternal succession."

The Honorable Shi then succeeded to the marquisate, and Yuan Xuan became his prime minister. Sima Man, Sun Yan, Zhou Chuan, Ye Jin, and a whole host of other civil and military officials set to work, and the situation within the state became somewhat more stable.

If you want to know what happened to the state of Wey in the end, READ ON.

Chapter Forty-three

Clever Ning Yu uses a poisoning scare to restore the ruling house of Wey.

Old Zhu Wu is let down from the city walls to persuade the Lord of Qin.

When King Xiang of Zhou had completed the ceremonies attendant on receiving court, he wanted to go home to Luoyang. The assembled lords escorted King Xiang as far as the north bank of the Yellow River, at which point Xian Mie was ordered to take the Marquis of Wey in chains to the capital. Lord Cheng of Wey was suffering from some minor indisposition, and Lord Wen of Jin ordered his own physician, Yan, to attend to him. He pretended that this was to cure him of the disease, but in fact the doctor had been given orders to poison the Marquis of Wey to assuage the anger that His Lordship felt. "If you do not do this for me, I will kill you!" He also instructed Xian Mie: "The sooner you get this over with the better. Once it is done, you can bring Doctor Yan back to report."

After King Xiang had gone, but before all the lords went their separate ways, Lord Wen of Jin said: "I have received an order from the Son of Heaven to punish miscreants. Xu is now the only state that still serves Chu wholeheartedly and has nothing to do with the Central States. When His Majesty announced his personal attendance, the other lords all came as quickly as they could, but the state of Xu ignored the summons even though they are located nearby. How can such behavior be acceptable? I am willing to lead you in a campaign against Xu."

"We will respectfully follow your orders!" the aristocrats all declared.

With the Marquis of Jin as their leader, the rulers of the eight states of Qi, Song, Lu, Cai, Chen, Qin, Ju, and Zhu all assembled their armies and received their marching orders, setting off together in the direction of Yingyang, the capital city of Xu. The only person who was unhappy about this was Jie, Marquis Wen of Zheng, who was the brother-in-law of the king of Chu. He only obeyed Jin because he was afraid of them. He was of the opinion that the punishment that Lord Wen of Jin had meted out to Cao and Wey was far too severe, and thought to himself, "When the Marquis of Jin was in exile, we did not treat him very well. I heard him promise that he would restore the rulers of Cao and Wey to power, but he shows no signs of actually doing so. If he holds on to his grudges so strongly, is it likely that he will forget about Zheng? I had better be sure to maintain good relations with Chu, so that I have a way out of this imbroglio. If the worst really does come to the worst, I have someone to rely on for support."

The senior minister Shu Zhan realized that the Earl of Zheng was vacillating and perhaps intended to betray his alliance with the state of Jin. He came forward and remonstrated: "We are indeed fortunate that Jin has decided not to punish Zheng. You must not betray them, my lord! If you do so, you will bring disaster down upon yourself and they will not forgive you."

The Earl of Zheng paid no attention to him. He sent someone to spread the rumor: "Pestilence has broken out in the capital!" With the excuse that he needed to offer prayers for the well-being of his people, he said goodbye to the Lord of Jin and went home early. In secret he sent someone to give his regards to the king of Chu: "The Marquis of Jin is disgusted by the way that the state of Xu remains allied with you, and hence he is leading the feudal lords in campaign against them. I am too frightened of Jin to dare to take my army home, but I thought I should inform you of this development."

When the people of Xu heard that the army of the feudal lords was on the way, they also sent someone to report this emergency to Chu.

"My army has just been defeated; there is no way that they can fight with Jin," King Cheng of Chu said. "We will have to wait until they are exhausted and then ask for a peace treaty."

For this reason, he did not go to the rescue of Xu. The armies of the feudal lords then laid siege to Yingyang, to the point where not even a drop of water could escape from the city.

• • •

At this time Xiang, Lord Gong of Cao, was still imprisoned at the city of Wulu. When he did not receive a pardon from the Marquis of Jin, he wanted someone whom he knew to be a persuasive speaker to go and talk to Lord Wen. One of his junior ministers, Hou Nou, asked permission to offer generous bribes, and Lord Gong of Cao agreed to this. When Hou Nou discovered that the lords were all in Xu, he set off in the direction of Yingyang and asked permission to have an audience with Lord Wen of Jin. Just at that time Lord Wen was suffering from flu, having been laid low by overwork. In his dreams he saw a ghost wearing an official hat and robe, which begged him for something to eat, then bit him and went away. After that he got even sicker and lay in bed, unable to get up. He summoned the Grand Astrologer Guo Yan and asked him to divine if this was auspicious or not. Hou Nou presented Guo Yan with a cart full of gold and silk while making an appeal to his better feelings, asking that he use the appearance of this ghost to get Cao out of trouble and instructing him in what to say. Guo Yan took the bribe and agreed to make the plea on their behalf.

When he had an audience with the Marquis of Jin, Lord Wen told him all about his dream. When the milfoil divination was performed, he obtained the two trigrams "Heaven" and "Lake," in which *yin* changes into *yang*. Guo Yan presented this result to Lord Wen and said, "When *yin* reaches its zenith it creates *yang*, thus the locusts spread their wings. When an amnesty is offered to the world, the bells and drums resound."

"What does this mean?" Lord Wen asked.

"The hexagram tallies with your dream," Guo Yan replied. "There must be a ghost or spirit that is not receiving sacrifice who has come to beg Your Lordship for clemency."

"I have always done my utmost to ensure that sacrifices are performed properly," Lord Wen said. "I would never allow one to be discontinued. What has happened that a ghost or spirit comes to me to ask for clemency?"

"Might this not refer to Cao?" Guo Yan suggested. "The founder of the ruling house of Cao, Prince Zhenduo, was a son of King Wen of Zhou. The founder of the ruling house of Jin, Prince Tangshu, was a son of King Wu of Zhou. In the past Lord Huan of Qi held interstate meetings to ensure the territorial integrity of the states of Xing and Wey, even though their ruling houses held a different surname from his own. Today you have convened an interstate meeting with a view to destroying Cao and Wey, even though these states are ruled by your own cousins. Besides which, you have already agreed to the restoration of the rulers of these two states. At the covenant at Jiantu, you restored Wey but did not restore Cao; thus you have punished two people differently for the same crime. Prince Zhenduo is no longer in receipt of sacrifice, so is it not only too appropriate that he appears in your dreams? If you were to restore the Earl of Cao to power, that would comfort the prince's soul. If you were to issue orders that demonstrate your magnanimity, you would enjoy the music of bells and drums performing songs of praise. Why would you ever suffer again from dreams in which you are bitten?"

As he spoke, Lord Wen relaxed and felt much better. He immediately sent someone to summon the Earl of Cao from Wulu and restored him to power. He also ordered that the lands that had been given to the state of Song should all be returned to Cao. Once the Earl of Cao was released, he felt like a caged bird that has been allowed to soar into the sky, like a monkey escaping from behind bars to return to the forest. He immediately gathered his troops and headed off to Yingyang at all speed to thank the Marquis of Jin in person for his generosity in allowing him to return home and to assist the other feudal lords in the siege of Xu. Lord Wen then gradually recovered from his ill health. When Lord Xi of Xu realized that Chu would not be sending troops to relieve him, he went out to the Jin army to surrender with his hands tied and a jade disc in his mouth. He offered vast quantities of gold and silk to reward the attacking troops. Lord Wen and the other aristocrats then lifted the siege and went home.

Just before Lord Mu of Qin set off, he came to an agreement with Lord Wen of Jin: "In the future in any military engagement, if Qin mobilizes its army, then Jin must come to their assistance; if Jin mobilizes its army, then Qin must support them. Our two states will be united in strength and will never sit by and let the other be attacked." Once the two lords had made this agreement, they each went their separate ways. As Lord Wen of Jin made his way home, he heard that the state of Zheng had reopened communications with Chu. He was absolutely furious about this and wanted to move his troops to attack Zheng. Zhao Cui remonstrated with him: "Your Lordship has barely recovered from a serious illness; you cannot possibly stand any further exertion. Besides which, your army is worn out and your supporters among the feudal lords have all gone home. You had better go back to Jin and allow one year for recovery, then make plans for how you are going to deal with them."

Accordingly, Lord Wen went home.

• • •

Let us now turn to another part of the story. When King Xiang of Zhou returned to the royal capital, his assembled ministers met to congratulate him. Once that ceremony had been completed, Xian Mie kowtowed and begged that the Marquis of Wey be handed over to the minister of justice, just as the Marquis of Jin had ordered him to. At that time Yue, Duke of Zhou, was chancellor and in charge of the government. He asked permission to allow the Marquis of Wey to lodge in an official guesthouse while he made his appeal.

"It would be too harsh to put him in prison," King Xiang said. "On the other hand, allowing him stay in a guesthouse is letting him off too lightly."

An empty house was found in the city, and he was kept prisoner there. King Xiang intended to protect the Marquis of Wey, but Lord Wen of Jin was so angry with him and had sent Xian Mie there to supervise his incarceration, so His Majesty became frightened and felt he had to place him under house arrest. Although in name he was imprisoned, in fact things were not too bad. Ning Yu kept close by his lord, sleeping next to him at night and never stirring more than a step away during the day. When it came to food and drink, he tasted everything himself first, only then allowing His Lordship to have any. Xian Mie ordered Doctor Yan to strike many times, but there was nothing he could do that could get past Ning Yu's strict precautions.

Since Doctor Yan found himself helpless, he told Ning Yu everything: "You know what the Marquis of Jin is like. Anyone who offends him, he kills. Anyone he hates, he will take revenge upon. When I came with you, I was given orders to poison His Lordship, otherwise I would myself be judged to have committed a crime. If you have a plan that can get me out of this mess, please tell me!"

Ning Yu leaned over and whispered in his ear: "Since you have told me the truth and asked for my help, naturally I will do my very best for you. The Marquis of Jin is getting old; he is no longer interested in the affairs of men but in the afterlife. I have heard that the Earl of Cao was pardoned entirely thanks to the words of an astrologer. If you feed His Lordship tiny quantities of poison and then put the blame for his survival upon the ghosts and spirits, not only will the Marquis of Jin not blame you, he will reward you."

Doctor Yan understood what it was he had to do and left. Subsequently, Ning Yu pretended to have received an order from the Marquis of Wey and went to collect some medicine from the doctor to cure his illness. This was handed over sealed in a jade casket.

"The Marquis of Wey is doomed," Doctor Yan assured Xian Mie. There was indeed some poison in the bottle that went to the marquis, but the quantities were very small and it was mixed in with other drugs that served as an antidote.

Ning Yu asked permission to taste the medicine, and Doctor Yan made a play of refusing to allow this and forcing the Marquis of Wey to swallow it. Once he had swallowed two or three mouthfuls, the doctor opened his eyes wide and stared fixedly into the courtyard, then suddenly screamed and fell to the ground, spitting out a quantity of blood. While he was carrying on, he made sure that the bottle of medicine was dashed to the ground, so that the poison it contained went everywhere. Ning Yu pretended to be absolutely amazed and summoned the servants to assist the doctor to his feet. When after a long time he finally came to and they asked him what had happened, Doctor Yan said, "When I was forcing the drugs down His Lordship's throat, I suddenly caught sight of a spirit quite ten feet tall with a head as large as a barrel coming down from the sky. He looked really imposing! He came straight into the room and said, 'I have received an order from Prince Tangshu to come here to save the life of the Marquis of Wey.' Then he swung his golden cudgel and smashed the medicine bottle, throwing me into a complete panic!"

The Marquis of Wey claimed that he had seen exactly the same thing as Doctor Yan. Ning Yu pretended to be angry and said, "You were going to poison His Lordship. If it were not for the intervention of the gods, he would be dead by now! I am going to kill you!" He started punching Doctor Yan, only to be held back by the servants present.

When Xian Mie heard what had happened, he came as quickly as he could. He said to Ning Yu, "Since your lord was protected by a spirit, his allotted span is clearly not yet ended. I will have to report this to His Lordship."

The Marquis of Wey had only swallowed a tiny amount of poison, so he was not badly affected; he recovered from the effects pretty quickly. Xian Mie and Doctor Yan went back to Jin, where they reported what had happened to Lord Wen. He believed every word that they said and pardoned the doctor.

A historian wrote a poem about this:

How could poison be used to kill the Marquis of Wey?
His instructions to Doctor Yan resulted in him breaking the bottle.
Although Lord Wen's anger burned like a flame,
How could he escape being caught up in Ning Yu's plot?

The marquises of Lu and Wey had been allied and intermarried for many generations. When Lord Xi of Lu heard that Doctor Yan's attempt to poison the marquis had failed, and that Lord Wen of Jin clearly had no intention of punishing the man, he asked Zangsun Chen, "Will the Marquis of Wey ever be restored to power?"

"Yes," Zangsun Chen declared.

"How do you work that out?" Lord Xi asked.

"The most severe of the five punishments sees the criminal beheaded with an axe under armed guard, while the second most severe sees him tattooed, right down to the lightest where he is merely whipped, sent into exile, or exposed in the marketplace so that the people will know his crime," Zangsun Chen replied. "Now, the Marquis of Jin has applied none of these punishments to the Lord of Wey, but has tried to poison him in secret. He has not punished Doctor Yan, because he is trying to avoid besmirching his reputation by becoming openly responsible for an attempted murder. If the Marquis of Wey survives, is it likely that he is going to spend the rest of his life in Zhou? If the feudal lords request it, the Marquis of Jin will have to pardon him. If the Marquis of Wey returns to his state, he will become even closer to Lu, my lord, and everyone will praise your sense of justice!"

Lord Xi was thrilled by this idea and sent Zangsun Chen to present ten pairs of white jade discs to King Xiang of Zhou and beg for the release from captivity of the Marquis of Wey.

"The Marquis of Jin is responsible for this," King Xiang said. "If Jin has no problem with releasing him, I certainly have no quarrel with the Marquis of Wey!"

"My lord intends to send me to ask for clemency from Jin, but without Your Majesty's order, I would not dare to go," Zangsun Chen said.

King Xiang accepted the white jade discs, making clear that he agreed. Zangsun Chen proceeded on to the state of Jin, where he had an audience with Lord Wen and presented him with a further ten white jade discs and said: "My lord and the Marquis of Wey are as close as brothers. Now that the Marquis of Wey has angered you, my lord cannot simply stand by. Now that we have heard that Your Lordship has already restored the Earl of Cao, we present these humble gifts to you, in atonement for the offense that the Lord of Wey has committed against you."

"The Marquis of Wey is at present in the capital, where he is held prisoner by His Majesty the king," Lord Wen replied. "How can I make a decision on my own authority?"

"You represent His Majesty in commanding the lords of the Central States," Zangsun Chen responded. "If Your Lordship were to pardon him, is that any different from receiving a royal order?"

Xian Mie came forward and said, "Lu and Wey are very close. If you were to pardon Wey for the sake of Lu, then both states would submit to your authority. Is that not exactly what you want?"

Lord Wen agreed and ordered Xian Mie to escort Zangsun Chen back to Zhou, where they would make a formal request for release from King Xiang. Lord Cheng of Wey was then released from captivity, and he returned to his own country.

...

At this time, Yuan Xuan had already installed the Honorable Shi as the new lord. He repaired the city walls and made every suitable preparation, with anyone attempting to enter or leave the capital subject to extremely strict interrogation. Lord Cheng of Wey was concerned that, on the day he returned to his state, Yuan Xuan would use force to prevent him from entering the capital, so he secretly plotted his return with Ning Yu.

"I have heard that Zhou Chuan and Ye Qin were both involved in the accession of the Honorable Shi, but when they asked for ministerial positions, they were refused," Ning Yu remarked. "They are both deeply resentful of this, so they could be recruited to help you from inside the state. I also have a close associate named Kong Da, a descendant of the Song loyal minister Kong Fu, who is a most brilliant man. Both Zhou Chuan and Ye Qin were close friends of Kong Fu. If you order Kong Da to take a message from you promising them ministerial office and ordering them to kill Yuan Xuan, there is nothing for you to worry about."

"Would you secretly instruct them on my behalf that if this matter is successfully accomplished, I will not begrudge them both a ministerial position?" the Marquis of Wey said.

Ning Yu sent some trusted servants to spread the following rumor: "Although the Marquis of Wey has now been released from captivity, he is too embarrassed to return to his state, so he has gone into exile in the kingdom of Chu." He likewise took the letter from the Marquis of Wey and instructed Kong Da to go in secret and make a deal with Zhou Chuan and Ye Qin, with precise orders about what he should tell them.

The two of them then came up with a plan: "Yuan Xuan patrols the ramparts in person every single night, so if we place soldiers in ambush by the curtain wall, they can leap out and murder him. Afterwards we can go to the palace and kill its occupants. The two of us will then have played the most important role in assuring the restoration of the Marquis of Wey." Both of them assembled their servants and ordered them to set an ambush.

Just as dusk was falling, Yuan Xuan was on patrol by the East Gate, when he caught sight of Zhou Chuan and Ye Qin coming towards him. Yuan Xuan was surprised by this and asked, "What are you doing here?"

"We have received a message from outside that the former Marquis of Wey has already crossed the border and will arrive any moment now," Zhou Chuan said. "Didn't you know?"

Yuan Xuan was deeply alarmed and cried out, "Who told you that?"

"According to my information," Ye Qin said, "Grandee Ning Yu has already sent someone into the city to arrange a delegation of ministers to greet His Lordship. What are you going to do?"

"This is all just rumor," Yuan Xuan declared. "I don't believe a word of it. Besides, we have already established a new lord, so why should anyone want the old one back?"

"You are the most senior minister and ought to have your eyes open," Zhou Chuan said. "If you don't even hear about such an important thing as this, what is the point of keeping you at all?"

Ye Qin grabbed hold of both Yuan Xuan's arms. Yuan Xuan tried to fight back as hard as he could, but Zhou Chuan drew his sword and with a great bellow brought it down on his head, cleaving his skull in two. The soldiers in ambush all rose up, as Yuan Xuan's entourage scattered in panic. Zhou Chuan and Ye Qin then led their servants to walk up and down the streets of the city, shouting: "The Marquis of Wey is outside the city walls with an army from Qi and Lu. You must stay at home and not interfere in what happens!" Everyone went home when this curfew was announced, bolting the shutters and barring the doors. The officials serving in court were not at all sure what to believe, but since they had no idea what was going on, they stayed quietly at home, waiting for news.

Zhou Chuan and Ye Qin then entered the palace to kill the inhabitants. Just at that moment, the Honorable Shi was in the palace drinking with his younger brother, the Honorable Yi, when they heard that a coup was underway. The Honorable Yi drew his sword and went out of the palace to find out what was going on. He ran straight into Zhou Chuan, who killed him. They searched for the Honorable Shi but could not find him. The palace was ripped apart overnight, but it was only when the next day dawned that they discovered that the Honorable Shi had committed suicide by throwing himself into a well. Zhou Chuan and Ye Qin then proclaimed the message that they had received from the Marquis of Wey and assembled all the officials at court with a view to welcoming Lord Cheng back into the city and restoring him to power.

Later on, people praised Ning Yu's wisdom in accepting humiliation in order to be able to restore Lord Cheng of Wey to the marquisate. However, in the circumstances that pertained at that time it would have been much better if he had either persuaded the marquis to abdicate in favor of the Honorable Shi or, since the Honorable Shi did not greet the news of the Marquis of Wey's return by mobilizing the army, to persuade him to return to his former subordinate position. By allowing Zhou Chuan and Ye Qin to go on the rampage, this resulted in a massacre in which family members murdered one another. Although ultimate responsibility rests with Lord Cheng of Wey, Ning Yu cannot escape criticism.

There is a poem that bewails this:

In the past, the Honorable Chuanquan murdered Shuwu with a single arrow.
Now again a new ruler is forced to descend to the Yellow Springs.
Time and again jealousy brought about disaster, which he did nothing to prevent;
There is no good reason for anyone to claim that Ning Yu was a wise man.

After Lord Cheng of Wey was restored to the marquisate, he selected an auspicious day to hold a sacrifice at the ancestral temple. Just as he had promised, he appointed Zhou Chuan and Ye Qin to ministerial positions and instructed them to accompany him to the ancestral sacrifices wearing full official robes. That day at the fifth watch Zhou Chuan got into his chariot and headed off, but when he arrived at the gates to the temple in advance of the others, his eyes suddenly started out of his head and he shouted: "Zhou Chuan, you wicked thief, you are as vicious as a cobra in working your evil ends! My son and I were totally loyal to the state, but you killed me because you coveted the glory of a ministerial position. My son and I have taken our innocent souls down to the Underworld, but you are not going to live to enjoy attending this sacrifice in your new ceremonial robes! I am going to take you down to have an audience with the Honorable Shuwu and Shi and see what you have to say for yourself! I am Grandee Yuan Xuan!" When he had finished speaking, blood spurted from every orifice and he fell dead upon his chariot.

Ye Qin was the second to arrive and was absolutely appalled at this turn of events. He quickly stripped off his ministerial robes and went back home, with the excuse that he was not feeling at all well. When Lord Cheng of Wey arrived at the temple, he ordered Ning Yu and Kong Da to accompany him instead. When he returned to the court, Ye Qin's formal letter declining his ministerial appointment arrived. The Marquis of Wey was aware of the mysterious circumstances in which Zhou Chuan had died and did not feel able to force him to accept the post. A few months later, Ye Qin too became sick and died.

It is indeed pitiful that Zhou Chuan and Ye Qin coveted the position of ministers so much that they were prepared to behave so wickedly. Neither of them enjoyed a single day in office, and yet for this they were prepared to be cursed for a thousand generations. Is this not stupid?

The Marquis of Wey remembered all that Ning Yu had done to protect him, and so he wanted to appoint him to the office of a senior minister. Ning Yu refused this honor and insisted that it be given to Kong Da instead, so Kong Da then became the senior minister and Ning Yu became a middle-ranking minister. Kong Da came up with a plan whereby the Marquis of Wey put all the blame for the deaths of Yuan Xuan and the Honorable Shi onto the deceased Zhou Chuan and Ye Qin. He then sent an ambassador to explain the situation to the Marquis of Jin. Lord Wen did not pursue the matter any further.

• • •

In the twelfth year of the reign of King Xiang of Zhou, the Jin army had been resting for more than a year. One day when Lord Wen was sitting in the court, he said to his assembled ministers: "I have not yet avenged the insults that I suffered from the people of Zheng. Today they have yet again betrayed me by throwing in their lot with the kingdom of Chu. Do you think it would be a good idea if I summoned the lords to punish them?"

"The lords have come to your call time and time again," Xian Zhen said. "Now because of Zheng you want to go out on campaign again; this is not the way in which to bring peace to the Central States. Besides which, we have an excellent army with fine generals and officers. Why do we need assistance from abroad?"

"Just before I left, I made an agreement with the Lord of Qin that henceforward we would be joined in a military alliance," Lord Wen said.

"Zheng is a crucial member of the Central States," Xian Zhen replied. "When Lord Huan of Qi wanted to make himself hegemon, every battle was fought over Zheng. If you launch an attack as part of a joint force with Qin, you are going to come to grief over Zheng. It would be far better if we just used our own army."

"Zheng shares a border with us but is located far from Qin," Lord Wen pointed out. "What possible benefit could it be to them to dispute the spoils of this campaign?"

He sent someone to set a date with Qin, whereby they agreed that in the first week of the ninth month they would meet at the border with the state of Zheng. When Lord Wen set off, he took the Honorable Lan with him. The Honorable Lan was the younger half-brother of the present Earl of Zheng, who had fled to Jin some years earlier and accepted appointment there as a grandee. When Lord Wen of Jin succeeded to the marquisate, he often had to deal with the Honorable Lan, who was a most loyal and honest man, as a result of which Lord Wen had become extremely fond of him. On this occasion he was hoping that the Honorable Lan would serve as a guide and advisor, but he refused outright: "I have heard it said: 'Even when a gentleman goes abroad, he never forgets his home.' You are going on campaign against Zheng, my lord, and that is something that I cannot be involved in."

"Your resolution is admirable," Lord Wen replied. He instructed the Honorable Lan to stay at the border, for he fully intended that one day soon he would become the new Earl of Zheng.

Just as the Jin army entered the borders of Zheng, Lord Mu of Qin led a force of two hundred chariots to meet him, together with his advisor Baili Xi, the commander-in-chief of his forces Meng Mingshi, and the assistant generals Qi Zi, Pang Sun, Yang Sun, and so on. The two armies launched a joint attack on the border passes and then marched straight on Quwei, which they fortified with a huge palisade. The Jin army made camp at Hanling, west of the Zheng capital city, while the Qin army made camp at Fannan to the east. Soldiers patrolled the area day and night, making it impossible for anyone to get in or out to collect firewood. Lord Wen of Zheng was so terrified that he had no idea what to do.

Grandee Shu Zhan came forward and said: "Now that Qin and Jin have joined forces, their army is invincible and we cannot possibly fight them. The only thing we can do is to find a persuasive speaker to go and talk to the Earl of Qin and make him withdraw his army. If Qin leaves, Jin's might will be much reduced and we will have nothing to worry about."

"Who can persuade the Lord of Qin to withdraw?" the Earl of Zheng asked.

"Shi Zhi Hu can," Shu Zhan told him.

The Earl of Zheng then summoned Shi Zhi Hu to give him his orders. Shi Zhi Hu said: "I cannot possibly carry out this mission successfully. However, I can recommend someone to replace me. This man can launch a raging torrent or flatten a mountain using nothing but his words. However, he has grown old without ever being employed in any senior office. If you give him an official title and send him out to speak for you, there is no need to worry that the Lord of Qin will not listen."

"Who is this person?" the Earl of Zheng demanded.

"His name is Zhu Wu and he comes from Kaocheng," Shi Zhi Hu said. "He is already more than seventy years of age. He has served the state of Zheng as a stables supervisor through three generations of rulers. I hope that you will send him on his way with full honors."

The Earl of Zheng summoned Zhu Wu to court, and all the servants present laughed when they saw his white head, his hunchback, and his tottering walk. Zhu Wu bowed to the Earl of Zheng and said, "Why have you summoned me, my lord?"

"Shi Zhi Hu has recommended you as a most able speaker, and so I want you to persuade the Lord of Qin to withdraw his army," the Earl of Zheng explained. "If you succeed, I will grant you half my state."

Zhu Wu bowed twice and refused this commission, saying, "I am neither learned nor talented. Even when I was young, I never achieved anything of note, so now that I am old and tired, and stammer in my speech, is it likely that I could persuade anyone to do anything, let alone the lord of a thousand chariots?"

"You have served three generations of the Zheng ruling house, and the fact that you never received high office is our mistake," the Earl of Zheng said. "I now appoint you to the position of a middle-ranking minister and hope that you will undertake this mission for me."

Shi Zhi Hu also put in his word of praise from one side: "When a man grows old without ever having an opportunity to show his mettle, he can only bewail his fate. His Lordship now appreciates you and is determined to give you an official position, so you really should not refuse." Zhu Wu then accepted the order and left the court.

• • •

At that time the two states were laying extremely close siege to the capital, and Zhu Wu knew that Qin was on the east and Jin on the west. Though the two armies cooperated, they did not interfere with each other. Therefore, that night he ordered some strong knights to let him down on a rope from the top of the East Gate to the city. He was on his way towards the Qin camp when he was stopped by a sentry on patrol. This soldier refused to allow him to see the Earl of Qin, so Zhu Wu began to cry and scream outside the encampment. The guards then arrested him and dragged him in front of Lord Mu for questioning.

"Who are you?" Lord Mu demanded.

"I am Grandee Zhu Wu of Zheng."

"Why have you been crying like that?"

"I am bewailing the coming fall of Zheng!"

"Zheng is doomed," Lord Mu said flatly. "But why are you wailing outside my camp?"

"I was bemoaning the fate of Zheng, but also that of Qin," Zhu Wu declared. "I am not particularly upset by the fall of Zheng, but there is much to be concerned about in the fate of Qin!"

Lord Mu was infuriated. "What is wrong with my country?" he shouted. "If you do not explain yourself immediately, I will have your head cut off!"

Zhu Wu was not moved in the least by this threat.

Indeed:

His speech could make a stone idol open its eyes;
He could talk until even a terracotta warrior would nod its head.
He could make the shining sun rise during the night,
Or the Yellow River change direction and flow to the west.

"Qin and Jin have joined forces to attack Zheng, so there is no point in discussing whether Zheng is doomed or not, that is obvious," Zhu Wu explained. "If there were any advantage for Qin in the destruction of Zheng, why would I be here talking to you? However, not only will this campaign not bring you any advantage, it will actually harm you a great deal. Why are you wasting your resources and getting your soldiers killed in order to see someone else walk off with all the benefits?"

"When you say that this will not only not benefit me but actually harm my state, what do you mean?" Lord Mu asked curiously.

"Zheng is located on the eastern border of the state of Jin while Qin is located on the western border of the state of Jin, and in between the two there is a journey of one thousand *li*," Zhu Wu replied. "Qin is bordered to the east by Jin and to the south by Zhou; how do you imagine that you are going to pass these two states to take possession of Zheng? If Zheng is destroyed, their lands will be entirely taken over by

Jin. Are they going to give anything to you? Jin and Qin are not only neighbors but also rivals; the stronger Jin becomes, the weaker Qin will be. No one sensible would devise a plan that not only gives a great deal of land to someone else but also weakens your own state in the process. Besides which, as I am sure you remember, Lord Hui of Jin once promised to give you five cities beyond the Yellow River, but once he had assumed power he betrayed this agreement. Everyone in the world knows how much you have done for Jin, but what have they ever done to pay you back? Ever since the Lord of Jin returned to his state, he has increased the size of his army and recruited ever more generals into his service, getting stronger day by day. At the moment he is trying to expand his land holdings to the east by destroying Zheng, but the day may come when he wants to expand to the west, and that means Qin! Has Your Lordship not heard of what happened to Yu and Guo? They tricked the ruler of Yu into helping to destroy the state of Guo, then they went and attacked Yu. The ruler of Yu was stupid enough to help Jin to destroy his own state; is that not enough of a warning to you? You have done much to help Jin, but that means nothing to them, for Jin has deep-laid plans to make use of Qin. In spite of all your goodness and wisdom, you have fallen into their trap. That is why I said, 'This will not benefit you but can only bring you harm,' and why I have been crying."

Lord Mu had been sitting listening quietly for a long time, but now he leapt up with an expression of alarm. Nodding his head over and over again, he said, "You are absolutely right!"

Baili Xi came forward and said, "This Zhu Wu is here because he wants to destroy the alliance between our two countries. You must not listen to him, my lord!"

"If Your Lordship would be prepared to lift the siege," Zhu Wu said, "I will swear a blood covenant with you that sees the Earl of Zheng abandon his alliance with Chu and throw his lot in with Qin. If Your Lordship has any business in the east, as your ambassadors come and go, they can pick up the necessary formal gifts in Zheng, just as if it were your own treasury."

Lord Mu was very pleased with this idea, and the two men then smeared their mouths with blood to seal the oath of allegiance. He ordered his three generals, Qi Zi, Feng Sun, and Yang Sun, to stay behind and help guard Zheng with a force of two thousand soldiers. Then without saying a word to Jin, he secretly stood down his army and left.

A historian wrote a poem about this:

A cloud of dust rose up above Fannan and Hanling;
An old minister waggled his tongue to great effect.
Supposing that someone other than Zhu Wu had been sent,
These mountains and rivers would all have belonged to Qin or Jin.

This news was quickly reported to the Jin camp by spies. Lord Wen of Jin was absolutely furious. Hu Yan was standing beside him and offered to go and attack the Qin army.

Do you know whether Lord Wen agreed to this? READ ON.

Chapter Forty-four

Shu Zhan grabs hold of a cauldron and defies the Marquis of Jin.

Xian Gao fakes an order to feast the Qin army.

After Lord Mu of Qin made his private covenant with Zheng, he withdrew his army in direct contravention of his earlier agreement with Jin. Lord Wen of Jin was absolutely furious.

Hu Yan came forward and said, "Qin cannot have gone far. I ask your permission, my lord, to take an army to attack them. Their soldiers will be thinking about going home, so they will have no stomach for a fight. We will be able to defeat them in a single battle. Once we have defeated Qin, Zheng will be terrified. They will then surrender without a fight."

"No," Lord Wen said. "It was only thanks to the Qin army that I was able to bring an end to the civil war in Jin. Without the Lord of Qin, would I be here today? When Cheng Dechen behaved so badly towards me, I still withdrew three stages to avoid him to thank Chu for their generosity towards me when I was in exile. And in the case of Qin, our two houses are joined by marriage alliances! We will continue the siege of Zheng without them."

He sent one half of the army to make camp at Hanling and continued the assault on Zheng as before.

The Earl of Zheng spoke to Zhu Wu about this. "It is thanks to you that the Qin army has gone home. What can we do about the fact that the Jin army is still here?"

"I have heard that the Honorable Lan is much loved by the Marquis of Jin," Zhu Wu replied. "If you send an ambassador to invite him home and then request a peace treaty with Jin, they are sure to agree."

"No ambassador could be more suitable than yourself," the Earl of Zheng said.

"Zhu Wu has already done enough," Shi Shenfu declared. "Let me go in his stead."

He left the city with a great quantity of treasure and marched straight at the Jin encampment, where he requested an audience with the Marquis of Jin. Lord Wen ordered that he be admitted to his presence. Shi Shenfu bowed twice and presented the treasure to His Lordship. As he had been instructed by the Earl of Zheng, he said: "His Lordship is in secret communication with the southern barbarians, because he does not dare to risk an open breach. However, he has no intention of betraying you, my lord. Now that you have made your feelings on the subject known, His Lordship is aware of having offended against you, so he does not begrudge any of the treasures accumulated by his ancestors, but presents them to your entourage. His Lordship's younger brother, the Honorable Lan, is known to be close to you, so we beg that you will forgive us for his sake if nothing else. Why do you not send the Honorable Lan back to Zheng, that he may be present day and night at our court? Surely that would prevent any implication of disloyalty."

"You have been able to alienate us from Qin," Lord Wen responded, "which was clearly done in the belief that without them we will not be able to force Zheng to surrender. Now you have come here to ask for a peace treaty, so I imagine that you have had news of an army coming to your relief. Are you waiting for Chu to rescue you? If you want me to withdraw my army, you are going to have to do two things for me."

"Please explain," Shi Shenfu said.

"You are going to have to appoint the Honorable Lan as the heir to the earldom of Zheng," Lord Wen told him, "and you are going to have to hand over Shu Zhan as a sign of your sincerity."

Shi Shenfu went back to the capital to report what the Marquis of Jin had said to the Earl of Zheng. The Earl of Zheng said, "I do not have any children, and I have heard that there have been good omens about the Honorable Lan. If he becomes scion, the country will flourish. However, Shu Zhan is like my own arms or legs; how can he possibly leave me?"

"I have heard it said that a good subject is ashamed if his ruler suffers unnecessary worry and will die to prevent his ruler from feeling humiliation," Shu Zhan exclaimed. "Now Jin is demanding that I be handed over to them. If I do not go, then their armies will continue to besiege us. Even if they kill me, it would be disloyal of me to try and avoid this fate; I cannot allow Your Lordship to suffer worry and humiliation! I am willing to go."

"If you go, they will kill you," the Earl of Zheng wailed. "I cannot bear it!"

"You can't bear the prospect of my death," Shu Zhan told him, "but what about the suffering of your people? The destruction of your state? If giving me up can save your people and bring peace to the country, what is the point of keeping me?"

The Earl of Zheng sent him on his way with tears in his eyes. Shu Zhan was escorted to the Jin army by Shi Shenfu and Hou Xuanduo. They said, "His Lordship is deeply in awe of the Marquis of Jin and would not dare to refuse his two requests. Shu Zhan now awaits your decision as to how to punish him outside your tent. Please, will you hand over the Honorable Lan that he may be appointed the scion of our state, so that we may carry out the second of Your Lordship's wishes?"

The Marquis of Jin was very pleased. He ordered Hu Yan to summon the Honorable Lan from the eastern border. Meanwhile, he commanded Shi Shenfu and Hou Xuanduo to stay at the camp to wait for him.

The Marquis of Jin had an audience with Shu Zhan, at which he shouted: "You were in control of the government of Zheng, and yet you allowed your ruler to behave rudely to a passing visitor. That is your first crime. You swore a blood covenant and then betrayed it; that is your second crime." He ordered his servants to bring in a huge cauldron in which he proposed to boil Shu Zhan.

Shu Zhan's expression did not change in the slightest. He folded his hands respectfully and said to Lord Wen, "Once I have said my final words, you can kill me."

"What have you got to say?" Lord Wen demanded.

"When you came to us in trouble," Shu Zhan answered, "I regularly told His Lordship: 'The Honorable Chonger of Jin is a clever man, and his companions would all make excellent ministers. If he returns to his state, he is sure to become hegemon over the feudal lords.' At the covenant at Wen, I again urged His Lordship: 'You must serve Jin to the best of your abilities. If you anger them, they will not pardon you.' Heaven sent down this disaster upon us and ensured that His Lordship would not listen to my advice. Today you are in a position to punish us, and my lord, knowing that I am innocent, did not want to deliver me into your hands. However, I believe in the principle that a subject should die to save his ruler from humiliation, and that is why I accept any punishment you care to mete out, providing that it may save my fellow citizens from danger. A person who correctly weighs up a situation is wise. A person who does his very best to save his country is loyal. A person who does not run away when disaster threatens is brave. A person who accepts his own death in order to save the lives of others is good. I have done my very best to be good, brave, loyal, and wise, but apparently according to the laws of Jin that means that I deserve to be boiled to death." He grabbed hold of one of the lugs on the cauldron and shouted, "From here on, let others take warning from my example!"

Lord Wen was shocked and immediately gave orders that he be pardoned. He said, "I was just testing you. You really are a most remarkable man!" He rewarded him with lavish gifts.

That same day the Honorable Lan arrived, and Lord Wen explained to him why he had been summoned. He instructed Shu Zhan, Shi Shenfu, and Hou Xuanduo to greet the Honorable Lan using all the protocol appropriate for an audience with the scion. Afterwards, these men left for the capital. The Earl of Zheng did indeed appoint the Honorable Lan as his heir, and the Jin army subsequently withdrew. However, from this time onwards the alliance that had existed between Jin and Qin was over.

A bearded old man wrote a poem that bemoans this:

The military alliance between Qin and Jin was going strong,
Only to be destroyed by a few words from Zhu Wu.
Simply for the sake of some minor territorial gains to the east,
A treaty that would have brought years of peace was broken.

It was at some point during this year that Wei Chou got drunk and fell off his chariot, breaking his arm. This accident caused old internal injuries to break open, as a result of which he vomited up great quantities of blood and died. Lord Wen allowed his son, Wei Ke, to succeed to his title. Not long after that Hu Mao and Hu Yan died, one after the other. Lord Wen of Jin was terribly upset and said, "That I was able to escape from trouble and reach my current eminence is really thanks largely to my two uncles. I was never expecting that they would leave me like this! I feel as though I have lost my right arm. This is terrible!"

Xu Chen stepped forward and said, "I know that Your Lordship regrets the loss of these two talented men. I would like to recommend someone who deserves appointment as a minister, and I hope that you will appreciate his abilities!"

"Whom would you like to recommend?" Lord Wen inquired.

"When I was heading one of Your Lordship's embassies, I happened to pass through the wilds of Ji and noticed a man who was ploughing the fields," Xu Chen explained. "When his wife brought him his lunch, she presented it to him with both hands and he took it with a reverent expression. He then performed a sacrifice before eating, while his wife stood in attendance to one side. After some time when his meal was finished, this man waited until his wife had gone before he went back to his ploughing. At no time did he relax the solemn expression on his face. If a man can make himself so respected by his wife, he will have no problem with other people. I have heard it said that a man who is respected by others is sure to be virtuous. I asked his name and discovered that this is Xi Que, the son of Xi Rui. If he were to obtain office in Jin, I am sure that he would prove in no way inferior to Hu Yan."

"His father was guilty of terrible crimes," Lord Wen said. "How am I supposed to employ him?"

"The sage-kings Yao and Shun had such wicked children as Danzhu and Shangjun, while the evil Gun produced the virtuous Yu," Xu Chen replied. "You cannot tell whether someone is going to be good or bad by looking at their parentage. Why should you miss the opportunity to employ such a brilliant man purely because you hated his father?"

"You are right," Lord Wen declared. "Would you summon him to court for me?"

"I was worried that he might run away to another country and end up serving one of our enemies, so I brought him home with me," Xu Chen explained. "If you wish to command him to come here, you had better behave with all the ceremony required when meeting an exceptionally clever man."

Lord Wen took his advice and ordered the palace servants to prepare an official hat and robe, which he then sent to Xi Que with the summons. Xi Que bowed twice, kowtowed, and refused to accept them: "I am just a farmer from the wilds of Ji. It is already extremely generous of His Lordship not to execute me on account of my father's crimes. I would not dare to befoul the court with my presence!"

The palace servants urged him over and over again to get into the carriage, and in the end Xi Que did put on the official regalia and go to court. Xi Que was a tall man with a prominent nose and strong jaw; his voice was bell-like in its resonance. At this first meeting, Lord Wen was extremely pleased. He immediately appointed Xu Chen as commander-in-chief of the Lower Army and ordered Xi Que to be his deputy. He also changed the name of the two "infantry divisions" to recognize the fact that they were actually armies, and he called them the New Upper Army and the New Lower Army. Zhao Cui was the general in command of the New Upper Army with Qi Zheng as his deputy. Xu Chen's son, Xu Ying, was placed in command of the New Lower Army with Xian Du as his deputy. Jin already had three armies, and with the addition of these two, there were five in total, the same as the Zhou Son of Heaven. Brave soldiers and brilliant strategists having flocked to his standard, the army was amazingly strong. When King Cheng of Chu heard this news, he became frightened and sent Grandee Dou Zhang to Jin to request a peace treaty. Lord Wen of Jin remained appreciative of how kindly he had been treated by Chu in the past and agreed to this. He sent Grandee Yang Chufu to head an embassy back to Chu. No more of this.

. . .

In the twenty-fourth year of the reign of King Xiang of Zhou, Jie, Lord Wen of Zheng died. The ministers then supported the succession of his younger brother, the Honorable Lan, to the earldom. He became Lord Mu. Everything corresponded with the omen of the orchid before he was born. That winter, Lord Wen of Jin became seriously ill. He summoned Zhao Cui, Xian Zhen, Hu Shegu, and Yang Chufu to hear his last will proclaimed. He instructed them to support the accession of Scion Huan as the new lord, but not to try and continue the hegemony. Because he was afraid that his other sons would not be prepared to simply live in peace at home, he sent the Honorable Yong to serve in Qin and the Honorable Le to seek office in Chen. The Honorable Yong was the son of Lady Qi of Du, while the Honorable Le was the son of Lady Ying of Chen. He sent his youngest son, the Honorable Heitun, to go and serve in Zhou that he might become close to the royal family. Lord Wen died at the age of sixty-eight, after eight years in power.

A historian wrote a poem in praise:

After nineteen years spent wandering in exile,
This dragon returned to his lair to take power.
In his dealings with the Zhou king he was always respectful and loyal;
At the battle of Chengpu the righteousness of his armies became manifest.
He expunged the humiliations he had suffered and honored his benefactors,
He was completely impartial in issuing rewards and punishments.
Although his great abilities were a gift from Heaven,
He was helped by his advisors and relied upon the wisdom of his companions.

Scion Huan presided over his father's funeral and then succeeded to the marquisate as Lord Xiang. His Lordship escorted Lord Wen's catafalque for burial in Quwo, but when they left the capital city of Jiang, the coffin suddenly emitted a loud bellow, like the lowing of an ox. At the same time the coffin suddenly became as heavy as Mount Tai, so that the cart carrying it could not possibly move. All the ministers present were deeply alarmed. Grand Astrologer Guo Yan performed a divination about this and obtained the following message: "A rat from the west has climbed over our wall. With one blow of my huge stick I will injure it in three places."

"Within the next couple of days there is sure to be news of an army coming from the west," Guo Yan announced. "If we attack them, we will win a great victory. The soul of His Late Lordship has given us these instructions." The ministers all bowed, and the noise from the coffin ceased and it became light again, so they were able to proceed as before.

"Qin is in the west," Xian Zhen said thoughtfully. He sent someone to go there secretly and discover what was going on.

• • •

Let us now turn to another part of the story. As mentioned previously, the Qin generals Qi Zi, Feng Sun, and Yang Sun had been left camped at the North Gate of the Zheng capital city. When Jin escorted the Honorable Lan back to Zheng and he was established as the scion, they were furious and said, "We stayed on guard here to prevent any trouble from the Jin army. However, the Earl of Zheng has now surrendered to Jin, making it clear that our presence here is pointless." A secret message concerning these developments was sent back to Qin. Lord Mu was also extremely angry about this, but because it involved the Marquis of Jin, he did not dare to express his resentment.

When the Honorable Lan succeeded to the title, he did not treat Qi Zi and the others with any special ceremony. Qi Zi discussed the situation with Feng Sun and Yang Sun: "We have been camped here far from home with no indication of when our service is supposed to end. We had better encourage His Lordship to launch a surprise attack upon Zheng, that we may all obtain lavish booty before we go home."

Just as they were discussing this, they heard that Lord Wen of Jin had died. Qi Zi raised his hands to his head and said, "Heaven wants me to succeed!" He then sent a trusted messenger back to Qin, to tell Lord Mu: "Zheng has entrusted me with the keys to the North Gate. If you were to send troops here in secret and make a surprise attack upon them, I could assist you from inside the walls of the city. Zheng will then be destroyed. Jin is caught up in national mourning, so they cannot possibly come to the rescue. Besides which, the Lord of Zheng has only just succeeded to the title, so they will be totally unprepared. This opportunity should not be lost!"

When Lord Mu of Qin received this letter, he discussed it with Jian Shu and Baili Xi. The two ministers both remonstrated: "Qin is a thousand *li* away from Zheng; we cannot take over their territory, and the most we can hope for is to obtain some prisoners of war and booty. If you have to send your army such a distance, the journey is sure to take a great deal of time. How can you keep it a secret? If they hear about what we have planned, they will be prepared. If the massive effort of launching such a campaign is all in vain, are you not worried about possible attacks on your authority? If you first send your troops to garrison a city and then change your mind and conspire against them instead, everyone will consider you untrustworthy. If you take advantage of a period of national mourning to attack, you are behaving most ungenerously. If you engage in such a risky endeavor for such a tiny prospect of gain, you are most unwise. How can you possibly afford to run such a risk?"

"I have established three lords of Jin," Lord Mu said crossly, "I have pacified two civil wars in Jin, and my awe-inspiring reputation is known to all the world. It is only because the Marquis of Jin defeated Chu in the battle of Chengpu that I had to yield the hegemony to him. Now that the Marquis of Jin has gone, is there anyone who is my match? Zheng is like a caged bird—where can they go? Let us take advantage of this opportunity to destroy Zheng and then offer to exchange their lands for the territory Jin holds east of the Yellow River; Jin is sure to agree to that. What can possibly go wrong?"

Jian Shu tried again. "Why do you not send an ambassador to condole with Jin and also with Zheng? That way you can discover if Zheng is indeed vulnerable to attack, rather than being misled by Qi Zi's baseless remarks!"

"If I have to wait until after an ambassador has offered formal condolences before sending out my army," Lord Mu complained, "by the time he has gone and come back, almost a year will have passed. When commanding troops, they must strike like lightning, catching the enemy unaware. What does an old idiot like you know about it?" He then secretly issued orders to Qi Zi: "In the first week of the second month, our army will be waiting at the North Gate. You must make no mistake in our joint attack!"

He summoned Baili Shi and appointed him commander-in-chief with Xiqi Shu and Jian Bing to assist him. He selected an army of more than three thousand crack troops, with three hundred chariots. They left the Qin capital by the East Gate. Baili Shi was the son of Baili Xi, while Jian Bing was Jian Shu's son. On the day that they left, Jian Shu and Baili Xi saw them off with tears in their eyes. "How terrible! How sad! We watch you leave, knowing that we will not see you come back!"

When Lord Mu heard this, he was absolutely furious and sent someone to upbraid his two ministers: "Why are you crying over my army? Are you deliberately trying to destroy their morale?"

"We are not crying over your army," Jian Shu and Baili Xi replied. "We are crying about our sons!"

When Jian Bing saw how upset his father was, he wanted to refuse to go. Jian Shu said, "We both of us enjoy a generous salary from the Qin state. Even if you have to die for them—that is what they are paying for." He secretly handed over a bamboo document sealed very tightly and instructed him: "You must do exactly what it says here." Jian Bing accepted the letter and set off, but he was upset and frightened. Baili Shi, on the other hand, was entirely convinced that his bravery and intelligence were equal to any challenge, so he was sure that he could make a success of this mission. He paid no attention to his father's distress.

Once the army had set off, Jian Shu excused himself from attending court on the grounds of ill health and requested permission to retire. Lord Mu wanted to force him to continue working, but Jian Shu insisted that he was far too unwell and begged to be allowed to return to Zhi Village. Baili Xi visited him at home to ask after his health and said to Jian Shu, "It is not that I am ignorant of the danger threatening this country. The only reason I am prepared to stay here is that I still hope that my son will come back alive. Do you have any final instructions for me?"

"This time the Qin army is going to be defeated," Jian Shu told him. "I hope that you will inform Noble Grandson Qi of this and get him to station boats on the Yellow River. That way anyone who survives will be able to make their way home. Remember this! Remember this!"

"I will do as you say immediately!" Baili Xi declared.

When Lord Mu realized that Jian Shu was determined to go home, he rewarded him with twenty pounds of gold and one hundred bolts of silk. All the officials gathered in the suburbs to see him off.

Baili Xi grabbed hold of Noble Grandson Qi's hand and told him exactly what Jian Shu had said: "He could not entrust this mission to anyone else; you are the only person who can carry it out! You are brave and loyal enough to deal with the danger that threatens our country. You must not let anyone else know! You will have to make all your plans to deal with this in secret."

"I will do everything that I can," the Noble Grandson Qi said. He then began the preparation of boats, which does not need to be described.

. . .

Baili Shi had witnessed Jian Bing being given the secret document by his father, and he thought that it must contain some kind of cunning plan to destroy Zheng, so that evening when they made camp he went and demanded to see what it said. Jian Bing opened and read it. The letter consisted of two lines:

> Zheng poses no threat to you; the danger is all from Jin. You must be very careful of the passes around Mount Xiao, which is where I will go to collect your body.

Baili Shi rushed out, his hands over his eyes, saying over and over again: "Bah! What a fool! And how unlucky! How inauspicious!" Indeed, Jian Bing was himself not at all sure that his father was right.

The Qin generals had led their army out of the capital on Bingxu day in the twelfth month, and in the first month of the following year they passed the North Gate of the Zhou capital city. "The Son of Heaven is present here," Baili Shi said. "Although we are engaged in a military campaign, which makes it inappropriate for us to seek an audience with His Majesty, there is no reason to be disrespectful!" He ordered his entourage to remove their armor and get down from their chariots to walk.

The junior general in charge of the vanguard, Bao Manzi, was the bravest of all the warriors present. As they were passing the gates to the capital city, as his chariot moved at full speed across the plain, he ran as fast as he could and leapt into it. Baili Shi sighed and said, "If only all my officers were like Bao Manzi . . . is there anything I could not accomplish?"

The generals muttered to each other, "How can we be seen to be inferior to Bao Manzi?" They fought amongst themselves to be the first to come forward and have a go. They shouted and waved their arms: "Anyone who cannot leap into a moving chariot will have to make their way to join our rearguard."

In an infantry army, the rearguard is the weakest part; it is only when the army has been defeated that it becomes important. To be sent to the back of the rearguard was therefore a humiliation.

There were three hundred chariots in this army, and all of the generals and officers successful leapt into theirs. Once they had jumped in, the chariots moved at even greater speed, disappearing in a cloud of dust.

At this time King Xiang of Zhou sent Prince Hu and Royal Grandson Man to observe the Qin army. Once they had passed, they went back to report to King Xiang.

Prince Hu sighed and said, "The Qin army is incredibly powerful; who can withstand them? I am afraid that this time Zheng is not going to survive!"

Royal Grandson Man was still very young, but he laughed and said nothing.

"What do you think, kid?" King Xiang asked.

"According to the rules of ritual propriety, when passing the gates of the Son of Heaven, you should remove all your weapons and hurry on," Royal Grandson Man replied. "Today they only took off their armor, which means that they have behaved very rudely. To get into your chariot by jumping up is to disrespect your equipment. Such open disrespect means that they do not understand the seriousness of what they are trying to do; such a failure in ritual propriety means that they will be easily put to flight. Accordingly, Qin is going to suffer a humiliating defeat. They will bring no harm to other people, only to themselves."

. . .

There was a merchant from the state of Zheng whose name was Xian Gao, who made a living by trading in cattle. In the past Prince Tui of Zhou had been particularly enamored of cattle, and merchants from Zheng and Wey had made a great profit selling their animals in Zhou. At this time Xian Gao was still engaged in this business. Although he was only a merchant, he was entirely loyal to his lord and very patriotic. He had many plans for how to resolve problems and prevent disaster, but having failed to find anyone to recommend him for office, he was reduced to making his living from trade. On this occasion, he was going to Zhou to sell a couple of hundred animals. As he approached the Liyang Ford, he spotted an old friend named Jian Ta, who had just arrived from the state of Qin.

When Xian Gao had exchanged greetings with Jian Ta, he asked, "What is happening in Qin nowadays?"

"Qin has sent their three generals to make a surprise attack on Zheng," Jian Ta replied. "They set out on Bingxu day in the twelfth month, so they will be here any minute now."

Xian Gao was very shocked. "My country is suddenly in terrible danger. If I did not know anything about it, then whatever happens would not be my fault. But now that I have heard about it, if I do nothing to prevent disaster and the state altars collapse, how could I ever face going home?" He then came up with a plan.

Once he had said goodbye to Jian Ta, he sent someone to go back to report to Zheng as quickly as possible, to instruct His Lordship to prepare for battle. At the same time, he selected twenty prime beasts to offer as a feast for the Qin army, leaving the remaining animals behind. Xian Gao rode in a light chariot as he headed out to find the Qin army. When he passed through the state of Hua, he ran into their advance guard at the Yan River. Xian Gao blocked the road, shouting, "I am an ambassador from the state of Zheng! I am here to have an audience with your generals!"

The advance guard went back to report this to the main camp. Baili Shi was amazed and thought to himself, "How did Zheng find out that our army was on the way? And they have managed to send their ambassador here to meet us! Let us see what he has to say for himself." He had Xian Gao brought before his chariot.

Xian Gao pretended that he had received an order from the Earl of Zheng, and said to Baili Shi: "When my lord heard that three Qin generals were coming to our humble country, he immediately sent me out to meet you and to present you with meat for a banquet, not begrudging any expense. We are caught between a couple of great states and are regularly bullied and humiliated by them; that is why you have been forced to garrison us for so long and from such a distance. We were afraid that some mistake or misapprehension had caused you to become angry with us. His Lordship is now busy day and night making preparations for your reception. I hope that you can forgive him!"

"If the Earl of Zheng has indeed sent you here to offer this gift," Baili Shi asked, "why do you not have any official credentials?"

"When you left the Qin capital on Bingxu day in the twelfth month," Xian Gao responded, "His Lordship was immediately aware of the nature of the force sent against him, and he was afraid that if he waited for all the documentation to be prepared, I might not be in time to intercept you. He therefore gave me oral instructions that I should apologize to you on my knees. He did not mention anything else."

Baili Shi leaned over and said in his ear, "My lord's objective this time is Hua and not Zheng." He issued orders: "The army is to make camp at the Yan River."

Xian Gao expressed his thanks and left.

Xiqi Shu asked Baili Shi, "Why are we making camp at the Yan River?"

"We have advanced one thousand *li* towards Zheng," Baili Shi replied, "but we could only attack them successfully if they were not anticipating our arrival. The people of Zheng knew that we were coming on the very day that we set out, so they will be fully prepared. If we attack them, we will find their fortifications impossible to break down; if we besiege them, we will find that we do not have enough soldiers to make it watertight. However, the state of Hua is completely unprepared, so we had better make a surprise attack and conquer them. With the captives and booty that we obtain, we can go back and report to our lord. Our mission will then not have been entirely pointless."

That night at the third watch, the three Qin generals each took their troops in a different direction and united in a surprise attack upon the city-state of Hua. The Lord of Hua fled to the Di. The Qin army robbed and plundered to their hearts' content, taking all the jade and silk as well as all the people they could find.

When historians talk about these events, they suggest that the commander-in-chief of the Qin army had never intended to attack Zheng. However, if it had not been for Xian Gao pretending to have received an order to give the army meat for a feast, according to the original plan it would have been Zheng that was destroyed and not Hua.

There is a poem that praises him:

After a journey of a thousand *li*, these soldiers were still as fierce as wolves;
It was no simple trick to blunt the edge of these weapons!
If Xian Gao had not faked an order offering this banquet to the invaders,
Would the state of Zheng have been able to avoid destruction?

After the state of Hua was destroyed, its ruler found it impossible to return to his country. These lands were eventually incorporated into the state of Wey. However, this is not part of our story.

• • •

When Lord Mu of Zheng received the secret message from the merchant Xian Gao, he did not entirely believe it. Nevertheless, in the first week of the second month he sent someone to the guest house to spy on what Qi Zi, Feng Sun, and Yang Sun were up to, only to discover that they had collected a large number of chariots, weapons, and well-fed horses. The Qin soldiers of the garrison were in the middle of their training, so clearly once the main army arrived, they were prepared to open the gate for them.

When his servant reported back, the Earl of Zheng was deeply shocked. He then sent Grandee Zhu Wu to visit Qi Zi, Feng Sun, and Yang Sun, to offer them a parting gift of silk. He said to them: "You have spent a long time in our humble country. We have nothing particular to offer you, the treasures of our Yuan Palace having long ago been exhausted. However, observing your preparations today, I can see that you are planning to leave. Since Baili Shi is at present on campaign between Zhou and Hua, why don't you go and join him?"

Qi Zi was alarmed by this. "Our plan is known!" he thought to himself. "Even if the army comes here, nothing will come of it; what is more, I am likely to be punished for this failure. I certainly cannot stay in Zheng any longer, but I also cannot go home to Qin!" He came up with a speech of thanks to Zhu Wu, then immediately fled into exile in the state of Qi with several dozen family members. Feng Sun and Yang Sun ran away to the state of Song, thus avoiding any punishment for this turn of events. Their soldiers were left leaderless and congregated at the North Gate, wanting to cause trouble. Lord Mu of Zheng sent Shi Zhi Hu to give them food. After the crowds had been broken up by being sent to different locations, they were escorted home. Lord Mu of Zheng rewarded Xian Gao's achievements with an appointment as a military commandant. From this time onward, the state of Zheng was at peace.

. . .

Lord Xiang of Jin was at Quwo, preparing for his father's funeral, when spies reported: "General Baili Shi of the state of Qin is leading his army east, but we do not know where he is going!" Lord Xiang was deeply alarmed and immediately sent his servants to summon his ministers to discuss the situation. Xian Zhen had already made his own investigations and discovered that the Lord of Qin was planning to attack Zheng. He came to have an audience with Lord Xiang.

Do you know how Xian Zhen planned to deal with this situation? READ ON.

Chapter Forty-five

Lord Xiang of Jin defeats Qin while still in mourning.

Commander-in-Chief Xian Zhen removes his armor to be killed by the Di.

The commander-in-chief of the Central Army of Jin, Xian Zhen, was aware from the beginning that the state of Qin was planning to make a surprise attack upon Zheng, so he had an audience with Lord Xiang, at which he said: "Qin has ignored the remonstrance of Jian Shu and Baili Xi and come one thousand *li* to attack their prey. This is what Astrologer Guo Yan meant when he said, 'A rat from the west has climbed over our wall.' We must attack them as soon as possible. You cannot let this opportunity slip."

Luan Zhi came forward and said, "Qin behaved with great kindness towards His Late Lordship; we have not yet done anything to repay them but instead plan to attack their army. How would His Late Lordship feel about that?"

"It is just what he would have wanted us to do!" Xian Zhen replied. "When he died, the other lords who had covenanted with him came to pay their last respects and condole with us as soon as they could, but Qin did nothing. What is more, they have now taken their forces through our territory to attack a state whose ruling house is closely related to us; what could be more disrespectful than that? In the circumstances, His Lordship cannot possibly rest in peace, let alone feel that we should be requiting their kindness! Besides which, our two states made an agreement that we would form a military alliance. During the siege of Zheng, they betrayed that alliance and went home. That is quite enough to prove what kind of people we are dealing with! Since they don't seem to feel any need to keep faith with us, why should we treat them with any consideration?"

"Qin has not yet entered our territory," Luan Zhi responded. "Surely it would not be right to attack them."

"When Lord Mu of Qin put His Late Lordship in power in Jin," Xian Zhen replied, "it was not because he wanted the best for our state, but to improve his own position. When His Lordship became hegemon over the feudal lords, Qin put a good face on things, but they were in fact terribly jealous. Now they are taking advantage of our being involved in a period of national mourning to attack; this is clearly done to humiliate us for not being able to protect Zheng. We have to send our army out or we will appear incapable! They may well not carry out their assault on Zheng, for they are quite strong enough to attack us instead. As the proverb goes: 'It takes only an instant to make an enemy, but several lifetimes to undo the damage.' If we do not attack Qin, how will we survive?"

"Even if you are right in your assertion that we should attack Qin," Zhao Cui said, "Lord Xiang is at present in mourning for his father. If he were to raise an army and go to war, I am afraid that it would contravene every rule of ritual propriety."

"Ritual propriety demands that a son who is mourning the death of his father should move out of the family home to live in a hut at the site of his father's grave, that he may perform his last act of filial piety," Xian Zhen said. "However, what act could be more filial than defeating a powerful enemy and bringing peace to the country? Even if the rest of you all refuse to have anything to do with this, I will go alone."

Xu Chen and the others supported his plan, and Xian Zhen then requested that Lord Xiang raise an army while still in mourning.

"When do you think that the Qin army will return?" Lord Xiang inquired. "What route will they take?"

Xian Zhen calculated it on his fingers and said: "I am working on the principle that the Qin army will not be able to conquer Zheng and they cannot stay long away from home since they have made no arrangements for support. They will come back in the fourth month at the latest, so at the beginning of summer they will cross Lake Mian. Lake Mian is the border between Qin and Jin. To the west lie the two peaks of Mount Xiao. It is thirty-five *li* from the West Peak to the East Peak, and that is the route that the Qin army will have to take when they go home. Mount Xiao is very densely wooded and the rocky outcrops are extremely precipitous; they will have great difficulty in getting their chariots across this terrain, so they will have to unyoke the trace-horses. If we have troops waiting in ambush there to attack them when they least expect it, we will be able to capture the entire army and their generals."

"We will follow your plan," Lord Xiang agreed.

Xian Zhen then sent his son, Xian Qieju, to take five thousand soldiers and set an ambush on the left side of Mount Xiao together with Tu Ji. He ordered Xu Chen's son, Xu Ying, to take another five thousand soldiers and set an ambush on the right side of Mount Xiao together with Hu Juju. They were to wait until the Qin army arrived and then attack in a pincer formation. He ordered Hu Yan's son, Hu Shegu, to take five thousand soldiers and wait in hiding at the West Peak of Mount Xiao, together with Han Ziyu. They had instructions to cut down trees beforehand, which they could use to block the road. He ordered Liang Yaomi's son, Liang Hong, to wait in hiding at the East Peak of Mount Xiao with five thousand soldiers, together with Lai Ju. They had instructions to remain there until after the whole of the Qin army had passed and then go in pursuit. Xian Zhen and the other generals—Zhao Cui, Luan Zhi, Xu Chen, Yang Chufu, Xian Mie, and so on—all followed Lord Xiang of Jin to make camp twenty *li* away. Each of them was in command of his own troops, who would support the attack. As the saying goes: "Stationed by the mouth of the cave, you can shoot the fiercest tiger; having prepared delicious bait, you can hook both fish and turtles."

. . .

The Qin army conquered Hua in the second month, capturing a rich booty. They then set off home with groaning baggage carts. Although they had not succeeded in making a surprise attack on Zheng, they were nevertheless hoping to be able to excuse this failure. In the first week of the fourth month, they arrived at Lake Mian.

"West of Mian Lake is the narrow pass between the two peaks of Mount Xiao," Jian Bing said to Baili Shi. "My father warned me that we should be extremely cautious there. I hope that you will not just rush in."

"I have not been scared by anything in our journey of one thousand *li*," Baili Shi boasted. "Once we have passed Mount Xiao, we are at the borders of Qin and in reach of home. What disaster can possibly overtake us there?"

"We all know how brave you are, but it never hurts to be careful," Xiqi Shu said. "Supposing that Jin has set ambushes there and we get attacked. How will you stop their onslaught?"

"If you are that frightened of Jin, I will go on ahead," Baili Shi declared. "If there are any ambushes, I will deal with them."

He then ordered Cavalry General Bao Manzi to unfurl his battle standard and go on ahead to clear the route. Baili Shi headed the second division, Xiqi Shu the third, and Jian Bing the fourth. Each division of the army proceeded just a *li* or two ahead of the next. Bao Manzi was used to fighting with a spear that weighed eighty pounds, which he could move as fast as the wind. He believed himself to be the world's finest warrior. Once his advance guard had crossed Mian Lake, they moved westwards until they arrived at the Eastern Peak of Mount Xiao. Suddenly thunderous drumming shook the mountain valley, and a chariot appeared out of nowhere. A great general was standing on the chariot, and he moved to block the road. He asked, "Are you the Qin general Baili Shi? I have waited a long time to meet you!"

"And who might you be?" Bao Manzi asked.

"I am General Lai Ju of Jin," he answered.

"Tell Luan Zhi or Wei Chou to come here and fight a few rounds with me," Bao Manzi replied. "You are nobody—how dare you block my route home? Get out of the way! If you delay any longer, I will kill you with a single blow from my spear!"

Lai Ju was enraged by this, and, grabbing hold of his spear, he stabbed straight at Bao Manzi's chest. With a deft movement, Bao Manzi parried the blow and reposted with his own thrust. Lai Ju got out of the way as quickly as he could, but the blow was delivered with such force that it struck the railing in front of his chariot. With this single thrust of his spear, Bao Manzi cut the railing in two. Lai Ju was impressed by his bravery and could not stop himself from sighing with admiration: "Your reputation is well deserved, Baili Shi."

Bao Manzi laughed and said, "I am Bao Manzi, one of Commander-in-Chief Baili Shi's junior generals. Our commander-in-chief would hardly be willing to cross swords with someone like you. You had better get out of the way as quickly as you can, because otherwise, when the commander-in-chief gets here, you are a dead man."

Lai Ju was terrified out of his wits and thought, "If the junior general is like this, what on earth is Baili Shi like?" He shouted out, "If I let you pass, you must not harm any of my troops." He moved his chariot to one side of the road and let Bao Manzi and the rest of the vanguard through.

Bao Manzi sent an officer to report back to Commander-in-Chief Baili Shi: "There was a small ambush of Jin soldiers, but they have already been forced to retreat. You had better unite the army in one place and get them through the Mount Xiao passes as quickly as possible. Everything will be fine."

Baili Shi was very happy to get this news, and he instructed Xiqi Shu and Jian Bing to move their armies up to allow them to proceed all together. Lai Ju took his troops back to report to Liang Hong and praised Bao Manzi's bravery.

Liang Hong laughed: "Even if he is a whale or an alligator, he is already caught in our iron net and will not be able to escape. We will wait here until they have all gone past and then come up from behind. That way we will win a complete victory."

. . .

Baili Shi and the three other generals advanced to the East Peak of Mount Xiao, where in the space of a couple of *li* were the Ladder to Heaven, the Falling Horse Cliff, the Peak of Death, the Lost Soul Gulf, the Ghostly Sadness Cave, and the Cloud Covered Valley. These were all famous danger-spots that their carts found impossible to pass. Bao Manzi and the rest of the advance guard were already far ahead.

"If Bao Manzi has gotten past, there cannot be any ambushes here!" Baili Shi declared. He instructed his soldiers to unyoke the horses and take off their armor. Some dragged the carts and some pushed them, stumbling every step of the way. It was an extremely difficult journey, marred by many halts, and during the course of it the soldiers' professional pride was severely damaged. Someone asked, "When we set out, we came through the Mount Xiao pass and it didn't seem so dangerous. Why do we have to be so careful on the way back?"

There were a number of reasons for this; first, when the Qin army set out, they were fired up for battle and, what is more, they did not have to face opposition from the Jin army. In addition to that, their chariots were light and their horses moved quickly, so they could advance at speed and get through the pass without noticing quite how dangerous it was. This time, however, they were at the end of a long journey and both men and horses were exhausted. Furthermore, they had plundered many people as well as much gold and silk in the sack of Hua, so their baggage was much encumbered. Finally, they had already encountered the Jin army presence in these mountains, and even though they had gotten through this first challenge, they were afraid that there might be further ambushes ahead. It is entirely natural that they should have become frightened, making the scene before their eyes seem much worse than it actually was.

When Baili Shi and his companions had made their way through the first narrow defile in the Ladder to Heaven, he suddenly heard the sound of muffled drumming, and someone came up to report from the rear-guard: "The Jin army are coming up behind us!"

"If it is difficult for us to get through this, it is also difficult for them," Baili Shi said. "We need to be worried about ambushes ahead of us, for there is nothing to be frightened of in soldiers behind us! Tell all divisions to move as quickly as they can. That should be enough." He told Jian Bing to go on ahead: "I will move to protect the rear and prevent any trouble from these soldiers pursuing us."

Once they had made their way past the Falling Horse Cliff and were approaching the Peak of Death, everyone started shouting, and the report came back: "There is a pile of logs blocking the road, and there is no way that we can get past. What do we do now?"

"Where do these logs come from?" Baili Shi asked himself. "Is there an ambush up ahead?" He decided to go and look at the situation in person, only to catch sight of a stone stele set up by one side of the peak, with words inscribed upon it: "King Wen of Zhou Escaped the Rain Here." A red flag had been planted to one side of the stele on a pole some thirty feet high. The flag bore the single word "Jin." This banner was held in position by a couple of logs placed across one another.

"This is just a trick," Baili Shi proclaimed. "But in the current situation, even if there is an ambush up ahead, we have no choice but to push on." He gave orders to his officers to take the flag down and move the logs out of the way so that they could proceed. What he did not know was that the red flag bearing the word "Jin" was the signal to the troops waiting in ambush. They were hidden all over the mountain and valley, but once they saw the flag come down they knew that the Qin army had arrived and would go and attack. Just when the Qin soldiers had started moving the logs out of the way, they heard the sound of drumming up ahead resounding like thunder, and far in the distance they could see a host of flags and banners fluttering in the light. They had no idea how large an army they would have to face, but Jian Bing gave orders to prime their weapons with a view to fighting their way out of this corner.

One general was standing high up on a mountain peak; that was Hu Shegu, also known by the style-name of Jiaji. He shouted: "Your entire advance guard, including Bao Manzi, has been taken prisoner already. You had better surrender to prevent unnecessary bloodshed."

When Bao Manzi advanced so bravely, he was simply throwing himself into a trap. Having been neatly separated from the rest of the Qin forces by the cunning of the Jin troops, he now found himself in chains in a prison cart. Jian Bing was most alarmed by this development and sent someone to report to Xiqi Shu and Baili Shi, to discuss joining forces to cut their way out.

Baili Shi looked at how narrow the road was, only a foot or two across, with a stone cliff on one side and a precipice a thousand feet deep on the other. This was the so-called Lost Soul Gulf. Even if you had a massive army with tens of thousands of horses, there was simply no room to deploy them. He came up with the best plan he could and gave the following orders: "There is no way that we can fight a battle here. Let the whole army move back to the East Peak of Mount Xiao, where we have room to maneuver. Once the battle is over, we can plan our next move."

Jian Bing took this order and started to retreat with his soldiers, with the sound of bells and drums ringing in his ears the whole way. When he got back to Falling Horse Cliff, he could see an unbroken line of battle standards lining the road to the east; this was the attacking force of five thousand men headed by General Liang Hong and Lai Ju, which had marched up behind them. There was no way that the Qin army would be able to get past Falling Horse Cliff, so they had to turn back again. Just like ants on a hot plate, they twisted this way and that, unable to find anywhere to make a stand.

Baili Shi ordered his officers to scale the mountains and plumb the gulfs on both sides to see if they could find a way out, but immediately he heard the sound of bells and drums resounding from the top of the left-hand peak; the division stationed there shouted down to them: "General Xian Qieju is already in possession here. You had better surrender as soon as you can!" On the right-hand side there was the sound of siege engines, and the battle standard of General Xu Ying was raised over both the mountain and valley. Baili Shi felt as if ten thousand arrows had struck his heart. He had no idea what to do, besides which his officers had scattered in panic, looking for a way to escape. As they scrambled across the mountainside, they were all taken prisoner by the Jin army. Baili Shi was furious and fought his way back to Falling Horse Cliff together with Xiqi Shu and Jian Bing. The logs blocking the road had been spread with saltpeter and other easily flammable substances; now Han Ziyu set light to them and the flames roared up, shooting smoke high into the heavens. The crimson flames scattered showers of sparks across the ground. Given that Liang Hong's troops had already cut off their retreat, Baili Shi and the other generals were left totally powerless to prevent disaster. They were now completely surrounded by the Jin army on all sides.

Baili Shi said to Jian Bing: "Your father really was amazingly accurate in his prognostications. I have now reached the point of no return; today I am going to die. You and Xiqi Shu must dress as ordinary soldiers and try to escape. If by some miracle one of you is able to return to the state of Qin, tell His Lordship to raise an army to avenge us. That way I can rest in peace in the Underworld!"

Xiqi Shu and Jian Bing wept and said, "Let us live or die together. Even if by splitting up we can improve our chances of survival, how could either of us bear to return to Qin alone?"

Before they had even finished speaking, the last of the soldiers under their command disappeared from view; piles of abandoned weapons and equipment blocked the road. Baili Shi and the other generals had no idea how they were going to get away, so they just sat down together on the mountainside and waited. The Jin soldiers drew ever closer, until they surrounded the Qin generals as tightly as stuffing in a bun. The three men held out their hands so they could be put in chains. In this terrible massacre, blood flowed like a river and bodies were scattered everywhere through the mountain paths, alongside their horses and chariots. No one was able to escape.

A bearded old man wrote a poem about this:

A long and successful campaign was ruined in an instant;
There was no return from the massacre at the West Peak of Mount Xiao.
Do not bother to praise the cunning plan carried out by the Jin army,
For Jian Shu had already grasped it and wept bitter tears.

Xian Qieju and the other generals gathered at the foot of the East Peak of Mount Xiao, whereupon the three generals joined Bao Manzi in the prison cart. The officers, chariots, and horses that they had captured, together with many of the people, the treasure, and the silk plundered at the fall of Hua, were all presented to Lord Xiang of Jin's main camp. Lord Xiang received the captives dressed in full mourning, and his army acclaimed his arrival with resounding shouts.

Lord Xiang asked the three generals their names and inquired, "Who is this Bao Manzi?"

"Even though he is only a junior general, he is unusually brave," Liang Hong explained. "Lai Ju lost his fight with him, so if he had not fallen into our trap, we would have found it very difficult to take him prisoner."

Lord Xiang was quite amazed. "If we were to spare the life of such a great warrior, I am afraid that he will pose a serious threat to us in the future." He summoned Lai Ju into his presence and said, "You lost to him yesterday. Today you can behead him in my presence to assuage the resentment that you feel."

Lai Ju accepted this command and tied Bao Manzi to one of the tent poles. He held a huge saber in one hand, but just as he was about to strike the blow, Bao Manzi shouted, "I defeated you in battle, how dare you do this to me!" His words came like a bolt from the blue, startling everyone present. As Bao Manzi shouted, he flexed the muscles of his arms and burst the bonds that tied him. Lai Ju was so shocked that his hand started to shake and the saber dropped from his grasp. Just as Bao Manzi was about to grab this weapon, a junior officer named Lang Shen, who had been standing to one side watching the proceedings, wrenched the sword away. With the first blow he brought Bao Manzi to his knees; the second blow carried off his head. He presented this to the Marquis of Jin.

"Lai Ju seems not to be as brave as this junior officer!" Lord Xiang said happily. He dismissed Lai Ju for incompetence and appointed Lang Shen as his chariot guard. Lang Shen thanked him for his kindness and withdrew. Since he felt that he owed everything to His Lordship, he did not bother to go and bow to the commander-in-chief, Xian Zhen. Xian Zhen was not happy about this.

The following day, Lord Xiang led his generals home in a triumphant procession. Since His Late Lordship's funeral was underway at Quwo, that was the city that they went to. It was Lord Xiang's intention to wait until they had returned to the capital city of Jiang to present the three captured Qin generals at the ancestral temple and then execute them. He first reported his victory over the state of Qin in front of his father's coffin, then completed the arrangements for the funeral. Lord Xiang attended the burial wearing full mourning and made a formal announcement of his success in battle. His Lordship's mother, Lady Wen Ying, was at Quwo in order to attend her husband's funeral.

When she heard the news of the capture of the three generals, she went to ask Lord Xiang, "I have heard that our forces have been victorious and Baili Shi and the other generals were all captured alive. This is wonderful news for our country. Have they already been executed?"

"Not yet," Lord Xiang said.

"The states of Qin and Jin have been linked by marriage alliances for many generations, and both sides have been very happy with this arrangement," Lady Wen Ying continued. "Baili Shi and the others were greedy for the honors that come with success in battle, so they forced the state of Qin to war. It is their fault that the good relationship between our two countries has been destroyed. I would imagine that the ruler of Qin is deeply angry with these three men. There is no point in our killing them. Why do you not release them and let them go back to Qin, so that Lord Mu can punish them? That way you will resolve the bad feeling that at present exists between our two countries. Would that not be wonderful?"

"Those three generals all serve the state of Qin," Lord Xiang said. "If I were to release them after having taken them captive, I am afraid that they will cause trouble for Jin."

"We all know the legal position," Lady Wen Ying reminded him. "A defeated general is executed. When the Chu army was defeated, did not Cheng Dechen die? Is Qin the only country in the world not to follow this principle? Besides which, when Lord Hui of Jin was taken prisoner by Qin, did they not treat him with all proper ritual propriety and send him home? Qin has behaved very well to us. If we were to insist on executing people as unimportant as these defeated generals for our own petty reasons, everyone will be justified in despising us."

At first Lord Xiang was not willing to agree to her point of view, but when she mentioned the return of Lord Hui, he started to come around, so he ordered his officials to release the three generals and send them home to Qin. When Baili Shi and the others were freed from their chains, they did not even go to court to thank His Lordship, but ran away as fast as they could.

Xian Zhen was at home eating with his family when he heard that the Marquis of Jin had set the three generals free. Having spat the mouthful of food he was chewing out across the table, he went immediately to court and had an audience with His Lordship, at which he angrily demanded: "Where are the Qin prisoners?"

"My mother asked that they be set free and sent home for punishment," Lord Xiang said, "so that is what I have done."

Xian Zhen was so angry that he spat in Lord Xiang's face and said, "Bah! You really have no idea, do you kid? Our soldiers suffered enormously to be able to take those three generals captive; how can the whole thing be wrecked simply by this woman's interference? You have let three extremely dangerous men go home. When in the future you come to regret this, it will be far too late!"

Lord Xiang realized what he had done and thanked Xian Zhen for his advice as he wiped the spittle from his face. He said, "This was my mistake!" He demanded of his assembled warriors, "Who dares to track down the Qin prisoners?"

Yang Chufu said that he would go. "You must do your best," Xian Zhen told him. "If you succeed, you will be rewarded with the very highest honors!"

Yang Chufu hitched the very fastest horses he could find to his chariot and drove out of the West Gate of Quwo in pursuit of Baili Shi, his sword in his hand.

A historian wrote a poem praising the fact that Lord Xiang was able to forgive Xian Zhen, which enabled him to continue the hegemony. This poem says:

A woman's stupidity ruined the army's efforts;
Xian Zhen was right to be so angry.
By his magnanimity when he wiped his face,
We know that the hegemony rightfully belonged to Lord Xiang.

Baili Shi and the two other generals had escaped from what seemed certain disaster. As they advanced along the road, they discussed what they should do next. "If we can get across the Yellow River, we will be safe. Otherwise there is still the possibility that we will be hunted down by the Lord of Jin, in which case there is nothing that we can do!"

When they arrived at the Yellow River, there was not a single boat in sight. They sighed and said, "Heaven wants us dead!"

Before they had finished their lamentations, they caught sight of a fisherman poling a light skiff, coming from the west. He was singing a song:

The imprisoned monkey has escaped its bars,
The imprisoned bird has left its cage.
Anyone who meets me will escape from disaster.

Baili Shi was amazed by these words and shouted, "Fisherman, take us across!"

"I will only ferry people from Qin, not people from Jin!" the fisherman declared.

"We are all from Qin," Baili Shi bellowed. "Now take us across as fast as you can!"

"Are you survivors of the battle at Mount Xiao?" the fisherman asked.

"Yes," Baili Shi said.

"Noble Grandson Qi gave me orders to wait here some time ago," the fisherman explained. "However, this skiff is far too small to take many passengers. If you go another half *li* you will find a big boat. You had better go there as fast as you can."

When he had finished speaking, the fisherman turned his craft around and poled off back to the west, moving so fast that it seemed as if he were flying. The three generals walked along the riverbank, and when they had gone less than half a *li*, just as the fisherman had said, there were several huge boats anchored in the Yellow River, less than a bow-shot from the bank. The fisherman was ready to transport them out there, but just as Baili Shi, Xiqi Shu, and Jian Bing stepped barefoot onto the boat, before the captain had even been able to cast off, a general arrived on the east bank of the river riding in a chariot. This was Yang Chufu.

"Stop!" he shouted.

Baili Shi and the others were all terrified. A moment later, Yang Chufu's chariot had pulled up on the bank. When he saw that the three generals were already onboard one of these great ships, he came up with a plan. He untied the left trace-horse from his chariot and presented it to Baili Shi, pretending to have received an order from Lord Xiang to do so. "His Lordship was afraid that you would not have a suitable horse to ride, so he sent me after you to give you this fine animal. This represents His Lordship's respectful good wishes and I hope that you will take it!"

Yang Chufu's idea was to entice Baili Shi onto the bank to take receipt of the horse and thank His Lordship, for then he would be able to arrest him. However, Baili Shi had only just been able to escape with his life. As the saying goes: "A fish that has been able to slip the hook never comes back for a second bite." Given his state of mind, there was no way he was prepared to set foot on the riverbank again. He stood at the prow of the boat and looked back at Yang Chufu. Then he kowtowed and apologized with the words: "His Lordship's generosity in pardoning me from the death penalty is already more than I could possibly expect. How could I accept this gift of a horse? If my lord does not kill me for my role in this disastrous campaign, I will return in three years' time to repay Lord Xiang for all that he has done!"

Yang Chufu wanted to expostulate, but the captain of the great ship had ordered his sailors to weigh anchor and set to the oars, and the boat was already beginning to make its way downriver. Yang Chufu felt bereft, as if he had lost something precious. He returned unhappily to Jin and reported to Lord Xiang exactly what Baili Shi had said.

Xian Zhen stepped forward angrily and said, "When he says 'I will return in three years' time to repay Lord Xiang for all that he has done,' what he means is that he is going to attack Jin to take revenge. You had better take advantage of the upheaval caused by their recent defeat to attack them, to prevent them from conspiring against you in the future."

Lord Xiang thought that he was right, and they began discussing an attack on Qin.

• • •

Let us turn now to another part of the story. When Lord Mu heard that his three generals had been captured, he was both angry and depressed, finding it difficult to sleep or eat. After several days like this, he heard that the three generals had been released and were on their way home, so he looked a lot happier. However, his entourage reminded him: "Baili Shi and the others are responsible for the deaths of the soldiers under their command, and they have humiliated our country. This crime deserves the death penalty. In the past Cheng Dechen was killed in order to strike fear into the three armies of Chu; today you, my lord, will have to follow that legal precedent."

"I did not listen to the advice I received from Jian Shu and Baili Xi," Lord Mu said. "That is why the three generals were defeated. If anyone is to blame here, it is me." He went out to meet the three men in the suburbs, dressed in plain clothes. He wept and expressed the most profound remorse, restoring them to their positions at the head of the army and treating them with the greatest respect and consideration.

Baili Xi sighed and said, "It is almost unbelievable that my son should have survived to come back to me!"

He subsequently retired from office on the grounds of old age. Lord Mu appointed two of his closest advisors, Yao Yu and Noble Grandson Qi, to replace Jian Shu and Baili Xi. There will be more of this story later on.

• • •

Just when Lord Xiang of Jin was discussing the possibility of an attack on Qin, suddenly border officials reported: "The chief of the Di people, Baibuhu, has brought his army across the border. He has already reached the city of Ji. Please send troops as soon as possible to defend us!"

Lord Xiang was horrified. "We have a good relationship with the Di. Why would they want to attack us?"

"His Late Lordship went to live with the Di people in exile, and their chief gave him Lady Wei as his bride," Xian Zhen explained. "He lived there for twelve years and they treated him really well. When His Lordship came back to Jin, the chief of the Di sent an ambassador to congratulate him and escort Lady Wei here. During His Late Lordship's lifetime, we did not give the Di as much as a single bundle of silk, but the chief of the Di remembered his long-standing friendship with Lord Wen and accepted the situation without saying a word. Now his son, Baibuhu, has inherited the chiefdom. He has a reputation for bravery to uphold, and that is why he is taking advantage of a time of national mourning to attack us."

"His Late Lordship served His Majesty the Zhou Son of Heaven, never letting private relationships interfere with the greater good," Lord Xiang proclaimed. "The Di chief has now attacked us while we are in mourning; that makes him our enemy. Get rid of him for me!"

Xian Zhen bowed twice and refused, saying: "I was so angry over the release of the three Qin generals that in a moment of madness I spat in your face. That is the most disrespectful thing I could have done! I have heard it said that an army relies on the proper distinction between ranks for its effectiveness, for it is only by the observance of ritual propriety that you can govern the people. A man who behaves disrespectfully cannot be an effective commander-in-chief. You must dismiss me from office and select a better general!"

"You were worried about the country and behaved as you did out of an excess of loyalty," Lord Xiang said. "How could I fail to forgive you? You are the only person who can get rid of the Di for me. You cannot refuse!"

Xian Zhen had no choice but to accept his command and leave the court. He sighed and said, "I would much have preferred to die at the hands of Qin! Who would have imagined I will be killed by the Di!" None of those who heard him understood what he was talking about. Afterwards, Lord Xiang returned to Jiang, the capital city of Jin.

When Xian Zhen arrived at the commander-in-chief's tent in the Central Army, he summoned the other generals and asked, "Who is willing to lead the vanguard?"

One man stepped out arrogantly and said, "I will go."

Xian Zhen looked at him. This was the newly appointed General of the Left, Lang Shen. Xian Zhen had already been offended by his failure to thank him for his promotion, and now he was requesting permission to lead the vanguard, which made him even more irritated. He cursed at him and said, "You are just a newly promoted officer who happened to get rewarded for killing a prisoner. A major enemy is almost at our gates, and you have no idea that you ought to be hanging back and letting more competent people take charge. Do you really imagine that all the senior generals in this army are useless?"

"I want to do my best to protect the country," Lang Shen retorted. "Why are you trying to stop me?"

"Every single person present here wants to do their best to protect the country," Xian Zhen replied. "What is so wonderful about you that you want to be put in charge of them?" He shouted at him to leave and not come back. Hu Juju had achieved great success in the battle at Mount Xiao, so he was placed in command of the vanguard. Lang Shen withdrew, hanging his head and not daring to express how angry he was.

On his way home he met a friend named Xian Bo, who asked him: "I have heard that the commander-in-chief is currently selecting the generals who will lead this campaign against the enemy. What are you doing wandering about here?"

"I asked to be given command of the vanguard, because I thought that would be the best way to do my bit for the country," Lang Shen responded. "I had no idea that Xian Zhen was going to completely blow his top. He asked me what was so wonderful about me and said I did not deserve to be put in such an important command ahead of the others. He has already dismissed me from my post and told me to go home!"

Xian Bo got really angry and said, "Xian Zhen is simply jealous of your abilities. Let us get our servants together and go and kill him. That way we can show him exactly what we think of him. Even if we are punished for it, it will have been worth it!"

"No! No!" Lang Shen shouted. "A good man dies for a worthy cause. It would not be right to get oneself killed over something like this! It was my bravery that first got me noticed by His Lordship and appointed to be his bodyguard in his battle chariot. Xian Zhen has gotten rid of me in the belief that I am useless, so if I were to die in an unjust cause, then it would simply prove that he was right to throw me out of the army. I am determined to prove my detractors wrong. You just wait and see."

Xian Bo sighed and said, "You have thought much more deeply into the matter than I have." He went home with Lang Shen, but no more of this now.

Later on someone wrote a poem explaining why it was wrong of Xian Zhen to get rid of Lang Shen like this. This poem runs:

He picked up his spear and beheaded the general just like a knight of old,
He was appointed to the position of bodyguard by his lord's favor.
Having done his best, he did not deserve to be dismissed in this way;
Many loyal and brave men have suffered such discrimination.

Having appointed his son, Xian Qieju, to lead the vanguard, Xian Zhen placed Luan Zhi and Xi Que in charge of the left and right wings of the army, while Hu Shegu and Hu Juju were made responsible for commanding the rearguard. The army of four hundred chariots then headed out of the North Gate of the capital, in the direction of the city of Ji. The two opposing armies met and made camp opposite to each other. Xian Zhen summoned his generals and came up with a plan of campaign: "There is a place near the city of Ji that is called the Great Valley. It is very broad and spacious, making it perfect for chariot warfare. The sides of the valley are heavily wooded, so we can set ambushes there. Generals Luan Zhi and Xi Que will be responsible for this. Qieju will meet the Di when they come to provoke battle, after which he will pretend to be defeated and trick them into the valley. The soldiers in ambush can then rise up and take the Di chief prisoner. The two generals from the Hu family will be in charge of ensuring that the remaining Di forces cannot come to his aid." The generals followed this plan. Xian Zhen moved the main camp back ten *li*, where a stockade was built.

The following morning, the two armies went into battle formation. The Di chief, Baibuhu, came in person to provoke battle. Xian Qieju fought a couple of rounds with him and then turned his chariot around and retreated. Baibuhu led more than one hundred cavalrymen in pursuit, only to be tricked by Xian Qieju into entering a great valley where the Jin army lay in ambush on both sides. Baibuhu fought bravely, charging now to the left, then making an attack on the right. The cavalry under his command fought to the last man, and the Jin army also suffered terrible casualties. After some time, Baibuhu was finally able to cut his way out of the surrounding forces in a frenzied attack that they were simply unable to withstand. When he arrived at the mouth of the valley, he ran into a senior general who let fly a single arrow that hit Baibuhu in the face. He twisted around and fell from his horse, the Jin troops advancing to take him prisoner. The person who shot the arrow was Grandee Xi Que, the general in command of the New Lower Army.

Baibuhu died instantly, the arrow piercing his skull. Xi Que recognized the chief of the Di and cut his head off to present it to His Lordship. At that time Xian Zhen was in the main camp, but when he heard that Baibuhu had been captured, he lifted his head up to the heavens and shouted: "Long live the Marquis of Jin! Long live the Marquis of Jin!" He called for paper and brush and wrote a letter, which he left on his desk. Then, without telling any of his generals and accompanied only by a couple of trusted officers from the main camp, Xian Zhen headed out in a single chariot towards the Di army.

Baibuhu's younger brother, Baitun, was still unaware that his older brother was dead. He was just about to move his army in support of Baibuhu's attack, when he suddenly caught sight of a single chariot racing towards him. Under the impression that these men were here to trick him into a disadvantageous situation, Baitun quickly grabbed a sword and went out to intercept them. Xian Zhen was carrying a spear across his shoulders, but before he could deploy it, he shouted out with staring eyes. Something within his eyes burst and blood came pouring down his face. Baitun was horrified and stepped back a couple of paces. When he realized that this warrior was not coming after him, he ordered his archers to surround and shoot him. Xian Zhen gathered his wits and attacked them, killing three officers and a couple dozen foot soldiers with his bare hands, without sustaining a single wound himself. The archers were so scared by Xian Zhen's attack that their hands shook too much to be able to shoot him. Besides which, Xian Zhen was wearing double armor; how could an arrow possibly pierce it? Xian Zhen was completely uninjured by the hail of arrows fired at him. He sighed and said, "I have spent my entire life killing the enemy in order to show what a great warrior I am. Now that everyone knows of my bravery, what is the point of killing any more people? I might as well die here and now."

He then took off his armor in order to allow the arrows to strike him. He died in a hail of arrows that stuck him as full of spines as a hedgehog. In spite of this, his corpse remained upright. Baitun wanted to cut his head off, but when he observed the angry glare from the dead man's eyes, the same as when he was alive, he became frightened. One of the army officers recognized him and said, "That is the commander-in-chief of the Jin army, Xian Zhen!"

Baitun led his soldiers in making a deep bow. He sighed and said, "A truly remarkable man!" He performed an incantation for him: "If your soul is willing to allow me to go home to Di territory, then fall to the ground!" The corpse remained upright. He then changed the words of the incantation and said, "Do you not want to return to the state of Jin? Let me send you back!" As he finished chanting, the body collapsed to the floor of the chariot.

If you want to know how Xian Zhen's corpse was sent back to the state of Jin, READ ON.

Chapter Forty-six

Prince Shangchen of Chu assassinates his father in the palace.

Lord Mu of Qin collects the bodies from the battlefield at Mount Xiao.

Those warriors who escaped with their lives informed Baitun of the death of his older brother, the chief of the Di, Baibuhu. Baitun wept and said, "I done told him: 'Heaven is helping the state of Jin; you must not attack them.' He did not listen and now this has happened!" He wanted to exchange Xian Zhen's head for that of Baibuhu, so he sent someone to the Jin army to suggest this option. When Xi Que and the other generals arrived back at the main camp and wanted to show Baibuhu's head to Xian Zhen, they discovered that the commander-in-chief was missing.

The officers guarding the camp said, "The commander-in-chief left the camp riding in a single chariot. All he said was, 'Guard the entrance to the stockade with your life!' We have no idea where he went."

Xian Qieju started to become worried. Then he noticed the letter lying on the table. He picked it up and read it:

> This report is respectfully submitted by Grandee Xian Zhen, general in command of the Central Army. I know myself to have behaved with great rudeness to His Lordship, who not only refused to punish me but even restored my command. I have been so fortunate as to be victorious in this battle, which means that I will receive rewards. If I were to go home and refuse to accept my reward, this would mean that my achievements would not receive their just recognition. On the other hand, if I went home and took my reward, the disrespect I have shown to His Lordship would simply be glossed over. If your merits are not recognized, how can you be spurred on to further efforts? If your disrespectful behavior is glossed over, how can you punish

the guilty? If rewards and punishments are administered in a confused fashion, how can you govern the country? I am going to attack the Di army, forcing them to kill me, since His Lordship will not. My son, Qieju, is a brilliant commander and he can replace me. That way, I will rest in peace.

"My father has gone to the Di army to die!" Xian Qieju exclaimed. He started to wail loudly; then he demanded command of a division of the army, so that he could go to the Di and demand to know his father's whereabouts.

By this time Xi Que, Luan Zhi, Hu Juju, Hu Shegu, and the others had all assembled at the main camp, and they begged him not to go. They said, "First let us send someone to find out if the commander-in-chief is still alive. Then, if necessary, we can send the army in."

Suddenly a report arrived: "The younger brother of the Di chief, Baitun, has sent someone to speak to you."

When this individual was summoned in and questioned, they discovered that he had come to discuss an exchange of bodies, so Xian Qieju was no longer in any doubt that his father was dead. He began to cry bitterly. The deal was made: "Tomorrow morning the bodies will be exchanged in front of our two respective armies."

Once the Di emissary had left, Xian Qieju said, "The Rong and the Di are notoriously tricky, so tomorrow we will have to be very careful." After further discussion he gave orders that Xi Que and Luan Zhi should remain in command of the left and right wings of the army. If there was any sign of trouble, they should attack in a pincer movement, while the two generals of the Hu family remained behind to guard the main camp.

The following day the two sides opened up their battle formations in order to allow the exchange. Xian Qieju got into a chariot wearing plain clothes and headed out alone in front of the army to collect his father's body. Baitun, out of fear of the power of Xian Zhen's spirit, had ordered all the arrows to be removed from his body, and it had been washed in perfumed waters. He then took off his own brocade gown and had the body dressed in it. The corpse was placed in a chariot, looking just as he had when he was alive. This was then sent out in front of the Di battle ranks. Xian Qieju accepted the return, and the Jin army restored Baibuhu's head to the Di. Now, what the Di handed back was a whole body that had been most respectfully treated, while what they received in return from Jin was a blood-stained head.

Baitun was terribly upset and shouted, "How dare you treat us like this! Why don't you give us back his whole body?"

Xian Qieju sent someone out to reply: "If you want to collect the rest of his body, you will have to go and look for it in the valley among all the other corpses."

Baitun was furious and grabbed hold of his great battle-axe. He ordered the Di cavalry into a murderous charge. However, the Jin battle formation was protected by military chariots that formed an impenetrable wall. Although they charged several times, they could not break through. This made Baitun hopping mad, but there was nothing he could do about it. Suddenly the sound of drums could be heard from the Jin Central Army, and the battle formation moved to create an entrance. A general came out, grasping a spear. This was Hu Shegu. Baitun fought a couple of rounds with him, only to find Xi Que ranged against him on the left-hand side and Luan Zhi on the right. He was completely surrounded by the army officers from the two wings. Baitun realized that the Jin army was numerically superior, so he turned his horse's head around as quickly as he could. The Jin army then attacked from behind, leaving countless Di warriors dead.

Hu Shegu had recognized Baitun and pursued him closely. Baitun was afraid that he might charge his ranks, so he whipped his horse up and broke through the encircling spears. Hu Shegu was not prepared to let him go and came in hot pursuit. Baitun turned around and looked at him, then he turned his horse around.

"I recognize you!" he exclaimed. "Aren't you Hu Shegu?"

"That's right," he replied.

"How've you been?" Baitun asked. "You and your father lived in our country for twelve years and we treated you very well. If you spare my life, I am sure that in the future we will meet again. My name is Baitun, and I am Baibuhu's younger brother."

At this mention of the past, Hu Shegu could not bear to kill him, so he promised him: "I will let you live. You had better get back to your army as quickly as you can, because this is not a place that is healthy for you to stay."

When he had finished speaking, he turned his chariot around and went back to the main camp. Since the Jin army was victorious, no one said anything about the fact that he had failed to capture Baitun. That night Baitun led his army home. Baibuhu did not have any sons, so after the period of official mourning was completed, Baitun was installed as the new chief. This happened sometime later on.

. . .

The Jin army returned home in a triumphal procession and was received by Lord Xiang. At this audience, they presented Xian Zhen's suicide note. Lord Xiang was very grieved by Xian Zhen's death and went to see his body in person. The eyes of the dead man were wide open and full of anger.

Lord Xiang patted the body and said, "You died protecting the country and your heroic spirit will live forever. The wording of your letter demonstrates your great sense of loyalty. I will not forget this!" In front of the coffin, he appointed Xian Qieju to be the commander-in-chief of the Central Army, replacing his father. The eyes then closed.

Later on, people built a temple at the city of Ji to perform sacrifices for him.

Lord Xiang was very pleased with Xi Que for his success in killing Baibuhu, so he rewarded him with the tax revenues of Xi Rui's former manor with the words: "Whatever crimes your father committed you have atoned for, so I now return his fief to you!" He also gave him the lands of Xianmao County as a reward. When the other generals saw how Lord Xiang rewarded his success in battle, they were all deeply impressed.

A historian wrote a poem:

The father was executed for his crimes, the son was praised.
Promoting the wise and giving rewards are glorious achievements.
If a great man had not emerged from the wilderness,
How could this great victory at the city of Ji ever have been won?

After the death of Lord Wen of Jin, the two states of Xu and Cai restored their alliance with Chu. Lord Xiang of Jin appointed Yang Chufu as general, and he led an army to attack first Xu and then Cai. King Cheng of Chu ordered Dou Bo and Cheng Daxin to take an army to rescue them. When they arrived at the Zhi River, they saw the Jin army on the opposite bank, so they quickly made camp. The Jin army was entrenched on the north bank of the Zhi River, so the two opposing armies were only separated by a narrow band of water. They were so close that they could hear the sound of the watchman's rattle as he made his rounds in the opposing camp. The Jin army found their advance was blocked by the Chu army, and the standoff lasted for almost two months. As the end of the year approached, the Jin army began to run low on food. Yang Chufu wanted to withdraw his army, but he was afraid that Chu would take advantage of this to attack them. He was also concerned that he would be humiliated if he was thought to have run away from them. He therefore sent someone across the Zhi River to go to the Chu camp and take the following message to Dou Bo: "According to the popular saying: 'If you come, that shows you aren't scared, because a coward wouldn't dare.' If you want to do battle with me, then I will withdraw one day's march to allow you to cross over the river and go into battle formation on this side. We can then fight to the death. If you do not want to cross the river, then you should withdraw by one stage to allow us onto the south bank, whereupon we can then decide a suitable day for battle. If neither of us withdraws or advances, we are just wasting our time and resources, and what is the point of that? Yang Chufu is even now hitching up his horses; he awaits your decision. Please make up your mind as quickly as possible!"

Dou Bo was angry and said, "Does Jin really think that we would not dare to cross the Zhi River?" He was determined that they should go across and fight.

Cheng Daxin quickly stopped him and said, "You cannot trust the people of Jin. They may say that they are going to withdraw by one stage, but that might simply be a trick. If they attack us when we are halfway across the river, we are going to find it very difficult to either advance or retreat. We had better move back ourselves and allow Jin to cross the river. That way we are in control of the situation, which is much better for us."

Dou Bo realized that this was very sensible advice and said: "You are absolutely right!" He ordered the army to retreat thirty *li* and then make camp, thereby allowing Jin to cross the river, and sent someone to inform Yang Chufu of his decision.

Yang Chufu put his own gloss on the situation and announced to the assembled troops: "General Dou Bo of Chu is too frightened of Jin to cross the Zhi River, so he has already begun his retreat." This news spread through the army like wildfire.

"The Chu army has already withdrawn," Yang Chufu said, "but why should we cross the river after them? Winter is here and the weather is really cold. We had better go home and recoup, awaiting a second mobilization." He stood down his army and returned to Jin.

Dou Bo waited for two days at his new camp without seeing hide nor hair of the Jin army. He sent someone to find out what was going on, but by that time they were already long gone. He too gave orders to stand down the army and went home.

. . .

The oldest son of King Cheng of Chu was named Shangchen. The king wanted to appoint him as his crown prince and asked Dou Bo his opinion.

"The throne of the kingdom of Chu has always been inherited by the youngest son," Dou Bo said, "so it is not appropriate that it should go to the oldest. This has been true for many generations. Besides which, having observed Prince Shangchen's appearance, he has waspish eyes and a wolfish tone of voice, not to mention a violent personality. If you establish him as crown prince today and at some point in the future you dismiss him over an offense, there is certain to be a civil war."

King Cheng did not listen to this advice but appointed him as his crown prince, with Pan Chong as his tutor. Prince Shangchen heard that Dou Bo had opposed his appointment and hated him from the bottom of his heart. Later on when Dou Bo rescued Cai and returned home without having done battle, Prince Shangchen slandered him to King Cheng, saying, "Dou Bo took bribes from Yang Chufu, and that is why he ran away. It is his fault that Jin has such an amazing reputation." King Cheng believed what the prince said and would not allow Dou Bo to have an audience with him; instead, he sent someone to bestow a sword upon him. Dou Bo was given no opportunity to exculpate himself; he committed suicide by cutting his throat with this sword.

Cheng Daxin kowtowed and wept in front of King Cheng, explaining exactly why they had been forced to retreat. "This has nothing to do with having been given bribes! If anyone was to blame for the retreat of our army, it was myself."

"You should not blame yourself," the king told him. "I really regret this turn of events."

After this, King Cheng became very suspicious of what Crown Prince Shangchen was up to.

After his beloved son, Prince Zhi, was born, King Cheng wanted to depose Shangchen and make Zhi his crown prince instead. However, he was afraid that Prince Shangchen would cause a civil war. He therefore decided to look for evidence of wrongdoing and use that to justify executing him. The palace servants knew exactly what was going on, and thus news filtered out into the capital as a whole. Prince Shangchen was not at all convinced of the genuineness of these rumors, but he did speak about them to his tutor, Pan Chong.

"I have a plan that will tell us if they are true or not," Pan Chong said.

"What plan?"

"His Majesty's younger sister, Princess Mi, is married to the ruler of the state of Jiang," Pan Chong replied. "She is at present on a visit to her family here in Chu, so she has been spending much time in the palace and must know what is going on. Princess Mi is a very hot-tempered woman; if you arrange a banquet in her honor and then treat her rudely, thereby provoking her anger, she will speak the truth in her rage."

Prince Shangchen followed this advice and arranged a banquet for Princess Mi. When she arrived at the East Palace, Shangchen bowed very respectfully. However, after three rounds of drinks had been served, he became more and more lax in his behavior. He had the food served by the cooks without getting up, and he intentionally flirted with the maids serving the wine. Princess Mi asked him a couple of questions that he simply did not bother to answer.

The princess became absolutely furious. Thumping the table, she got up and shouted: "If you are always this rude, no wonder His Majesty wants to kill you and appoint Prince Zhi instead!"

Prince Shangchen pretended that he was sorry and apologized, but Princess Mi paid no attention to him. She insisted on her carriage being called immediately so that she could go home. All the way she cursed and swore at him.

That very night, Prince Shangchen reported what had happened to Pan Chong and begged him to come up with some kind of plan to save him.

"Could you accept a subordinate position serving Prince Zhi?" Pan Chong asked.

"I will not serve my younger brother," Shangchen told him.

"Well, if you are not prepared to accept the humiliation of becoming your younger brother's vassal," Pan Chong replied, "then how about going into exile in another country?"

"That would be very difficult," Prince Shangchen said.

"Those are the only two options," Pan Chong said. "There is nothing else left!" Shangchen kept on asking him what to do, so he continued: "There is one other plan that would work out very well for you, but I am afraid that you could not bear to actually carry it out."

"My life is trembling in the balance!" Prince Shangchen cried. "There is nothing that I could not bear to do!"

Pan Chong whispered in his ear: "The only way you will survive this crisis is by launching a coup."

"I can do that," the prince asserted.

At midnight, the crown prince's guard surrounded the royal palace on the pretext that there was some trouble in the palace. Pan Chong grasped a sword and led a couple of brave knights into the palace, whereupon they made their way into King Cheng's presence. His entourage fled in panic.

"Why are you here?" the king asked.

"Your Majesty has been on the throne for forty-seven years," Pan Chong replied, "and it is time for you to go. Your subjects want a new ruler, so you had better hand the throne over to the crown prince!"

King Cheng was terrified and said, "I will abdicate immediately, but will I be able to survive?"

"When one king dies, another comes to the throne; no country has ever had two kings!" Pan Chong said. "Besides which, Your Majesty is old and does not have long to live anyway!"

"Let me order the cooks to prepare me a dish of bear's paws," King Cheng requested. "Once I have eaten them, I am prepared to die!"

"Bear's paws take a very long time to cook," Pan Chong said sharply. "You are just trying to spin things out, Your Majesty, in the hope that troops will arrive from outside to rescue you. I hope that you will make your own arrangements rather than forcing me to kill you!"

When he had finished speaking, he took off his belt and laid it down in front of the king. King Cheng shouted up at the sky: "Dou Bo! Dou Bo! I did not listen to your excellent advice and brought this disaster down upon myself. What more is there to say?" He wound the belt around his neck. Pan Chong ordered the soldiers to tighten the garrote, and a short time later King Cheng ceased breathing.

"It is my fault that my brother was killed!" Princess Mi screamed, and she hanged herself. This happened in the twenty-sixth year of the reign of King Xiang of Zhou, on Dingwei day in the tenth month.

An old man, discussing this matter, pointed out that King Cheng assassinated his older brother in order to come to the throne; now he was himself murdered by his son, Prince Shangchen. You could describe this as a kind of karmic revenge.

There is a poem that bewails this:

In the past the king of Chu assassinated Prince Xiongxi;
Today Prince Shangchen revenged the death of his innocent uncle.
Heaven sent down Pan Chong to instruct his pupil to act in this wicked way;
The deluded king still hoped to go on enjoying his old privileges.

Once Prince Shangchen had murdered his father, he reported his sudden death due to disease to the lords of the Central States and had himself crowned King Mu. Pan Chong was granted the title of Grand Preceptor and head of the Palace Guard. He was also given the crown prince's house to be his own home. The Grand Vizier Dou Ban and the other officials were all well aware of the fact that King Cheng had been murdered, but they did not dare to say anything. When Dou Yishen heard about the murder of King Cheng, he used the excuse of a family funeral to come to the capital city of Ying and plot the assassination of King Mu with Grandee Zhong Gui. The plot was discovered, and King Mu sent Emir Dou Yuejiao to arrest Dou Yishen and Zhong Gui and kill them. The shaman from Fan, Yusi, once said: "As long as King Cheng has Cheng Dechen and Dou Yishen by his side, he will not die." His words were proved absolutely correct.

. . .

Dou Yuejiao had his eye on becoming Grand Vizier, and said to King Mu: "Dou Ban is going around telling people, 'My father and myself have controlled the government of Chu for generations, and His Late Majesty's kindness to us is more than we can ever repay. My greatest regret is not being able to carry out His Late Majesty's wishes.' This means that he wants Prince Zhi to become king. Dou Yishen came here because Dou Ban summoned him; now that Dou Yishen has been executed, Dou Ban must be very concerned about his own position. I am afraid that he is involved in some conspiracy against you . . . You must be very careful."

King Mu was a paranoid man at the best of times, so he summoned Dou Ban and ordered him to kill Prince Zhi. Dou Ban refused and said that he could not possibly do such a thing.

"Are you still hoping to carry out His Late Majesty's wishes?" King Mu demanded angrily. He personally beat Dou Ban to death with a metal baton. Prince Zhi attempted to flee to Jin, but he was chased down by Dou Yuejiao and murdered outside the suburbs. King Mu appointed Cheng Daxin to be his new Grand Vizier. However, not long after that, Cheng Daxin died. He then appointed Dou Yuejiao as Grand Vizier and Wei Jia became Emir. Later on, King Mu came to remember how much the Dou family had done for Chu, so he appointed Dou Kehuang as his majordomo. Dou Kehuang had the style-name Ziyi—he was the son of Dou Ban and the grandson of the great Ziwen.

. . .

When Lord Xiang of Jin heard of the death of King Cheng of Chu, he asked Zhao Dun, "Is this Heaven's way of destroying Chu?"

"Although the king of Chu is a violent man," Zhao Dun replied, "he might yet be able to atone for the circumstances in which he came to the throne by behaving with ritual propriety and justice. However, given that Prince Shangchen did not love his own father, it is unlikely that he feels much concern for anyone else! I am afraid that disaster threatens the feudal lords!"

Within the next couple of years, King Mu sent his armies out in all directions, destroying first the state of Jiang, then Liu, then Liao. He also turned his troops against Chen and Zheng, causing the Central States a great deal of trouble. In fact, it was all just as Zhao Dun had said. However, this all happened much later on.

. . .

In the second month of the twenty-seventh year of the reign of King Xiang of Zhou, the Qin general Baili Shi requested permission from Lord Mu to raise an army and attack Jin, to avenge the defeat at Mount Xiao. Lord Mu admired his resolution and agreed. Baili Shi, Xiqi Shu, and Jian Bing then led an army of four hundred chariots to attack Jin. Lord Xiang of Jin was concerned that Qin would take revenge, and so every day he sent spies out to investigate what was going on. Once he got this news, he laughed and said, "The prisoners that I released are on their way back." He appointed Xian Qieju as commander-in-chief with Zhao Cui as his deputy and Hu Juju as his bodyguard. They went to intercept the Qin army at the border. Just as the army set out, Lang Shen requested permission to go along with a small private force of his own men, and Xian Qieju agreed. At this time Baili Shi still had not yet crossed the border.

"What is the point of waiting until the Qin army has arrived before we do battle?" Xian Qieju demanded. "Why not just invade Qin?"

He advanced westwards until he reached Pengya, where he encountered the Qin army and the two sides each went into battle formation. Lang Shen requested permission of Xian Qieju: "Our former commander-in-chief dismissed me from the army on the grounds that he thought I was useless. I now ask permission to prove myself, not because I am hoping for any kind of official position or reward, but because I want to expunge this insult." When he had finished speaking, he and his friend Xian Bo, together with about one hundred other men, launched a frontal assault on the Qin army. The enemy forces scattered, and countless Qin soldiers were killed. However, Xian Bo was killed by Jian Bing himself.

When Xian Qieju climbed up into his chariot, he could see that the Qin battle formations were disintegrating, so he spurred on the main army to attack. Baili Shi and his other generals could do nothing in the face of this onslaught. Having suffered a terrible defeat, they ran away. When Xian Qieju rescued Lang Shen from the midst of the battle, his body was covered in wounds. He vomited large quantities of blood, and the following day he died. The Jin army returned to the capital singing songs of triumph.

Xian Qieju reported to Lord Xiang: "This victory is entirely down to Lang Shen. It is nothing to do with me." Lord Xiang ordered that Lang Shen should be buried outside the western city wall, with all the honors appropriate to a senior grandee. He also ordered all his officials to attend the funeral. This was how Lord Xiang was hoping to encourage talented men into his service.

A historian wrote a poem praising Lang Shen's bravery:

How brave was Lang Shen!
He beheaded a prisoner with the same insouciance as if he were killing a chicken.
When dismissed from his post, he did not express pointless anger,
He assaulted the enemy with no thought for his own safety.
His death expressed the principles by which he had lived;
The Qin army was put to flight by him.
If the dead have any awareness,
Xian Zhen should hang his head in shame.

When Baili Shi returned home, he was sure that he was going to be executed. He could never have imagined that Lord Mu would sympathize with his difficulties and never say a single word of blame. Just like before, he came out to the suburbs in person to comfort his defeated generals and restored them to their original offices. Baili Shi was deeply ashamed that he had been defeated, so he improved the government of the country, as well as taking every single penny from his family's coffers to succor the families of the bereaved. Every day he trained his officers, encouraging them to behave with loyalty and justice, because the following year he intended to raise another great army to attack Jin.

That winter, Lord Xiang of Jin ordered Xian Qieju to lead an attack on Qin in concert with Grandee the Honorable Cheng of Song, Grandee Yuan Xuan of Chen, and Grandee the Honorable Guisheng of Zheng. They captured the two cities of Jiang and Pengya before returning home. As a joke, he said: "This was just a little trip to see my prisoners." In the past when Guo Yan performed a divination, he got the result "With one blow I will injure it in three places" and interpreted this as meaning that the Qin army would be defeated three times in a row. This is in fact exactly what happened. When Baili Shi did not request permission to lead the army to resist the invasion by Jin, everyone thought it was because he was afraid. Lord Mu was the only person who really trusted him. He told his ministers: "Baili Shi will take revenge upon the Jin army; the right opportunity has not yet come along."

In the fifth month the following year, Baili Shi had assembled exactly the army that he wanted with the right number of chariots, and their training had been completed. He requested that Lord Mu should join them to see how they performed in battle. "If this time I cannot expunge the humiliation that we have suffered, I swear that I will not come back alive!"

"I too have been defeated three times by Jin," Lord Mu said. "If this time we are not victorious, how can I bear to go home!"

After Lord Mu had reviewed the army of five hundred chariots, an auspicious day was selected for them to set off. An enormous amount of money was dispersed among the families of both officers and foot soldiers. Everyone in the three armies was amazed, and they were willing to die to repay this generosity. The army advanced through the Pujin Pass and then crossed the Yellow River. Baili Shi gave orders that all their boats should be burned.

Lord Mu thought that this was a bizarre command, and asked him: "What do you mean by burning our boats?"

Baili Shi presented his opinion: "A victory is guaranteed by the morale of the army. Having been defeated several times in a row, morale is very low. If we are so fortunate as to be victorious in the coming campaign, our soldiers will be equal to any challenge. I want them to know that there is no going back, to force them to pull themselves together."

"Good," Lord Mu said.

Baili Shi then took personal command of the vanguard and advanced at top speed, breaking through the walls of the city of Wangguan and capturing it. When spies reported this development to the capital, Lord Xiang of Jin summoned his ministers to discuss mobilizing the army to meet the enemy.

"Qin's aggression is at its height," Zhao Cui said. "This time they have raised an incredibly powerful army and they have come here to kill us. Besides which, His Lordship has come along personally. We cannot resist them, so we had better avoid them. If we allow them to achieve some success in this campaign, it might serve to improve relations between our two countries."

Xian Qieju also said: "Even a cornered rat will fight, not to mention a great state! The Lord of Qin is humiliated by these defeats, and his three generals—all of whom are brave men—are determined to defeat us. Never-ending warfare is a terrible thing. Zhao Cui is right in what he says."

Lord Xiang sent a message to the officials guarding every corner of his realm to tell them not to fight Qin. Yao Yu said to Lord Mu, "Jin is afraid of us. Your Lordship should take advantage of your army's might to go and collect the bones of the soldiers who died at Mount Xiao, that you may expunge the humiliation of that defeat."

Lord Mu followed this advice and led his army across the Yellow River to the upper bank, where he then took his army across the Mao Ford and made camp at the Eastern Peak of Mount Xiao. Not a single Jin soldier or cavalryman dared to approach. Lord Mu ordered his officers to collect all the bodies strewn around Falling Horse Cliff, the Peak of Death, and Lost Soul Gulf. The bones were wrapped in hay and buried on the slopes of the mountain valley. Horses and oxen were then killed and a great sacrifice performed, which Lord Mu attended dressed in plain clothes. He poured a libation for their souls and wept bitterly. Baili Shi and the other generals lay face down upon the ground, unable to get up. Their sadness affected the whole army, and everyone shed tears.

A bearded old man wrote a poem:

Having once blamed two fathers for mourning the fate of our army,
Why today do you cry yourself?
If you had done the right thing in the first place,
Mount Xiao, no matter how precipitous, would not have taken a single life.

When the people of Jiang and Pengya heard that Lord Mu had defeated Jin, they got together and threw out the generals whom Jin had left behind, restoring their allegiance to Qin. Lord Mu of Qin led his army home in triumph, whereupon he appointed Baili Shi to a senior ministerial position, giving him the same authority in the government as the two prime ministers. Xiqi Shu and Jian Bing were both rewarded with even bigger fiefs. Lord Mu changed the name of Pujin Pass to Victory Pass, to encourage his army to even greater efforts.

. . .

The chief of the Western Rong people, Chiban, was aware that the Qin army had been defeated several times in succession and he wanted to kick them while they were down, so he intended to lead the Rong in an attack against them. However, once they had come back from the attack on Jin, Lord Mu decided to turn his army against the Rong. Yao Yu asked permission to send a message to the Rong requesting tribute from them; if it did not arrive, then Qin would attack them. After Chiban heard about Baili Shi's victory, he became terrified, and when the message arrived, he led a delegation representing more than twenty states to pay court and honor Lord Mu as the hegemon of the Western Rong.

When historians talk about the history of Qin, they often cite the saying: "Obtaining a thousand soldiers is easy, getting one good general is difficult." Lord Mu trusted in Baili Shi's abilities and insisted on employing him come what may. That is why in the end he became a hegemon.

There is a poem that testifies to this:

When Cheng Dexin was executed, Lord Wen of Jin triumphed;
When Baili Shi was restored to office, Lord Xiang worried.
How amazing his achievements in making himself hegemon of the West!
Why should he care about avenging this old humiliation?

At this time Qin's awe-inspiring reputation was also known in the Zhou capital. As King Xiang said to Lord Wu of Yin, "Qin and Jin are states of equal status—their ancestors both performed signal services to the Zhou royal house. In the past Chonger was the Central States' Master of Covenants, so I appointed him as hegemon. Now, Renhao, the Earl of Qin, is certainly just as powerful as Jin, and I wish to make him the new hegemon. What do you think about that?"

"Although Qin is now hegemon of the Western Rong, they have never served Your Majesty the way that Jin has," Lord Wu of Yin replied. "At present relations between Jin and Qin are extremely tense, and moreover the new Marquis of Jin is perfectly capable of taking over his father's honors. If you were to transfer the hegemony to Qin, you would seriously offend Jin. It would be better if you were to send an ambassador to Qin and present them with gifts to congratulate him, for that way they will appreciate your gesture and yet Jin will have no reason to be angry with us."

King Xiang followed his advice.

If you want to know what happened after that, READ ON.

Chapter Forty-seven

Nongyu plays the flute and rides off on the back of a phoenix.

Zhao Dun installs Lord Ling in the teeth of all opposition from Qin.

Lord Mu of Qin united twenty countries and became hegemon of the Western Rong, so King Xiang of Zhou commanded Lord Wu of Yin to present him with a golden drum to congratulate him. The Earl of Qin said that he was too old to go to court, but he sent Noble Grandson Qi to Zhou to thank His Majesty for his kindness. That year Yao Yu became sick and died. Lord Mu was very upset by this and subsequently appointed Baili Shi as the Militia General of the Left. When Noble Grandson Qi returned from Zhou and realized how much Lord Mu had come to rely upon Baili Shi, he resigned his government post on the grounds of old age. However, no more of this now.

. . .

Lord Mu of Qin had a young daughter, who was born at the same time as someone presented a raw gemstone to His Lordship. When it was polished, it turned out to be an exceptionally fine piece of green jade. When the baby was one year old, the tray ceremony in which various objects were placed in front of the child to divine her future was held in the palace. The only thing she showed any interest in at all was this jade, which she grabbed and would not let go. Accordingly, they named her Nongyu or "Jade-holder." When she grew up, she turned out to be exceptionally beautiful and extremely clever. What is more, she was very good at playing the flute, though she had no musician to instruct her. Lord Mu commanded one of his craftsmen to carve the jade stone into a flute, and when his daughter played it, it sounded like phoenix-song. Lord Mu adored his daughter and built a special house for her to live in; this was called the Phoenix Belvedere. In front of the tower there was a great terrace, which was called Phoenix Terrace. When Nongyu was fifteen, Lord Mu began to think about finding her a suitably brilliant husband. Nongyu had her own requirements: "It must be someone who is good at playing the flute and can accompany me. That is all I want!"

Lord Mu sent people everywhere to search, but they could not find anyone suitable.

One day Nongyu rolled up the blinds around the belvedere where she lived and looked out into the cloud-covered skies, where the moon shone like a mirror. She called for her servants to light a stick of incense, and then she took her green jade flute and started to play it as she looked out of the window. The sound was pure and sweet, penetrating to the far horizon, and as the melody unfolded, it suddenly seemed as though there was someone harmonizing with her. Sometimes the sound seemed to be coming from nearby, sometimes from far away. Nongyu thought that this was strange, so she stopped playing to listen, whereupon the other player also immediately stopped, though the echoes continued to resound for some time. Nongyu was surprised and leaned out of the window. She all of a sudden felt as though she had lost something. Having paced restlessly around the room until the moon had swung around to the west and the incense was burned to ash, she laid her jade flute down upon her pillow and forced herself to sleep. In her dreams she saw the gates of Heaven swing open in the southwest, as a handsome man dressed in a plumed hat and crane-feather robe came down from the sky, riding on the back of a multicolored phoenix, through a bright pearlescent haze such as is sometimes seen at dawn.

He landed on the Phoenix Terrace and said to Nongyu, "I am the Master of Mount Taihua. God on High has commanded me to come here to marry you. On the day of the Mid-Autumn Festival we will meet, and your destiny will be completed." He pulled a red-jade pipe from his waistband, and, leaning against the railings, he began to play. The phoenix stretched its wings and danced, singing in harmony to the sound of the pipe, the music and birdsong merging into one. The notes of the melody filled her ears.

Nongyu was entranced, and without thinking, she asked: "What is this tune?"

"This is the first movement of the 'Mount Taihua Plaint'!" the handsome man replied.

"Will you teach it to me?" Nongyu asked.

"Given that we are engaged, there is no difficulty about that!" the handsome stranger said. When he had finished speaking, he took hold of Nongyu's hand. She woke up abruptly, with all that she had seen in her dream dancing before her eyes.

Once it got light, she reported her dream to Lord Mu, who accordingly sent Baili Shi to Mount Taihua to investigate. There, a local man told him: "There is a most unusual man who lives at Bright Star Cliff in these mountains. He arrived here on the fifteenth of the seventh month and built himself a hut in which he lives alone; every day he comes down the mountain to buy himself wine to drink. In the evening he always plays the pipe, and the sound can be heard all around here. Anyone who hears it forgets how tired they are. I do not know where this man came from originally!"

Baili Shi climbed Mount Taihua and arrived at the foot of Bright Star Cliff. Just as he had been told, there was a man wearing a plumed hat and crane-feather robe, of exceptional good looks and with something otherworldly about him. Baili Shi realized that this was no ordinary person, so he came forward and greeted him politely, asking his name.

"My name is Xiao Shi," he replied. "Who are you? Why have you come here?"

"I am the Militia General of the Left, Baili Shi," he explained. "His Lordship is trying to find a suitable husband for his favorite daughter. She loves playing the flute, and so she wants someone who can match her in skill. Having heard of your musical abilities, His Lordship would like very much to meet you. He commanded me to come here and invite you."

"I know a little bit about music but have no other quality to bring me to your attention," Xiao Shi said modestly. "I would not like to let you down."

"When you see His Lordship," Baili Shi said, "everything will become clear." They traveled back together, riding on the same chariot.

Baili Shi went on ahead to have an audience with Lord Mu, at which he reported everything he had discovered. After that, Xiao Shi was brought in. Lord Mu was sitting on Phoenix Terrace. Xiao Shi bowed twice and said, "I am just an ordinary man from the mountains; I know nothing about ritual propriety or the law. I hope that you will forgive me for any lapse."

Lord Mu looked at Xiao Shi's handsome face; noticing his refined and elegant appearance, he was already really pleased with him. He ordered that he sit down by his side and asked, "I have heard that you are good at playing the pipe. Are you also good at playing the flute?"

"I can only play the pipe," Xiao Shi said. "I cannot play the flute."

"I was hoping to find someone who can play the flute," Lord Mu said. "However, the flute and the pipe are completely different instruments. I am afraid that you are not right for my daughter!"

He turned his head to glance at Baili Shi, wanting him to take Xiao Shi away. However, Nongyu ordered one of her servants to take the following message to Lord Mu: "The pipe and the flute are the same kind of instrument. Since our visitor is good at playing the pipe, why not test his skills? Surely you are not going to throw him out without even giving him this opportunity?"

Lord Mu thought that she was right, and so he commanded that Xiao Shi play him a tune. Xiao Shi took out his red-jade pipe. The color of the stone glowed warmly with a soft crimson light—this was truly a treasure rarely seen in this world. When he played the first movement, a gentle wind began to blow. When he played the second movement, colored clouds gathered in the sky. When he played the third movement, a pair of white cranes began to spread their wings and dance, many pairs of peacocks gathered in the nearby trees, and all the birds sang in harmony with this melody, dispersing once it was over. Lord Mu was absolutely delighted.

Nongyu, who was present sitting behind a screen, stole a glance at the remarkable Xiao Shi and said happily, "This man really is my husband-to-be!"

"Do you know why the flute and the pipe were created?" Lord Mu asked. "When does their history begin?"

"The flute is the earliest of musical instruments," Xiao Shi answered. "It was created by the goddess Nüwa and represents creative ability. It is tuned to the note Taicu. Pan-pipes, on the other hand, are the most respected of musical instruments. They were created by Fuxi and represent peaceful existence. They are tuned to the note Zhonglü."

"Please, could you explain in more detail?" Lord Mu asked.

"My knowledge and skill is all focused upon pipes, so let me speak about them," Xiao Shi responded. "In high antiquity, Fuxi tied together a bunch of bamboo tubes, arranged in order of length so that they looked like a phoenix wing. Their sound was so beautiful and harmonious, it was like phoenix-song. He created the Elegant Pipes, the largest variety, which consisted of twenty-three tubes of which the longest was one foot and four inches. He also created the Hymn Pipes, the smallest kind, which consisted of sixteen tubes of which the longest was one foot and two inches. These are both types of pan-pipes. The pipes where the end is not sealed are called Hollow Pipes. Later on, the Yellow Emperor ordered Ling Lun to cut down the bamboos growing along the Kun Stream and fashion a flute with seven holes, which, when he played it, also sounded like phoenix-song but was much simpler than the old form of pan-pipes. Later generations disliked the complexity of the pan-pipes, and so only the single-pipe variety continued to be played. The long version is called a pipe, the short one a whistle. The pipes that people play today are not at all the same as the pan-pipes of antiquity."

"When you played your pipe, how were you able to gather all these rare varieties of birds?" Lord Mu inquired.

"Although the skill of making pipes has deteriorated, the sound remains the same," Xiao Shi assured him. "This instrument was created to mimic phoenix-song. The phoenix is the king of birds; that is why they all gather when they hear its song. In the past, the sage-king Shun composed the tune 'Xiaoshao' and phoenixes came in response to this music. If even phoenixes answer this call, how can other birds ignore it?"

Xiao Shi answered every question that was put to him so fluently and the sound of his voice was so melodious that Lord Mu was even more pleased with him. He said to Xiao Shi, "My favorite daughter's name is Nongyu, and she is very interested in music. I did not want to entrust her to a tone-deaf husband. I would be happy to marry her to you."

Xiao Shi bowed twice and refused this offer, a serious expression on his face: "I am just a peasant from the mountains. How could I possibly marry into a noble family?"

"My daughter has already sworn that she will only marry a man who is good at playing the flute," Lord Mu said. "Your playing of the pipe is truly amazing—you have convinced me that it is superior to the flute in every way! Besides which, your arrival corresponds to my daughter's dream that you would come here on the day of the Mid-Autumn Festival. Your match has been arranged by Heaven: you cannot refuse!"

Xiao Shi then bowed and thanked him. Lord Mu ordered the Grand Astrologer to select an auspicious day for the wedding, and the Grand Astrologer reported back that today was the most auspicious date of all, for the full moon above would bless the happy couple below Lord Mu ordered his entourage to prepare a bath to allow Xiao Shi to purify his body before changing into the new robe and official hat he had been awarded. The bridegroom was then escorted to the Phoenix Belvedere, where he married Nongyu. Their happiness on this occasion does not need to be described.

The following morning, Lord Mu appointed Xiao Shi a mid-ranking grandee. Although Xiao Shi now held a rank at court, he had nothing to do with the government of the country, spending every day at the Phoenix Belvedere. He would not eat cooked food, though every now and then he would drink a couple of cups of wine. Nongyu learned this habit and gradually ceased eating grain herself. Xiao Shi taught Nongyu to play the pan-pipes and composed the song "Summoning the Phoenix" for her. About six months after they were married, suddenly one night as they were playing music together under the moon, a purple phoenix alighted on the left side of the terrace and a red dragon coiled up on the right side.

"I was originally a heavenly immortal," Xiao Shi told her. "God on High became concerned that the historical records kept by people were becoming too confused and chaotic, so he ordered me to sort the situation out. That is how it came about that on the fifth day of the fifth month, in the seventeenth year of the reign of King Xuan of Zhou, I was born into the Xiao family of the Royal Domain as their third son. In the last year of King Xuan's reign, the court historians all lost their jobs, but I continued working, filling the gaps in the historical records. The people of Zhou appreciated the efforts that I had made in maintaining their documents, and that is why they called me Xiao Shi or 'Historian Xiao.' That is more than one hundred and ten years ago. God on High has now commanded me to become the Master of Mount Taihua, but we were predestined to meet by a fate determined many generations ago, which is why I played my pipes to attract your attention. However, we cannot stay long in the world of men. Today this dragon and phoenix have come to collect us, so it is time for us to go!"

Nongyu wanted to say goodbye to her father, but Xiao Shi would not allow her to do so: "You have already become an immortal. You should show no hesitation in sloughing off your worldly preoccupations. There is no way for you now to be caught up in the toils of human affections!"

Xiao Shi then rode on the back of the red dragon and Nongyu on the back of the purple phoenix as they flew up into the clouds.

Today when people call an exceptionally fine son-in-law a "dragon-rider," they are referring to this story.

That night someone heard a phoenix sing at Mount Taihua. The following morning the palace servants reported this to Lord Mu. The Earl of Qin was amazed, and said with a sigh: "There really are such things as spirits and immortals! If a dragon and a phoenix came right now to collect me, I would abandon my country just as easily as throwing away a pair of worn-out shoes!"

He ordered people to go to Mount Taihua to track them down, but no one ever saw either of them again.

A temple was constructed at the foot of Bright Star Cliff, at which annual offerings were made of wine and fruit. Right up to the present day this place is known as Lady Xiao's Temple, and the sound of phoenix-song is heard within its precincts from time to time.

During the Six Dynasties, Bao Zhao wrote the "Song of Xiao Shi:"

Xiao Shi was a handsome young man,
Thus a daughter of the ruling house of Ying fell madly in love with him.
She was willing to cease eating cooked food and grain,
That she might climb with him into the Empyrean.
A flying dragon can traverse the roads of Heaven,
A soaring phoenix can escape the borders of Qin.
Once gone, she never returned,
Only her flute-song can be heard from time to time.

Jiang Zong also wrote a poem on the same theme:

Nongyu was a daughter of the Qin ruling house,
Xiao Shi a handsome young immortal.
He arrived as the moon became full,
They departed leaving the Phoenix Tower desolate.
Smiles exchanged in secret formed their bond,
The haunting strains of their melody can sometimes still be heard.
They came together in a blaze of glorious color,
They flew off into the purple mists.

From this time onwards, Lord Mu found it increasingly difficult to show any interest in warfare, for his mind turned more and more to otherworldly matters. The running of the country was entrusted entirely to Baili Shi, as Lord Mu devoted himself to purification and self-cultivation. Not long after this, Noble Grandson Qi died. Baili Shi recommended the three sons of the Che family for office; Yanxi, Zhonghang, and Zhenhu were all virtuous and talented men, who were known to one and all as the "Three Good Men." Lord Mu appointed all three of them as grandees and treated them very generously. Three years later, on the fifteenth day of the second month of the thirty-first year of the reign of King Xiang of Zhou, Lord Mu was sitting on the Phoenix Terrace gazing at the moon and missing his daughter Nongyu. He had no idea where she had gone or if they would ever meet again. He suddenly fell asleep. In his dream he saw Nongyu and Xiao Shi coming to meet him, riding on a phoenix, and they took him on a journey to the moon, where the cold pierced his bones. When he woke up, he turned out to have contracted pneumonia, from which he died a couple of days later. People said that he had become an immortal. He had been in power for thirty-nine years and died at the age of sixty-nine. Lord Mu's first wife was the daughter of Lord Xian of Jin, and her son was the Scion of Qin who now succeeded to the title as Lord Kang. He buried Lord Mu at Yongzhou. According to the custom of the Western Rong, human sacrifices formed part of the funeral ceremonies in which one hundred and seventy-seven people died; the three sons of the Che family were among their number. The people of the capital were most upset about this and composed the song "The Yellow Birds."

This song can be found in the "Airs of the States" section of the Book of Songs. *When later generations discussed the fact that Lord Mu had the "Three Good Men" used as human sacrifice at his funeral, they seemed to be under the impression that Lord Mu regarded his own death as more important than the loss of these men to the government of the country, and argued that he had completely lost any sense of planning for the future. Only Su Dongpo of the Song dynasty, in his writings on the tomb of Lord Mu of Qin, raises the possibility that this might have been their own wish.*

He says:

> The Hidden Springs Palace is located in the eastern part of the city, and the tomb is not one hundred paces from the city wall. Although in antiquity this wall had not yet been built, it nevertheless serves as a landmark allowing the people of Qin to recognize the location of Lord Mu's tomb. Originally he refused to execute Baili Shi on numerous occasions, so surely it is not possible that he could order the deaths of the other good men when he died? This suggests that the three men died out of a sense of public duty, just like the two men who died in Qi for Tian Heng. People in antiquity seem to have felt that being given a meal created such a debt of honor that only death could repay it. Since we no longer have people like this, it leads us to doubt their very existence. But just because we do not understand the people of the past, does that make modern people more invulnerable?

• • •

Let us now turn to another part of the story. In the sixth year of Lord Xiang of Jin, he appointed his son, the Honorable Yigao, as scion and sent his younger half-brother, the Honorable Le, to serve in Chen. That same year, Zhao Cui, Luan Zhi, Xian Qieju, and Xu Chen died one after the other. Losing four ministers in succession meant that a number of key positions became vacant simultaneously. The following year a great muster was held of men and chariots in Yi; they gave up two armies and went back to the old standard of having just three. Lord Xiang wanted to appoint Shi Hu and Liang Yier as generals in command of the Central Army, with Ji Zhengfu and Xian Du in command of the Upper Army.

Xian Qieju's son, Xian Ke, came forward and said: "The Hu and the Zhao families have done great things for Jin; you cannot remove them from office. Besides which, Shi Hu already holds senior office as the minister of works, and neither he nor Liang Yier has any military experience. If you insist on appointing them as generals, I am afraid that the people will not support your choice."

Lord Xiang followed his advice and appointed Hu Shegu as commander-in-chief of the Central Army with Zhao Dun to assist him; Ji Zhengfu became commander-in-chief of the Upper Army with Xun Linfu to assist him; and Xian Mie became commander-in-chief of the Lower Army with Xian Du to assist him. Hu Shegu climbed onto the command platform and gave his orders, placing everyone just as he wished, without apparently even noticing the other officers.

One of his subordinates, the cavalry commander Yu Pian, remonstrated with him: "I have heard it said that a successful commander-in-chief relies upon harmonious relations with his officers. The generals in command of all three armies are all excellent men and come from families who have served in the government for many generations. You should treat them politely and ask their opinions. It was because he was too inflexible and arrogant that Cheng Dechen was defeated by Jin. You should take this as a warning!"

Hu Shegu was furious and shouted at him: "I have already given my orders; how dare you interfere! You are destroying military discipline!" He screamed at his entourage to whip him one hundred times. After that everyone had lost their respect for him.

• • •

When Shi Hu and Liang Yier heard that it was Xian Ke who had prevented their promotion, they were absolutely furious. Xian Du was also angry because he had not received the position of commander-in-chief of the Upper Army. At this time the Grand Tutor Yang Chufu was on a diplomatic mission to Chen, so he had nothing to do with all of this, but when he returned to the country and discovered that Hu Shegu had been appointed as commander-in-chief, he secretly presented his opinion to Lord Xiang: "Hu Shegu is a hard man and very competitive, not to mention abrasive in his relationship with other people. He is never going to make a great general. I served many years in the army under Zhao Cui's command, and his son, Zhao Dun, is someone whom I know well. He is extremely clever. It has always been our abiding principle to respect the wise and employ the capable. If you wish to appoint a new commander-in-chief, Zhao Dun would be best."

Lord Xiang followed his recommendation and ordered Yang Chufu to hold another set of military exercises at Dong. Hu Shegu knew nothing about the decision to appoint someone else as commander-in-chief, and he was happily employed arranging the divisions in the Central Army. Lord Xiang called his name: "Hu Shegu! In the past I had Zhao Dun support you, now I would like you to help Zhao Dun." Hu Shegu did not dare to say a single word; he just mumbled his agreement and withdrew. Lord Xiang then appointed Zhao Dun formally as commander-in-chief of the Central Army with Hu Shegu as his deputy. The commanders of the Upper and Lower Army remained the same as before. From this time onwards Zhao Dun took charge of the country, instituting major reforms that deeply pleased the people.

Someone said to Yang Chufu, "Zhao Dun always speaks his mind and seems very loyal, but is it not a problem that he seems to arouse people's enmity so easily?"

"If what he does benefits the country," Yang Chufu asked, "why should he not make a few enemies?"

The following day, Hu Shegu had a private audience with Lord Xiang, at which he asked: "Your Lordship appointed me to the ministry of war in recognition of the services performed for the state by my ancestors and in spite of my own meager abilities. However, suddenly I have been removed from office, and I have no idea what I have done wrong! Does this mean that what my father did for the country is thought to be less than what Zhao Cui did? Or is there some other reason?"

"You don't understand," Lord Xiang replied. "Yang Chufu explained to me that you are not someone the people trust and respect, therefore you cannot be the most senior military commander. That is why I removed you from office."

Hu Shegu withdrew in silence.

• • •

In the eighth month, Lord Xiang of Jin became ill, and it quickly became apparent that he was dying. He summoned the Grand Tutor Yang Chufu and the senior minister Zhao Dun to his bedside, as well as various other close advisors, and instructed them: "My attacks on the Di and the state of Qin were merely continuations of my father's struggles; I have never yet prosecuted a war abroad. I am going to die soon, so I will have to say goodbye to you forever. Scion Yigao is very young, so you will all have to do your very best to support him and find allies among our neighbors. You must not let the position of Master of Covenants fall into other hands!"

The assembled ministers bowed twice and accepted his commands. Shortly afterwards Lord Xiang died. The following day, the ministers wanted to install the scion as the new marquis, but Zhao Dun said: "The country is in a lot of trouble. The Di and the state of Qin are our inveterate enemies—we cannot have a young ruler in power. Now Lady Qi of Du's son, the Honorable Yong, is currently employed in a government position in Qin. What is more, he is an adult and a good man. We should bring him back and let him assume the marquisate."

None of the ministers said a word. Then Hu Shegu responded: "It would be even better if we appointed the Honorable Le. His mother was the late Lord Wen's favorite wife. Le has been attached to the court of Chen, as a result of which he persuaded them to make peace with Jin. We have nothing like the problems with them that we do with Qin. If we invite him back, he can set out in the morning and be here by dusk."

"No!" Zhao Dun exclaimed. "Chen is too small and too far away. Qin is big and much closer by. If we bring in a lord from Chen it will do nothing for us, whereas bringing one in from Qin means that we can put an end to the enmity between our two countries and create an important strategic alliance. We must have the Honorable Yong!"

That put an end to the discussion. They appointed Xian Mie as ambassador with Shi Hui to assist him. He was to go to Qin to report the death of His Lordship and bring the Honorable Yong back to become the next lord.

Just as Xian Mie was about to set out, Xun Linfu stopped him and said, "Her Ladyship and the scion are both here, and yet you want to bring in a new lord abroad. I am afraid that this will not work, and it will simply provoke a coup. Why do you not refuse this commission on the grounds of ill health?"

"The government is entirely in the hands of the Zhao family," Xian Mie replied. "How can there possibly be a coup?"

Afterwards Xun Linfu remarked to someone else, "If you serve together as officials in the same government, then you are colleagues; Xian Mie and I have now been colleagues for a long time. I have expressed my innermost thoughts, but he has not listened to me. I am afraid that he will go, never to return!"

. . .

Let us not speak of Xian Mie's journey to Qin, but turn instead to the subject of Hu Shegu's audience with Zhao Dun, which led to the latter ignoring his advice. "The Hu and Zhao clans are equally distinguished," Hu Shegu said angrily. "Is it possible that today the Zhao family has completely eclipsed the Hus?"

He secretly sent someone to summon the Honorable Le from Chen, with the intention of disputing the succession. Naturally, someone immediately informed Zhao Dun of this development. Zhao Dun sent one of his men, Gongsun Chujiu, to lie in ambush on the road at the head of a small force of one hundred men. They waited until the Honorable Le came past and then killed him.

Hu Shegu was even more furious and said, "Yang Chufu put Zhao Dun in power. This family is weak and without powerful support, and he has now gone to live outside the suburbs to take charge of the arrangements for all the ambassadors who will attend His Late Lordship's funeral—it will be easy enough to assassinate him! Zhao Dun has killed the Honorable Le; now I am going to kill Yang Chufu, what could be fairer than that?"

He conspired with his younger brother, Hu Juju, who said, "I can do this!" He and a number of other members of the Hu family dressed up as robbers and broke into Yang Chufu's house at midnight, climbing over the wall. Yang Chufu was sitting reading by lamplight when Hu Juju attacked him, stabbing him in the shoulder. Yang Chufu fled in terror, but Hu Juju chased after him and killed him, after which he cut off his head and took it home. One of Yang Chufu's servants recognized Hu Juju and reported this to Zhao Dun, who pretended not to believe a word of what he was saying. "Grand Tutor Yang was murdered by robbers!" he yelled. "How dare you slander anyone else?" He ordered the servants to collect the body for burial. This happened in the middle of the ninth month.

. . .

In the tenth month, Lord Xiang was buried at Quwo. Lord Xiang's widow, Lady Mu Ying, attended the funeral with Scion Yigao, and she said to Zhao Dun: "What did His Late Lordship do wrong? What crime has his son and heir committed? Why have you set his claims aside and brought in a new lord from abroad?"

"This is an important matter of state," Zhao Dun replied. "It was not done for my own selfish reasons!"

Once the funeral was over and His Lordship's name-tablet had been placed in the ancestral temple, Zhao Dun announced to all the ministers present: "His Late Lordship was the only person who could wield the two handles of power—rewards and punishments—and that is how he was able to dominate the other feudal lords. Now His Lordship is lying in his coffin, and so Hu Juju has dared to murder Yang Chufu. In circumstances like this, is anyone safe? We must punish him!"

Hu Juju was arrested and handed over to the minister of justice, who read out a list of his crimes and had him beheaded. When a search was carried out of his house, they discovered Yang Chufu's head, which was then sewn back onto his neck before the body was buried. Hu Shegu was afraid that Zhao Dun knew of his role in the conspiracy, so that very night he got into a light chariot and fled to the Di, where he threw in his lot with the Di chief, Baitun.

• • •

At that time there was a giant among the Di people whose name was Qiaoru. He was over two meters tall, and everyone called him the "Tall Di." He was also strong enough to be able to lift a thousand pounds, and he was tough enough to be able to break bricks with his head without injuring himself in the slightest. Baitun appointed him as general and ordered him to invade Lu. Lord Wen sent Shusun Dechen to command the army that would resist them. By that time it was deep into the winter months and snow clouds filled the skies.

Grandee Fufu Zhongsheng, realizing that it was about to start snowing, came up with the following plan: "Qiaoru is unusually brave. We can counter him with cunning, not with brute force."

They therefore dug deep pits along the main road and covered them with straw, which they then daubed with mud. That night, just as they had anticipated, it snowed heavily, carpeting the ground so that it was impossible to see the traps. Fufu Zhongsheng led one division of his army to attempt to break into Qiaoru's encampment. Qiaoru came out to attack, and Fufu Zhongsheng pretended to be defeated. This resulted in Qiaoru setting off in hot pursuit. Fufu Zhongsheng had left secret markers allowing him and his men to recognize and pass safely by the pits in the road, but when Qiaoru followed him, he fell into their trap. Shusun Dechen and the soldiers waiting in ambush then rose up and killed the Di warriors. Fufu Zhongsheng killed Qiaoru by stabbing him through the throat with his spear. Then he loaded his body into a huge cart. Everyone who saw the corpse was amazed, thinking it was the giant god Fangfeng. When Shusun Dechen's oldest son was born, he was named Shusun Qiaoru, to commemorate this great victory.

After this the states of Lu, Qi, and Wey launched a combined attack on the Di that resulted in the death of Baitun and the destruction of his country. Hu Shegu then traveled to the Red Di state of Loo, where he threw himself upon the mercies of Grandee Feng Shu of Loo.

"My father and Hu Yan went into exile together at the same time," Zhao Dun said, "and they both served His Late Lordship devotedly. I executed Hu Juju as a warning to Hu Shegu; he became frightened and fled into exile. However, it would not be right to leave him all alone among the Di!"

He ordered Yu Pian to escort Hu Shegu's wife and family to Loo. Yu Pian summoned his servants because they were going to accompany him. As they were about to set out, these man complained: "During the muster of the army at Yi, you behaved with the utmost loyalty to Commander-in-Chief Hu, which he repaid by humiliating you. You must take revenge! Now Zhao Dun has ordered you to escort his wife and children to the Di, which is a Heaven-sent opportunity. Kill all of them to avenge the insult that you have suffered!"

Yu Pian said over and over again, "No! No! Zhao Dun has entrusted me with Hu Shegu's wife and children as a sign of favor. If he wants them sent to the Di and I kill them, will he not be angry with me? It would not be benevolent to take advantage of someone else's troubles to attack them; equally, it would not be wise to provoke the anger of a man like Zhao Dun!" He put Hu Shegu's wife and the rest of his family in a carriage and having carefully checked the lists of the family property, he personally escorted them across the border without any incident.

When Hu Shegu heard this, he sighed and said, "I had this clever man right beside me and did not realize it; no wonder that I am now in exile!"

Zhao Dun came to esteem Yu Pian greatly as a result of his behavior on this occasion, and he decided to entrust him with important commissions.

• • •

When Xian Mie and Shi Hui arrived in Qin, they informed the Honorable Yong that he was now the new marquis. Lord Kang of Qin was delighted and said, "My father established two lords of Jin, and now I have established the Honorable Yong. The lords of Jin have now come from Qin for many generations!" He ordered Jian Bing to escort the Honorable Yong to Jin with a guard of four hundred chariots.

When Lord Xiang's widow, Lady Mu Ying, returned to the capital after the funeral, she would get up at dawn every day. Holding Scion Yigao in her arms, she would go to court and cry, asking the assembled grandees, "This is His Late Lordship's legitimate heir. Why have you abandoned him?"

Once court was dismissed, she would order her carriage to take her to the Zhao family mansion, where she would kowtow to Zhao Dun and say, "Just before he died, His Late Lordship instructed you to do everything in your power to help this child. Even though His Lordship is dead, how could you establish someone else with his words still ringing in your ears? Where can this wretched child go? Given that my son has been dispossessed, we may as well die!" When she had finished speaking, she carried on wailing and crying.

When the people of the capital heard this, they felt deeply sorry for Lady Mu Ying, and everyone blamed Zhao Dun. The grandees also started talking about the appointment of the Honorable Yong as a bad idea, and Zhao Dun became increasingly worried. He discussed the situation with Xi Que: "Xian Mie has already gone to Qin to welcome our new lord; how can we possibly install the scion?"

"At the moment you have decided that we need an adult ruler," Xi Que replied, "and so you have set aside this child's claims. However, he will grow up, and one day he is sure to launch a coup. You had better quickly send someone to Qin to stop Xian Mie."

"We will establish the new lord first and then call off the embassy," Zhao Dun said, "for that way we have legal sanction for our actions."

He immediately ordered all the ministers to assemble, and they installed Scion Yigao as Lord Ling of Jin. At that time he was not yet seven years of age.

When the officials had finished offering their formal congratulations, suddenly a spy from the borders reported: "Qin has sent a huge army to escort the Honorable Yong home. They have already arrived at the Yellow River."

"We have behaved very badly to Qin," the grandees exclaimed. "What on earth are we going to say to them?"

"If we were going to install the Honorable Yong as our next ruler, then Qin would be our honored guests," Zhao Dun announced. "However, since we are not going to put him in power, they are our enemies. If we were to send an ambassador to apologize to them, they would have a good excuse to attack us. We had better send our army to deal with them!"

He ordered the general in command of the Upper Army, Ji Zhengfu, to remain behind to protect Lord Ling; Zhao Dun himself took command of the Central Army with Xian Ke as his deputy, filling the position left vacant by Hu Shegu. Xun Linfu commanded the Upper Army alone, while Xian Du commanded the Lower Army alone, since Xian Mie had gone to Qin. Once the three armies had been organized, they advanced to meet the Qin army and camped at Jinyin. The Qin army had already crossed the Yellow River and was moving eastwards, making camp when they reached Linghu. On discovering the Jin army in front of them, they still thought that they had come to welcome the Honorable Yong and were completely unprepared for any trouble.

Xian Mie went on ahead to the Jin camp to see Zhao Dun, who then informed him that Scion Yigao had already become the new ruler. Xian Mie opened his eyes wide and glared at him, saying, "Whose idea was it to bring back the Honorable Yong anyway? Are you going to prevent us from going any further because you have already installed the scion?" He brushed down his sleeves and left. When he saw Xun Linfu, he said, "I really regret not listening to your advice—now I am in a pretty fix!"

Xun Linfu stopped him and said, "You are a minister of the state of Jin. If you leave here, where can you go?"

"I was ordered to go to Qin to bring back the Honorable Yong," Xian Mie said, "so he is now my lord. Qin will not go back on their word to support him. Although I enjoyed wealth and nobility in Jin, that is nothing to me now!" He rushed back to the Qin encampment.

"Since Xian Mie is not willing to stay in Jin," Zhao Dun said, "the Qin army will attack us. We had better launch an assault on the Qin camp overnight, when they are least expecting it, for that is the only way that we can win."

He gave orders that a full ration of hay should be given to the horses, while the army officers rested and ate their fill. Then they marched silently but quickly on the Qin camp, arriving just after midnight. With a great shout the drums were sounded and they attacked the main gate. The Qin army woke from their dreams in a panic; they had no time to saddle their horses, they had no time to grab their spears, they rushed here and there trying to escape. The Jin army pursued them right up to Kushou. Jian Bing was able to escape only after a desperate struggle, but the Honorable Yong was killed in the confusion.

Xian Mie sighed and said, "Zhao Dun has betrayed me, but I will not betray Qin!" He fled into exile in Qin.

Shi Hui also sighed and said, "I have served in the government with Xian Mie for a long time. Now that he has gone to Qin, I am not going to go home alone!" He too followed the Qin army back to their capital, whereupon Lord Kang of Qin appointed both these men as grandees.

Xun Linfu spoke to Zhao Dun. "When Hu Shegu fled to the Di, you remembered your long-standing working relationship and sent his wife and children to join him. Now another of your old colleagues, Xian Mie, has followed his example. I hope that you will do exactly the same as you did before!"

"You are a very righteous man," Zhao Dun replied. "That is exactly what I intend."

He ordered Wei Shi to escort the families of the two men and all their portable wealth to Qin.

Master Hu Zeng wrote a poem about this:

Who would escort another man's wife and children abroad?
Only someone who really respects the relationship between old colleagues.
Nowadays when people are so suspicious and jealous,
How could this kind of friendly feeling exist?

A bearded old man also wrote a poem criticizing Zhao Dun for his frivolous decision to make the Honorable Yong the new ruler of Jin, which resulted in friends becoming enemies:

When advancing your pawns in chess, you have to consider the consequences;
With a legitimate heir at home, why did you need to go abroad?
Turning old friends into enemies in the blink of an eye,
What on earth was Zhao Dun thinking of?

Each of the generals in this battle took some prisoners. However, one of Xian Ke's subordinates, a man named Kuai De, was so determined to advance that he ignored all the possible dangers, as a result of which he was not only defeated by Qin but also lost the division of five chariots he commanded. Xian Ke wanted to execute him in accordance with military law. The other generals asked for clemency, and Xian Ke then spoke to Zhao Dun about it. He stripped him of his lands and emoluments. Kuai De was absolutely furious about this.

. . .

Ji Zhengfu, Shi Hu, and Liang Yier were all close friends. Once Zhao Dun was appointed as commander-in-chief of the Central Army, Shi Hu and Liang Yier were stripped of power. Even Ji Zhengfu was unhappy about the situation. At this time Ji Zhengfu was guarding the capital, and Shi Hu and Liang Yier would join him and complain: "Zhao Dun appoints and dismisses people at a whim; he really does not care what anyone else thinks. The word is that Qin has sent an enormous army to escort the Honorable Yong here, and if push comes to shove, it is not at all clear who is going to win. If we lead an uprising against Zhao Dun, we can get rid of Yigao and put the Honorable Yong in power, which means that in the future all power within the state will be in our hands."

That was their decision, but were they successful? READ ON.

Chapter Forty-eight

After assassinating Xian Ke, five generals cause trouble in Jin.

In order to summon back Shi Hui, Wei Shouyu lies to Qin.

The three men, Ji Zhengfu, Shi Hu, and Liang Yier, discussed the situation. They decided to wait until the Qin army really made itself felt, and then they would start a revolt inside the city, with a view to getting rid of Zhao Dun. What they were not expecting was that Zhou Dun would make a surprise attack upon the Qin army and defeat them, returning home in triumph. They were enraged by this development. Xian Du was in command of the Lower Army since the senior general, Xian Mie, had been betrayed by Zhao Dun and fled to Qin. He too was deeply angry with Zhao Dun, which only became worse when he met Kuai De and discovered that Xian Ke had taken over all of his lands and emoluments as well as gaining control of the army. He discussed this situation with Shi Hu.

"Xian Ke relies on the protection that he receives from Zhao Dun," Shi Hu told him, "and that is why he dares to behave so arrogantly. Zhao Dun is able to monopolize power because he controls the Central Army. If there were one brave man who could come forward to kill Xian Ke, Zhao Dun would find himself isolated and at our mercy. We need Xian Du!"

"Xian Du hates Zhao Dun too because of how he treated Xian Mie!" Kuai De shouted.

"If that is the case," Shi Hu said, "then Ke will not be difficult to deal with!" He leaned over and whispered, "If you undertake the mission, everything will be fine."

"I will go and speak to him immediately!" Kuai De said happily.

He went to see Xian Du, but it was actually Xian Du who broached the subject first: "Zhao Dun betrayed Xian Mie and made a surprise attack on the Qin army that resulted in their defeat. He has behaved in a completely untrustworthy and unjust way. It is impossible to work with someone like that!"

Kuai De reported to Xian Du what Shi Hu had said. Xian Du answered, "If he can indeed accomplish this, it would be a great thing for the state of Jin!"

At this time winter was already over and spring was on its way. Xian Ke traveled to the city of Ji in order to pray at the shrine dedicated to the memory of his grandfather, Xian Zhen. Xian Du had arranged for his guards to lie in ambush outside the city walls of Ji and wait until Xian Ke had gone past. They followed him at a distance, looking for an opportunity to strike. Once it came, they fell on him and stabbed him to death; Xian Ke's followers scattered in panic. When Zhao Dun heard that Xian Ke had been murdered by rebels, he was very angry and gave strict orders that the minister of justice should capture those responsible within the next five days. Xian Du and the others now became frightened and discussed what to do with Kuai De, who encouraged Shi Hu and Liang Yier to strike as soon as possible. When he was drunk, Liang Yier let slip the secret to Liang Hong.

Liang Hong was terrified and said, "This is the kind of thing that will get your whole clan killed!"

He secretly reported all that he knew to Yu Pian, who in turn reported it to Zhao Dun. Zhao Dun gathered his forces and instructed them to await his orders.

When Xian Du realized that Zhao Dun was gathering his forces, he suspected that the plot was known. He rushed around to Shi Hu's house and told him to act as quickly as he could. Ji Zhengfu wanted to make use of the festival of Shangyuan on the fifth day of the first month, when the Marquis of Jin held a great banquet, to start their uprising; they argued for ages without coming to any decision. Zhao Dun sent Yu Pian to go first to Xian Du's house and surround it, whereupon he arrested Xian Du and carted him off to prison. Liang Yier and Kuai De now started to panic, and they came up with a plan whereby they would join forces with Ji Zhengfu and Shi Hu, break Xian Du out of prison, and then launch their uprising together. Zhao Dun sent someone to Ji Zhengfu to tell him about Xian Du's conspiracy and invited him to court to discuss the situation.

"If Zhao Dun has summoned me," Ji Zhengfu said, "he cannot suspect me of involvement in the plot!" He set off perfectly happily. In fact Zhao Dun was concerned about the fact that Ji Zhengfu was the commander-in-chief of the Upper Army and he was afraid that he might incite his troops to foment rebellion, which is why he pretended that he needed to consult him. Ji Zhengfu had no idea that this was a plot and went off to court without a care in the world. Zhao Dun invited him into a council chamber on the grounds that he wanted to discuss Xian Du's conspiracy. He secretly ordered Xun Linfu, Xi Que, and Luan Dun to take the soldiers under their command and arrest Shi Hu, Liang Yier, and Kuai De. Once they had all been transferred to prison, Xun Linfu and the others came to the council chamber to report.

"Ji Zhengfu was also one of the rebels," Xun Linfu shouted. "Why hasn't he been arrested yet?"

"I have guarded the capital with my life!" Ji Zhengfu screamed. "When the three armies were out on campaign, I was left alone here. Now that everyone has come back, how can you suddenly decide to kill me?"

"The reason that your rebellion was delayed was because you were waiting for Xian Du and Kuai De," Zhao Dun retorted. "I already know all about it! I will not believe your prevarications!" Ji Zhengfu hung his head as he was bundled off to prison.

Zhao Dun reported what had happened to Lord Ling, with the intention of executing Xian Du and the four other men. Lord Ling was only a child, and so he had to agree. When Lord Ling returned to the palace, his mother had already heard about the arrest and imprisonment of the five men, so she asked him: "How does the prime minister plan to punish them?"

"The prime minister says their crime deserves the death penalty," Lord Ling replied.

His mother, Lady Xiang, said, "This whole thing came about in a competition over power in the state. They never had any intention of usurping the lord's authority. Only one or two of these men were actually involved in the plan to assassinate Xian Ke. Given that some of them masterminded this and others were just following orders, why should all of them be executed? In recent years many senior ministers have passed away, leaving us with a serious dearth of administrative talent. If one morning we execute five ministers, that will leave the court empty. Surely this should also be considered!"

The following day, Lord Ling reported Lady Xiang's words to Zhao Dun. Zhao Dun presented his opinion: "You, my lord, are very young, and the country is not at peace. If senior ministers murder one another and go unpunished, how can we keep order in the future?"

The five men, Xian Du, Shi Hu, Ji Zhengfu, Liang Yier, and Kuai De, were all found guilty of the crime of lèse-majesté and beheaded in the marketplace. Xian Ke's son, Xian Hu, was appointed as a grandee. The people of the Jin capital were terrified of Zhao Dun and trembled in his presence.

Hu Shegu was living in the state of Loo when he heard what had happened. He was shocked and said, "How lucky I am to have escaped death!"

Shortly afterwards, it happened that Grandee Feng Shu of Loo asked Hu Shegu, "Who is cleverer, Zhao Cui or Zhao Dun?"

"Zhao Cui was like the sun in winter," Hu Shegu said, "while Zhao Dun is like the sun in summer. In the winter you rely upon its warmth, in the summer you fear its heat."

Feng Shu laughed: "You are a general, but you too are afraid of Zhao Dun!"

Master Qian Yuan wrote a poem:

Zhao Cui yielded and gave way, refusing supreme power,
How could the summer sun be as valued as the winter one?
A moment's anger saw his colleagues ripped to pieces,
And the people of Jin found they could no longer sleep soundly at night.

. . .

Let us now turn to another part of the story. After King Mu of Chu usurped the throne, his ambition was aroused to fight for hegemony over the Central Plain. He heard from his spies: "The Lord of Jin has only just been appointed and Zhao Dun monopolizes power in the government, leading the grandees to fight and kill each other." He then summoned his ministers and discussed the situation, for he wanted to attack Zheng.

Grandee Fan Shan came forward and said, "The Lord of Jin is young, and his ministers are quarreling among themselves—they have no attention to spare for the feudal lords. If you were to take advantage of this situation to advance your troops and invade the north, who can resist you?"

King Mu was very pleased. He appointed Dou Yuejiao as the senior general and Wei Jia as his deputy, and ordered them to attack Zheng in command of a force of three hundred chariots. He personally led the finest troops from the Guangxi and Guangdong regions to camp at

Langyuan, from where reinforcements could be issued as required. In addition to that, he appointed Prince Zhu as senior general with Prince Fei as his deputy, with orders to lead a force of three hundred chariots to attack Chen.

When Lord Mu of Zheng heard that the Chu army had arrived at his borders, he immediately sent Grandee the Honorable Jian, the Honorable Pang, and the Honorable Yue'er to take the army to intercept them there, with instructions that they were to defend the fortifications and not to go out to do battle. In addition, he sent someone to report this emergency to Jin. Dou Yuejiao tried to provoke battle day after day, but the Zheng army would not leave their fortresses.

Wei Jia spoke secretly to Dou Yuejiao: "After the battle of Chengpu, the Chu army left Zheng in peace. Zheng is relying on receiving help from Jin, so they are refusing to fight us. If we take advantage of the fact that the Jin army still has not arrived to trick them and take them prisoner, we will be able to avenge the humiliating defeat that we suffered then. Otherwise, if things drag out much longer, the feudal lords will eventually assemble. We will simply repeat what happened to Cheng Dechen, and there will be nothing that we can do to change things!"

"You want to trick them," Dou Yuejiao said, "so what is your plan?"

Wei Jia whispered in his ear: "This is what we have to do . . ."

Dou Yuejiao followed his plan and gave the following orders to his army: "We are starting to run out of food, so you should go and steal what we need from neighboring towns and villages so that we have enough supplies." Afterwards he had the drums sounded in the main tent and drank wine, holding parties every day, which did not break up until late into the night. Someone reported this to Langyuan, but King Mu of Chu was sure that Dou Yuejiao was trying to trick the enemy in some way. He wanted to go in person to see the battle, but Fan Shan said, "Dou Yuejiao is a brilliant commander, and I am sure that he has a good plan. In a few days news of his victory will reach us!"

The Honorable Jian and the others became concerned when the Chu army did not come anymore to try and make them fight, so they sent someone to investigate. He reported back: "The Chu army are busy plundering for food all over the place while Commander-in-Chief Dou and the rest of the Central Army spend every day drinking and playing music. When they are drunk they curse us, saying that the people of Zheng are useless and there is no point in killing us."

The Honorable Jian was delighted and said, "If the Chu army is robbing the neighborhood, their food supplies must be exhausted; if the

Chu generals are drinking and playing music, they must be terribly overconfident. If we make a surprise attack on their camp overnight, we will win a famous victory."

The Honorable Pang and Yue'er thought this was a splendid plan. That night after they had eaten their fill, the Honorable Pang wanted to divide his forces into three groups—front, middle, and rear—to advance in order. The Honorable Jian said, "Attacking a camp is not at all the same as going into battle against troops drawn up in formation; a surprise attack requires everyone to launch their assault at the same time, so you divide into left and right wings, not into advance and rearguards!" The three generals accordingly proceeded together.

As they moved towards the Chu camp, in the distance they could see the glittering light of lamps, and the clear sound of flutes floated out towards them. The Honorable Jian said, "It is time for them to die!" His battle chariot plunged forward, and the Chu army was completely unable to counter this attack. The Honorable Jian was the first to rush into the encampment, and the musicians fled in all directions. Dou Yuejiao was the only person to remain in his seat, not moving at all. When Jian came forward and looked more closely, in a moment of absolute horror he realized it was a scarecrow dressed up in Dou Yuejiao's clothes.

The Honorable Jian called out in panic: "We have fallen into a trap!"

Just as they were trying to make their way out of the encampment, they suddenly heard the rumbling of siege engines and a general led his troops to attack them, shouting: "Dou Yuejiao is right here!"

The Honorable Jian realized that he would not be able to escape easily, so he joined with the Honorable Pang and the Honorable Yue'er to cut their way out. Before they had even gone one *li*, they heard the sound of siege engines in front of them. Wei Jia and his troops were lying in ambush on the main road, and now they too attacked the Zheng army. With Wei Jia in front of them and Dou Yuejiao behind them, the two wings of the Chu army were able to advance in a pincer movement, inflicting a terrible defeat on the Zheng army. The Honorable Pang and Yue'er were both captured. The Honorable Jian risked his own life to try and rescue them; however, his horses stumbled and his chariot overturned, so he too was taken prisoner by the Chu army.

Terribly shocked, Lord Mu of Zheng asked his ministers, "Our three generals have been taken prisoner and help from Jin has not yet arrived. What are we going to do?"

"Chu is becoming increasingly powerful," they replied, "so we had better surrender before they raze our city walls and moats. Even Jin cannot match these people!"

Lord Mu of Zheng sent the Honorable Feng to the Chu camp to apologize for their crimes and offer bribes in the hope of being allowed to make a peace treaty. He swore that he would never betray Chu again. Dou Yuejiao sent someone to ask for a decision from King Mu of Chu, who agreed. He then released the Honorable Jian, Pang, and Yue'er from captivity and sent them back to Zheng.

King Mu of Chu gave the order to stand down the army, but just as he was on his way home, Prince Zhu of Chu attacked the Chen army and was defeated, his deputy general, Prince Fei, being taken prisoner by Chen. The survivors had followed King Mu's route from Langyuan because they wanted to ask for more troops with which to avenge this defeat. King Mu was furious and wanted to attack Chen. Suddenly a report came in: "An ambassador has arrived from Chen to return Prince Fei to us and beg permission to surrender." King Mu ripped open the letter and read it:

> I live in a small and remote country, making it impossible for me to serve Your Majesty. However, I hope that you will have a peaceful journey. My border officials are stupid and violent men who have taken a couple of your princes prisoner. I was so deeply alarmed at this news that I could not sleep. I respectfully send this messenger to return your chariots and horses to you. I wish to surrender to you in the hope of thereby receiving your protection. I hope that Your Majesty will stoop to taking me in.

King Mu laughed and said, "Chen is afraid that we would punish them, and that is why they are begging to be allowed to surrender. His Lordship could be said to understand the situation!" He agreed to the surrender and sent an invitation to the lords of Chen and Zheng, as well as the Marquis of Cai, to attend a meeting at Juehao on the first day of the tenth month.

. . .

When Zhao Dun of Jin received the message from the people of Zheng reporting the emergency, he sent envoys to assemble a coalition from Song, Lu, Wey, and Xu to rescue Zheng. However, before they had even arrived at the borders of Zheng, they were informed of the surrender and the departure of the Chu army. In addition, they discovered that Chen had also surrendered to Chu. Grandee Hua Ou of Song and Grandee the

Honorable Sui of Lu both asked permission to attack Chen and Zheng, but Zhao Dun said, "These two countries were lost because we could not save them. In what way is this their fault? We had better go home and put our own houses in order." He then stood down his army.

An old man wrote a poem bewailing these events:

Who was in control of the country? Who was the master of the feudal lords?
How could you allow the barbarians from Chu to get away with this!
Today as both Zheng and Chen were lost,
The hegemony of the Central Plain silently collapsed.

At the end of autumn, both Shuo, Marquis of Chen, and Lan, Earl of Zheng, arrived at Xi to await the arrival of King Mu of Chu. Once the ceremonial greetings had been concluded, King Mu asked, "We originally agreed to meet at Juehao, so why are you waiting here?"

The Marquis of Chen and the Earl of Zheng said with one voice: "Having agreed to meet Your Majesty, we were afraid of being punished for arriving late, so we waited here to meet you before proceeding." King Mu was very pleased.

Suddenly a report came in from his spies: "Jiawu, Marquis of Cai, has already arrived at Juehao."

King Mu and the two lords of Chen and Zheng got back on their chariots and set off at full speed. The Marquis of Cai welcomed King Mu at Juehao with the rituals of a subject greeting a king, bowing twice and kowtowing. The Marquis of Chen and the Earl of Zheng were very shocked and spoke secretly to one another: "If Cai has humbled himself like this, Chu will think that we are being rude!"

They went and made the following suggestion to King Mu: "Your Majesty has come all this way, but the Lord of Song has not come to see you. You should attack him!"

King Mu laughed and said, "The reason why I am camped here is exactly because I intend to attack Song." This news was quickly reported back to the state of Song.

. . .

By this time Wangchen, Lord Cheng of Song, was already dead, and his son Wujiu had been established as Lord Zhao for some three years. He put all his trust in flattering and fawning advisors and had become completely alienated from the noble clans. The supporters of the descendants of Lord Mu and Lord Xiang brought about a civil war, in which they succeeded in killing the minister of war, the Honorable Yang, and forcing his deputy, Tang Yizhu, into exile in Lu. The state of Song then descended into chaos. Fortunately the minister of justice, Hua Yushi, was able to bring some measure of order to the government and bring back Tang Yizhu, which stabilized the situation a little. Just at that moment they heard that Chu was holding an international meeting at Juehao with a view to attacking Song.

Hua Yushi informed the Duke of Song: "I have heard it said: 'If a small country does not serve a large one, it will be destroyed.' Chu has already forced Chen and Zheng to submit to their authority; only Song has escaped. Let me go to welcome them. If we wait until we have been attacked before we ask for a peace treaty, it will be too late."

The Duke of Song thought that this was a good idea and went in person to Juehao to see the king of Chu. Furthermore, he prepared hunting equipment and suggested that they enjoy the pleasures of the chase in the Mengzhu Marshes. King Mu was very pleased. The Marquis of Chen asked permission to go on ahead to clear the road, while the Duke of Song headed the right flank and the Earl of Zheng the left flank. The Marquis of Cai brought up the rear. Thus, they all followed the king of Chu out hunting. King Mu gave orders commanding the feudal lords who followed him out on this hunt to set off before dawn and make sure that they carried a brazier on their chariots, so that they could light fires if necessary. When the battue had been in progress for some while, King Mu rode out to the right and happened to flush out a family of foxes. The foxes bolted for a deep hole and King Mu turned his head to look at the Duke of Song, expecting him to light a fire to smoke them out. However, he had forgotten to put a brazier in his chariot.

The Chu minister of war, Shen Wuwei, presented his opinion: "The Duke of Song has disobeyed Your Majesty's orders, but you cannot punish him. Let his servant suffer in his stead." The Duke of Song's charioteer was then beaten three hundred blows, which struck terror into the hearts of the lords. The Duke of Song was deeply shocked and ashamed. This happened in the second year of the reign of King Qing of Zhou. From this time on, Chu was by far the most powerful state, and when His Majesty sent Dou Yuejiao on diplomatic missions to Qi and Lu, the king of Chu was treated as if he were the hegemon of the Central States. There was nothing that Jin could do to prevent this.

• • •

In the fourth year of the reign of King Qing of Zhou, Lord Kang of Qin summoned his ministers and announced to them: "I have swallowed the bitterness of our defeat at Linghu for five years. Now Zhao Dun tortures and executed senior ministers, pays no attention to the issue of reforming the government, and has lost the states of Chen, Cai, Zheng, and Song to Chu one after the other. Jin has been completely unable to prevent this, which tells us something about their weakness. If we do not attack Jin now, are we ever going to get a better opportunity?"

The other grandees all said, "Let us fight!"

Lord Kang then held a huge muster of men and chariots. Leaving Baili Shi behind to guard the capital, he appointed Xiqi Shu as the commander-in-chief and Jian Bing as his deputy. Shi Hui was appointed the chief strategist for the army, and they set off with a force of five hundred chariots, in a magnificent procession. They crossed the Yellow River and headed east, attacking Jima and razing its walls to the ground. When Zhao Dun heard this news, he quickly came up with a plan to counter the enemy. He took personal command of the Central Army and promoted Grandee Xun Linfu from the Upper Army to be his deputy, thereby filling the vacancy left by Xian Ke. He appointed Ti Miming to be his bodyguard on his chariot, and ordered Xi Que to replace Ji Zhengfu as commander-in-chief of the Upper Army.

Zhao Dun had a younger cousin named Zhao Chuan who had been Lord Xiang of Jin's favorite son-in-law. He recommended himself to serve as the assistant general in command of the Upper Army.

"In spite of your youth, you are an extremely brave man," Zhao Dun commended him. "However, you completely lack experience. You will have to wait for your chance in the future." He appointed Yu Pian to this position instead.

Luan Dun became commander-in-chief of the Lower Army, filling the vacancy left by Xian Mie. Xu Chen's son, Xu Jia, became his deputy, thereby filling the place left empty by Xian Du. Zhao Chuan again asked permission that he should be allowed to lead his own private forces as a detachment of the Upper Army, to gain experience in battle. Zhao Dun agreed to this. There was still no minister of war, but Han Ziyu's son, Han Jue, had been brought up in Zhao Dun's family since an early age and had later joined his staff. He was a very clever and talented man, so Zhao Dun recommended him to Lord Ling, who agreed to his appointment.

The three armies left the city of Jiang and were proceeding in strict order, but before they had even gone ten *li*, a carriage suddenly forced its way into the Central Army. Han Jue sent someone to ask what was going on, and the driver replied, "The prime minister forgot his drinking cup, so he ordered me to go back and collect it. I had special instructions to catch up with you."

"The order of the carriages was strictly settled," Han Jue said angrily. "How could you just force your way in? You will be beheaded according to military law!"

The driver said in tears. "It was the prime minister's command!"

"Since I became minister of war, the only thing I care about is military law," Han Jue shouted. "I do not care about the prime minister!" He beheaded the driver and had his carriage broken up.

The other commanders reported this to Zhao Dun. "You recommended Han Jue for office, and now he has destroyed your carriage. He has betrayed your generosity to him, so you should not employ him."

Zhao Dun smiled slightly and sent someone to summon Han Jue. The generals were all expecting that Zhao Dun would humiliate Han Jue to assuage his anger. What actually happened was that when Han Jue arrived, Zhao Dun got down from his seat and greeted him politely, saying, "I have heard it said that a man who serves his ruler should be friendly but not biased. That you have been able to uphold the law in this way means that you are entirely worthy of my recommendation. You are forgiven!"

Han Jue bowed his thanks and left. Zhao Dun then said to the assembled generals, "One day, Han Jue will be in charge of the government of Jin. The Han family has a glorious future in front of it!"

The Jin army made camp at Hequ. Yu Pian presented his plan as follows: "The Qin army has been stockpiling weapons and supplies for many years to prepare for this campaign; we will not be able to withstand a direct onslaught. Let us take advantage of the deep valleys and sheer cliffs to hold firm and not do battle. They will not be able to stay here forever, and eventually they will have to withdraw. Once they leave, we should attack them. That way victory is guaranteed." Zhao Dun followed his advice.

Lord Kang of Qin attempted to provoke battle but was repulsed. He asked Shi Hui to come up with a plan.

"The Zhao family has recently employed a new man whose name is Yu Pian," Shi Hui replied. "He is very clever. Today they are guarding the hilltops and refusing to fight with us; this must be his idea. They are trying to tire us out. There is a commoner son of the Zhao family whose name is Zhao Chuan—he was the favorite son-in-law of His Late

Lordship of Jin. I have heard that he asked to be appointed the second-in-command of the Upper Army and that Zhao Dun refused and gave this position to Yu Pian instead. Chuan is sure to have been deeply angered by this. When Zhao Dun decided to use Yu Pian's strategy, Chuan was even angrier, which is why he has come with his own private forces in an attempt to establish some kind of merit independently of Yu Pian. If you send some lightly armored troops to provoke battle with the Upper Army, Yu Pian will not respond. However, Zhao Chuan will certainly be confident enough to come out and fight, and you can then do battle with him. How would that be?"

Lord Kang of Qin followed his plan. He sent Jian Bing in command of one hundred chariots to make a surprise attack on the Upper Army and provoke them into fighting. Xi Que and Yu Pian both held firm and did not move, but when Zhao Chuan heard that the Qin troops had arrived, he led out his own force of one hundred chariots to meet them. Jian Bing turned his chariot around and fled. His force moved so quickly that even though Zhao Chuan chased them for more than ten *li*, he was not able to catch up with them and had to go home. He was really angry that Yu Pan and the others were not willing to help him chase them down. He summoned the army officers and cursed them: "We put on our armor to fight! Now the enemy is here and you don't go out to meet them—is the Upper Army entirely composed of women?"

The army officers said, "The commander-in-chief has his own plan for how to defeat the enemy, but the time is not yet ripe."

Zhao Chuan cursed again and said, "What kind of plan can a rat like that come up with? He is scared witless. Everyone else here is petrified of Qin, but I am not! I will go and fight the Qin army on my own, even if it kills me, to wipe out the humiliation of this defensive strategy!" He whipped up his team and shouted to the assembled multitude: "Does anyone have the guts to come with me?"

No one from the three armies responded. Only Xu Jia, the deputy general in command of the Lower Army, sighed and said, "This man really is a great warrior and we ought to help him." He really wanted to send the army out in support.

By this time, the commander-in-chief of the Upper Army, Xi Que, had already sent someone at top speed to report what Zhao Chuan had done to Zhao Dun.

Zhao Dun was amazed and said, "If that madman goes out on his own, he will be taken prisoner by Qin. We have to save him!" He gave orders to the three armies to set out together and do battle with Qin.

Zhao Dun hurled himself at the wall of the Qin army, whereupon Jian Bing came out to fight him. The pair of them crossed swords more than thirty times, inflicting serious injuries on each other. Xiqi Shu wanted to join in the attack from one side, only to see the main body of the army drawing up opposite him. He did not dare to advance recklessly. Both sides sounded bells to order the two warriors to retreat.

When Zhao Chuan rejoined his own side, he asked Zhao Dun, "I was going to destroy the Qin army on my own to avenge the humiliation that all of the generals have suffered. Why did you sound the bells for a retreat?"

"Qin is a great state and cannot be engaged lightly," Zhao Dun replied. "I have a plan to defeat them."

"Well, use it then before I explode!" Chuan shouted.

Before he had finished speaking, a report came in: "The state of Qin has sent someone with the articles of war." Zhao Dun sent Yu Pian to deal with this. Once the envoy handed over the document, Yu Pian transmitted it to Zhao Dun. He opened the letter and read it:

> Since the officers of both our armies are on their mettle, let us decide victory and defeat tomorrow!

"I respectfully agree!" Zhao Dun answered.

After the envoy had departed, Yu Pian said to Zhao Dun: "Even though the Qin envoy said that he was here to provoke battle, his eyes kept roaming around as if he were nervous of something. If they are afraid of us, they will try and withdraw under cover of darkness. Let us place some soldiers in ambush around the mouth of the river to attack them, just as they are preparing to cross. That way you are sure to win a complete victory."

"That is a wonderful plan!" Zhao Dun exclaimed.

He was just about to give the orders to set the ambush when Xu Jia heard about the plan and reported it to Zhao Chuan. They went together to the gates of the army camp and shouted: "Army officers, listen to me! Here in Jin we have strong soldiers and good generals; surely we are not inferior to Qin! Qin has come to arrange a battle, and we have already agreed. Now they want to set an ambush at the mouth of the river, because they are planning to make a surprise attack on them. Is that the kind of thing that a gentleman would do?"

Zhao Dun heard about this and summoned Zhao Chuan. "This was originally not my idea," he told him. "Can you stop disturbing the morale of the army?"

Qin spies heard what Zhao Chuan and Xu Jia had said by the gates to the army camp, so that very night they withdrew. They broke through the defenses of Xiayi and made their escape through the pass at Taolin. Zhao Dun also stood down his army. Zhao Chuan was guilty of leaking a military secret to the enemy, but he was His Late Lordship's son-in-law as well as being Zhao Dun's cousin, so he was spared any punishment. The only person who was punished was Xu Jia, who lost his title and was sent to guard the state of Wey. As Zhao Dun said, "Xu Chen achieved so much that it would not be appropriate to behead his son!" From this time on, Xu Jia's son, Xu Ke, was employed as the deputy general of the Lower Army.

A bearded old man wrote a poem criticizing Zhao Dun's partiality:

They shouted together at the army gates, but their punishment was different:
Only General Xu Jia suffered the proper penalty.
It is not right for a prime minister to protect his own family;
Just ask Dong Hu about what happened at the Peach Garden!

In the fifth year of the reign of King Qing of Zhou, Zhao Dun was afraid that the Qin army would return, so he sent Grandee Zhan Jia to Xiayi to guard the border pass at Taolin. Yu Pian stepped forward and said, "The strategy of the battle of Hequ was the brainchild of Shi Hui. As long as this man is in Qin, how can any of us rest easy?" Zhao Dun agreed with him. He then summoned the six ministers to discuss this matter at his Zhufu villa.

Who were these six ministers? They were Xi Que, Luan Dun, Xun Linfu, Yu Pian, and Xu Ke.

On the appointed day, the six ministers all assembled. Zhao Dun opened the discussion by saying: "Hu Shegu is now living with the Di people and Shi Hui is in Qin. Both these two men are plotting the destruction of the state of Jin. What is your plan for dealing with this situation?"

"Summon Hu Shegu and give him his old job back," Xun Linfu suggested. "Hu Shegu is extremely knowledgeable about our enemies, in addition to which he is Hu Yan's son; it would be entirely appropriate for you to restore his high office!"

"No!" Xi Que said. "While it is perfectly true that as Hu Yan's son, Hu Shegu deserves some consideration, he was responsible for the murder of a senior minister. If you now restore his position, how will you control him in the future? It would be much better if you summoned Shi

Hui home. Shi Hui is a gentle and intelligent man, and his decision to go into exile in Qin can hardly be considered his fault. The Di are far away from us, but Qin is close by. If you wish to neutralize the threat posed by Qin, you will first have to remove their supporters. That is why it would be a good idea to recall Shi Hui."

"Qin has treated Shi Hui with great generosity and employed him in a senior position," Zhao Dun replied. "Even if we invite him back, he will not agree. What plan do you have to make him return?"

"I have a good friend, Wei Shouyu, who is the grandson of the late minister Bi Wan," Yu Pian commented. "He is a nephew of Wei Chou. At present he is living in his fief at Wei. Even though he comes from a famous aristocratic family, he has never held office. He is very good at manipulating events in his favor, so if you want to summon Shi Hui back to your service, he is the only person who can do it." He whispered in Zhao Dun's ear: "We could do this . . ."

"Please go ahead!" Zhao Dun said happily.

Afterwards the six ministers went their separate ways. Yu Pian knocked that very night on Wei Shouyu's door. He welcomed Yu Pian and invited him in. Yu Pian suggested that they talk in a secret room, whereupon he revealed the plan to summon Shi Hui. Wei Shouyu agreed to his role. Afterwards Yu Pian went back to report to Zhao Dun.

The following day, Zhao Dun presented his opinion to Lord Ling: "The people of Qin have repeatedly invaded Jin, so we should order the officials in towns east of the Yellow River to train soldiers and build a chain of fortresses on the banks of the Yellow River, so that they can reinforce each other. We should also appoint an official who has a fief in the region to oversee this matter, because such a person would have a personal interest in seeing it succeed. He would want to make very careful preparations."

Lord Ling agreed to this submission, and Zhao Dun continued: "Wei is a huge fief. If Wei supports this plan, then none of the others will dare to refuse!"

He summoned Wei Shouyu in Lord Ling's name and ordered him to take charge of this, mustering troops to guard the fortresses.

Wei Shouyu presented his opinion: "Thanks to His Lordship's kindness in rewarding the labors of my ancestors, I enjoy the benefits of a large domain, but I know nothing at all about military matters. Besides which, the Yellow River meanders for several hundred *li*, and it is possible to cross it at any point. There is no point in trying to defend it against invasion."

"How dare you try and prevent me from carrying out my plan!" Zhao Dun shouted angrily. "You have three days in which to take the military rolls and begin your preparations. If you still refuse, you will be punished according to military law!"

Wei Shouyu could only sigh and leave. When he got home he was very depressed, and his wife asked him what the matter was.

"Zhao Dun is a complete ignoramus, who wants me to guard the riverbanks," Wei Shouyu complained. "How is such a thing possible? You had better go and pack, and we will run away to Qin to join Shi Hui."

He instructed his servants to prepare his carriage and horses. That night he got drunk and whipped the cook more than one hundred lashes for sending in some food that was not properly prepared. This did not appease his rage, and he threatened to kill him. The cook ran to the Zhao mansion, where he reported that Wei Shouyu wanted to betray Jin and go into exile in Qin. Zhao Dun then ordered Han Jue to take his troops to arrest him. Han Jue allowed Wei Shouyu to escape, but arrested his wife and children and put them in prison.

Wei Shouyu escaped to the state of Qin under cover of darkness. He had an audience with Lord Kang, at which he reported all that Zhao Dun had done and how wicked he was: "My wife and children are all in prison now; only I was able to escape. I have come here to throw in my lot with yours."

Lord Kang asked Shi Hui, "Is this true?"

"Jin people are very tricky and not to be trusted," Shi Hui said. "However, if Wei Shouyu really has come here to join you, what present has he brought?"

Wei Shouyu took a document out of his sleeve. This described the geography and population of Wei in full. He presented this to Lord Kang with the words: "If you are willing to take me in, my lord, then I will hand over my fief in Jin to you."

Lord Kang asked Shi Hui, "Can we capture Wei?"

Wei Shouyu looked at Shi Hui and made a movement with his foot. Even though Shi Hui had indeed fled into exile in Qin, he still thought of himself as a Jin vassal. Now he saw what Wei Shouyu was doing and had some idea of why. He replied: "For the sake of the marriage alliance with Jin, Qin abandoned their claim to the five cities east of the Yellow River. Today the armies of your two countries have attacked each other ceaselessly for many years, capturing each other's towns and cities, making brute force the most important thing. Of all the cities east of the Yellow River, Wei is by far the largest. Once you have occupied

Wei, you can gradually take over the remaining land in the region; that should be your long-term plan. However, I am worried that the officials in Wei are afraid of being punished by Jin, and they will not be willing to switch their allegiance to you!"

"It is true that the officials in Wei are public servants of the state of Jin, but this is in fact my family's private land," Wei Shouyu said. "If Your Lordship were to send your army to camp on the west side of the Yellow River, making sure that news of this move spreads far and wide, I can deal with the rest."

Lord Kang of Qin turned his head to look at Shi Hui and said, "You know all about things in Jin; you had better come with me!"

He appointed Xiqi Shu as the senior general and Shi Hui as his deputy, personally joining the army on campaign. When they arrived at the mouth of the river, they made camp. Then the spies sent out ahead of the main army reported back: "There is an army camped east of the Yellow River, but we don't know why."

"It must be that the people of Wei have heard that the Qin army was on its way and so they have made preparations," Wei Shouyu said. "They did not realize that I have joined Qin. We need someone who has spent some time in Qin but who also understands the situation in Jin to go with me to talk to them in their best interests. The Wei officials are sure to agree with my assessment of the situation!"

Lord Kang ordered Shi Hui to go, but Shi Hui kowtowed and refused, saying: "The people of Jin are like tigers and wolves—it is very difficult to know what they are up to. If I go and speak to them and persuade them to our side, that would of course be a great blessing for the country. However, if they do not agree and take me prisoner, you may blame me for being incompetent and punish my wife and children. That would not benefit you in any way, and it would bring disaster down upon my family. But once they are dead, it is too late for regrets!"

Lord Kang had no idea quite how devious Shi Hui was, so he said, "I just want you to do your best. If you obtain the lands of Wei, you will be generously rewarded. If, on the other hand, you are taken prisoner by Jin, I will send your family to join you to show my deep affection for you!" He swore an oath with Shi Hui facing the Yellow River.

Grandee Rao Zhao of Qin remonstrated with him: "Shi Hui is a strategist from the state of Jin; if you let him go, it will be like allowing a whale to return to the ocean—he will never come back! Why do you trust what Wei Shouyu says to the point where you are prepared to make a present of this man to our enemies?"

"I know what I am doing in this matter," Lord Kang replied. "Don't be so suspicious!"

Shi Hui and Wei Shouyu said goodbye to Lord Kang together and set off. Rao Zhao quickly set off after them in a chariot. He gave a whip to Shi Hui and said, "Do not think that the state of Qin is completely devoid of men of intelligence. The problem is that His Lordship does not listen to my advice. You had better take this whip and use it to get home as soon as possible, for any delay will cause disaster for you!"

Shi Hui bowed and thanked him; then he whipped up his horses.

A historian wrote a poem that says:

Traveling in haste back down this road,
He respectfully presented his friend with a long whip.
Do not say that the state of Qin lacked talented men,
But criticize Lord Kang for not listening to his advice.

Shi Hui and the others crossed the Yellow River and proceeded eastwards.

Do you know if they were able to return to Jin? READ ON.

Chapter Forty-nine

The Honorable Bao buys a country with lavish gifts.

Lord Yi of Qi is assassinated among the lakeside bamboos.

Shi Hui and Wei Shouyu crossed the Yellow River and advanced eastward. Before they had reached Lixu, they caught sight of a young general who had led a detachment of cavalry to meet them. He stood on top of his chariot, bowed, and said, "I hope that you are well!" Shi Hui came forward and looked at him. This was General Zhao Shuo, son of the prime minister, Zhao Dun. The three men then all got off their chariots to greet one another. Shi Hui asked why he was here, and Zhao Shuo said: "My father ordered me to come here to meet you and take you back to court. The main body of the army is on its way!"

Just as he spoke, with a great rumbling sound, a vast body of chariots moved forward like a cataract, sweeping Shi Hui and Wei Shouyu back to Jin. Lord Kang of Qin had ordered someone to watch what was happening from the far side of the river, and he now returned and reported this. Lord Kang was furious and wanted to cross the river to attack Jin. His advance guard then reported: "We have spotted a huge army on the east side of the river, commanded by General Xun Linfu and Xi Que."

"If the Jin army is here in such numbers," Xiqi Shu commented, "they will not allow us to cross the Yellow River. We had better go home." His Lordship stood down the army. Xun Linfu watched the Qin army leave, before returning to the state of Jin.

Shi Hui had spent three years in Qin. Now on returning to the city of Jiang, he could not help feeling awkward. When he went in to have an audience with Lord Ling, he assumed the posture of a captive and apologized for his crimes.

"You have done nothing wrong," Lord Ling declared. He ordered that he be ranked among the six senior ministers.

Zhao Dun was impressed by what Wei Shouyu had done and spoke of it to Lord Ling, who rewarded him with ten chariots. Lord Kang of Qin sent someone to escort Shi Hui's wife and children back to Jin with the message: "I have not betrayed the oath that I swore at the Yellow River." Shi Hui was deeply impressed by Lord Kang's generosity and wrote a letter to apologize. He encouraged him to rest his troops and pay attention to improving the lot of his people, keeping to within his own borders. Lord Kang followed this advice, and hence there was no warfare between Qin and Jin for several decades.

• • •

In the sixth year of the reign of King Qing of Zhou, His Majesty died. Crown Prince Ban came to the throne as King Kuang. This occurred in the eighth year of Lord Ling of Jin. At this time King Mu of Chu also died, and Crown Prince Lü came to the throne as King Zhuang. Zhao Dun decided that since Chu was involved in national mourning, it would be a shame not to take advantage of this opportunity to renew the position of Master of Covenants formerly held by the marquises of Jin. He assembled the feudal lords at Xincheng, and this meeting was attended by Chujiu, Lord Zhao of Song; Xing, Lord Wen of Lu; Pingguo, Lord Ling of Chen; Zheng, Lord Cheng of Wey; Lan, Lord Mu of Zheng; and Xiwo, Lord Zhao of Xu. The lords of Song, Chen, and Zheng all explained that they had followed Chu in the past simply because they had no choice. Zhao Dun comforted them one by one, and they began to submit to Jin's authority again. Only the Marquis of Cai still served Chu as of old and refused to attend this meeting. Zhao Dun sent Xi Que to attack them with his army. The people of Cai asked for a peace treaty, and they then turned back.

Pan, Lord Zhao of Qi, originally intended to attend the meeting, but when the time came, he was too ill. Before the covenant could be held, Lord Zhao had died. Scion She then succeeded to the marquisate. His mother was a daughter of the Lu ruling house, and her name was Lady Zhao Ji. Although Lady Zhao Ji was the Marquis of Qi's principal wife, he had never been particularly fond of her. Scion She was also a very ordinary young man, and the people of the capital did not respect him. The Honorable Shangren, the son of Lord Huan of Qi by his concubine,

Lady Mi Ji, had always intended to usurp the title, but because he was treated with such generosity and kindness by Lord Zhao, he gradually gave up the idea. Now that Lord Zhao was dead, it was time to launch his rebellion. In the last year of Lord Zhao's life, he summoned the Honorable Yuan from Wey and entrusted the government of the country to him. Shangren was aware of the Honorable Yuan's talents, so he wanted to ensure that the people supported him. He therefore exhausted the wealth of his family on charitable projects to succor the poor. If he did not have enough money himself, he would borrow it so that his work could continue. The people of Qi were deeply moved by this. He also collected a large number of brave warriors in his household, and they trained day and night. Every time he went out, they followed close behind.

Shortly after Scion She succeeded to the title, a comet appeared in the vicinity of the Dipper constellation. The Honorable Shangren ordered someone to perform a divination about this, and he said: "The rulers of Song, Qi, and Jin are all going to die in civil wars."

"If there is a rebellion in Qi," Shangren said to himself, "it will be by me!"

He ordered his knights to go to the funerary hut and stab Scion She to death. Shangren remembered that the Honorable Yuan was his senior in the family, so he lied to him: "Scion She did not have the authority to govern others, nor could he possibly occupy a senior position. I killed him in order to allow you to succeed to the title!"

The Honorable Yuan was deeply shocked and said, "I know that you have wanted to become the ruler for a long time; why are you dragging me into this? I can serve you loyally, but you could not possibly serve me. Once you have become the Marquis of Qi, I hope that you will allow me to live the ordinary life of a commoner to the end of my days. That is all that I ask!"

When Shangren became the marquis, he took the title of Lord Yi. The Honorable Yuan was disgusted by Shangren's actions, so he shut his gates and pretended that he was too ill to go to court. This was very sensible of the Honorable Yuan.

Lady Zhao Ji was devastated by the murder of her son and cried day and night, to the annoyance of Lord Yi. He kept her prisoner in one of the side chambers of the palace and gave orders that she should not be given food or drink. However, Lady Zhao Ji was able to bribe one of the palace servants to take a message to Lu. Lord Wen of Lu was frightened of the military might of Qi, so he ordered Grandee Dongmen Sui to go to Zhou and report this matter to King Kuang. He was hoping that His

Majesty would be kind enough to demand the release of Lady Zhao Ji from captivity.

King Kuang ordered the Earl of Shan to go to Qi, where he spoke to Lord Yi: "You have already murdered the son, so what is the point of keeping the mother? Why do you not release her and let her go back to Lu, in order to demonstrate the magnanimity and virtue of Qi?"

Lord Yi had forbidden anyone to mention the death of Scion She, so when he heard the words "murdered the son" his cheeks went bright red and he was completely silent. The Earl of Shan withdrew and went back to the guesthouse. Meanwhile, Lord Yi moved Lady Zhao Ji to one of the other palaces and sent someone to trick the Earl of Shan: "His Lordship would hardly dare to treat the dowager marchioness badly! Now that the Son of Heaven has spoken about this matter, how could he not obey orders? Why don't you ask to see Her Ladyship, to make it clear that the Son of Heaven is deeply concerned about the affairs of all states in the confederacy and every branch of his clan?"

The Earl of Shan thought this was a good idea and rode with the messenger to the palace to ask to be allowed to see Lady Zhao Ji. Her Ladyship wept as she told of her sufferings, but before the Earl of Shan could open his mouth to reply, Lord Yi had rushed in from outside cursing and shouting: "What are you doing in my palace without an invitation? How dare you meet the dowager marchioness in secret! Are you trying to seduce her or what? I am going to make a formal complaint to the Son of Heaven!"

He then had the Earl of Shan arrested and imprisoned in the same cell as Lady Zhao Ji. He was angry that Lu had tried to put pressure on him by going to the Zhou king, so he raised an army to attack them.

Lord Yi assassinated a young ruler, imprisoned the dowager marchioness, laid violent hands upon an ambassador from the Son of Heaven, and bullied his neighbors, acting with extreme cruelty; how could this be acceptable? The court at Qi was full of members of the Guo and Gao families who had served the ruling house for many generations—why did they not support the Honorable Yuan and punish Shangren? Why did they let him get away with these wicked things without even saying a word? It really is very upsetting.

There is a poem about this:

If you want to usurp a title and murder a child ruler,
First spend your family money buying the hearts and minds of the people.
It is painful to have to admit that the officials and bureaucrats
Simply followed the common rabble in admiring this criminal!

The senior minister, Jisun Xingfu of Lu, went to Jin to report the emergency. Zhao Dun of Jin—representing Lord Ling—then met the feudal lords of Song, Wey, Cai, Chen, Zheng, Cao, and Xu at Hudi to discuss an attack on Qi. Lord Yi of Qi gave bribes to Jin, released the Earl of Shan to return to Zhou, and sent Lady Zhao Ji back to Lu, whereupon the lords all returned to their own states. When Lu heard that Jin had not in fact attacked Qi, they sent the Honorable Sui with bribes to ask for a peace treaty with Qi. No more of this now.

• • •

Lady Wang Ji, the principal wife of Lord Xiang of Song, was the older sister of King Xiang of Zhou and the mother of Wangchen, Lord Cheng of Song, which made her the grandmother of Chujiu, Lord Zhao of Song. When Lord Zhao was the scion, he would enjoy himself by going hunting and having fun with his three boon companions: the Honorable Ang, Noble Grandson Kongshu, and Noble Grandson Zhongli. After he succeeded to the title, he would only listen to them, paying no attention to the six senior ministers. He did not go to visit his grandmother, and he kept all the other members of the family at a distance. He had no interest in governing the people and only enjoyed going out hunting. The minister of war, Yue Yu, understood that a civil war was imminent in Song, so he resigned his job in favor of the Honorable Ang. The minister of works, Noble Grandson Shou, was also aware that disaster was just about to overtake them, so he left the government on the grounds of old age. Lord Zhao allowed his son, Dang Yizhu, to inherit his office.

Lady Wang Ji, the Grand Dowager Duchess, had a powerful sexual appetite in spite of her age. Lord Zhao had a half-brother, the Honorable Bao, who was much more beautiful than any woman. The Grand Dowager Duchess adored him to the point of madness. She forced him into an affair and agreed that she would support him to become the next ruler. She wanted to depose Lord Zhao and establish the Honorable Bao in his place. Lord Zhao was afraid that the clans descended from Lord Mu and Lord Xiang were too powerful, so he ordered the Honorable Ang to expel them from the country. Lady Wang Ji secretly reported his plans to the families concerned, and they began an uprising in which they surrounded the Honorable Ang and Noble Grandson Zhongli at the gates of the palace and killed them. The minister of works, Dang Yizhu, became frightened and fled into exile in Lu. The Honorable Bao had always shown a great deal of respect to the six ministers, and now he was able to make peace with the officials and the noble clans, promising them that he would not punish them for the murders of these two men. He summoned Dang Yizhu back from Lu and restored him to office.

The Honorable Bao had heard the story of how the Honorable Shangren of Qi had been able to buy the support of the populace by lavish generosity and thus usurped the title of marquis, and he thought this was a very useful model. He began to disburse his family wealth among the poor. In the seventh year of Lord Zhao's rule, there was a famine in the state of Song, and the Honorable Bao handed out every single grain of rice in his storehouses to the needy. He also showed respect to the old and wise, giving a set quantity of grain and silk every month to every single person in the state who was over seventy years of age, together with food and drink. He would also send people to ask how they were. Every person of talent whom he could find was collected into his household and generously rewarded with a stipend. He also sent gifts every month to the houses of ministers and grandees. Every time there was a birth, marriage, or funeral of a member of his clan, no matter how remotely related, he was sure to empty his purse to help.

In the eighth year of Lord Zhao's reign, there was a further great famine. By this time the Honorable Bao had completely exhausted his reserves, but the Grand Dowager Duchess sent out all the grain stored in the palace to help him. She made sure that the whole country was singing the praises of the Honorable Bao and that everyone, whether a close or distant relative, noble or commoner, was in favor of seeing him become their ruler. The Honorable Bao knew that he had the full support of the people of the capital, so he sent a secret message to the Grand Dowager Duchess to plot the assassination of Lord Zhao.

"I have heard that Chujiu is going to go hunting at the Mengzhu Marshes," the Grand Dowager Duchess said, "so we can take advantage of his departure to have the Honorable Xu close the gates of the city against him, while you lead the people of the capital to attack him. We will succeed!" The Honorable Bao followed her advice.

The minister of works, Dang Yizhu, was a wise man, and the Honorable Bao had always treated him with respect and ritual propriety. However, when he heard the Grand Dowager Duchess's plan, he reported it to Lord Zhao. "You must not go hunting, my lord, for if you do, I am afraid that you will not be able to return."

"If they are going to rise in rebellion," Lord Zhao pointed out, "what can I do to stop them even if I am in the capital?"

He ordered the General of the Left, Hua Yuan, and the General of the Right, Noble Grandson You, to guard the city. He loaded all the treasures from the storehouses into his carriages, and, accompanied by a train of servants, he set out for Mengzhu in November. Once he had left the city, the Grand Dowager Duchess summoned Hua Yuan and Noble Grandson You to the palace and ordered the Honorable Xu to close the gates.

The Honorable Bao ordered Marshal Hua Ou to announce to the army: "The Grand Dowager Duchess commands, 'Today, let us put the Honorable Bao in power.' We must get rid of this useless ruler and replace him with someone better. What do you think?"

The army officers all jumped for joy. "We are happy to obey!" Everyone in the capital was delighted.

Hua Ou led the people out of the city and set off in pursuit of Lord Zhao. En route, Lord Zhao heard that a rebellion had broken out. Dang Yizhu urged him to flee into exile abroad, so that he might yet be able to return in the future.

"Both my grandmother and the people of the capital see me as their enemy," Lord Zhao said. "Who among the feudal lords would be prepared to take me in? I would rather die at home than in exile among strangers!" He gave orders that the chariots should stop so everyone could prepare lunch, so all the people following him on this hunt could eat their fill. Once they had finished, Lord Zhao told his companions: "Any fault is mine alone and has nothing to do with you. You have followed me for many years without receiving anything for your pains. The treasures of the state of Song are all here. Divide them among yourselves and run for your lives; do not die here with me!"

His servants all wept and said, "Please go on ahead. If anyone comes after you, we will fight to the death."

"There is no point in your getting yourselves killed," Lord Zhao said. "I will die here. Do not waste your time here with me!"

A short while later, Hua Ou's troops arrived and surrounded Lord Zhao. They told him the Grand Dowager Duchess's orders: "Just kill the wicked lord; it is nothing to do with anyone else."

Lord Zhao waved away his servants hastily, and more than half of them did indeed run off. Dang Yizhu stood beside Lord Zhao with his sword in his hand. Hua Ou had orders from the Grand Dowager Duchess to summon Dang Yizhu back to the palace alone. Dang Yizhu sighed and said, "I would rather die than leave His Lordship to face this on his own."

Hua Ou threatened Lord Zhao with his spear, only to have Dang Yizhu throw himself in the way. As the two men grappled, the soldiers closed in, killing first Dang Yizhu and then Lord Zhao. Those servants who had stayed behind were all butchered. How sad!

A historian wrote a poem about this:

In the past Hua Du assassinated Lord Shang,
Now Hua Ou helps another murderer.
Traitors and rebels come from the same families,
As distinct from the rest of us as pears are from plums.

Hua Ou led the army back and reported to the Grand Dowager Duchess. The General of the Right, Hua Yuan, and the General of the Left, Noble Grandson You, both presented their opinion in concert: "The Honorable Bao is much loved by the people for his kindness; he should take the title." They supported the Honorable Bao's accession to the dukedom, and he took the title Lord Wen.

After Hua Ou had attended court to offer congratulations, he returned home and had a heart attack of which he died. Lord Wen was very appreciative of the loyalty shown by Dang Yizhu, so he appointed his younger brother, Dang Kui, to be the marshal, replacing Hua Ou. His own younger brother, the Honorable Xu, was appointed to be the minister of works, filling the vacancy left by Dang Yizhu.

. . .

When Zhao Dun heard that the ruler of Song had been assassinated, he appointed Xun Lunfu as general and attacked Song at the head of an allied army with the forces of Wey, Chen, and Zheng. Hua Yuan, the General of the Right of Song, went to the Jin army and explained the reasons why the people of the capital wanted the Honorable Bao to become their ruler. He also brought along several carts of gold and silk as a reward for the army when he requested a peace treaty from Jin. Xun Linfu wanted to accept this, but Lord Mu of Zheng said, "We have sounded our bells and struck our drums in order to follow you here to Song to punish their wicked overthrow of the legitimate ruler. If you agree to their request, the traitors will have escaped unpunished!"

"What happened in Song is exactly the same as what happened in Qi," Xun Linfu said. "If we could accept the situation in Qi, why should we only punish Song? Besides which, if the people of the capital want this man to become their ruler, what is wrong with that?"

He swore a blood covenant with Hua Yuan of Song, agreed to accept the accession of Lord Wen of Song, and went home. Lord Mu of Zheng withdrew and said, "Jin was greedy for the bribes on offer. All these fine words were completely empty. They will never be able to restore the hegemony. The king of Chu is newly enthroned, and he will want to go out on campaign soon. I had better abandon the alliance with Jin in order to follow Chu, to keep us all safe." He accordingly sent someone to restore the relationship with Chu, and there was nothing that Jin could do about it.

A bearded old man wrote a poem:

To support the cause of justice and prevent evildoing is the act of a hegemon;
Having raised an army, they suddenly decided to support a traitor.
Shangren was safe and Bao was secure in his title;
Laughingly they acknowledged that the Central States were powerless.

Shangren, Lord Yi of Qi, was a very violent and greedy man. When his father, Lord Huan, was in power, he had a dispute over the boundary of his property with that of Grandee Bing Yuan. Lord Huan ordered Guan Zhong to sort this out. Guan Zhong was not impressed by the evidence that the Honorable Shangren was able to produce and decided in favor of the Bing family. Shangren was furious about this and did not forget it. When he assassinated Scion She and established himself, he stole all the lands of the Bing family. He was still angry that Guan Zhong had supported them, so he reduced their fief by half. The Guan family were afraid that they would suffer further punishment, so they fled to the kingdom of Chu, serving there as ministers from one generation to the next. Lord Yi's hatred of Bing Yuan had still not been assuaged, but by this time the man was already dead. He knew that his tomb was located in the eastern suburbs of the capital, so he arranged to go there one day when out hunting, ordering his soldiers to dig up the grave and take the body out of its coffin to cut off its feet. Bing Yuan's son, Bing Chu, was part of the train following His Lordship.

"Did your father's crime deserve the penalty of having his feet cut off?" Lord Yi asked. "Are you angry with me?"

"My father was able to escape punishment while he was alive and is now forever beyond your reach," Bing Chu replied. "Why should I mind what you do to this heap of rotten bones?"

Lord Yi was very pleased: "You have atoned for all your father's crimes!" He ordered all the lands that he had taken to be returned to the Bing family. Bing Chu asked permission to rebury his father, and Lord Yi agreed.

Lord Yi was also busy acquiring all the beautiful women he could find and was sunk in irredeemable debauchery. Someone happened to mention that the wife of Grandee Yan Zhi was extremely beautiful, and so on New Year's Day he ordered the wives of all the grandees of state to come to court to visit the ladies of the harem. Yan Zhi's wife was one of them, and Lord Yi was delighted the moment he set eyes on her. He kept her in his palace, not allowing her to go home. He sent a message to Yan Zhi: "My ladies enjoy having the companionship of your wife. Marry someone else." Yan Zhi was furious, but he did not dare to complain.

Near the Southwest Gate of the capital city of Qi, there was a place named Shen Lake. The waters of this lake were very pure and were popular for bathing; the bamboos that grew along the banks were extremely lush. That year in the fifth month, Lord Yi wanted to go to Shen Lake to avoid the summer heat, and he commanded Bing Chu to drive his chariot and Yan Zhi to accompany him.

The General of the Right, Hua Yuan, remonstrated in private: "You cut the feet off Bing Chu's father, my lord, and you stole Yan Zhi's wife. Is it possible that these two men do not hate you? And yet Your Lordship keeps them in close attendance! Qi has never lacked for good men; why do you have to have this pair?"

"They would never dare to be angry with me," Lord Yi replied. "Do not worry!"

He rode his chariot to Lake Shen, where he drank wine and enjoyed himself. Lord Yi became really drunk and found the heat oppressive, so he ordered that his silk couch be carried deep into the bamboo forest so that he could lie there and cool down. Bing Chu and Yan Zhi went swimming in the lake. Bing Chu loathed Lord Yi and had long wanted to kill him to avenge what had been done to his father. However, he did not have anyone to join him in this conspiracy. He knew that Yan Zhi was angry about the loss of his wife, so he wanted to discuss the matter with him, though he found it very difficult to start. When they were bathing together in the lake, he came up with a plan. He broke off a stave of bamboo and deliberately hit Yan Zhi over the head with it.

"Why are you hitting me?" Yan Zhi asked crossly.

Bing Chu laughed and said, "You weren't angry when you lost your wife, so what is the problem with me hitting you?"

"Losing a wife is indeed humiliating for me," Yan Zhi retorted, "but compared to having to see the feet cut off one's own father's body, it's nothing! You put up with what happened to your father and yet you blame me for swallowing the insult of losing my wife; what kind of logic is that?"

"There is something that I want to say to you," Bing Chu said, "but I have been keeping it secret out of fear that you have forgotten the humiliation that you suffered, in which case it would be pointless for me to say anything."

"We both care," Yan Zhi returned, "and neither of us has forgotten, but there is nothing that we can do about it!"

"The person responsible is lying dead drunk among the bamboos, and we are the only two people who followed him on this journey," Bing Chu pointed out. "Heaven has given us this opportunity to take revenge, and we must not let it slip!"

"If you can do it," Yan Zhi said, "I will help you."

The two men then got dressed and walked into the bamboo forest. When they found him, Lord Yi was fast asleep and snoring loudly with just a few servants standing nearby.

"When His Lordship wakes up he will want something to drink," Bing Chu told them. "You had better prepare some soup and have it waiting ready."

The servants went off to make some soup. Yan Zhi grabbed hold of Lord Yi's hands and Bing Chu gripped his throat, using his sword to saw through his neck. His head fell to the ground. The two men picked up the body and hid it deep in the heart of the bamboo forest, throwing his head into the lake.

Lord Yi was in power for only four years.

When the servants came back with the soup, Bing Chu told them: "Shangren assassinated the ruler and put himself in power. The former rulers of Qi would want us to punish him. The Honorable Yuan is a wise and filial man, and he should be our next ruler!" The servants nodded, none of them daring to say a word.

Bing Chu and Yan Zhi rode back to the capital city, whereupon they held a banquet to celebrate and congratulated each other happily. Someone had already reported what had happened to the senior ministers Gao Qing and Guo Guifu.

"Should we not execute them for the crime that they have committed as a warning to others?" Gao Qing asked.

"We could not punish the man who assassinated our lord," Guo Guifu replied. "Now someone else has done it for us; what crime are they guilty of?"

When Bing Chu and Yan Zhi had finished their celebrations, they ordered that all their family possessions should be loaded onto large carts and that their wives and children should get into carriages. They left the city by the southern gate. Their relatives sent someone to urge them to leave as soon as possible.

"Shangren was a wicked man, and everyone in the capital is delighted that he is dead," Bing Chu said. "Why should we be afraid?"

They eventually set off and all made their way to the kingdom of Chu. Gao Qing and Guo Guifu summoned the remaining officials to discuss the situation. Afterwards, they invited the Honorable Yuan to become their ruler, taking the title of Lord Hui.

A bearded old man wrote a poem that says:

How can you go for a journey with your enemy?
Letting them get close gives them the opportunity to take revenge.
It is not that the murderous Shangren lacked a long-term plan,
But chance meant that two mistakes resulted in a terrible vengeance.

...

Let us now turn to another part of the story. Lord Wen of Lu had the personal name Xing and was the son of Lady Sheng Jiang, the principal wife of Lord Xi. He succeeded to the title in the twenty-sixth year of the reign of King Xiang of Zhou. Lord Wen married the daughter of Lord Zhao of Qi as his principal wife, and she gave birth to two sons named Wu and Shi. He also had a favorite concubine, Lady Jing Ying. She was a member of the Qin ruling house, and she too gave birth to two sons, named Jie and Shuxi. Of these four sons, Ai was the oldest but Wu was the son of the principal wife, so Lord Wen appointed Wu as scion.

At this point, the government of the state of Lu was dominated by the Three Huan clans—that is, the descendants of the sons of Lord Huan of Lu. The head of the Mengsun family was Noble Grandson Ao, who had two sons named Gu and Nan. The head of the Shusun family was Noble Grandson Ci, whose sons were named Shusun Pengsheng and Shusun Dechen. Lord Wen appointed Shusun Pengsheng as Grand Tutor to the Heir Apparent. The head of the Jisun family was named Wuyi, and he was the son of the Honorable You of Lu. Jisun Wuyi was the father of Jisun Xingfu, also known by the name Jisun Wenzi. Lord Zhuang of Lu had a son by a commoner woman named the Honorable Sui, who was the second child of the family. From his residence by the East Gate of the capital, he took the name Dongmen or "East Gate" Sui. When Lord Xi was alive, he did everything in accordance with the wishes of the Three Huan clans. When you are thinking of seniority within the family, Noble Grandson Ao and the Honorable Sui were his cousins, while Jisun Xingfu was in the same generation as his nephews. However, Noble Grandson Ao happened to annoy Dongmen Sui and was forced into exile, where he died. As a result, the Mengsun family completely lost power. It was the three families of Dongmen, Shusun, and Jisun that controlled the government.

Let me explain how Noble Grandson Ao annoyed his relative. Noble Grandson Ao married Lady Dai Ji of the ruling house of Ju as his principal wife, and she was the mother of Mengsun Gu. Her younger sister, Lady Sheng Ji, was the mother of Mengsun Nan. Lady Dai Ji became ill and died. Ao was a sexually voracious man and wanted to ask for another daughter of the Ji family as his new wife, but the people of Ju refused and said, "You still have Lady Sheng Ji, so why don't you promote her to being your second wife."

"My cousin, Dongmen Sui, is not yet married," Noble Grandson Ao remarked. "Let me offer these betrothal gifts on his behalf!" The people of Ju agreed to this.

In the seventh year of Lord Wen of Lu's rule, Noble Grandson Ao was ordered to go to Ju to arrange the marriage by His Lordship and to collect Dongmen Sui's bride. When he arrived at Yanling, Noble Grandson Ao climbed the city walls in order to look into her house, at which point he discovered that this Lady Ji was extremely beautiful. He spent that night with her himself and afterwards married her. When Dongmen Sui discovered that his bride had been stolen from him, he was absolutely furious and complained to Lord Wen, asking permission to take troops to attack him.

Shusun Pengsheng remonstrated and said: "You must not do that. I have heard it said that using troops inside the country results in civil war, using them outside results in banditry. Since we are lucky enough to be at peace, how can we deliberately foment a civil war?"

Lord Wen summoned Noble Grandson Ao and ordered him to return Lady Ji to Ju, to assuage Dongmen Sui's resentment. Noble Grandson Ao and Dongmen Sui subsequently got along as well as they had before. However, Ao continued to think about Lady Ji, and the following year, when he was sent to Zhou to attend the funeral of King Xiang, he did not go to the capital but threw aside his mourning garb and ran away to the state of Ju, where he was reunited with Lady Ji. Lord Wen of Lu did not make any move to punish him, and he established his son, Gu, as the master of sacrifices at the Mengsun family shrine.

Some years later, the Noble Grandson suddenly missed his old home and sent someone to take a message to this effect to Gu. Mengsun Gu mentioned this to his uncle, Dongmen Sui.

"If your father wants to come home, he will have to agree to my three conditions," Sui told him. "He cannot come to court; he cannot become involved in the government of the country; and he cannot bring Lady Ji back with him."

Gu sent a messenger to report this to Noble Grandson Ao, who was so desperate to go home that he happily agreed. For the first three years after his return to Lu, he did indeed close his gates and not appear in public. However, suddenly one day he collected all the treasures, the gold, and silk that his family possessed and went back to the state of Ju. Mengsun Gu was devastated by his father's disappearance, and within the year he got sick and died. His son, Mengsun Mie, was still very young, so his younger brother, Mengsun Nan, took over his ministerial position. Not long after that, Lady Ji died, and the Noble Grandson turned his thoughts to going home to Lu for a second time. He gave all his property to Lord Wen and Dongmen Sui, and also asked his son, Mengsun Nan, to speak on his behalf. Lord Wen agreed and he came back again. However, by the time he arrived in Qi he was already too ill to move, and he died at Tangfu. Mengsun Nan insisted that he wanted his father to be buried in Lu, but since Mengsun Nan was the son of such a notorious individual, it was impossible for him to do anything. Even though he was nominally in charge of the ancestral sacrifices, in fact he was merely acting on behalf of Mengsun Mie.

Jisun Xingfu decided to give up his official positions to allow Dongmen Sui, Shusun Pengsheng, and Shusun Dechen to take over, given that they were of a senior generation to himself. In every matter he was careful not to be seen to act on his own authority. Shusun Pengsheng was a very kind and generous man, who held office as a military strategist. His younger brother, Shusun Dechen, took control of the army on a number of occasions, so power in the country was evenly divided between Dongmen Sui and Shusun Dechen.

Lady Jing Ying was Lord Wen of Lu's favorite consort, and she was furious that her son would not become the heir to the title. She offered enormous bribes to Dongmen Sui and entrusted her son, Jie, to his care. She said, "If in the future the Honorable Jie becomes the ruler, he will share the state of Lu with you!" Dongmen Sui understood exactly what she meant and started to think about how to put him in power. However, he knew that Shusun Pengsheng was the tutor of Scion Wu, so there was no way that he would agree to be part of a conspiracy against him. On the other hand, Shusun Dechen was a greedy and corrupt man who could be tempted with bribes. From time to time he would take out some of the things that Lady Jing Ying had given him and hand them over, saying: "Her Ladyship ordered me to present this to you." He would also periodically send the Honorable Jie to Shusun Dechen's house to ask after him most respectfully. This made sure that Shusun Dechen was favorably disposed to him.

The fourth year of the reign of King Kuang of Zhou was the eighteenth year of Lord Wen of Lu's rule. In the spring of this year, Lord Wen died and Scion Wu presided over the funeral before succeeding to the title. Every state sent an ambassador to offer formal condolences. Yuan, Lord Hui of Qi, had only just acceded to the title himself and wanted to make a complete break with the violent government of Shangren, so he specially sent an ambassador to Lu to attend Lord Wen's funeral obsequies.

Dongmen Sui said to Shusun Dechen: "Qi and Lu have been hereditary allies for many generations now. Lord Huan of Qi and Lord Lu of Xi were as close as brothers. However, the relationship went sour during the rule of Lord Xiao and continued to the time of Shangren, whereby we have become enemies. Now the Honorable Yuan has succeeded to the title and we have not yet sent anyone to congratulate him, but they have sent someone to attend the funeral. This is an excellent augury for the prospects of restoring the relationship between us. We must go and thank them and take advantage of this opportunity to press for an alliance with Qi. This is the first step towards seeing the Honorable Jie established!"

"If you go," Shusun Dechen replied, "I will go with you."

When the two men went to Qi, what happened? READ ON.

Chapter Fifty

Dongmen Sui helps to establish the Honorable Jie.

Zhao Dun offers serious remonstrance at the Peach Garden.

Dongmen Sui and Shusun Dechen went to Qi to congratulate the new ruler and thank him for his kindness in sending an ambassador to attend the funeral of Lord Wen. When the ceremonies had been completed, Lord Hui of Qi held a banquet in their honor. He happened to ask about the new ruler of the state of Lu: "Why is he called Wu, meaning 'Bad'? There are so many auspicious names—why did they have to use one which is so unpleasant?"

"When this son was born to His Late Lordship," Dongmen Sui explained, "he asked the Grand Astrologer to perform a divination, and it said: 'He will die a bad death and will never enjoy possession of the country.' His Lordship therefore decided to name him Wu in order to turn his luck, but he was never particularly fond of his son. His Late Lordship loved his oldest son, named Jie, who is a clever and filial young man who has always shown great respect to the senior ministers. The people of the country wanted to establish him as our new ruler, but they were prevented by the fact that he is not the son of His Late Lordship's principal wife."

"Since antiquity the rule has been that the oldest son should be established," Lord Hui said, "and it is even better if he is also the favorite."

"In the past the state of Lu has always established the son of the principal wife," Shusun Dechen assured him. "It is only if there is no such person that we establish the oldest son. His Late Lordship insisted against all advice on upholding the usual practices of our state, whereby he established Wu at the expense of Jie, but no one in the capital is happy about it. If you would help us to establish a wise ruler in his place, we would be delighted to form a marriage alliance with you, and we will serve you by paying court to you and offering gifts every year without fail."

Lord Hui was delighted and said, "If you are determined to do this, I will follow your recommendations. How could I dare to refuse?"

Dongmen Sui and Shusun Dechen smeared their mouths with blood as they swore an oath together. When they proposed a marriage alliance, Lord Hui agreed.

After Dongmen Sui and his companion returned, he explained to Jisun Xingfu: "Jin's hegemony has now collapsed, but Qi is becoming powerful again. They would like to marry a daughter of their ruling house to the Honorable Jie; such a wonderful opportunity should not be lost."

"His Lordship is the nephew of the Marquis of Qi," Jisun Xingfu said. "If the Marquis of Qi has a daughter, why does he not marry her to His Lordship rather than to the Honorable Jie?"

"The Marquis of Qi has heard much about how wonderful Jie is," Dongmen Sui informed him, "and he is determined that they should become good friends—that is why he is insisting on this marriage. The dowager marchioness is Lady Jiang, the daughter of Lord Zhao of Qi. The children of Lord Huan of Qi have been attacking each other as if they were mortal enemies; on four occasions a younger brother has succeeded to the older brother's titles. Since they treat even their own brothers so badly, is that the kind of person that you want as His Lordship's father-in-law?"

Jisun Xingfu was silent, but when he got home he sighed and said, "Dongmen Sui is up to something."

It is because the Honorable Sui lived next to the East Gate that he was known as Dongmen Sui.

Jisun Xingfu secretly reported this conversation to Shusun Pengsheng, who said: "The succession has already been determined, who would dare to rebel?" He really did not think anything of the matter.

Dongmen Sui and Lady Jing Ying secretly came up with a plan whereby they would have some army officers lying in ambush in the stables. One of the grooms would trick Scion Wu there with a false report: "One of your mares has given birth to a particularly fine foal." Lady Jing Ying told the Honorable Jie to go and look at it with Wu and the Honorable Shi. When they went to the stables to see the foal, the officers rushed out and beat Wu to death with wooden clubs. They also killed the Honorable Shi.

"The Grand Tutor to the Heir Apparent, Shusun Pengsheng, is still here," Dongmen Sui declared. "Until we have gotten rid of this man, this is not over."

He sent a eunuch with a message purporting to be from His Lordship, summoning Shusun Pengsheng into the palace. Pengsheng was just about to set out when his servant Gongran Wuren, who knew that Dongmen Sui was involved in some kind of conspiracy with the harem and suspected that there was some trickery here, stopped him and said, "You must not go! If you go they will kill you!"

"It is His Lordship's order," Shusun Pengsheng replied. "Even if I die, how can I refuse to obey his command?"

"If it is indeed His Lordship's command," Gongran Wuren said, "then you are not going to die. If you die obeying something that is not actually His Lordship's order, what is the point of that?"

Pengsheng did not listen to him. Gongran Wuren grabbed hold of his sleeve and wept. Pengsheng ripped his sleeve off and got into his chariot, heading straight for the palace.

"Where is His Lordship?" he asked.

The eunuch lied: "One of the horses in the stables has given birth to a foal, and he is there inspecting it." He led Shusun Pengsheng to the stables, where he was attacked and killed by the army officers, who hid his body under a pile of manure.

Lady Jing Ying sent someone to report to Lady Jiang: "His Lordship and the Honorable Shi have both been kicked and bitten to death by a stallion in the stables!"

Lady Jiang wept bitterly and went to the stables to look at the bodies, but by that time they had already been removed from the palace. When Jisun Xingfu heard that Wu and Shi were both dead, he knew that this was Dongmen Sui's deed, but he did not dare to speak out about the matter. He said in private to Dongmen Sui, "It was a terrible thing to do! I could hardly bear to listen to the news!"

"This is all Lady Jing Ying's fault," Dongmen Sui declared. "It has nothing to do with me!"

"If Jin comes to punish us, what are we going to do?" Jisun Xingfu asked.

"Everyone knows what happened in Song and Qi," Dongmen Sui answered. "In both cases their rulers were assassinated and nothing happened to the perpetrators. Now that the two kids are dead, why should they punish us?"

Jisun Xingfu stroked His Lordship's body—then he burst out crying and wailed until he lost his voice.

"A senior minister ought to save his voice for discussing matters of state," Dongmen Sui sneered. "What is the point of wailing and weeping like a woman?"

Xingfu dried his tears. Shortly afterwards, Shusun Dechen arrived, asking where his brother Pengsheng was. Dongmen Sui said that he did not know. Dechen laughed and said, "My older brother died to prove his loyalty to His Lordship. That was his greatest ambition. You don't need to lie to me!"

Dongmen Sui gave him whispered instructions as to the location of the body. He added: "The most important thing we need to do now is to establish a new lord. The Honorable Jie is a good man and he is the oldest son, so he should succeed to the title!"

All the officials simply agreed to this, and so the Honorable Jie became their new ruler under the title of Lord Xuan. The officials offered formal congratulations to him.

Master Hu Zeng wrote a historical poem about this:

A powerful official and a harem favorite joined together in a vicious conspiracy;
An innocent ruler was overthrown without warning.
How sad that Jisun Xingfu simply sat on the fence,
His native caution no match for a good plan.

Shusun Dechen dug through the horse manure to find Pengsheng's body. Afterwards he buried it, but that is not part of this story.

Lady Jiang, the Dowager Marchioness of Lu, beat her breast and wept when she heard that her two sons had both been murdered and Dongmen Sui had installed the Honorable Jie as the new lord. She fainted several times in succession and was only brought around with difficulty. Dongmen Sui wanted to ingratiate himself with Lord Xuan, and so, claiming that a mother should be ennobled on account of her son, he recommended that Lady Jing Ying should become the dowager marchioness. The officials of Lu all offered their congratulations to His Lordship. Dowager Marchioness Jiang could find no peace in the palace, and so she wept and wailed day and night. She ordered her servants to pack a couple of carriages, for she wanted to go home to Qi.

Dongmen Sui sent a messenger to her pretending that he wanted her to stay: "While it is true that our newly established lord is not your son, you are nevertheless the dowager marchioness, and he will treat you according to the demands of filial piety. Surely you do not have to throw yourself on the charity of your own relatives?"

Lady Jiang cursed: "You bastard, Sui! What had my son ever done to you that you murdered him so cruelly? How dare you use these weasel words to try and make me stay! If there are such things as ghosts and spirits, they will not let you get away with this!"

Lady Jiang did not go to say farewell to Lady Jing Ying, but went straight to the palace gates and got into a carriage. As she passed through the marketplace and along the main roads, she wailed and shouted: "Heaven! Heaven! What crime did my poor children commit? What have I done wrong? How could that traitor Sui go against every principle and murder the true heir to put a concubine's son in power? Today I say goodbye forever to the people of the capital; I will never return to the state of Lu again!"

Those passers-by who heard what she said were all deeply upset, and many of them shed tears. On that day, no market was held anywhere in the state of Lu as a mark of respect. The dowager marchioness was originally called Lady Ai Jiang, but after she went home to Qi, she was known by the name Lady Chu Jiang. When Lady Chu Jiang arrived in Qi, she was greeted by her mother, the dowager marchioness and widow of Lord Zhao of Qi, and both of them wept bitterly over the terrible deaths of their innocent sons. Lord Hui of Qi had a strong aversion to hearing the sound of people crying, so he built a separate residence for the mother and daughter and moved them there. Lady Chu Jiang lived the rest of her life in Qi.

...

Lord Xuan of Lu had a younger brother by the same mother named Shuxi who had a very direct and loyal character. When he realized that his older brother had availed himself of Dongmen Sui's power to murder their half-brother and establish himself, he was horrified and did not go to court to congratulate him. Lord Xuan sent someone to summon him, because he was intending to give him high office. Shuxi stubbornly refused to go, and when a friend asked him why, he said: "It is not that I have a rooted objection to wealth and nobility; the problem is that every time I see my brother, I think about how the Honorable Wu died. I can't bear it!"

"If you are so upset by your brother's injustice," his friend said, "should you not go into exile abroad?"

"Since my older brother has not disowned me," Shuxi replied, "I would not dare to abandon him."

Whenever Lord Xuan sent an official to ask after him, or presented him with grain or silk, Shuxi would bow to the messenger and decline, saying, "I am so lucky as to be neither hungry nor cold. I would not like to see His Lordship's property being wasted on me!" If the messenger insisted, Shuxi would say, "Let us wait until I need something, and then I will go and collect it. Right now I simply cannot accept this gift!"

"You have already made your determination clear by refusing to accept titles or emoluments," his friend said. "You are not wealthy, and taking a few scraps from your brother's table would allow you to eat your fill twice a day without hurting your principles. Surely it is too much to refuse everything!"

The Honorable Shuxi laughed and did not reply. His friend sighed and left. The messenger did not dare to stay any longer and returned to report to Lord Xuan. Lord Xuan said, "My brother does not have any money; how on earth does he survive?" That night the messenger went back to spy on him and discovered that overnight he would weave sandals and in the morning he would go and sell them, thus making enough money to keep himself fed. Lord Xuan sighed and said, "My brother wants to imitate Boyi and Shuqi, and go and pick vetch at the foot of Mount Shouyang. I will just have to let him get on with it." The Honorable Shuxi died in the last year of Lord Xuan's rule, without ever taking so much as an inch of silk or a grain of rice from his older brother. On the other hand, he also never said a word of criticism about his brother during his whole life.

A historian wrote a poem praising this:

The Honorable Shuxi was a wise and good man;
When deeply moved, he cried tears of blood.
He wove sandals in order to support himself,
Taking nothing from his lord.
Just like the Shang loyalists, ashamed to take service under the Zhou,
He lived out his years by picking vetch.

Only the Honorable Shuxi remembered the rightful heir,
He could touch pitch and yet not be defiled.
Though they sprang from the same branch,
The older brother was a shameless opportunist and the younger pure and honest.
As for Dongmen Sui,
Even mentioning him would sully my tongue.

The people of Lu were most impressed by the Honorable Shuxi's sense of justice and praised him greatly for it. In the first year of the rule of Lord Cheng, he appointed his son, Noble Grandson Yingqi, as a grandee. From this time on there was not just the Shusun family, but also the Shu clan. Shu Lao, Shu Gong, Shu Zhe, Shu An, and Shu Zhi—these were all his descendants. However, this is something that happened much later on, so for the moment it will have to be put to one side.

. . .

The fifth year of the reign of King Kuang of Zhou was the first year of the rule of Lord Xuan of Lu. On New Year's Day, when the formal ceremony of congratulation had been concluded, Dongmen Sui presented his opinion: "Your Lordship is still unmarried, but the Marquis of Qi and I have arranged a match for you, and it should not be long delayed."

"Who will go to Qi to conclude the arrangements on my behalf?" Lord Xuan asked.

"This was my idea, so let me go on my own," Dongmen Sui replied.

The Marquis of Lu then sent Dongmen Sui to Qi to present the bridal gifts. He arrived in Qi the first month, and in the second month he returned with the bride, Lady Jiang. He secretly advised Lord Xuan: "Even though you are now joined in a marriage alliance with Qi, it is not clear whether the relations between your two countries in the future will be good or bad. However, the most important thing now is to ensure that you can attend covenants and meetings and are ranked among the lords of the Central States. For that reason I have already made a blood covenant with the Marquis of Qi, at which I swore that we would pay court to them every year and send diplomatic gifts, without fail. I also promised that once you came to power, you would obey him. Now, you must not begrudge heavy bribes to invite Qi to attend a meeting. If they take our bribes and agree to the meeting, you must serve them with the utmost respect. In that way the alliance between our two countries will be as firm as that between lips and teeth, and your position will be as secure as Mount Tai."

Lord Xuan thought that this was good advice, and so he sent Jisun Xingfu to go to Qi to thank them for agreeing to the match and convey the following message:

> Thanks to Your Lordship's benevolence, the shrines of my ancestors are now secure. However, I cannot feel at ease, for I am afraid that I will not be ranked among the feudal lords, which would be most humiliating for the ruler of a country. If you feel any sympathy for my plight, you will agree to a meeting.

> Under the circumstances I do not begrudge the fields of Jixi, which were a present from Lord Wen of Jin to our former lord. I am willing to give them to you, and I hope that you will humble yourself to receive them.

Lord Hui of Qi was very pleased and agreed that in the fifth month he would meet the Lord of Lu at Pingzhou.

On the appointed day, Lord Xuan of Lu was the first to arrive, and the Marquis of Qi followed him. First they greeted each other affectionately as father-in-law and son-in-law, and then they performed the proper ceremonies for two rulers meeting. Dongmen Sui presented the documentation concerning the lands of Jixi, and the Marquis of Qi did not refuse them. When this had been arranged, Lord Xuan said farewell to the Marquis of Qi and returned to Lu.

"I can now sleep easy," Dongmen Sui declared.

From this time onwards Lu regularly paid court and sent diplomatic gifts to Qi, and they served them as a subject would a ruler, with complete sincerity. There was no order that they did not follow, no campaign that they refused to participate in. In the last year of Lord Hui of Qi's life, in recognition of the loyal service of the Marquis of Lu, he returned the lands of Jixi to him. This happened much later on.

• • •

Let us turn now to another part of the story. During the first three years after Prince Lü had succeeded to the title as King Zhuang of Chu, he gave no orders and spent every day in hunting. When he returned to the palace, he would spend day and night drinking with his wives and would have a notice hung from the door to the court: "Anyone who dares to remonstrate will be executed with no possibility of pardon!" Grandee Shen Wuwei went in to have an audience with His Majesty and found King Zhuang hugging Lady Ji of Zheng with his right arm and cuddling a woman from Cai with the other. He was sitting with legs sprawled among the rows of bells and drums.

"Since you are here, why don't you have something to drink?" His Majesty asked. "How about we listen to some music? Or is there something that you want to say?"

"I am not here to drink or listen to music," Shen Wuwei declared. "Recently I was traveling in the suburbs and someone told me a riddle that I cannot solve. I wonder if Your Majesty would like to hear it?"

"Oh!" King Zhuang exclaimed. "What kind of riddle is it that you cannot solve but that you want me to hear?"

"There is a great bird with a multicolored body that has perched on top of a mountain in Chu for three years without anyone seeing it fly or hearing it sing," Shen Wuwei said. "What kind of bird is this?"

King Zhuang knew that this was a covert criticism of himself, but he just laughed and said, "I know that this is no ordinary bird. It has not flown for three years, but when it does, it will soar high into the sky; it has not sung for three years, but when it does, it will strike fear into all who hear it. You just wait and see!" Shen Wuwei bowed twice and withdrew.

Over the next couple of days, King Zhuang was just as sunken in debauch as he had been before. Grandee Su Cong requested an audience with King Zhuang, and when it was granted, he started to wail.

"Why are you so upset?" His Majesty inquired.

"I am crying because I am about to die," Su Cong replied, "and the kingdom of Chu will be destroyed!"

"Why are you going to die?" King Zhuang asked. "Why should the kingdom of Chu be destroyed?"

"I am going to remonstrate with Your Majesty and you are going to refuse to listen and kill me," Su Cong told him. "Once I am dead, no one in the kingdom of Chu will dare to remonstrate with you. When everyone just flatters and fawns over you, the government of Chu will collapse. The destruction of the country is imminent!"

King Zhuang flushed with anger and said, "I have given orders: 'Anyone who dares to remonstrate with me will die!' You clearly know that remonstrance will bring about your death, but you still insist on coming here to annoy me—is that not really stupid?"

"I may be stupid," Su Cong retorted, "but I am not as stupid as Your Majesty!"

King Zhuang became even more furious. "In what way am I really stupid?" he demanded.

"Your Majesty has command of an army of ten thousand chariots, you enjoy the tax revenue of a realm one thousand *li* across, you have strong knights and trained horses, the lords fear you and submit to your authority and they send in tribute every season and come regularly to court," Su Cong replied. "These are blessings for ten thousand generations. However, you are sunk in drunken debauchery, you amuse yourself with music, you pay no attention to the government, you make no effort to befriend wise and talented men, and you suffer attacks from great foreign powers and rebellions among your allies. You are having fun now, but disaster will strike you down. Are you really prepared to lose blessings for ten thousand generations simply for the sake of a moment's pleasure? If this is not extremely stupid, what is it? I may be stupid, but that will just get me killed. Once Your Majesty has killed me, later generations will praise me as a loyal subject and I will be ranked with Guan Longfeng and Prince Bigan. What is wrong with that? Your kind of stupidity means that even if you want to be degraded to the status of a commoner, it will not be possible. I have now said everything that I want to. Please let me borrow your sword so that I can cut my throat right here and now, in accordance with Your Majesty's orders!"

King Zhuang got up quickly and said, "No! Every word that you have said is loyal advice, and I will listen to you!"

He cut the ropes holding the bells and drums in their frames, sent away Lady Ji of Zheng, ordered the woman from Cai to leave, and appointed Lady Ji of Fan as his queen to take charge of running the palace.

"I love hunting and Lady Ji of Fan remonstrated with me," King Zhuang announced. "When I paid no attention, she stopped eating the meat of birds or animals. This woman is the perfect partner to help me!"

He employed Wei Jia, Pan Wang, and Qu Dang as a balance to the power wielded by the Grand Vizier Dou Yuejiao. He would issue orders every morning and evening. He commanded the Honorable Guisheng of Zheng to attack Song and they did battle at Daji, where he captured alive the Song General of the Right, Hua Yuan. He ordered Wei Jia to rescue Zheng; they did battle with Jin at Beilin and captured alive the Jin general Jie Yang, returning home with him. He was only released the following year. From this point onwards Chu became much stronger, and King Zhuang began to think greedily of the possibility that he might be able to establish hegemony over the Central Plain.

People discussing this note that Zhao Dun took bribes from the two states of Qi and Song, and so Jin did not punish those who assassinated their rulers. Thus the Central States lost their moral compass, and the people of Chu took advantage of this to fight for hegemony. Whose fault is that?

The poem about this reads:

The Master of Covenants ought to uphold righteous principles;
How could he allow a subordinate state to destroy his lord's relatives?
Having taken bribes to let Qi and Song off the hook,
No wonder the barbarians felt free to do as they liked!

The senior minister of Jin, Zhao Dun, realized that Chu was becoming more powerful by the day and decided that they needed an alliance with Qin to block the advance of Chu. Zhao Chuan presented his opinion: "There is a state subordinate to Qin named Chong that has been their most long-standing ally. If we were to send an army to invade Chong, Qin would be certain to go to their rescue. We can then ask for a peace treaty from them. In these circumstances, we would be in a very favorable position!"

Zhao Dun followed his advice. He spoke to Lord Ling about the matter and then mobilized three hundred chariots, under the command of Zhao Chuan, to invade Chong.

"The enmity between Qin and Jin is already appalling," Zhao Shuo pleaded. "If we now invade one of their subordinate states, Qin will be even angrier. Is it likely that they will agree to a peace treaty with us?"

"I have already agreed to this plan!" Zhao Dun snapped.

Zhao Shuo then tried to talk to Han Jue about it. Han Jue laughed coldly and whispered in Zhao Shuo's ear: "This campaign is intended to build Chuan's authority and confirm the importance of the Zhao clan; it is not really about making peace with Qin!" Zhao Shuo withdrew in silence.

When Qin heard that Jin had invaded Chong, they did not bother to go to the rescue, they simply raised an army and invaded Jin, laying siege to the city of Jiao. Zhao Chuan had to turn his army around to rescue Jiao, whereupon the Qin army withdrew. From this time onwards, Zhao Chuan held many senior military appointments. When Yu Pian died, Zhao Chuan replaced him.

• • •

By this time Lord Ling of Jin had grown up and revealed himself to be a wicked and cruel man. He placed a heavy tax burden on his people while expanding his own landholdings, where he would enjoy himself. He particularly favored one of his grandees, a man named Tu'an Gu.

He was the son of Tu'an Ji and the grandson of Tu'an Yi.

Tu'an Gu knew exactly how to please His Lordship with flattery, so he always listened to what he said. Lord Ling ordered Tu'an Gu to build a garden inside the walls of the capital city, Jiang, and fill it with strange and rare plants. The peach trees were the most magnificent, and in spring when they flowered, they looked like a bolt of silk brocade. It was these trees that gave their name to this place: Peach Garden. In the middle of the garden he constructed a three-tier platform that was topped by the Falling Snowflakes Belvedere, with its painted pillars and carved beams, its vermillion lintels and inlaid roof-brackets. A red railing surrounded the building on all four sides so that you could lean out and admire the view. The main market of the city was well within view. Lord Ling enjoyed this place very much and would often climb up to look out on his capital. Sometimes he would bend his bow to shoot at birds, or he would amuse himself by betting with Tu'an Gu on how much they could drink.

One day he had summoned a troupe of actors to perform on the terrace there, and a number of ordinary people gathered outside the garden to watch. Lord Ling said to Tu'an Gu, "Shooting birds is not nearly so much fun as shooting people. Let us have a contest! The person who shoots someone in the eye is the winner. If you hit an arm or a leg, then you will not be punished. If you fail to hit your target at all, you will have to drink a large cup of wine."

Lord Ling stood on the right-hand side and Tu'an Gu on the left. The actors on the stage screamed, "Look out!" The bows were stretched till they looked like a full moon, and the cross-bow bolts fell like shooting stars. One person in the crowd had a bolt carry off half his ear; another was hit in the left shoulder. In terror, the people rushed this way and that, shouting in confusion and pushing each other. Then the cry went up: "Another round of bolts is coming!" Lord Ling was furious and ordered his entourage to join in; when they all shot together, the cross-bow bolts fell like rain. There was absolutely nowhere for people to hide—some were hit in the head, the bolt grazing their foreheads or plucking out an eye or knocking out their teeth. Heart-wrenching cries went up—some were calling for their fathers, others for their mothers, trying to find a way to escape, pushing and shoving and kicking and punching, rushing around in panic: it was an unendurable sight. Lord Ling stood watching this from his tower. Throwing his bow onto the ground, he burst out laughing.

"I have come to this tower to enjoy myself many times," he told Tu'an Gu, "but I have never had so much fun as today!"

From this time on, if people saw that there was someone on the terrace, they did not dare to walk anywhere near the Peach Garden. There was a saying current in the city: "If you look at the terrace, they will kill you for it. You may leave home happily, but you will return in tears and lamentations."

. . .

The people of Zhou presented the lord of Jin with a guard dog called Ling'ao, which was three feet tall and the color of hot coals. It was very good at understanding what people wanted, and if any of his entourage did something wrong, Lord Ling would call on Ling'ao to bite them. Ling'ao would hurl itself at their necks and bite them to death. There was a slave whose job it was to look after this mastiff, and every day he fed it a couple of pounds of lamb meat. The dog therefore also listened to his commands. This man was known as the Ling'ao Slave, and he enjoyed the same salary as a mid-level grandee.

Lord Ling decided that he could no longer be bothered to hold court, so he ordered his officials to attend him in the inner palace. Every time he held an audience or went out traveling, the Ling'ao Slave would be there in attendance, holding the dog on a fine chain. Everyone who saw it was terrified. By this time other countries had become alienated from Jin, and the people of Jin hated him. Zhao Dun and others repeatedly warned His Lordship and remonstrated with him, telling him to treat wise men with courtesy and keep away from sycophants. Lord Ling carried on as if his ears had been plugged and paid absolutely no attention to them—in fact, he became increasingly suspicious of their motives.

Suddenly one day, when Lord Ling dismissed his court and the officials all dispersed, Zhao Dun and Shi Hui happened to find themselves discussing some matter of state by the inner palace gates and arguing with one another. They noticed a pair of eunuchs carrying a wicker basket out of the side door to the palace.

"Why should they be taking a basket out of the palace?" Zhao Dun asked. "There must be something going on." He shouted to the servants: "Come over here! Over here!"

The eunuchs just lowered their heads and ignored him.

"What is in that basket?" Zhao Dun demanded.

"You are the prime minister," the eunuchs replied, "so if you want to look, of course you can. However, we would not dare to tell you."

Zhao Dun was now thoroughly suspicious and ordered Shi Hui to go and have a look. He had already noticed that a hand and a foot were hanging out of the basket. When the two men opened it up, they found that it contained a corpse. Zhao Dun was deeply shocked and asked who this was. The eunuchs were still not willing to answer, so Zhao Dun said, "If you don't tell me I will have you beheaded immediately!"

"He was a chef," the eunuchs said reluctantly. "His Lordship ordered him to cook bear's paws, but he was in a hurry to eat them as a snack while he was drinking, so he kept on sending messages to the kitchen telling them to hurry up. In the end the chef had to send in the paws as they were, and when His Lordship tasted them, he was angry because they were not properly cooked. He beat the chef to death with a bronze flagon and hacked his body into a couple of pieces. He ordered us to dump the remains somewhere in the wilds, and he told us that we had to be back in the palace by a certain time or he would execute us!"

Zhao Dun let the two eunuchs take the body away. "His Lordship is a wicked man who treats other people like dirt," he said. "The country is in terrible danger. Let us go and remonstrate seriously with him. What do you think?"

"The two of us have remonstrated many times but he does not listen," Shi Hui replied, "largely because no one ever follows up on it. Let me go and talk to him first. If he does not listen, then you can try."

At that time Lord Ling was still in the audience chamber, and when Shi Hui came in, Lord Ling looked at him and realized that he had come to complain of his behavior. Therefore, he greeted him with the words: "Don't say anything! I know I have behaved badly, and starting today I am going to reform."

Shi Hui kowtowed and said, "Everyone makes mistakes. If you recognize your faults and reform, it will be a great blessing for the whole country. I am absolutely delighted!" When he had finished speaking, he withdrew. When he reported this to Zhao Dun, the latter said, "If His Lordship genuinely regrets his mistakes, we should see some signs soon."

On the following day, Lord Ling decided not to hold court, but ordered his chariot to take him to the Peach Garden for a party.

"This move on His Lordship's part really does not look like reformation!" Zhao Dun remarked. "I will have to speak to him today myself!" He went on ahead to the gate to the Peach Garden and waited to Lord Ling to arrive. Then he came forward and requested an audience.

"I have not summoned you!" Lord Ling said suspiciously. "Why are you here?"

Zhao Dun kowtowed, bowed twice, and said: "I have committed a crime that deserves the death penalty! I have something to say and I hope that Your Lordship will listen to me. I have heard it said that a good ruler enjoys making other people happy; an evil ruler enjoys making himself happy. It is bad enough that you should make yourself happy with your wives and favorites amid the luxuries of the palace, or by going out hunting and amusing yourself. No one should make themselves happy by killing other people. You allow your dog to bite people; you personally shoot people dead; you kill your chef over a trifling misdemeanor: these are things that a good ruler would not do, but you have done them. Human life is paramount. If you kill people in such sadistic ways, you will find your populace in revolt against you at home and the feudal lords will oppose you abroad. Your Lordship is about to be overtaken by the same fate as the wicked kings Jie and Zhou. If I do not speak to you about this today, no one else will. I cannot bear to sit by idly, while you are murdered and the country destroyed. That is the reason why I have dared to speak out directly. I beg Your Lordship to turn your chariot around and go back to court, reform your previous behavior—do not engage in such sadistic amusements! Do not kill anyone else! If you can pull the state of Jin back from the brink of disaster, even if you kill me, I will have no regrets."

Lord Ling felt very ashamed of himself and hid his face behind his sleeve. "You can leave now," he said. "I will just enjoy myself today. In the future I will follow your advice!"

Zhao Dun blocked the way to the gate of the Peach Garden with his body and would not allow Lord Ling to enter. Tu'an Gu, who was standing to one side, said: "The prime minister has remonstrated out of the best of motives. However, since you are already here, people will laugh at you if you turn back. Why don't you tell the prime minister to go home for the moment? If there is some important government matter, you can discuss it tomorrow morning, when you hold court."

Lord Ling accordingly made the excuse: "I will hold court tomorrow morning and summon you then!"

There was nothing that Zhao Dun could do. He stood to one side and allowed Lord Ling to enter the garden. He glared at Tu'an Gu and said, "That is the kind of man who ruins his country and destroys his family!" He was absolutely furious.

Tu'an Gu followed Lord Ling in his revels, and when they were laughing heartily, Tu'an Gu suddenly sighed and said, "We will never have such fun again!"

"Why do you say that?" Lord Ling asked.

"Tomorrow morning Prime Minister Zhao is sure to put you under some form of restraint," Tu'an Gu reminded him. "Is it likely that he will let you out again?"

Lord Ling flushed with anger: "Ever since antiquity it has been rulers who control their subjects and not the other way round. This old man is really not convenient to have around. Do you have a plan to get rid of him?"

"One of the men in my service is called Xu Ni," Tu'an Gu said. "He comes from a poor family that relies entirely upon me for their survival. He is completely loyal and would do anything to repay me, even if it means his death. If I send him to assassinate the prime minister, you can do whatever you like in the future without fear of trouble."

"If you can really pull it off," Lord Ling declared, "you will have performed a signal service."

That evening, Tu'an Gu secretly summoned Xu Ni and gave him wine to drink. He instructed him: "Zhao Dun monopolizes power and bullies His Lordship. I have an official order from the Marquis of Jin to send you to assassinate him. If you wait in ambush at Prime Minister Zhao's gate, you can kill him when he leaves to attend court first thing in the morning. Make no mistakes!"

Xu Ni accepted this command and left. Having made his preparations, he lurked around the gate to the Zhao mansion until he heard the drums sounding the fifth watch, carrying his dagger, *Snow-Speckle*. He moved into position right next to the gate. He then saw the gate flung open and a chariot move out; in the distance he could see the lamps flickering in the main hall. Xu Ni took advantage of this opportunity to sneak through the main gate. Hiding in the shadows, he looked around and spotted an official sitting calmly in the main hall, wearing an official robe and hat, his belt knotted around his waist and his staff of office tucked firmly into it. This was none other than the prime minister, Zhao Dun. He was in such a hurry to get to court that he was ready long before it was light, so now he was waiting for the dawn.

Xu Ni was shocked and slipped out of the gate. He sighed and said, "What an honorable and respectful man! It would be disloyal of me to kill a good man, but having received His Lordship's order to do so, failure would show untrustworthiness. If I am neither loyal nor trustworthy, what is the point of being alive?" He shouted towards the gate: "I, Xu Ni, have failed to carry out His Lordship's command because I could not bear to kill a loyal minister. Instead I choose to kill myself. I am afraid that there will be more attempts on your life, so you had better be careful!" As he finished speaking, he noticed a huge pagoda tree and he hurled himself against its trunk, breaking open his skull and killing himself.

A historian wrote a poem of praise:

How brave was Xu Ni, the finest of knights-errant!
Justice was his motivation, he looked upon death as simply going home.
He repaid his debt to Tu'an Gu and protected Zhao Dun;
Though he died in the process, his name has been handed down in history.
As long as the pagoda tree throws a shade,
He will be remembered.

By this time all the guards and gatekeepers had been alarmed, and they reported what Xu Ni had said and done to Zhao Dun. Zhao Dun's bodyguard, Di Miming, said: "You had better not go to court today, Prime Minister, for I am afraid there is going to be trouble."

"His Lordship has demanded my appearance at morning court," Zhao Dun returned, "so if I do not go, I will fail in ritual propriety. Life and death are determined by fate; why should I worry?"

He instructed his family members to bury Xu Ni temporarily in a shallow grave next to the pagoda tree. Afterwards, Zhao Dun got in a chariot and rode to court, where he performed the usual ceremonies. When Lord Ling saw that Zhao Dun was still alive, he asked Tu'an Gu what had happened to Xu Ni.

"Xu Ni went out but did not come back," Tu'an Gu replied. "Someone told me that he dashed his head against a pagoda tree and killed himself, but I don't know why."

"Since this plan has not worked, what do we do now?" Lord Ling asked.

Tu'an Gu presented his opinion: "I have a plan that can definitely kill Zhao Dun."

"What plan?" Lord Ling demanded.

"In a day or two's time, my lord, you should summon Zhao Dun for a banquet in the palace," Tu'an Gu suggested. "We will have soldiers waiting in ambush behind the back wall. Once the three formal rounds of toasting have been performed, you can ask to see Zhao Dun's sword. He will certainly take it out to show it to you and I will then give the signal, shouting: 'Zhao Dun has drawn his sword in His Lordship's presence! He is plotting an assassination! Save His Lordship!' The soldiers will leap out, tie him up, and behead him. Everyone will say that Zhao Dun brought this punishment upon himself, and you will not have to bear the odium of executing a senior minister. What do you think?"

"Wonderful! Wonderful!" Lord Ling exclaimed. "That is exactly what we will do!"

The following day when he held court again, Lord Ling said to Zhao Dun, "Thanks to your earnest advice, I have decided to treat my ministers better. Let me begin by holding this little banquet for you, in honor of your achievements." He ordered Tu'an Gu to lead him into the palace and his bodyguard, Di Miming, followed him.

As they went up the steps, Tu'an Gu said, "His Lordship is holding a banquet in honor of the prime minister; no one else is allowed to come up these steps." Di Miming took his place below the stairs. Zhao Dun bowed twice and took his place on Lord Ling's right-hand side, while Tu'an Gu stood on His Lordship's left. The cooks presented their dishes and the wine circulated three times.

"I have heard that the sword you wear is particularly fine," Lord Ling said to Zhao Dun. "Would you mind taking it out, so that I can have a look at it?"

Zhao Dun did not know that this was a trap, so he was just about to unclasp his sword, when Di Miming realized what was going on and shouted: "When a subject is attending a banquet given by his lord, it is ritually correct that a maximum of three cups of wine should be drunk. Since when has it become acceptable to drink and then draw your sword in the presence of the ruler?"

Zhao Dun immediately came to his senses and stood up. Di Miming hurled himself into the hall in a frenzy, trying to get Zhao Dun out safely. Tu'an Gu ordered the Ling'ao Slave to release the dog to hunt down the man in a purple robe. Ling'ao ran like the wind and caught up with Zhao Dun just inside the palace gates. Di Miming was strong enough to lift a thousand pounds, and with his two hands he grabbed hold of Ling'ao and broke its neck. Seeing Ling'ao die like that made Lord Ling even more enraged, so he ordered the soldiers lying in ambush to attack Zhao Dun. Di Miming shielded him with his own body. He told Zhao Dun to run for his life. Di Miming fought them off alone, but he was just one against many. Having sustained injuries all over his body, he died of his wounds.

A historian praised this:

The lord had a mastiff, but the minister had his own guard dog.
The lord's mastiff could not defeat the minister's guard dog.
The lord's mastiff hurt people,
The minister's guard dog saved his life.
Alas! Which of the two would you rather have?

Thanks to Di Miming's determined fight with the attacking soldiers, Zhao Dun was able to escape. Suddenly someone came running up to him. Zhao Dun was petrified until the man said, "Do not be afraid, Prime Minister! I am here to rescue you, not to kill you!"

"Who are you?" Zhao Dun demanded.

"Do you not remember the starving man under the mulberry tree?" he replied. "I am Ling Zhe."

. . .

Some five years earlier, Zhao Dun had been hunting at Mount Jiuyuan and had rested under a mulberry tree. He noticed a man lying on the ground. Zhao Dun suspected that it was an assassin and ordered someone to arrest him. The man was so hungry that he could not stand upright, and when they inquired who he was, he replied, "My name is Ling Zhe. I was a student in Wey for three years, and I am now on my way home. I have no more food in my bag and it is three days since I last had anything to eat."

Zhao Dun felt sorry for him and gave him some food. Zhe accepted a little basket, of which he put one half away and ate the other half.

"Why have you put one half away?" Zhao Dun asked.

"I have an old mother living by the West Gate," Zhe replied. "I have been abroad for so long that I do not even know if my mother is alive or dead! I am now only a few *li* from home and I would like to keep some of the food that you have given me for her."

Zhao Dun sighed and said, "What a filial son!" He told him to eat up the food that he had given him and took out another basket containing meat and rice which he put in Ling Zhe's bag. Ling Zhe bowed his thanks and left.

To this day in Jiangzhou there is a place called Feeding the Starving Ridge, which takes its name from this incident.

. . .

Later on, Ling Zhe joined His Lordship's service and was numbered among his guards, but remembering how kind Zhao Dun had been to him in the past, he came specially to rescue him. By the time people realized what had happened, both of them had fled. Ling Zhe carried Zhao Dun out of the palace on his back. Once the guards had killed Di Miming, they set off in hot pursuit, but by then Zhao Shuo had roused all his family's troops and come out to meet Zhao Dun, helping him into a chariot. Zhao Dun summoned Ling Zhe to ride by his side and the pair of them fled. The pursuing soldiers, looking at how many people the Zhao clan had mobilized, did not dare to continue the chase.

"I cannot go home," Zhao Dun told Shuo. "I will have to go either to the Di or to Qin to try and find somewhere to survive!"

Thus the father and son rode out of the West Gate together. From there they proceeded on to the west.

Historians note that Zhao Dun was sympathetic and kind to others, and so they were prepared to die for him: that is how he escaped disaster on this occasion. There is a poem about this:

A mouthful of wine and a bit of meat was nothing to him,
But it was everything to this loyal knight.
If Zhao Dun had not helped the man under the mulberry tree,
How would he have escaped the closing net today?

Do you know where Zhao Dun went? READ ON.

Chapter Fifty-one

Dong Hu uses an upright brush to upbraid Zhao Dun.

After executing Dou Yuejiao, King Zhuang holds the Broken Tassel Banquet.

Once Lord Ling had decided to kill Zhao Dun, even though the plot did not succeed, he was nevertheless happy to have forced him to leave the city of Jiang. He felt like an ignorant pupil who has gotten away from his teacher, or a lazy slave escaped from his master; he could breathe easily for the first time. He was happier than he could say. He took his womenfolk and servants to stay at the Peach Garden, and they did not go home day or night.

When Zhao Chuan returned from hunting in the western suburbs, he happened to run into the chariot carrying Zhao Dun and his son, Shuo, so they both stopped to greet each other and explain what they were doing.

"Do not go out of the border, Uncle," Zhao Chuan said. "If you have not received a letter from me in the next couple of days, decide then whether you want to stay or leave."

"In these circumstances," Zhao Dun pronounced, "my one thought is to head into exile at Mount Shouyang and wait for better news. You must be very careful. Do not make things worse than they already are."

Zhao Chuan said goodbye to Zhao Dun and his son, and headed back to the city of Jiang. When he heard that Lord Ling was living in the Peach Garden, he pretended that he wanted to have an audience with him, whereupon he kowtowed and apologized: "I am ashamed of my traitorous family and would not dare to continue in your service. Please remove me from office!"

Lord Ling believed that he was sincere and comforted him: "Zhao Dun has humiliated and bullied me time and time again. I could not stand it a moment longer. But what has this to do with you? You can take up your job again knowing that you have my full confidence."

After Zhao Chuan had thanked him for his magnanimity, he presented his opinion: "I have heard it said that only a nobleman who is the ruler of a state can enjoy to the full life's pleasures of women and song. Although you have the bells and drums suspended here, your harem is inadequate; how can you possibly enjoy yourself? Lord Huan of Qi had a host of harem favorites—quite apart from his official wives, he had six junior consorts. Even though our former ruler, Lord Wen, was forced into exile and found himself in terrible danger, he still managed to marry many wives. When finally he returned to his country at past sixty years of age, he had countless women with him. You, my lord, have a grand palace and vast estates, quite sufficient to house a whole harem. Why do you not select some girls of good family to fill them and invite some famous instructors to teach them music and dancing? That way you can really enjoy yourself! Would that not be wonderful?"

"You took the words right out of my mouth," Lord Ling laughed. "Who would be the best choice to take the job of searching out the most beautiful women in the country?"

"Why don't you send Tu'an Gu?" suggested Zhao Chuan.

Lord Ling commanded Tu'an Gu to take charge of this matter. All good-looking women under the age of twenty and unmarried, whether they lived inside or outside of the city walls, had to report for selection within a month. Having ensured that Tu'an Gu was sent away on this task, Zhao Chuan presented his opinion to Lord Ling: "There are not many guards stationed at the Peach Garden. Let me select two hundred of the finest soldiers in the army to protect Your Lordship. I hope that you will agree to my proposal." Lord Ling did so.

Zhao Chuan returned to camp and selected two hundred of his best men.

"What mission do you have for us?" they asked.

"His Lordship does not care about the sufferings of his people, and he spends every day at the Peach Garden enjoying himself," Zhao Chuan declared. "He ordered me to select you so that you can patrol around and protect him. You all have families, but you are going to be taken from them to work day and night. Who knows when you will see them again?"

The soldiers were all furious: "Why doesn't this wicked ruler of ours die soon! If the prime minister were here, none of this would have happened!"

"I have something that I would like to say to you," Zhao Chuan said, "but I don't know if it would be a good idea . . ."

The soldiers all said, "If you can save us from this bitter fate, general, we will serve you as we would our own parents."

"The Peach Garden is not as strictly guarded and inaccessible as the palace," Zhao Chuan suggested. "If you were to wait until after midnight and then attack the Garden, you could claim that you have demands to make to His Lordship. I will signal to you by waving my sleeve, and you can kill the Marquis of Jin. I will then bring the prime minister back, and he will establish a new ruler. What do you think of this plan?"

"That would be wonderful!" the soldiers all agreed.

Zhao Chuan served them wine and food before lining them up outside the Peach Garden. He went in to speak to Lord Ling.

Lord Ling had climbed the terrace to review his troops, and when he saw how well turned out they were, each one stronger and braver than the last, Lord Ling was delighted. He kept Zhao Chuan with him, drinking wine. When it got past midnight, suddenly the sound of shouting could be heard outside. Lord Ling was alarmed and asked what was going on.

"It must be the guards on night patrol chasing away some miscreant," Zhao Chuan said. "I will go and speak to them and tell them not to alarm you."

Zhao Chuan ordered that lamps be brought, and then he made his way down the steps of the three-tier terrace. The two hundred soldiers had already forced their way in. Zhao Chuan calmed everyone down and then walked out in front of the terrace to call up to the main building: "The army officers discovered that Your Lordship was here holding a banquet, and they would like to hold their own feast with whatever you have left over. That is all!"

Lord Ling gave orders that the servants should bring out wine and give it to the soldiers. He leaned out on the railing to watch this being done. Zhao Chuan stood to one side and shouted, "His Lordship is treating you in this way, so you should accept with gratitude." When he had finished speaking, he waved his sleeve. The soldiers were all now aware of which one was the Marquis of Jin as they stormed the terrace.

Panic-stricken, Lord Ling asked Zhao Chuan, "What do they mean by climbing up here? Tell them to go away immediately!"

"Everyone wants to see the prime minister, Zhao Dun, brought back," Zhao Chuan shouted. "Summon him home, my lord!"

Before Lord Ling had even had a chance to reply, he had been stabbed repeatedly by halberds. He died immediately, his entourage fleeing in terror.

"The wicked lord is dead, so you must not kill anyone else," Zhao Chuan yelled. "Come with me and we will go to welcome the prime minister back to court."

Everyone hated the Marquis of Jin and thought that he deserved to die, for in recent years they all had lived in terror of their lives. When the soldiers murdered him, no one tried to save him. The ordinary people of Jin had suffered for a long time and were so happy that the marquis was dead that not a single person blamed Zhao Chuan for his actions. Seven years earlier, a comet had appeared in the Northern Dipper constellation, and this was divined as a sign that there would be a civil war in Qi, Song, and Jin, and that in each case a ruler would be murdered. Here was the proof.

A bearded old man wrote a poem:

As song and music resounded around the terrace,
A red belvedere was spotted with blood shed by rioting troops.
Do not blame others for the fact that they failed to rescue you;
After shooting people with crossbow bolts, you were no longer thought human.

Tu'an Gu was outside the suburbs, going from door to door looking for beautiful women. Suddenly he got the report: "The Marquis of Jin had been assassinated." He was terribly shocked. He was quite sure this was Zhao Chuan's doing, but he did not dare to say anything openly, returning home in secret. When Shi Hui and the other officials heard about the killing, they went as quickly as they could to the Peach Garden, but there was nobody there. They guessed that Zhao Chuan would have gone to meet the prime minister, so they locked the gates to the Peach Garden and waited quietly.

Within less than one day, Zhao Dun returned. When he entered the city of Jiang, he headed for the Peach Garden, where all the officials were awaiting him. Zhao Dun threw himself down upon the body of Lord Ling and cried bitterly. The heartbreaking sound could be heard far beyond the grounds. The people who heard it all said, "Look how loyal the prime minister is. The Marquis of Jin deserved everything that he got. This has nothing to do with the prime minister."

Zhao Dun gave orders that Lord Ling's body should be put in a coffin and transported to Quwo for burial. He then held a meeting for all the officials to discuss the appointment of a new ruler. Lord Ling did not have any children, so Zhao Dun said, "When our former ruler, Lord Xiang, died, I insisted that we needed to establish an adult as the next marquis, but you did not agree. Given the situation that we are in today, we must be very careful."

"If you could suggest an adult heir," Shi Hui declared, "that would indeed be a great blessing to the country. Whom do you recommend?"

"There is one surviving son of Lord Wen," Zhao Dun said. "When he was born, his mother dreamed that a god marked his buttocks with a black hand, and hence she named him Heitun or 'Black Buttock.' At present he holds office in the Zhou court, and he is certainly an adult, so in my opinion we ought to establish him. What do you think?"

None of the officials dared to suggest a different candidate, so they simply agreed: "The prime minister is absolutely right."

Zhao Dun pardoned Zhao Chuan for his crime of murdering the previous ruler and sent him to Zhou to bring the Honorable Heitun back to Jin. He was then formally presented to the ancestral shrines and succeeded to the title of the Marquis of Jin, taking the name Lord Cheng.

Once Lord Cheng was established, he entrusted the government to Zhao Dun and gave Zhao Shuo the hand of his daughter, Lady Zhuang Ji, in marriage. Zhao Dun presented his opinion: "My mother was a Di woman. Lord Wen of Jin's daughter made a wonderful gesture in giving up the title of principal wife and sent someone to collect my mother and me from the Di and bring us to Jin. It was only because of her generosity that I was able to become my father's heir and command the Central Army. I have three half-brothers—Tong, Kuo, and Ying—all of whom are now adults, and I would like to resign my offices in their favor!"

"I will love your brothers as if they were my own," Lord Cheng proclaimed. "However, they will take office with you and not instead of you. Do not try and yield your position, because they cannot do it better!" Zhao Tong, Zhao Kuo, and Zhao Ying were then all appointed to grandeeships, while Zhao Chuan returned to his old position of second-in-command of the Central Army.

Zhao Chuan spoke in private to Zhao Dun. "Tu'an Gu played a particularly egregious role in His Late Lordship's regime, and he hates the Zhao family. If we do not get rid of him, I am afraid that the Zhao family will suffer the consequences."

Tu'an Gu was the only person who was unhappy about the murder at the Peach Garden.

"He has done nothing to you, so why are you trying to cause trouble for him?" Zhao Dun asked. "The continued nobility and prosperity of our clan depends on getting along with other officials, not with trying to turn them into our enemies!"

Zhao Chuan gave up his representations. Tu'an Gu served the Zhao clan with the utmost circumspection in order to save his own skin.

. . .

To the very end of his life, Zhao Dun was uncomfortable about what had happened at the Peach Garden. One day he happened to go to the historian's office and saw the Grand Scribe, Dong Hu, looking at some documents. Dong Hu presented him with a historical work, and when Zhao Dun read the first bamboo strip, he saw the following words written bright and clear: "On Yichou day in the eighth month, Zhao Dun assassinated his ruler, Yigao, at the Peach Garden."

Zhao Dun was shocked and said, "You are wrong. At that time I was in exile in Hedong, more than two hundred *li* from the city of Jiang; how could I have had anything to do with the murder? Isn't it wrong of you to put the blame on me?"

"You are the prime minister, and from start to finish you were within the borders of the country," Dong Hu said. "Since your return to the capital, you have done nothing to punish the people responsible. If you say that you were not the moving spirit behind it, who will believe you?"

"Can't you change the entry?" Zhao Dun asked.

"Right is right and wrong is wrong, and that is how you create a trustworthy historical account," Dong Hu said proudly. "You can cut my head off, but this strip stays as it is!"

Zhao Dun sighed and said, "Alas! The power of a historian is much greater than that of a prime minister. Thanks to the fact that I was still inside the borders of the country, I will bear an evil reputation for ten thousand generations. However, it is now too late for regrets!" From this time onwards, Zhao Dun served Lord Cheng with redoubled respect.

Zhao Chuan thought that he had done much to be proud of, and he asked for a senior ministerial appointment. Zhao Dun was afraid of arousing public condemnation, so he refused this. Zhao Chuan was so enraged that he broke out in boils all over his back and died. His son, Zhao Zhan, asked permission to inherit his father's office. Zhao Dun said, "Wait until you have actually done something that deserves reward, and even a ministerial appointment is not beyond your grasp!"

Historians, when discussing Zhao Dun's refusal to treat Zhao Chuan and his son with anything other than the strictest impartiality, attribute this to Dong Hu's influence.

Someone wrote in praise:

An ordinary historian records events,
A good historian ascribes praise and blame.
Zhao Chuan assassinated his ruler,
Zhao Dun covered up the crime.
Who would rather lose his head,
Than dare to record anything other than the truth?
How impressive was Dong Hu!
How awe-inspiring his impartiality!

This happened in the sixth year of the reign of King Kuang of Zhou. That same year, King Kuang died and was succeeded by his younger brother, Prince Yu, who took the title King Ding.

• • •

In the first year of the reign of King Ding, King Zhuang of Chu raised an army to attack the Luhun Rong people, whereupon he crossed the Luo River and encroached upon the borders of the Zhou Royal Domain. He was trying to threaten the Son of Heaven in the hope of partitioning All-Under-Heaven. King Ding sent Grandee the Royal Grandson Man to make polite inquiries of King Zhuang.

"I have heard that the sage-king Yu made nine bronze *ding*-cauldrons that have been handed down through the three dynasties," King Zhuang said. "These great treasures are now in Luoyang. How big are they? How heavy are they? I would like to hear about them."

"What has been handed down through the three dynasties is a tradition of virtuous government," Royal Grandson Man said, "not nine *ding*-cauldrons! In ancient times when the sage-king Yu governed the world, the Nine Governors presented metal as tribute and the finest was selected to be made into these nine *ding*-cauldrons. When the wicked last king of the Xia dynasty, Jie, lost the Mandate of Heaven, they were transferred to the Shang. When the wicked last king of the Shang dynasty, Zhou, behaved so cruelly and violently, the *ding*-cauldrons were handed over to the present dynasty. If you govern virtuously, even if these bronzes are small, they are too heavy to move. If you govern badly, even if these bronzes are huge, they are easy to take away. King

Cheng ordered that the *ding*-cauldrons be kept at Jiaru, and after thirty generations and seven hundred years the Mandate of Heaven still rests with us. The time to make inquiries about them is not yet ripe!"

King Zhuang felt ashamed of himself and withdrew. After this he made no further attempt to encroach upon the Zhou.

• • •

The Grand Vizier of Chu, Dou Yuejiao, was angered by King Zhuang's decision to assume personal control of the government, which reduced his own power, and thus a breach sprang up between the two men. He soon began to plot a rebellion, relying on his own matchless bravery and might, the loyal service of his ancestors to earlier kings of Chu, and the trust and allegiance of the people. He would often say, "The only talented man in the whole of the kingdom of Chu is Emir Wei Jia; the rest don't count."

When King Zhuang attacked the Luhun Rong, he was worried that Dou Yuejiao might launch a coup against him, so he ordered Wei Jia to stay behind in the capital. When Dou Yuejiao saw King Zhuang take the army out on campaign, he decided that the time was right for his rebellion. He mobilized all the forces under the control of his family. Dou Ke opposed him, and so he was killed. Wei Jia was also killed. Wei Jia's son, Sunshu Ao, helped his mother to escape from danger by hiding in the Meng Marshes. Meanwhile, Dou Yuejiao had gone to camp in the wilds of Cheng in order to prevent King Zhuang from ever coming home.

King Zhuang heard that a coup was underway and came back by forced marches. When he arrived at Zhangshi, Dou Yuejiao led his forces to intercept him. His army was truly mighty and Dou Yuejiao himself rode out in front of his battle formations, armed to the teeth. When the Chu soldiers noticed this, they all looked terrified.

"The Dou family has served the kingdom of Chu loyally for many generations," King Zhuang declared. "They can betray me, but I will not turn against them!"

He ordered Grandee Su Cong to go to Dou Yuejiao's camp and make peace with him. He was pardoned for his crime in murdering Wei Jia, and they agreed to give him a prince as a hostage.

"I am ashamed to be merely the Grand Vizier," Dou Yuejiao said. "I am not expecting anyone to pardon me. If His Majesty thinks he can defeat me in battle, then bring it on!"

Su Cong tried to bring him to his senses several times, but he would not listen. After Su Cong had left, Dou Yuejiao ordered his army officers to beat the drums to signal an advance.

"Which one of you can make Dou Yuejiao retreat?" King Zhuang asked his generals.

General Le Bo responded and set off. Dou Yuejiao's son, Dou Bihuang, engaged him in combat. Pan Wang realized that Le Bo would not be able to defeat Dou Bihuang, so he quickly whipped up his chariot and sped out from the ranks. Dou Yuejiao's cousin, Dou Qi, met him in battle.

King Zhuang stood in his battle chariot. and he seized hold of the drumsticks and personally drummed forward his troops. Dou Yuejiao caught sight of him far in the distance, and like the wind he hurled himself in the direction of King Zhuang, grabbing his bow and letting a single arrow fly. This arrow passed straight over the horses to lodge itself in the drum stand. King Zhuang was so shocked that he dropped the drumsticks. His Majesty fled as quickly as he could; his entourage covered his retreat with their large straw hats. Dou Yuejiao now let fly another arrow, and this time it pierced the left-hand hat. King Zhuang was helped back to his chariot, and he sounded the bells to recall his troops. Dou Yuejiao was bursting with confidence and came forward, only to be beaten back by a combined assault by the General of the Right, Prince Ce, and the General of the Left, Prince Yingqi. When Le Bo and Pan Wang heard the sound of the bells, they both stood down their battle formations and retreated. The Chu army had suffered many losses, and they retreated as far as Gaoxu, where they made camp. When they inspected the arrows shot by Dou Yuejiao, they realized that they were half as long again as ordinary arrows, fletched with crane feathers and barbed with wildcat teeth—the point was also unusually sharp. Those who saw these arrows stuck their tongues out in amazement.

That night, King Zhuang went out on patrol around the camp, and he noticed his men were clustered together into little groups. They were all muttering: "Grand Vizier Dou's arrows are really scary. It will be hard for us to defeat him."

King Zhuang sent someone to spread rumors among his soldiery: "In the past during the reign of King Wen of Chu, he heard that the very best arrows in the world were made by the Rong barbarians. He sent someone to make inquiries and the Rong presented His Majesty with two arrows, called *Bone Piercing Winds*. He stored them in the ancestral temple, from where they were stolen by Dou Yuejiao. Now that he has shot both of them, there is nothing to be worried about. We will defeat him tomorrow." After that, people started to calm down a bit.

King Zhuang gave orders that his army should retreat to the state of Sui, spreading the word: "We are going to raise a great army in the states east of the Han River to punish the Dou clan!"

"We have a strong enemy right in front of us, and the minute we begin our withdrawal, there is going to be trouble," Su Cong said. "His Majesty's plan will put us all in terrible danger!"

"This is just a rumor that His Majesty has started," Prince Ce said. "We will go and talk to him and find out what he actually intends."

He went with Prince Yingqi to have an audience with King Zhuang that very night.

"The traitor Yuejiao is very powerful," the king of Chu said. "If we are going to defeat him, it cannot be done by brute force; trickery is the only way." He gave precise instructions to his two generals about where they were to wait in ambush. The two generals obeyed their orders.

The following morning at cockcrow, King Zhuang let his army out of the main camp in retreat. Dou Yuejiao heard this news and believed that it was true, so he sent his own forces in pursuit. The Chu army was moving quickly by forced marches. By this time they had already passed Jingling and were heading north. Dou Yuejiao advanced more than two hundred *li* in the space of twenty-four hours. When he arrived at the Qing River Bridge, the Chu army was making breakfast on the north bank. When they saw in the distance that the pursuing army had arrived, they fled, clutching their cooking pots. Dou Yuejiao gave orders: "You may eat breakfast once the king of Chu has been captured."

His troops were exhausted, and now they were told that they would have to endure hunger as well, as they forced themselves forward, heading off after Pan Wang's army. Pan Wang was standing in his chariot and shouted to Dou Yuejiao: "If you want to capture the king, why don't you hurry after him?"

Dou Yuejiao thought that this was a good idea, and so he stopped the attack on Pan Wang and advanced a further sixty *li*. When he arrived at Mount Qing he encountered the Chu general, Xiong Fuji, and asked him, "Where is the king of Chu?"

"He has not yet arrived," Xiong Fuji replied.

Dou Yuejiao became suspicious and said, "If you are willing to spy on His Majesty for me, once I have conquered the country, you will have an honored place in my government."

"I can see that your army is exhausted," Xiong Fuji said. "You need to give them something to eat or they will not be able to do battle."

Dou Yuejiao agreed, and so he stopped his chariots for them to set up their pots. Before their food was cooked, Prince Ce and Prince Yingqi arrived with their respective armies. Dou Yuejiao's forces could not possibly fight again, so they headed south until they arrived back at the Qing River Bridge. The bridge was broken. King Zhuang of Chu had led his own forces to hide around the bridge, and once Dou Yuejiao had crossed, they hacked through the supporting beams and cut off his retreat. Dou Yuejiao was now terrified and ordered his followers to find somewhere to ford the river. His only idea now was to get to the other bank. However, he heard the sound of siege engines on the far side of the river, and the Chu army shouted from the bank: "Le Bo is over here. Get off your horse, you traitor, and surrender!" Dou Yuejiao was furious and ordered his archers to shoot at the opposite side.

There was a junior officer in Le Bo's army who was an exceptionally fine archer. His name was Yang Yaoji, but everyone called him Archer Yang. He asked permission of Le Bo to go and hold an archery competition with Dou Yuejiao. He took up position on the riverbank and shouted: "With the river being so broad, who can possibly shoot across? I have heard that the Grand Vizier is a fine shot, and I would like to test just how good you really are! Let us each stand on the end of the bridge and shoot three arrows. If one or the other of us dies, that is Heaven's will!"

"Who are you?" Dou Yuejiao asked.

"I am one of General Le Bo's subordinates and my name is Yang Yaoji!" he replied.

Dou Yuejiao was not impressed by the fact that he did not have a title or senior position, and bellowed across: "If you want to shoot with me, you are going to have to let me shoot my three arrows first!"

"I don't care about three arrows," Yang Yaoji shouted back. "You could shoot a hundred and I would have nothing to fear! Anyone who moves out of the way will stand revealed as a coward!" They each ordered their soldiers to stand to the north and south of the remains of the bridge.

Dou Yuejiao drew back his bow and shot the first arrow, regretting as he did so that it would not be possible to shoot Yang Yaoji's head off with it and hurl it into the river. He had forgotten the old adage: "If you are in too much of a hurry, you can't do it. If you can do it, you don't need to hurry." When Yang Yaoji saw the arrow, he swiped it aside with his bow case, and it headed straight into the water. Yang Yaoji immediately shouted, "Shoot! Shoot again!" Dou Yuejiao nocked his second arrow to the string and sighted carefully, letting this arrow go with a whistle. Yang Yaoji bobbed down and the arrow passed over his head.

"I thought you said that no one was allowed to get out of the way!" Dou Yuejiao called out. "You are a coward!"

"You have one more arrow and this time I promise I will not dodge it," Yang Yaoji replied. "However, if you don't hit me, it is my turn!"

Dou Yuejiao thought to himself, "Providing he does not get out of the way, this arrow will get him!" He picked up the third arrow, and as he shot it, he shouted: "Got you!" Yang Yaoji did not move his feet at all, but as the arrow sped towards him he opened his mouth and caught it between his teeth. None of Dou Yuejiao's arrows having hit the target, he was now starting to panic. However, having given his word, it was impossible to draw back. He shouted across, "It is now your turn to shoot three arrows. If none of them hit me, it is my turn again!"

"Only a rank beginner would need three arrows to shoot you," Yang Yaoji yelled. "I will only use one. It was your bad luck that you ran into me today!"

"So far I have only heard you talk big," Dou Yuejiao bellowed. "If you really are that good, why don't you shoot me to prove it?" He thought to himself, "How can he get me with just a single arrow? If he doesn't hit me first time around, I will give orders to arrest him!" He pulled himself together and stood up to be the target.

The Grand Vizier had no idea that Yang Yaoji hit the target with every arrow. When Yang Yaoji picked up his arrow he called out, "Grand Vizier! Watch this!" He drew back the bow and released, but in fact he did not let go of the arrow. Dou Yuejiao heard the twang of the bow string and thought that the arrow was on its way, so he wiggled to the left to get out of the way.

"The arrow is here in my hand," Yang Yaoji shouted. "I never nocked it to the bow. It was you who said that anyone who gets out of the way is a coward, so why did you dodge just now?"

"A really good archer does not need to worry about people getting out of the way," Dou Yuejiao responded.

Yang Yaoji again pretended to put his arrow to the bow and release; this time Dou Yuejiao dodged to the right. Yang Yaoji took advantage of his movement to actually shoot an arrow and Dou Yuejiao, caught unawares, was unable to get out of the way. It struck him right through the head. How sad that Dou Yuejiao, after so many years of service as Grand Vizier of the kingdom of Chu, should die this day from a single arrow shot by Yang Yaoji!

A bearded old man wrote a poem:

It is best when people are happy to be themselves.
This Grand Vizier's greed brought him to contemplate making himself king;
By competing in archery with the finest of shots,
Dou Yuejiao fell dead on the Qing River Bridge.

Dou's army was already exhausted and hungry. Now they saw their commander-in-chief fall, struck by an arrow, and they ran away in panic. The two generals, Prince Ce and Prince Yingqi, set off in pursuit and killed an enormous number of them, their blood running in a red stream. Yuejiao's son, Dou Bihuang, fled into exile in the state of Jin. The Marquis of Jin appointed him to a grandeeship and gave him lands in Miao. From this time onwards he was known as Miao Bihuang.

King Zhuang had now won a total victory, and he gave orders to stand down his army. His captives were immediately beheaded in front of the army. They returned to the capital city of Ying singing songs of triumph. The Dou family was beheaded to the last man, regardless of age. However, Dou Ban's son, Dou Kehuang, was at that time an official in charge of remonstrance, and he had been sent on a diplomatic mission by King Zhuang to visit the states of Qi and Qin. Having completed his duties in Qi, Dou Kehuang was on his way home and traveling through Song when he heard that Dou Yuejiao had launched a coup.

"You must not go home!" his servants said.

"A ruler is like Heaven," Dou Kehuang responded. "How can you disobey Heaven's orders?"

He ordered them to return to Ying as quickly as possible. When he had finished making his report on his mission, he went in person to see the emir and asked to be imprisoned. He said: "My grandfather, Ziwen, once said, 'Dou Yuejiao bears all the hallmarks of a traitor; he is sure to bring about the deaths of our entire clan.' Just before he died, he told my father to go into exile abroad. My father could not bear to obey, remembering how much we owed to generations of Chu kings, and ended up being killed by Dou Yuejiao, just as my grandfather predicted. I am so unlucky as to belong to a traitor's family, and I have disregarded the teaching of my ancestors. In either case I deserve to die. How could I dare to try to avoid punishment?"

When King Zhuang heard this, he sighed and said, "Ziwen really was a most remarkable man who governed the kingdom of Chu with exceptional ability. How could I bear to kill every last one of his descendants?" He pardoned Dou Kehuang, saying: "You would rather die than avoid punishment, so it is clear you are a loyal subject." He restored his official position to him and changed his name to Dou Sheng, meaning "Life."

This commemorated the fact that he survived in spite of the fact that he should have been executed.

King Zhuang was very impressed by Yang Yaoji's one shot, so he rewarded him lavishly and gave him command of the royal guard. Yang Yaoji was also appointed the king's own bodyguard, standing at his right on the chariot. However, he had no idea who should be appointed as the new Grand Vizier. When he heard of the wisdom of Yu Qiu, prime minister of Shen, he appointed him to take charge of matters of state and arranged for a great banquet to be held at the top of the Zhe Tower, at which he would feast all his officials with his own wives and concubines in attendance.

"It is six years since I last listened to music," King Zhuang said. "Now the rebel has been executed and my country is at peace, I would like to hold a day-long party for my ministers, which we will call the 'Banquet of Eternal Peace.' There is a seat arranged for every single official, civil and military, and I want everyone to enjoy himself to the utmost."

The officials all bowed twice and took their appointed seats. The cooks presented the viands, the Grand Scribe presided over the choice of music, and they drank until the sun had sunk behind the western hills. King Zhuang then ordered the lamps to be lit to allow the party to carry on and commanded his favorite wives, Lady Ji of Xu and Lady Jiang, to serve wine to his grandees. They all got up from their seats to offer a toast when suddenly there was a gust of wind that blew out every lamp in the room. Before the servants had arrived with fires to relight them, one of the men present—attracted by Lady Ji of Xu's unusual beauty—reached out in the dark and took hold of her sleeve. Lady Ji of Xu ripped the sleeve free with her left hand, while with her right she grabbed hold of the tassel hanging from his hat and broke it off. The man was shocked into letting go.

Lady Ji of Xu kept tight hold of the tassel and crept around to where King Zhuang was sitting. She whispered in his ear, "As Your Majesty had commanded me, I went around to pour wine for your ministers. However, one of them so far forgot himself as to take advantage of the lamps being blown out to grab hold of my sleeve. I broke one of the tassels off his hat. When the lamps are relit, Your Majesty can find out who it was!"

King Zhuang immediately gave orders to the servants holding the lamps: "Do not light them! I have held this party today to enjoy myself with my ministers. Anyone who is having a good time should break a tassel off his hat. Anyone who refuses is not welcome here."

All the officials promptly broke a tassel off their hats, and so when the king finally allowed the lamps to be lit again, it was impossible to tell who had groped his concubine. When the party was over and they returned to the palace, Lady Ji of Xu asked: "I have heard it said that men and women should preserve a proper distance, not to mention that which should be maintained between a ruler and a subject! Your Majesty ordered me to serve wine to the ministers as a sign of your respect. However, you did not investigate who it was who grabbed hold of me. Does this maintain the proper distinction between superiors and inferiors? Is this the correct way for men to behave towards women?"

King Zhuang laughed and said, "How could a woman possibly understand? Since antiquity, when rulers and subjects feast together, a maximum of three toasts should be offered. However, this rule only applies during the day and not at night. I wanted my ministers to have a really good time, and that is why I continued the banquet by lamplight. For people to behave badly when they are drunk is perfectly normal. If I had investigated this offense and punished the guilty party, it would have shown how virtuous my wives are at the expense of upsetting my most important officials. When I gave orders to hold the banquet in the first place, it was not done with a view to making all my officials unhappy." Lady Ji of Xu accepted this argument.

Later generations called this the Broken Tassel Banquet.

A bearded old man wrote a poem:

In the dark, a man overcome by drunken emotion grabs hold of a sleeve;
A pale hand, quick as a flash, breaks off a tassel.
Let us praise His Majesty's understanding,
His intimate knowledge of the minds of men.

One day His Majesty was discussing matters of government with Yu Qiu, and thus it was only after dark that he returned to the palace.

His queen, Lady Ji of Fan, asked him, "What happened at court today that you finished so late?"

"I was talking to Yu Qiu about the government and I did not notice how late it was getting," King Zhuang explained.

"Who is Yu Qiu?" the queen asked.

"One of the wisest men in Chu," His Majesty declared.

"In my opinion, Yu Qiu is not clever at all!"

"How do you know?"

"A minister serves his ruler just like a wife serves her husband." Lady Ji of Fan said thoughtfully. "I know my place within the harem and make sure that beautiful women are regularly presented to Your Majesty. Today, Yu Qiu was discussing government matters with you until it got dark, but apparently he did not recommend a single wise man to your service. There is a limit to what one man can achieve, no matter how clever, and there are countless brilliant scholars in the kingdom of Chu. Apparently Yu Qiu is prepared to use only his own brains and would like to keep everyone else in nameless obscurity. How can that be considered wise?"

King Zhuang was delighted with her advice, and the following morning he reported what Lady Ji of Fan had said to Yu Qiu. "I am clearly not as clever as I thought myself," he said. "We will have to come up with a further plan to take account of Her Majesty's advice."

He went around and asked the other ministers for recommendations. Dou Sheng suggested that Wei Jia's son, Sunshu Ao, was a wise man. "To get away from the trouble caused by Dou Yuejiao's rebellion, he went to live in the Meng Marshes. He would make a worthy Grand Vizier one day!"

Yu Qiu mentioned this to King Zhuang, and His Majesty said: "Wei Jia was a most excellent man, and I am sure that his son will be far from ordinary. I had almost forgotten Dou Sheng's earlier advice!" He ordered Yu Qiu and Dou Sheng to go to the Meng Marshes in their chariot and bring Wei Sunshu Ao back to court for his appointment.

Sunshu was actually his style-name, but everyone called him Sunshu Ao.

When he and his mother fled the troubles, they went to live in the Meng Marshes and made a living by tilling the land. One day as he set out with his hoe, he saw a snake with two heads in the field. He said in alarm: "I have heard that a snake with two heads is a terrible omen. Anyone who sees it will die. I am doomed!" Then he thought: "If I leave this snake alive, later on someone else might also see it and they will die too. It would be better if it was just me." He lifted his hoe and killed the snake, which he buried on the path running between his fields. Afterwards he ran home to see his mother and cried.

His mother asked him the reason for this, and Sunshu Ao explained: "I have heard that anyone who sees a two-headed snake will die. I saw one today myself, and I am afraid that I will not live to look after you for the rest of your life. That is why I was crying."

"Where is the snake now?" his mother inquired.

"I was afraid that someone else might see it, so I have killed it and buried it," Ao answered.

"Since you have been so thoughtful, I am sure that Heaven will protect you," his mother said. "You saw the two-headed snake and were afraid that it might cause trouble to others, so you killed and buried it. That was a good deed. I am sure that you will not die, and indeed that you will be blessed by your action!"

A couple of days later, Yu Qiu and the others arrived according to His Majesty's command to employ Sunshu Ao in the government. His mother laughed and said, "This is your return for burying the snake!" Ao and his mother then went back to Ying with Yu Qiu.

King Zhuang gave his first audience to Sunshu Ao and talked with him for the whole day. He was very pleased and said, "There is not a single minister in the whole kingdom of Chu that can compare!" He immediately appointed him Grand Vizier.

Sunshu Ao refused. "I gave up all my honors in order to go and till the fields, so how could I now persuade people to support me if I were to take sole charge of the government? Please let me be numbered among the least of your grandees."

"I know what you are capable of," the king of Chu said, "and I will not allow you to decline."

Sunshu Ao insisted on refusing the job another two or three times, but in the end he accepted his command and assumed the office of Grand Vizier. He conducted research into the government of the kingdom of Chu and established military law. When the army advanced, the right-hand battalions would be responsible for checking all equipment and making sure that they were ready to do battle. The left-hand battalions would be responsible for finding hay and other building materials so that they could make camp. There were also the standard-bearers, officers of the Central Army, and crack troops. The standard-bearers were to advance with their flags and probe the enemy's weaknesses, while the officers of the Central Army planned the campaign in such a way that it was difficult for unknown factors to cause trouble. The job of the crack troops was twofold. In battle, they were to make surprise attacks on the enemy, while in retreat they were to prevent attacks from the rear.

The king's own personal guard was divided into two wings, and each wing consisted of fifteen chariots. Each chariot had one hundred infantry attached to it and later on twenty-five marines as well. The left wing was responsible for security during one lot of six two-hour watches; the right wing was responsible during the other lot of six two-hour watches. Starting at cockcrow every morning, the right wing would harness their horses to be prepared to head out; at midday they would be replaced by the left wing, who would serve until sunset. The inner guard was divided into groups that would patrol during the night, to prevent any problems arising. Sunshu Ao appointed Yu Qiu to command the Central Army; Prince Yingqi commanded the Army of the Left; Prince Ce commanded the Army of the Right; Yang Yaoji commanded the right wing; and Qu Dang commanded the left wing. Every four hours there was a roll call, and since everyone knew exactly what he had to do, the three armies were kept in strict good order and the people were untroubled. Sunshu Ao also constructed a dam at Quebo with a view to improving irrigation; it was used to water ten thousand hectares of fields in the region of Liu and Liao. The people all praised this. When the ministers of Chu saw how King Zhuang favored Sunshu Ao, they were deeply unhappy; when they realized how competent he was, they all sighed and said, "The kingdom of Chu is very lucky to have such a wise minister. He is Ziwen risen again!"

Many years earlier Grand Vizier Ziwen had governed the kingdom of Chu well; now they had Sunshu Ao, and it was as if Ziwen had come back to life.

• • •

It was just at this time that Lan, Lord Mu of Zheng, died and Scion Yi succeeded to the title as Lord Ling. The Honorable Song and the Honorable Guisheng were in charge of the government of Zheng. They were hesitating between throwing in their lot with either Jin or Chu, but had not yet made a decision. King Zhuang of Chu and Sunshu Ao were discussing the possibility of raising an army to attack Zheng when they suddenly heard that Lord Ling of Zheng had been assassinated by the Honorable Guisheng. King Zhuang said, "There is our excuse to attack Zheng!"

Do you know why the Honorable Guisheng murdered his lord? READ ON.

Chapter Fifty-two

The Honorable Song is forced into rebellion by tasting a turtle.

Lord Ling of Chen uses underwear to make a joke at court.

The Honorable Guisheng had the style-name Zijia, and the Honorable Song had the style-name Zigong. Both these men were members of the ruling house of Zheng and served as ministers in its government. In the first year of the rule of Lord Ling of Zheng, it happened one day that the Honorable Song and the Honorable Guisheng had agreed in advance that they would get up early and go and have an audience with Lord Ling. Suddenly the Honorable Song's "eating finger" started twitching uncontrollably.

Why is it called an "eating finger"? Well, the first digit on your hand is the thumb. The third is your middle finger, the fourth is the "nameless" finger and the fifth is your little finger. Your forefinger is one that you have to use when picking up food, and that is why it has come to be known as the "eating finger."

When the Honorable Song's "eating finger" started moving about, he and Guisheng both looked at it. The Honorable Guisheng thought this very odd.

"There can be no other explanation," Song said. "Every time my finger moves like that, it means that the same day I get something really unusual to eat. When I was sent as an ambassador to Jin I got to eat Shihua carp, while later on, when on an embassy to Chu, I got to eat swan and Hehuan oranges. Each time my finger moved just like that. It is clearly some kind of omen. I wonder what remarkable and unusual food I will get to eat today?"

When they went to the inner gate of the palace, a eunuch was busy shouting at the chefs to hurry up.

"Why are you shouting at the chefs?" the Honorable Song asked.

"A visitor has arrived from the Han River with an enormous soft-shell turtle weighing more than two hundred pounds," the eunuch explained. "He presented it to His Lordship, for which he was rewarded. It is now waiting tied up below the main hall. His Lordship ordered me to get the chefs to cut it up and steam it as a delicacy for you to try."

"With such an unusual taste sensation coming, how could my 'eating finger' not be twitching?" the Honorable Song said happily. When they went into court, they saw a huge soft-shell turtle tied to one of the pillars of the main hall. The two men looked at each other and laughed. Throughout their audience with His Lordship, they carried on chuckling.

"Why are the pair of you so happy today?" Lord Ling asked.

The Honorable Guisheng replied: "When I was on my way to court today with Song, his finger suddenly started to twitch and he said, 'Every time this happens, I get something unusual to eat.' We saw the huge soft-shell turtle in the main hall and we guessed that once it was steamed for Your Lordship to eat, we would also be allowed to try some. The finger-omen has proved right yet again. That is why we were laughing."

Lord Ling joked with them. "It is up to me whether the omen is proved right or not!"

The two men then withdrew. Guisheng said to Song, "Even though there is this unusual food in the offing, if His Lordship does not summon you to enjoy it, what will you do?"

"If he shares it among everyone," Song said, "would it be possible to leave me out?"

As it began to get dark, the servants summoned all the grandees just as the Honorable Song had predicted. He went in happily and said to the Honorable Guisheng with a smile, "I knew that His Lordship would invite me to join him."

Once all of the ministers were in attendance, Lord Ling ordered them to take their appointed seats and said, "The soft-shell turtle offers us the finest flavor of any river creature. I did not dare to enjoy this treat alone, so I am going to share it with you."

The ministers all thanked him and said, "You even remember us when eating, my lord. What can we do to repay you?"

Once they had taken their seats, the chef announced that the turtle was perfectly cooked and ready to eat. The first portion was given to

Lord Ling, who tasted it and pronounced it delicious. He ordered that everyone should be given an individual bronze *ding* filled with turtle soup and a pair of ivory chopsticks. The guests were served in the reverse order of precedence, so that when it got to the very last couple of places, there was only one *ding* of soup left.

The chef announced: "There is still one *ding* of soup left. To whom should it be presented?"

Lord Ling said, "Give it to the Honorable Guisheng."

The chef then placed the soup in front of him. Lord Ling laughed and said, "I ordered the soup to be given to all of my ministers, but there is not enough for the Honorable Song. I am afraid that he is not going to be able to eat turtle, regardless of what his finger does!"

In fact Lord Ling had deliberately ordered his cooks to make one *ding* too few, so that the Honorable Song's finger would fail in its prediction. He thought this was a great joke. He did not know just how much the Honorable Song had boasted to Guisheng.

That day, all the officials were given turtle to eat and the Honorable Song was the only person left out. His humiliation quickly turned to anger. He strode up to Lord Ling, dipped his fingers into his *ding* and fished out a lump of turtle meat, which he swallowed. He said: "I have now tasted it. My finger is accurate, as always." When he had finished speaking, he walked out.

It was now Lord Ling's turn to be angry. He threw down his chopsticks and said, "Song has never really respected me, and now he is openly rude to me! Can it be true that the state of Zheng is so lacking in weapons that I cannot cut off his head?"

Guisheng and the others all got down from their seats and threw themselves on the ground. They said, "Song knows that you love every member of your family. Aware of how good-natured you are, he came up with this little joke. How would he dare to behave badly to Your Lordship? Please forgive him!"

Lord Ling remained furious, and the ministers dispersed unhappily. Guisheng went straight to the Honorable Song's home and told him about His Lordship's anger. "Tomorrow you are going to have to go to court to apologize."

The Honorable Song said, "I have heard that someone who is rude to others will be treated badly himself. His Lordship was rude to me first. Why does he blame me rather than looking at his own behavior?"

"That may be true," Guisheng replied, "but as a subject you still ought to apologize to His Lordship."

The following day, the two men went to court together. The Honorable Song performed the usual ceremonies but said not a single word of apology. This made Guisheng extremely uneasy. He presented his opinion: "The Honorable Song is afraid that Your Lordship will punish him for polluting your food with his fingers, so he has come here specially to apologize. He is so much in awe of you that he cannot find the words to express his anguish. I hope Your Lordship will forgive him."

"It is more likely that I would be afraid of upsetting the Honorable Song than that he would be concerned about annoying me!" Lord Ling snapped. He got up, drawing his robe around him.

The Honorable Song left the court and went straight around to the Honorable Guisheng's mansion. He spoke in private with him: "His Lordship is very angry with me, and I am afraid that I will be executed. I had better strike first, for if I am successful at least I will not die."

Guisheng clapped his hands over his ears. "People cannot bear to kill even animals that they have looked after for a long time. How dare you speak so lightly of assassinating the ruler of a country?"

"It was just a joke," Song said, "but you had better not tell anyone." Guisheng then said goodbye to him.

The Honorable Song was aware of the fact that Guisheng was a close friend of Lord Ling's younger brother, the Honorable Quji, and they often spent time together. Therefore, he said loudly at court, "The Honorable Guisheng is spending day and night with the Honorable Quji. I do not know what they are plotting, but it bodes no good for the country."

Guisheng grabbed the Honorable Song by the arm and dragged him off to a quiet corner. "Why do you say that?" he demanded.

"If you will not join in my conspiracy," Song told him, "I am going to make sure that you die before I do!"

Guisheng was a weak man and could not make up his mind about what to do. When he heard the Honorable Song's words on this occasion, he was deeply shocked and said, "What do you mean?"

"You can see how useless His Lordship is from the way he behaved over the turtle. Once he has been dealt with, you and I can put the Honorable Quji in power and resume our alliance with Jin. That way the state of Zheng will be at peace for many years to come."

The Honorable Guisheng thought about this for a moment, and then he agreed. "Whatever you do, I will not betray you."

After that, the Honorable Song secretly convened his private forces. He took advantage of Lord Ling's overnight fast for the autumn sacrifices to offer heavy bribes to his attendants to allow them to sneak in. They murdered Lord Ling by suffocating him with sandbags. The word was given out that he had suffered some kind of fit and died. Guisheng knew exactly what had happened but did not dare to say a word about it.

In the Spring and Autumn Annals, Confucius wrote: "The Honorable Guisheng of Zheng assassinated his ruler, Yi." He did not mention the Honorable Song, putting all the blame on Guisheng. That was because he was in charge of the government and went along with this assassination out of fear. This is what is meant when it says, "If you are employed in an important position, you have to take responsibility." The sage wrote this in order to warn later generations of ministers not to be afraid.

There is a poem that reads:

> Ever since antiquity, lords and ministers have been warned against joking;
> The terrible fate of Lord Ling was occasioned by a turtle.
> Guisheng controlled the government, but did nothing about it,
> He sat by and watched as his ruler was killed.

The following day, Guisheng and the Honorable Song discussed the matter together and decided that the Honorable Quji should become the next ruler. Quji was shocked and refused: "His Late Lordship had a total of eight sons. If you want to establish the best, it is certainly not me. If you want to establish the oldest, that is the Honorable Jian. I would rather die than usurp the title."

The Honorable Jian was accordingly invited to succeed to the title, and he became Lord Xiang. In fact, Lord Mu had thirteen sons altogether: some born to his main wife and others to concubines. Once Yi, Lord Ling of Zheng, had been assassinated, Jian succeeded as Lord Xiang. However, there were a further eleven sons. There was the Honorable Qiji, whose style-name was Ziliang; the Honorable Xi, whose style-name was Zihan; the Honorable Xun, whose style-name was Zisi; the Honorable Fa, whose style-name was Ziguo; the Honorable Jia, whose style-name was Zikong; the Honorable Yan, whose style-name was Ziyou; the Honorable Shu, whose style-name was Ziyin; in addition to them there were the Honorable Feng, Yu, Ran, and Zhi. Lord Xiang was concerned that his younger brothers might form their own factions and he was afraid that they might later launch coups against him, so he discussed the situation privately with the Honorable Quji and decided that he would be the only one to be allowed to stay; all the others would have to leave the country.

"His Late Lordship was born after his mother dreamed of an orchid," the Honorable Qiji said, "and when a divination was performed about this, it said, 'He will bring glory to the Ji clan.' The relationship of your brothers to the earldom can be compared to that of the branches and leaves of a luxuriant tree: they add glory to the trunk. If you were to cut off the branches and strip away the leaves, while it is true that the trunk would then be revealed, it would simply stand there, withered and bare. If you could permit them to stay, they will do great things for you; if you refuse, I will leave with the rest since I could not endure to stay here on my own. If I did, then in the future how could I face our former lord in the Underworld?"

Lord Xiang came to his senses and appointed his eleven younger brothers as grandees. They were all involved in the government of the state of Zheng. The Honorable Song was sent to ask for a peace treaty with Jin, with a view to ensuring the stability of the country. This happened in the second year of the reign of King Ding of Zhou.

The following year, which was the first year of the rule of Lord Xiang of Zheng, King Zhuang of Chu appointed Prince Yingqi as commander-in-chief, and he led his army to attack Zheng. He asked, "Why have you murdered your lord?" Jin sent Xun Linfu to rescue them and Chu then moved their army to attack Chen. Lord Xiang of Zheng subsequently swore a covenant with Lord Cheng of Jin at Heirang.

. . .

In the third year of the reign of King Ding of Zhou, the prime minister of Jin, Zhao Dun, died. Xi Que took over his position as commander-in-chief of the Central Army. When he heard that Chen and Chu had made peace, he mentioned this to Lord Cheng. His Lordship, assisted by Xun Linfu, led his army to attack Chen with the allied states of Song, Wey, Zheng, and Cao. During this journey, Lord Cheng of Jin died. The army had to stand down. Scion Ru succeeded to the title and became Lord Jing. In the same year, King Zhuang of Chu took personal command of the Central Army when he attacked Zheng, meeting them in battle at Liufen. Xi Que of Jin led his forces to rescue them. He defeated the Chu army in a surprise attack. The people of Zheng were delighted. The Honorable Quji was the only one to look worried. Lord Xiang thought this was strange and asked him the reason.

The Honorable Quji explained: "It was pure accident that Jin was able to defeat Chu. Chu will take out their anger on Zheng, and I am not sure that Jin can be relied on to save us next time! You will soon see the Chu army in our suburbs!"

The following year, King Zhuang of Chu attacked Zheng again, camping with his army north of the Ying River. The Honorable Guisheng became sick and died. This finally gave the Honorable Quji his opportunity to punish someone for the death of Lord Ling, so he killed the Honorable Song and exposed his body at court. He had the Honorable Guisheng's coffin broken open and forced his entire family into exile. Afterwards, he sent an ambassador to apologize to the king of Chu: "His Lordship has finally been able to execute both the traitors, the Honorable Guisheng and the Honorable Song. His Lordship is now able to follow the example set by the Marquis of Chen and swear a blood covenant with your great country."

King Zhuang agreed to this. He decided that he would make a covenant with both Chen and Zheng at Chenling, so he sent an ambassador to summon the Marquis of Chen to this meeting. The ambassador came back from Chen and reported: "The Marquis of Chen has been assassinated by Grandee Xia Zhengshu. The capital is in uproar."

There is a poem that testifies to this:

Ever since the Zhou capital moved to the east there had been disorder,
Every year there were usurpations and assassinations.
The comet in the Dipper constellation brought chaos to three countries.
Now they reported the Marquis of Chen had fallen victim to Xia Zhengshu.

The Honorable Pingguo, the son of Shuo, Lord Gong of Chen, succeeded to his father's title and was installed as Lord Ling in the sixth year of the reign of King Qing of Zhou. He was a frivolous and silly man, without any of the awe-inspiring characteristics that a ruler needs. His only interests were alcohol and women; his only pursuit was of enjoyment. He paid no attention whatsoever to the government of the country. There were two grandees whom he particularly favored: Kong Ning and Yi Xingfu. Both encouraged and assisted him in his drunken debauchery. The ruler and his two subjects found themselves to be birds of a feather; there was no restraint in their words or actions. At this time there was one wise minister at the Chen court, a man named Xie Ye, who was loyal and upright, and who dared to speak his mind on every occasion. The Marquis of Chen and his cronies were scared stiff of him. There was also a certain Grandee Xia Yushu. His father was the Honorable Shaoxi, the son of Lord Ding of Chen.

The Honorable Shaoxi had the style-name Zixia, therefore his descendants used the word Xia as their surname, though sometimes they were also called the Shaoxi clan.

The Xia family held office as Minister of War in the state of Chen as a hereditary prerogative, and they enjoyed the revenues of a fief at Zhulin. Grandee Xia Yushu was married to Lady Xia Ji, the daughter of Lord Mu of Zheng. Lady Xia Ji had a face like an almond with cheeks of coral; her slanted phoenix eyes were topped by elegantly curved eyebrows. She was as beautiful as Lady Li Ji or Lady Xi Gui, and as seductive as Da Ji or Lady Wen Jiang. She seemed to hook the soul of every man who saw her out of his body, causing him to go raving mad. There was a further remarkable thing about her: at the age of fifteen, she had dreamed that she saw a man dressed in a hat covered with stars and a robe of feathers who proclaimed that he was an immortal from the realms above. When they engaged in sexual relations, he instructed her in the skills of sucking out a man's essence and moving his *qi*, so that every time she had sex, not only would she enjoy great pleasure, she would also be able to use her partner's *yang* to boost her own *yin*, thereby never growing old. This is the so-called "Plain Girl's Fighting Technique." Before she was married, Lady Xia Ji engaged in an incestuous relationship with Lord Ling of Zheng's older half-brother, born to a concubine mother: the Honorable Man. Within three years the Honorable Man had died in his prime. Later on, she married Xia Yushu and gave birth to a son named Zhengshu. Xia Zhengshu, styled Zinan, was only twelve years of age when his father became sick and died. Lady Xia Ji was having an affair, so she left Zhengshu behind in the capital where he could receive instruction from his teachers, while she herself went to live in Zhulin.

Kong Ning and Yi Xingfu were both acquainted with Xia Zhengshu from their dealings at court, and, having spied on his beautiful mother, they each conceived the idea of seducing her. Lady Xia Ji had a maid named Hehua, wise in the ways of the world, who played a key role in introducing her mistress to suitable lovers. One day Kong Ning was out hunting beyond the suburbs with Xia Zhengshu, whereupon they journeyed as far as Zhulin and spent the night in his house. Kong Ning put a bit of thought into how to seduce Hehua first. He gave her a hairpin and a pair of earrings and then begged her to present him to Her Ladyship. Having seduced her too, he left, having stolen her brocade vest to wear under his own clothes. He paraded around in front of Yi Xingfu, showing off about it. That made Yi Xingfu envious and so he offered generous bribes to Hehua as well, to put him in contact with Her Ladyship. Lady

Xia Ji had already noticed how tall and handsome Yi Xingfu was and was deeply attracted by him, so she sent Hehua to arrange a secret meeting between them. Yi Xingfu had invested in some aphrodisiacs in the hope of pleasing Lady Xia Ji, and she loved him twice as much as Kong Ning.

Yi Xingfu said to Lady Xia Ji: "Grandee Kong has the brocade vest that you gave him, and now I hope that you will give me something too as a sign of your affection."

"He stole my brocade vest," Lady Xia Ji said with a laugh. "I did not give it to him." Then she whispered in his ear: "Although I have slept with both of you, do you really think that I can't tell which one is better?"

She took off her green silk underpants and gave them to him. Yi Xingfu was very pleased. From this time onwards, Yi Xingfu came and went in great secrecy, and Kong Ning naturally found himself somewhat left out.

There is an old poem that testifies to this:

What happened in Zheng to make its people so debauched?
The transformation wrought by Lord Huan and Lord Wu crumbled away.
Young men and women run away together,
The common people lose all sense of right and wrong.
When Zhongzi sees a wall he wants to leap over it;
Zichong is a crafty youth.
By the East Gate I remember the madder that grew here,
Out in the wilds there grows a creeping grass.
The girls lift their skirts when they see their lovers far away;
Though they yoke their chariots, where can they go to find their men?
His blue collar comes ever to their mind,
Agate and jade love-tokens never change, though people grow old.
In the wind and the rain when the cocks crow in unison,
The secret trysts are already over.
Flood waters may carry away a bundle of firewood,
But rumor can never be trusted.
The customs of the country affect everyone who lives there;
How can you be sure that you too are pure?

Yi Xingfu had once been envious because Kong Ning got the brocade vest, but now that he had her green silk underpants, he could vaunt his position in front of Kong Ning. Kong Ning went in secret to visit Hehua and discovered that Yi Xingfu was having an affair with Lady Xia Ji. He was very jealous but had no idea of how to get back at him. Then he thought of a plan: the Marquis of Chen was a greedy and debauched man who had long heard tell of Lady Xia Ji's remarkable beauty. He had mentioned her several times and would obviously like to number her among his many conquests.

"If he starts having an affair with her too, the Marquis of Chen is sure to be grateful to me for making it possible. However, His Lordship suffers from a disease in his private parts that medical textbooks call the 'Fox Stink' or 'Armpit Effluvium'; Lady Xia Ji is not going to like that at all. I will act as a go-between and try and strike up a relationship between the two of them, thereby making sure that I come out on top. At the very least, Yi Xingfu will find himself being ignored a little, which will be an adequate penalty for the jealousy he has made me suffer. What a plan! What an excellent plan!"

He went alone to see Lord Ling, and as they were gossiping, he casually mentioned that Lady Xia Ji was the most beautiful woman in the world.

"I too have long heard her name mentioned," Lord Ling said, "but she must now be over forty. Surely she is long past her prime!"

"Lady Xia Ji is exceptionally well-versed in the bedroom arts," Kong Ning explained, "and her face has preserved all its beauty. To look at her you might think her seventeen or eighteen years old! She is also unusually skilled in sexual techniques. If you try her, I can guarantee that you will lose your heart to her."

Lord Ling felt desire coursing through his veins, his face turning purple. "Can you arrange for me to meet Lady Xia Ji?" he asked. "I promise I will not forget how helpful you have been!"

Kong Ning presented his opinion: "The Xia family live at Zhulin, a place well-known for its magnificent bamboos and trees, so you can go there to admire them. If you announce tomorrow morning that you are going to visit Zhulin, the Xia family will be sure to arrange a banquet in your honor. Lady Xia Ji has a maid named Hehua, who knows all about her mistress's amorous adventures. I will communicate Your Lordship's wishes to her. That way, everything can easily be arranged."

"I am relying on you to make this happen," Lord Ling said with a laugh.

The following day he ordered his chariot to be prepared and traveled to Zhulin in plain clothes. Only Grandee Kong Ning was allowed to accompany him. Kong Ning had already sent a letter on ahead to Lady Xia Ji instructing her to make suitable preparations. He also made sure that Hehua was aware of what was in the wind, so that she was ready to play her role. Lady Xia Ji was not the kind of woman to be flustered by having to entertain a nobleman at such short notice, and every arrangement was made well ahead of time. Lord Ling thought about nothing except Lady Xia Ji: as far as he was concerned, this trip was all about the conquest of a famous beauty. As the saying goes: "An affair with a beautiful woman is everything and makes even the most magnificent scenery meaningless."

Within a short time, they arrived at the Xia family mansion. Lady Xia Ji came out to greet them wearing her official robes. She invited His Lordship to take the seat of honor in the main hall, then she bowed and said politely: "My son, Zhengshu, is away from home. Not knowing that Your Lordship intended to honor us with a visit, he is not present to receive you." Her voice, like the fluting of an oriole, was utterly delightful to listen to. Lord Ling looked at her: she really was divinely beautiful! Among all the concubines in his six palaces there was no one who could compare.

"I happened to be passing and thought that I would visit your mansion," Lord Ling declared. "I do hope that I am not disturbing you."

Lady Xia Ji straightened her robe and said, "It is a great honor to be able to receive Your Lordship in my humble home. I have prepared some simple snacks and wine, but I do not dare to present them to you."

"Since you have already put your cooks to this trouble," Lord Ling returned, "let us not bother with a formal banquet. I have heard that your mansion has an exceptionally beautiful garden attached to it, which I would very much like to see. How about serving the meal there, Your Ladyship?"

"Since the death of my husband," Lady Xia Ji replied, "the garden has become overgrown and desolate. I am afraid that you will not enjoy it, my lord. Let me apologize now for its poor condition!"

Lady Xia Ji's modest and respectful replies made Lord Ling even more anxious to seduce her. He ordered Lady Xia Ji: "Change out of your formal robes and show me around your garden!"

Lady Xia Ji then removed her official robes, revealing herself in a simple dress, like pear blossom below the moon or plum petals in the snow. She really was exceptionally lovely. Her Ladyship led the way into the garden. Although it did not cover a huge area, it contained elegant pine trees and fine cypresses, unusual rocks and rare plants—there was a lake to one side and several painted pavilions scattered here and there. In the middle of the garden there was a belvedere placed on a high promontory; its pillars were painted red and its beams hung with silk, all very beautiful and refined: this was where the banquet would be held. Rooms were set aside for the servants to be entertained as well. Behind this belvedere was a covered walkway winding up and down, leading to a separate cluster of buildings; these were the bedrooms. There was also a stable in the garden, where fine horses were raised. West of the garden there was an area of open ground, which was used for target archery.

Lord Ling looked at everything, and then a banquet was served in the belvedere. Lady Xia Ji had arranged the seating in order of precedence, so when Lord Ling told her to sit down beside him, she declined politely.

"How can Your Ladyship refuse to sit down in your own house?" Lord Ling asked. He ordered Kong Ning to sit on his right-hand side and Lady Xia Ji to sit on his left. "Today let us make none of the distinctions between ruler and subject, but just enjoy ourselves!"

While he was drinking, Lord Ling never took his eyes off her, and Lady Xia Ji returned his glances. His Lordship was a heavy drinker at the best of times, and with Kong Ning sitting beside him and encouraging him, he poured the wine down his neck without noticing how much he was consuming. As the sun set behind the western hills, the servants brought in lamps and washed the drinking cups before pouring in new wine. Lord Ling was now very drunk and lay slumped across his seating mat, snoring.

Kong Ning whispered to Lady Xia Ji, "His Lordship has heard a great deal about how lovely you are and came here today because he is hoping to enjoy you. You cannot refuse."

Lady Xia Ji smiled and said nothing. Kong Ning made the necessary arrangements quickly; he went out to tell the servants to go to bed, then he went to sleep himself. Lady Xia Ji had a brocade coverlet and embroidered pillow taken to the belvedere. She herself went off to bathe in perfumed waters in preparation for receiving His Lordship's amorous advances. She made Hehua stay behind and look after him.

A short time later, Lord Ling awoke. As he opened his eyes, he asked, "Who are you?"

"I am Hehua, my lord," she said, sinking to her knees. "Her Ladyship ordered me to take care of you." Accordingly, she offered him some sour plum hangover soup.

"Who made this soup?" Lord Ling asked.

"I did," Hehua replied.

"If you are serving me plum soup, does that mean you are also ready to serve as my go-between?"

Hehua pretended that she did not understand what he was talking about and said, "I have never been a go-between before, but I do know how to run errands and take messages. However, I do not know who has taken Your Lordship's fancy."

"Her Ladyship has sundered my soul!" Lord Ling exclaimed dramatically. "If you can arrange this for me, I will reward you generously."

"Her Ladyship is a widow, so I am afraid she cannot join your harem," Hehua replied. "However, if you do not object to the idea, an affair might be possible . . ."

Lord Ling was delighted and immediately ordered Hehua to carry a lamp and light his way. By twists and turns they made their way to the women's quarters. Lady Xia Ji was sitting alone beside a lamp, as if she were waiting for someone. When she suddenly heard the sound of footsteps, she made as if she was about to call out, but Lord Ling was already inside the room. Hehua carried the silver lamp away. Lord Ling did not bother to say anything; he just wrapped his arms around Lady Xia Ji and carried her towards the bed, stripping her of her clothes along the way. Her skin was so soft and delicate, and yet her body was burning with desire. When he penetrated her, he could have sworn that she was a virgin. Lord Ling was amazed and asked her about it.

"I know how to look after myself," Lady Xia Ji explained. "Even though I have given birth to a child, after three days I was as good as new."

Lord Ling sighed and said, "If I encountered a genuine goddess, she would not be as lovely as you!" Lord Ling's sexual techniques were far inferior to those of either Kong Ning or Yi Xingfu, in addition to which he had an unpleasant disease, so there was no pleasure to be gained by sleeping with him. On the other hand, he was the ruler of a country and hence in a position of great power, so Lady Xia Ji did not dare to complain. She pretended to enjoy his fumbling, and Lord Ling thought that he was engaged in an earth-shattering romance.

There is a song to the tune "A Crow Cries in the Night," which speaks of this kind of illicit relationship:

A rakish woman will have experienced many men;
What is to be done when they are all so desirable?
First slow then quick she entices her lover,
Showing off her skills at "The Phoenix in the Swallow's Nest."
Her delicate petals parted,
Her "lotus" ready for dotting,
She lets him put his plaything there.
With a shower of silvery rain,
Her pleasure reaches its height!

They slept until cockcrow, and then Lady Xia Ji shook Lord Ling awake.

"Having met you," Lord Ling told her, "I look upon the women of my six palaces as so much dross. However, I do not know if you have any feeling in your heart for me."

Lady Xia Ji was concerned that Lord Ling already knew about her affairs with Kong Ning and Yi Xingfu, so she said, "I would not dare to deceive Your Lordship. After my husband died, I was not able to control myself and I ended up having a number of affairs. Now that I have served Your Lordship, I will refuse all other relationships in the future. If I betray my word, you can punish me as you wish!"

"Tell me who your other lovers are," Lord Ling said cheerfully. "I do not want you to conceal any of them."

"My lovers are Grandee Kong and Grandee Yi," Lady Xia Ji said. "No one else!"

"No wonder that Kong Ning praised your unusual sexual prowess," Lord Ling said. "How could he have known if he had not experienced it himself?"

"I apologize," Lady Xia Ji said humbly. "Please forgive me!"

"Kong Ning did a wonderful thing in recommending you," Lord Ling stated. "I am grateful to him, have no doubts about that! I want to see you regularly in the future, to continue our affair. You can do whatever you like the rest of the time; I would not dream of interfering with you."

"If you come here often, my lord, will you not be able to see me regularly?" Lady Xia Ji asked coquettishly.

A short time later, Lord Ling got up, and Lady Xia Ji removed her own undershirt and gave it to him to wear. "When you look on this shirt, my lord," she said, "you can imagine that you are looking at me!" Hehua picked up a lamp and led His Lordship back to the belvedere the same way that they had come.

When it got light, breakfast was laid out in the main hall. Kong Ning ordered the servants to prepare the carriages. Lady Xia Ji invited Lord Ling to take the seat of honor and asked if he had slept well. The cooks presented the viands, and everyone ate and drank their fill. When the meal was over, Kong Ning drove His Lordship back to court. The officials knew that the Marquis of Chen had spent the night out in the countryside, so they had all assembled at the inner door of the palace to ask after him. Lord Ling gave orders: "No court will be held today." He went straight in through the main door of the palace. Yi Xingfu dragged Kong Ning off to one side and asked him where His Lordship had spent the night. Kong Ning could not lie, so he told him the truth.

Yi Xingfu realized that Kong Ning was behind all of this, so stamping his foot, he burst out: "How could you monopolize His Lordship's favor in this way!"

"His Lordship is really thrilled," Kong Ning replied. "However, next time I will leave it to you to make the recommendation."

The two men laughed heartily and went their separate ways.

At that time there was a village song about these kinds of threesomes:

A single river and three eels,
Many eels in a narrow stream make for a tight fit.
No eels would make the river sad,
It's lucky they found their way in!

The following day, Lord Ling held court in the morning. Once the ceremony was over, the ministers dispersed. His Lordship summoned Kong Ning into his presence and thanked him for recommending Lady Xia Ji. He also summoned Yi Xingfu and asked him, "You should have let me in on this secret much earlier. How could you keep it to yourselves?"

Kong Ning and Yi Xingfu both said, "There is no secret."

"She told me about it herself," Lord Ling said. "There is no need for you to lie."

"I guess you could compare this to a subject acting as a taster for his lord, or a son for his father," Kong Ning replied. "If we were not sure that she was wonderful, how could we dare to recommend her to Your Lordship?"

Lord Ling laughed and said, "Not so. Supposing that a bear's paw was served, I think letting me have first taste would not hurt anyone." Kong Ning and Yi Xingfu both burst out laughing, and His Lordship continued: "You may have gotten there first, but unlike the two of you, I have a memento of the occasion." He took out the undershirt and showed it to them. "This was a present from her. What have you two got to say about that?"

"I have my own memento," Kong Ning told him.

"What did she give you?" Lord Ling asked.

Kong Ning loosened his clothing to reveal his brocade vest and said: "Lady Xia Ji gave me this. It is not just me either, Yi Xingfu also has something."

"So, what do you have?" Lord Ling inquired teasingly.

Yi Xingfu took out the green silk underpants and showed them to His Lordship. Lord Ling laughed heartily. "All three of us have a token of our victory on our persons. Someday we should all go to Zhulin together for an orgy!"

Word that the lord and the two grandees were making disgusting jokes together in the main hall spread beyond the palace gates, thereby angering an upright minister beyond measure. This man, Xie Ye, gritted his teeth and shouted: "Court is where the laws and regulations are determined. If such wickedness is to be countenanced, the state of Chen will collapse at any moment!" He straightened his robes and grabbed his staff of office before heading in through the gates to confront them.

Who was this minister? READ ON.

Chapter Fifty-three

King Zhuang of Chu, after remonstrance, restores the state of Chen.

Lord Jing of Jin sends his army to rescue the country of Zheng.

Lord Ling of Chen and his two grandees, Kong Ning and Yi Xingfu, were all wearing items of intimate clothing that they had been given by Lady Xia Ji, when they discussed their sexual exploits in the main audience hall of the palace. When Grandee Xie Ye heard about this, he arranged his clothing properly and grasped his staff of office tightly before heading back to the gate to the inner court. Kong Ning and Yi Xingfu were afraid of Xie Ye's direct reproaches, and seeing him barge in without any announcement, they knew that he was going to remonstrate with them. Therefore, they bade hasty farewells to Lord Ling and left. Lord Ling was just about to leave his throne when Xie Ye stormed in and grabbed him by the sleeve. He knelt down and said, "I have heard that a vassal should respect his ruler and that men and women should maintain a proper segregation. Now you have caused a widow to lose her chastity, and what is more, you and your boon companions boast of your wicked exploits, encouraging each other to go even further. It is completely inappropriate that such vile things should be discussed at court—you have destroyed every vestige of honesty and shame, violating our traditions. Your subjects no longer respect you, no woman is safe—our moral order has collapsed! A lack of respect leads to dissolution, dissolution leads to chaos, and chaos leads to the ruin of the country. You must reform!"

Lord Ling could feel the sweat breaking out on his forehead. He covered his face with his sleeve and replied, "Say no more! I regret everything that I have done!"

Xie Ye said goodbye and walked out of the palace gates. Kong Ning and Yi Xingfu were standing out there, attempting to find out what was going on inside. When they saw Xie Ye marching out in a rage, they tried to hide in the crowd. However, Xie Ye had already spotted them and called the two men forward, upbraiding them to their faces: "When a ruler does a good deed, his subjects should publicize it; when a ruler does something wrong, his subjects ought to conceal that fact. Now, you not only behave badly but encourage His Lordship to do likewise and make sure that everyone far and wide has heard of your wicked deeds. What does that look like? Are you not ashamed of yourselves?"

The two men had nothing to say, so they just apologized weakly.

When Xie Ye had left, Kong Ning and Yi Xingfu went to see Lord Ling, and they told him of Xie Ye's parting shot: "His Lordship must never go to Zhulin again!"

"Are you going to go back?" Lord Ling asked.

"Xie Ye was complaining about your behavior, my lord, and that has nothing to do with us," they said. "We can go again, but you can't!"

"I would rather annoy Xie Ye than give up my pleasures there," Lord Ling said crossly.

"If you go back again, my lord, I am afraid that you will find it difficult to withstand Xie Ye's tongue-lashing," they pointed out. "What are you going to do?"

"Do you have a plan for silencing Xie Ye?" His Lordship asked.

"If you want to shut Xie Ye up," Kong Ning said, "you are going to have to prevent him from opening his mouth."

Lord Ling laughed at that: "His mouth is his own. How am I supposed to stop him from opening it?"

"I know exactly what Ning means," Yi Xingfu said. "If he is dead, he won't be able to speak. Why don't you just give orders, my lord, to have Xie Ye killed? That way you can enjoy yourself without restraint!"

"I could not possibly do that!" Lord Ling exclaimed.

"How about I send an assassin after him?" Kong Ning suggested.

Lord Ling nodded and said, "Do whatever you like!"

The two men then said goodbye and left the palace, going somewhere private to discuss the matter. They hired an assassin, ordering him to lie in ambush on the main road to wait until Xie Ye went to court, then he leapt out and killed him. The people of Chen believed that the marquis was behind this assassination, for they were unaware of the two grandees' role in the conspiracy.

A historian wrote a poem about this:

Every principle of virtue was humbled into the dust in Chen;
The ruler and his subjects proclaimed their vices proudly.
Their official hats and robes were polluted by women's underwear,
They behaved as if the court had moved its home to Zhulin.
How brave was Xie Ye!
He alone remained as straight as an arrow, speaking his mind.
Though he died, his reputation was unsullied,
As loyal as Guan Longfeng or Prince Bigan!

After Xie Ye was murdered, neither ruler nor ministers were afraid of anyone anymore, so they would regularly go together to Zhulin. The first couple of times they went in secret, but as it became a common occurrence they made no pretense of trying to hide. The people of the capital composed the song "Zhulin" to criticize them. This song runs:

Why does His Lordship go to Zhulin?
He follows Xia Nan.
If he is in Zhulin,
He follows Xia Nan!

Xia Zhengshu's style-name was Zinan. The people who composed this song were loyal subjects who deliberately chose not to mention the name of Lady Xia Ji. Instead they spoke of "Xia Nan," suggesting that His Lordship went to visit the son rather than the mother.

. . .

The Marquis of Chen was a worthless man, and with the full and active support of Kong Ning and Yi Xingfu, he paid no attention to the demands of propriety or any sense of shame. What is more, Lady Xia Ji was good at arranging things to everyone's satisfaction, so they came to an agreement whereby the three men would share her, enjoying themselves together. They saw nothing to be surprised at in their mode of living. Xia Zhengshu gradually grew up and became aware of his mother's behavior, which cut him to the heart. However, an open breach was impossible because of the Marquis of Chen's noble position, so there was really nothing he could do. Every time he heard that the Marquis of Chen was going to visit Zhulin, he made some kind of excuse not to be present, on the principle that what the eye does not see, the heart does not grieve after. This debauched foursome thus found themselves unrestrained by Xia Zhengshu's presence. Time flew like an arrow until Zhengshu was eighteen, by which time he had grown up into a handsome and strapping young man, a fine warrior and impressive archer. In order to please Lady Xia Ji, Lord Ling appointed him to the office formerly held by his own father, which gave him complete control over the army. When Zhengshu had finished offering thanks for His Lordship's benevolence, he went back to Zhulin to see his mother, Lady Xia Ji.

"How terribly kind of His Lordship!" she said. "You must do your utmost to fulfill the demands of your office and take responsibility for the security of the state. Do not worry about what is going on at home!"

Zhengshu said goodbye to his mother and returned to court to take up his new office.

It happened that one day Lord Ling of Chen was visiting Zhulin with Kong Ning and Yi Xingfu, and they stayed overnight at the Xia family mansion. Xia Zhengshu came home especially in order to hold a banquet in Lord Ling's honor, to thank His Lordship for his kindness in allowing him to inherit his father's office. Since her son was present, Lady Xia Ji did not dare to come out and keep the men company. As they got drunk, His Lordship and his boon companions were making their usual smutty jokes, waving their hands about and stamping their feet. Xia Zhengshu was disgusted by their appearance and withdrew to the far side of the screens, where he listened in secret to what they were saying.

"Zhengshu is a handsome young man and he looks a little like you," Lord Ling joked with Yi Xingfu. "Are you sure he is not your son?"

Yi Xingfu laughed and said: "The sparkle in Zhengshu's eyes reminds me of Your Lordship. I think that he is your son."

Kong Ning then broke into the conversation: "His Lordship and Grandee Yi are both far too young to be his father. However, there are lots of possible candidates for the paternity of that little bastard. I bet even Lady Xia herself can't remember who it really is!"

The three men clapped their hands and roared with laughter. It would have been a good thing if Xia Zhengshu had not heard this. However, since he did, his anger and humiliation were indeed hard to bear. As the saying goes: "Rage and disgust are born deep within!" He went and quietly locked Lady Xia Ji in her chambers, then slid out of one of the side gates and instructed his guards: "I want you to surround the mansion and prevent the Marquis of Chen, Kong Ning, and Yi Xingfu from leaving."

The officers accepted these orders and shouted out their instructions. The Xia mansion was now completely cut off from the outside world.

Xia Zhengshu now donned his armor and clasped a cloak around his neck. With a sword in his hand, he led the strongest of his private guard on an attack through the main gate of the residence. "Arrest the rapists!" he shouted.

Lord Ling of Chen was still cracking foul jokes, laughing and drinking, but Kong Ning realized that something was terribly wrong and shouted: "My lord! Zhengshu has tricked you into coming here. He is leading his soldiers in an attack. Run!"

"The front gate is surrounded," Yi Xingfu screamed. "Let us try the back!"

The three men had spent a lot of time in the Xia mansion and knew the place very well. The Marquis of Chen thought of going to the women's quarters, to beg Lady Xia Ji to save him. When he discovered that the door to that part of the residence was locked, it only added further terror to his panic. Now he ran in the direction of the garden, with Xia Zhengshu in hot pursuit. His Lordship remembered that the stables on the east side were surrounded by a low wall that he would be able to climb over, so he ran in that direction.

"You are not going anywhere!" Xia Zhengshu shouted. He drew his bow and sent an arrow whistling after him, but it did not hit him. When the Marquis of Chen got to the stables, his first idea was to find somewhere to hide, but the frightened horses started to neigh. Running back as quickly as he could, he came within range of Xia Zhengshu. He shot a second arrow, and this time it killed him. How sad that the Marquis of Chen should rule for fifteen years only to die so ignominiously in a stable!

Master Qian Yuan wrote the following poem, expressing sympathy with Xia Zhengshu for assassinating his ruler:

> This lord and his ministers were each more lascivious than the next;
> In their disgusting debauchery they showed not the slightest sense of shame.
> Even though he knew that he would be punished for it,
> At least he gave vent to his anger and feelings of humiliation.

When Kong Ning and Yi Xingfu saw the Marquis of Chen heading eastward, they knew Zhengshu would chase after him, so instead they ran westward towards the archery ground. Just as they had anticipated, Zhengshu went after the Marquis of Chen. Kong Ning and Yi Xingfu then managed to squeeze out through a dog-flap. Not daring to go home, they fled penniless to the kingdom of Chu.

After shooting dead the Marquis of Chen, Xia Zhengshu led his troops into the capital city. He gave out that the Marquis of Chen had been struck down by a violent illness after drinking too much wine and died. According to His Lordship's dying wishes, Scion Wu was to succeed him: he took the title of Lord Cheng. Lord Cheng loathed Xia Zhengshu, but he was too powerful to control, so he had to endure the situation in silence. Xia Zhengfu was afraid that the other feudal lords might try to punish him, so he forced the new Marquis of Chen into going to pay court to Jin, in order to cement the alliance between their two states.

• • •

As it happened, an ambassador from the kingdom of Chu had been ordered to go and make a blood covenant with the Marquis of Chen at Chenling. Before he had even arrived, he heard about the murder and turned back. It was at this time that Kong Ning and Yi Xingfu arrived in exile in Chu. When they had an audience with King Zhuang, they kept completely quiet about the vices that they and His Late Lordship had been engaged in, and simply said: "Xia Zhengshu launched a coup and assassinated Pingguo, the Marquis of Chen." This accorded exactly with what the ambassador had said.

King Zhuang summoned his ministers to discuss this situation. There was a hereditary grandee of the kingdom of Chu named Qu Wu, styled Ziling, who was the son of Qu Dang. This man was very handsome and skilled in all the arts of war as well as literature, but he had one flaw: he was excessively libidinous and an expert in techniques for improving longevity and sexual performance. A few years earlier he had been sent on a mission to the state of Chen, during which time he had met Lady Xia Ji and seen how beautiful she was. He had also heard of her skills in bed and how she never seemed to grow old, for which he admired her greatly. When he heard that Xia Zhengshu had assassinated his ruler, he decided to take advantage of this situation to steal Lady Xia Ji, so he encouraged King Zhuang to raise an army and attack Chen.

The Grand Vizier, Sunshu Ao, also said, "We must punish this murder in Chen!"

King Zhuang agreed. This happened in the ninth year of the reign of King Ding of Zhou, which was the first year of Lord Cheng of Chen's rule.

King Zhuang began by sending a formal declaration of intent to the state of Chen:

> The king of Chu says to you: A member of the Xia family has assassinated his ruler, something that both gods and men hold in abomination. You cannot punish him, so I will do it for you. He is the only person guilty

> of this crime, so everyone else can rest assured that they will not be harmed.

When this text reached the Chen capital, everyone blamed Xia Zhengshu and was perfectly happy to see him punished by Chu. As a result, there was no plan forthcoming for resisting the enemy.

King Zhuang of Chu personally took control of the three armies, which were headed by the senior generals Prince Yingqi, Prince Ce, and Qu Wu. They raced to the Chen capital with the speed of lightning, without encountering the slightest opposition. So as to maintain order among the populace, strict orders were given to avoid causing trouble. Xia Zhengshu knew that the people of Chen had turned against him, so he fled to Zhulin. At that time Lord Cheng of Chen had still not returned from the state of Jin.

Grandee Yuan Po discussed the situation with the other ministers: "The king of Chu is here to punish the guilty on our behalf. He is not planning to execute anyone other than Xia Zhengshu. We had better arrest Zhengshu and hand him over to the Chu army, then send an ambassador to ask for a peace treaty, for that way we will preserve the state altars safe and sound. That would be the best plan."

The other ministers all agreed with him. Accordingly, Yuan Po ordered his son, Qiaoru, to lead the army to Zhulin and arrest Xia Zhengshu. Before Qiaoru could set out, the Chu army had already arrived below the walls of the capital. The government of Chen had ceased to function effectively many years earlier, and the marquis was abroad, so the people of the capital opened the gates of their own accord and welcomed the Chu army. King Zhuang led his troops into the city in good order.

When Grandee Yuan Po and his colleagues were brought before King Zhuang, His Majesty asked, "Where is Zhengshu?"

"At Zhulin," Yuan Po replied.

"You are all subjects of His Late Lordship," King Zhuang pointed out. "Why have you let this traitorous bastard get away with murder? Why didn't you punish him?"

"It is not that we did not want to punish him," Yuan Po explained. "We were not powerful enough."

Immediately King Zhuang ordered Yuan Po to lead the way as the main body of the army advanced towards Zhulin under the command of His Majesty himself. Prince Yingqi stayed behind with his forces, camped inside the city walls.

Xia Zhengshu had collected all his family's portable wealth, with the intention of going into exile in the state of Zheng with his mother, Lady Xia Ji. Just moments before they were due to set off, the Chu army surrounded their mansion at Zhulin and arrested Zhengshu. King Zhuang ordered that he be placed in a prison cart. "Why don't I see Lady Xia Ji?" he asked. He had his officers search the mansion, and they found her in the garden.

Lady Xia Ji bowed twice before King Zhuang and said, "With my country in chaos and my family ruined, my life is now in your hands, Your Majesty. If you allow me to live, I will happily serve you as a slave."

Lady Xia Ji was so beautiful and her voice so elegant that King Zhuang found himself bewitched by the very sight of her. He said to his generals, "Even though there are many women in my harem, there are few who are as lovely as Lady Xia Ji. I would like to take her into my own household as a concubine. What do you think?"

"You must not do that!" Qu Wu remonstrated. "You turned the army against Chen, Your Majesty, in order to punish Xia Zhengshu for his crime. If you now take Lady Xia Ji into your harem, it shows that you only really care about her beauty. It is righteous to punish the guilty, but taking a woman into your household like this would be wicked. You must not start righteously and end up in the wrong. This is not the kind of thing that a hegemon would do."

"You are absolutely right!" King Zhuang exclaimed. "I would not dare take her in the teeth of your advice. However, she really is amazingly lovely, and if she crosses my path again, I am afraid that I will not be able to control myself."

Prince Ce was standing by the king's side throughout this exchange, and he too was deeply struck by Lady Xia Ji's beauty. When he realized that King Zhuang was not going to keep her for himself, he knelt and said, "Although I am now middle-aged, I have never been married. Please give her to me as my wife."

Again, Qu Wu remonstrated: "You must not agree to this, Your Majesty!"

"Why don't you want me to marry Lady Xia Ji?" Prince Ce demanded angrily.

"This woman is ill-starred," Qu Wu declared. "Let us look at the evidence: she brought the Honorable Man of Zheng to an early grave, caused the murder of Xie Ye, the assassination of the Marquis of Chen, the execution of her son, the exile of Grandees Kong Ning and Yi Xingfu, and the destruction of the state of Chen. What more proof of her evil nature do you want? There are many beautiful women in the world, so why do you have to pick this disgusting creature who will cause you nothing but regrets?"

"If it is indeed as you say, that is horrifying!" King Zhuang exclaimed.

"In that case I won't have her," Prince Ce said. "So far you have said that His Majesty cannot marry her and I cannot marry her. Are you planning to take her on yourself?"

"No! I wouldn't dare!" Qu Wu protested.

"Everyone fights over things that don't have an owner," King Zhuang said thoughtfully. "If I remember correctly, Sirdar Xiang Lao has recently lost his wife. I will give her to him as a second one!"

At this time Xiang Lao was out on campaign with the auxiliaries. Now King Zhuang summoned him and gave Lady Xia Ji into his care. The couple thanked His Majesty for his benevolence and withdrew. Prince Ce put the whole business out of his mind. However, when Qu Wu remonstrated with King Zhuang and prevented Prince Ce from taking the woman over, it was with the intention of getting her himself. When King Zhuang bestowed her upon Xiang Lao, he said to himself, "What a shame! What a loss!" Then he considered the matter further: "How can such an old man cope with a woman like that? Within six months to a year, she is going to be a widow and fresh arrangements will have to be made."

Qu Wu had his own plans for the woman but said nothing whatsoever about them. King Zhuang spent one night at Zhulin and then went back to the capital city of Chen. He entered the city in state with Prince Yingqi. King Zhuang ordered that Xia Zhengshu should be taken out of the Li Gate in chains and torn to pieces by chariots.

A historian wrote a poem:

> The Lord of Chen brought his doom upon himself by wickedness
> and lust,
> Nevertheless it was wrong of Xia Zhengshu to assassinate him.
> King Zhuang's attack came like timely rain;
> Above the Si River the feudal lords could see his pennants flying.

Once King Zhuang had given orders about how Xia Zhengshu was to be dealt with, he had a good look at the maps and official documentation to do with the state of Chen. He decided that in future Chen would be a county in the kingdom of Chu, and he appointed Prince Yingqi as Duke of Chen, to look after this territory. He took Grandee Yuan Po and all his colleagues back to his capital city of Ying. A number of subordinate states in the south, when they heard that the king of Chu had destroyed Chen, came to pay court. The dukes of counties in the kingdom of Chu naturally did likewise. The only person who did not do so was Shen Shushi, who was on a diplomatic mission in Qi and had not yet returned. At this time Lord Hui of Qi died and was succeeded by the Honorable Wuye, who became Lord Qing. Qi and Chu were allies, so King Zhuang had sent Shen Shushi on this mission to condole on the death of the old lord and congratulate the new one on his accession before the whole issue of the attack on Chen came up. Three days after King Zhuang arrived back in Chu, Shen Shushi also returned. He reported on the successful completion of his mission and withdrew, without uttering a single word of congratulation.

King Zhuang sent a eunuch to upbraid Shen Shushi for his omission: "The traitor Xia Zhengshu assassinated his lord, and so His Majesty executed him for his crime. Chen was thus brought under Chu's control. The whole world has heard of His Majesty's reputation for justice, and the lords of the counties have all congratulated him. You are the only one to keep silent. Surely you do not think that His Majesty was wrong to launch this campaign against Chen?"

Shen Shushi subsequently requested permission to have an audience with King Zhuang to explain himself face-to-face. The king of Chu agreed to this.

"Has Your Majesty ever heard of the legal case whereby they took away an ox for trampling the fields?" Shen Shushi asked.

"No," King Zhuang replied.

"One day someone was leading an ox along the path between fields belonging to someone else, and the animal trampled down some rice," Shen Shushi began. "The owner of the fields got angry and demanded possession of the ox as compensation. If a case like this landed before Your Majesty, how would you decide it?"

"If the ox that was being led along the path got into the fields and trampled them about a bit," King Zhuang said thoughtfully, "it cannot have done very much damage. Taking away the ox is much too harsh! If I had to decide this case, I would speak severely to the person in charge of the ox and give it back to him. Do you think that would be appropriate?"

"Your Majesty's judgment about the ox is enlightened, but that about Chen is muddled," Shen Shushi returned. "While it is true that Xia Zhengshu committed a crime, all he did was to assassinate his ruler; he did not bring the country to ruin. Executing him is enough; why did you have to take the country? What is the difference between what you did and the man who demanded a whole ox as compensation? Do you see now why I did not congratulate you?"

King Zhuang stamped his foot: "You are absolutely right. I had no idea!"

"If you think that I am right," Shen Shushi said, "why don't you hand back the ox?"

King Zhuang summoned Grandee Yuan Po of Chen and asked him, "Where is the Lord of Chen?"

"He went to the state of Jin," Yuan Po replied, "but I have no idea where he is now." As he finished speaking, tears began to drip down his cheeks.

King Zhuang said shamefacedly, "I am going to restore your country, and you should make every effort to bring back the Lord of Chen and install him in power. I hope that in the future you will be allied with Chu from one generation to the next, keeping firmly within your own borders. Do not betray my generosity." He also summoned Kong Ning and Yi Xingfu to tell them: "I am going to send you back home. Do your best to support the Lord of Chen."

Grandee Yuan Po was well aware of all the trouble that Kong Ning and Yi Xingfu had caused, but he did not dare to speak plainly in front of the king of Chu. He therefore kept his mouth shut and left after bowing and thanking His Majesty. Just as they left the borders of Chu, they met the Marquis of Chen. On his way home from Jin, he had heard that his country had been destroyed, and so he headed for Chu to have an audience with the king. Grandee Yuan Po reported all that the king of Chu had done for them, and ruler and minister then returned together to Chen. Prince Yingqi, in command of the defense of this territory, had already received new orders from the king of Chu summoning him back home. He therefore returned all the maps and official documents to Chen and set off. This was the first of King Zhuang of Chu's real triumphs.

An old man wrote a poem:

> Having made Chen a county, who would have guessed it would be restored?
> King Zhuang went from being Robber Zhi to the sage-king Shun in a single leap!
> The righteous reputation of Chu spread out within the four seas,
> Thus we know that a good king relies on his wise ministers!

After Kong Ning returned to the capital, one day in broad daylight he saw Xia Zhengshu come to take his life. In a complete panic, he jumped into a pond and drowned. After he died, Yi Xingfu dreamed that he saw Lord Ling of Chen, Kong Ning, and Xia Zhengshu arrive to drag him to the Heavenly Court to answer for his crimes. This dream shocked him so much that he became ill and died. That was the retribution for his wickedness.

• • •

When Prince Yingqi returned home to Chu, he had an audience with King Zhuang, at which he referred to himself as the Duke of Chen.

"I have already restored the state of Chen," King Zhuang informed him. "I will find some other way to reward you."

Prince Yingqi asked for the lands of Shen and Lü, and King Zhuang agreed.

Qu Wu presented his opinion: "These are your northern marches and you rely on them to prevent Jin from invading your territory. You cannot give them away!"

King Zhuang then withheld the grant. When Grandee Shen Shushi resigned his office on the grounds of old age, King Zhuang gave Qu Wu the title of Duke of Shen, and he did not refuse. From this time onwards, Prince Yingqi was alienated from Qu Wu. This happened in the tenth year of the reign of King Ding of Zhou, which was also the seventeenth year of the reign of King Zhuang of Chu.

King Zhuang was pleased that Chen was now his ally. However, Zheng still followed Jin; its people were not willing to give their allegiance to Chu. He discussed this situation with his grandees.

"If we attack Zheng," Grand Vizier Sunshu Ao said, "Jin is sure to go to their rescue, so we will need the whole army."

"That is just what I was thinking," King Zhuang replied.

He mobilized the three armies and two wings, and in a huge procession they marched on Yingyang. Sirdar Xiang Lao was in the vanguard. Just before they were about to set out, one of the army officers, Tang Jiao, said: "Zheng is a small country, and we don't actually need to take this enormous force against them. Let me lead the one hundred men under my command out one day in advance, and I will make sure that the road is clear for the three armies."

Xiang Lao was impressed by his ambition and agreed to this. Tang Jiao was an excellent soldier, and anyone who got in his way was sent packing with their tails between their legs. He and his troops kept moving forward, making sure that every evening a well-prepared campsite was waiting for the army. King Zhuang led his troops straight into the suburbs of Zheng without seeing a single enemy soldier try to stop them. King Zhuang was amazed at how quickly they had managed to advance, and said to Xiang Lao: "I was not expecting you to prove quite so hale and hearty at your age, that you can sweep all opposition before you like this!"

"This has nothing to do with me," he replied. "It is Tang Jiao whom you have to thank!"

King Zhuang immediately summoned Tang Jiao and wanted to reward him lavishly.

"I have already received generous rewards from Your Majesty, and today I am doing my best to repay you," Tang Jiao told him. "I would not dare to expect anything more!"

King Zhuang was curious and said, "I do not know you at all. When did I reward you?"

"At the Broken Tassel Banquet, it was I who grabbed hold of Her Ladyship's sleeve," Tang Jiao replied. "I will repay you for your kindness in refusing to punish me on that occasion, even if it costs me my life."

"Ah!" King Zhuang sighed. "If I had lit the lamps and insisted on punishing whoever was guilty, would this man have been prepared to work so hard for me today?" He ordered that Tang Jiao's achievements should be mentioned in dispatches and promised him a senior position after Zheng was pacified.

Tang Jiao said to someone, "His Majesty could rightly have executed me for the crime that I committed against him and yet he covered it up and did nothing to punish me. This is what I have done to pay him back. However, I have already made it completely clear that as a criminal, I do not expect to receive any rewards in the future."

That night he slipped out of the camp in secret and disappeared. When King Zhuang heard this, he sighed and said, "What a hero!"

The main army attacked and broke through the passes guarding the way to Zheng, arriving below the city walls. King Zhuang gave orders to lay siege to the capital, and for the next seventeen days it underwent bombardment day and night. Lord Xiang of Zheng was waiting for relief from Jin, so he made no attempts to make peace. An enormous number of officers and men were killed or injured. The northeastern corner of the city wall began to crumble, but just as the Chu army were about to climb in, King Zhuang heard the sound of weeping and wailing rising up from inside. He could not bear it and ordered that his army retreat ten *li*.

Prince Yingqi came forward and said, "We should take advantage of the collapse of that section of the city wall to press on. Why have you withdrawn our troops?"

"Zheng knows about my military might," the king of Chu explained, "but they do not know about my magnanimity. I have withdrawn in order to show how generous I can be. Let us see how they react to this and then decide whether to advance or withdraw!"

. . .

When Lord Xiang of Zheng heard that the Chu army was retreating, he thought this must mean that relief troops had arrived from Jin, and so he sent his people out to repair the city walls and entrenchments. Men and women were all sent out to patrol the tops of the walls. When King Zhuang realized that Zheng had no intention of surrendering, he moved his army back to besiege them again. Zheng held out for three months, but then they could resist no longer. The Chu general, Le Bo, led his forces over the wall near the Huang Gate, opening up every gate of the city. King Zhuang gave strict orders to prevent looting and rape, and the three armies maintained good discipline.

As they marched along the main road, Lord Xiang of Zheng came forward to welcome the Chu army, dressed as a prisoner and leading a sheep. "Thanks to my limited abilities," he said, "I have not been able to serve Your Majesty's great kingdom, making you angry with me. Now that you have led your army to my country, I realize the crime I have committed against you. My life and death will be determined by a single word from Your Majesty. If you remember the alliance that pertained between our two states in the past and hence do not destroy my country, allowing the sacrifices at my ancestral temples to continue, I will serve you as a subordinate lord and remember forever Your Majesty's kindness."

Prince Yingqi came forward and said, "Zheng surrendered because they could hold out no longer. If you pardon them, they will simply rebel again. You had better destroy their country!"

"If Shen Shushi were here," King Zhuang replied, "he would complain again about me taking away an ox because it trampled a field!"

He immediately withdrew the army thirty *li*. Lord Xiang of Zheng paid a personal visit to the Chu encampment, at which he apologized for his crimes and requested a blood covenant. He left his younger brother, the Honorable Quji, behind as a hostage.

King Zhuang stood down his army and proceeded northwards, making camp at Yan. His spies reported: "The state of Jin has appointed Xun Linfu as senior general and Xian Hu as his second-in-command, and they have set off to rescue Zheng with a force of six hundred chariots. They have already crossed the Yellow River."

King Zhuang asked his generals, "The Jin army is here. Do we go home? Or do we fight?"

"Before we had made peace with Zheng," Grand Vizier Sunshu Ao said, "we would have been in a good position to do battle with Jin. However, Zheng is now allied with us and there is no point in forcing Jin to become our enemy. You had better take the army home, Your Majesty. That is the best plan."

King Zhuang's favorite servant, Wu San, presented his opinion: "The Grand Vizier is wrong. Zheng has always claimed that they allied with Jin because we were not strong enough to defend them. If once the Jin army turns up we simply avoid them, we really are not strong enough to defend anybody! Besides which, when Jin discovers that Zheng is now allied with us, they will turn their troops against them. Jin came to rescue them; we can also come to rescue them. What is wrong with that?"

"Last year we fought in Chen," Sunshu Ao retorted. "This year we are fighting in Zheng. The Chu army is exhausted. If we do battle and are defeated, even if we eat your flesh it will hardly atone for the crime you have committed!"

"If we do battle and are victorious," Wu San returned, "that will mean that you have failed in your strategic calculations. If we are defeated, it is the Jin army that will eat my flesh. Is it likely that they will spare a mouthful for the Chu army?"

King Zhuang decided to put the issue to a vote among his generals. Each of them wrote one word on the palm of his hand. Those in favor of doing battle wrote "Fight"; those in favor of going home wrote "Withdraw." When the generals had finished writing, King Zhuang ordered them to hold up their hands so he could have a look. Four men—the commander-in-chief of the Central Army, Yu Qiu; Sirdar Xiang Lao; and Generals Cai Jiuju and Peng Ming—had written "Withdraw." The other twenty or so, including Prince Yingqi, Prince Ce, Prince Guchen, Qu Dang, Pan Dang, Le Bo, Yang Yaoji, Xu Bo, Xiong Fuji, and Xu Yan, had all written "Fight."

"My old minister, Yu Qiu, agrees with the Grand Vizier," King Zhuang declared. "We are going home!" He gave orders to turn the chariots around and move the battle standards. His troops were told that the following day they should water their horses at the Yellow River and then head for home.

Wu San went that night and asked for an audience with King Zhuang. "Why are you so afraid of Jin, Your Majesty, that you abandon Zheng to them?" he asked.

"I will never abandon Zheng to them!" the king of Chu declared.

"The Chu army was camped below the walls of Zheng for ninety days before they surrendered," Wu San said. "Now Jin is here and we are leaving, which means that they will take over under the pretext of 'rescuing' Zheng. Chu will not be able to do anything about it. If that is not abandoning Zheng to them, what is it?"

"The Grand Vizier says that if we fight Jin we cannot be assured of victory. That is why we are leaving."

"I have already made my own inquiries," Wu San told him. "Xun Linfu has only recently been appointed as commander-in-chief of the Central Army, and he is not yet trusted or obeyed by his men. His deputy, Xian Hu, is the grandson of Xian Zhen and the son of Xian Qieju. He received this position purely due to the achievements of his ancestors. He is a bad-tempered and unpleasant man and will not make a good general. The Luan and Zhao families have produced many famous generals over the generations, but they each have their own ideas and their orders conflict with each other. The Jin army is large, but they will be easily defeated. Furthermore, Your Majesty is a king, so for you to run away to avoid these vassals will make you a laughingstock to the whole world, not just in Zheng!"

"I am certainly not a great general," King Zhuang said angrily, "but that does not mean I am in any way inferior to these men from Jin! Let us go out and fight them!"

That very night he sent someone to inform Grand Vizier Sunshu Ao of his decision, and he ordered that the shafts of all the chariots should be turned around to face north. They would advance to the city of Guan and wait for the Jin army.

Do you know if they were victorious or not? READ ON.

Chapter Fifty-four

Xun Linfu's lax discipline leads his army into a defeat.

Dwarf Meng uses his acting skills to remind his king of an obligation.

It was in the third year of the rule of Lord Jing of Jin that he heard that the king of Chu was personally commanding an attack on Zheng. He wanted to rescue them, and so he appointed Xun Linfu as the commander-in-chief of the Central Army and Xian Hu as his deputy. Shi Hui was appointed as the commander-in-chief of the Upper Army with Xi Ke to assist him; Zhao Shuo was appointed as commander-in-chief of the Lower Army with Luan Shu to assist him. Zhao Kuo and Zhao Yingqi became grandees of the Central Army; Gong Shuo and Han Chuan became grandees of the Upper Army; Xun Shou and Zhao Tong became grandees of the Lower Army. Han Jue was appointed minister of war, and there were a further ten or more junior generals appointed, including Wei Qi, Zhao Zhan, Xun Ying, Feng Bo, and Bao Kui. In the sixth month they set out from Jiang with a force of six hundred chariots. When they arrived at the mouth of the Yellow River, the advance guard had discovered that after a long siege by the forces of Chu with no relief, Zheng could no longer hold out and thus had already surrendered to Chu. The enemy army was reported to be moving north. Xun Linfu summoned his generals to discuss whether they should proceed or not.

"We are already too late to save Zheng," Shi Hui declared, "so there is no benefit to doing battle with Chu. We had better stand down the army and wait for another opportunity."

Xun Linfu agreed with this suggestion and gave orders to stand down. One of the senior generals got up and said, "No! You must not do this! The reason that Jin's authority as hegemon has been recognized by our peers for so long is because we support those in danger and rescue those in trouble. Zheng was waiting for our help and we did not come, so they found themselves forced to surrender to Chu. If we were to attack Chu, Zheng would certainly return to the Jin fold. If we abandon Zheng today and flee in the face of the Chu army, on whom will little countries rely in the future? We will never be able to assume hegemony over the feudal lords again! If the commander-in-chief insists upon standing down the army, I will take just the forces under my own command into battle."

Xun Linfu looked at him; the speaker was Xian Hu, styled Zhizi, second-in-command of the Central Army. "The king of Chu is presently with his army," Xun Linfu said. "He has excellent generals and fine troops at his disposal. If you were to proceed alone with your tiny force, would that not be like throwing a lump of meat into the jaws of a hungry tiger? What do you think you would achieve?"

"If I do not go," Xian Hu shouted, "then people will say that in the whole of the great state of Jin there is not a single person who dares to go out and fight. What a humiliation! Even if I die in front of their battle formations, at least I will not have let anyone down!"

When he had finished speaking, he stormed out of the gates to the encampment. He bumped into the Zhao brothers—Zhao Tong and Zhao Kuo—and told them, "The commander-in-chief is terrified of the Chu army. I am going across the river on my own!"

"That is what a man should do!" they said. "We will join forces with you!"

The three men took their soldiers across the Yellow River in direct contravention of military orders. When Xun Shou could not find Zhao Tong, one of his officers reported: "He has already gone with General Xian to fight the Chu army." Xun Shou was shocked and reported this to the minister of war, Han Jue. He went especially to the Central Army to see Xun Linfu, and said: "Are you aware that Xian Hu has already crossed the Yellow River? If he meets the Chu army, he is sure to be defeated. You have ultimate responsibility for the Central Army, and if Xian Hu gets his troops killed, you will have to take all the blame for it. What are you going to do?"

Xun Linfu quickly asked if the minister of war had any suggestions.

"With the situation as it is," Han Jue told him, "you had better advance your three armies. If you are victorious, you will be rewarded. If by some misfortune you are defeated, you can share the blame equally among the six senior commanders. Surely that is better than taking sole responsibility."

Xun Linfu bowed and said: "You are right."

He gave orders that the three armies should cross the Yellow River and establish a camp between Mount Ao and Mount Hao. Xian Hu said happily, "I knew that the commander-in-chief would follow my recommendations."

• • •

Let us now turn to another part of the story. When Lord Xiang of Zheng discovered from his spies that the Jin troops had arrived in force, he was afraid that once they were victorious, they would punish Zheng for their surrender to Chu. He gathered his ministers to discuss the situation.

Grandee Huang Rong came forward and said, "I will go to the Jin army on Your Lordship's behalf and encourage them to do battle with Chu. If Jin is victorious, then we will ally with Jin; if Chu is victorious, we will ally with Chu. We have nothing to worry about providing we are on the strongest side!"

The Earl of Zheng thought that this was an excellent plan, so he sent Huang Rong as his envoy to the Jin army. In accordance with the instructions that he had received from the Earl of Zheng, Huang Rong said: "His Lordship was waiting for your relief troops with the expectancy of a farmer hoping for seasonal rain. It was only the extreme danger of the situation that forced him to make peace with Chu. That surrender allowed us to survive the crisis, but His Lordship still remembers our alliance with Jin. The Chu army has been made arrogant by their victory over Zheng; they have also been on campaign for a long time and are exhausted. If Jin attacks them, we will provide support."

"In a single battle," Xian Hu declared, "we will be able to defeat Chu and restore our alliance with Zheng!"

"Zheng keeps changing sides," Luan Shu said. "We cannot trust them!"

Zhao Tong and Zhao Kuo said, "If our allies are prepared to help us, this is a wonderful opportunity that should not be lost! Xian Hu is absolutely right!"

Without waiting for Xun Linfu's approval, Xian Hu and the Zhao brothers arranged to do battle with Chu, with Huang Rong's support. They had no idea that Lord Xiang of Zheng had sent another envoy to the Chu army, to encourage them to do battle with Jin. It was his intention to set the two sides to fighting while he stood by and watched.

Sunshu Ao was worried about the size of the Jin army. He said to the king of Chu, "The people of Jin do not look like they want to force a fight, so you had better ask for a peace treaty. If they refuse, you can then do battle, knowing that they have put themselves in the wrong."

King Zhuang thought this was a good idea, and so he sent Cai Jiuju to go to Jin and ask them to make peace rather than fight. Xun Linfu was delighted and said, "What a blessing to our two countries!"

Xian Hu cursed Cai Jiuju: "First you steal one of our allies, and then you come here to talk about a peace treaty in the hope of dragging things out. The commander-in-chief may be willing to make peace, but I am not! I am going to see to it that your army is cut to pieces! Go back and tell the Chu king that if he runs away now he might still escape with his life!"

Cai Jiuju left after having been yelled at, only to run into Zhao Tong and Zhao Kuo at the gates of the army camp. The brothers drew their swords and said, "If you come back, it will be over our dead bodies!"

After Cai Jiuju left the Jin camp, the Jin general Zhao Zhan also drew a bow and aimed at him with the words: "I have sighted you, and sooner or later I am going to kill you. Take a message for me and tell your barbarian king to be very careful!"

When Cai Jiuju returned to his own stockade, he reported what had happened to King Zhuang. His Majesty was furious and asked his generals, "Which one of you dares to go out and provoke battle?"

The senior general, Le Bo, stepped forward from the ranks and responded, "I will go!" He got into a single chariot, driven by Xu Bo, with She Shu as his bodyguard. Xu Bo drove the chariot at high speed in the direction of the Jin entrenchments. Le Bo then purposely took over the reins and had Xu Bo get off the chariot to inspect the horses' harness, which would show how relaxed and off-guard they were. That got about a dozen guards out on patrol to come over. Without any sign of panic or hurry, Le Bo shot and killed one of them. She Shu jumped down from the chariot and took one of the men prisoner, using only his bare hands. He leapt back into the chariot as the remainder of the patrol ran away screaming and shouting. Xu Bo took over the reins again and sped back to their own encampment.

The Jin army knew that the Chu general had come to provoke battle, so they divided into three columns and set off in pursuit. Bao Kui commanded the central column, Feng Ning the one on the left, and Feng Gai the one on the right. Le Bo shouted, "I will shoot down horses from the left column and men from the right column. If I make a mistake, then I lose!" He drew his bow back and shot arrows here and there, as fast as he could. His accuracy was devastating. Within the next few minutes he had shot down three or four horses from the left-hand column. Once the horses were dead, the chariots could no longer move. Feng Gai, at the head of the right-hand column, took an arrow full in the face. A large number of his officers had also been injured. Neither the right nor left column dared to advance any further, but Bao Kui was still pressed close behind him. As he watched them approach, Le Bo realized that he only had one arrow left. He decided to shoot Bao Kui and gripped his bow tightly. However, then he thought: "If this arrow does not hit him, I will be killed by the Jin forces!"

Just as he was turning this thought over in his mind, the mass of chariots and horses approaching him put up a deer. The animal ran across in front of Le Bo. He now had a new idea and brought down the deer with a single arrow. This shot went straight into the deer's heart. He ordered She Shu to get down from the chariot and collect the deer, which he presented to Bao Kui with the words: "I hope you and your men enjoy eating this!"

When Bao Kui realized how impressive Le Bo's archery was, he was more than a little scared. On being given the deer, he sighed and said, "That is very kind of you. I would not dare to refuse!" He turned his chariots around, and Le Bo also went home.

There is a poem that testifies to this:

In a single chariot going to provoke battle, a general displays his bravery;
His chariot moves with a rumble like thunder, his horses prance like dragons.
What does such a brilliant archer have to fear?
The pursuing troops turn tail and scatter as fast as they can.

When the Jin general Wei Qi heard that Bao Kui had set Bo Le free, he was very angry. "Chu came here to provoke battle," he said. "Since not a single Jin soldier dared to appear, the Chu army must have been laughing themselves sick. Let me take a single chariot and find out how strong the Chu army really is."

"I would like to go with General Wei," Zhao Zhan announced.

"Chu came to ask for peace, and it was only after that failed that they tried to provoke battle," Xun Linfu said. "If you go to the Chu army, it must be to discuss the terms of a peace treaty between us. This is our formal reply to their initial embassy."

"I will go and open negotiations," Wei Qi replied.

Zhao Zhan helped Wei Qi into his chariot and said, "You can pay back Cai Jiuju, I will pay back Le Bo. It will be great fun!"

When the commander-in-chief of the Upper Army, Shi Hui, heard that Zhao Zhan and Wei Qi had been sent on a mission to the Chu army, he rushed as quickly as he could to see Xun Linfu to stop them before things could go any further. By the time he arrived at the Central Army, the two generals had already left. Shi Hui spoke privately to Xun Linfu. "Wei Qi and Zhao Zhan have their present positions purely on account of their ancestors' great service to the state; you cannot give them any important jobs to do. They are angry and stubborn men who have no idea of strategy and deployment, so they are sure to annoy Chu. If Chu were to attack us suddenly, how would we defend ourselves?"

At that moment his assistant, General Xi Ke, chimed in: "We have no idea what Chu is really up to. We had better be prepared for the worst."

"We will just kill them," Xian Hu shouted. "Why do we need to be prepared?"

Xun Linfu could not make up his mind about what to do. Shi Hui withdrew and said to Xi Ke, "Xun Linfu is nothing but a puppet! We should make our own plans!"

He sent Xi Ke to talk to the grandees of the Upper Army, Gong Shuo and Han Chuan, after which each of them took his own troops and lay in ambush in three different places around Mount Ao. The grandee of the Central Army, Zhao Yingqi, was also worried that the Jin army was heading towards defeat, so he sent his people to make sure a boat was ready for him at the mouth of the Yellow River.

. . .

Let us now turn to another part of this story. Wei Qi had always been jealous of Xun Linfu's position, and he was determined to wreck his reputation as a commander. In Xun Linfu's presence he promised that he would sue for peace, but when he arrived at the Chu army, he told them they would have to do battle and then set off home. The Chu general Pan Dang was aware that when Cai Jiuju had gone on his mission to the Jin encampment, he had been humiliated by the Jin generals. Now that Wei Qi was here, he wanted to take revenge. He rushed around to the Central Army, but by that time Wei Qi had already departed. He whipped up his horse and set off in pursuit. Wei Qi had gotten as far as the marshes when he realized that someone was coming after him. He decided to fight. All of a sudden he caught sight of six deer in the marshes and remembered how the Chu general had shot just such an animal in order to escape. He drew back his bow and shot one of the deer, ordering his charioteer to present it to Pan Dang with the words: "In thanks for General Le's gift of fresh meat, I now respectfully return this."

"You are trying to pull that old trick on me," Pan Dang said with a laugh. "If I were to pursue you now, it would look as though we Chu people did not understand how to behave properly." He ordered his charioteer to turn around and headed homewards.

When Wei Qi got back to the entrenchments, he lied about his mission: "The king of Chu would not agree to a peace treaty, so we are going to have to fight to decide the victor."

"Where is Zhao Zhan?" Xun Linfu asked.

"I went on ahead and he was somewhere behind me," Wei Qi said. "I don't know what has happened to him."

"Since Chu has refused the peace treaty," Xun Linfu said in alarm, "General Zhao is in a very dangerous position." He ordered Xun Ying to take twenty heavy chariots and five hundred foot soldiers and go and find Zhao Zhan.

Zhao Zhan arrived at the Chu army camp under cover of darkness. He put down his seating mat somewhere outside the gates of the stockade and took a bottle of wine out of his chariot. While he sat there and drank his wine, he ordered twenty of his men to wander around pretending to speak the Chu language, in the hope of obtaining the password, after which they were to try and break into the Chu encampment. Some of the Chu officers realized that they were imposters and started to interrogate them. They drew their swords and fought. In a moment the camp was in uproar. Guards carrying torches searched the place for intruders. More than a dozen of Zhao Zhan's men were taken prisoner, while the remainder fled. They ran back to find Zhao Zhan still sitting comfortably on his mat. They lifted him up and got him into his chariot. However, when they tried to find the charioteer, they realized that he was one of the prisoners back at the Chu stockade. By that time, it was already starting to get light. Zhao Zhan had to take the reins himself, but the horses were too hungry to move fast.

When King Zhuang of Chu heard that intruders had been discovered, he rode in a battle chariot and set off in pursuit with his own troops. They advanced at top speed. Zhao Zhan was afraid that he would be captured, so he abandoned his chariot and fled on foot into the pine forests. The Chu general Qu Dang spotted this move and got down from his own chariot to hunt him down. Zhao Zhan took off his armor and hung it from the branch of a small pine tree; now that he was no longer so encumbered, he was able to get away. Qu Dang presented the armor and the chariot to King Zhuang. Just as they were about to head back to base, they caught sight of a single chariot coming towards them at high speed. When they looked more closely, they realized that this was Pan Dang. Pointing to a cloud of dust rising in the north, he said, "The main body of the Jin army is on its way!" This dust was being kicked up by the heavy chariots that Xun Linfu had sent to help out Zhao Zhan. Looking at it from far away, Pan Dang had been deceived into thinking that this meant that the main body of the army was on the move. As a result, he made this misleading report and scared King Zhuang of Chu so badly that he went as pale as a sheet.

Suddenly they heard an earth-shattering drumming coming from the south, and a body of chariots advanced with a great minister at the head. Who was this man? It was Grand Vizier Sunshu Ao. King Zhuang started to feel a bit better and asked, "How did you know that the Jin army had arrived so you could come here in time to rescue me?"

"I did not know anything about it," Sunshu Ao replied. "However, I was concerned that Your Majesty might have advanced without fully considering the consequences and that by mistake you might fall into the hands of the Jin army. I came on ahead to save Your Majesty, but the three armies are right behind!"

King Zhuang looked northwards again and realized the dust cloud was not very big. "This is not the whole army," he said.

"*The Art of War* says: 'In all situations it is better for you to put the enemy under pressure than to allow the enemy to put pressure on you,'" Sunshu Ao said. "Since all your generals are here, give orders to advance, Your Majesty! If we can break their Central Army, the other two will not stand alone!"

King Zhuang gave orders that Prince Yingqi and Cai Jiuju should take the Army of the Left to attack Jin's Upper Army; Prince Ce and Gongyin Qi should take the Army of the Right to attack Jin's Lower Army; while His Majesty would personally lead the Central Army and the two wings in an assault on Xun Linfu's main camp. King Zhuang picked up the drumsticks and sounded the battle drums, and every division of the army responded with its own drumming. The noise was like thunder. The horses and chariots raced forward as the foot soldiers charged into battle behind them, running like the wind.

The Jin army was caught completely unprepared. When Xun Linfu heard the sound of the drums he wanted to find out what was going on, but by that time the Chu army had already spread out through the mountains and across the plain, their battle divisions drawn up in front of the camp. This was worse than anything he could have imagined! Xun Linfu panicked, and having no plan to deal with this situation, he gave orders that his men were to fight as best they could. Each soldier in the Chu army was well-disciplined and properly equipped, and they fell upon the Jin army like a crushing avalanche. The Jin troops were moving in a daze, as if drunk, and without any sense of direction. When two such armies meet, it is obvious who will win and who will lose! Caught like rats in a trap, they were butchered by the Chu forces. All was death and confusion.

Xun Ying, who had ridden out in a heavy chariot to find Zhao Zhan, not only could not get to him but even worse, he ran straight into the Chu general Xiong Fuji. The pair of them fought until the Chu army arrived en masse, at which point the small Jin force could no longer withstand their onslaught. The foot soldiers started to cut and run. Xun Ying's left-hand trace-horse was brought down by an arrow, after which he was taken prisoner by Xiong Fuji.

. . .

The Jin general Feng Bo got into a small chariot with his two sons—Feng Ning and Feng Gai—and tried to escape. It was just at that moment that Zhao Zhan arrived, his feet cut and bleeding. When he saw the chariot, he shouted, "Who are you? Take me with you!"

Feng Bo recognized Zhao Zhan's voice and instructed his sons: "Keep going as fast as you can and don't look back!" His two sons did not understand what their father meant, and they did look back.

"Take me with you!" Zhao Zhan screamed.

The two young men said to their father, "It is Grandee Zhao Zhan back there, calling to us."

"Since you have seen that it is Grandee Zhao Zhan," Feng Bo said angrily, "you had better give up your places in this chariot to him!"

He ordered the two young men to get off and give the reins to Zhao Zhan. Once he had gotten into the chariot, they drove off. Feng Ning and Feng Gai, having lost their chariot, were killed in the subsequent fighting.

Xun Linfu and Han Chuan got into a chariot in the rear encampment and led the scattered remnants of their defeated army along a track through the mountains, which ended up taking them to the banks of the Yellow River. Along the way they abandoned countless chariots and a vast amount of equipment. Xian Hu caught up with them. He had taken an arrow in his forehead and blood was dripping down, soaking the surcoat that he had wrapped around his head. Xun Linfu pointed to him and said, "You wanted this battle, and now look!"

When they arrived at the mouth of the Yellow River, Zhao Kuo arrived and discovered that his brother, Zhao Yingqi, had secretly arranged for a boat to be made ready, and he had already crossed the river.

"Why didn't he tell anyone else about this?"

"Whether we are going to live or die depends on what happens in the next couple of minutes," Xun Linfu pointed out. "We do not have time to ask questions!"

Zhao Kuo was furious and never forgave his brother for running away.

"My troops cannot possibly fight again!" Xun Linfu declared. "The most important thing now is to get across the river!"

He ordered Xian Hu to walk along the bank and collect some boats. However, what watercraft there were lay scattered all over the place and could not be brought together quickly. Just as they were busy with this, countless men and horses arrived at the top of the riverbank, in a ceaseless stream. When Xun Linfu looked closely, he discovered that these were the two generals from the Lower Army, Zhao Shuo and Luan Shu. Having been defeated by Prince Ce, they had gathered up the remnants of their forces and retreated to the river. There were now two armies gathered on the riverbank with no way to get across. The number of boats that they had collected was totally inadequate. Looking south, they could see clouds of dust rising into the sky.

Xun Linfu was afraid that the Chu army would take advantage of their victory and come in pursuit, so he drummed his soldiers forward and announced: "The first man across the river will be rewarded!" The two armies fought to get to the ships, killing and injuring each other. Even after the boats were full, those behind them kept clambering in, overturning the vessels. In this way more than thirty boats were wrecked.

Xian Hu gave orders from his position in one of the ships: "Cut the hands off anyone who tries to climb in or who grabs hold of an oar!"

The other boats followed suit in giving similar orders. Hands and fingers fell into the bottom of the vessels like flower petals. A number of soldiers who were unable to hold on found their resting place at the bottom of the river. The sound of screaming and shouting rose from the riverbank behind them and the mountains and valleys resounded with their lamentations. At such a terrible tragedy, even though the sun still shone, the sky seemed to have gone dark.

A historian wrote a poem that reads:

As boats capsize, great waves drag even the sails under;
As men drown, the waters carry a stream of blood.
How sad that tens of thousands of Jin soldiers
Were left to die on the banks of the Yellow River!

Yet another dust cloud rose up behind them. This time it was the defeated generals Xun Ying, Zhao Tong, Wei Qi, Feng Bo, and Bao Kui who arrived one after the other. Xun Shou had already managed to get into one of the boats, but not seeing his son, Xun Ying, he sent someone to the bank to call him. One officer had seen Xun Ying being taken prisoner by the Chu army and reported this to Xun Shou.

"If my son has been captured," he declared, "I will not go home alone!" He climbed back up the riverbank and got into a chariot, ready to set off.

Xun Linfu stopped him: "Ying has already been captured. There is no point in your going anywhere!"

"I will capture one of their general's sons and use him to exchange for mine!" Xun Shou shouted.

Wei Qi had always been a good friend of Xun Ying and volunteered to go with him. Xun Shou was extremely pleased and collected up his clan's private forces, numbering several hundred men. Since he was a good commanding officer and very thoughtful about his men, he was popular in the army. As a result, all of the soldiers from the Lower Army who had made their way to the riverbank decided that they wanted to go along too. There were some who had managed to get into the boats, but now that they heard that Grandee Xun of the Lower Army wanted to go to the Chu army to find his son, they all went back on land and promised to rescue Xun Ying even at the risk of their own lives. The determination to fight spread among the men, so that their morale was higher than when they had first pitched camp.

Xun Shou was the finest archer in all of Jin, so armed with a number of high-quality arrows he launched his assault on the Chu army. The first senior officer he encountered was Sirdar Xiang Lao, who was picking up abandoned materiel and chariots. He was not expecting to be subjected to a ferocious attack by the Jin army and was completely unprepared. Xun Shou shot a single arrow, which hit him in the cheek, knocking him to the floor of his chariot. When Prince Guchen saw that Xiang Lao had been struck, he whipped up his horses and came to the rescue. Wei Qi intercepted him, and the two men began to fight. Xun Shou was observing this from one side and, sighting carefully, he shot a second arrow, which hit Prince Guchen in the forearm. The prince, ignoring the pain, pulled the arrow out of his flesh, but Wei Qi took advantage of this opportunity to take him prisoner. They loaded Xiang Lao's body onto the chariot too.

"This pair should be enough to ransom my son!" Xun Shou declared. "The Chu army is too strong for us to be able to withstand them!" He whipped up his horses and headed off at top speed. By the time that the rest of the Chu army realized what had happened and wanted to set off in pursuit, they were long gone.

• • •

Prince Yingqi had been placed in command of the attack on the Upper Army. However, Shi Hui realized that this was likely and got news of his arrival well ahead of time, so that his troops were ready and waiting in battle formation. They forced the enemy to fight every step of the way. Prince Yingqi advanced to the foot of Mount Ao when suddenly he heard the sound of siege engines as an army marched forward to attack them. The general at the head of these forces shouted: "I am Gong Shuo, and I have been waiting a long time for this!"

Prince Yingqi was absolutely appalled. Gong Shuo fought with the prince, crossing swords more than twenty times. However, not daring to engage in protracted fighting, he withdrew together with Shi Hui. Prince Yingqi was not prepared to give up so easily and set off in pursuit, only to hear the sound of siege engines yet again as Han Chuan led his forces in attack. General Cai Jiuju led his chariot forward to intercept the enemy, but before they were engaged, the mountains and valleys resounded with the sound of siege engines as battle standards rose up like clouds. This time it was the senior general Xi Ke who led his army on the attack. Prince Yingqi realized that an enormous number of troops were waiting in ambush here and he was afraid that he had fallen into Jin's trap, so he sounded the bells to recall his army. Shi Hui held a quick roll call of his generals and officers only to discover that he had not lost a single man. They had built a chain of seven little forts on the precipices of Mount Ao, arranged like seven stars in a constellation. The Chu army did not dare to approach. When the Chu army gave up and withdrew, they struck their flags and went home. This happened somewhat later on.

• • •

When Xun Shou's troops arrived at the mouth of the Yellow River, Xun Linfu's army had still not all made their way across. He was very worried by this. Luckily, Zhao Yingqi, who had sailed across to the north bank of the river, thought to send an empty boat back to the southern bank to collect them. By that time it was already dark, and the Chu army had advanced to the city of Bi. Wu San asked permission to pursue the Jin army.

"Chu's state altars were humiliated by our defeat at the battle of Chengpu," King Zhuang said. "This battle wipes the slate clean. Sooner or later we will make peace with Jin. What is the point of killing any more people?" He gave orders that the army should stay in their encampments. The Jin army crossed the river under cover of darkness in terror and confusion. The panic endured until the last men crossed just before dawn.

Historians criticize Xun Linfu as a clever man who was completely unable to understand the enemy's actions and had no idea how to control his own generals. He could neither advance nor withdraw, and when he suffered this defeat, the last vestiges of Jin's hegemony over the Central States were transferred to the kingdom of Chu. Is this not tragic?

There is a poem that reads:

The commander-in-chief, away from home, found himself helpless.
Who could have imagined that his junior generals would ignore his orders?
How dreadful to cut off men's clutching fingers to keep them out of the boats;
To cross the Yellow River in such a way is indeed shameful!

When Lord Xiang of Zheng heard that the Chu army had been victorious, he went in person to the city of Bi to reward them. He traveled with the king of Chu to Hengyong, where he had built a royal palace. A great banquet was held there to celebrate this victory. Pan Dang asked permission to collect the bodies of the fallen Jin soldiers and build an artificial hill with them, in order that Chu's martial power should be remembered for ten thousand generations.

"Jin had done nothing wrong that they deserved such punishment," King Zhuang said. "I was lucky enough to be able to defeat them, but this cannot be ascribed to any special martial merit!"

He ordered his officers to bury the dead and hold a sacrifice to the river god. When he returned home in triumph, he issued rewards to the deserving. In appreciation of Wu San's plan, he appointed him a grandee.

Wu Ju, Wu She, Wu Shang, and Wu Zixu were all descended from this man.

Grand Vizier Sunshu Ao sighed and said, "The plan that brought us this great victory over the Jin army was presented by a favorite servant. I really am humiliated by this!" He was so depressed that he became sick.

. . .

Let us now turn to another part of the story. When Xun Linfu led his defeated troops back and had an audience with Lord Jing, at first the Marquis of Jin wanted to behead him. One of his ministers, Li Bao, said: "Xun Linfu has served the ruling house of Jin loyally under the rule of several lords. Even though he has now been defeated in battle, that is all because Xian Hu deliberately disobeyed orders. Your Lordship should behead Xian Hu to set an example to others and no more! In the past, Lord Wen was delighted when Chu executed Cheng Dechen; Lord Xiang was terrified when Qin kept Baili Shi. We hope that Your Lordship will forgive Xun Linfu's crime and let him atone for it by victories in the future."

Lord Jing followed this advice and beheaded Xian Hu, restoring Xun Linfu to his former position. He ordered his six ministers to pay special attention to the training of officers and men, that one day he would be able to avenge his defeat. This all took place in the tenth year of the reign of King Ding of Zhou.

. . .

In the second month of spring, in the twelfth year of the reign of King Ding of Zhou, the Grand Vizier of Chu, Sunshu Ao, became critically ill. He instructed his son, An: "I have made my last testament. Once I am dead, you should give it to the king of Chu. If His Majesty offers you titles or official positions, you must not accept them, for you are not particularly clever and lack the kind of skills that would enable you to survive in the cutthroat world at court. If His Majesty wants to give you a great estate, you must resolutely refuse. You must ask His Majesty for the lands of Qinqiu. No one else would want a place that is so mountainous and where the soil is so thin. However, these estates will keep our family from want for many generations into the future." He died soon after he had finished speaking. Sunshu An took his father's testament and presented it to the king. When King Zhuang of Chu opened and read it, it said:

> In spite of my problematic background, Your Majesty honored me with the position of Grand Vizier. For many years I have done my best to make up for my deficiencies and shouldered this heavy responsibility. Thanks to Your

> Majesty's beneficence, I will die in my own bed. I am very lucky! I only have one son, who is not particularly intelligent, so you must not trust him with a senior position. My nephew Wei Ping is a clever and capable man, whom you could employ. Jin has held the hegemony over the Central States for many generations, so even though they have now been defeated, you must not underestimate them. The people have suffered many years of warfare; now is the time for you to let them rest. When a man is about to die, his last words should be taken seriously. I hope that Your Majesty will consider this.

When King Zhuang of Chu had finished reading this missive, he sighed and said, "Even when he was dying, Sunshu Ao did not forget his country. How unlucky I am that Heaven should take this excellent minister away from me!" He decided to go in person to attend the funeral, at which he touched the coffin and wept bitterly. All his attendants shed tears too.

The following day, he appointed Prince Yingqi as the new Grand Vizier and made Wei Ping an emir. He was the founder of the Wei clan. King Zhuang wanted to make Sunshu An the vizier in charge of public works, but mindful of his father's dying words, An refused. He left the capital and took to ploughing the fields.

. . .

King Zhuang had a particular favorite actor, Dwarf Meng, who was also occasionally known as Actor Meng. He was less than five feet tall and made jokes all day long, poking fun at His Majesty's entourage. One day he happened to leave the palace for the suburbs, where he saw Sunshu An carrying home a large bundle of firewood that he had just chopped down.

Dwarf Meng greeted him and asked, "Why are you putting yourself to the trouble of carrying your own firewood, sir?"

"Although my father was Grand Vizier for many years," Sunshu An replied, "not a single coin of public money entered our purse. After the funeral we had no money left, so how could I do otherwise than carry my own firewood?"

Dwarf Meng sighed and said, "Carry on working hard, sir, for when His Majesty goes on his next progress, he will summon you to his side!"

The dwarf found Sunshu Ao's official hat and robe, his shoes and his sword, and practiced the way that the late Grand Vizier had spoken and walked for three days until he felt that he had it down pat. His uncanny abilities made it seem that Sunshu Ao had come to life again. He waited until His Majesty was holding a banquet in the palace and summoned his actors to perform. Dwarf Meng got another actor to dress up as the king of Chu, who made a play of missing Sunshu Ao's sagacious presence. He then took his place on stage dressed as the late Grand Vizier. When the king of Chu saw this he said in shock, "Sunshu Ao has returned safe and sound! It must be that I missed you so much that you have come back to help me!"

"I am not Sunshu Ao," Dwarf Meng replied. "I am just dressed up like him."

"I have been so worried by being deprived of the late Grand Vizier's counsel," the king of Chu said, "that even though you are just dressed up as Sunshu Ao, you can still relieve my mind of some of its concerns. I will make you Grand Vizier! Do not refuse!"

"If you want to give me a job," Dwarf Meng replied, "I would be delighted. However, I have a wife at home who is very wise in the ways of the world, so I would like to go and discuss the matter with her before I accept Your Majesty's commands."

He went away, and when he came back again, he said, "I have talked it over with my wife, and she says that I should refuse."

"Why?" King Zhuang asked.

"My wife taught me a song," the dwarf said. "Let me sing it for Your Majesty."

This song ran:

There are bad corrupt officials and good ones.
There are good incorrupt officials and bad ones.
A bad corrupt official is greedy and incompetent,
A good corrupt official leaves his descendants to live in the lap of luxury!
A good incorrupt official is high-minded and pure,
A bad incorrupt official leaves his children in poverty and want!

Just look at Chu's Grand Vizier, Sunshu Ao,
During his lifetime he never touched a single coin of public money!
Once dead, his family suffers hunger and want,
His children reduced to begging for their bread and living in a hut!
Do not follow in the footsteps of that Sunshu Ao;
His Majesty does not remember the hard work of the dead!

King Zhuang, sitting in the seat of honor, looked at Dwarf Meng during their conversation and noted how uncannily like Sunshu Ao he appeared. He felt most upset. When Dwarf Meng finished his song, His Majesty was in tears: "How could I forget all that Sunshu Ao did!"

He ordered Dwarf Meng to summon Sunshu An, who arrived dressed in coarse clothes and straw sandals. He bowed his greetings to King Zhuang, and His Majesty asked, "Are you really so very poor?"

Dwarf Meng chimed in from one side: "If he were not so very poor, would you know how honest the late Grand Vizier was?"

"If you do not want to take office, let me give you a grant of ten thousand households," King Zhuang said. Sunshu An resolutely refused to accept this, but the king said: "My mind is made up. I will not let you refuse."

Sunshu An petitioned His Majesty: "Since you remember my father's service to the state and are determined to give me a grant of land, let it be in Qinqiu. That is all that I ask."

"The lands of Qinqiu are dangerously mountainous," King Zhuang said in a puzzled voice. "What good will they do you?"

"Such was my late father's wish," Sunshu An declared. "I would not dare to accept any other grant of land."

King Zhuang agreed to his demands.

Later on people realized that because Qinqiu was poor land, no one came to try and take it away from them, so the Sunshu family held it for many generations. From this you can understand how clever Sunshu Ao was.

A historian wrote a poem about Dwarf Meng. It reads:

An honest official is forced to leave his family in poverty;
After his death, their future rests entirely with the sovereign.
If it had not been for the pointed reminder from his dwarf,
Would King Zhuang ever have remembered his old minister?

When Xun Linfu heard about the death of Sunshu Ao, he knew that the Chu army would not be able to go out on campaign in the near future, and so he asked permission to raise an army to attack Zheng. He pillaged the suburbs of the Zheng capital before returning with his troops. The other generals suggested laying siege to Zheng.

"If we lay siege to them," Xun Linfu said, "we are not assured of a speedy victory. If by some mischance the Chu army were to turn up suddenly to rescue them, we would be in real trouble. Let us just scare Zheng and see what they do."

Lord Xiang of Zheng was indeed terrified out of his wits, so he sent an ambassador to Chu to request that his younger brother, the Honorable Zhang, should be offered as a hostage instead of the Honorable

Quji. The Honorable Quji was needed back at home, to help govern the country.

"If Zheng keeps faith with us," the king of Chu declared, "it will be for other reasons than because we have their hostages!"

He sent both of the men home and then summoned all of his ministers for a discussion.

Do you know what they talked about? READ ON.

Chapter Fifty-five

Hua Yuan climbs into bed and takes Prince Ce prisoner.

An old man knots the grass to put an end to Du Hui.

King Zhuang of Chu held a great meeting of his ministers to discuss the attack on Jin.

Prince Ce came forward and said, "Our staunchest ally is the state of Qi, while Jin's strongest supporter is the state of Song. If we were to raise an army and attack Song, Jin would be forced to go to their rescue. Would they dare to dispute Zheng with us?"

"Your plan has its points, but there are certain problems," His Majesty replied. "In the past King Cheng of Chu succeeded in defeating them at the battle of Hong, wounding Lord Xiang of Song in the leg. Song simply swallowed this humiliation. Later on at the meeting at Juehao, the Duke of Song came in person to support us. Later still Lord Zhao was assassinated, and his son, the Honorable Bao, succeeded to the title, but that was eighteen years ago. What excuse can we possibly make for going to war?"

"That is not difficult at all," Prince Yingqi responded. "The ruler of Qi has repeatedly sent embassies to us, but we have never done anything in return. You should send an ambassador to Qi armed with diplomatic gifts. Naturally, his route would lie through the territory of the state of Song. He ought to be stopped and searched at the border, since we will not have bothered to ask for passage for him. If they make no attempt to interfere with our ambassador, that means that they are afraid of us, and in the future they will come to all Your Majesty's meetings and covenants. If they do arrest our man because he has broken diplomatic conventions, we can use this as an excuse to attack them. What more do we need?"

"Who should be the ambassador?" King Zhuang asked.

"Shen Wuwei was part of your train at the meeting at Juehao," Prince Yingqi replied. "You should send him."

King Zhuang ordered Shen Wuwei to lead the embassy to the state of Qi, whereupon he presented his opinion: "The route will have to pass through the territory of the state of Song, so I must have full accreditation and permission from them to go through all the passes."

"Are you afraid that they will not let you through?" the king asked.

"In the past, at the meeting at Juehao," Shen Wuwei replied, "the feudal lords all went hunting together at Mengzhu. The Duke of Song disobeyed Your Majesty's orders, and hence I had to arrest his servants and execute them. Song resents me greatly for this. If I do not have proper accreditation, they are going to kill me."

"On the official paperwork we have changed your name to Shen Zhou. Do not use your old name of Wuwei."

Shen Wuwei was still not willing to go. "It is easy enough to change your name but changing your appearance is impossible."

King Zhuang shouted angrily: "If they kill you, I will raise an army and destroy their entire country in revenge!"

Shen Wuwei did not dare make any more objections, but the following day he took his son, Shen Xi, to have an audience with King Zhuang. He said, "If I am killed in the service of my country, that is part of my job. However, I hope that Your Majesty will treat my son well."

"That is my business," King Zhuang said. "Don't worry about it!"

Shen Wuwei collected the official gifts he was to present, and, having said goodbye, he went out of the city. Shen Xi escorted him as far as the suburbs. Shen Wuwei instructed his son: "This time I am going to die in Song. You must ask His Majesty to avenge my death. Remember my words!" Father and son said farewell, the tears streaming down their cheeks.

After less than one day's travel, he arrived at Suiyang. The border official realized he was an important official from the kingdom of Chu and requested to see his letter of permission to travel.

"In accordance with the king of Chu's command," he explained, "I have only been given official accreditation; I do not have any documents concerning my permission to travel."

The border official insisted that Shen Wuwei stay there while he sent an urgent message to Lord Wen of Song. At that time Hua Yuan was in charge of the government, and he presented his opinion to Lord Wen: "Chu has been our enemy for many generations now. They have sent an ambassador to go openly through Song but without showing the courtesy of requesting a document giving him permission to travel. They are trying to humiliate us. Kill him!"

"If we kill him," the Duke of Song pointed out, "Chu will attack us. What do we do then?"

"Humiliating us like this is worse than attacking us," Hua Yuan declared. "Besides which, if they are bullying us in this way, it is because they know that they are in a position to attack us. Let them move against us openly, so we can expunge all the insults that we have suffered!"

He ordered his men to arrest this "Shen Zhou" and take him to Songyan. The moment Hua Yuan clapped eyes on him, he recognized Shen Wuwei. Now he was even more angry. He shouted at him: "You murdered His Lordship's servants, and now it appears that you have changed your name in the hope of escaping just punishment!"

Shen Wuwei knew that he was about to die, so he responded by cursing the Duke of Song: "You committed incest with your grandmother and murdered your nephew; how you have managed to escape punishment, Heaven only knows! Now it seems that you want to murder an ambassador from a powerful country. When the Chu army arrives, they will crush you and all your ministers to pulp!"

Hua Yuan gave orders that his tongue be cut out before execution. The letter of accreditation as an ambassador to Qi and all the presents he was carrying were burned outside the suburbs.

• • •

Shen Wuwei's entourage had fled when he was arrested, and they now returned to report what had happened to King Zhuang. His Majesty was eating lunch when he heard that Shen Wuwei had been killed. He threw his chopsticks down upon his mat and got up. His Majesty immediately appointed Pasha Prince Ce as commander-in-chief and ordered Shen Shushi to be his deputy. A grand muster of chariots was held, and His Majesty decided that he would be personally present at the attack on Song. He appointed Shen Xi to a military position that he too might participate in this campaign. Shen Wuwei was killed in the fourth month, and the Chu army arrived at the borders of Song in the ninth month, from which their speed of action can be seen.

Qian Yuan wrote a poem:

Although he knew from the start that humiliating Song would result in disaster,
A ruler's order is like a heavenly command—impossible to disobey.
Raising an army in haste as the storm clouds gather,
By now Hua Yuan ought to regret murdering this traveler.

Once the Chu army had surrounded Suiyang, they began to tighten the noose, constructing siege towers as high as the city walls, which allowed them to attack on all four sides. Hua Yuan led his soldiers and the ordinary people to patrol the tops of the walls; at the same time, he sent Grandee Yue Yingqi to go as quickly as he could to Jin to report this emergency. Lord Jing of Jin wanted to send his army to rescue them. However, his advisor, Bo Zong, remonstrated against this: "Xun Linfu was defeated at Bi in spite of the fact that he commanded a force of six hundred chariots; this means that Heaven is supporting the kingdom of Chu. If you go to the assistance of Song, you will not necessarily succeed in helping them."

"At present Song is our only ally," Lord Jing declared. "If we do not save them, we will lose them too."

"Chu is located more than two thousand *li* from Song," Bo Zong reminded him, "and they have no means of transporting grain so far; they will not be able to remain there for any length of time. All you have to do is to send an ambassador to Song and tell them Jin has raised an enormous army that is on its way to assist them, so they must hold firm. The Chu army will leave within a couple of months. That way we will not be put to the trouble of having to fight Chu, but we will still succeed in saving Song."

Lord Jing thought this was very sensible advice. He asked, "Who is prepared to go as my ambassador to the state of Song?"

Grandee Xie Yang asked permission to undertake this mission. "Xie Yang is the perfect person to do this successfully!" Lord Jing said happily.

. . .

Xie Yang dressed in plain clothes and traveled to the suburbs of the Song capital. There he was stopped by a roving patrol of Chu soldiers, who first interrogated and then arrested him. He was taken before King Zhuang. His Majesty recognized that this was General Xie Yang of Jin and asked, "What are you doing here?"

I have received an order from the Marquis of Jin," he replied, "to come here and instruct the state of Song that they are to hold firm and wait for our troops to rescue them."

"Ah, you are an ambassador from Jin," King Zhuang said. "At the time of the battle of Beilin, you were captured by my general, Wei Jia. I did not have you killed but allowed you to go home . . . yet here you are throwing yourself back into my net. What have you got to say for yourself?"

"Jin and Chu are enemies, so you are going to kill me," Xie Yang said. "I have nothing to say on this subject."

King Zhuang had him searched and discovered the letter that he was carrying. When he had finished reading it, he said: "The Song capital is going to fall within the next couple of days. I want you to tell them the opposite of what it says in this letter. Tell them that your state faces an internal crisis and cannot possibly come to their aid, for that will cause disaster for your own country, and hence you have agreed to take them a special message on my behalf. That will make the people of Song lose heart. They will surrender, thereby preventing further tragedy as our forces massacre each other. On the day that this is successfully accomplished, I will immediately appoint you to a dukedom, and you can stay with me to serve the kingdom of Chu."

Xie Yang lowered his head and said nothing. "Do this or I will have you beheaded!" the king of Chu threatened.

Xie Yang did not want to agree, but he was afraid that if he was killed amidst the Chu army, there would be no one to carry out the Marquis of Jin's orders. He therefore pretended to accept the situation and said: "All right."

King Zhuang sent Xie Yang to the top of one of the siege towers and ordered his men to push it close to the city walls. Xie Yang shouted out to the people of Song, "I am an ambassador from the state of Jin, and I have been captured by the Chu army. They want me to trick you into surrendering, but you must not! My lord has taken personal command and he is leading an enormous army to rescue you! He will be here shortly!"

When King Zhuang heard what he said, he ordered his soldiers to pull the tower back. He complained: "First you promise me you will do it and then you betray me. You have let me down, so you cannot blame me for what happens to you now!" He shouted to his entourage: "Report back when you have beheaded him!"

Xie Yang did not appear in the least bit frightened. He replied calmly, "I have never let anyone down. If I were to be loyal to you, it would mean disloyalty to Jin. Would you be happy if a minister in the kingdom of Chu betrayed you for the sake of bribes from a foreign state? Or would you regard such a person as fundamentally untrustworthy? Have me executed to demonstrate that in Chu you only care about external appearances and not principles!"

King Zhuang sighed and said, "When they say that a loyal minister does not fear death, they were talking about a man like you!" He released Xie Yang and sent him home.

• • •

Once Hua Yuan of Song had heard what Xie Yang had to say, he defended the city with even greater energy. Prince Ce instructed his officers to build a pounded-earth artificial mountain just outside the city walls, the same height as the siege towers. He placed his own encampment there, from which he could look into the city. That way he would spy on their every move. Hua Yuan built a similar artificial mountain inside the city walls in order to counter this. The siege began in the ninth month, and the following year in the fifth month they were still locked in a stalemate. By this time, all the food in Suiyang had been eaten and many people had died from starvation. All Hua Yuan could do was to try and encourage his subordinates with speeches about loyalty and righteousness as the people wept. Although by this time they had been reduced to exchanging their children in order to eat them and collecting bones to cook for food, their determination to resist the invaders never faltered. There was nothing that King Zhuang could do.

"Our men have only got enough food left for seven days!" his officers reported.

"I had no idea that the state of Song could put up such resistance!" King Zhuang said. He climbed into his chariot and drove off to inspect the walls of the capital city of Song, only to discover that the defenders were lined up in good order. He sighed and summoned Prince Ce, with a view to giving the order to stand down the army.

Shen Xi cried as he bowed down in front of His Majesty's horses: "My father carried out your orders even though it cost him his life; will you now betray him?"

King Zhuang looked very ashamed of himself. At that moment Shen Shushi was holding the reins on King Zhuang's behalf, and he now took the opportunity to suggest a plan: "The reason that Song does not surrender is that they have calculated that we cannot keep up the siege for any length of time. If you were to order your soldiers to start building houses and ploughing the fields, that would demonstrate that we are here for the long term, in which case Song is sure to panic."

"That is a wonderful plan!" the king of Chu declared. He gave orders that his troops should build a camp at the foot of the city walls, which was constructed by tearing down people's houses in the suburbs for material, as well as cutting down stands of bamboo and trees. Out of every ten soldiers, five stayed behind to continue the attack on the city, while the other five went to plough the fields. Every ten days they would change places. The officers were charged with communicating this change of plan to their men.

When Hua Yuan heard about this, he told Lord Wen of Song: "The king of Chu does not plan to leave! What can we do when the promised support from Jin does not arrive? Let me go to the Chu encampment and speak to Prince Ce face-to-face, for then I may be able to force him to make a peace treaty with us, or perhaps find some other way to resolve the situation."

"Be careful!" Lord Wen of Song warned him. "The very survival of our country depends on you!"

Hua Yuan had discovered that Prince Ce was living in the encampment on top of the artificial mountain that they had constructed, and he made careful inquiries about the names of his entourage and the security arrangements made for guarding this place. That night, he dressed up as an official messenger and had himself let down from the top of the city wall on a rope, landing at a carefully chosen secluded spot just near the hill. He bumped into a patrol, sounding their clappers.

"Is the commander-in-chief in residence?" Hua Yuan inquired.

The patrol replied: "He is."

"Is he asleep?"

"Seeing as he had worked so hard for so many days, this evening His Majesty gave him a pot of wine. Once he had drunk it, he went to bed."

Hua Yuan walked up the artificial mountain until he was stopped by one of the officers on guard.

"I am the official messenger, Yong Liao," Hua Yuan declared. "His Majesty has an urgent and top-secret matter that he wishes to convey to the commander-in-chief. Since he had previously bestowed wine upon the commander, he was afraid that he might be drunk. That is why he sent me to explain the matter in person and then return to make my report." The officer believed what he said and allowed Hua Yuan up the mountain.

The lamps in His Royal Highness's tent were still lit, for Prince Ce had fallen asleep fully dressed. Hua Yuan went over to his bed and gently shook him. Prince Ce awoke, but just as he was about to turn over, he found that Hua Yuan was sitting on his sleeves in such a way that he could not move. In a panic, he asked, "Who are you?"

Hua Yuan replied in a low voice: "Do not be alarmed, Commander. I am the General of the Right of the state of Song, and my name is Hua Yuan. I have received an order from His Grace to come here especially tonight to make peace. If you agree, we can make a blood covenant to this effect immediately. If you do not accept, the two of us will die right here and now!" When he finished speaking, he held the prince fast with his left hand, while with his right hand he took from his sleeve a dagger. Its blade was as white as snow, and it flashed and shone in the lamplight.

"Let us discuss this matter in a civilized fashion," Prince Ce replied quickly. "There is no need to resort to violence!"

Hua Yuan put the dagger away and apologized. "I am not expecting to leave here alive. With things having reached this pass, we do not have time to waste."

"What is the situation inside the city like?" Prince Ce asked.

"People are exchanging their children in order to eat them and collecting bones to be cooked for food. It is more dreadful than you can imagine!"

Prince Ce was shocked. "I had no idea things were going so badly for you! I have heard that in military matters people try and make you distrust the facts and believe whatever fiction they have invented. Why don't you tell me the truth?"

"A gentleman is considerate when other people are in danger," Hua Yuan said, "where a rogue would try to profit from it. I believe that Your Royal Highness is a gentleman and not a rogue. It is for that reason that I would not dare to try and deceive you."

"If you really are in such dire straits, why don't you surrender?" the prince asked.

"The country may be in difficulties, but the people's morale is still high. My lord and his people would rather die with their city than be forced into a treaty at the point of a sword! If you are prepared to show benevolence to those in danger and withdraw your army twenty *li*, His Lordship will restore his alliance with you. That is all that we want."

"I would not want to deceive you," Prince Ce said. "We only have enough food left for seven days. Once that time has passed, if the city does not surrender, we will have to stand down our army. Building houses and ploughing fields was done just to scare you! Tomorrow I will report to the king of Chu and recommend withdrawing the army by one day's travel. However, you must keep your side of the bargain!"

"I am willing to offer myself as a hostage and swear an oath with you, Commander-in-Chief, so that neither of us can go back on our word!"

After they had sworn a solemn oath together, Prince Ce and Hua Yuan also swore an oath of brotherhood. His Royal Highness entrusted a military tally to Hua Yuan, instructing him to set off as quickly as possible. Once Hua Yuan had the tally, he was able to travel openly, walking straight up to the city walls. Once he had given the secret code word, a basket was let down from the top of the walls and Hua Yuan was hoisted into the city. He went straight back to report to the Duke of Song. The two of them celebrated as they waited for dawn and the news that the Chu army had withdrawn.

A bearded old man wrote a poem:

He walked alone at night through a forest of spears,
He climbed onto the bed and persuaded the enemy to a private covenant.
Without this man, how could they have escaped disaster?
A dagger would soon have been called into action.

First thing the following day, Prince Ce did indeed report to King Zhuang what Hua Yuan had told him the previous night. "I almost fell victim to his dagger! I only survived because Hua Yuan is a good man. He told me the truth about the situation inside the city and begged me to withdraw our army. I have already agreed. Please give the order, Your Majesty!"

"Since Song is in such a terrible state," King Zhuang said, "I will wait until I have forced them to surrender and then go home."

Prince Ce kowtowed. "I have already told them that we only have enough food left for seven days."

King Zhuang was furious at this. "Why did you reveal such crucial information to the enemy?"

"A weak little state like Song still has some honest ministers," Prince Ce replied. "How can a great country like Chu be seen to be lacking in such men? It would not be appropriate for me to have lied!"

King Zhuang's face cleared as he said, "You are absolutely right, Pasha." He immediately gave orders that his army should withdraw thirty *li*. When Shen Xi discovered that orders to this effect had already been issued, he did not dare to try and stop this again, but he beat his breast and wailed loudly. King Zhuang sent someone to console him with the words: "Do not be so sad! At least you have been able to show that you are a filial son!"

. . .

When the Chu army had settled in their new camp, Hua Yuan arrived bearing the Duke of Song's order of permission to participate in a blood covenant. Prince Ce then followed Hua Yuan into the city where he and Lord Wen of Song both smeared their mouths in blood. The Duke of Song ordered that Hua Yuan return Shen Wuwei's coffin to the Chu encampment, staying behind himself as a hostage. After that King Zhuang stood down his army and returned to Chu, where he buried Shen Wuwei with full honors. The entire court escorted his coffin to the grave. Once the funeral ceremony was over, His Majesty announced that Shen Xi would inherit his father's office as a grandee.

When Hua Yuan was resident in Chu, thanks to the good offices of Prince Ce, he was introduced to Prince Yingqi and the two men became close friends. One day they met, and the conversation turned to contemporary political issues. Prince Yingqi sighed and said, "Right now Jin and Chu are caught up in constant conflict, both of us locked in an arms race. When will the world ever know peace?"

"In my humble opinion," Hua Yuan replied, "there is really nothing much to choose between your two countries. If someone could bring peace to both countries, so that you can each restrict yourselves to maintaining good relations with your subordinate states, resting your troops and sparing your people from disaster, that would indeed be wonderful!"

"Do you think that you could accomplish such a feat?" Prince Yingqi asked.

"I am a friend of General Luan Shu of Jin," Hua Yuan explained. "When I was sent on a diplomatic mission to Jin some years ago, we discussed the possibility. Unfortunately, there was then no one to mediate with your side . . ."

The following day, Prince Yingqi reported what Hua Yuan had said to Prince Ce, who replied: "Our two countries have both mobilized our armies—it is not yet time to discuss this further."

Hua Yuan spent a total of six years in Chu. In the eighteenth year of the reign of King Ding of Zhou, on the death of Bao, Lord Wen of Song, Hua Yuan requested permission to go home to attend the funeral. They allowed him to return to Song. No more of this now.

. . .

When Lord Jing of Jin realized that the siege of Song by the Chu army had lasted for more than a year, he said to Bo Zong: "The defenses of the Song capital must be crumbling! I cannot break my word to Song. I will have to go and rescue them." Just as he was about to begin raising an army, a report suddenly came in: "A secret message has arrived from the state of Loo."

The state of Loo was a branch of the Red Di, and its ruling house had the title of viscount and was part of the Wei clan. This country bordered upon the state of Li. In the time of King Ping of Zhou, the ruler of the state of Loo was a follower of the Marquis of Li who eventually took over his territory. From this time onwards the Red Di became much stronger.

The Viscount of Loo was called Ying'er, and he had married Lady Bo Ji, the older sister of Lord Jing of Jin, as his principal wife. Ying'er was a weak and pusillanimous man, so all power was wielded by his prime minister, Feng Shu. When in the past Hu Shegu had fled to this country, he was a famous minister in the state of Jin with considerable ability and a great breadth of knowledge, so Feng Shu was more than a little frightened of him and did not dare to behave improperly. After Hu Shegu died, Feng Shu became increasingly reckless. He was determined that the Viscount of Loo should break off his alliance with Jin, and so he slandered Lady Bo Ji, accusing her of all sorts of crimes. Eventually he succeeded in forcing the viscount to have her hanged.

On another occasion he went out hunting with the Viscount of Loo beyond the suburbs, and after they had gotten drunk, the ruler and the minister decided that it would amuse them to have a crossbow competition, betting on who would hit the flying birds. Feng Shu released his bolt, but by some mischance he managed thereby to injure the Viscount of Loo's eye. He threw his crossbow down upon the ground and tried to pass it off with a laugh: "Since my shot went wide, let me drink a cup of wine as a penalty." The Viscount of Loo was now unable to suppress his rage, but he was not able to do anything about it other than to write a secret missive and send it to Jin. He begged the marquis to raise an army and come and punish Feng Shu.

Bo Zong came forward and said: "If you go and punish Feng Shu, you can incorporate all the lands of Loo into your own. The states bordering them are all peopled by the Di. As we spread out towards the southwest, we will gain greatly in terms of both men and taxation revenue. This is an opportunity that cannot be let slip!"

Lord Jing was furious with Ying'er, Viscount of Loo, for failing to protect his wife. He therefore ordered Xun Linfu to take command of the army with Wei Ke as his deputy. They attacked Loo with a force of three hundred chariots.

Feng Shu led his forces to intercept the enemy at Quliang. He did battle with them only to suffer a defeat, after which he fled to Wey. Su, Lord Mu of Wey, was determined to make peace with Jin, so he simply arrested Feng Shu and handed him over to the Jin army. Xun Linfu gave orders that he should be taken in chains to the capital city of Jiang and executed there. The Jin army advanced on Loo. Ying'er, Viscount of Loo, welcomed them at Mashou. Xun Linfu enumerated his crimes in listening to slanderous accusations and murdering his wife, Lady Bo Ji, after which he arrested him and took him back to Jin. The excuse made for all of this was that the people of Li had been left without a ruler for too long. They found a descendant of the original Marquis of Li, set up a fief of five hundred households, and fortified a city in which he could live. This was called "restoring the marquisate of Li," but in fact what they were doing was destroying the state of Loo. Ying'er was so devastated by the loss of his country that he committed suicide by cutting his own throat. The people of Loo mourned him and established a shrine in his memory.

To the present day, fifteen li *south of the city of Li, you will find Mount Loo Shrine.*

A bearded old man wrote a poem about this:

Below the Mount Loo Shrine you hear the sound of weeping;
This may be Ying'er crying in his agony.
How could Feng Shu expect to get away with it?
A strong minister and a weak ruler cannot coexist.

Lord Jing of Jin was concerned that Xun Linfu might not be able to accomplish the mission with which he had been entrusted, so he personally took command of the main army and led them to camp at Mount Ji. Xun Linfu went to Mount Ji to report his success, leaving his deputy general, Wei Ke, behind to determine the distribution of the Red Di territory. Just as they were passing through the Fushi Marshes, suddenly they saw something the shape of a deer's head pass in front of the sun, while the heavens echoed with screams and shouts. The Jin army had no idea what on earth was going on. The scouts reported: "The state of Qin has sent their commander-in-chief, Du Hui, to intercept you with an enormous army!"

• • •

Lord Kang of Qin had died in the fourth year of the reign of King Kuang of Zhou, and his son, the Honorable Tao, had succeeded him as

Lord Gong. After Zhao Chuan had invaded the state of Chong and mobilized Xin, the Qin army had laid siege to Jiao but without result. For this reason, they had offered lavish bribes to Feng Shu, in the hope of organizing a joint attack on the state of Jin. Lord Gong died in the fourth year of his rule and was succeeded by his son, the Honorable Ying, who took the title of Lord Huan. In the eleventh year of the rule of Lord Huan of Qin, he raised an army and came to rescue Feng Shu when he heard that Jin had attacked him. However, on being informed that Jin had already killed Feng Shu and arrested the Viscount of Loo, he sent Du Hui to take his army on ahead and capture as much Loo territory as possible.

This Du Hui was a well-known warrior from the state of Qin. He was born with silver marks on his teeth and his eyes had golden irises. His fists were like bronze cudgels and his face like an iron bowl. He had a thick beard and long curly hair, standing nearly two meters tall. He was strong enough to lift a thousand pounds, and it was his custom to carry a huge mountain-splitting axe into battle, which weighed one hundred and twenty pounds. Ethnically he was a member of the White Di people. One day in the Qingmei Mountains, he killed five tigers and came home with their skins. Lord Huan of Qin had heard of his bravery and appointed him Cavalry General of the Right. With just three hundred men at his command he had wiped out a band of ten thousand bandits at Mount Emei, making him famous. For this feat he was promoted to commander-in-chief.

Wei Ke ordered his men to go into battle formation and waited for the vanguards of the two respective armies to clash. Du Hui did not bother to send out his cavalry—with a huge axe in his hand, he marched at the head of his three hundred battle-hardened warriors as they strode in the direction of the enemy forces. Some cut the feet of the Jin chargers while others cleaved the armor of their officers. It was as if a troop of demons had gone into action. The Jin troops had never sustained such a ferocious attack, and they had no way to resist it; they sustained a bad defeat. Wei Ke gave orders to retreat to their fortifications, forbidding anyone to go out and fight. Du Hui led a group of men wielding sabers and axes to shout and scream abuse outside the camp for three days, but from start to finish Wei Ke did not dare to go out and respond. Suddenly he received a report that further troops had arrived from his own country and that Wei Qi, his younger brother, was the general in command.

"His Lordship was worried about the possibility that the Red Di might be in cahoots with the state of Qin to cause trouble for us," Wei Qi explained, "so he sent me to help you out."

Wei Ke reported on the difficulties that they had faced dealing with the Qin general, Du Hui, who was so brave that he was impossible to fight. He told his brother that he had been intending to ask for reinforcements anyway. Wei Qi could not believe his ears. "What can that kind of peasant bandit do? Tomorrow I will go and oversee our troops; I am sure that I can defeat him!"

The following morning, Du Hui came out to provoke battle. Wei Qi responded angrily, riding out at the head of his troops. Wei Ke tried to stop him, but he did not listen. He commanded all the fresh troops to ride forward, advancing on the enemy. The Qin forces scattered in all directions, whereupon Wei Qi divided his troops up to chase after them. Suddenly there was a whistling sound and three hundred hardened troops advanced as one, all under the command of Du Hui. Carrying their sabers and battle-axes, they set to, cutting the horses' legs off and scything through the soldiers' ranks. On the northern edge of the battlefield, there was a large group of infantry massed around the chariots. Battle chariots are not easy to turn at the best of times, but this made it doubly difficult. They were simply cut to pieces by the enemy, attacking from all sides. Wei Qi sustained a terrible defeat. Fortunately, Wei Ke brought his troops out in support, taking the survivors back to camp.

That night, Wei Ke sat sunk in depression in the middle of the camp, pondering his next move, but he was totally unable to come up with a good plan. Slumped there until past midnight, he was exhausted and fell into a fitful sleep. Just then by his ear, it seemed as though someone whispered the words "Green grass bank." When he woke up, he did not understand what this could mean. He went back to sleep again and exactly the same thing happened. This time he mentioned it to Wei Qi, and his younger brother said, "Some ten *li* west of here there is a large hill that is locally known as Green Grass Bank; perhaps the Qin army can be defeated there. Let me take my troops there and arrange an ambush. If you trick the enemy forces into moving in that direction, we can trap them in a pincer movement. Perhaps we will be able to defeat them."

Wei Qi set off to lay the ambush. Meanwhile, Wei Ke gave orders to strike camp and spread the word: "We are going back to the city of Li." Just as he had anticipated, Du Hui came out in pursuit. Wei Ke fought several engagements; then he turned his chariot around and fled, gradually drawing the enemy towards Green Grass Bank. With a roar of siege engines going into action, Wei Qi's troops rose up from ambush. Wei Ke now turned his chariot around again as they proceeded to encircle Du Hui and his army. Du Hui did not panic. As he swirled his gigantic battle-axe through the air, hacking here and sweeping sideways there, anyone who came within his orbit was immediately killed. Even though some of his men were injured, this was far from being a victory for the Jin army. The two Wei brothers repeatedly led their troops forward to attack, but Du Hui did not retreat.

When the fighting moved to the middle of Green Grass Bank, Du Hui suddenly stumbled, as if he had slipped on a patch of ice. He seemed to find it impossible to regain his footing. The army started shouting. When Wei Ke looked closely, he caught sight of an old man dressed in cotton clothes and hemp sandals, looking for all the world like a farmer, holding a knotted length of grass that he was winding around Du Hui's feet. Wei Ke and Wei Qi's chariots arrived at the scene simultaneously—they raised their spears in unison and pinned Du Hui to the ground, capturing him alive. When his troops saw that their general had been taken prisoner, they started to run away, only to be pursued and captured by the Jin army. Of the three hundred warriors under his command, only forty or fifty escaped.

Wei Ke asked Du Hui, "You call yourself a hero, so why have you been captured?"

"It felt as though something was tying up my feet," Du Hui replied. "I could not move them. Heaven must have decided that it is time for me to die! There is nothing that I can do about it!" Wei Ke found the whole thing extremely strange.

"That man is capable of amazing feats," his brother, Wei Qi, said. "If we keep him here in the army, I am afraid that there will be problems."

"That is exactly what I am worried about," Wei Ke replied. He immediately had Du Hui beheaded before setting off to Mount Jie to see the Marquis of Jin.

That evening, when Wei Ke fell asleep, he dreamed that an old man came forward, bowed, and said: "Do you know why Du Hui was captured, general? It was I who knotted the grass in order to stop him. That is why he stumbled and was taken prisoner!"

Wei Ke was very surprised. "I don't know you, so why should you help me? What are you expecting to gain in return?"

"I am Lady Zu Ji's father," the old man explained. "You followed your father's instructions and found my daughter a good husband. My soul, even down by the Yellow Springs, felt overjoyed by the news that you had saved my daughter's life, and that is why I decided to help you to the best of my abilities, assisting you to success in this campaign. Carry on working hard, General, for your descendants will know great glory from one generation to the next. One day, they will be ranked among the kings and marquises! Do not forget my words!"

. . .

It so happened that Wei Ke's father, Wei Chou, had a favorite concubine whose name was Lady Zu Ji. Every time Wei Chou went out on campaign, he would always instruct his son: "If I die in battle, you must be sure to pick a good husband for Lady Zu Ji. I don't want any mistakes! Then I can rest in peace." However, when Wei Chou lay sick and was dying, he said to his son, "I love Lady Zu Ji very much. When I am dead, you must kill her and bury her with me, so I can have her company in my journey to the Yellow Springs."

When he had finished saying this, he died. Wei Ke interred his father at the military camp, but he did not kill Lady Zu Ji and bury her with him.

"Don't you remember what Father said as he lay dying?" Wei Qi asked.

"Throughout his life," his brother replied, "Father told me that he wanted her to marry someone else afterwards; what he said when he was dying were the words of a sick and confused man. A filial son should follow his father's instructions, but not when they are wrong."

After the funeral was completed, he selected an officer to become the woman's husband. Thanks to this virtuous action, he was repaid by the old man knotting the grass.

When Wei Ke woke up, he told his younger brother about his dream. "I was criticized a great deal at the time for not killing the woman. But who could have guessed that her father's soul would show such great appreciation of my generosity!" Wei Qi sighed.

An old man wrote a poem:

Who was the old man who knotted the grass that put an end to Du
Hui?
In a dream he explained he had come to repay a generous action.
Let this encourage people to do many good deeds,
For then you will find happiness and luck to be your share.

When the remnants of Qin's defeated forces limped home to Yongzhou, they informed their ruler of Du Hui's death in battle. Everyone was much saddened by this. Lord Jing of Jin was delighted with Wei Ke's success and enfeoffed him with the lands of Linghu. He also ordered that a great bell be cast to commemorate this occasion, recording the year and month of the victory. Since it was cast by Lord Jing of Jin, it later became known as the Jing Bell. The Marquis of Jin also sent Shi Hui to lead his troops to attack and conquer various branches of the Red Di peoples. In all, he succeeded in destroying three states—Shenshi, Liuyu, and a subordinate state of Liuyu called Duochen. From this time on, all the lands formerly occupied by the Red Di peoples belonged to Jin.

. . .

At this time, the state of Jin suffered famine for successive years, whereupon robbers and bandits rose up like hornets. Xun Linfu searched the country for someone who could bring these criminals to book, and he discovered a member of the Xi family with the personal name of Yong. This man had truly remarkable talents for making bandits return to their original peaceful occupations. One day he was walking through the marketplace and suddenly pointed to a man and said that he was a robber. He ordered someone to arrest and interrogate this man, who sure enough proved to genuinely be a thief.

"How did you know?" Xun Linfu asked.

"I was looking at his eyes," Xi Yong explained. "When he looked at objects for sale in the market, he seemed covetous. When he looked at the people in the market, he seemed ashamed. When he looked at me, he seemed afraid. That is how I knew what he was."

Xi Yong arrested dozens of robbers every day, striking terror into the people in the marketplace, and yet the number of bandits only increased. Grandee Yangshe Zhi said to Xun Linfu, "You have set Xi Yong to catch thieves, but he is going to be dead long before he has arrested them all!"

"How can that be?" Xun Linfu asked in alarm.

If you don't know what Yangshe Zhi said in reply, READ ON.

Chapter Fifty-six

The Dowager Marchioness of Qi, Lady Xiao, ascends a tower to laugh at her guests.

Feng Choufu changes his clothes in order to allow His Lordship to escape from danger.

As mentioned above, Xun Linfu employed Xi Yong to deal with the menace posed by bandits, only to have Yangshe Zhi claim that he would soon die. Xun Linfu asked him his reasoning.

Yangshe Zhi replied: "There is a famous proverb: 'The man whose sight is so keen that he can see the fish resting in the depths of the gulf will come to a bad end; the man whose intelligence is so incisive that he can see the secrets of other men's hearts will find himself murdered.' Xi Yong is investigating these criminals on his own, which makes it impossible for him to deal with the vast number of bandits threatening the realm; the minute they gang up against him, there will be nothing that he can do. They will just kill him!"

Some three days later, Xi Yong happened to be on patrol outside the suburbs, whereupon a group of several dozen bandits attacked him en masse. They cut off his head and then dispersed. Xun Linfu was so shocked and troubled that he fell ill. Shortly afterwards he died.

Lord Jing of Jin was informed of what Grandee Yangshe Zhi had said and summoned him for an audience. "You already foretold the fate of Xi Yong—do you have any plan for dealing with the bandits?"

"If you attempt to use an intelligent means to deal with these cunning men," Yangshe Zhi replied, "it will be like attempting to cut grass with a stone hoe—the grass will simply regrow from the roots. If you attempt to use violent means to deal with these brutal men, it will be like hitting one stone with another—both sides will be irreparably damaged in the process. If you really wish to get rid of them, changing the way they think is the only way: you must teach them to understand the principles of honesty and shame. You must not imagine arresting a large number of bandits qualifies as a success! Your Lordship must select a good man and exalt him as a model for the people; he will lead these wicked men to transform themselves. In the future you will not have to worry about bandits ever again!"

"Of all the good men that we have living in Jin, whom would you consider to be the best?" Lord Jing asked.

"You will have to appoint Shi Hui," Yangshe Zhi said. "He is famously trustworthy in his speech and righteous in his actions; he knows how to get along with other people without resorting to flattery, he is modest without being irritatingly self-abasing, he is honest without being abrasive, he is respected by others but not feared by them—this is the man that you must send!"

When Shi Hui returned from his mission to pacify the Red Di, Lord Jing of Jin presented the prisoners of war to the Zhou capital and proclaimed Shi Hui's great merit in a memorial to King Ding of Zhou. His Majesty rewarded Shi Hui with a full set of ceremonial robes and appointed him to the rank of a senior minister. He replaced Xun Linfu as commander-in-chief of the Central Army; simultaneously, he held office as the Grand Tutor to the Heir Apparent and received a new grant of land in Fan.

Shi Hui was the founder of the Fan clan.

Shi Hui threw himself enthusiastically into this plan to get rid of the bandit menace—instructing the people and transforming their moral values. Those determined to pursue an evil course then moved over the border into the state of Qin. Thus the state of Jin became well-governed and there was not a single criminal to be found within its borders.

At this time, Lord Jing revived his ambition to become hegemon. His advisor, Bo Zong, came forward and said: "Our former ruler, Lord Wen, held his first covenant at Jiantu and the feudal lords all flocked to his banner. When Lord Xiang was in power, he held a blood covenant at Xincheng and no one dared to disobey him. However, when Linghu failed to keep his word, our long-standing alliance with Qin was irrevocably damaged. That was followed by a series of assassinations and usurpations in Qi and Song that we could do nothing about—the states east of the mountains abandoned their alliance with us and threw in their lot with the kingdom of Chu. Subsequently, we were unable to rescue the state of Zheng, and we tried to save Song but failed; having lost those two states, we are just left with Wey and Cao and a couple of other tiny countries as our allies! At the moment, Qi and Lu are the most important states in the Zhou confederacy—if Your Lordship intends to become the next Master of Covenants, you will have to create an alliance with them. If you were to send ambassadors loaded with gifts to Qi and Lu, to create a good relationship, you can wait for the moment a breach opens up with Chu. Then you can achieve your ambition!"

Lord Jing of Jin thought that this was an excellent plan and ordered Xi Ke, the commander-in-chief of the Upper Army, to visit first Lu and then Qi, armed with expensive gifts.

• • •

Lord Xuan of Lu had only been able to take power thanks to the support offered to him by Lord Hui of Qi, so he was extremely cautious in all his actions, sending regular diplomatic missions and gifts to his neighbor. When the Honorable Wuye succeeded as Lord Qing of Qi, he continued according to the old rules, never missing a single occasion. When Xi Ke arrived in Lu to reestablish diplomatic relations, a formal ceremony of greeting was carried out, and afterwards—since it was time for Lord Xuan of Lu to send his own diplomatic mission to Qi—he arranged that the senior minister Jisun Xingfu would travel with Xi Ke. When they arrived at the suburbs of the Qi capital, they discovered that their mission had coincided with those of a senior minister in Wey, Sun Liangfu, and Grandee the Honorable Shou of Cao. When these four men saw each other, they realized that although each of them had arrived by a different route, this unexpected meeting showed that they all had the same aim in mind. These four senior officials all spent the night in an official guesthouse, and the following day they were offered a court audience, at which each expressed his master's intention. After the audience was over, Lord Qing of Qi surveyed the four ambassadors with a sudden sense of shock. Nevertheless, he said politely, "Please return temporarily to the guesthouse, gentlemen, where a banquet is waiting for you." The four senior officials then left by the main gate to the palace.

When Lord Qing returned to his palace, he went to see his mother, Dowager Marchioness Xiao, in an uncontrollable fit of laughter. The dowager marchioness was the daughter of the lord of Xiao, who had married Lord Hui of Qi. After the death of Lord Hui, Her Ladyship had been devastated, weeping day and night. Lord Qing was a very filial son, who tried to please his mother in everything. If he heard some amusing joke or funny story that was making the rounds, he would be sure to tell it to his mother, in the hope of cheering her up. On this occasion, Lord Qing was hooting with laughter and would not say why.

"What has happened outside that has amused you like this?" the dowager marchioness inquired.

"There is nothing particularly amusing going on in the main palace," Lord Qing said, "but I saw something most bizarre today. The four states of Jin, Lu, Wey, and Cao have each sent a senior government official here on an embassy. Grandee Xi Ke of Jin has only one eye; Grandee Jisun Xingfu of Lu is completely bald; Grandee Sun Liangfu of Wey has a clubfoot; and the Honorable Shou of Cao is a hunchback. Of course, I know that many people get sick and suffer from other problems, so not everyone has their full complement of limbs and faculties, but for each one of these afflicted men to arrive in my country at the same time and stand there together at court like a collection of horrors—it just struck me as deeply amusing!"

The dowager marchioness did not believe that such a thing was possible, so she said, "I want to see them for myself."

"Before they return home," Lord Qing said, "I have to host a state banquet for them. In addition, I will also hold a private party. I'll give orders that this party is to be held in the rear garden of the palace. In that case their route will take them past the Chong Tower. If you wait up on top of the tower, Mother, you can see them through the curtains. What is the difficulty in that?"

. . .

Let us now skip over the events at the state banquet to speak only of the private party. Dowager Marchioness Xiao was lying in wait on top of the Chong Tower. According to the customs of the time, when an ambassador arrived, the chariot and horses, even the servants who accompanied him, all were to be provided by the host country in order to diminish the troubles faced in undertaking a diplomatic mission. In the hope of wringing a laugh from his mother, Lord Qing had decided to secretly assemble a one-eyed, bald, club-footed, and hunch-backed man with a view to having them act as the four senior officials' charioteers. Since Xi Ke only had one eye, his chariot was driven by a one-eyed man; since Jisun Xingfu was bald, his charioteer was also completely bald; Sun Liangfu had a clubfoot, and so did the man driving him; the Honorable Shou was hunchbacked, and so was his charioteer.

Guo Zuo, a senior minister in the state of Qi, remonstrated with His Lordship: "A formal diplomatic visit is a very serious matter of state.

You should show respect to your visitors and treat them with all due ceremony—do not make fun of them!"

Lord Qing ignored him. When first two one-eyed men, then two bald men, then two club-footed men, and finally two hunchbacks passed beneath the tower, the dowager marchioness peered at them through the curtains. Without realizing what she was doing, she burst into giggles. Her entourage and servant girls all followed suit, and the sound of their rollicking laughter could be heard outside.

Xi Ke had of course noticed that his charioteer was a one-eyed man, but originally he had just dismissed this as a coincidence and had not thought to blame the Lord of Qi for it at all. However, when he heard the sound of shrieks of feminine laughter proceeding from the tower, he became very suspicious. He drank a couple of cups of wine in a very perfunctory manner and then hurriedly got up from his seat and returned to the official guesthouse. When he arrived, he sent someone to make inquiries: "Who was up on the tower?"

"Dowager Marchioness Xiao!"

A short time later the ambassadors from Lu, Wey, and Cao also arrived back, and they all complained to Xi Ke: "The Marquis of Qi deliberately picked those drivers to make fun of us, apparently with a view to amusing his womenfolk. What kind of behavior is that?"

"We came here on a diplomatic mission with sincere good will," Xi Ke said, "and they humiliate us. We must have our revenge!"

Jisun Xingfu and the others declared, "If you raise an army and attack Qi, we will send memorials to our own rulers to encourage them to help you."

"Since we are all agreed," Xi Ke said, "let us swear a blood covenant. If on the day of the attack on Qi there is anyone who does not do his utmost, may the Bright Spirits punish him!"

The four senior officials got together and discussed the matter throughout the night. When it got light, they each got onto their chariots and ordered their charioteers to drive off as quickly as they could, without bothering to offer a formal farewell to the Marquis of Qi. They returned to their own home countries. Guo Zuo sighed and said, "A terrible disaster for the state of Qi begins here!"

A historian wrote a poem:

A host should treat his visitors with respect—
How could he make fun of his crippled and sick guests like this?
Before the shrieks of laughter from the tower had stilled,
War beacons were lit on all four sides.

By this time, the Lu ministers Dongmen Sui and Shusun Dechen were both dead and Jisun Xingfu was the senior official in charge of the government. After he had been so humiliated in Qi, he swore that he would have his revenge. He knew that Xi Ke had requested troops from the Marquis of Jin, but because of a dispute with Grand Tutor Shi Hui, the Marquis of Jin had refused. Jisun Xingfu was now even more anxious, so he sent a memorial to Lord Xuan to inform him that he had requested an army from the kingdom of Chu. At around this time, King Zhuang of Chu fell ill while away from home and died—Crown Prince Shen succeeded to the throne at the age of just ten and was crowned King Gong.

A historian wrote the following in praise of King Zhuang of Chu:

How illustrious was King Zhuang, who put an end to the evils of his father's reign!
At first he was silent; in the end he brought great glory to the kingdom of Chu.
With the assistance of Lady Ji of Fan in his harem, and Sunshu Ao at court,
He justly punished the guilty, defeating Jin to proclaim his military might!
He made the Zhou king obey his orders—he besieged the state of Song,
He prowled hither and yon with the fearsome might of a tiger!
This barbarian came to be ranked with Lord Huan of Qi and Lord Wen of Jin!

Since King Gong of Chu was busy with his father's funeral, he refused to send an army to Lu. Jisun Xingfu remained just as upset and angry as before, but just then someone arrived from the state of Jin to report: "Xi Ke speaks to His Lordship day and night of the benefits to be gained from attacking the state of Qi, claiming that it will be difficult to become hegemon without this, and the Marquis of Jin was finally moved by his arguments. Shi Hui discovered how determined Xi Ke is about this and announced that he was retiring on the grounds of old age: he has now left the government. Xi Ke is therefore the commander-in-chief of the Central Army and in sole charge of the government of the state of Jin, so any day now he will raise an army to take revenge on Qi."

Jisun Xingfu was delighted with this news and sent Dongmen Sui's son—Noble Grandson Guifu—on a diplomatic mission to Jin, with a view to making a formal response to Xi Ke's embassy and setting a date for the attack on Qi.

Lord Xuan of Lu knew that he owed his position entirely to the actions of Dongmen Sui, so he showed special favor to Noble Grandson

Guifu and treated him in a completely different manner from other ministers. At this time in Lu, three hereditary ministerial families of Mengsun, Shusun, and Jisun entirely dominated the government. Lord Xuan was deeply worried about this, for he was well aware that sooner or later his own sons or grandchildren would fall victim to their machinations. Therefore, the day before Noble Grandson Guifu set out on his mission, Lord Xuan took hold of his hand and secretly instructed him: "The three clans descended from Lord Huan grow more powerful by the day, while our own house declines; you know this as well as I do. During your mission, if you could find an opportunity to explain the situation in secret to the Marquis of Jin and his ministers, you might be able to borrow an army from them. This would allow us to get rid of them. I would be happy to pay the state of Jin an annual tithe of silk in gratitude for their assistance and support them loyally in everything they do. Please be careful and do not reveal to anyone else the words that I have just spoken to you!"

Noble Grandson Guifu accepted this mission and took the lavish diplomatic gifts with which he had been entrusted to Jin. On his arrival, he discovered that Tu'an Gu was in great favor with Lord Jing, thanks to his flattery and fawning attitude, and so he held office as minister of justice. He gave bribes to Tu'an Gu, suggesting to him that His Lordship would be grateful for any assistance that helped him to get rid of the three hereditary ministerial clans. Tu'an Gu had already suffered a total breach with the hitherto powerful Zhao clan, so he had been forced to contract alliances with the Luan and Xi families, though their dealings were still kept a complete secret. However, when he heard what Noble Grandson Guifu had to say, Tu'an Gu discussed the matter with Luan Shu.

"The commander-in-chief of the Central Army and Jisun Xingfu are both obsessed with the same enemy," Luan Shu said, "so I am afraid that he will not support us. Let me go and see what he says about the idea."

Luan Shu then took advantage of a private moment together to ask Xi Ke what he thought.

"This man seems to be trying to start a civil war in Lu," Xi Ke said. "Don't listen to him!"

He wrote a secret missive that a trusted messenger carried to Jisun Xingfu in Lu under cover of darkness. Xingfu was absolutely furious: "It was Dongmen Sui who was the chief conspirator behind the assassinations of the Honorable Wu and the Honorable Shi. All I wanted was to see the country at peace, so I put up with his machinations and did my best to protect him from any consequences. Now his son is trying to get rid of me! That really is biting the hand that feeds you!"

He showed Xi Ke's secret missive to Shusun Qiaoru, who said: "His Lordship has not attended court for the past month. He says that he is unwell, but this may be just an excuse. Let us all go and ask after his health. If we can make representations directly to His Lordship, what will he be able to do to us?"

A further message to this effect was sent to Zhongsun Mie. He refused to go, saying, "It would not be right for ministers to quarrel openly with the ruler. I am not going to have any part of this." Because of this, they took the minister of justice, Zang Sunxu, with them instead.

When the three men arrived at the palace gates, they were told that Lord Xuan was sinking. Since it was not possible for them to see him, they went home after expressing their concern. The following day, Lord Xuan died. This happened in the sixteenth year of the reign of King Ding of Zhou. Jisun Xingfu and the other ministers then installed the thirteen-year-old Scion Heigong as Lord Cheng. He was only a child, so all the power was gathered in the hands of the Jisun family. Jisun Xingfu gathered all the ministers together at court and announced: "His Lordship is very young and our country is weak—in such circumstances it is vital that the state be well-governed. When the legitimate ruler was killed and the child of a concubine set up in his place, it was done entirely at the behest of Qi: this was how we lost our long-standing alliance with Jin. This is all the Honorable Sui's fault. Dongmen Sui has committed a terrible crime, bringing the country to the brink of destruction, so we must punish him."

The ministers simply agreed. Jisun Xingfu ordered the minister of justice, Zang Sunxu, to launch a witch hunt against the family of the Honorable Sui. Noble Grandson Guifu was on his way home to Lu from Jin, completely unaware of Lord Xuan's death and the Jisun clan's intention of punishing all his late father's connections. This forced him to seek exile in Qi, where the surviving members of his family joined him.

Later on, Confucian scholars wrote of how Dongmen Sui murdered many people in order to assist Lord Xuan in coming to power, but that shortly after he died, his sons and grandsons were forced into exile—what is the point of doing evil if no one benefits from it?

An old man wrote a poem bewailing this:

Having helped Lord Xuan to power, he was wealthy and noble beyond compare.
Who would have guessed he would make an enemy of the ministerial clans?

Once the Dongmen family had fallen and his descendants scattered,
All that remained was an evil reputation recorded in books of history.

In Lord Cheng of Lu's second year in power, Lord Qing of Qi discovered that Lu and Jin were plotting a joint attack on his country. He thereupon made overtures to the kingdom of Chu with a view to creating a defensive alliance, whereby they would come to the aid of Qi if they were attacked. Furthermore, he began to raise his own army, that he might launch a preemptive strike on Lu. From Pingyang, he advanced his army straight to Longyi, well within the borders of Lu. A favorite of the Marquis of Qi—Lupu Jiukui—advanced incautiously and was taken prisoner by army officers guarding the North Gate.

Lord Qing sent someone to stand on top of a chariot and shout to the people inside the walls: "If you return General Lupu, I will immediately order a retreat!"

The people of Longyi did not believe a word of this; they killed Lupu Jiukui and hung his corpse from the top of the city walls. Lord Qing was furious and ordered his three armies to attack all four sides of the city at once; they did not let up for three days and nights. When the city was captured, Lord Qing went straight to the northern quarter and had everyone there killed, regardless of whether they were soldiers or civilians, in revenge for the death of Lupu Jiukui. He was planning to continue his advance, but just then spies reported that the senior general of the state of Wey, Sun Liangfu, was approaching the border of Qi with his army.

"Wey realized that we were forced to leave the country virtually undefended," Lord Qing said, "and hence they have come to raid our borders. We will have to turn around and go home to deal with them."

He left some of his soldiers behind, guarding the city of Longyi, while the remainder marched southwards.

When they arrived at Xinzhu, a city on the border between Wey and Qi, they happened to run into the advance guard of the Wey army, under the command of General Shi Ji, which was already well ensconced. The two armies made camp opposite each other. General Shi Ji went to the Central Army to inform Sun Liangfu of this development: "In accordance with your orders, I invaded Qi, taking advantage of the fact that their army was out on campaign. However, now the Qi army has returned with His Lordship at their head. I think it would be a bad idea to underestimate the enemy. My suggestion would be to withdraw and let them return to their country. We can then wait until Lu and Jin launch their joint attack, for then we are assured of victory."

"The whole point was to take revenge for the way in which the Marquis of Qi made fun of us," Sun Liangfu said. "Now the enemy is directly ahead, why should we run away?"

For this reason he did not listen to Shi Ji's well-meant advice, but moved the Central Army to attack the Qi encampment that very night. The Qi army had a suspicion that the Wey forces would attempt a surprise attack on them, so they had made preparations against this eventuality. Sun Liangfu fought his way in through the gate, only to find the main camp deserted. Just as he turned his chariot around, he found Guo Zuo in position on his right-hand side, and Gao Gu in position on the left; these two great generals advanced in an encircling formation. The Marquis of Qi personally led the main force of the army on the attack, shouting: "Hopalong! Leave your head right here!"

Sun Liangfu fought as though his life depended on it, but he could not find a way to break out. Just as things were in this critical position, Ning Xiang and Xiang Qin led their forces in support, rescuing Sun Liangfu and escaping northward. Nevertheless, the Wey army suffered a terrible defeat. The Marquis of Qi ordered his two generals to go in pursuit. By that time, General Shi Ji of Wey had also arrived on the scene. He told Sun Liangfu, "You go on ahead, Commander. I will defend the rear." Sun Liangfu led the army's retreat in full flight, but before they had even traveled one *li*, they saw a plume of dust rising into the air ahead of them and heard the rumbling thunderous sound of chariots. Sun Liangfu sighed and said, "Qi set an ambush for me. I will die here!"

As they watched the chariots approach, they realized that one of the generals was bowing to them. "I did not realize you had already joined battle, Commander, so I am afraid that I have arrived too late to be able to assist. I do apologize!"

"Who are you?" Sun Liangfu asked.

The general replied, "I am the grandee in charge of Xinzhu—my name is Zhongshu Yuxi. I have mobilized all the forces at my disposal, some one hundred chariots, and brought them here. We will be able to fight a good battle! Do not worry, Commander!"

Sun Liangfu was much relieved by this information and said to Zhongshu Yuxi, "General Shi is located somewhere to the rear. You should go and help him!"

Zhongshu Yuxi raised his battle standard and set off with his troops.

The Qi soldiers by this time had caught up with Shi Ji's remaining forces and were just about to do battle, when they saw a plume of dust rising up in the north and their spies reported that Zhongshu Yuxi had arrived with reinforcements. Lord Qing of Qi was fighting in Wey territory, and he was concerned that his troops' morale would not hold up for any length of time, so he had the bells sounded to order a retreat. They contented themselves with plundering the Wey baggage train before they began their journey home. Shi Ji and Zhongshu Yuxi did not bother to pursue them—they only returned home after they had fought in Jin's victorious campaign against Qi. The Marquis of Wey was deeply impressed by Zhongshu Yuxi's valiance in saving the life of Sun Liangfu and wanted to reward him with a fief.

He refused: "I cannot accept such a lavish gift. If you wish to make me a present, then give me a Quxian and a Fanying, which will be quite sufficient favor and glory to mark me out among my peers!"

According to the Rites of Zhou, the orchestra of the Son of Heaven was arranged in a square; this was called Gongxian. The orchestra of an aristocrat was arranged in a U-shape with the south side being left empty; this was called Quxian (also occasionally given as Xuanxian). Grandees were only allowed a small orchestra, arranged on left and right. Fanying was the name of a kind of caparison for aristocrats' horses. The two things that he asked for were both special privileges granted only to members of the aristocracy, but Zhongshu Yuxi made this request, knowing that His Lordship thought so highly of him.

The Marquis of Wey smilingly acceded to his request.

When Confucius discussed this in the Spring and Autumn Annals, he noted that the different nomenclature and position of the items reflected the social status of the owner and should not be given to someone not entitled to it. The Marquis of Wey therefore failed to give a suitable reward.

This all happened somewhat later on, and does not need to be described further.

. . .

Having collected the remnants of his defeated army, Sun Liangfu entered the city of Xinzhu and rested there for a few days. His generals requested that he set a date for their return, but Sun Liangfu said: "My original intention was to take revenge on Qi. Now I have led our forces into a terrible defeat—how can I go home and face His Lordship? Let me beg for an army from the state of Jin with which we can capture the Marquis of Qi alive; that is the only way to assuage the anger swelling in my breast!"

He ordered Shi Ji and the others to remain encamped at Xinzhu, while he went in person to the state of Jin to ask for the loan of an army.

When he arrived, he discovered that the minister of justice of the state of Lu, Zang Sunxu, was there on a similar mission. The two of them discussed the situation with Xi Ke first, then they had an audience with Lord Jing of Jin. Given that both his allies and his own senior ministers were in complete agreement, and every argument one put forward was backed up by the others, Lord Jing found he had no choice but to agree. Xi Ke was concerned about the military might of Qi, so he requested a force of eight hundred chariots, to which the Marquis of Jin agreed. Xi Ke was placed in command of the Central Army, with Jie Zhang as his charioteer and Zheng Qiuhuan as his bodyguard and right-hand man. Shi Xie was appointed to command the Upper Army, Luan Shu was appointed general of the Lower Army, and Han Que was the minister of war. In the sixth month of summer in the eighteenth year of the reign of King Ding of Zhou, the army marched out of Jiang and headed eastward. Zang Sunxu had already returned home to report the appointed day for the attack. Jisun Xingfu and Shusun Qiaoru led their forces to meet the Jin army as they all converged on Xinzhu. Sun Liangfu had already made arrangements with the Honorable Shou of Cao. The armies gathered at Xinzhu, whereupon the chain of command was decided and the order of battle formation set out. The combined army column stretched for thirty *li* without a break.

Lord Qing of Qi had already sent his spies to the border with Lu to investigate what was going on, so he was aware of the fact that Zang Sunxu had gone to Jin to beg for the loan of an army.

"If we wait until the Jin army invades," Lord Qing said, "that will cause great trouble and distress to our people. We will have to launch our counterattack at the border."

He mustered a large army, from which he selected five hundred chariots. In the course of the next three days and nights, they advanced more than five hundred *li*. When he arrived at Anhua, he ordered his troops to make camp. His scouts reported: "The Jin army is already encamped at the foot of Mount Moji."

Lord Qing sent a messenger to arrange for a date to do battle, and Xi Ke agreed they would fight on the following day. The senior general Gao Gu suggested to Lord Qing: "Qi and Jin have never fought against each other, so we have no idea what their army is like. I would like to test them."

He rode a single chariot in the direction of the Jin encampment with the intention of provoking battle. A junior general immediately got on his chariot and came out through the gates of the camp. Gao Gu picked up a huge stone and threw it at him, hitting him right in the middle of the chest. He fell to the floor, and his charioteer fled in terror. Gao Gu leapt from his own chariot into that of the Jin general, and with his foot holding his captive firmly in place, he tied him up thoroughly, before racing back to the Qi encampment. He rode around it once, shouting: "This one was let down by being too brave!"

The Qi soldiers hooted with laughter. When the Jin soldiers realized what he was up to, they came in pursuit, but none of them were able to catch up with him. Gao Gu informed Lord Qing: "The Jin army is numerous but very few of them know how to fight a battle. You have nothing to worry about!"

The following day, Lord Qing of Qi put on his armor and went out to do battle. Bing Xia drove his chariot and Feng Choufu served as his bodyguard. The two armies went into battle formation at An. Guo Zuo was in command of the Army of the Right, with orders to deal with Lu; Gao Gu was in command of the Army of the Left, with orders to deal with Wey and Cao. The two sides held their positions, with no one being prepared to be the first to engage their troops. They were waiting for news from the Central Army. The Marquis of Qi was very proud of his own bravery and had no time for the Jin army—he was wearing a brocade silk robe and fancy armor, riding in a golden chariot. He ordered his troops to draw their bows and wait. He declared: "When you see the direction in which my horses are traveling, fire!"

The drums sounded, his horses galloped in the direction of the Jin battle lines, and arrows flew like hornets: vast numbers of Jin soldiers died in the first assault. Jie Zhang's wrist and elbow were both struck by arrows, and the blood from his wounds dripped down to soak the wheels of the chariot. Nevertheless, he endured the pain and kept tight hold of the reins. When Xi Ke drummed the army forward, he too received an arrow wound in the left thigh. The blood poured down his leg and into his shoes, so his beats began to falter.

"The eyes and ears of every one of your soldiers are trained upon the battle standards and drums of the Central Army," Jie Zang told him, "for they determine whether the Three Armies will advance or retreat. As long as you are alive, whatever happens, you must not let up!"

"Jie Zhang is right," Zheng Qiuhuan declared. "Life and death are determined by fate!"

Xi Ke grabbed hold of the drumsticks again and carried on banging; Jie Zhang whipped up his horses and advanced through a hail of arrows; Zheng Qiuhuan held a shield in his left hand, which he used to protect

Xi Ke, while with his right he swung a halberd with which to kill the enemy. As the left and the right wing advanced, the sound of drumming shook the heavens and the Jin army knew that their forces had won. It was time to rush into battle: their forces advanced and fell upon the hapless Qi army like a crushing wave, an irresistible force. Having suffered a terrible defeat, the Qi army turned tail and fled. Han Jue realized that Xi Ke had sustained a serious injury, and said: "Let the commander-in-chief rest for now. The rest of us can go in pursuit of these bastards!" When he had finished speaking, he set off after them, leading his own division of men. The Qi army had scattered in every direction, while Lord Qing escaped by skirting Mount Huabuzhu. Han Jue spotted the golden chariot in the distance and chased it down as fast as he possibly could.

Feng Choufu turned his head to speak to Bing Xia. "Get out of here as quickly as you can, General, and round up some troops to help us out. I will take the reins for you!" Bing Xia got down from the chariot and headed off.

A vast number of Jin soldiers had now arrived, surrounding Mount Huabuzhu in three concentric circles. Feng Choufu told Lord Qing: "This is the crucial moment to act! You must take off your brocade robe and patterned armor immediately, my lord, and let me wear them. I will pretend to be you while you're wearing my clothes and holding the reins by my side. That is the only chance we have to deceive the Jin soldiers, though it is very dangerous and may not work. I will die to save you, my lord! Take your clothes off now!"

Lord Qing did as he was told. Having exchanged garments, they were just about to reach Hua Spring. By this time, Han Jue's chariot had drawn level with Lord Qing's horses' heads. He observed the brocade robe and fancy armor and imagined that this was the Marquis of Qi. He drew up his own horses, bowed twice, and said: "His Lordship was not able to refuse the requests made by Lu and Wey, so he sent us here to punish you. You had better let me onto your chariot so that I can drive you. Do not let this situation become any more humiliating."

Feng Choufu pretended that his mouth was too dry to speak, so he handed a calabash to the Marquis of Qi and said, "Choufu, go and get me something to drink!"

The Marquis of Qi got down from his chariot and headed off to Hua Spring to get something to drink. When the water arrived, the "Marquis of Qi" pretended to be annoyed at how muddy it was and demanded to be brought something fresher—Lord Qing then skirted the mountain and escaped. By chance he bumped into the Qi general, Zheng Zhoufu, driving his auxiliary chariot, who said, "Bing Xia has already fallen amid the Jin army. Their forces are enormous; this route is the only one that is still comparatively clear. Get into this chariot now before it is too late!" He gave the reins to Lord Qing, who was then able to get away.

Han Jue had by this time sent a messenger to report to the Jin army: "We have already captured the Marquis of Qi!"

Xi Ke was thrilled. When Han Jue presented his captive, Xi Ke looked at him and said, "This is not the Marquis of Qi!"

Xi Ke had at one time been sent as an ambassador to the state of Qi, and hence he was perfectly well aware of what the real man looked like; Han Jue did not recognize him and thus fell into his trap. He angrily questioned Feng Choufu: "Who are you?"

"I am Feng Choufu, General of the Right. If you want to know where His Lordship is, he went off to collect water from the Han Spring!"

Xi Ke was more and more angry. "According to military law, anyone who cheats the Three Armies will be punished by death. You have pretended to be the Marquis of Qi to deceive our army—do you still expect to live?" He shouted to his entourage: "Tie up Feng Choufu and drag him out to behead him!"

"Listen to me, soldiers of Jin!" Feng Choufu shouted. "From here on in, none of you should help your lord to escape from danger! I helped the Marquis of Qi to escape and now I am going to be executed for it!"

Xi Ke ordered that his bonds be untied and said, "It would be inauspicious for me to kill such a loyal man!" He rode away, with Feng Choufu in one of the following chariots.

The recluse Qian Yuan wrote a poem that says:

At the foot of the mountain stood serried ranks of pikes;
The lord in his patterned armor was almost captured by them.
The Han Spring is so deep that it never runs dry,
Yet Feng Choufu's plans ran even deeper.

Later on, people renamed Mount Huabuzhu the "Golden Chariot" Mountain, in honor of the gold carriage that the Marquis of Qi had driven there.

When Lord Qing escaped from danger and made his way back to his own camp, he was deeply grateful to Feng Choufu for saving his life. He rode a fast chariot straight into the middle of the Jin army, to try and see if he could save him; three sorties were made with no result. The two generals, Guo Zuo and Gao Gu, heard that the Central Army had been defeated and were afraid that something might have happened to the Marquis of Qi, so they both led their forces to rescue him. When they saw the Marquis of Qi emerge from the middle of the Jin army, they were deeply shocked. "How can you treat your position as the lord of one thousand chariots so lightly?" they asked him. "Why do you go yourself into the tiger's den?"

"Feng Choufu saved my life," Lord Qing said, "at the cost of being captured by the enemy. I do not know if he is alive or dead! How can I possibly rest easy when I do not know what has happened to him? That is why I came to save him!"

Before he had finished speaking, a scout reported: "The Jin army has divided into five groups, and they are on the march in this direction!"

Guo Zuo presented his opinion: "Our army's morale has already collapsed; you cannot stay here a moment longer, my lord! Go home and defend the capital, my lord, for providing you can hold out until reinforcements arrive from Chu, everything will be fine!"

The Marquis of Qi followed this advice and led his great army back to Linzi. Xi Ke led his great force, supported by the armies of the three states of Lu, Wey, and Cao deep into Qi territory, destroying every pass and fortress that they went through, advancing until they reached the capital. It was his intention to destroy Qi.

Do you know how Qi dealt with the enemy? READ ON.

Chapter Fifty-seven

Having married Lady Xia Ji, Wu Chen flees to Jin.

After the siege of the Lower Palace, Cheng Ying hides an orphan.

The Jin army pursued the Marquis of Qi for four hundred and fifty *li*, until they arrived at a place called Yuanlou, where they made camp and planned their attack upon the capital. Lord Qing of Qi was panic-stricken and summoned all his ministers for a consultation.

Guo Zuo came forward and said, "I would recommend sending the Marquis of Ji's bronze ceremonial vessel and a set of jade chime-stones as a bribe to Jin, requesting a peace treaty with them. You had also better return the lands that we have captured from the two states of Lu and Wey to their original owners."

"Were I to do as you suggest, sir, I might as well be dead," Lord Qing returned. "But if I do not follow your advice, we will have to go to war."

Guo Zuo, in accordance with His Lordship's instructions, took the Marquis of Ji's bronze vessel and the jade chime-stones and went to the Jin army, where he first had an audience with Han Jue, at which he expressed the Marquis of Qi's intentions.

"The states of Lu and Wey have suffered ceaseless incursions by Qi," Han Jue said. "His Lordship was deeply affected by their situation and came here to assist them. His Lordship certainly has no personal quarrel with the Marquis of Qi . . ."

"And if I were to speak to His Lordship," Guo Zuo responded, "and make him agree to return the territory that we have conquered from Lu and Wey?"

"The commander-in-chief of the Central Army is present in the field," Han Jue said, "so I would not like to make such an important decision on my own authority."

Han Jue took Guo Zuo to speak to Xi Ke, who treated him with considerable aggression, but Guo Zuo remained extremely respectful in all that he said and did.

"Your country's fate is trembling in the balance, and yet you are still trying this last-ditch attempt to divert me from my purpose with cunning words," Xi Ke said menacingly. "If you really want peace, you are going to have to do two things for me!"

"Please tell me what they are, sir." Guo Zuo replied.

"First, you will have to send the daughter of the ruler of Xiao as a hostage to Jin," Xi Ke demanded. "Secondly, I want you to construct a series of highways running east-west within the borders of Qi. That way, should Qi ever turn their backs upon this peace treaty in the future, we will be able to kill the hostage and attack your country along these highways, which will take us straight to your capital."

Guo Zuo was by now absolutely furious. "This is completely unacceptable, Commander-in-Chief! The daughter of the ruler of Xiao is none other than His Lordship's mother. Given that the states of Qi and Jin are of equal rank, that makes her equivalent to the Marquis of Jin's own mother. Since when has it been acceptable to demand the ruler's mother as a hostage? As for the position of our roads, they follow the natural contours of the landscape. If we are to change them purely at the whim of the Jin people, why don't we simply hand over our country to you now? From your responses, sir, I imagine that you are not in the least interested in discussing this peace treaty!"

"I am not," Xi Ke retorted. "So what?"

"Do not think that you can get away with kicking us around like this!" Guo Zuo shouted. "Qi may be a comparatively small state, but His Lordship can still put an army of one thousand chariots in the field. Were we to include the private forces of various senior ministers, that would be another couple of hundred. While it is true that we have sustained some losses in the recent campaign, we are far from being crippled by them. If you are determined not to accept this peace treaty, Commander-in-Chief, then we will simply have to gather our remaining forces and fight to the death at the foot of the city walls. If we do not win the first battle, there is always the second. If we do not win the second, there is always the third. If we are defeated in the third battle, then Qi will simply fall to Jin and you can do whatever you like without having to take Her Ladyship hostage or mess about with our road network. Goodbye!"

Placing the bronze vessel and the jade chime-stones on the ground, Guo Zuo bowed once and stalked out of the camp.

Jisun Xingfu and Sun Liangfu had heard every single word from their position behind the curtains. Now they came out and said to Xi Ke, "Qi hates us and will do everything in their power to kill us. In these circumstances, I am not sure that we can win. Why don't you agree to the peace treaty?"

"The Qi ambassador has already left," Xi Ke returned. "What do you expect me to do about it?"

"How about I go after him and bring him back?" Jisun Xingfu suggested. He had a fine horse yoked to his chariot and set off in pursuit. Some dozen *li* later, he caught up with Guo Zuo and dragged him back to the Jin encampment.

Xi Ke then had audience with him in the company of Jisun Xingfu and Sun Liangfu, and announced: "I am afraid that His Lordship will be angry with me if I return unsuccessful; that is why I could not easily accede to your request. However, both the grandees of Lu and Wey have spoken up in your favor, and I cannot ignore their representations—I agree!"

"Since you have accepted our humble request, Commander-in-Chief, let us hold a blood covenant to demonstrate our good faith," Guo Zuo replied. "In the future, Qi will recognize the suzerainty of Jin and pay court to you, while returning the territory that we have conquered from the states of Lu and Wey. In return, Jin will withdraw their army without causing any further damage. Let each party swear a binding oath."

Xi Ke gave orders that a beast be ceremonially sacrificed, and they all smeared their mouths with blood. Having sworn this blood covenant, he left, releasing Feng Choufu and allowing him to return home to Qi. Lord Qing of Qi promptly appointed Feng Choufu to the position of a senior minister. The armies of Jin, Lu, and Wey each returned to their own countries.

When Song dynasty Neo-Confucian scholars discussed this covenant, they mentioned that Xi Ke was made arrogant by his victory, which is why he gave such inappropriate orders that upset Guo Zuo deeply. Even though a peace treaty was made here, the circumstances were hardly such that the people of Qi were going to accept it.

When the Jin army presented their booty seized in Qi, Lord Jing was absolutely delighted and rewarded Xi Ke and the other generals with even greater fiefs. In the wake of this victory, he established the Three New Armies. Han Jue became the commander-in-chief of the New Central Army, with Zhao Tuo to assist him; Gong Shuo became the commander-in-chief of the New Upper Army, with Han Chuan to assist him; Xun Zhui became the commander-in-chief of the New Lower Army, with Zhao Zhan to assist him. All six held ministerial rank. From this point onwards, Jin always had six armies, and they again began to dominate over their peers. When the minister of justice, Tu'an Gu, realized that the Zhao family was becoming powerful again, his jealousy and suspicion were correspondingly deepened. Day and night he was looking for evidence of misdeeds committed by members of the Zhao clan, so that he might report them with embellishments to Lord Jing. These developments also forced him into a close alliance with the Luan and Xi families, because they might help him out when the time came.

For the moment this story will have to be set to one side, but we will return to it shortly.

Lord Qing of Qi was deeply shocked by the defeat his army had sustained, so he divided his time between condoling with the bereaved and comforting their families, while succoring his people and reforming the government—his aim in all of this was revenge. The ruler of Jin and his ministers were afraid that they would be attacked by Qi, thereby losing the chance to seize hegemony. Therefore, making the excuse that Qi was behaving so well, they forced the countries that had lost territory and had it returned to give it back to Qi. This made all the aristocrats regard Jin as untrustworthy and unjust, causing them to become gradually alienated from their former allies. This became a serious issue later on.

• • •

Less than a year after Lady Xia Ji of Chen married Sirdar Xiang Lao, her husband was sent on campaign in Bi. This allowed Lady Xia Ji to embark upon an incestuous relationship with her stepson, Heiyao. When Xiang Lao died in battle, Heiyao was so besotted with Lady Xia Ji that he did not even go and collect his father's body for burial—this was much criticized by the people of the capital. Lady Xia Ji felt humiliated by all the gossip that this caused, so she made the excuse that she would like to go and collect her husband's body herself, but in fact she was hoping to go home to Zheng. Qu Wu now bribed her servants to carry the following message to her: "I have heard so much about you that it has awakened my deepest interest—if you return to the state of Zheng, I will join you there as soon as I can that we may get married."

In addition to that, he sent a further message to Lord Xiang of Zheng: "Her Ladyship would like to return home. Would you send someone to meet her?" Lord Xiang of Zheng then did indeed send an ambassador to escort Lady Xia Ji.

King Zhuang of Chu questioned his ministers about this development: "Why should Zheng send someone to collect Lady Xia Ji?"

Qu Wu was the only person to try to answer him. "Her Ladyship has expressed the wish to collect Xiang Lao's body for burial. Zheng must be aware of this and imagine that she will succeed, so they have sent someone to meet her."

"The body is in Jin," King Zhuang said in puzzlement. "What on earth has it got to do with Zheng?"

"Xun Ying is Xun Shou's beloved son," Qu Wu replied, "and he is at present a prisoner in Chu. His father is worried sick about him. Xun Shou has been appointed as deputy general in command of the New Central Army, and he is a close friend of Grandee Huang Shu of Zheng. Xun Shou is going to employ Huang Shu as an intermediary, to try and get Chu to release Ying from custody. He would be happy to exchange the bodies of Prince Guchen and Sirdar Xiang Lao to ensure the return of his son. Ever since the battle of Bi, the ruler of Zheng has been terrified lest Jin come and punish him. He is going to try and use this opportunity to establish a better relationship with Jin. That is what is actually going on here."

While he was still speaking, Lady Xia Ji arrived at court to bid His Majesty farewell, and report that she was going home to Zheng. Her tears fell like rain as she said, "If I cannot find my husband's body, I swear I will never return to Chu!"

King Zhuang felt sorry for her and allowed her to leave.

When Lady Xia Ji had gone, Qu Wu wrote a letter to Lord Xiang of Zheng begging his permission to be allowed to marry her. Lord Xiang did not know that both King Zhuang of Chu and Prince Yingqi had once hoped to marry this woman; he thought that this would be an excellent match because Qu Wu was an important minister in the kingdom of Chu, so he accepted his betrothal gifts, and no one in Chu was any the wiser. Meanwhile, Qu Wu sent another messenger to Jin to take a letter to Xun Shou, instructing him to offer to exchange the two bodies for Xun Ying, just as he had said. Xun Shou accordingly got in touch with Huang Shu, begging him to act as an intermediary. King Zhuang was determined to get back the remains of his son, Prince Guchen, so he sent Xun Ying home to Jin. Afterwards, Jin returned the two bodies to

Chu. The people of Chu believed that every word Qu Wu had said was true and did not suspect him of any ulterior motive.

Later on, when the Jin army attacked Qi, Lord Qing of Qi requested assistance from Chu. However, Chu was engaged in national mourning following the death of King Cheng and hence could not mobilize its army. Subsequently they heard that the Qi army had suffered a terrible defeat and Guo Zuo had made a blood covenant with Jin.

"Qi has made this alliance with Jin because we failed to protect them," King Gong of Chu declared. "This does not reflect their real wishes. I am going to attack Lu and Wey on Qi's behalf to expunge the humiliation that has been inflicted upon them. Who will convey my intentions to the Marquis of Qi?"

"I will go!" Qu Wu shouted.

"Your route will take you through the state of Zheng," King Gong said. "You had better inform the Zheng army that we expect them to arrive at the borders of Wey in support of Qi in the first week of the tenth month. You can also tell the Marquis of Qi that this is the date we have set!"

Qu Wu accepted this command and went home. On the pretext of visiting Xinyi to collect taxes, he gathered up his household and all his property, to the tune of more than a dozen carts, and sent them out of the capital. He himself set off afterwards, driving his light chariot in the direction of Zheng, speeding along as fast as he could, in accordance with his mission from the king of Chu. On his arrival, he married Lady Xia Ji in a ceremony conducted at the official guesthouse. The joy the couple felt can readily be imagined!

There is a poem that testifies to this:

This beauty was a famous whore,
Her affairs were notorious wherever she went.
This precious pair made the perfect couple;
It is hard to know which one of them was worse.

When they were in bed together, Lady Xia Ji asked Qu Wu: "Have you informed the king of Chu about this?"

Qu Wu explained that both King Zhuang and Prince Yingqi had both wanted to marry her, concluding with the words: "I went to a lot of trouble in order to be able to get my hands on you. Now that we are married, I regard that as my crowning achievement! However, I do not dare go back to Chu. Tomorrow we will have to find somewhere else to live, a place where we can grow old together. Wouldn't that be wonderful?"

"Now I understand," Lady Xia Ji said. "But if you don't go back to Chu, how will you complete your mission to the state of Qi?"

"I am not going anywhere near the state of Qi!" Qu Wu declared. "Right now, the only state that can deal with Chu on equal terms is Jin. You and I are going there!"

The following morning, having written a letter of explanation, he instructed his servants that they should deliver it to the king of Chu. Then Qu Wu and Lady Xia Ji fled into exile in the state of Jin.

. . .

Lord Jing of Jin was still feeling profoundly humiliated by the defeat that he had suffered at the hands of the Chu army, so when he heard that Qu Wu had arrived, he said happily, "This man really is a gift from Heaven!" He immediately appointed him to the position of a grandee and gave him the lands of Xing as his fief. Qu Wu then decided to give up using the surname Qu and took the name of Wu instead, with the personal name Chen.

Today he is better known by this later name: Wu Chen.

He took up residence in the state of Jin.

Meanwhile, King Gong of Chu had received Wu Chen's letter. He opened and read it:

> When the ruler of Zheng offered me Lady Xia Ji's hand in marriage, I was unfortunately not able to refuse. I was afraid that Your Majesty would be angry about this, so I have temporarily taken up residence in the state of Jin. As for the embassy to Qi, you will have to find someone else to send. I do apologize for all the trouble that I am causing!

King Gong was furious when he read this letter. He summoned Prince Yingqi and Prince Ce and ordered them to read it too.

"Jin and Chu are hereditary enemies," Prince Ce said. "Now that he has gone over to Jin, he has utterly betrayed us. We must punish him!"

Prince Yingqi was struck by a different aspect of the matter: "Heiyao committed incest with his stepmother, and that is a crime. You ought to punish him too!"

King Gong followed this advice. He sent Prince Yingqi to take his soldiers to confiscate everything the Qu clan owned, while Prince Ce took his troops to arrest Xiang Heiyao and execute him. The property of these two aristocratic clans was then partitioned by the two princes. When Wu Chen heard that his family had been executed, he wrote a letter to the two princes:

> You may claim to be serving His Majesty but in fact you are just greedy and sycophantic swine. Having killed so many innocent people, I am looking forward to the day when I see you starving to death in the gutter!

Prince Yingqi and his brother kept the contents of this letter a secret, and did not mention it to the king of Chu. Wu Chen came up with a plan for Jin whereby they would develop an alliance with the kingdom of Wu. He went as a military advisor to that kingdom, to train their troops in chariot warfare. His son Huyong ended up staying behind in Wu as a government advisor, to keep avenues of communication open. As a result, the power of the kingdom of Wu grew day by day as they picked off all of Chu's subordinate states in the east. It was at this point that their ruler, Shoumeng, first adopted the title of king. They raided the Chu border area constantly, not allowing them a moment's peace.

A historian wrote a poem about this:

> Why begrudge someone else possession of a lascivious woman?
> As the whole court fought to marry her, brother turned against brother.
> Thus the kingdom of Wu was able to fight for hegemony,
> And Chu could only regret losing an able minister!

Later on, when Wu Chen died, his son Huyong started to use the surname Qu again. Qu Huyong spent the rest of his life in the service of the kingdom of Wu, eventually becoming the prime minister, entrusted with the most important affairs of state. However, this all happened much later on.

. . .

In the tenth month of that year, the king of Chu appointed Prince Yingqi as the senior general. He attacked Wey in concert with the Zheng army, destroying the suburbs of the capital. He then moved his army to attack Lu, making camp at Yangqiao. Zhongsun Mie received permission from the Marquis of Lu to offer bribes. He presented one hundred fine craftsmen, one hundred weaving maids, and one hundred embroiderers to the Chu army; they then agreed to a blood covenant and withdrew. Jin then sent an ambassador to suggest a joint attack on the state of Zheng to the Marquis of Lu, and Lord Cheng of Lu agreed to this.

In the twentieth year of the reign of King Ding of Zhou, Jian, Lord Xiang of Zheng, died. Scion Fei succeeded to the title and became Lord Dao. He became involved in a territorial dispute with the state of Xu over the precise position of their boundaries. The ruler of Xu reported this to Chu, whereupon King Gong of Chu sent someone to make strong representations to Zheng, on the grounds that he believed Xu to be in the right. Lord Dao of Zheng was deeply irritated by this, so he abandoned his alliance with Chu and made a new treaty with Jin. That very same year, Xi Ke was forced to resign because he had failed to recover from the arrow wound that he had received, which resulted in his losing the use of his left arm. Shortly after this, he died. Luan Shu replaced him as commander-in-chief of the Central Army. The following year, Prince Yingqi of Chu led his army in an attack on Zheng, but Luan Shu rescued them.

. . .

Lord Jing of Jin was delighted that he had gained alliances with Qi and Zheng, so he was feeling very pleased with himself. He was very fond of Tu'an Gu, and the two of them would go out hunting and then spend time drinking together, just like in the time of Lord Ling. Tu'an Gu did not get along at all with Zhao Tong, Zhao Tuo, or his older brother, Zhao Yingqi. He slandered them, accusing them of corruption and sedition, forcing them into exile in Qi. Lord Jing could do nothing to prevent this. It was around this time that Mount Liang suddenly collapsed for no reason, blocking the waters of the Yellow River for three days before they worked their way past the obstruction. Lord Jing ordered the Grand Astrologer to perform a divination about this. Tu'an Gu bribed the Grand Astrologer to give the reading that this was because punishments were not meted out to the right people.

"I have never punished anyone," Lord Jing said in surprise, "so why would it say that I am not punishing the right people?"

Tu'an Gu presented his opinion: "When the oracle speaks of punishments not being meted out to the right people, it could mean that the innocent are suffering, but it could also mean that people who ought to be punished are escaping scot-free. Zhao Dun assassinated Lord Ling in the Peach Garden; this is written in our historical records. This is an unforgivable crime, and yet your father, Lord Cheng, not only did not execute him, he entrusted the government of the country to him. This situation has carried on to the present day—the sons and grandsons of this traitor fill the court. Is this how you warn later generations against following their example? I have heard that Zhao Shuo, Zhao Tong, and Zhao Tuo are all engaged in treasonous conspiracies, backed by their powerful clan. Mount Liang crumbled because Heaven wants you to punish the murder of Lord Ling—this is the crime of the Zhao family!"

Lord Jing had already been deeply offended by the arrogance shown by Zhao Tong and Zhao Tuo, so he was swayed by Tu'an Gu's words. Therefore, he discussed the matter further with Han Jue.

"I do not think that Zhao Dun can be held responsible for what happened at the Peach Garden," Han Jue said thoughtfully. "Furthermore, every generation of the Zhao family has done great things in the service of the state. I do not understand why you doubt the loyalty of the descendants of such a great minister merely at the word of some jumped-up little jack-in-office!"

Lord Jing could not make up his mind what to do. He asked Luan Shu and Xi Yi about it. The two of them had already received full instructions from Tu'an Gu as to what to say. They stuck to the script and would not admit any positive achievement by any member of the Zhao clan. Lord Jing was now convinced that every word Tu'an Gu had said was the truth. He therefore proclaimed Zhao Dun guilty of murder and instructed Tu'an Gu: "You deal with this! All I ask is that you do not alarm the people of the capital!"

Han Jue knew that Tu'an Gu was up to something, so that very night he went to the Lower Palace to warn Zhao Shuo and tell him to get ready to flee.

"My father prevented the late Lord Ling from carrying out his threat to execute him, and the only thing he gained thereby was an evil reputation," Zhao Shuo said. "Tu'an Gu has received an order from His Lordship to kill me; how could I dare to run away? However, my wife is pregnant and will give birth any day now. It does not matter if she gives birth to a daughter, but if Heaven blesses us with a son, the ancestral sacrifices of the Zhao clan may yet continue. In that case, I beg you to save the baby. Even if I die, at least let my son survive!"

Han Jue spoke through his tears. "I know that everything I have achieved is thanks to your father's assistance; Zhao Dun treated me as if I were his own son. I am afraid that today there is nothing I can do to help you—I cannot cut off the bastard's head! Given that it is His Lordship's order, I have no choice but to obey! This wicked man has been holding back his resentment for a long time: now the floodgates have burst and we are on the verge of a cataclysm! There is nothing I can do to stop it. But why don't you go send your wife secretly into the palace now, before the troops arrive? At least there she should be safe. When your son is grown, the day for revenge will have come!"

"I will do just as you suggest," Zhao Shuo said. The two men dried their tears and said goodbye.

Zhao Shuo secretly made the following agreement with his wife, Lady Zhuang Ji: "If you give birth to a daughter, then I want her to be named Wen, meaning 'Cultured.' If you give birth to a son, then I would like him to be named Wu, or 'Martial.' Cultured people are completely useless, but a martial son will avenge us!"

The only person who knew about this was Cheng Ying, Zhao Shuo's close associate. He smuggled Lady Zhuang Ji out the back door and into a covered carriage, which he then conveyed to the palace of Jin, where he placed her in the care of her mother, Lady Cheng, the Dowager Marchioness of Jin. The bitterness and pain that the couple felt in parting does not need to be described.

. . .

When it got light, Tu'an Gu ordered armed guards to surround the Lower Palace. He had the document that Lord Jing had written concerning the Zhao clan's crimes suspended from the main gate, and put out the word that he had received His Lordship's orders to punish the guilty. He then executed Zhao Shao, Zhao Tong, Zhao Tuo, and Zhao Zhan, together with all their family: young and old, male and female. Bodies lay everywhere in the main halls of the house and the blood poured down the steps and soaked the courtyards. When they counted the dead, they discovered that Lady Zhuang Ji was missing.

"Her Ladyship is not a source of concern," Tu'an Gu said. "The problem is that I have heard that she is expecting a baby. If by some mischance she were to give birth to a boy, leaving this villainous spawn alive would simply be storing up trouble for the future!"

Someone reported: "A covered carriage entered the palace in the middle of the night."

"That must be Lady Zhuang Ji," Tu'an Gu decided. Immediately he presented his opinion to the Marquis of Jin. "The traitor's family has now been executed, but Her Ladyship has now gone to the palace. I beg you to make a decision on the matter!"

"Mother loves my older sister," Lord Jing said. "You cannot possibly expect me to do anything to harm her!"

Tu'an Gu then presented his opinion: "Her Ladyship is pregnant. If she were to give birth to a boy and we let this last remnant of the traitor's family survive, when he grows up he will take revenge upon us. We will just see a repeat of the murder at the Pear Garden. You need to think about this very carefully!"

"If the baby is a boy, kill him!" Lord Jing commanded.

Tu'an Gu sent out spies to keep watch day and night for any news of Lady Zhuang Ji's baby. A couple of days later, Lady Zhuang Ji did indeed give birth to a son. The dowager marchioness gave instructions to everyone in the palace to pretend that the baby was a girl. Tu'an Gu did not believe this, so he sent a nurse from his own household into the palace to inspect the child. Lady Zhuang Ji was terrified and discussed the matter with her mother, the dowager marchioness. They decided to say that the baby girl had died. At this time Lord Jing of Jin spent all his time sunk in drunken debauch, and the government of the state was entrusted to Tu'an Gu, leaving him free to do exactly as he pleased. Tu'an Gu suspected that the baby was neither female nor dead, so he personally escorted maids from his own household to search the palace from top to bottom.

Lady Zhuang Ji tied the baby under her own voluminous robes and prayed to Heaven: "If Heaven is determined to destroy the Zhao clan, let my son wake up and cry. If the Zhao family is destined to continue, let my baby remain silent!"

When the maids dragged Lady Zhuang Ji out of her rooms so that they could be searched, they discovered nothing. The baby tied under his mother's clothing did not make a sound. Although Tu'an Gu had searched the palace from one end to the other, he remained suspicious.

Someone suggested: "Perhaps the orphan has already been smuggled out of the palace!"

Tu'an Gu had the following reward posted on the gates: "Anyone who reports the location of the orphan will be rewarded with one thousand pieces of gold. Anyone who knows his whereabouts and conceals this information will be punished according to the law on hiding a traitor, and his whole family will be executed!" He also ordered that anyone going in or out of the palace should be interrogated.

. . .

Zhao Dun had two particularly close subordinates: Gongsun Chujiu and Cheng Ying. When the pair of them first heard that Tu'an Gu had surrounded the Lower Palace, Gongsun Chujiu suggested that they should go and rescue them.

"That man is claiming that he is simply carrying out His Lordship's orders," Cheng Ying replied. "He says he is punishing traitors. If we go there he will just kill us, which will not help the Zhao family at all!"

"I know it won't help," Gongsun Chujiu wailed, "but they are in danger and I cannot bear to just stand by and watch!"

"Her Ladyship is pregnant," Cheng Ying informed him. "If she gives birth to a son, the two of us can support him. If she gives birth to a daughter, it will not be too late to die for our master then."

When they heard that Lady Zhuang Ji had given birth to a daughter, Gongsun Chujiu wept and said, "Does Heaven really want bring the Zhao clan to an end?"

"I don't believe it," Chen Ying declared. "Let me make further investigations."

He gave lavish bribes to one of the palace maids, who then took a letter through to Lady Zhuang Ji. Her Ladyship knew of Cheng Ying's strong sense of loyalty and honor, so she smuggled out a message consisting of a single word: "Wu." Cheng Ying was thrilled: "Her Ladyship has given birth to a boy!"

When Tu'an Gu searched the palace without finding the baby, Cheng Ying said to Gongsun Chujiu: "The orphan of the Zhao family is in the palace but they have not found him, thank Heaven! However, they will not be able to keep his existence a secret for much longer. The minute word gets out, that bastard Tu'an Gu is going to be back for another search. We must come up with a plan to get him out of the palace and hide him somewhere far away—that is the only way to keep him safe!"

Gongsun Chujiu was sunk in deep thought for a time, then he asked Cheng Ying: "It will be difficult to save the orphan, but it would also be hard to die. Which do you think is worse?"

"In this situation, getting yourself killed is easy. It is saving the orphan that is going to be difficult."

"You take the difficult job," Gongsun Chujiu proposed, "and I will take the easy one."

"Do you have a plan?"

"We will find some other baby and pretend that he is the orphan of the Zhao clan," Gongsun Chujiu said. "I will take that baby to Mount Shouyang; you can then go to the authorities and tell them where the child is hidden. Once that bastard Tu'an Gu has gotten his hands on the pretend orphan, the real one will be able to escape."

"Swapping the babies is easy," Cheng Ying agreed. "However, we must find a way to get the real orphan out of the palace, so that we can keep him safe."

"Of the generals serving in the Jin army, Han Jue has always been the closest to the Zhao family," Gongsun Chujiu said thoughtfully. "He could be entrusted with the task of smuggling the baby out of the palace."

"My son was born at about the same time as the orphan," Cheng Ying said. "He can replace him. After all, if we are discovered to have been involved in the conspiracy to hide the orphan, our whole families will be executed anyway." Then he burst into tears: "It is unbearable, though, that my son should have to die before me!"

"You are doing the right thing," Gongsun Chujiu said angrily. "Why are you crying?"

Cheng Ying then dried his tears and left. That very night, he carried his son in his arms and placed him in the hands of Gongsun Chujiu. Immediately afterwards, he went to have an audience with Han Jue. First, he showed him the message with the word "Wu," then he explained what he and Gongsun Chujiu had planned.

"Her Ladyship is complaining about feeling ill, so I have been commanded to find her a doctor," Han Jue explained. "If you can persuade that criminal lunatic Tu'an Gu to head off on a wild-goose chase around Mount Shouyang, I have a plan for how to get the orphan out of the palace."

Cheng Ying started to spread the word: "If the minister of justice, Tu'an Gu, wants to lay hands on the orphan of the Zhao clan, why is he messing around in the palace?"

When one of Tu'an Gu's subordinates heard this, he asked, "Do you know where the orphan of the Zhao clan is?"

"Give me a thousand pieces of gold and I will tell you," Cheng Ying said. The man took him to meet Tu'an Gu, who began by asking his name.

"I am Cheng Ying," he replied. "Gongsun Chujiu and I used to work for the Zhao family. When Her Ladyship gave birth to a boy, she had one of her women to take him out of the palace and instructed us to hide him. I was afraid that sooner or later someone would find out and go to the authorities. He would then be rewarded with a thousand pieces of gold, but my whole family would be executed. That is why I have come to hand myself in."

"Where is the orphan now?" Tu'an Gu demanded.

"Send your entourage away," Cheng Ying said, "and I will tell you."

Tu'an Gu immediately ordered his servants to withdraw.

"He is hidden deep in Mount Shouyang," Cheng Ying whispered. "If you hurry you will be able to catch him, otherwise in a few days' time he will be taken to the state of Qin. I am afraid that you are going to have to go yourself, sir, for so many people owe a great deal to the Zhao family and might be tempted to let the child go. This is not a task that you can entrust to anyone else."

"You are coming with me!" Tu'an Gu said. "If you are telling the truth you will receive great rewards. If you are lying, I am going to kill you!"

"I have just come from the mountains," Cheng Ying told him, "and I am practically starving. Please give me something to eat!" Tu'an Gu had him served food and wine. When Cheng Ying had finished eating, he told him that they needed to be on their way as quickly as possible.

Tu'an Gu led his own force of three thousand armed guards in the direction that Cheng Ying indicated, heading straight for Mount Shouyang. Once they had traveled a few *li*, the road began to get narrower and more difficult. They saw a small thatched cottage located overlooking the stream, its wicker gate firmly closed. Cheng Ying pointed to it and said, "That is where Gongsun Chujiu has the orphan hidden." When Cheng Ying knocked on the door, Gongsun Chujiu came to greet him. Seeing how many soldiers there were, he made as if to run away and hide. Cheng Ying shouted, "There is nowhere to go! The minister of justice already knows that you have the orphan here and has come to collect him. Hand him over immediately!" Before he had finished speaking, the guards had laid violent hands upon Gongsun Chujiu and dragged him in front of Tu'an Gu.

"Where is the orphan?" he demanded.

Chujiu tried to deny the whole thing: "I know nothing about it."

Tu'an Gu gave orders that the hut be searched. There was a very strong lock on one of the doors; the soldiers broke it open and went into the room. It was pitch dark, but they could hear the sound of a baby crying hysterically, coming from a bamboo-frame bed. They carried the baby out and discovered that he was wrapped in fine embroidered silk clothes: this was certainly the child of a noble family. When Gongsun Chujiu caught sight of the baby, he tried to snatch it away from them, but he was held back by his bonds and could not move.

"You bastard, Cheng Ying!" he cursed. "When the Lower Palace was surrounded, I wanted us to die together. It was you who said that Her Ladyship was pregnant and that if we died there would be nobody to protect the orphan! Her Ladyship entrusted her son to the two of us, so we hid in these mountains. We plotted this together! Now you are so greedy for the reward of one thousand pieces of gold that you have gone to the authorities and told them everything! It doesn't matter if I get killed, but I have betrayed Zhao Dun's trust in me!" He cursed on and on, using the worst swear words that he could.

Cheng Ying looked deeply ashamed and humiliated. He said to Tu'an Gu, "Why don't you kill him?"

Tu'an Gu shouted his order: "Behead Gongsun Chujiu!" He lifted up the baby and dashed him against the ground. The baby gave a sobbing sound and died. How sad!

An old man wrote a poem:

Even in the midst of the palace no member of the Zhao family was safe;
They were lucky that Cheng Ying put his own son in the orphan's place.
Tu'an Gu was determined that he would not escape his net,
But he could not have imagined Gongsun Chujiu's trick!

When Tu'an Gu headed to Mount Shouyang to capture the orphan, the capital was rocked by rumors. There were some people who were pleased at the rise of the Tu'an family, while others bewailed the fall of the Zhao clan. In the absence of the minister of justice, the palace guards did not bother with questioning people. Han Jue ordered one of his most trusted confidantes to dress up as a doctor and enter the palace to treat Her Ladyship's illness. The one-word message that he had been given by Cheng Ying, "Wu," was pasted inside his medicine chest. When Lady Zhuang Ji saw that, she knew exactly what was afoot. After he had checked her pulse, he asked her some questions about her health before and after giving birth. Lady Zhuang Ji's attendants on this occasion were all servants devoted to her interests, and they immediately placed the baby inside the chest. The baby started to cry. Lady Zhuang Ji placed her hand on top of the medicine chest and prayed: "Zhao Wu! Zhao Wu! More than a hundred innocent members of our family are dead—you are the only survivor! When you leave the palace, you must not cry!"

When she finished speaking, the baby gradually stopped crying. When they left the palace, there was no one there to interrogate the "doctor." Once Han Jue had the orphan in his possession, he felt as if he had been given an invaluable treasure, and hid him away in the most secluded part of his mansion in the care of a single wet-nurse. Even his closest relatives knew nothing about what was going on.

. . .

When Tu'an Gu returned to his mansion, he gave Cheng Ying the reward of one thousand pieces of gold. Cheng Ying refused to take it.

"You went to the authorities because of this reward," Tu'an Gu said, "so why do you now refuse it?"

"I worked for the Zhao family for a long time," Cheng Ying explained. "Now I have killed the orphan to save my own skin—I have already behaved unforgivably! What would it look like if I were also to accept this enormous reward! If you really appreciate the small contribution that I have made, let this money be used to bury the dead Zhaos properly. At least I can show them this last bit of respect."

Tu'an Gu was very pleased about this: "You really are a good man! There is no problem with letting you collect the bodies of the Zhao family for burial. If you want to use this money for the funeral, you can."

Cheng Ying then bowed and took the reward. He collected the bones of each family member and had them formally encoffined; afterwards they were buried in graves arranged around the tomb of Zhao Dun. Once that was done, he went back again to thank Tu'an Gu. He wanted him to stay behind and work for him, but Cheng Ying burst into tears and said: "A moment's greed and fear of death led me to commit a terrible injustice. I cannot bear to stay another moment in Jin and face the people here. Let me go and make my living somewhere far away." Cheng Ying bade farewell to Tu'an Gu, before going to have an audience with Han Jue. The general entrusted the orphan and his wet-nurse to Cheng Ying's care. Cheng Ying treated him as if he were his own baby son. They went away to live hidden in Mount Yu.

Later on people called this place the Hidden Mountain, to commemorate the fact that the orphan of the Zhao clan was concealed here.

• • •

Three years later, Lord Jing of Jin was out hunting in Xintian when he noticed that the land was very fertile and the waters sweet, so he moved his capital there. The officials all came to court to offer their congratulations to His Lordship. Lord Jing held a banquet in honor of his senior ministers in the inner palace. As it began to get dark, his servants lit the lamps. Suddenly a strange gust of wind came roiling through the main hall, forcing people away with its icy blast. Those present were all panic-stricken. A short time later the wind fell. Lord Jing was then the only person present to see the ghost that walked in: a tall man with long hair that trailed upon the ground. He clenched his fist and shouted: "Heaven! What crime had my sons and grandchildren committed that you should murder them like that? My complaints have been heard by God on High and so I have come to take your life!" When he had finished speaking, he struck Lord Jing with a bronze cudgel.

"Save me!" Lord Jing screamed. He drew his sword and tried to strike at the ghost, but in his panic all he managed to do was to slice through his own fingers. The ministers present had no idea what was going on, but in spite of all the confusion, they managed to overpower His Lordship and wrench the sword out of his grasp. Lord Jing spat a mouthful of blood before crumpling to the floor, unconscious.

Did he survive? READ ON.

Chapter Fifty-eight

Having persuaded the Earl of Qin, Wei Xiang takes a doctor home.

In taking revenge on Wei Yi, Yang Yaoji shows great skill.

When Lord Jing of Jin was attacked by the ghost, he spat a mouthful of blood and collapsed to the floor. The palace eunuchs lifted him up and carried him into his bedchamber, but it was a long time before they were able to bring him around. The ministers eventually dispersed, deeply concerned about what had happened. Lord Jing was now too ill to get out of bed.

One of his entourage suggested: "The Great Shaman from Sangmen can see ghosts even in broad daylight—why don't we summon her?"

The Great Shaman arrived in response to the Marquis of Jin's summons and was taken directly into His Lordship's chamber. She immediately announced that it was haunted.

"What does the ghost look like?" Lord Jing asked.

"It is a tall man with long, unbound hair," the Great Shaman replied. "He beats his breast and looks deeply enraged!"

"That is exactly the same as what I saw!" Lord Jing exclaimed. "He claims that I murdered his innocent children and grandchildren. I wonder who this ghost could be!"

"How about, it is a minister who did great things in the service of your ancestors," the Great Shaman suggested, "only to have his sons and grandsons murdered by you in a particularly cruel and appalling way?"

Shocked, Lord Jing said, "Do you think this really is the ancestor of the Zhao clan?"

Tu'an Gu was standing to one side and immediately presented his opinion: "This shaman once worked for the Zhao family, and now she is taking advantage of this situation to complain about what happened to them. Do not believe a word she says, Your Lordship!"

Lord Jing was silent for a long time; then he asked another question: "Can you exorcise this ghost?"

"This ghost is so angry that an exorcism will be of no use," the Great Shaman declared.

"Does that mean that I am going to die?" asked Lord Jing.

"I will tell you the truth even at the risk of my own life," the Great Shaman responded. "In your current state of health, I am afraid that Your Lordship will not live to taste this year's freshly harvested barley!"

"The barley is only a month from harvest!" Tu'an Gu exclaimed. "Even though His Lordship is ill, his mind is still perfectly clear: it is not possible that he will die any day now! If His Lordship does live to eat fresh barley, I am going to kill you!"

He did not wait for Lord Jing to give the order, but shouted at the servants to throw the shaman out.

After the Great Shaman left, Lord Jing's condition worsened. Every doctor in Jin was called in to consult, but none of them were able to recognize the condition that was killing him, and they did not dare prescribe any drugs.

Grandee Wei Yi's son, Wei Xiang, spoke to the ministers: "I have heard that there are two famous doctors in Qin: Gao He and Gao Yuan. They are trained in the tradition of the great Bian Que. They understand the principles of human anatomy and have had great success in treating all kinds of diseases, and they have both been appointed as court physicians in Qin. These are the only people who can cure His Lordship's illness. Why don't I go and ask them to come here?"

"Qin is an enemy state," the ministers responded. "Why on earth would they send their best doctors to help cure His Lordship?"

"Neighboring countries ought to help in times of trouble," Wei Xiang replied. "Even though I am not a talented man, I am prepared to go and try to persuade them to let their doctors come to Jin."

"If you can do that," the ministers said, "we will all be deeply grateful to you."

• • •

That very day, Wei Xiang packed his bags and set off for Qin at full speed, traveling day and night. Lord Huan of Qin asked the reason for his journey. Wei Xiang respectfully said, "My lord is suffering from a terrible illness. I have heard that your country has two excellent doctors—Gao He and Gao Yuan—both of whom can bring the dead back to life. I have come specially to beg you to save my lord's life."

"The state of Jin has repeatedly defeated our army in unprovoked attacks," Lord Huan returned. "We may have fine doctors, but why would we want to save your lord?"

"You are wrong!" Wei Xiang said sternly. "Qin and Jin are neighboring countries—in the past our Lord Xian and your Lord Mu were allies and relatives by marriage, and our states remained on good terms from one generation to the next. Your Lord Mu put our Lord Hui in power; then your invasion caused the battle of Hanquan. Next he put Lord Wen in power; then your side betrayed the covenant at Fannan. The reason that this alliance has not endured is all the fault of Qin! After Lord Wen died, your Lord Mu made a terrible mistake and tried to bully our little Lord Xiang, sending your army to Mount Xiao and attacking our subordinate states. Any defeat and humiliation that you suffered there, you brought upon yourselves! We captured the generals of your three armies, but we did not execute them and in the end they were pardoned. The response Qin made to this was to betray your promise and steal our royal office! In the reigns of Lord Ling and Lord Kang, when we invaded Chong, you responded by immediately attacking Jin. When our Lord Jing tried to punish Qi, you ordered Du Hui to raise an army to rescue them. When you are defeated, you lack basic discipline; when you are victorious, you do not know when to stop. If anyone is responsible for breaking our alliance and making us into your enemies, it is Qin! Please consider: Is it Jin that has caused trouble for Qin? Or Qin that has caused trouble for Jin? Now His Lordship is terribly ill and he wants to borrow a qualified doctor from your country. The other ministers all said, 'Qin hates us and they will not agree.' I said, 'No. The ruler of Qin may have done many things wrong in the past, but perhaps he now regrets this! My mission is to use the doctors as an excuse to reaffirm the long-standing good relationship between our two countries.' If you do not agree, my lord, all that will happen is that you confirm our ministers' poor opinion! Neighboring countries ought to assist each other in time of trouble, but you are refusing to do so! Doctors try and save people's lives, but you, my lord, are preventing them! Let me say that I think this a very bad idea."

Lord Huan of Qin was rendered acutely uncomfortable by Wei Xiang's incisive analysis. He felt an increasing admiration for the man, and said, "You are quite right to criticize me, sir. I have no choice but to grant your request." He immediately ordered the court physician, Gao Yuan, to go to Jin. Wei Xiang bowed and thanked His Lordship. He and Gao Yuan then departed from Yongzhou, traveling day and night in the direction of the Jin capital.

There is a poem that testifies to this:

> Having once been allied by marriage, they have now become enemies,
> Sitting by and enjoying the moments when the other suffers disaster.
> If it were not for Wei Xiang's persistence and eloquence,
> Would this famous doctor ever have set out for Jin?

By this time, Lord Jing of Jin was critically ill; day and night he looked for the Qin doctors, but they did not come. One day he had a dream in which two little boys jumped out of his nose. One child said, "Gao Yuan of Qin is one of the most famous doctors of our times. If he comes here and starts his treatment, we are going to be very seriously injured. How can we avoid him?" The second little boy said, "If we hide above the heart and below the top of the ribcage, there is nothing that he can do about us!" A short time later, Lord Jing screamed in agony because of the terrible pain in his chest. He was uncomfortable whether he sat up or lay down.

A short time later, Wei Xiang arrived with Gao Yuan. When he entered the palace, he began by feeling His Lordship's pulse. When that was done, Gao Yuan declared, "I can do nothing about this disease!"

"Why not?" Lord Jing asked.

"This disease is lodged above your heart and below the top of your ribcage," Gao Yuan replied. "Under such circumstances, I cannot get at it with moxibustion, and acupuncture will also not work. Even if I were to try and use drugs, they would not reach it. I am afraid that this is the will of Heaven!"

Lord Jing sighed and said, "What you have said accords exactly with my dream. You really are a wonderful doctor!" He gave him a large present of money and had the doctor escorted back to the state of Qin.

. . .

There was a young eunuch named Jiang Zhong. Exhausted by the work of looking after Lord Jing, he fell asleep in the morning. He dreamed that he carried Lord Jing on his back and the two of them flew off into the sky. When he woke up, he told the other servants about this. Even Tu'an Gu, coming to the palace to ask after His Lordship's health, heard about the dream. He congratulated Lord Jing and said, "Heaven represents light and disease represents darkness. If you fly up into the sky, it means that you are going to move towards the light, leaving darkness behind you. You will soon recover from this illness, my lord!"

The Marquis of Jin was feeling somewhat better that day, and when he heard these words he was absolutely delighted. Suddenly a report came in: "The superintendent of farms has come to present freshly harvested barley.

Lord Jing announced that he would like to taste some. He ordered his cooks to take half of it and pound it up to make porridge for him. Tu'an Gu was still furious about the complaints that the Grand Shaman of Sangmen had made concerning the violent deaths of the innocent members of the Zhao clan, so he presented his opinion as follows: "The shaman said that Your Lordship would not live to taste the barley harvested this year. You have now proved her wrong, my lord, so let us summon her and show her how mistaken she was."

Lord Jing did as he suggested and summoned the Grand Shaman of Sangmen to the palace. Tu'an Gu shouted at her: "Here is the fresh barley! Do you think His Lordship is going to be unable to eat it?"

"That remains to be seen," the shaman replied.

Lord Jing changed color.

"How dare you curse His Lordship?" Tu'an Gu screamed. "Behead this woman immediately!" He shouted at his entourage to drag the shaman away.

The shaman sighed and said, "Because of my ability to foretell the future, I have brought disaster down upon my own head. Is that not tragic?"

The servants brought back the dead shaman's head to present to His Lordship just as the cooks sent in the porridge. It was exactly midday. Lord Jing was just about to taste the dish, when suddenly he felt the onset of a bout of diarrhea gripping his guts. He shouted to Jiang Zhong: "Lift me onto the privy!" As he was placed on the privy seat, he felt a terrible pain around his heart. He was not able to keep his balance and fell into the privy. Jiang Zhong lifted him out, paying no attention to the disgusting filth, but Lord Jing had already died.

He did not live to taste the newly harvested barley. The death of the Great Shaman of Sangmen, who had accurately foretold his fate, can be laid entirely at the door of Tu'an Gu.

The senior minister Luan Shu led the other officials to assist Scion Zhoupu in taking charge of the funeral. Afterwards, he took the title of

Lord Li of Jin. Everyone was discussing Jiang Zhong's dream in which he had taken His Lordship on his back and flown up into the sky—this seemed to correspond with the fact that he had lifted Lord Jing out of the privy. Thanks to this connection, Jiang Zhong was selected to be one of the human sacrificial offerings in Lord Jing's tomb.

If right at the beginning Jiang Zhou had said nothing about his dream, this horrible fate would not have befallen him. You can bring great harm upon yourself by speaking incautiously—this is something to be on guard against!

Ever since Lord Jing had been killed in an attack by a powerful ghost, the state of Jin was riven with gossip about the unjust fate of the Zhao clan. However, thanks to the good relationship that still pertained between Tu'an Gu and the Luan and Xi families, Han Jue remained completely isolated. For this reason, he did not dare to speak out about the deaths of so many innocent people.

• • •

At this time Lord Gong of Song sent his senior minister, Hua Yuan, to offer his condolences to Jin and congratulate the new marquis. He discussed recent events with Luan Shu, for he was hoping to develop an alliance between Jin and Chu, which would prevent further north-south conflict and allow the populace time to recover.

"We cannot trust Chu." Luan Shu declared.

"I am a close friend of Prince Yingqi," Hua Yan said. "Let me see what can be done about this matter."

Luan Shu then sent his younger son, Luan Qian, to accompany Hua Yuan on a mission to Chu. The first thing they did was to attend an audience with Prince Yingqi. Prince Yingqi noticed the young and handsome Luan Qian and asked Hua Yuan who he was—that is how he discovered that this was the son of the commander-in-chief of the Central Army of Jin. He wanted to find out more about him, so he asked, "How does the country of Jin deal with military matters?"

"We maintain good order at all times," Luan Qian replied.

"What is your strong point?"

"We remain calm at all times," Luan Qian told him.

"When the enemy is in confusion you are in good order," Prince Yingqi mused. "When the enemy is busy, you remain calm. No wonder you have won so many victories! These two principles are simple, but they are vital for military success!" From this time onwards, he treated the young man with redoubled respect. He agreed to accompany the pair of them to an audience with the king of Chu. They concluded the following agreement: "Let our two countries make peace; let the people living on the border recover from their wounds. Anyone who touches a weapon again will be punished by the Bright Spirits!"

A date was set for a blood covenant to be sworn. Shi Xie of Jin and Prince Ba of Chu smeared their mouths with blood outside the West Gate of the Song capital.

Marshal Prince Ce of Chu was not part of these discussions, and he said angrily: "North and south have now been at war for ages! How dare Prince Yingqi take all the credit for making peace between us! I am going to get him for this!"

Thanks to his spies, he knew that Wu Chen had brought King Shoumeng of Wu into this alliance and that His Majesty was at present meeting with grandees from the states of Jin, Lu, Qi, Song, Wey, and Zheng at Zhongli. Prince Ce said to the king of Chu, "Jin has concluded an alliance with Wu, which means that they must be plotting to attack us. Song and Zheng have already joined them; our allies are all deserting us!"

"I would like to attack Zheng," King Gong replied, "but what about the blood covenant we swore at the West Gate?"

"Song and Zheng are our long-standing allies," Prince Ce said. "They have betrayed us to join with Jin. Nowadays people only care about profit—who cares about blood covenants?"

King Gong then ordered Prince Ce to attack Zheng. Zheng promptly abandoned its alliance with Jin to return to the Chu fold. This happened in the tenth year of the reign of King Jian of Zhou.

• • •

Lord Li of Jin was furious at this development and summoned his ministers to discuss an attack on Zheng. At this time Luan Shu and the three senior members of the Xi clan completely dominated the government. These three men were Xi Yi, Xi Chou, and Xi Zhi. Xi Yi was the commander-in-chief of the Upper Army, Xi Chou was the deputy general in command of the Upper Army, and Xi Zhi was the deputy general in command of the New Army. Chou's son, Xi Yee, and Zhi's younger brother, Xi Qi, were both employed in the government as grandees.

Bo Zong was the kind of man who dared to speak out directly. He repeatedly warned Lord Li: "The Xi clan is too powerful. You really ought to find pretexts for weeding out the incompetent, that thereby you may gradually reduce their power while preserving the positions of able descendants of a loyal minister."

Lord Li did not listen. The three senior members of the Xi family loathed Bo Zong and slandered him, accusing him of engaging in a treasonous conspiracy aimed at destabilizing the government. Lord Li believed them and executed Bo Zong. His son, Bo Zhouli, fled to Chu. In Chu he rose to the eminence of chancellor and was given the job of planning the attack on Jin.

Lord Li was an idle and dissolute young man, with a host of boon companions inside and outside the court. His favorites outside the court included Xu Tong, Yiyang Wu, Changyu Jiao, and the young men from the Jinli family—His Lordship appointed them all to the position of grandees. He had countless concubines, as well as seducing a host of maids about the palace. Given his debauchery and concomitant refusal to listen to good advice, the government went to the dogs, his officials refusing to do any work.

Shi Xie realized how badly things had gone wrong and tried to stop the attack on Zheng.

"If we do not attack Zheng," Xi Zhi said, "how can we get the other aristocrats to obey us?"

"We have already lost Zheng," Luan Shu said, "and that means that Lu and Song will also be planning to leave us. Xi Zhi is absolutely right."

General Miao Benhuang, who had surrendered to Jin from Chu, also urged an attack on Zheng. Lord Li followed these men's advice. Leaving only Xun Ying behind to guard the capital, His Lordship led an army of six hundred chariots, with Commander-in-Chief Luan Shu, Shi Xie, Xi Yi, Xun Yan, Han Jue, Xi Zhi, Wei Yi, and Luan Qian in attendance, out of the city in a magnificent procession and advanced towards the state of Zheng. Meanwhile, Xi Chou was sent to Lu and Wey to request troops in support.

• • •

When Lord Cheng of Zheng heard what a strong force Jin had mustered against him, his first thought was to surrender. Grandee Yao Gou'er said, "Zheng is a small state sandwiched between two great countries. Our only choice is to pick one powerful neighbor to defend us. Surely we cannot serve Chu at one moment and Jin the next, under constant attack year after year?"

"What should I do?" Lord Cheng of Zheng asked.

"In my humble opinion, the best policy would be to request assistance from Chu," Yao Gou'er replied. "If they come to help us, we can launch a joint attack with them, inflicting a great defeat upon the Jin army. That should buy us a couple of years of peace."

Lord Cheng then sent Grandee Yao Gou'er to Chu to request their assistance. King Gong of Chu was still smarting from the blood covenant at the West Gate and did not want to raise troops. He asked Prince Yingqi, the Grand Vizier of Chu, for his opinion.

"We do not trust Zheng," Prince Yingqi replied, "so why should we have to support them against the Jin army? Furthermore, if in protecting Zheng we are put in a position where we have to do battle, that will put our own people in a bad situation. We will not necessarily be able to guarantee victory, so it would be better to just wait and see what happens."

Prince Ce stepped forward and said: "The people of Zheng do not want to break their alliance with Chu; that is why they have come to report this emergency. We have already abandoned Qi to their fate, now it seems that we are also going to lose Zheng—clearly we want our allies to feel that we have totally forgotten them! I may be a stupid man, but give me just one division and I will go on ahead to protect them. Your Majesty will not even have to lift a finger."

King Gong of Chu was delighted. He appointed Marshal Prince Ce as commander-in-chief of the Central Army. The Grand Vizier, Prince Yingqi, was placed in command of the Army of the Left; Prince Renfu, the Minister of the Right, was placed in command of the Army of the Right. His Majesty personally took command of the two divisions of the Royal Guard, and they advanced northwards, heading out to rescue the state of Zheng. Each day they advanced one hundred *li*, moving as fast as the wind. Spies immediately reported this development to the Jin army.

Shi Xie spoke privately to Luan Shu about this. "His Lordship is a child who knows nothing about governing a country. We must pretend to be scared of Chu and run away, to try and instill the principles of caution in His Lordship's heart. If we can get him to feel frightened, there is still time to make peace."

"I refuse to have my reputation besmirched by people thinking that I got scared and ran away," Luan Shu said crossly.

Shi Xie had no choice but to withdraw. He sighed and said, "It would be a great thing if we lost this battle. If by some horrible mischance we win, there is going to be a civil war. That really is something to be scared of!"

By this time the Chu army had already passed Yanling, so the Jin army could not advance any further. They decided to make camp at Pengzugang. The two armies both set up their encampments. The following day, Jiawu day in the sixth month, was the last day of the month. On such days it is unlucky to move your troops, so the Jin army did not make any defensive preparations. Drums were sounded throughout the night, but then, before it even got light, the sound of shouting suddenly rose up outside the encampment. The officers in charge of guarding the camp rushed in to report: "The Chu army is attacking us! They have gone into battle formation!"

Luan Shu was deeply shocked. "If they really have gone into battle formation just outside the gates of our camp, we have nowhere to put our own soldiers. We cannot fight them under these circumstances! Let us stay inside the fortifications and try and come up with some sort of plan to defeat them!"

The whole army was abuzz with suggestions for what to do next. Some people suggested selecting a small band of battle-hardened soldiers and making a sudden assault on the Chu army; others spoke up in favor of a retreat. At this time Shi Xie's son, Shi Gai, was only sixteen years of age. Realizing that none of these people could make up their minds, he burst into the middle of the Central Army and went straight up to Luan Shu to say: "Are you worried about the fact that we don't have a place to fight, Commander-in-Chief? That is easily fixed."

"You have a plan?" Luan Shu asked.

"Give orders to close the gate of the camp and keep it shut," Shi Gai said. "The soldiers can then secretly dismantle all our food storage facilities, leaving a large area of level ground. The wells can be covered with planks of wood. Within about an hour, we should have enough space to put our troops into battle formation. When we are ready, you can open the gates and move out. What will the Chu army be able to do about that?"

"The wells and food storage are absolutely crucial for the army," Luan Shu pointed out. "If you cover the former and flatten the latter, how are we going to eat?"

"Order each soldier to prepare enough food and water for a couple of days in advance," Shi Gai instructed him. "Once the main force of the army has gone into battle formation, you can send the older and weaker troops out of the back of the camp to dig us a new set of wells and food-storage areas."

Shi Xie had never wanted to do battle in the first place, and now he saw his son suggest a feasible plan of campaign. He was absolutely furious and yelled: "Victory and defeat in battle are a reflection of the will of Heaven! What does a kid like you know that you dare to speak up on such an important occasion?" He grabbed hold of a halberd and started chasing his son. The other generals restrained Shi Xie, allowing his son to escape.

Luan Shu laughed and said, "This kid is much cleverer even than his father!" He followed Shi Gai's advice and ordered each soldier to collect enough food to last him for a few days, after which the wells were covered and the food storage was flattened. The soldiers were then drawn up in battle formation, and they prepared to fight the following day.

Hu Zeng in his "Historical Poem" says:

To line up your soldiers in battle formation inside the camp was an amazing idea,
Yet Shi Xie reacted by seizing a halberd and trying to strike his son!
Surely it was not his intention to chastise his own flesh and blood?
His fears for the country led him to take this desperate step!

When the king of Chu moved his army into position just outside the enemy camp and then went into battle formation, he thought that this would be a most unexpected move for them, whereby they would be thrown into confusion. What he was not expecting was total silence and a complete lack of movement. He asked Pasha Bo Zhouli about this. "The Jin army is sitting behind their fortifications without moving. You are a Jin person, so you must have some idea of what they are up to."

"Why don't you get onto a battle tower and have a look for yourself, Your Majesty?" Bo Zhouli suggested.

The king of Chu then climbed the mobile tower, and Bo Zhouli stood by his side. "The Jin army is rushing about, some heading left and some heading right," the king said thoughtfully. "What are they doing?"

"They are collecting the army officers together," Bo Zhouli said.

"Now a group of them has gathered by the Central Army," the king noted.

"They are discussing a plan together," Bo Zhouli said.

The king of Chu looked out into the distance and remarked, "Now they are putting up a tent. What is that for?"

"That means they are going to report their decision to the ancestors of our ruling house," Bo Zhouli informed him.

Looking out again, His Majesty remarked, "Now they are taking the tent down."

"That means that they are going to give orders."

Staring into the distance, His Majesty said, "What on earth are they doing? Why is there so much dust?"

"They don't have enough space to go into battle formation, so they are closing up their wells and food storage areas, in order to make room to fight."

The king looked out again. "Horses are being hitched to chariots and soldiers are getting on board," he said.

"They are going to go into battle formation."

A little bit later, the king remarked: "Why are the people who climbed onto the chariots getting off again?"

"Since they are about to do battle," Bo Zhouli responded, "they are praying to the gods."

Looking out, the king said, "The Central Army seems to be exceptionally strong; is His Lordship present?"

"The Luan and Fan families have sent their forces to fight side-by-side with the Marquis of Jin. This is an enemy that you do not want to underestimate."

When the king of Chu had placed himself in full command of the situation inside the Jin camp, he issued his own warnings to his troops and planned the attack for the following day. Miao Benhuang, who had surrendered from the Chu army, stood in attendance on the Marquis of Jin and informed him: "Ever since the death of Sunshu Ao, there have been big problems in the Chu army. The so-called crack troops of the Royal Guard have been in service for too long; there are many of them who are now too old to fight. Furthermore, the generals in command of the armies of the left and right hate each other. You should be able to defeat Chu in one battle."

A bearded old man wrote a poem:

Chu employed Bo Zhouli, once an aristocrat in Jin;
Jin employed Miao Benhuang, who originally came from Chu.
It is hard enough to find a really talented man,
You don't want to lose them to an enemy country!

That day, the two armies both kept to their encampments, holding firm and not fighting. The Chu general, Pan Dang, was practicing his archery in the rear camp, hitting the middle of the target with three successive arrows. The other generals present all praised his marksmanship. Then Yang Yaoji arrived, and the generals said, "The best archer we have is here!"

"In what way is my archery inferior to yours?" Pan Dang asked crossly.

"You have just hit the middle of an archery target," Yang Yaoji told him. "That is nothing to be particularly proud of. I can send an arrow through a willow at one hundred paces."

The assembled generals asked him, "What do you mean by sending an arrow through a willow at one hundred paces?"

"If you send someone to mark a single willow leaf, I will shoot an arrow through that leaf at one hundred paces," Yang Yaoji told them. "That is my target."

"There are a great many willow trees around here," the generals said. "Would one of them be suitable?"

"Why not?" Yang Yaoji asked.

The generals exclaimed happily, "Now we are really going to get to see some fine shooting!" They picked out a single leaf that was marked with a black spot, and Yang Yaoji moved one hundred paces away and drew his bow. No one saw where the arrow went; however, when the generals went to inspect the target, they saw that the arrow had pierced the leaf, the point having struck the mark exactly.

"That is just a coincidence," Pan Dang declared. "In my opinion, it is only when you can hit the marks on three leaves in succession that you can be considered a truly great archer."

"I am not sure that I can do it," Yang Yaoji said thoughtfully. "However, I am willing to give it a try."

Pan Dang marked three different leaves, hanging down at different levels, with the numbers one, two, and three. Yang Yaoji took note of their position, then moved back one hundred paces. He had three arrows, which were also numbered one, two, and three. He hit each target with the correct arrow, one after the other, without the slightest mistake. The generals present all clapped their hands and exclaimed, "What an amazing archer you are, Mr. Yang!"

Pan Dang could not prevent himself from feeling a certain shock, but he was nevertheless determined to try and show off his own skills. Therefore, he said to Yang Yaoji, "Your archery is deeply impressive! However, when killing a man, you need real strength behind the bow. I can pierce several layers of armor with a single shot—let me show you gentlemen what I mean."

"We would love to see that!" the generals all exclaimed.

Pan Dang ordered several soldiers in armor to take it off and piled them up in five layers. The generals said, "Surely that is enough?" Pan Dang added another two layers, making seven in total. The generals present thought to themselves, "Seven layers of armor is almost a foot thick—how can an arrow pass through that?" Pan Dang had these seven layers hung from an archery target. He too stood one hundred paces away and grabbed his black lacquer bow, nocking his wolf-tooth arrow to the string. His left hand was held as hard as if he were pushing back Mount Tai, his right hand as gentle as if he were holding a baby. He stood firm, and then put all the force at his command into the arrow. He released the bow with a shout: "Hit!" No one saw the arrow arch up into the air; no one saw it come down again. All the generals had their eyes fixed on the target, and then with one voice they started to shout: "How amazing! How wonderful!" With the force that Pan Dang had put behind that arrow, he had managed to pierce seven layers of armor. The arrow had nailed them to the target, piercing straight through.

Pan Dang looked very pleased with himself. He instructed an officer to take down the armor but leave the arrow in place, so that it could be shown around the army camp.

"Don't move it," Yang Yaoji said. "I would like to have a go!"

"Why not?" the generals said.

Yang Yaoji picked up his bow and made as if to shoot, then he stopped. The generals asked, "Why do you not shoot?"

"There is nothing special about whacking an arrow through many layers of armor," Yang Yaoji declared. "I have another idea." When he had finished speaking, he drew his bow and shot.

The shout rose up: "Beautiful!" This arrow moved neither up nor down, not to the left or to the right; it simply curved along exactly the same trajectory that General Pan Dang's arrow had carved through the air and tracing it straight into the target. Yang Yaoji's arrow split the first one, following the hole that it had drilled through the seven layers of armor. When they saw this, the generals were truly amazed. Even Pan Dang had to admit that this was a remarkable thing to be able to do. He sighed and said, "You really are a great archer, Mr. Yang! I do not even come close!"

Master Qian Yuan wrote a poem:

> There are many archers who have shot down birds or sent an arrow
> through a rat;
> Hitting a willow leaf at one hundred paces is a much rarer feat!
> To shoot an arrow through many layers of armor is nothing to be
> amazed about;
> For every powerful man there is someone even stronger!

"Jin and Chu are now locked in a standoff," the generals said. "Now is the time that we need men of talent. You are both remarkable archers, gentlemen, so let us tell His Majesty that such fine officers should not be hidden away!" They ordered an officer to take down the suits of armor with the two arrows through it and carry this into the presence of King Gong of Chu. Yang Yaoji and Pan Deng went with them. The generals explained how the two men had competed over their archery skills, first one and then the other, after which they flattered the king of Chu with the suggestion: "With such remarkable archers in our country, why should we worry about Jin's huge army?"

The king of Chu was furious. "If you want to win a battle, a single fine shot will not do it for you! If you are this arrogant, you are going to get yourselves killed!" He took away Yang Yaoji's arrows and would not allow him to shoot again. Yang Yaoji withdrew feeling deeply humiliated.

The following day at the fifth watch, the two armies sounded their drums and moved their armies forward. Xi Yi, the commander-in-chief of the Jin Upper Army, attacked the Army of the Left of Chu, whereby he was pitched against Prince Yingqi. The commander-in-chief of the Lower Army, Han Jue, was ordered to attack the Army of the Right of Chu, to do battle with Prince Renfu. Luan Shu and Shi Xie each commanded their own divisions and fought with the Central Army, protecting His Lordship. They found themselves doing battle with King Gong and Prince Ce. On the Jin side, Lord Li had Xi Yi as his charioteer and Luan Qian as the auxiliary general and bodyguard. Xi Zhi was in command of the New Army, which brought up the rear. On the Chu side, when King Gong rode out from the battle formation, he ought to have been followed by the Right division of the Royal Guard. However, the Right division was commanded by Yang Yaoji. Since King Gong was angry with Yang Yaoji for showing off his archery, he did not use the Right division, but was accompanied by the Left. Peng Ming drove the king of Chu's chariot, while Qu Dang was his auxiliary general and bodyguard. Lord Cheng of Zheng led his own forces to bring up the rear.

• • •

Lord Li of Jin wore a helmet topped with a plume made of pheasant feathers, battle dress consisting of a red brocade gown with a design of coiling dragons and serpents, a precious sword hung from his waist, and he grasped a great spear in his hand. Furthermore, he was riding in a battle chariot decorated with gilded bronze panels. Luan Shu held his position on the right, Shi Xie held his position on the left, as they threw open the gates to the army camp and fell upon the Chu soldiers drawn up in tight formation. Who could have imagined that there would be a marshy patch of ground located right in front of the Chu army? In the faint predawn light, it was impossible to see clearly. The Marquis of Jin's charioteer whipped up his horses and sent them charging into battle, driving the wheels of the chariot straight into the mud, so that the horses found it impossible to move.

Prince Xiongpei, King Gong of Chu's son, was still a very young man but also extremely brave, and he had been placed in command of the vanguard. Looking into the distance, he realized that the Marquis of Jin's chariot had become bogged down, so he immediately launched his attack, spurring on his horses to full speed. On the Jin side, Luan Qian got down from the chariot as quickly as he could. Standing in the mud, he used every ounce of strength to lift up the body of the chariot with his two bare hands. As the chariot came free, the horses moved forward; step by step they dragged the chariot out of the quagmire. Prince Xiongpei of Chu was now within striking distance, but Luan Shu's forces had also caught up with them.

"General, do not think you can get away with this!" he shouted.

Prince Xiongpei saw the flags for the commander-in-chief of the Central Army and realized that this represented the main body of the Jin army. Horrified at the situation into which he had gotten himself, he turned around and raced for his own side. Luan Shu set off in pursuit, trying his best to capture him. By this time the Chu army had realized that Prince Xiongpei was in danger, so they came out en masse to rescue him. Shi Xie now led his troops on the attack, and Xi Zhi arrived with reinforcements. The Chu army was afraid that they might be drawn into a trap, so they collected their forces and retreated back into their encampment. The Jin army did not pursue them. Both sides returned to camp. Luan Shu presented his captive, Prince Xiongpei, and the Marquis of Jin wanted to kill him.

Miao Benhuang stepped forward and said, "When the king of Chu hears that his son has been captured, he will come out to fight himself. You had better send Prince Xiongpei out with the vanguard, so that we can force them to attack in an unfavorable position."

"Good idea!" the Marquis of Jin declared.

Nothing more happened that night.

At dawn the following day, General Luan Shu of Jin ordered the gates to be opened so that they might do battle again. The senior general, Wei Yi, reported to Luan Shu: "Last night I dreamed that the moon floated high in the sky, whereupon I drew my bow and shot at it. Just as my arrow hit the center, a beam of golden light shone down. I was in a great hurry to get away from it, but my foot slipped and I became bogged down in the marshy patch in front of the encampment. That gave me such a shock that I woke up. I wonder if this is an auspicious omen or not?"

Luan Shu thought about this carefully for a moment and then said, "Relatives of the Zhou ruling house are represented by the sun, other ruling houses by the moon. If you shot the moon and hit it, that must refer to the king of Chu. However, mud comes from the mixing of earth and water. You stepped backwards and got stuck in the mud—that is not an auspicious omen! You had better be very careful!"

"If we can defeat Chu, I don't care if I die!" Wei Yi said.

Luan Shu then agreed that Wei Yi could go out in advance of the main body of the troops. The Chu general, Gongyin Xiang, came out to meet him. The two of them crossed swords a couple of times, then the Jin army moved a prison wagon out in front of their battle ranks. King Gong of Chu realized that his son, Prince Xiongpei, was inside it in chains; he was so angry and panic-stricken that it was as if flames were licking his heart. He shouted, "Peng Ming, whip up your horses and see if we can capture that wagon!"

Wei Yi noticed this maneuver and, shaking off Mirza Xiang, set off in pursuit of the king of Chu. He let fly a single arrow, which struck the king of Chu in his left eye. Pan Dang fought him off while supporting the king of Chu inside the chariot. The king of Chu endured the pain of plucking out the arrow himself; his eyeball came out on the point of the arrow and dropped to the ground. One of the ordinary soldiers picked it up and handed it back to him. "This is Your Majesty's eyeball. It should not just be thrown away!" The king of Chu took it from him and dropped it into his quiver.

The Jin army realized that Wei Yi had pulled off a remarkable feat, so they now attacked all together. Prince Ce led his own forces to defend against this, thereby allowing King Gong of Chu to escape. Xi Zhi's army surrounded Lord Cheng of Zheng's forces. Thanks to his charioteer, who hid his battle standard in his bow case, Lord Cheng was also able to escape. By this time the king of Chu was as furious as he had ever been in his life, and he quickly shouted for General Yang Yaoji to get him out of there. When Yang Yaoji heard the summons, he came immediately. Naturally, he did not have a single arrow on him. The king of Chu handed him two arrows and said, "The man who shot me was wearing a green robe and had a heavy beard; I want you to take revenge for me, general! With your remarkable skills, I am sure you do not need any more arrows than this!"

Yang Yaoji ordered a fast chariot to take him within range of the Jin army. He immediately caught sight of a man wearing a green robe, who had a heavy beard, whom he recognized as Wei Yi. "Who do you think you are, you bastard?" he shouted. "How dare you shoot at His Majesty!" Wei Yi was just about to respond when he was struck by Yang Yaoji's arrow. It hit him in the neck. He fell back upon his bow-case and died. Luan Shu ordered that his soldiers recover the body. Meanwhile, Yang Yaoji had returned the remaining arrow to the king of Chu. He announced: "According to Your Majesty's commands, I have shot and killed the general with a beard, wearing a green robe." King Gong was very pleased. He personally presented him with a brocade robe and one hundred wolf-tooth arrows. The whole army took to calling him "One-Arrow Yang" since he did not need a second one to hit the target.

There is a poem that testifies to this:

Whipping up his horses, the chariot speeds into battle.
At first sight, the Jin troops feel their blood run cold.
Where everyone else had failed to kill this famous general,
Yang Yaoji returned in triumph having downed him with one shot!

The Jin army followed the Chu troops in hot pursuit. Yang Yaoji drove out in front of the rest of the army, nocked an arrow to the string and let fly, killing a whole host of pursuing troops dead. The Jin troops did not dare to get close. When Prince Yingqi and Prince Renfu heard that the king had been shot, they both brought their troops out in support. After a short but chaotic battle, the Jin army withdrew. Luan Qian spotted the Grand Vizier of Chu's flag fluttering in the distance, and he knew that this was Prince Yingqi's army. He said to the Marquis of Jin, "Some time ago, Your Lordship, you sent me on an embassy to Chu, and the Grand Vizier questioned me about the way in which the state of Jin conducted warfare. I told him that the two most important principles were maintaining good order and remaining calm. In the messy battle that we fought today, we had no opportunity to show good order, and with everyone running around there has been no sign of us remaining calm. I would like to take some soldiers and go to offer the Grand Vizier of Chu a cup of wine, so that he may see what we can really do!"

"Why not?" the Marquis of Jin said.

Luan Qian then ordered his servants to prepare a presentation cup of wine, which he sent over to Prince Yingqi's army with the following message: "My lord lacks good men, so he has ordered me to act as his bodyguard and right-hand man on his chariot; that is why I am not able to serve you this wine in person. However, I have sent a servant in my stead."

Prince Yingqi remembered how Luan Qian had spoken of the good order and calmness of the Jin army. He sighed and said, "The general is very thoughtful!" He took the cup and drank it in the presence of the servant. Then he sent the following message back: "One day I will thank you in person when we meet in front of our troops!"

The messenger returned and reported these words. Luan Qian said, "The king of Chu has been hit by an arrow, but still his army does not retreat. What do we do now?"

"We significantly augmented our forces in the recent muster of troops," Miao Benhuang said. "We have well-fed horses and well-trained troops, so we should use them in the most advantageous battle formations. Tomorrow at cockcrow, we can have the army eat their fill and then send them out to fight. Surely Chu does not pose a serious threat to us."

Just at that moment, Xi Chou and Luan Yan returned from their mission to collect forces from Lu and Wey. They said, "Both states have raised an army for you, and they are now only twenty *li* from here." The Chu spies spotted this development and reported it to the king.

"The Jin army is already enormous," His Majesty declared in alarm. "Now that Lu and Wey are here too, what on earth are we going to do?"

He ordered his servants to summon the commander-in-chief of the Central Army, Prince Ce, for a consultation.

If you do not know what happened next, READ ON.

Chapter Fifty-nine

The favor shown to Xu Tong takes the state of Jin to the brink of civil war.

Having executed Tu'an Gu, the Zhao clan rises again.

Prince Ce, the commander-in-chief of the Central Army of Chu, was an alcoholic. Once he started, he would not stop until he had drunk one hundred calabashes dry; once he got drunk, he would not wake up for days. King Gong was well aware of this failing, and every time they went out on campaign, he would warn his servants to keep him off the drink. During the tense standoff between Jin and Chu, because he had such an important role to play, he did not touch a drop of any kind of liquid all day.

On the day when the king of Chu returned to the camp having had his eye shot out, he was feeling both angry and deeply humiliated. Prince Ce came forward and said, "Both armies are now exhausted. Let us rest tomorrow! Let your ministers have time to come up with a new plan of campaign, so that we can expunge the humiliation inflicted upon Your Majesty!"

Prince Ce bade His Majesty farewell and returned to the Central Army. He sat in his tent until the middle of the night, trying and failing to come up with a plan. One of his servants, a man named Gu Yang, was very much favored by His Royal Highness, who kept him constantly about his person. When he saw that the commander-in-chief was looking troubled and exhausted, he took out the triple-distilled *meijiu* that he had secreted away and warmed one bottle before presenting it to the prince. When Prince Ce smelled the liquid, he was startled and said, "Is this alcoholic?"

Gu Yang knew that His Royal Highness wanted a drink but was afraid that his servants might report it to the king. Therefore, he lied and said, "It is not alcoholic. This is a pepper soup."

Prince Ce understood exactly why he was saying this and downed the cup in a single gulp. He felt its sweet fragrance spread through his mouth and was more delighted than he could say. "Is there any more pepper soup?" he asked.

"There is," Gu Yang assured him.

Since he was claiming that it was entirely innocuous, this time he served a whole bowl to His Royal Highness. Prince Ce was feeling absolutely parched anyway. He remarked, "This pepper soup is delicious! How thoughtful of you to prepare it for me!" As soon as the bowl arrived, he drained it in one swallow and asked for more, until he had no idea how many bowls he had drunk. He was now too sodden with drink to be able to stand up, so he was lolling against his seating mat.

The king of Chu was informed that Jin would do battle at cockcrow, and they had received reinforcements from Lu and Wey. He immediately sent one of the palace servants to summon Prince Ce and discuss a plan for countering the enemy attack. He had no idea that Prince Ce was now so drunk that he was comatose! They shouted at him but he did not respond, they tried to lift him up but couldn't, and the smell of alcohol was overpowering. They realized that he was drunk again and went back to report this to the king of Chu. His Majesty sent a dozen messengers to the commander-in-chief in succession, trying to wake him up. The more they tried to wake Prince Ce, the sounder he seemed to sleep. The servant Gu Yang said tearfully, "I love the commander-in-chief, and that is why I gave him something to drink. I had no idea that I would cause such a disaster! When the king of Chu finds out, he will probably order my execution. I had better run away now!"

When the king of Chu realized that Prince Ce was not coming, there was nothing that he could do about it. He had to order the Grand Vizier, Prince Yingqi, to discuss strategy with him instead. Prince Yingqi had never been close to Prince Ce. He now presented his opinion: "I told you that the Jin army was very powerful and that if we fought them we could not be assured of victory. That is why in our initial discussions I opposed this campaign. This was all Prince Ce's idea. Now he is too drunk to continue the campaign—I have no plan to offer. Why don't you stand down your army overnight and head for home? That way, at least we will not suffer the humiliation of sustaining a second such defeat!"

"If we were indeed to do that and leave the prince drunk in his tent with the Central Army, he would be taken prisoner by Jin," the king of Chu said. "That would also be a humiliation for our country." He summoned Yang Yaoji and said, "You are a very fine archer. It will be your mission to bring His Highness home safe and sound." He secretly gave orders to strike camp and leave.

Yang Yaoji was left behind alone to cover the retreat, and he thought to himself, "There is no saying when His Royal Highness will wake up." He gave orders to the servants to lift Prince Ce and tie him onto the back of a chariot with leather straps. His troops then headed off. Yang Yaoji and the three hundred archers he had with him retreated slowly. Prince Ce of Chu only woke up fifty *li* into the journey. He realized that he had been tied up, so he shouted, "Who has trussed me up like this?"

"You were drunk," his servants told him, "and General Yang was worried that you would not be able to keep your footing on a moving chariot, so he tied you up in this way." They immediately cut the leather thongs off him.

Prince Ce was bristling with rage. "Where are we going?" he asked.

"We are on the way home," his servants informed him.

"Why are we going home?"

"Last night the king of Chu sent many messengers to try and summon you, but you were so drunk that you were dead to the world. The king of Chu was afraid that if the Jin army attacked us, there would be no one to lead the defense, so he had no choice but to stand down the army!"

Prince Ce wept bitterly. "Gu Yang might as well have killed me!" He immediately called for Gu Yang, but he was long gone and no one knew where.

King Gong of Chu moved his army two hundred *li*, but since there were no signs of pursuit, he then started to relax. He was afraid that Prince Ce might be so frightened of punishment that he would commit suicide, so he sent an envoy to tell him: "The failure of this campaign rests solely with me, the king. It is not your fault."

Prince Yingqi was afraid that Prince Ce might fail to commit suicide, so he sent a messenger to tell him: "You know the law: a defeated general deserves the death penalty. His Majesty cannot bear to order your execution, but do you really think you can ever face the Central Army again?"

Prince Ce sighed and said, "The Grand Vizier is correct when he blames me for this defeat. In the circumstances, how can I survive?" He promptly hanged himself. The king of Chu was devastated by this news. These events occurred in the eleventh year of the reign of King Jian of Zhou.

A bearded old man wrote a poem about the way in which things can be ruined by alcohol:

When king or lord suddenly demands a new plan,
What hero would be willing to refuse?
A servant's love brought about his master's death,
When all that was needed was some sensible advice.

• • •

Let us now turn to another part of the story. When Lord Li of Jin returned to court after his defeat of the Chu army, he imagined that he was the greatest warrior in the world and behaved with ever-increasing arrogance and extravagance. Shi Xie was sure that the state of Jin was heading for a civil war, and the depression that this induced ended up making him ill. Nevertheless, he was not willing to seek treatment from doctors. Instead, he had the Grand Supplicator beg the spirits to grant him an early death. Not long afterwards, he did indeed die. His son, Shi Gai—better known as Fan Gai—succeeded to his titles and emoluments.

At this time Xu Tong was the Marquis of Jin's favorite boon companion, thanks to his cunning flattery. Lord Li was determined to appoint him to a ministerial position, but there was no vacancy. Xu Tong presented his opinion: "The three senior members of the Xi family are in total control of the army, and their clan is very powerful. They are in a position to do just exactly what they feel like without reference to Your Lordship. In the future they are sure to try and rebel, so you should get rid of them now. If you do get rid of the Xi clan, you will have a lot of empty government posts to play with. You can choose your own people to fill them, and nobody will be able to object!"

"The Xi clan has done nothing to justify an accusation of treason," Lord Li said. "If I were to execute them, I am afraid that my ministers would disapprove."

"At the battle of Yanling," Xu Tong responded, "Xi Zhi had the Lord of Zheng surrounded, but then he drew up his chariot close by and the two of them chatted for a long time, after which he let the Earl of Zheng go. I am sure that he is engaged in treasonable communication with Chu and has been so for a long time. If you ask Prince Xiongpei about this, you will get to the truth of the matter."

Lord Li ordered Xu Tong to go and get Prince Xiongpei. Xu Tong asked the prince, "Would you like to go home to Chu?"

"I would love to be able to go home, but I am afraid that it is impossible," the prince replied.

"If you will do one thing for me," Xu Tong told him, "I promise that you will be sent back."

"Tell me what I have to do!"

Xu Tong leaned over and whispered in his ear: "If, when you have an audience with the Marquis of Jin, His Lordship asks you about Xi Zhi, then you must say exactly what I tell you."

Prince Xiongpei agreed. Xu Tong took him to the palace, where he had an audience with Lord Li of Jin. He sent away his entourage and asked, "Is Xi Zhi in secret communication with Chu? If you tell me the truth, I will let you go home."

"If you promise to pardon me for the crime that I am about to commit," Prince Xiongpei said, "then I will tell you what is going on."

"I want you to tell me the truth," Lord Li said. "There is no crime in that!"

"Xi Zhi and Prince Yingqi from my country are very close friends and often send letters back and forth," Prince Xiongpei told him. "He said, 'The Marquis of Jin does not trust any of his senior ministers and is sunk in drunken debauchery. The people hate him deeply. I refuse to regard such a man as my ruler. Everyone remembers Lord Xiang with great affection. Lord Xiang's grandson, Zhou, is at present living in the royal capital. Let us hope that at some point in the future when north and south do battle, our army is defeated. If Zhou comes to power, I will ensure that he serves the kingdom of Chu well.' That is all that I know about this situation. There may be more going on that I have not heard of."

• • •

Lord Xiang of Jin's oldest son, born to a concubine, was named Tan. When Zhao Dun placed Lord Ling in power, the Honorable Tan went into exile in Zhou, where he joined the household of Lord Xiang of Dan. Later on, he had a son who was named Zhou because he was born within the borders of the Zhou Royal Domain. When Lord Ling was murdered, the people of Jin thought back with great affection and respect to Lord Wen of Jin, which is why they established the Honorable Heitun. When Heitun died, the Honorable Ru succeeded to the title. When Ru died, the Honorable Zhoupu inherited the marquisate. Right up to the present time, in spite of the fact that Zhoupu, Lord Li of Jin, had seduced countless women, he had no son to succeed him. In the circumstances, it is not surprising that people's hearts turned to affectionate memories of Lord Xiang. The reason why Xu Tong had instructed Prince Xiongpei of Chu to mention Noble Grandson Zhou was in the hope of enflaming Lord Li's anger even further.

Before Prince Xiongpei had finished speaking, Xu Tong chimed in: "No wonder that at the battle of Yanling, when Xi Chou's chariot drew level with that of Prince Yingqi, neither side shot a single arrow! It is quite clear that they are conspiring together. Furthermore, Xi Zhi's motives in letting the ruler of Zheng escape are now perfectly clear! If you do not believe me, my lord, all you have to do is to send Xi Zhi to present the prisoners we have captured to the Zhou king and send someone else to watch him. If he is indeed involved in some treasonous plot, he will take this opportunity to make contact with Noble Grandson Zhou."

"That is a great idea," Lord Li said. He ordered Xi Zhi to present the Chu prisoners of war to the king.

Meanwhile Xu Tong secretly send someone to communicate with Noble Grandson Zhou: "Fully half the government of Jin is dominated by appointees selected from the Xi clan. Now Xi Zhi is coming to the royal capital to present captives from the recent war, so why don't you try and meet with him? If in the future you were ever to return to your home country, that would be a very useful connection."

Noble Grandson Zhou thought that this was a very good idea. Xi Zhi arrived in the Royal Domain and carried out his formal duties. After they were completed, Noble Grandson Zhou went to the official guesthouse to meet him, and naturally asked about the situation in Jin. Xi Zhi explained many things to him in considerable detail—the two of them talked together for many hours. When the spy Lord Li had sent came back and reported this, it seemed that every word that Prince Xiongpei of Chu had said was true. The Marquis of Jin made up his mind that he had to get rid of the Xi clan, but he had not yet given an order to this effect.

One day, Lord Li and his wife were drinking wine together when they demanded some venison as a snack. The eunuch Meng Zhang was sent to the market to purchase some. As it transpired, there was none for sale in the market anywhere, but just at that moment Xi Zhi arrived from outside the suburbs with a dead deer slung over the back of his chariot. As he drove through the marketplace, Meng Zhang grabbed the deer off him without pausing to explain the reason. Xi Zhi was most offended by this barefaced theft and shot him with his bow and arrow, killing Meng Zhang stone dead. Xi Zhi then took his deer back.

When Lord Li heard about this, he said angrily, "Xi Zhi has annoyed me for the last time!" He summoned Xu Tong, Yiyang Wu, and all his other closest boon companions to discuss how to kill him.

"If you murder Xi Zhi," Xu Tong pointed out, "that will force Xi Yi and Xi Chou to rebel against you. It would be better to get rid of all of them at the same time."

"Your Lordship has eight hundred guards at your disposal," Yiyang Wu reminded him. "If you were to send them out one night to attack the Xi clan, we could take advantage of the fact that they will be completely unprepared to kill them all."

"The private army commanded by the three senior members of the Xi family is twice the size of His Lordship's guard," Changyu Jiao warned them. "If we fight them and do not win, that will put His Lordship in serious danger. At the moment Xi Zhi holds the office of minister of justice, while Xi Chou is the chief judge. Why not pretend that there is some serious uprising underway and trick them into a position where we can stab them to death? You can then use your troops to support us."

"Wonderful!" Lord Li exclaimed. "I will send one of my guards, Qing Feitui, to help you."

Changyu Jiao investigated their movements and discovered that the three senior members of the Xi family were in a meeting at the Hall of Military Discussions. He and Qing Feitui smeared their faces with chicken's blood, so that it would look as if they had been fighting. They rushed into the Hall of Military Discussions, naked swords in their hands, to report that they were under attack. Xi Chou had no idea that this was all part of a plot, so he got down from his seat to ask them what was going on. Qing Feitui pretended that he was about to make a report—he stepped forward and then made a sudden lunge, stabbing Xi Chou in the stomach. He fell to the ground. Xi Yi immediately drew his sword and attacked Qing Feitui, only to have his move countered by Changyu Jiao; the two men fought down the middle of the hall and out into the open air. Xi Zhi spotted his opportunity and started running. He jumped into a chariot and fled the scene. Qing Feitui struck Xi Chou twice with his sword. Realizing that the man was now dead, he joined in the fight against Xi Yi.

Xi Yi was a general, but Qing Feitui was a fine warrior too. Even though Changyu Jiao was only a young man without much military experience, it was not possible for one person to fight off the two of them, and Qing Feitui cut him down. Just at that moment Changyu Jiao realized that Xi Zhi had fled. "Damn!" he shouted. "I will have to chase him down!"

While the Xi family were fighting for their lives, Xu Tong and Yiyang Wu brought up eight hundred troops in support. They gave their orders: "The Marquis of Jin has given an edict to say that every member of the traitorous Xi clan must be arrested; do not let anyone escape!"

Xi Zhi realized that having escaped one set of enemies, he had run headlong into another. He turned his chariot around, only to encounter Changyu Jiao, who leapt into his vehicle with a single bound. Xi Zhi was in such a panic that he did not counter this move in time—Changyu Jiao cut him to pieces. Afterwards, he chopped off his head. Meanwhile, Qing Feitui had cut off the heads of Xi Yi and Xi Chou. These three heads, dripping with blood, were carried in through the palace gates.

There is a poem that testifies to this:

A wicked ruler encourages evil ministers,
A host of idle sycophants monopolize the court.
Having once made the mistake of listening to malicious slander,
The Hall of Martial Discussions became a battlefield.

Xun Yan, the deputy general of the Upper Army, heard that his commander-in-chief, Xi Yi, had been murdered at the Hall of Martial Discussions, though he did not know who by. He immediately got into his chariot and rode to court, with the intention of obtaining permission to punish the guilty. En route, he happened to meet the commander-in-chief of the Central Army, Luan Shu. When they arrived at the palace gates, they bumped into Xu Tong and his guards.

Luan Shu and Xun Yan said angrily, "All we knew is that someone was trying to cause trouble—so it is this little bastard! How dare you take soldiers into the presence of His Lordship! Why don't you just crawl back into whatever hole you came from?"

Xu Tong did not bother to reply. He shouted to the guards: "Luan Shu and Xun Yan were part of the Xi family's treasonous conspiracy! Arrest them! Anyone who captures them will be generously rewarded!"

The guards advanced boldly and surrounded Luan Shu and Xun Yan. They forced the two of them into the main hall of the palace.

When Lord Li heard that Changyu Jiao and the others were back, having finished their work, he immediately went to the main hall of the palace. When he got there, he found it stuffed with soldiers milling about, which gave him a terrible shock. He asked Xu Tong, "The criminals are dead. What are all these soldiers doing here?"

"They have arrested the conspirators Luan Shu and Xun Yan," Xu Tong replied. "Please give the order to execute them, my lord!"

"This has nothing to do with Luan Shu and Xun Yan!" Lord Li declared.

Changyu Jiao knelt down before the Marquis of Jin and whispered, "The Luan and the Xi family are part of the same political faction; Xun Yan was Xi Yi's subordinate. Now that the Xi clan has been killed, the Luan and Xun clans are certain to become restive. Sooner or later they will start thinking about avenging the Xis. If you do not kill them now, the court will not know a moment's peace!"

"I have already executed three senior ministers in a single day," Lord Li said. "Now you are telling me that I have to kill more people! I cannot bear it!" He pardoned Luan Shu and Xun Yan, confirming them in their original official positions. The two men thanked His Lordship for his kindness and went home.

Changyu Jiao sighed and said, "His Lordship could not bear to hurt the two of them, but will they feel the same way about His Lordship?" That very same day he fled into exile with the Western Rong people.

Meanwhile, Lord Li rewarded his guards. He gave orders that the heads of the three senior members of the Xi family should be hung from the gates of the palace for three days, after which their families could collect them for burial. All other members of the Xi clan who held positions at court were told that they would not be killed, but they would lose their jobs. Xu Tong was appointed commander-in-chief of the Upper Army, to replace Xi Yi. Yiyang Wu was appointed as commander-in-chief of the New Army, to replace Xi Chou. Finally, Qing Feitui was appointed as deputy general in command of the New Army, to replace Xi Zhi. Prince Xiongpei of Chu was released and allowed to return home. Xu Tong now also held ministerial rank, but Luan Shu and Xun Yan regarded the idea of working with him as too humiliating, so they kept claiming to be ill and hence refused to go to court. Xu Tong believed that the Marquis of Jin's favoritism rendered him immune to criticism, so he paid no attention to this.

. . .

One day, Lord Li and Xu Tong were out visiting another of the Marquis of Jin's boon companions—a member of the Jiangli family—at home. This man lived south of Mount Taiyin, some twenty or more *li* away from the capital city. They were to be gone for three days.

Xun Yan then communicated secretly with Luan Shu: "As you well know, His Lordship is a wicked and vicious man. We are refusing to go to court on the grounds of ill health: this is keeping us safe in the short term, but the minute that Xu Tong becomes suspicious, he will slander us in some foul way and we will suffer the same fate as the ministers from the Xi clan. We really need to think carefully about what we are going to do!"

"I agree with you," Luan Shu said, "but where do we go from here?"

"For any senior minister, it is the good of the country that comes first," Xun Yan declared. "The lord is much less important. We have the people in the palms of our hands. If we kill His Lordship and establish a wiser and better man in his place, who would dare to object?"

"How do we proceed?" Luan Shu asked.

"When a dragon is lurking at the bottom of a deep pool, not even the finest diver can reach it," Xun Yan said cryptically. "However, when a dragon leaves the pool and reaches dry land, even a child can catch it. His Lordship is off on a visit to the Jiangli family and will be gone for three days—he is a dragon that has left its pool. There is nothing to worry about here!"

Luan Shu sighed and said, "My family have been loyal servants to the Jin ruling house for many generations. Now with the fate of our country trembling in the balance, I am forced to take desperate measures. Even though later generations will describe me as a traitor to my ruler, I cannot stand aside and let him continue like this!" They accordingly agreed their plan.

The two of them suddenly announced that they had recovered and needed to speak urgently to the Marquis of Jin. Meanwhile, they had sent the junior general, Cheng Hua, in command of three hundred men, to lie in ambush around the foot of Mount Taiyin. When the two ministers arrived at the Jiangli mansion, they requested an audience with Lord Li and said, "Your Lordship has left the capital for three days to have fun without thinking anything of the government problems that urgently need a decision. Your ministers and people are deeply troubled by this. We have come to collect you because you need to come back to court right now!"

Lord Li was much flustered by all of this and agreed to get into the chariot. Xu Tong went on ahead, with Luan Shu and Xun Yan bringing up the rear. When they skirted the foot of Mount Taiyin, the sound of siege engines was heard on both sides of the road, and the troops that had been waiting in ambush rose up. Cheng Hua cut Xu Tong to pieces.

Lord Li was so terrified that he fell off his chariot. Luan Shu and Xun Yan ordered the soldiers to arrest Lord Li. They made camp at the foot of Mount Taiyin, holding Lord Li prisoner on his own chariot.

"I am concerned that the Fan and Han clans might in the future not agree with our version of events," Luan Shu said. "I am going to summon them with a forged edict from His Lordship."

"Good idea!" Xu Yan exclaimed.

He sent two fast chariots to collect the two generals: Fan Gai and Han Jue. When the messenger arrived at Fan Gai's house, he asked, "Why does His Lordship want to see me?" The messenger was not able to reply. "There is something suspicious going on here!" Fan Gai said.

He sent a trusted servant to find out whether Han Jue was going or not. Han Jue had announced that he was far too unwell to go anywhere. Fan Gai remarked, "Clearly the two of us have exactly the same idea!" When Luan Shu realized that neither Fan Gai nor Han Jue was coming, he asked Xun Yan, "What do we do now?"

"You are already riding on the tiger's back," Xu Yan said. "Did you expect it would be easy to get off?"

Luan Shu nodded his head in understanding. That night, he ordered Cheng Hua to give Lord Li poisoned wine. The Marquis of Jin drank it and died. A rough-and-ready funeral was immediately organized by the army, and he was buried outside the East Gate of the city of Yi. When Fan Gai and Han Jue heard that His Lordship was dead, they both came out of the city to perform a formal ceremony of mourning, but neither of them asked what he had died from.

Once the funeral was over, Luan Shu convened a meeting of all the officials to discuss appointing a new ruler.

"When the three senior ministers from the Xi clan died," Xun Yan said, "it was because Xu Tong had slandered them, claiming that they were plotting to put Noble Grandson Zhou in power. Let us make this slander a prophecy! When Lord Ling died in the Pear Garden, it seemed as though Lord Xiang's line of descent was doomed. This is the will of Heaven! Let us go and meet him!"

The ministers were all delighted with this suggestion. Luan Shu sent Xun Ying to the Royal Domain to meet Noble Grandson Zhou and bring him back to be the new ruler. At that time he was still only fourteen years of age, but he had already shown signs of remarkable intelligence and great ambition. When he heard that Xun Ying had come to take him back to Jin, he inquired very carefully into what had happened. Afterwards, he said goodbye to Lord Xiang of Shan and journeyed to Jin with Xun Ying. When he arrived at Qingyuan, Luan Shu, Xun Yan, Fan Gai, Han Jue, and all the other ministers and grandees came out to meet him.

Noble Grandson Zhou was the first to speak. "I have spent all my life abroad and never expected to be able to return to my home country, let alone become the ruler. However, now that I am the lord, it is my duty to take command. If my ministers claim to be carrying out my orders but in fact do not respect them, I might as well not bother. Now is your opportunity to demonstrate whether you are serious or not in agreeing to accept my commands. If you are not, you need to find yourselves a different marquis. I am not prepared to be a puppet like my cousin Zhoupu!"

Luan Shu and the others were all so shocked that they bowed and said, "We are all delighted to serve such an enlightened ruler. How would we dare to disobey your orders?"

As they left, Luan Shu said to his companions, "This new marquis is not at all like the old one. We are going to have to be careful!"

When Noble Grandson Zhou arrived at the city of Xinjiang, he held court at the Great Ancestral Shrine, at which he succeeded to the position of Marquis of Jin, taking the title of Lord Dao. The day after he formally took office, Lord Dao announced that Yiyang Wu, Qing Feitui, and their like were guilty of the crime of leading His Late Lordship astray. He ordered his servants to drag them out of the court and behead them. Their families were all expelled from the country. What is more, he condemned Cheng Hua to death for the murder of Lord Li, and had him ripped to pieces by animals in the marketplace. This gave Luan Shu such a shock that he was not able to sleep all night. The next day he announced his retirement on the grounds of old age, suggesting that Han Jue should be appointed to replace him. Not long after, the stress and fear that he had suffered brought about his death. Lord Dao had heard much about Han Jue's good qualities, so he did indeed appoint him commander-in-chief of the Central Army to replace Luan Shu.

Han Jue came to court to thank His Lordship for his kindness, and then he found a way to speak privately to Lord Dao. "There are many of us here at court who keep our positions thanks to the meritorious service of our ancestors. However, when it comes to performing great deeds in the service of the state of Jin, there is no one who can compare to the Zhao clan; Zhao Cui served Lord Wen, Zhao Dun served Lord Xiang—both of them were totally loyal and worked incredibly hard to make our country powerful and our rulers respected by their peers. It is a terrible shame that Lord Ling lost control of the government and trusted the wicked Tu'an Gu: that is why he plotted to murder Zhao Dun, It was only by going into exile that he was able to escape. Lord Ling was murdered at the Pear Garden by mutinous soldiers, whereupon Lord Jing was established. He too favored Tu'an Gu. Although Zhao Dun was by that time dead, Tu'an Gu still pretended that the Zhao family were involved in murder and sedition. This led to the deaths of the entire Zhao clan; right up to the present day, the people are still in uproar over this. A single member of the Zhao family, the orphan Zhao Wu, has survived. Today you have rewarded the virtuous and punished the wicked, my lord. You have undertaken a great reform of the government of Jin. Already we have seen Yiyang Wu and his coterie being punished, but surely you are not going to forget to reward the great deeds of the Zhao family?"

"I heard my father speak about this," Lord Dao said. "Where is the orphan now?"

"When Tu'an Gu was searching everywhere for the orphan of the Zhao clan, two of their old subordinates got involved," Han Jue explained. "One was called Gongsun Chujiu and the other Cheng Ying. Gongsun Chujiu smuggled a fake orphan out of the city, for which he was executed, thereby allowing Zhao Wu to escape. Later on Cheng Ying took the orphan to hide at Mount Yu, where they have been living for the last fifteen years!"

"Bring them back for me!" Lord Dao said.

"Tu'an Gu is still here at court," Han Jue pointed out. "You must keep this secret, my lord!"

"I will!" Lord Dao said firmly.

Han Jue left the palace and, driving himself in a fast chariot, went to find Zhao Wu in his place of hiding at Mount Yu. When Cheng Ying had smuggled the baby to safety, he had left the city of Gujiang. Now it was Xinjiang that he was traveling to. Everything about the city was completely different and his feelings were deeply pained.

Han Jue took Zhao Wu into the palace, where he had an audience with Lord Dao. The Marquis of Jin kept him hidden inside the palace, while announcing that he himself was sick. The following morning, Han Jue led the officials into the palace as part of a formal delegation to ask after His Lordship's health; Tu'an Gu was also present.

"Do you know why I am so worried?" Lord Dao asked. "Those who have performed meritorious deeds should be reported to the ruler. However, in one case this has not happened, and I am most unhappy about it!"

The ministers kowtowed and asked, "Who has performed a meritorious deed without it being reported?"

"Zhao Cui and Zhao Dun both performed great deeds in the service of our country, so how can their family line be cut off?" Lord Dao asked.

Everyone present said the same thing: "The entire Zhao clan was murdered fifteen years ago. Although today you remember the great deeds that they did, my lord, there is no one left to take charge of their family sacrifices!"

Lord Dao then called Zhao Wu out and had him greet the generals present. "Who is this young man?" they asked.

"This is the real orphan of the Zhao clan: Zhao Wu," Han Jue explained. "The child that was killed was in fact the son of Cheng Ying, one of the Zhao clan's subordinate officials."

Tu'an Gu felt his soul leave his body. He collapsed to the ground as if drunk. He could not find a single word to say.

"This is Tu'an Gu's crime," Lord Dao declared. "If today the Tu'an clan gets off scot-free, how will the souls of his innocent victims in the Underworld ever be appeased?" He shouted to his guards: "Arrest Tu'an Gu, drag him out and behead him!"

He ordered Han Jue and Zhao Wu to take their soldiers to Tu'an Gu's house and surround it, killing everyone inside regardless of age or sex. Zhao Wu asked permission to sacrifice Tu'an Gu's head on the grave of his father, Zhao Shuo. Everyone in the country was delighted by the fall of Tu'an Gu.

Master Qian Yuan wrote a poem about this:

First Tu'an Gu killed the entire Zhao clan,
Today the Zhao clan gets to execute them.
For the wheel to turn completely in only fifteen years
Means they did not have to wait too long for their revenge.

After Lord Dao of Jin executed Tu'an Gu, he summoned Zhao Wu to court, where a capping ceremony was held, marking his advent into manhood. Afterwards, he appointed Zhao Wu minister of justice, replacing Tu'an Gu. All the lands that had previously been held by the Zhao clan were now returned to him. In appreciation of what Cheng Ying had done, the Marquis of Jin also wanted to appoint him to an officer's rank in the army.

"I could not die before the orphan of the Zhao clan had been restored to his rightful heritage," Cheng Ying said. "Now his family has been avenged and his official position confirmed, but that is no reason for me to become greedy for titles and riches! I let Gongsun Chujiu die alone; now it is time for me to join him to report our success!"

He cut his throat and died. Zhao Wu cradled his body and wept bitterly. He begged Lord Dao for permission to bury him with full honors. He was interred at Mount Yunzhong with Gongsun Chujiu, in a tomb known as the Grave of the Two Gentlemen. Zhao Wu wore mourning clothes for three years, just as he would for his own father, to show his appreciation for all that Cheng Ying had done for him.

There is a poem that testifies to this:

Fifteen years were spent in hiding far away,
Thus the baby lived to revenge the deaths of his innocent parents.
Cheng Ying and Gongsu Chujiu were both good men;
Who cares which one of them died first and left the other to live?

After Lord Dao of Jin had restored Zhao Wu to his rightful position, he summoned Zhao Sheng back from Song, returning his fief in Handan to his possession. A root-and-branch reform was carried out in the government—the wise were shown all due respect and the able promoted to suitable office—while His Lordship also rewarded those who had achieved much in the service of the state and pardoned those guilty of only minor infractions of the law. Thus, all the officials found themselves working within very precisely defined positions. Some famous men found themselves holding high office in this new administration: Han Jue became the commander-in-chief of the Central Army with Fan Gai as his deputy. Xun Ying became commander-in-chief of the Upper Army with Xun Yan as his deputy. Luan Yan became commander-in-chief of the Lower Army with Shi Fang as his deputy. Zhao Wu became commander-in-chief of the New Army with Wei Xiang as his deputy. Qi Xi became commandant of the Central Army, with Yangshe Zhi as his deputy. Wei Jiang became marshal of the Central Army; Zhang Lao became the head of the Palace Guard; Han Wuji became the Grandee Director of the Ruling House; Shi Wo became the Grand Tutor; Jia Xin became minister of works; Luan Jiu became the Marquis of Jin's personal charioteer; Xun Bin became general in charge of the defense of His Lordship's person; Cheng Zheng became the Grand Admonisher; Duo Yikou became commandant of the cavalry; and Ji Yan became marshal of the cavalry. Once these officials were all confirmed in their new office, the government underwent a profound change as taxes were remitted, corvée labor was reduced, repairs and reforms conducted and widows and orphans were cared for. The people of Jin were very happy about this. When the states of Song and Lu heard about this, both sent delegations to the court. It was only Lord Cheng of Zheng, mindful of the fact that King Gong of Chu had lost his eye trying to save him, who was not willing to serve Jin.

. . .

King Gong of Chu was very happy when he heard that Lord Li had been murdered. His thoughts immediately turned to the possibility of revenge. Then he was told that a new ruler had been appointed who rewarded the wise and punished the guilty, employing able men in the government of the country, conducting himself in a moderate and restrained fashion, and who was much loved inside and outside the country to the point where people were talking about him as a future hegemon. At this point King Gong's happiness turned to concern. He immediately summoned his ministers to discuss this situation. He was determined to cause trouble among the Central States, to prevent Jin from achieving hegemony. The Grand Vizier, Prince Yingqi, had no idea how to achieve this. Prince Renfu then came forward and suggested: "Song holds the noblest title of any of the aristocrats of the Central States, and his country is also the largest. Furthermore, his state is sandwiched between Jin and the kingdom of Wu. If you wish to cause trouble and prevent Jin from achieving hegemony, you must start from Song. There are five grandees in Song—Yu Shi, Xiang Weiren, Lin Zhu, Xiang Dai, and Yu Fu—who hold serious grudges against the commander-in-chief of the Army of the Right, Hua Yuan. The situation became so poisonous that they were forced to seek sanctuary in Chu. If you give them a military force with which to attack Song, you can promise to enfeoff them with any towns that they capture. This is using an enemy to attack an enemy. If Jin does not go to the rescue, then they will lose the trust of the other aristocrats. If they do go to the rescue of the Duke of Song, they will be forced into open conflict with Yu Shi and the others. We can just sit by and watch which one of them wins. That is my plan."

King Gong decided to follow his advice, and so he appointed Prince Renfu as the senior commander, while telling Yu Shi and his companions to lead the way. A great host then marched on Song.

Do you know whether they won or lost? READ ON.